TONY HILLERMAN

Leaphorn, Chee, and More

The Fallen Man
The First Eagle
Hunting Badger

ALSO BY TONY HILLERMAN

Fiction
Skeleton Man
The Sinister Pig
The Wailing Wind
Hunting Badger
The First Eagle
The Fallen Man
Finding Moon
Sacred Clowns
Coyote Waits
Talking God
A Thief of Time
Skinwalkers
The Ghostway
The Dark Wind
People of Darkness
Listening Woman
Dance Hall of the Dead
The Fly on the Wall
The Blessing Way
The Boy Who Made Dragonfly (for children)
Buster Mesquite's Cowboy Band (for children)

Nonfiction
Seldom Disappointed
Hillerman Country
The Great Taos Bank Robbery
Rio Grande
New Mexico
The Spell of New Mexico
Indian Country
Talking Mysteries (with Ernie Bulous)
Kilroy Was There
The American Detective
The Best American Detective Stories of the Century

TONY HILLERMAN

Leaphorn, Chee, and More

The Fallen Man
The First Eagle
Hunting Badger

HarperCollins*Publishers*

TONY HILLERMAN: LEAPHORN, CHEE, AND MORE. Copyright © 2005 by Tony Hillerman. All rights reserved. Printed in the United States of America. No part of this book may be used or reproduced in any manner whatsoever without written permission except in the case of brief quotations embodied in critical articles and reviews. For information, address HarperCollins Publishers, 10 East 53rd Street, New York, NY 10022.

HarperCollins books may be purchased for educational, business, or sales promotional use. For information, please write: Special Markets Department, HarperCollins Publishers, 10 East 53rd Street, New York, NY 10022.

The Fallen Man, The First Eagle, and *Hunting Badger* were originally published in 1996, 1998, and 1999 respectively by HarperCollins Publishers Inc.

FIRST EDITION

Printed on acid-free paper

Library of Congress Cataloging-in-Publication Data

Hillerman, Tony.
    Leaphorn, Chee, and more / Tony Hillerman.—1st ed.
      p. cm.
    Contents: The fallen man—The first eagle—Hunting badger.
    ISBN-10: 0-06-082078-0
    ISBN-13: 978-0-06-082078-7
    1. Detective and mystery stories, American.   2. Leaphorn, Joe, Lt. (Fictitious character)—Fiction.   3. Chee, Jim (Fictitious character)—Fiction.   4. Police—Southwestern States—Fiction.   5. Indian reservation police—Fiction.   6. Southwestern States—Fiction.   7. Navajo Indians—Fiction.   I. Title.

PS3558.I45A6   2005
813'.6—dc22   2005046254

05 06 07 08 09 WBC/RRD 10 9 8 7 6 5 4 3 2 1

Contents

The Fallen Man   1

The First Eagle   205

Hunting Badger   411

The Fallen Man

This book is dedicated to members of the Dick Pfaff Philosophical Group, which for the past quarter-century has gathered each Tuesday evening to test the laws of probability and sometimes, alas, the Chaos Theory.

Acknowledgments

IN WRITING FICTION involving Navajo Tribal Police, I lean upon the professionals for help. In this book, it was provided by personnel of both the N.T.P. and the Navajo Rangers, and especially by old friend Captain Bill Hillgartner. My thanks also to Chief Leonard G. Butler, Lieutenants Raymond Smith and Clarence Hawthorne, and Sergeants McConnel Wood and Wilfred Tahy. If any technical details are wrong, it wasn't because they didn't try to teach me. Robert Rosebrough, author of *The San Juan Mountains*, loaned me his journal of a Ship Rock climb and gave me other help.

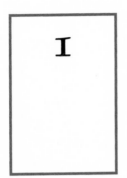

I

FROM WHERE BILL Buchanan sat with his back resting against the rough breccia, he could see the side of Whiteside's head, about three feet away. When John leaned back, Buchanan could see the snowcapped top of Mount Taylor looming over Grants, New Mexico, about eighty miles to the east. Now John was leaning forward, talking.

"This climbing down to climb back up, and climbing up so you can climb back down again," Whiteside said. "That seems like a poor way to get the job done. Maybe it's the only way to get to the summit, but I'll bet we could find a faster way down."

"Relax," Buchanan said. "Be calm. We're supposed to be resting."

They were perched on one of the few relatively flat outcrops of basalt in what climbers of Ship Rock call Rappel Gully. On the way up, it was the launching point for the final hard climb to the summit, a slightly tilted but flat surface of basalt about the size of a desktop and 1,721 feet above the prairie below. If you were going down, it was where you began a shorter but even harder almost vertical climb to reach the slope that led you downward with a fair chance of not killing yourself.

Buchanan, Whiteside, and Jim Stapp had just been to the summit. They had opened the army surplus ammo box that held the Ship Rock climbers' register and signed it, certifying their conquest of one of North

America's hard ones. Buchanan was tired. He was thinking that he was getting too old for this.

Whiteside was removing his climbing harness, laying aside the nylon belt and the assortment of pitons, jumars, etriers, and carabiners that make reaching such mountaintops possible.

He did a deep knee bend, touched his toes, and stretched. Buchanan watched, uneasy.

"What are you doing?"

"Nothing," Whiteside said. "Actually, I'm following the instructions of that rock climber's guide you're always threatening to write. I am getting rid of all nonessential weight before making an unprotected traverse."

Buchanan sat up. He played in a poker game in which Whiteside was called "Two-Dollar John" because of his unshakable faith that the dealer would give him the fifth heart if he needed one. Whiteside enjoyed taking risks.

"Traversing what?" Buchanan asked.

"I'm just going to ease over there and take a look." He pointed along the face of the cliff. "Get out there maybe a hundred feet and you can see down under the overhang and into the honeycomb formations. I can't believe there's not some way to rappel right on down."

"You're looking for some way to kill yourself," Buchanan said. "If you're in such a damn hurry to get down, get yourself a parachute."

"Rappelling down is easier than up," Whiteside said. He pointed across the little basin to where Stapp was preparing to begin hauling himself up the basalt wall behind them. "I'll just be a few minutes." He began moving with gingerly care out onto the cliff face.

Buchanan was on his feet. "Come on, John! That's too damn risky."

"Not really," Whiteside said. "I'm just going out far enough to see past the overhang. Just a peek at what it looks like. Is it all this broken-up breccia or is there, maybe, a big old finger of basalt sticking up that we could scramble right on down?"

Buchanan slid along the wall, getting closer, admiring Whiteside's technique if not his judgment. The man was moving slowly along the cliff, body almost perfectly vertical, his toes holding his weight on perhaps an inch of sloping stone, his fingers finding the cracks, crevices, and rough spots that would help him keep his balance if the wind gusted. He was doing the traverse perfectly. Beautiful to watch. Even the body was perfect for the purpose. A little smaller and slimmer than Buchanan's. Just bone, sinew, and muscle, without an ounce of surplus weight, moving like an insect against the cracked basalt wall.

And a thousand feet below him—no, a quarter of a mile below him lay what Stapp liked to call "the surface of the world." Buchanan looked out at it. Almost directly below, two Navajos on horseback were riding along the base of the monolith—tiny figures that put the risk of what Whiteside was doing into terrifying perspective. If he slipped, Whiteside would die, but not for a while. It would take time for a body to drop six hundred feet, then to bounce from an outcrop, and fall again, and bounce and fall, until it finally rested among the boulders at the bottom of this strange old volcanic core.

Buchanan looked away from the riders and from the thought. It was early afternoon, but the autumn sun was far to the north and the shadow of Ship Rock already stretched southeastward for miles across the tan prairie. Winter would soon end the climbing season. The sun was already so low that it reflected only from the very tip of Mount Taylor. Eighty miles to the north early snows had already packed the higher peaks in Colorado's San Juans. Not a cloud anywhere. The sky was a deep dry-country blue; the air was cool and, a rarity at this altitude, utterly still.

The silence was so absolute that Buchanan could hear the faint sibilance of Whiteside's soft rubber shoe sole as he shifted a foot along the stone. A couple of hundred feet below him, a red-tailed hawk drifted along, riding an updraft of air along the cliff face. From behind him came the click of Stapp fastening his rappelling gear.

This is why I climb, Buchanan thought. To get so far away from Stapp's "surface of the earth" that I can't even hear it. But Whiteside climbs for the thrill of challenging death. And now he's out about thirty yards. It's just too damn risky.

"That's far enough, John," Buchanan said. "Don't press your luck."

"Two more feet to a handhold," Whiteside said. "Then I can take a look."

He moved. And stopped. And looked down.

"There's more of that honeycomb breccia under the overhang," he said, and shifted his weight to allow a better head position. "Lot of those little erosion cavities, and it looks like some pretty good cracking where you can see the basalt." He shifted again. "And a pretty good shelf down about—"

Silence. Then Whiteside said, "I think I see a helmet."

"What?"

"My God!" Whiteside said. "There's a skull in it."

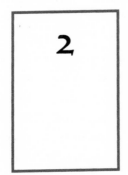

2

T HE WHITE PORSCHE looming in the rearview mirror of his pickup distracted Jim Chee from his gloomy thoughts. Chee had been rolling southward down Highway 666 toward Salt Creek Wash at about sixty-five miles per hour, which was somewhat more than the law he was paid to uphold allowed. But Navajo Tribal Police protocol this season was permitting speeders about that much margin of error. Besides, traffic was very light, it was past quitting time (the mid-November sunset was turning the clouds over the Carrizo Mountains a gaudy pink), and he saved both gasoline and wear on the pickup's tired old engine by letting it accelerate downhill, thereby gathering momentum for the long climb over the hump between the wash and Shiprock.

But the driver of the Porsche was making a lot more than a tolerable mistake. He was doing about ninety-five. Chee picked the portable blinker light off the passenger-side floorboard, switched it on, rolled down the window, and slapped its magnets against the pickup roof. Just as the Porsche whipped past.

He was instantly engulfed in cold air and road dust. He rolled up the window and jammed his foot down on the accelerator. The speedometer needle reached 70 as he crossed Salt Creek Wash, crept up to almost 75, and then wavered back to 72 as the upslope gravity and engine fatigue took their toll. The Porsche was almost a mile up the hill by now. Chee reached for the mike, clicked it on, and got the Shiprock dispatcher.

"Shiprock," the voice said. "Go ahead, Jim."

This would be Alice Notabah, the veteran. The other dispatcher, who was young and almost as new on the job as was Chee, always called him Lieutenant.

"Go ahead," Alice repeated, sounding slightly impatient.

"Just a speeder," Chee said. "White Porsche Targa, Utah tags, south on triple six into Shiprock. No big deal." The driver probably hadn't seen his blinker. No reason to look in your rearview when you pass a rusty pickup. Still, it added another minor frustration to the day's harvest. Trying to chase the sports car would have been simply humiliating.

"Ten four," Alice said. "You coming in?"

"Going home," Chee said.

"Lieutenant Leaphorn was in looking for you," Alice said.

"What'd he want?" It was actually former lieutenant Leaphorn now. The old man had retired last summer. Finally. After about a century. Still, retired or not, hearing that Leaphorn was looking for him made Chee feel uneasy and begin examining his conscience. He'd spent too many years working for the man.

"He just said he'd catch you later," Alice said. "You sound like you had a bad day."

"Just a total blank," Chee agreed. But that wasn't accurate. It was worse than blank. First there had been the episode with the kid in the Ute Mountain Tribal Police uniform (Chee balked at thinking of him as a policeman), and then there was Mrs. Twosalt.

Cocky kid. Chee had been parked high on the slope below Popping Rock where his truck was screened from view by brush and he had a long view of the oil field roads below. He'd been watching a mud-spattered blue two-ton GMC pickup parked at a cattle guard about a mile below him. Chee had dug out his binoculars and focused them, and was trying to determine why the driver had parked there and if anyone was sitting on the passenger's side. All he was seeing was dirt on the windshield.

About then the kid had said "*Hey!*" in a loud voice, and when Chee had turned, there he was, about six feet away, staring at him through dark and shiny sunglasses.

"What's you doing?" the kid had asked, and Chee had recognized that he was wearing what looked like a brand-new Ute Mountain Tribal Police uniform.

"I'm watching birds," Chee said, and tapped the binoculars.

Which the kid hadn't found amusing.

"Let's see some identification," he'd said. That was all right with Chee. It was proper procedure when you run across something that maybe looks suspicious. He'd fished out his Navajo Tribal Police identification folder, wishing he hadn't made the smart-aleck remark about bird-watching. It was just the sort of wisecrack cops heard every day and resented. He wouldn't have done it, he thought, if the kid hadn't sneaked up on him so efficiently. That was embarrassing.

The kid looked at the folder, from Chee's photograph to Chee's face. Neither seemed to please him.

"Navajo police?" he'd said. "What's you doing out here on the Ute reservation?"

And then Chee politely explained to the kid that they weren't on the Ute reservation. They were on Navajo land, the border being maybe a half mile or so east of them. And the kid had sort of smirked and said Chee was lost, the border was at least a mile the other way, and he'd pointed down the slope. The argument that might have started would have been totally pointless, so Chee had said good-bye and climbed back into his truck. He had driven away, thoroughly pissed off, remembering that the Utes were the enemy in a lot of Navajo mythology and understanding why. He was also thinking he had handled that encounter very poorly for an acting lieutenant, which he had been now for almost three weeks. And that led him to think of Janet Pete, who was why he'd worked for this promotion. Thinking of Janet always cheered him up a little. The day would surely get better.

It didn't. Next came Old Lady Twosalt.

Just like the Ute cop, she'd walked right up behind him without him hearing a thing. She caught him standing in the door of the school bus parked beside the Twosalt hogan, and there wasn't a damn thing he could do but continue standing there, stammering and stuttering, explaining that he'd honked his horn, and waited around and hollered, and did all the polite things one does to protect another's privacy when one visits a house in mostly empty country. And then he'd finally decided that nobody was home. Finally, too, he stopped talking.

Mrs. Twosalt had just stood there, looking politely away from him while he talked instead of looking into his eyes—which is the traditional Navajo way of suggesting disbelief. And when he'd finally finished, she went right to the heart of it.

"I was out looking after the goats," she said. "But what are you looking for in my school bus? You think you lost something in there, or what?"

What Chee was looking for in the school bus was some trace of cow manure, or cow hair, or wool, or any other evidence that the vehicle had been used to haul animals other than schoolkids. It involved the same problem that had him peering through his binoculars at the big pickup over by Popping Rock. Cattle were disappearing from grazing land in the jurisdiction of the Shiprock agency, and Captain Largo had made stopping this thievery the first priority of Chee's criminal investigation division. He put it ahead of dope dealing at the junior college, a gang shooting, bootlegging, and other crimes that Chee felt were more interesting.

He'd rolled out of the cot in his trailer house in the cold dawn this morning, put on his jeans and work jacket, and fired up the old truck intending to spend the day incognito, just prowling around looking for the kind of vehicles into which those cattle might be disappearing.

The GMC pickup was a natural. It was a fifth-wheel model designed to pull heavy trailers and known to be favored by serious rustlers who like to do their stealing in wholesale, trailer-load lots. But he'd just happened to notice the school bus while jolting down the trail from Popping Rock, and just happened to remember the Two salt outfit not only raised cattle but had a shaky reputation, and just happened to wonder what they would want with an old school bus anyway. None of that helped him come up with the answer for which Mrs. Twosalt had stood there waiting.

"I was just curious," Chee said. "I used to ride one of these things to school when I was a kid. I was wondering if they'd changed them any." He produced a weak laugh.

Mrs. Twosalt hadn't seemed to share his amusement. She waited, looked at him, waited some more—giving him a chance to change his story and to offer a more plausible explanation for this visit.

In default of a better idea, Chee had fished out his identification folder.

He'd said he'd come by to learn if the Twosalts were missing any cattle or sheep or had seen anything suspicious. Mrs. Twosalt said she kept good track of all their animals. Nothing was missing. And that had been the end of that except for the lingering embarrassment.

It was almost dark as he topped the hill and looked down at the scattering of lights of Shiprock town. No sign of the Porsche. Chee yawned. What a day! He turned off the pavement onto the gravel road, which led to the dirt road, which led to the weedy track down to his trailer under the cottonwoods beside the San Juan River. He rubbed his eyes, yawned again. He'd warm up what was left of his breakfast coffee, open a can of chili, and hit the sack early. A bad day, but now it was over.

No, it wasn't. His headlights reflected off a windshield, off a dusty car parked just past his trailer. Chee recognized it. Former lieutenant Joe Leaphorn, as promised, had caught him later.

3

CHEE'S TRAILER HAD been chilly when he left it at dawn. Now it was frigid, having leaked what little warmth it had retained into the chill that settled along the San Juan River. Chee lit the propane heater and started the coffee.

Joe Leaphorn was sitting stiff and straight on the bench behind the table. He put his hat on the Formica tabletop and rubbed his hand through his old-fashioned crew cut, which had become appropriately gray. Then he re-placed the hat, looked uneasy, and took it off again. To Chee the hat looked as weatherworn as its owner.

"I hate to bother you like this," Leaphorn said, and paused. "By the way, congratulations on the promotion."

"Thanks," Chee said. He glanced around from the coffeepot, where the hot water was still dripping through the grounds, and hesitated. But what the hell. It had not seemed plausible when he'd heard it, but why not find out?

"People tell me you recommended me for it."

If Leaphorn heard that, it didn't show on his face. He was watching his folded hands, the thumbs of which he had engaged in circling each other.

"It gets you lots of work and worry," Leaphorn said, "and not much pay goes with the job."

Chee extracted two mugs from the cabinet, put the one advertising the *Farmington Times* in front of Leaphorn, and looked for the sugar bowl.

"How you enjoying your retirement?" Chee asked. Which was a sort of oblique way of getting the man to the point of this visit. This wouldn't be a social call. No way. Leaphorn had always been the boss and Chee had been the gofer. One way or another this visit would involve law enforcement and something Leaphorn wanted Chee to do about it.

"Well, being retired there's a lot less aggravation," Leaphorn said. "You don't have to put up with—" He shrugged and chuckled.

Chee laughed, but it was forced. He wasn't used to this strange new version of Leaphorn. This Leaphorn, come to ask him for something, hesitant and diffident, wasn't the Lieutenant Leaphorn he remembered with a mixture of puzzlement, irritation, and admiration. Seeing the man as a supplicant made him uneasy. He'd put a stop to that.

"I remember when you told me you were retiring, you said if I ever needed to pick your brains for anything, to feel free to ask," Chee said. "So I'm going to ask you what you know about the cattle-rustling business."

Leaphorn considered, thumbs still circling. "Well," he said, "I know there's always some of it going on. And I know your boss and his family have been in the cow business for about three generations. So he probably doesn't care much for cow thieves." He stopped watching his thumbs and looked up at Chee. "You having a run of it up here? Anything big?"

"Nothing very big. The Conroy ranch lost eight heifers last month. That was the worst. Had six or seven other complaints in the past two months. Mostly one or two missing, and some of them probably just strayed off. But Captain Largo tells me it's worse than usual."

"Enough to get Largo stirred up," Leaphorn said. "His family has grazing leases scattered around over on the Checkerboard."

Chee grinned.

"I'll bet you already knew that," Leaphorn said, and chuckled.

"I did," Chee said, and poured the coffee.

Leaphorn sipped.

"I don't think I know anything about catching rustlers that Captain Largo hasn't already told you," Leaphorn said. "Now we have the Navajo Rangers, and since cattle are a tribal resource and their job is protecting tribal resources, it's really their worry. But the rangers are a real small group and they tend to be tied up with game poachers and people vandal-izing the parks, or stealing timber, or draining off drip gasoline. That sort of thing. Not enough rangers to go around, so you work with whoever the New Mexico Cattle Sanitary Board has covering this district, and the Ari-zona Brand Inspection Office, and the Colorado people. And you keep an eye out for strange trucks and horse trailers." Leaphorn looked up and shrugged. "Not much you can do. I never had much luck catching 'em, and the few times I did, we could never get a conviction."

"I don't think I'm going to get much return on the time I've been in-vesting in it either," Chee said.

"I bet you're already doing everything I suggested." Leaphorn added sugar to his coffee, sipped, looked at Chee over the rim. "And then, of course, you're getting into the ceremonial season, and you know how that works. Somebody's having a sing. They need to feed all those kinfolks and friends who come to help with the cure. Lots of hungry people and maybe you have them for a whole week if it's a full-fledged ceremony. You know what they say in New Mexico: nobody eats his own beef."

"Yeah," Chee said. "Looking through the reports for the past years I noticed the little one or two animal thefts go up when the thunderstorms stop and the sings begin."

"I used to just snoop around a little. Maybe I'd find some fresh hides with the wrong brands on 'em. But you know there's not much use ar-resting anybody for that. I'd just say a word or two to let 'em know we'd caught 'em, and then I'd tell the owner. And if he was Navajo, he'd figure that he should have known they needed a little help and butchered some-thing for them and saved 'em the trouble of stealing it."

Leaphorn stopped, knowing he was wasting time.

"Good ideas," Chee said, knowing he wasn't fooling Leaphorn. "Any-thing I can do for you?"

"It's nothing important," Leaphorn said. "Just something that's been sort of sticking in my mind for years. Just curiosity really."

Chee tried his own coffee and found it absolutely delicious. He waited for Leaphorn to decide how he wanted to ask this favor.

"It was eleven years this fall," Leaphorn said. "I was assigned to the Chinle office then and we had a young man disappear from the lodge at Canyon de Chelly. Fellow named Harold Breedlove. He and his wife were there celebrating their fifth wedding anniversary. His birthday, too. The way his wife told it, he got a telephone call. He tells her he has to meet someone about a business deal. He says he'll be right back and he drives off in their car. He doesn't come back. Next morning she calls the Arizona Highway Patrol. They call us."

Leaphorn paused, understanding that such a strong reaction to what seemed like nothing more sinister than a man taking a vacation from his wife needed an explanation. "They're a big ranching family. The Breedloves. The Lazy B ranch up in Colorado, leases in New Mexico and Arizona, all sorts of mining interests, and so forth. The old man ran for Congress once. Anyway, we put out a description of the car. It was a new green Land Rover. Easy to spot out here. And about a week later an officer spots it. It had been left up an arroyo beside that road that runs from 191 over to the Sweetwater chapter house."

"I'm sort of remembering that case now," Chee said. "But very dimly. I was new then, working way over at Crownpoint." And, Chee thought, having absolutely nothing to do with the Breedlove case. So where could this conversation possibly be leading?

"No sign of violence at the car, that right?" Chee asked. "No blood. No weapon. No note. No nothing."

"Not even tracks," Leaphorn said. "A week of wind took care of that."

"And nothing stolen out of the car, if I remember it right," Chee said. "Seems like I remember somebody saying it still had an expensive audio system in it, spare tire, everything still there."

Leaphorn sipped his coffee, thinking. Then he said, "So it seemed then. Now I don't know. Maybe some mountain climbing equipment was stolen."

"Ah," Chee said. He put down the coffee cup. Now he understood where Leaphorn was heading.

"That skeleton up on Ship Rock," Leaphorn said. "All I know about it is what I read in the *Gallup Independent*. Do you have any identification yet?"

"Not that I know of," Chee said. "There's no evidence of foul play, but Captain Largo got the FBI laboratory people to take a look at everything. Last I heard, they hadn't come up with anything."

"Nothing much but bare bones to work with, I heard," Leaphorn said.

"And what was left of the clothing. I guess people who climb mountains don't take along their billfolds."

"Or engraved jewelry," Chee added. "Or anything else they're not using. At least this guy didn't."

"You get an estimate on his age?"

"The pathologist said between thirty and thirty-five. No sign of any health problems which affected bone development. I guess you don't expect health problems in people who climb mountains. And he probably grew up someplace with lots of fluoride in the drinking water."

Leaphorn chuckled. "Which means no fillings in his teeth and no help from any dental charts."

"We had lots of that kind of luck on this one," Chee said.

Leaphorn drained his cup, put it down. "How was he dressed?"

Chee frowned. It was an odd question. "Like a mountain climber," he said. "You know. Special boots with those soft rubber soles, all the gear hanging off of him."

"I was thinking about the season," Leaphorn said. "Black as that Ship Rock is, the sun gets it hot in the summer—even up there a mile and a half above sea level. And in the winter, it gets coated with ice. The snow packs in where it's shaded. Layers of ice form."

"Yeah," Chee said. "Well, this guy wasn't wearing cold-weather gear. Just pants and a long-sleeved shirt. Maybe some sort of thermal underwear, though. He was on a sort of shelf a couple of hundred feet below the peak. Way too high for the coyotes to get to him, but the buzzards and ravens had been there."

"Did the rescue team bring everything down? Was there anything that you'd expect to find that wasn't there? I mean, you'd expect to find if you knew anything about the gear climbers carry."

"As far as I know nothing was missing," Chee said. "Of course, stuff may have fallen down into cracks. The birds would have scattered things around."

"A lot of rope, I guess," Leaphorn said.

"Quite a bit," Chee said. "I don't know how much would be normal. I know climbing rope stretches a lot. Largo sent it to the FBI lab to see if they could tell if a knot slipped, or it broke, or what."

"Did they bring down the other end?"

"Other end?"

Leaphorn nodded. "If it broke, there'd be the other end. He would have had it secured someplace. A piton driven in or tied to something secure. In case he slipped."

"Oh," Chee said. "The climbers who went up for the bones didn't find it. I doubt if they looked. Largo asked them to go up and bring down the body. And I remember they thought there'd have to be two bodies. Nobody would be crazy enough to climb Ship Rock alone. But they didn't find another one. I guess our fallen man was that crazy."

"Sounds like it," Leaphorn said.

Chee poured them both some more coffee, looked at Leaphorn and said, "I guess this Harold Breedlove was a mountain climber. Am I right?"

"He was," Leaphorn said. "But if he's your fallen man, he wasn't a very smart one."

"You mean climbing up there alone."

"Yeah," Leaphorn said. "Or if he wasn't alone, climbing with someone who'd go off and leave him."

"I've thought about that," Chee said. "The rescue crew said he'd either climbed up to the ledge, which they didn't think would be possible without help, or tried to rappel down from above. But the skeleton was intact. Nothing broken." Chee shook his head.

"If someone was with him, why didn't they report it? Get help? Bring down the body? You have any thoughts about that?"

"Yeah," Chee said. "Makes no sense either way."

Leaphorn sipped coffee. Considered.

"I'd like to know more about this climbing gear you said was stolen out of Breedlove's car," Chee said.

"I said it might have been stolen, and maybe from the car," Leaphorn said.

Chee waited.

"About a month after the guy vanished, we caught a kid from Many Farms breaking into a tourist's car parked at one of the Canyon de Chelly overlooks. He had a bunch of other stolen stuff at his place, car radios, mobile phones, tape decks, so forth, including some mountain climbing gear. Rope, pitons, whatever they call those gadgets. By then we'd been looking for Breedlove long enough to know he was a climber. The boy claimed he found the stuff where runoff had uncovered it in an arroyo bottom. We had him take us out and show us. It was about five hundred yards upstream from where we'd found Breedlove's car."

Chee considered this.

"Did you say the car hadn't been broken into?"

"It wasn't locked when we found it. The stuff kids usually take was still there."

Chee made a wry face. "You have any idea why he'd just take the climbing gear?"

"And leave the stuff he could sell? I don't know," Leaphorn said. He picked up his cup, noticed it was empty, put it down again.

"I heard you're getting married," he said. "Congratulations."

"Thanks. You want a refill?"

"A very pretty lady," Leaphorn said. "And smart. A good lawyer." He held out his cup.

Chee laughed. "I never heard you use that adjective talking about a lawyer before. Anyway, not about a defense lawyer." Janet Pete worked for Dinebeiina Nahiilna be Agaditahe, which translates more or less literally as "People who talk fast and help people" and was more likely to be called DNA, or public defenders, or with less polite language by Navajo Police.

"Has to be a first time for everything," Leaphorn said. "And Miss Pete—" Leaphorn couldn't think of a way to finish that sentence.

Chee took his cup and refilled it.

"I hope you'll let me know if anything interesting turns up on your fallen man."

That surprised Chee. Wasn't it finished now? Leaphorn had found his missing man. Largo's fallen man was identified. Case closed. What else interesting would there be?

"You mean if we check out the Breedlove identification and the skeleton turns out to be the wrong size, or wrong race, or Breedlove had false teeth? Or what?"

"Yeah," Leaphorn said. But he still sat there, holding his replenished coffee cup. This conversation wasn't finished. Chee waited, trying to deduce the way it would be going.

"Did you have a suspect? I guess the widow would be one?"

"There seemed to be a good reason for it in this case. But that didn't pan out. Then there was a cousin. A Washington lawyer named George Shaw. Who just happened to also be a mountain climber, and just happened to be out here and looked just perfect as the odd man in a love triangle if you wanted one. He said he'd come out to talk to Breedlove about some sort of mineral lease proposal on the Lazy B ranch. That seemed to be true from what I could find out. Shaw was representing the family's business interests and a mining company was dickering for a lease."

"With Harold? Did he own the place?"

Leaphorn laughed. "He'd just inherited it. Three days before he disappeared."

"Well, now," Chee said, and thought about it while Leaphorn sipped his coffee.

"Did you see the report on the shooting over at Canyon de Chelly the other day?" Leaphorn asked. "An old man named Amos Nez shot apparently by somebody up on the rim?"

"I saw it," Chee said. It was an odd piece of business. Nez had been hit in the side. He'd fallen off his horse still holding the reins. The next shot hit the horse in the head. It had fallen partly across Nez and then four more shots had been fired. One hit Nez in the forearm and then he had pulled himself into cover behind the animal. The last Chee'd seen on it, six empty 30.06 cartridges had been recovered among the boulders up on the rim. As far as Chee knew that's where the trail in this case ended. No suspects. No motive. Nez was listed in fair condition at the Chinle hospital— well enough to say he had no idea why anyone would want to shoot him.

"That's what stirred me up," Leaphorn said. "Old Hosteen Nez was one of the last people to see this Hal Breedlove before he disappeared."

"Quite a coincidence," Chee said. When he'd worked for Leaphorn at Window Rock, Leaphorn had told him never to believe in coincidences. Told him that often. It was one of the man's cardinal rules. Every effect had its cause. If it seemed to be connected and you couldn't find the link it just meant you weren't trying hard enough. But this sounded like an awfully strained coincidence.

"Nez was their guide in the canyon," Leaphorn said. "When the Breedloves were staying at the lodge he was one of the crew there. The Breedloves hired him to take them all the way up Canyon del Muerto one day, and the main canyon the next. I talked to him three times."

That seemed to Leaphorn to require some explanation.

"You know," he said. "Rich guy with a pretty young wife disappears for no reason. You ask questions. But Nez told me they seemed to like each other a lot. Having lots of fun. He said one time he'd been up one of the side canyons to relieve himself and when he came back it looked like she was crying and Breedlove was comforting her. So he waited a little before showing up and then everything was all right."

Chee considered. "What do you think? It could have been anything?"

"Yep," Leaphorn said, and sipped coffee. "Did I mention they were celebrating Breedlove's birthday? We found out that he'd turned thirty just the previous week, and when he turned thirty he inherited. His daddy left him the ranch but he put it into a family trust. It had a provision that the trustee controlled it until Breedlove got to be thirty years old. Then it was all his."

Chee considered again. "And the widow inherited from him?"

"That's what we found out. So she had a motive and we had the logical suspect."

"But no evidence," Chee guessed.

"None. Not only that. Just before Breedlove drove away, our Mr. Nez arrived to take them on another junket up the canyon. He remembered Breedlove apologized for missing out, paid him in advance, and gave him a fifty-dollar tip. Then Mrs. Breedlove and Nez took off. They spent the day sight-seeing. Nez remembered she was in a hurry when it was getting dark because she was supposed to meet Breedlove and another couple for dinner. But when they got back to the lodge, no car. That's the last Nez saw of her."

Leaphorn paused, looked at Chee, and added, "Or so he says."

"Oh?" Chee said.

"Well, I didn't mean he'd seen her again. It's just that I always had a feeling that Nez knew something he wasn't telling me. That's one reason I kept going back to talk to him."

"You think he had something to do with the disappearance. Maybe the two of them weren't up the canyon when Breedlove was supposed to be driving away?"

"Well, no," Leaphorn said. "People staying at the lodge saw them coming out of the canyon in Nez's truck about seven P.M. Then a little after seven, she went over to the lodge and asked if Breedlove had called in. About seven-thirty she's having dinner with the other couple. They remembered her being irritated about him being so late, mixed with a little bit of worry."

"I guess that's what they call an airtight alibi," Chee said. "So how long did it take her to get old Hal declared legally dead so she could marry her coconspirator? And would I be wrong if I guessed that would be George Shaw?"

"She's still a widow, last I heard," Leaphorn said. "She offered a ten-thousand-dollar reward and after a while upped it to twenty thousand and didn't petition to get her husband declared legally dead until five years later. She lives up near Mancos, Colorado. She and her brother run the Lazy B now."

"You know what?" Chee said. "I think I know those people. Is the brother Eldon Demott?"

"That's him."

"He's one of our customers," Chee said. "The ranch still has those public land leases you mentioned on the Checkerboard Reservation and they've been losing Angus calves. He thinks maybe some of us Navajos might be stealing them."

"Eldon is Elisa Breedlove's older brother," Leaphorn said. "Their daddy was old man Breedlove's foreman, and when their daddy died, I think Eldon just sort of inherited the job. Anyway, the Demott family lived on the ranch. I guess that's how Elisa and the Breedlove boy got together."

Chee stifled a yawn. It had been a long and tiring day and this session with Leaphorn, helpful as it had been, didn't qualify as relaxation. He had accumulated too many memories of tense times trying to live up to the man's high expectations. It would be a while before he could relax in Leaphorn's presence. Maybe another twenty years would do it.

"Well," Chee said. "I guess that takes care of the fallen man. I've got a probable identification of our skeleton. You've located your missing Hal Breedlove. I'll call you when we get it confirmed."

Leaphorn drained his cup, got up, adjusted his hat.

"I thank you for the help," he said.

"And you for yours."

Leaphorn opened the door, admitting a rush of cold air, the rich perfume of autumn, and a reminder that winter was out there somewhere, like the coyote, just waiting.

"All we need to do now—" he said, and stopped, looking embarrassed. "All that needs to be done," he amended, "is find out if your bones really are my Breedlove, and then find out how the hell he got from that abandoned Land Rover about a hundred fifty miles west, and way up there to where he could fall off of Ship Rock."

"And why," Chee said. "And how he did it all by himself."

"If he did," Leaphorn said.

THE STRANGE TRUCK parked in one of the Official Visitor slots at the Shiprock headquarters of the Navajo Tribal Police wore a New Jersey license and looked to Jim Chee anything but official. It had dual back wheels and carried a cumbersome camper, its windows covered by decals that certified visitation at tourist traps from Key West to Vancouver Island. Other stickers plastered across the rear announced that A BAD DAY FISHING IS BETTER THAN A GOOD DAY AT WORK, and declared the camper-truck to be OUR CHILDREN'S INHERITANCE. Bumper decals exhorted viewers to VISUALIZE WHIRLED PEAS and to TRY RANDOM ACTS OF KINDNESS, and endorsed the National Rifle Association. A broad band of silver duct tape circled the camper's rear panel, sealing the dust out of the joint and giving the camper a ramshackle, homemade look.

Chee stuck his head into Alice Notabah's dispatcher office and indicated the truck with a nod: "Who's the Official Visitor?"

Notabah nodded toward Largo's office. "In with the captain," she said. "And he wants to see you."

The man who drove the truck was sitting in the comfortable chair Captain Largo kept for important visitors. He held a battered black hat with a silver concha band in his lap and looked relaxed and comfortable.

"I'll catch you later," Chee said, but Largo waved him in.

"I want you to meet Dick Finch," Largo said. "He's the New Mexico brand inspector working the Four Corners, and he's been getting some complaints."

Chee and Finch shook hands. "Complaints?" Chee said. "Like what?"

"'Bout what you'd expect for a brand inspector to get," Finch said. "People missing their cattle. Thinking maybe somebody's stealing 'em."

Finch grinned when he said it, eliminating some of the sting from the sarcasm.

"Yeah," Chee said, "we've been hearing some of that, too."

Finch shrugged. "Folks always say that nobody likes to eat his own beef. But it's got a little beyond that, I think. With bred heifers going at sixty dollars a hundred pounds, it just takes three of 'em to make you a grand larceny."

Captain Largo was looking sour. "Sixty dollars a hundred, like hell," he said. "More like a thousand dollars a head for me. I've been trying to raise purebred stock." He nodded in Chee's direction. "Jim here is running our criminal investigation division. He's been working on it."

Largo waited. So did Finch.

"I'm here on something else now," Chee said finally. "I think we may have an identification on that skeleton that was found up on Ship Rock."

"Well, now," Largo said. "Where'd that come from?"

"Joe Leaphorn remembered a missing person case he had eleven years ago. The man disappeared from Canyon de Chelly but he was a mountain climber."

"Leaphorn," Largo said. "I thought old Joe was supposed to be retired."

"He is," Chee said.

"Eleven years is a hell of a long time to remember a missing person case," Largo said. "How many of those do we get in an average month?"

"Several," Chee said. "But most of 'em don't stay missing long."

Largo nodded. "So who's the man?"

"Harold Breedlove was the missing man. He used to own the Lazy B ranch south of Mancos. Or his family owned it."

"Fella named Eldon Demott owns it now," Finch said. "Runs a lot of Herefords down in San Juan County. Has some deeded land and some BLM leases and a big home place up in Colorado."

"What have you got beyond this Breedlove fella's been missing long enough to become a skeleton and him being a climber?" Largo asked.

Chee explained what Leaphorn had told him.

"Just that?" Largo asked, and thought a moment. "Well, it could be right. It sounds like it is and Joe Leaphorn never was much for being wrong. Did Joe have any notion why this guy left his wife at the canyon? Or why he'd be climbing Ship Rock all by himself?"

"He didn't say, but I think he figures maybe Breedlove wasn't alone up there. And maybe the widow knew more than she was telling him at the time."

"And what's that about Amos Nez getting shot last week down at Canyon de Chelly? You lost me on that connection."

"It was sort of thin," Chee said. "Nez happened to be one of the witnesses in the disappearance case. Leaphorn said he was the last person known to have seen Breedlove alive. Except for the widow."

Largo considered. Grinned. "And she was Joe's suspect, of course," he said. And shook his head. "Joe never could believe in coincidences."

"They still had that mountain climbing gear in the evidence room at Window Rock and I had them send it up," Chee said. "It looks to me a lot like the gear they found on our Fallen Man, so I called Mrs. Breedlove up at Mancos."

"What'd she say?"

"She'd gone into town for something. The housekeeper said she'd be back in a couple of hours. I left word that I was coming up this afternoon to show her some stuff that might bear on her missing husband."

Finch cleared his throat, glanced up at Chee. "While you're there why not just kind of keep your eyes open? Tell 'em you've heard good things about the way they run their place. Look around. You know?"

Finch looked to Chee to be about fifty. He had a hollowed scar high on his right cheek (resulting, Chee guessed, from some sort of surgery), small, bright blue eyes, and a complexion burned and cracked by the Four Corners weather. He was waiting now for Chee's response to this suggestion.

"You think Demott's sort of augmenting his herd with some strangers?" Chee asked.

"Well, not exactly," Finch said, and shrugged. "But who knows? People losing their cattle. Maybe the coyotes are getting 'em. Maybe Demott's got fifteen or twenty head he's shipping off to the feedlot and he thinks it would be nice to round it off at twenty or twenty-five. No harm in looking. Seeing what you can see."

"I'll do that," Chee said. "But were you telling me you don't have anything specific against Demott?"

Finch was studying Chee, looking quizzical. He's trying to decide, Chee thought, how stupid I am.

"Nothing I could take in to a judge and get a search warrant with. But you hear things." With that, Finch broke into a chuckle. "Hell, you hear things about everybody." He jerked a thumb at Largo. "I've even been told that your captain here has some peculiar-looking brands on some of his stock. That right, Captain?"

"I've heard that myself," Largo said, grinning. "We have a barbecue over at the place, all the neighbors want to go out and take a look at the cowhides."

"Well, it's a lot cheaper than buying beef at the butcher shop. So maybe somebody's eating Demott's sirloin and the Demotts are eating theirs."

"Or mutton," added Largo, who was missing some ewes as well as a calf or two.

"How about me going along for the ride?" Finch said. "I mean up to the Lazy B?"

"Why not?" Chee said.

"You wouldn't have to introduce me, you know. I'll just sort of get out and stretch my legs. Look around a little bit. You never know what you might see."

5

THEY CAME INTO view of the headquarters of the Lazy B with the autumn sun low over Mesa Verde, producing shadow patterns on Bridge Timber Mountain. Chee had been thinking more of home sites lately and he thought now that this little valley would be a beautiful place for Janet and him. The house in the cluster of cottonwoods below them would be far, far too large for him to feel comfortable in. But Janet would love it.

Finch had been doing the talking on the drive up from Shiprock. After the first fifty miles of that, Chee began listening just enough to nod or grunt at the proper intervals. Mostly he was thinking about Janet Pete and the differences between what they liked and what they didn't. This house, for example. Women usually had most to say about living places, but if he retained veto power, theirs certainly wouldn't be anything as huge as the fieldstone, timber, and slate mansion the Breedlove family had built for itself. Even if they could afford it, which they certainly never would.

That reminded Chee of the white Porsche that had zipped past him yesterday. Why did he connect it to Janet? Because it had class, as did she. And was beautiful. And, sure, she'd like it. Who wouldn't? So why did he resent it? Was it because it was a part of the world she came from in which he would never be comfortable? Or understand? Maybe.

But now he was about to walk in and see if he could get a widow to identify a bunch of stuff that would tell her that her husband was truly dead. Tell her, that is, unless she already knew—having killed him herself. Or arranged it. He'd worry about the Porsche later. The Breedlove mansion was now just across the fence.

According to Finch, old Edgar Breedlove had built it as a second home—his first one being in Denver, from which he ran his mining operations. But he'd never lived in it. He'd bought the ranch because his prospectors had found a molybdenum deposit on the high end of the property. But the ore price fell after the war and somehow or other the place got left to a grandson, Harold. Hal had adopted his granddad's policy of overgrazing it and letting it run down.

"That ain't happening now," Finch had told him. "This place ain't going to go to hell while Demott's running it. He's sort of a tree-hugger. That's what people say. Say he never got married 'cause he's in love with this place."

Chee parked under a tree a polite distance from the front entrance, turned off the ignition, and sat, killing the time needed by hosts to get decent before welcoming guests. Finch, another empty-country man, seemed to understand that. He yawned, stretched, and examined the half dozen cows in the feedlot beside the barn with a professional eye.

"How do you know all this about the Breedlove ranch, and Demott and everything?" Chee asked. "This is Colorado. It's not your territory."

"Ranching—and stealing cows off of ranches—don't pay much attention to state lines," Finch said, not taking his eyes off the cows. "The Lazy B has leases in New Mexico. Makes 'em my business."

Finch extracted a twenty-stick pack of chewing gum from his jacket pocket, offered it to Chee, extracted two sticks for himself, and started chewing them. "Besides," he said, "you got to have something going to make the job interesting. I got one particular guy I keep looking for. Most of these cow thieves are 'hungries.' Folks run out of eating money, or got a payment due, and they go out and get themselves a cow or two to sell. Or, on the reservation, maybe they got somebody sick in the family, and they're having a sing for the patient, and they need a steer to feed all the kinfolks coming in. I never worried too much about them. If they keep doing it, they get careless and they get caught and the neighbors talk to them about it. Get it straightened out. But then there's some others who are in it for business. It's easy money and it beats working."

"Who's this one you're specially after?"

Finch laughed. "If I knew that, we wouldn't be talking about it, now would we?"

"I guess not," Chee said, impressed with how insulting Finch could be even when he was acting friendly.

"We'd just go out and get him then, wouldn't we?" Finch concluded. "But all I know about him is the way he operates. Modus operandi, if you know your Latin. He always picks the spread-out ranches where a few head won't be missed for a while. He always takes something that he can sell quick. No little calves that you have to wean, no big, expensive, easy-to-trace breeding bulls. Never messes with horses, 'cause some people get attached to a nag and go out looking for it. Has some other tricks, too. Like he finds a good place beside a back road where there wouldn't be any traffic to bother him and he'll put out feed. Usually good alfalfa hay. Do it several times so the cattle get in the habit of coming up and looking for it when they see his truck parking."

Finch stopped, looked at Chee, waited for a comment.

"Pretty smart," Chee said.

"Yes, sir," Finch agreed. "So far, he's been smarter than me."

Chee had no comment on that. He glanced at his watch. Another three minutes and he'd go ring the doorbell and get this job over with.

"Then I've found a place or two where he fixed up the fence so he could get 'em through it fast." He paused again, seeing if Chee understood this. Chee did, but to hell with Finch.

"You could cut the wire, of course," Finch explained, "but then the herd gets out on the road and somebody notices it right away and they do a head count and know some are missing."

Chee said, "Really?"

"Yeah," Finch said. "Anyway, I've been after this son of a bitch for years now. Every time I take off from home to come out this way, he's the one I'm thinking of."

Chee didn't comment.

"Zorro," Finch said. "That's what I call him. And this time I think I'll finally get him."

"How?"

Silence, unusual for Finch, followed. Then he said, "Well, now, that's sort of complicated."

"You think it might be Demott?"

"Why you say that?"

"Well, you wanted to come up here. And you've collected all that information about him."

"If you're a brand inspector you learn to pick up on all the gossip you can hear if you want to get your job done. And there was some talk that Demott paid off a mortgage by selling a bunch of calves nobody knew he owned."

"So what's the gossip about the widow Breedlove?" Chee asked. "Who was the lover who helped her kill her husband? What do the neighbors say about that?"

Finch was wearing a broad smile. "People I know up in Mancos have her down as the brokenhearted, wronged, abandoned bride. The majority of them, that is. They figured Hal ran off with some bimbo."

"How about the minority?"

"They think she had herself a local boyfriend. Somebody to keep her happy when Hal was off in New York, or climbing his mountains or playing his games."

"They have a name for him?"

"Not that I ever heard," Finch said.

"Which bunch you think is right?"

"About her? I never thought about it," Finch said. "None of my business, that part of it wasn't. Talk like that just means that folks around here didn't like Hal."

"What'd he do?"

"Well, for starters he got born in the East," Finch said. "That's two strikes on you right there. And he was raised there. Citified. Preppy type. Papa's boy. Ivy Leaguer. He didn't get any bones broke falling off horses, lose a finger in a hay baler. Didn't pay his dues, you know. You don't have to actually do anything to have folks down on you."

"How about the widow? You hear anything specific about her?"

"Don't hear nothing about her, except some fellas guessing. And she's a real pretty woman, so that was probably just them wishing," Finch said.

He was grinning at Chee. "You know how it works. If you're behaving yourself it's not interesting."

The front door of the Breedlove house opened and Chee could see someone standing behind the screen looking out at them. He picked up his evidence satchel and stepped out of the vehicle.

"I'll wait here for you," Finch said, "and maybe scout around a little if I get too stiff from sitting."

Mrs. Elisa Breedlove was indeed a real pretty woman. She seemed excited and nervous, which was what Chee had expected. Her handshake grip was hard, and so was the hand. She led him into a huge living room, dark and cluttered with heavy, old-fashioned furniture. She motioned him into a chair, explaining that she'd had to run into Mancos "to get some stuff."

"I got back just before you drove up and Ramona told me you'd called and were coming."

"I hope I'm not—" Chee began, but she cut him off.

"No. No," she said. "I appreciate this. Ramona said you'd found Hal. Or think so. But she didn't know anything else."

"Well," Chee said, and paused. "What we found was merely bones. We thought they might be Mr. Breedlove."

He sat on the edge of the sofa, watching her.

"Bones," she said. "Just a skeleton? Was that the skeleton they found about Halloween up on Ship Rock?"

"Yes, ma'am. We wanted to ask you to look at the clothing and equipment he was wearing and see if—tell us if it was the right size, and if you thought it was your husband's stuff."

"Equipment?" She was standing beside a table, her hand on it. The light slanting through windows on each side of the fireplace illuminated her face. It was a small, narrow face framed by light brown hair, the jaw muscles tight, the expression tense. Middle thirties, Chee guessed. Slender, perfectly built, luminous green eyes, the sort of classic beauty that survived sun, wind, and hard winters and didn't seem to require the disguise of makeup. But today she looked tired. He thought of a description Finch had applied to a woman they both knew: "Been rode hard and put up wet."

Mrs. Breedlove was waiting for an answer, her green eyes fixed on his face.

"Mountain climbing equipment," Chee said. "I understand the skeleton was in a cleft down the face of a cliff. Presumably, the man had fallen."

Mrs. Breedlove closed her eyes and bent slightly forward with her hips against the table.

Chee rose. "Are you all right?"

"All right," she said, but she put a hand against the table to support herself.

"Would you like to sit down? A drink of water?"

"Why do you think it's Hal?" Her eyes were still closed.

"He's been missing for eleven years. And we're told he was a mountain climber. Is that correct?"

"He was. He loved the mountains."

"This man was about five feet nine inches tall," Chee said. "The coroner estimated he would have weighed about one hundred and fifty pounds. He had perfect teeth. He had rather long fingers and—"

"Hal was about five eight, I'd say. He was slender, muscular. An athlete. I think he weighed about a hundred and sixty. He was worried about gaining weight." She produced a weak smile. "Around the belt line. Before we went on that trip, I let out his suit pants to give him another inch."

"He'd had a broken nose," Chee continued. "Healed. The doctor said it probably happened when he was an adolescent. And a broken wrist. He said that was more recent."

Mrs. Breedlove sighed. "The nose was from playing fraternity football, or whatever the boys play at Dartmouth. And the wrist when a horse threw him after we were married."

Chee opened the satchel, extracted the climbing equipment, and stacked it on the coffee table. There wasn't much: a nylon belt harness, the ragged remains of a nylon jacket, even more fragmentary remains of trousers and shirt, a pair of narrow shoes with soles of soft, smooth rubber, a little rock hammer, three pitons, and a couple of steel gadgets that Chee presumed were used somehow for controlling rope slippage.

When he glanced up, Mrs. Breedlove was staring at them, her face white. She turned away, facing the window but looking at nothing except some memory.

"I thought about Hal when I saw the piece the paper had on the skeleton," she said. "Eldon and I talked about it at supper that night. He thought the same thing I did. We decided it couldn't be Hal." She attempted a smile. "He was always into derring-do stuff. But he wouldn't try to climb Ship Rock alone. Nobody would. That would be insane. Two great rock men were killed on it, and they were climbing with teams of experienced experts."

She paused. Listening. The sound of a car engine came through the window. "That was before the Navajos banned climbing," she added.

"Are you a climber?"

"When I was younger," she said. "When Hal used to come out, Eldon started teaching him to climb. Hal and his cousin George. Sometimes I would go along and they taught me."

"How about Ship Rock?" Chee asked. "Did you ever climb it?"

She studied him. "The tribe prohibited that a long time ago. Before I was big enough to climb anything."

Chee smiled. "But some people still climbed it. Quite a few, from what I hear. And there's not actually a tribal ordinance against it. It's just that the tribe stopped issuing those 'back country' permits. You know, to allow non-Navajos the right to trespass."

Mrs. Breedlove looked thoughtful. Through the window came the sound of a car door slamming.

"To make it perfectly legal, you'd go see one of the local people who had a grazing permit running up to the base and get him to give you permission to be on the land," Chee added. "But most people even don't bother to do that."

Mrs. Breedlove considered this. Nodded. "We always got permission. I climbed it once. It was terrifying. With Eldon, Hal, and George. I still have nightmares."

"About falling?"

She shuddered. "I'm up there looking all around. Looking at Ute Mountain up in Colorado, and seeing the shape of Case del Eco Mesa in Utah, and the Carrizos in Arizona, and Mount Taylor, and I have this dreadful feeling that Ship Rock is getting higher and higher and then I know I can never get down." She laughed. "Fear of falling, I guess. Or fear of flying away and being lost forever."

"I guess you've heard our name for it," Chee said. "Tse´ Bit´ a´i´—the Rock with Wings. According to the legend it flew here from the north bringing the first Navajos on its back. Maybe it was flying again in your dream."

A voice from somewhere back in the house shouted: "Hey, Sis! Where are you? What's that Navajo police car doing parked out there?"

"We've got company," Mrs. Breedlove said, barely raising her voice. "In here."

Chee stood. A man wearing dusty jeans, a faded jean jacket with a torn sleeve, and well-worn boots walked into the room. He held a battered gray felt hat in his right hand.

"Mr. Chee," said Mrs. Breedlove, "this is my brother Eldon. Eldon Demott."

"Oh," Demott said. "Hello." He shifted his hat to his left hand and offered Chee the right one. His grip was like his sister's and his expression was a mixture of curiosity, worry, and fatigue.

"They think they've found Hal," Elisa Breedlove said. "You remember talking about that skeleton on Ship Rock. The Navajo police think it must be him."

Demott was eyeing the little stack of climbing equipment on the table. He sighed, slapped the hat against his leg. "I was wrong then, if it really is Hal," he said. "That makes him a better climber than I gave him credit for, climbing that sucker by himself and getting that high." He snorted. "And a hell of a lot crazier, too."

"Do you recognize any of this?" Chee asked, indicating the equipment.

Demott picked up the nylon belt and examined it. He was a small man. Wiry. A man built of sun-scorched leather, bone, and gristle, with a strong jaw and a receding hairline that made him look older than he probably was.

"It's pretty faded out but it used to be red," he said, and tossed it back to the tabletop. He looked at his sister, his face full of concern and sympathy. "Hal's was red, wasn't it?"

"It was," she said.

"You all right?"

"I'm fine," she said. "And how about this jumar? Didn't you fix one for Hal once?"

"By God," Demott said, and picked it up. It reminded Chee of an oversized steel pretzel with a sort of ratchet device connected. Chee had wondered about it and concluded that the ratchet would allow a rope to slip in one direction and not the other. Thus, it must be used to allow a climber to pull himself up a cliff. Demott obviously knew what it was for. He was examining the place where the ratchet had been welded to the steel.

"I remember I couldn't fix it. Hal and you took it into Mancos and had Gus weld it," Demott said to Elisa. "It sure looks like the same one."

"I guess we can close this up then," Chee said. "I don't see any reason for you going down to Shiprock to look at the bones. Unless you want to."

Demott was inspecting one of the climbing shoes. "The soles must be all the same," he said. "At least all I ever saw was just soft, smooth rubber like this. And his were white. And he had little feet, too." He glanced at Elisa. "How about the clothing? That look like Hal's?"

"The jacket, yes," she said. "I think that's Hal's jacket."

Something in her tone caused Chee to glance back at her. She held her lips pressed together, face tense, determined somehow not to cry. Her brother didn't see that. He was studying the artifacts on the table.

"It's pretty tore up," Demott said, poking the clothing with a finger. "You think coyotes? But from what the paper said, it would be too high for them."

"Way too high," Chee said.

"Birds, then," Demott said. "Ravens. Vultures and—" He cut that off, with a repentant glance at Elisa.

Chee picked up the evidence valise and stuffed the tattered clothing into it, getting it out of Elisa's sight.

"I think I should go to Shiprock," Elisa said. She looked away from Chee and out the window. "To take care of things. Hal would have wanted to be cremated, I think. And his ashes scattered in the San Juan Mountains."

"Yeah," Demott said. "Over in the La Plata range. On Mount Hesperus. That was his very favorite."

"We call it Dibe Nitsaa," Chee said. He thought of a dead man's ashes drifting down on serene slopes that the spirit called First Man had built to protect the Navajos from evil. First Man had decorated the mountain with jet-black jewelry to fend off all bad things. But what could protect it from the invincible ignorance of this white culture? These were good, kind people, he thought, who wouldn't knowingly use corpse powder, the Navajo symbol for the ultimate evil, to desecrate a holy place. But then climbing Ship Rock to prove that man was the dominating master of the universe was also a desecration.

"It's our Sacred Mountain of the North," Chee said. "Was that what Mr. Breedlove was trying to do? Put his feet on top of all our sacred places?" Having said it, Chee instantly regretted it. This was not the time or place to show his resentment.

He glanced at Demott, who was looking at him, surprised. But Elisa Breedlove was still staring out the window.

"Hal wasn't like that," she said. "He was just trying to find some happiness," she said. "Nobody had ever taught him anything about sacred things. The only god the Breedloves ever worshiped was cast out of gold."

"I don't think Hal knew anything about your mythology," Demott agreed. "It's just that Hesperus is over thirteen thousand feet and an easy climb. I like them high and easy and I guess Hal did, too."

Chee considered that. "Why Ship Rock, then? I know it's killed some people. I've heard it's one of the hardest climbs."

"Yeah," Demott said. "Why Ship Rock? And why by himself? And if he wasn't by himself, how come his friends just left him there? Didn't even report it."

Chee didn't comment on that. Elisa was still staring blindly out the window.

"How high did he get?" Demott asked.

Chee shrugged. "Close to the top, I think. I think the rescue party said the skeleton was just a couple hundred feet down from the crest."

"I knew he was good, but if he got that high all by himself he was even better than I thought," Demott said. "He'd gotten past the hardest parts."

"He'd always wanted to climb Ship Rock," Elisa said. "Remember?"

"I guess so," Demott said thoughtfully. "I remember him talking about climbing El Diente and Lizard's Head. I thought they were next on his agenda." He turned to Chee, frowning. "Have you fellows looked into who else he might have climbed with? I have trouble believing he did that alone. I guess he could have and he was reckless enough to try it. But it damn sure wouldn't be easy. Not getting that high."

"It's not a criminal case," Chee said. "We're just trying to close up an old missing person file."

"But who the hell would go off and leave a fallen man like that? Not even report so the rescue people could go get him? You think they was afraid you Navajos would arrest 'em for trespassing?" He shook his head. "Or the way things are now, maybe they thought they'd get sued." He laughed, put on his hat. "But I got to get moving. Good to meet you, Mr. Chee," he said, and was gone.

"I've got to be going, too," Chee said. He dumped the rest of the equipment in the valise.

She walked with him to the door, opened it for him. He pulled at the valise zipper, then stopped. He should really leave this stuff with her. She was the widow. It was her property.

"Mr. Chee," she said. "The skeleton. Were the bones all broken up?"

"No," Chee said. "Nothing broken. And all the joints were still articulated."

From Elisa's expression he first thought she didn't understand that anthropology jargon. "I mean, the skeleton was all together in one piece. And nothing was broken."

"Nothing was broken?" she repeated. "Nothing." And then he realized the expression reflected disbelief. And shock.

Why shock? Had Mrs. Breedlove expected her husband's body to be broken apart? Why would she? If he asked her why, she'd say it must have been a long fall.

He zipped the valise closed. He'd keep these artifacts from the Fallen Man, at least for a while.

6

H E MET JANET at the Carriage Inn in Farmington, halfway between his trailer at Shiprock and the San Juan County courthouse at Aztec where she had been defending a Checkerboard Reservation Navajo on a grand theft charge. He arrived late—but not very late—and her kidding about his watch being on Navajo time lacked its usual vigor. She looked absolutely used up, he thought. Beautiful but tired, and maybe the fatigue explained the diminution of the usual spark, of the delight he usually sensed in her when she first saw him. Or maybe it was because he was weary himself. Anyway, just being with her, seeing her across the table, cheered him. He took her hand.

"Janet, you work too hard," Chee said. "You should marry me and let me take you away from all this."

"I intend to marry you," she said, rewarding him with a weary smile. "You keep forgetting that. But all you do is keep making more work for me. Arresting these poor innocent people."

"That sounds to me like you won today," Chee said. "Charmed the jury again?"

"It didn't take any charm. This time it wouldn't have been reasonable to have even a reasonable doubt. His brother-in-law did it and the state cops totally screwed up the investigation."

"Do you have to go right back to Window Rock tomorrow? Why not take a day off? Tell 'em you are doing the post-trial paperwork. Maybe preparing a false arrest suit or something."

"Ah, Jim," she said. "I have to drive down there tonight."

"Tonight! That's crazy. That's more than two hours on a dangerous road," he said. "You're tired. Get some sleep. What's the hurry?"

She looked apologetic. Shrugged. "No choice, Jim. I'd love to stay over. Can't do it. Duty calls."

"Ah, come on," Chee said. "Duty can wait."

Janet squeezed his hand. "Really," she said. "I have to go to Washington. On a bunch of legal stuff with Justice and the Bureau of Indian Affairs. I have to be there day after tomorrow ready to argue." She shrugged, made a wry face. "So I have to pack tonight and drive to Albuquerque tomorrow to catch my plane."

Chee picked up the menu, said, "Like I've been telling you, you work way too hard." He tried to keep it out, but the disappointment again showed in his voice.

"And as I told you, it's the fault of you policemen," she said, smiling her tired smile. "Arresting too many innocent people."

"I haven't had much luck at arresting people lately," he said. "I can't even catch any guilty ones."

The Carriage Inn had printed a handsome menu on which nothing changed but the prices. Variety was provided by the cooks, who came and went. Chee decided to presume that the current one was adept at preparing Mexican foods.

"Why not try the chile rellenos?"

Janet grimaced. "That's what you said last time. This time I'm trying the fish."

"Too far from the ocean for fish," Chee said. But now he remembered that his last time here the cook had converted the rellenos to something like leather. Maybe he'd order the chicken-fried steak.

"It's trout," Janet said. "A local fish. The waiter told me they steal 'em out of the fish hatchery ponds."

"Okay then," Chee said. "Trout for me, too."

"You look totally worn-out," she said. "Is Captain Largo getting to be too much for you?"

"I spent the day with a redneck New Mexico brand inspector," Chee said. "We drove all the way up to Mancos with him talking every inch of the way. Then back again, him still talking."

"About what? Cows?"

"People. Mr. Finch works on the theory that you catch cattle rustlers by knowing everything about everybody who owns cattle. I guess it's a pretty good system, but then he passed all that information along to me. You want to know anything about anybody who raises cows in the Four Corners area? Or hauls them? Or runs feedlots? Just ask me."

"Finch?" she said. "I've run into him twice in court." She shook her head, smiling.

"Who won?"

"He did. Both times.

"Oh, well," Chee said. "It's too bad, but sometimes justice triumphs over you public defenders. Were your clients guilty?"

"Probably. They said they weren't. But this Finch guy is smart."

Chee did not want to talk about Finch.

"You know, Janet," he said. "Sometime we need to talk about . . ."

She put down the menu and looked at him over her glasses. "Sometime, but not tonight. What took you and Mr. Finch to Mancos?"

No. Not tonight, Chee thought. They would just go over the same ground. She'd say that if the police were doing their jobs properly there really wasn't a conflict of interest if a public defender was the wife of a cop. And he'd say, yeah, but what if the cop had arrested the very guy she was defending and was a witness? What if she were cross-examining her own husband as a hostile witness? And she'd fall back on her Stanford Law School lecture notes and tell him that all she wanted to extract from anyone was the exact truth. And he'd say, but sometimes the lawyer isn't after quite 100 percent of the truth, and she'd say that some evidence can't be admitted, and he'd say, as an attorney it would be easy for her to get a job with a private firm, and she'd remind him he'd turned down an offer from the Arizona Department of Public Safety and was a cinch for a job with the Bureau of Indian Affairs law-and-order division if he would take it. And he'd say, that would mean leaving the reservation, and she'd say, why not? Did he want to spend his life here? And that would open a new can of worms. No. Tonight he'd let her change the subject.

The waiter came. Janet ordered a glass of white wine. Chee had coffee.

"I went to Mancos to tell a widow that we'd found her husband's skeleton," Chee said. "Mr. Finch went along because it gave him an excuse to contemplate the cows in the lady's feedlot."

"All you found were dry bones? Her husband must have been away a lot. I'll bet he was a policeman," she said, and laughed.

Chee let that pass.

"Was it the skeleton they spotted up on Ship Rock about Halloween?" she asked, sounding mildly repentant.

Chee nodded. "He turned out to be a guy named Harold Breedlove. He owned a big ranch near Mancos."

"Breedlove," Janet said. "That sounds familiar." The waiter came—a lanky, rawboned Navajo who listened attentively to Janet's questions about the wine and seemed to understand them no better than did Chee. He would ask the cook. About the trout he was on familiar ground. "Very fresh," he said, and hurried off.

Janet was looking thoughtful. "Breedlove," she said, and shook her head. "I remember the paper said there was no identification on him. So how'd you get him identified? Dental chart?"

"Joe Leaphorn had a hunch," Chee said.

"The legend-in-his-own-time lieutenant? I thought he'd retired."

"He did," Chee said. "But he remembered a missing person case he'd worked on way back. This guy who disappeared was a mountain climber and an inheritance was involved, and—"

"Hey," Janet said. "Breedlove. I remember now."

Remember what? Chee thought. And why? This had happened long before Janet had joined the DNA, and become a resident reservation Navajo instead of one in name only, and entered his life, and made him happy. His expression had a question in it.

"From when I was with Granger-hyphen-Smith in Albuquerque. Just out of law school," she said. "The firm represented the Breedlove family. They had public land grazing leases, some mineral rights deals with the Jicarilla Apaches, some water rights arrangements with the Utes." She threw out her hands to signify an endless variety of concerns. "There were some dealings with the Navajo Nation, too. Anyway, I remember the widow was having the husband declared legally dead so she could inherit from him. The family wanted that looked into."

She stopped, looking slightly abashed. Picked up the menu again. "I'll definitely have the trout," she said.

"Were they suspicious?" Chee asked.

"I presume so," she said, still looking at the menu. "I remember it did look funny. The guy inherits a trust and two or three days later he vanishes. Vanishes under what you'd have to consider unusual circumstances."

The waiter came. Chee watched Janet order trout, watched the waiter admire her. A classy lady, Janet. From what Chee had learned about law firms as a cop, lawyers didn't chat about their clients' business to rookie interns. It was unethical. Or at least unprofessional.

He knew the answer but he asked it anyway. "Did you work on it? The looking into it?"

"Not directly," Janet said. She sipped her water.

Chee looked at her.

She flushed slightly. "The Breedlove Corporation was John McDermott's client. His job," she said. "I guess because he handled all things Indian for the firm. And the Breedlove family had all these tribal connections."

"Did you find anything?"

"I guess not," Janet said. "I don't remember the family having us intervene in the case."

"The family?" Chee said. "Do you remember who, specifically?"

"I don't," she said. "John was dealing with an attorney in New York. I guess he was representing the rest of the Breedloves. Or maybe the family corporation. Or whatever." She shrugged. "What did you think of Finch, aside from him being so talkative?"

John, Chee thought. John. Professor John McDermott. Her old mentor at Stanford. The man who had hired her at Albuquerque when he went into private practice there, and took her to Washington when he transferred, and made her his mistress, used her, and broke her heart.

"I wonder what made them suspicious?" Chee said. "Aside from the circumstances."

"I don't know," Janet said.

Their trout arrived. Rainbows, neatly split, neatly placed on a bed of wild rice. Flanked by small carrots and boiled new potatoes. Janet broke off a tiny piece of trout and ate it.

Beautiful, Chee thought. The perfect skin, the oval face, the dark eyes that expressed so much. He found himself wishing he was a poet, a singer of ballads. Chee knew a lot of songs but they were the chants the shaman sings at the curing ceremonials, recounting the deeds of the spirits. No one had taught him how to sing to someone as beautiful as this.

He ate a bite of trout.

"If I had been driving a patrol car yesterday instead of my old pickup," he said, "I could have given a speeding ticket to a guy driving a white Porsche convertible. Really flying. But I was driving my truck."

"Wow," Janet said, looking delighted. "My favorite car. I have a fantasy about tooling around Paris in one of those. With the top down."

Maybe she looked happy because he was changing the subject. Moving away from unhappy ground. But to Chee the trout now seemed to have no taste at all.

7

JOE LEAPHORN, UNEASILY conscious that he was now a mere civilian, had given himself three excuses for calling on Hosteen Nez and thereby butting into police business.

First, he'd come to like the old man way back when he was picking his brain in the Breedlove missing person case. Thus going to see him while Nez was recuperating from being shot was a friendly thing to do. Second, Canyon de Chelly wasn't much out of his way, since he was going to Flagstaff anyway. Third, a trip into the canyon never failed to lift Joe Leaphorn's spirits.

Lately they had needed a lift. Most of the things he'd yearned to do when retirement allowed it had now been done—at least once. He was bored. He was lonely. The little house he and Emma had shared so many years had never recovered from the emptiness her death had left in every room. That was worse now without the job to distract him. Maybe he was oversensitive, but he felt like an intruder down at the police headquarters. When he dropped in to chat with old friends he often found them busy. Just as he had always been. And he was a mere civilian now, no longer one of the little band of brothers.

Good excuses or not, Leaphorn had been a policeman too long to go unprepared. He took his GMC Jimmy with the four-wheel drive required in the canyon both by National Park Service rules and by the uncertain bottom up Chinle Wash. He had stopped at the grocery in Ganado and bought a case of assorted soda pop flavors, two pounds of bacon, a pound of coffee, a large can of peaches, and a loaf of bread. Only then did he head for Chinle.

Once there, he made another stop at the district Tribal Police office to make sure his visit wouldn't tread on the toes of the investigating officer. He found Sergeant Addison Deke at his desk. They chatted about family matters and mutual friends and finally got around to the shooting of Amos Nez.

Deke shook his head, produced a wry grin. "The people around here have that one all solved for us," he said. "They say old Nez was tipping us off about who was breaking into tourists' cars up on the canyon lookout points. So the burglars got mad at him and shot him."

"That makes sense," Leaphorn said. Which it did, even though he could tell from Deke's face that it wasn't true.

"Nez hadn't told us a damn thing, of course," Deke said. "And when we asked him about the rumor, it pissed him off. He was insulted that his neighbors would even think such a thing."

Leaphorn chuckled. Car break-ins at several of the Navajo Nation's more popular tourist attractions were a chronic headache for the Tribal Police. They usually involved one or two hard-up families whose boys considered the salable items left in tourist cars a legitimate harvest—like wild asparagus, rabbits, and sand plums. Their neighbors disapproved, but it wasn't the sort of thing one would get a boy in trouble over.

Leaphorn's next stop was seven-tenths of a mile up the rim road from the White House Ruins overlook—the point from which the sniper had shot Nez. Leaphorn pulled his Jimmy off into the grass at the spot where Deke had told him they'd found six newly fired 30.06 cartridges. Here the layer of tough igneous rock had broken into a jumble of room-sized boulders, giving the sniper a place to watch and wait out of sight from the road. He looked directly down and across the canyon floor. Nez would have been riding his horse along the track across the sandy bottom of the wash. Not a difficult shot in terms of distance for one who knew how to use a rifle, but shooting down at that angle would require some careful adjustment of the sights to avoid an overshot. Whoever shot Nez knew what he was doing.

The next stop was at the Canyon de Chelly park office on the way in. He chatted with the rangers there and picked up the local gossip. Relative to Hosteen Nez, the speculation was exactly what Leaphorn had heard from Deke. The old man had been shot because he was tipping the cops on the car break-ins. How about enemies? No one could imagine that, and they knew him well. Nez was a kindly man, a traditional who helped his family and was generous with his neighbors. He loved jokes. Always in good humor. Everybody liked him. He'd guided in the canyon for years and he could even handle the tourists who wanted to get drunk without making them angry. Always contributed something to help out with the ceremonials when somebody was having a curing sing.

How about eccentricities? Gambling? Grazing rights problems? Any odd behavior? Well, yes. Nez's mother-in-law lived with him, which was a direct violation of the taboo against such conduct. But Nez rationalized that. He said he and old lady Benally had been good friends for years be-fore he'd met her daughter. They'd talked it over and decided that when the Holy People taught that a son-in-law seeing his mother-in-law caused insanity, blindness, and other maladies, they meant that this happened when the two didn't like each other. Anyway, old lady Benally was still go-ing strong in her nineties and Nez was not blind and didn't seem to be any crazier than anyone else.

Indeed, Nez seemed to be feeling pretty good when Leaphorn found him.

"Pretty good," he said, "considering the shape I'm in." And when Leaphorn laughed at that, he added, "But if I'd known I was going to live so damn long, I'd have taken better care of myself."

Nez was sprawled in a wired-together overstuffed recliner, his head al-most against the red sandstone wall of a cul-de-sac behind his hogan. The early afternoon sun beat down upon him. Warmth radiated from the cliff behind him, the sky overhead was almost navy blue, and the air was cool and fresh, and smelled of autumn's last cutting of alfalfa hay from a field up the canyon. Nothing in the scene, except for the cast on the Nez legs and the bandages on his neck and chest, reminded Leaphorn of a hospital room.

Leaphorn had introduced himself in the traditional Navajo fashion, identifying his parents and their clans. "I wonder if you remember me," he said. "I'm the policeman who talked to you three times a long time ago when the man you'd been guiding disappeared."

"Sure," Nez said. "You kept coming back. Acting like you'd forgot something to ask me, and then asking me everything all over again."

"Well, I was pretty forgetful."

"Glad to hear that," Nez said. "I thought you figured I was maybe lying to you a little bit and if you asked me often enough I'd forget and tell the truth."

This notion didn't seem to bother Nez. He motioned Leaphorn to sit on the boulder beside his chair.

"Now you want to talk to me about who'd want to shoot me. I tell you one thing right now. It wasn't no car burglars. That's a lot of lies they're saying about me."

Leaphorn nodded. "That's right," he said. "The police at Chinle told me you weren't helping them catch those people."

Nez seemed pleased at that. He nodded.

"But you know, maybe the car burglars don't know that," Leaphorn said. "Maybe they think you're telling on 'em."

Nez shook his head. "No," he said. "They know better. They're my kinfolks."

"You picked a good place to get some sunshine here," Leaphorn said. "Lots of heat off the cliff. Out of the wind. And—"

Nez laughed. "And nobody can get a shot at me here. Not from the rim anyway."

"I noticed that," Leaphorn said.

"I figured you had."

"I read the police report," Leaphorn said, and recited it to Nez. "That about right?"

"That's it," Nez said. "The son of a bitch just kept shooting. After I sort of crawled under the horse, he hit the horse twice more." Nez whacked his hand against the cast. "Thump. Thump."

"Sounds like he wanted to kill you," Leaphorn said.

"I thought maybe he just didn't like my horse," Nez said. "He was a pretty sorry horse. Liked to bite people."

"The last time I came to see you it was also bad news," Leaphorn said. "You think there could be any connection?"

"Connection?" Nez said. He looked genuinely surprised. "No. I didn't think of that." But he thought now, staring at Leaphorn, frowning. "Connection," he repeated. "How could there be? What for?"

Leaphorn shrugged. "I don't know. It was just a thought. Did anybody tell you our missing man from way back then has turned up?"

"No," Nez said, looking delighted. "I didn't know that. After a month or so I figured he must be dead. Didn't make any sense to leave that pretty woman that way."

"You were right. He was dead. We just found his bones," Leaphorn said, and watched Nez, waiting for the question. But no question came.

"I thought so," Nez said. "Been dead a long time, too, I bet."

"Probably more than ten years," Leaphorn said.

"Yeah," Nez said. He shook his head, said, "Crazy bastard," and looked sad.

Leaphorn waited.

"I liked him," Nez said. "He was a good man. Funny. Lots of jokes."

"Are you going to play games with me like you did eleven years ago, or you going to tell me what you know about this? Like why you think he was crazy and why you thought he'd been dead all this time."

"I don't tell on people," Nez said. "There's already plenty of trouble without that."

"There won't be any more trouble for Harold Breedlove," Leaphorn said. "But from the look of all those bandages, there's been some trouble for you."

Nez considered that. Then he considered Leaphorn.

"Tell me if you found him on Ship Rock," Nez said. "Was he climbing Tse′ Bit′ a′i′?"

Absolutely nothing Amos Nez could have said would have surprised Leaphorn more than that. He spent a few moments re-collecting his wits.

"That's right," he said finally. "Somebody spotted his skeleton down below the peak. How the hell did you know?"

Nez shrugged.

"Did Breedlove tell you he was going there?"

"He told me."

"When?"

Nez hesitated again. "He's dead?"

"Dead."

"When I was guiding them," Nez said. "We were way up Canyon del Muerto. His woman, Mrs. Breedlove, she'd gone up a little ways around the corner. To urinate, I guess it was. Breedlove, he'd been talking about climbing the cliff there." He gestured upward. "You been up there. It's straight up. Worse than that. Some places the top hangs over. I said nobody could do it. He said he could. He told me some places he'd climbed up in Colorado. He started talking then about all the things he wanted to do while he was still young and now he was already thirty years old and he hadn't done them. And then he said—" Nez cut it off, looking at Leaphorn.

"I'm not a policeman anymore," he said. "I'm retired, like you. I just want to know what the hell happened to the man."

"Maybe I should have told you then," Nez said.

"Yeah. Maybe you should have," Leaphorn said. "Why didn't you?"

"Wasn't any reason to," Nez said. "He said he wasn't going to do it until spring came. Said now it was too close to winter. He said not to talk about it because his wife wanted him to stop climbing."

"Did Mrs. Breedlove hear him?"

"She was off taking a leak," Nez said. "He said he thought maybe he'd do it all by himself. Said nobody had ever done that."

"Did you think he meant it? Did he sound serious?"

"Sounded serious, yes. But I thought he was just bragging. White men do that a lot."

"He didn't say where he was going?"

"His wife came back then. He shut up about it."

"No, I mean did he say anything about where he was going to go that evening? After you came in out of the canyon."

"I remember they had some friends coming to see them. They were going to eat together."

"Not drinking, was he?"

"Not drinking," Nez said. "I don't let my tourists drink. It's against the law."

"So he said he was going to climb Tse´ Bit´ a´i´ the following spring," Leaphorn said. "Is that the way you remember it?"

"That's what he said."

They sat a while, engulfed by sunlight, cool air, and silence. A raven planed down from the rim, circled around a cottonwood, landed on a Russian olive across the canyon floor, and perched, waiting for them to die.

Nez extracted a pack of cigarettes from his shirt, offered one to Leaphorn, and lit one for himself.

"Like to smoke while I'm thinking," he said.

"I used to do that, too," Leaphorn said. "But my wife talked me into quitting."

"They'll do that if you're not careful," Nez said.

"Thinking about what?"

"Thinking about why he told me that. You know, maybe he figured I'd say something and his woman would hear it and stop him." Nez exhaled a cloud of blue smoke. "And he wanted somebody to stop him. Or when spring came and he slipped off to climb it by himself, he thought maybe he'd fall off and get killed and if nobody knew where he was nobody would find his body. And he didn't want to be up there dead and all alone."

"And you think he figured you'd hear about him disappearing and you'd tell people where to find him?" Leaphorn asked.

"Maybe," Nez said, and shrugged.

"It didn't work."

"Because he was already missing," Nez said. "Where was he all those months between when he goes away from his wife here, and when he climbed our Rock with Wings?"

Leaphorn grinned. "That's what I was hoping you'd know something about. Did he say anything that gave you ideas about where he was going after he left here? Who he was meeting?"

Nez shook his head. "That's a long time to stay away from that good woman," Nez said. "Way too long, I think. I guess you policemen haven't found out where he was?"

"No," Leaphorn said. "We don't have the slightest idea."

8

A MILD PRELUDE to winter had come quietly during the night, slipping across the Arizona border, covering Chee's house trailer with about five inches of wet whiteness. It caused him to shift his pickup into four-wheel drive to make the climb from his site under the San Juan River cottonwoods up the slope to the highway. But the first snow of winter is a cheering sight for natives of the high, dry Four Corners country. It's especially cheering for those doing Chee's criminal investigation division's job. The snow was making extra work for the troopers out on the highways, but for the detectives it dampened down the crime rate.

Lieutenant Jim Chee's good humor even survived the sight of the stack of folders Jenifer had dumped on his desk. The note atop them said: "Cap. Largo wants to talk to you right away about the one on top but I don't think he'll be in before noon because with this snow he'll have to get some feed out to his cows."

On the table of organization, Jenifer was Chee's employee, the secretary of his criminal investigation unit. But Jenifer had been hired by Captain Largo a long time ago and had seen lieutenants come and go. Chee understood that as far as Jenifer was concerned he was still on probation. But the friendly tone of the note suggested she was thinking he might meet her standards.

"Hah!" he said, grinning. But that faded away before he finished working through the folders. The top one concerned the theft of two more Angus calves from a woman named Roanhorse who had a grazing lease west of Red Rock. The ones in the middle involved a drunken brawl at a girl dance at the Lukachukai chapter house, in which shots were fired and the shooter fled in a pickup, not his own; a request for a transfer from this office by Officer Bernadette (Bernie) Manuelito, the rookie trainee Chee had inherited with the job; a report of drug use and purported gang activity around Hogback, and so forth. Plus, of course, forms to be filled out on mileage, maintenance, and gasoline usage by patrol vehicles, and a reminder that he hadn't submitted vacation schedules for his office.

The final folder held a citizen's complaint that he was being harassed by Officer Manuelito. What remained of Chee's high spirits evaporated as he read it.

The form was signed by Roderick Diamonte. Mr. Diamonte alleged that Officer Manuelito was parking her Tribal Police car at the access road to his place of business at Hogback, stopping his customers on trumped-up traffic violations, and using what Diamonte called "various sneaky tricks" in an effort to violate their constitutional protection against illegal searches. He asked that Officer Manuelito be ordered to desist from this harassment and be reprimanded.

Diamonte? Yes, indeed. Chee remembered the name from the days when he had been a patrolman assigned here. Diamonte operated a bar on the margin of reservation land and was one of the first people to come to mind when something lucrative and illegal was going on. Still, he had his rights.

Chee buzzed Jenifer and asked if Manuelito was in. She was out on patrol.

"Would you call her? Tell her I want to talk to her when she comes in. Please." Chee had learned early on that Jenifer's response time shortened when an order became a request.

"Right," Jenifer said. "I thought you'd want to talk to her. I guess you know who that Diamonte is, don't you?"

"I remember him," Chee said.

"And you had a call," Jenifer said. "From Janet Pete in Washington. She left a number."

Someday when he was better established Chee intended to talk to his secretary about her practice of deciding which calls to tell him about when. Calls from Janet tended to get low priority. Maybe that was because Jenifer had the typical cop attitude about defense lawyers. Or maybe not.

He called the number.

"Jim," she said. "Ah, Jim. It's good to hear your voice."

"And yours," he said. "You called to tell me you're headed out to National Airport. Flying home. You want me to pick you up at the Farmington Airport?"

"Don't I wish," she said. "But I'm stuck here a little longer. How about you? The job getting any easier? And did you get a snowstorm? The weather girl always stands in front of the Four Corners when she's giving us the news, but it looked like a front was pushing across from the west."

They talked about the weather for a moment, talked about love, talked about wedding plans. Chee didn't ask her about the Justice Department and Bureau of Indian Affairs business that had called her away. It was one of several little zones of silence that develop when a cop and a defense lawyer are dating.

And then Janet said: "Anything new developing on the Fallen Man business?"

"Fallen Man?" Chee hadn't been giving that any thought. It was a closed case. A missing person found. A corpse identified. Officially an accidental death. Officially none of his business. A curious affair, true, but the world of a police lieutenant was full of such oddities and he had too much pressing stuff on his desk to give it any time.

"No. Nothing new." Chee wanted to say, "He's in the dead file," but he was a little too traditional for that. Death is not a subject for Navajo humor.

"Do you know if anyone ever climbed up there—I mean after the rescue party brought the bones down—to see if they could find any evidence of funny stuff?"

Chee thought about that. And about Janet's interest in it.

"You know," she continued, talking into his silence. "Was there any suggestion that it might not have been an accident? Or that somebody was up there with him and just didn't report it?"

"No," Chee said. "Anyway, we didn't send anyone up." He found himself feeling defensive. "The only apparent motive would be the widow wanting his money, and she waited five years before getting him declared legally dead. And had an ironclad alibi. And—" But Chee stopped. Irked. Why explain all this? She already knew it. They'd talked about it the last time he'd seen her. At dinner in Farmington.

"Why—" he began, but she was already talking. A new subject. She'd gone to a dinner concert at the Library of Congress last night, some fifteenth-century music played on the fifteenth-century instruments. Very interesting. The French ambassador was there—and his wife. You should have seen her dress. Wow. And so it went.

When the call was over, Chee picked up the Manuelito file again. But he held it unopened while he thought about Janet's interest in the Fallen Man. And about how a dinner concert at the Library of Congress must have been by invitation only. Or restricted to major donors to some fund or other. Super exclusive. In fact he had no idea the Library of Congress even produced such events, no idea how he could wangle an invitation if he'd wanted to go, no idea how Janet had come to be there.

Well, yes, he did have an idea about that. Of course. Janet had friends in Washington. From those days when she had worked there as what she called "the House Indian" of Dalman, MacArthur, White and Hertzog, Attorneys at Law. One of those friends had been John McDermott. Her ex-lover and exploiter. From whom Janet had fled.

Chee escaped from that unhappy thought into the problem presented by Officer Bernadette Manuelito.

The Navajo culture that had produced Acting Lieutenant Jim Chee had taught him the power of words and of thought. Western metaphysicians might argue that language and imagination are products of reality. But in their own migrations out of Mongolia and over the icy Bering Strait, the Navajos brought with them a much older Asian philosophy. Thoughts, and words that spring from them, bend the individual's reality. To speak of death is to invite it. To think of sorrow is to produce it. He would think of his duties instead of his love.

Chee flipped open the Manuelito folder. He read through it, wondering why he could have ever believed he wanted an administrative post. That brought him back to Janet. He'd wanted the promotion to impress her, to make himself eligible, to narrow the gap between the child of the urban privileged class and the child of the isolated sheep camp. Thus he had made a thoroughly non-Navajo decision based on an utterly non-Navajo way of thinking. He put down the Manuelito file and buzzed Jenifer.

Officer Manuelito, it seemed, had come in early, and called in about nine saying she was working on the cattle-rustling problem. Chee allowed himself a rare expletive. What the hell was she doing about cattle theft? She was supposed to be finding witnesses to a homicide at a wild party.

"Would you ask the dispatcher to contact her, please, and ask her to come in?" Chee said.

"Want 'em to tell her why?" Jenifer asked.

"Just tell her I want to talk to her," Chee said, forgetting to say please.

But what would he say to Officer Manuelito? He'd have time to decide that by the time she got to the office. It would keep him from thinking about what might have provoked Janet's curiosity about Harold Breedlove, late of the Breedlove family that had been a client of John McDermott.

9

A S IT HAPPENED, Officer Manuelito didn't get to the office.
"She says she's stuck," Jenifer reported. "She went out Route 5010
south of Rattlesnake and turned off on that dirt track that skirts around
the west side of Ship Rock. Then she slid off into a ditch." This amused
Jenifer, who chuckled. "I'll see if I can get somebody to go pull her out."

"I think I'll just take care of it myself," Chee said. "But thanks anyway."

He pulled on his jacket. What the devil was Manuelito doing out in
that empty landscape by the Rock with Wings? He'd told her to work
her way down a list of people who might be willing to talk about gang
membership at Shiprock High School, not practicing her skill at driving
in mud.

Just getting out of the parking lot demonstrated to Chee how
Manuelito could manage to get stuck. The overnight storm had drifted
eastward, leaving the town of Shiprock under a cloudless sky. The temperature was already well above freezing and the sun was making short work
of the snow. But even after he shifted into four-wheel drive, Chee's truck
did some wheel-spinning. The ditches beside the highway were already
carrying runoff water and a cloud of white steam swirled over the asphalt
where the moisture was evaporating.

Navajo Route 5010, according to the road map, was "improved." Which

meant it was graded now and then and in theory at least had a gravel surface. On a busy day, probably six or eight vehicles would use it. This
morning, Officer Manuelito's patrol car had been the first to leave its
tracks in the snow and Chee's pickup was number two. Chee noted ap-
provingly that she had made a slow and careful left turn off of 5010 onto
an unnumbered access road that led toward Ship Rock—thereby leaving
no skid marks. He made the same turn, felt his rear wheels slipping, cor-
rected, and eased the truck gingerly down the road.

All muscles were tense, all senses alert. He was enjoying testing his
skill against the slick road surface. Enjoying the clean, cold air in his lungs,
the gray-and-white patterns of soft snow on sage and salt bush and
chamisa, enjoying the beauty, the vast emptiness, and a silence broken
only by the sound of his truck's engine and its tires in the mud. The immense basalt monolith of Ship Rock towered beside him, its west face still
untouched by the warming sun and thus still coated with its whitewash of
snow. The Fallen Man must have prayed for that sort of moisture before
his thirst killed him on that lonely ledge.

Then the truck topped a hillock, and there was Officer Bernadette
Manuelito, a tiny figure standing beside her stuck patrol car, representing
an unsolved administrative problem, the end of joy, and a reminder of how
good life had been when he was just a patrolman. Ah, well, there was a
bright side. Even from here he could see that Manuelito had stuck her car
so thoroughly that there would be no hope of towing it out with his vehicle. He'd simply give her a ride back to the office and send out a tow truck.

Officer Manuelito had seemed to Lieutenant Jim Chee to be both unusually pretty and unusually young to be wearing a Navajo Tribal Police
uniform. This morning she wouldn't have made that impression. She
looked tired and disheveled and at least her age, which Chee knew from
her personnel records was twenty-six years. She also looked surly. He
leaned across the pickup seat and opened the door for her.

"Tough luck," he said. "Get your stuff out of it, and the weapons, and
lock it up. We'll send out a tow truck to get it when the mud dries."

Officer Manuelito had prepared an explanation of how this happened
and would not be deterred.

"The snow covered up a little wash, there. Drifted it full so you couldn't
see it. And . . ."

"It could happen to anybody," Chee said. "Let's go."

"You didn't bring a tow chain?"

"I did bring a tow chain," Chee said. "But look at it. There's no traction now. It's clay and it's too soft."

"You have four-wheel drive," she said.

"I know," Chee said, feeling in no mood to debate this. "But that just means you dig yourself in by spinning four wheels instead of two. I couldn't budge it. Get your stuff and get in."

Officer Manuelito brushed a lock of hair off her forehead, leaving a streak of gray mud. Her lips parted with a response, then closed. "Yes, sir," she said.

That was all she said. Chee backed the pickup to a rocky place, turned it, and slipped and slid his way back to 5010 in leaden silence. Back on the gravel, he said:

"Did you know that Diamonte filed a complaint against you? Charged you with harassment."

Officer Manuelito was staring out the windshield. "No," she said. "But I knew he said he was going to."

"Yep," Chee said. "He did. Said you were hanging around. Bothering his customers."

"His dope buyers."

"Some of them, probably," Chee said.

Manuelito stared relentlessly out of the windshield.

"What were you doing?" Chee asked.

"You mean besides harassing his customers?"

"Besides that," Chee said, thinking that the very first thing he would do when they got back to the office was approve this woman's transfer to anywhere. Preferably to Tuba City, which was about as far as he could get her from Shiprock. He glanced at her, waiting for a reply. She was still focused on the windshield.

"You know what he runs out there?" she said.

"I know what he used to do when I was assigned here before," Chee said. "In those days he wholesaled booze to the reservation bootleggers, fenced stolen property, handled some marijuana. Things like that. Now I understand he's branched out into more serious dope."

"That's right," she said. "He still supplies the creeps who push pot and now he's selling the worse stuff, too."

"That's what I always heard," Chee said. "And most recently from Teddy Begayaye. The kid Begayaye picked up at the community college last week named Diamonte as his source for coke. But then he changed his mind and decided he just couldn't remember where he got it."

"I know Diamonte's selling it."

"So you bring in your evidence. We take it to the captain, he takes it to the federal prosecutors, or maybe the San Juan County cops, and we put the bastard in jail."

"Sure," Manuelito said.

"But we don't go out there, with no evidence, and harass his customers. There's a law against it."

Chee sensed that she was no longer staring at the windshield. She was looking at him.

"I heard that you did," she said. "When you were a cop here before."

Chee felt his face flushing. "Who told you that?"

"Captain Largo told us when we were in recruit training."

The son of a bitch, Chee thought.

"Largo was using me as a bad example?"

"He didn't say who did it. But I asked around. People said it was you."

"It just about got me kicked out of the police," Chee said. "The same thing could happen to you."

"I heard it got the place shut down, too," Manuelito said.

"Yeah, and about the time I got off suspension, he was going full blast again."

"Still . . ." Manuelito said. And let the thought trail off.

"Don't say 'still.' You stay away from there. It's Begayaye's job, looking into the dope situation. If you run across anything useful, tell Teddy. Or tell me. Don't go freelancing around."

"Yes, sir," Manuelito said, sounding very formal.

"I mean it," Chee said. "I'll put a letter in your file reporting these instructions."

"Yes, sir," Manuelito said.

"Now. What's this transfer request about? What's wrong with Shiprock? And where do you want to go?"

"I don't care. Anywhere."

That surprised Chee. He'd guessed Manuelito wanted to be closer to a boyfriend somewhere. Or that her mother was sick. Something like that. But now he remembered that she was from Red Rock. By Big Rez standards, Shiprock was conveniently close to her family.

"Is there something about Shiprock you don't like?"

That question produced a long silence, and finally:

"I just want to get away from here."

"Why?"

"It's a personal reason," she said. "I don't have to say why, do I? It's not in the personnel rules."

"I guess not," Chee said. "Anyway, I'll approve it."

"Thank you," Manuelito said.

"That's no guarantee you'll get it, though. You know how it works. Largo may kill it. And there has to be the right kind of opening somewhere. You'll have to be patient."

Officer Manuelito was pointing out the window. "Did you notice that?" she asked.

All Chee saw was the grassland rolling away toward the great dark shape of Ship Rock.

"I mean the fence," she said. "There where that wash runs down into the borrow ditch. Notice the posts."

Chee noticed the posts, two of which were leaning sharply. He stopped the pickup.

"Somebody dug at the base of the posts," she said. "Loosened them so you could pull them up."

"And lay the fence down?"

"More likely raise it up," she said. "Then you could drive cows down the wash and right under it."

"Do you know whose grazing lease this is?"

"Yes, sir," she said. "A man named Maryboy has it."

"Has he lost any cattle?"

"I don't know. Not lately, anyway. At least I haven't seen a report on it."

Chee climbed out of the truck, plodded through the snow, and tried the posts. They lifted easily but the snow made it impossible to determine exactly why. He thought about Zorro, Mr. Finch's favorite cow thief.

Manuelito was standing beside him.

"See?" she said.

"When did you notice this?"

"I don't know," Officer Manuelito said. "Just a few days ago."

"If I remember right, just a few days ago—and today, too—you were supposed to be running down that list of people at that dance. Looking for anyone willing to tell us about gang membership. About what they saw. Who'd tell us who had the gun. Who shot it. That sort of thing. Is that right? That was number one on the list you were handed after the staff meeting."

"Yes, sir," Officer Manuelito said, proving she could sound meek if she wanted to. She was looking down at her hands.

"Do any of those possible witnesses live out here?"

"Well, not exactly. The Roanhorse couple is on the list. They live over near Burnham."

"Near Burnham?" The Burnham trading post was way to hell south of here. Down Highway 666.

"I sort of detoured over this way," Manuelito explained uneasily. "We had that report that Lucy Sam had lost some cattle, and I knew the captain was after you about catching somebody and putting a stop to that and—"

"How did you know that?"

Now Manuelito's face was a little flushed. "Well," she said. "You know how people talk about things."

Yes, Chee knew about that.

"Are you telling me you just drove out here blind? What were you looking for?"

"Well," she said. "I was just sort of looking."

Chee waited. "Just sort of looking?"

"Well," she said. "I remembered my grandfather telling me about Hosteen Sam. That was Lucy's father. About him hating it when white people came out here to climb Ship Rock. They would park out there, over that little rise there by the foot of the cliff. He would write down their license number or what the car looked like and when he went into town he would go by the police station and try to get the police to arrest them for trespassing. So when I was assigned here, and one of the problems worrying the captain was people stealing cattle, I came out here to ask Hosteen Sam if he would keep track of strange pickups and trucks for us."

"Pretty good idea," Chee said. "What did he say?"

"He was dead. Died last year. But his daughter said she would do it for me and I gave her a little notebook for it, but she said she had the one her father had used. So, anyway, I thought I would just make a little detour by there and see if she had written down anything for us."

"Quite a little detour," Chee said. "I'd say about sixty miles or so. Had she?"

"I don't know. I noticed some other posts leaning over and I decided to pull off and see if they had been cut off or dug up or anything else funny. And then I got stuck."

It was a clever idea, Chee was thinking. He should have thought of it himself. He'd see if he could find some people to keep a similar eye on things up near the Ute reservation, and over on the Checkerboard. Wherever people were losing cattle. Who could he get? But he was distracted from that thought. His feet, buried to the ankles in the melting snow, were complaining about the cold. And the sun had now risen far enough to illuminate a different set of snowfields high above them on Ship Rock. They reflected a dazzling white light.

Officer Manuelito was watching him. "Beautiful, isn't it?" she said. "Tse´ Bit´ a´i´. It never seems to look the same."

"I remember noticing that when I was a little boy and I was staying for a while with an aunt over near Toadlena," Chee said. "I thought it was alive."

Officer Manuelito was staring at it. "Beautiful," she said, and shuddered. "I wonder what he was doing up there. All alone."

"The Fallen Man?"

"Deejay doesn't think he fell. He said no bones were broken and if you'd fallen down that cliff it would break something. Deejay thinks he was climbing with somebody and they just stranded him there."

"Who knows?" Chee said. "Anyway, it's not in the books as anything but an accidental death. No evidence of foul play. We don't have to worry about it." Chee's feet were telling him that his boots were leaking. Leaking ice water. "Let's go," he said, heading back for his truck.

Officer Manuelito was still standing there, staring up at the cliffs towering above her.

"They say Monster Slayer couldn't get down either. When he climbed up to the top and killed the Winged Monster he couldn't get down."

"Come on," Chee said. He climbed into the truck and started the engine, thinking that you'd have a better chance if you were a spirit like Monster Slayer. When spirits scream for help other spirits hear them. Spider Woman had heard and came to the rescue. But Harold Breedlove could have called forever with nothing but the ravens to hear him. The stuff of bad dreams.

They drove in silence.

Then Officer Manuelito said, "To be trapped up there. I try not to even think about it. It would give me nightmares."

"What?" Chee said, who hadn't been listening because by then he was working his way around a nightmare of his own. He was trying to think of another reason Janet Pete might have asked him about the Fallen Man affair. He wanted to find a reason that didn't involve John McDermott and his law firm representing the Breedlove family. Maybe it was the oddity of the skeleton on the mountain that provoked her question. He always came back to that. But then he'd find himself speculating on who had taken Janet to that concert and he'd think of John McDermott again.

IO

THE FIRST THING Joe Leaphorn noticed when he came through the door was his breakfast dishes awaiting attention in the sink. It was a bad habit and it demanded correction. No more of this sinking into slip-shod widower ways. Then he noticed the red light blinking atop his tele-phone answering machine. The indicator declared he'd received two calls today—pretty close to a post-retirement record. He took a step toward the telephone.

But no. First things first. He detoured into the kitchen, washed his ce-real bowl, saucer, and spoon, dried them, and put them in their place on the dish rack. Then he sat in his recliner, put his boots on the footstool, picked up the telephone, and pushed the button.

The first call was from his auto insurance dealer, informing him that if he'd take a defensive driving course he could get a discount on his liability rates. He punched the button again.

"Mr. Leaphorn," the voice said. "This is John McDermott. I am an at-torney and our firm has represented the interests of the Edgar Breedlove family for many years. I remember that you investigated the disappearance of Harold Breedlove several years ago when you were a member of the Navajo Tribal Police. Would you be kind enough to call me, collect, and discuss whether you might be willing to help the family complete its own investiga-tion of his death?"

McDermott had left an Albuquerque number. Leaphorn dialed it.

"Oh, yes," the secretary said. "He was hoping you'd call."

After the "thank you for calling," McDermott didn't linger long over formalities.

"We would like you to get right onto this for us," he said. "If you're available, our usual rate is twenty-five dollars an hour, plus your expenses."

"You mentioned completing the investigation," Leaphorn said. "Does that mean you have some question about the identification of the skeleton?"

"There is a question concerning just about everything," McDermott said. "It is a very peculiar case."

"Could you be more specific? I need a better idea of what you'd like to find out."

"This isn't the sort of thing we can discuss over the telephone," McDermott said. "Nor is it the sort of thing I can talk about until I know whether you will accept a retainer." He produced a chuckle. "Family business, you know."

Leaphorn discovered he was allowing himself to be irritated by the tone of this—not a weakness he tolerated. And he was curious. He produced a chuckle of his own.

"From what I remember of the Breedlove disappearance, I don't see how I could help you. Would you like me to recommend someone?"

"No. No," McDermott said. "We'd like to use you."

"But what sort of information would I be looking for?" Leaphorn asked. "I was trying to find out what happened to the man. Why he didn't come back to Canyon de Chelly that evening. Where he went. What happened to him. And of course the important thing was what happened to him. We know that now, if the identification of the skeleton is correct. The rest of it doesn't seem to matter."

McDermott spent a few moments deciding how to respond.

"The family would like to establish who was up there with him," he said.

Now this was getting a bit more interesting. "They've learned someone was up there when he fell? How did they learn that?"

"A mere physical fact. We've talked to rock climbers who know that mountain. They say you couldn't do it alone, not to the point where they found the skeleton. They say Harold Breedlove didn't have the skills, the experience, to have done it."

Leaphorn waited but McDermott had nothing to add.

"The implication, then, is that someone went up with him. When he fell, they abandoned him and didn't report it. Is that what you're suggesting?"

"And why would they do that?" McDermott asked.

Leaphorn found himself grinning. Lawyers! The man didn't want to say it himself. Let the witness say it.

"Well, let's see then. They might do it if, for example, they had pushed him over. Given him a fatal shove. Watched him fall. Then they might forget to report it."

"Well, yes."

"And you're suggesting the family has some lead to who this forgetful person might be."

"No, I'm not suggesting anything."

"The only lead, then, is the list of those who might be motivated. If I can rely on my memory, the only one I knew of was the widow. The lady who would inherit. I presume she did inherit, didn't she? But perhaps there's a lot I didn't know. We didn't have a criminal case to work on, you know. We didn't—and still don't—have a felony to interest the Navajo Police or the Federal Bureau of Investigation. Just a missing person then. Now we have what is presumed to be an accidental death. There was never any proof that he hadn't simply—" Leaphorn paused, looked for a better way to phrase it, found none, and concluded, "Simply run away from wife and home."

"Greed is often the motivation in murder," McDermott said.

Murder, Leaphorn thought. It was the first time that word had been used.

"That's true. But if I am remembering what I was told at the time, there wasn't much to inherit except the ranch, and it was losing money. Unless there was some sort of nuptial agreement, she would have owned half of it anyway. Colorado law. The wife's community property. And if I remember what I learned then, Breedlove had already mortgaged it. Was there a motive beyond greed?"

McDermott let the question hang. "If you'll work with this, I'll discuss it with you in person."

"I always wondered if there was a nuptial agreement. But now I've heard that she owns the ranch."

"No nuptial agreement," McDermott said, reluctantly. "What do you think? If you don't like the hourly arrangement, we could make it a weekly rate. Multiply the twenty-five dollars by forty hours and make it a thousand a week."

A thousand a week, Leaphorn thought. A lot of money for a retired cop. And what would McDermott be charging his client?

"I tell you what I'll do," Leaphorn said. "I'll give it some thought. But I'll have to have some more specific information."

"Sleep on it, then," McDermott said. "I'm coming to Window Rock tomorrow anyway. Why don't we meet for lunch?"

Joe Leaphorn couldn't think of any reason not to do that. He wasn't doing anything else tomorrow. Or for the rest of the week, for that matter.

They set the date for one P.M. at the Navajo Inn. That allowed time for the lunch-hour crowd to thin and for McDermott to make the two-hundred-mile drive from Albuquerque. It also gave Leaphorn the morning hours to collect information on the telephone, talking to friends in the ranching business, a Denver banker, a cattle broker, learning all he could about the Lazy B ranch and the past history of the Breedloves.

That done, he drove down to the Inn and waited in the office lobby. A white Lexus pulled into the parking area and two men emerged: one tall and slender with graying blond hair, the other six inches shorter, dark-haired, sun-browned, with the heavy-shouldered, slim-waisted build of one who lifts weights and plays handball. Ten minutes early, but it was probably McDermott and who? An assistant, perhaps.

Leaphorn met them at the entrance, went through the introductions, and ushered them in to the quiet corner table he'd arranged to hold.

"Shaw," Leaphorn said. "George Shaw? Is that correct?"

"Right," the dark man said. "Hal Breedlove was my cousin. My best friend, too, for that matter. I was the executor of the estate when Elisa had him declared legally dead."

"A sad situation," Leaphorn said.

"Yes," Shaw said. "And strange."

"Why do you say that?" Leaphorn could think of a dozen ways Breedlove's death was strange. But which one would Mr. Shaw pick?

"Well," Shaw said. "Why wasn't the fall reported, for one thing?"

"You don't think he made the climb alone?"

"Of course not. He couldn't have," Shaw said. "I couldn't do it, and I was a grade or two better at rock climbing than Hal. Nobody could."

Leaphorn recommended the chicken enchilada, and they all ordered it. McDermott inquired whether Leaphorn had considered their offer. Leaphorn said he had. Would he accept, then? They'd like to get moving on it right away. Leaphorn said he needed some more information. Their orders arrived. Delicious, thought Leaphorn, who had been dining mostly on his own cooking. McDermott ate thoughtfully. Shaw took a large bite, rich with green chile, and frowned at his fork.

"What sort of information?" McDermott asked.

"What am I looking for?" Leaphorn said.

"As I told you," McDermott said, "we can't be too specific. We just want to know that we have every bit of information that's available. We'd like to know why Harold Breedlove left Canyon de Chelly, and precisely when, and who he met and where they went. Anything that might concern his widow and her affairs at that time. We want to know everything that might cast light on this business." McDermott gave Leaphorn a small, deprecatory smile. "Everything," he said.

"My first question was what I would be looking for," Leaphorn said. "My second one is why? This must be expensive. If Mr. Shaw here is willing to pay me a thousand a week through your law firm, you will be charging him, what? The rate for an Albuquerque lawyer I know about used to be a hundred and ten dollars an hour. But that was long ago, and that was Albuquerque. Double it for a Washington firm? Would that be about right?"

"It isn't cheap," McDermott said.

"And maybe I find nothing useful at all. Probably you learn nothing. Tracks are cold after eleven years. But let us say that you learn the widow conspired to do away with her husband. I don't know for sure but I'd guess then she couldn't inherit. So the family gets the ranch back. What's it worth? Wonderful house, I hear, if someone rich wants to live in it way out there. Maybe a hundred head of cattle. I'm told there's still an old mortgage Harold's widow took out six years ago to pay off her husband's debts. How much could you get for that ranch?"

"It's a matter of justice," McDermott said. "I am not privy to the family's motives, but I presume they want some equity for Harold's death."

Leaphorn smiled.

Shaw had been sipping his coffee. He drained the cup and slammed it into the saucer with a clatter.

"We want to see Harold's killer hanged," he said. "Isn't that what they do out here? Hang 'em?"

"Not lately," Leaphorn said. "The mountain is on the New Mexico side of the reservation and New Mexico uses the gas chamber. But it would probably be federal jurisdiction. We Navajos don't have a death penalty and the federal government doesn't hang people." He signaled the waiter, had their coffee replenished, sipped his own, and put down the cup.

"If I take this job I don't want to be wasting my time," he said. "I would look for motives. An obvious one is inheritance of the ranch. That gives you two obvious suspects—the widow and her brother. But neither of them could have done it—at least not in the period right after Harold disappeared. The next possibility would be the widow's boyfriend, if she had one. So I would examine all that. Premeditated murder usually involves a lot of trouble and risk. I never knew of one that didn't grow out of a strong motivation."

Neither Shaw nor Breedlove responded to that.

"Usually greed," Leaphorn said.

"Love," said Shaw. "Or lust."

"Which does not seem to have been consummated, from what I know now," Leaphorn said. "The widow remained single. When I was investigating the disappearance years ago I snooped around a little looking for a boyfriend. I couldn't pick up any gossip that suggested a love triangle was involved."

"Easy enough to keep that quiet," Shaw said.

"Not out here it isn't," Leaphorn said. "I would be more interested in an economic motive." He looked at Shaw. "If this is a crime it's a white man's crime. No Navajo would kill anyone on that sacred mountain. I doubt if a Navajo would be disrespectful enough even to climb it. Among my people, murder tends to be motivated by whiskey or sexual jealousy. Among white people, I've noticed crime is more likely to be motivated by money. So if I take the job, I'd be turning on my computer and tapping into the metal market statistics and price trends."

Shaw gave McDermott a sidewise glance, which McDermott didn't notice. He was staring at Leaphorn.

"Why?"

"Because the gossipers around Mancos say Edgar Breedlove bought the ranch more because his prospectors had found molybdenum deposits on it than for its grazing. They say the price of moly ore rose enough about ten or fifteen years ago to make development profitable. They say Harold, or the Breedlove family, or somebody, was negotiating for a mineral lease and the Mancos Chamber of Commerce had high hopes of a big mining payroll. But then Harold disappeared and before you know it the price was down again. I'd want to find out if any of that was true."

"I see," McDermott said. "Yes, it would have made the ranch more valuable and made the motive stronger."

"What the hell," Shaw said. "We were keeping quiet about it because news like that leaks out, it causes problems. With local politicians, with the tree-huggers, with everybody else."

"Okay," Leaphorn said. "I guess if I take this job, then I'm safe in figuring the ranch is worth a lot more than the grass growing on it."

"What do you say?" Shaw said, his voice impatient. "Can we count on you to do some digging for us?"

"I'll think about it," Leaphorn said. "I'll call your office."

"We'll be here a day or two," Shaw said. "And we're in a hurry. Why not a decision right now?"

A hurry, Leaphorn thought. After all these years. "I'll let you know tomorrow," he said. "But you haven't answered my question about the value of the ranch."

McDermott looked grim. "You'd be safe to assume it was worth killing for."

11

TWISTING THE TAIL of a cow will encourage her to move forward," the text declared. "If the tail is held up over the back, it serves as a mild restraint. In both cases, the handler should hold the tail close to the base to avoid breaking it, and stand to the side to avoid being kicked."

The paragraph was at the top of the fourth-from-final page of a training manual supplied by the Navajo Nation for training brand inspectors of its Resource Enforcement Agency. Acting Lieutenant Jim Chee read it, put down the manual, and rubbed his eyes. He was not on the payroll of the tribe's REA. But since Captain Largo was forcing him to do its job he'd borrowed an REA brand inspector manual and was plowing his way through it. He'd covered the legal sections relating to grazing rights, trespass, brand registration, bills of sale, when and how livestock could be moved over the reservation boundary, and disease quarantine rules, and was now into advice about handling livestock without getting hurt. To Chee, who had been kicked by several horses but never by a cow, the advice seemed sound. Besides, it diverted him from the paperwork—vacation schedules, justifications for overtime pay, patrol car mileage reports, and so forth—that was awaiting action on his cluttered desk. He picked up the manual.

"The ear twitch can be used to divert attention from other parts of the body," the next paragraph began. "It should be used with care to avoid damage to the ear cartilage. To make the twitch, fasten a loop of cord or rope around the base of the horns. The rope is then carried around the ear and a half-hitch formed. The end of the rope is pulled to apply restraint."

Chee studied the adjoining illustration of a sleepy-looking cow wearing an ear twitch. Chee's childhood experience had been with sheep, on which an ear twitch wouldn't be needed. Still, he figured he could make one easily enough.

The next paragraph concerned a "rope casting harness" with which a person working alone could tie up a mature cow or bull without the risk of strangulation that was involved with usual bulldogging techniques. It looked easy, too, but required a lot of rope. Two pages to go and he'd be finished with this.

Then the telephone rang.

The voice on the telephone belonged to Officer Manuelito.

"Lieutenant," she said, "I've found something I think you should know about."

"Tell me," Chee said.

"Out near Ship Rock, that place where the fence posts had been dug out. You remember?"

"I remember."

"Well, the snow is gone now and you can see where before it snowed somebody had thrown out a bunch of hay."

"Ah," Chee said.

"Like they wanted to attract the cattle. Make them easy to get a rope on. To get 'em into a chute. Into your trailer."

"Manuelito," Chee said. "Have you finished interviewing that list of possible witnesses in that shooting business?"

Silence. Finally, "Most of them. Some of them I'm still looking for."

"Do they live out near Ship Rock?"

"Well, no. But—"

"Don't say but," Chee said. He shifted his weight in his chair, aware that his back hurt from too much sitting, aware that out in the natural world the sun was bright, the sky a dark blue, the chamisa had turned gold and the snakeweed a brilliant yellow. He sighed.

"Manuelito," he said. "Have you gone out to talk to the Sam woman about whether she's seen anything suspicious?"

"No, sir," Officer Manuelito said, sounding surprised. "You told me to—"

"Where are you calling from?"

"The Burnham trading post," she said. "The people there said they hadn't seen anything at the girl dance. But I think they did."

"Probably," Chee said. "They just didn't want to get the shooter into trouble. So come on in now, and buzz me when you get here, and we'll go out and see if Lucy Sam has seen anything interesting."

"Yes, sir," Officer Manuelito said, and she sounded like she thought that was a good idea. It seemed like a good idea to Chee, too. The tossing hay over the fence business sounded like Zorro's trademark as described by Finch, and that sounded like an opportunity to beat that arrogant bastard at his own game.

Officer Manuelito looked better today. Her uniform was tidy, hair black as a raven's wing and neatly combed, and no mud on her face. But she still displayed a slight tendency toward bossiness.

"Turn up there," she ordered, pointing to the road that led toward Ship Rock, "and I'll show you the hay."

Chee remembered very well the location of the loosened fence posts, but the beauty of the morning had turned him amiable. With Manuelito, he would work on correcting one fault at a time, leaving this one for a rainy day. He turned as ordered, parked when told to park, and followed her over to the fence. With the snow cover now evaporated, it was easy to see that the dirt had been dug away from the posts. It was also easy to see, scattered among the sage, juniper, and rabbit brush, what was left of several bales of alfalfa after the cattle had dined.

"Did you tell Delmar Yazzie about this?" Chee asked.

Officer Manuelito looked puzzled. "Yazzie?"

"Yazzie," Chee said. "The resource-enforcement ranger who works out of Shiprock. Mr. Yazzie is the man responsible for keeping people from stealing cattle."

Officer Manuelito looked flustered. "No, sir," she said. "I thought we could sort of stake this place out. Keep an eye on it, you know. Whoever is putting out this hay bait will be back and once he gets the cows used to coming here, he'll—"

"He'll rig himself up a sort of chute," Chee said, "and back his trailer in here, and drive a few of 'em on it, and . . ."

Chee paused. Her flustered look had been replaced by the smile of youthful enthusiasm. But now Chee's impatient tone had caused the smile to go away.

Acting Lieutenant Chee had intended to tell Officer Manuelito some of what he'd learned in digesting the brand inspector training manual. If they did indeed catch the cattle thief and managed to get a conviction, the absolute maximum penalty for his crime would be a fine "not to exceed $100" and a jail term "not to exceed six months." That's what it said in section 1356 of subchapter six of chapter seven of the Livestock Inspection and Control Manual. Reading that section just after Manuelito's call had fueled Chee's urge to get out of the office and into the sunlight. But why was he venting his bad mood on this rookie cop? Even interrupting her to do it—an inexcusable rudeness for any Navajo. It wasn't her fault, it was Captain Largo's. And besides, Finch had hurt his pride. He wanted to deflate that pompous jerk by catching Finch's Zorro before Finch got him. Manuelito looked like a valuable help in that project.

Chee swallowed, cleared his throat. ". . . and then we'd have an easy conviction," he concluded.

Officer Manuelito's expression had become unreadable. A hard lady to mislead.

"And put a stop to one cow thief," he added, conscious of how lame it sounded. "Well, let's go. Let's see if anyone's at home at the Sam place."

The Rural Electrification Administration had run a power line across the empty landscape off in the direction of the Chuska Mountains, which took it within a few miles of the Sam place, and the Navajo Communication Company had followed by linking such inhabited spots as Rattlesnake and Red Rock to the world with its own telephone lines. But the Sam outfit had either been too far off the route to make a connection feasible, or the Sam family had opted to preserve its privacy. Thus the fence posts that lined the dirt track leading to the Sam hogan were not draped with telephone wire, and thus there had been no way for Jim Chee to warn Ms. Sam of the impending visit.

But as he geared down into low to creep over the cattle guard and onto the track leading into the Sam grazing lease, he noticed the old boot hanging on the gate post was right side up. Someone must be home.

"I hope someone's here," Officer Manuelito said.

"They are," Chee said. He nodded toward the boot.

Officer Manuelito frowned, not understanding.

"The boot's turned up," Chee said. "When you're leaving, and nobody's going to be home, you turn the boot upside down. Empty. Nobody home. That saves your visitor from driving all the way up to the hogan."

"Oh," Manuelito said. "I didn't know that. We lived over near Keams Canyon before Mom moved to Red Rock."

She sounded impressed. Chee became aware that he was showing off. And enjoying it. He nodded, said: "Yep. You probably had a different signal over there." And thought it would be embarrassing now if nobody was home. The trouble with cattle guard signaling was that people forgot to stop and change the boot.

But Lucy Sam's pickup was resting in front of her double-wide mobile home and Lucy Sam was peering out of the screen door at them. Chee let the patrol car roll to a stop amid a flock of startled chickens. They waited, giving Ms. Sam the time required to prepare herself for receiving visitors. It also gave Chee time to inspect the place.

The mobile home was one of the flimsier models but it had been placed solidly on a base of concrete blocks to keep the wind from blowing under it. A small satellite dish sat on its roof, helping a row of old tires hold down the aluminum panels as well as bringing in a television signal. Beside this insubstantial residence stood the Sam hogan, solidly built of sandstone slabs with its door facing properly eastward. Chee's practiced eyes could tell that it had been built to the specifications prescribed for the People by Changing Woman, their giver of laws. Beyond the hogan was a hay shed with a plank holding pen for cattle, a windmill with attendant water tank, and, on top of the shed, a small wind generator, its fan blades spinning in the morning breeze. Down the slope a rusty and long-deceased Ford F100 pickup rested on blocks with its wheels missing. Farther down stood an outhouse. Beyond this untidy clutter of rural living, the view stretched away forever.

It reminded Chee of a professor he'd had once at the University of

New Mexico who had done a research project on how Navajos place their hogans. The answer seemed to Chee glaringly obvious. A Navajo, like a rancher anywhere, would need access to water, to grazing, to a road, and above all a soul-healing view of—in the words of one of the curing chants—"beauty all around you."

The Sam family had put beauty first. They had picked the very crest of the high grassy ridge between Red Wash and Little Ship Rock Wash. To the west the morning sun lit the pink and orange wilderness of erosion that gave the Red Rock community its name. Beyond that the blue-green mass of the Carrizo Mountains rose. Far to the north in Colorado, the Roman nose shape of Sleeping Ute Mountain dominated, and west of that was the always-changing pattern of lights and shadows that marked the edge of Utah's canyon country. But look eastward, and all of this was overpowered by the dark monolith of the Rock with Wings towering over the rolling grassland. Only five or six million years old, the geologists said, but in Chee's mythology it had been there since God created time or, depending on the version one preferred, had flown in fairly recently carrying the first Navajo clans down from the north.

Lucy Sam reappeared at her doorway, the signal that she was ready to receive her visitors. She had started a coffeepot brewing on her propane stove, put on a blouse of dark blue velveteen, and donned her silver and turquoise jewelry in their honor. Now they went through the polite formalities of traditional Navajo greetings, seated themselves beside the Sam table, and waited while Ms. Sam extracted what she called her "rustler book" from a cabinet stacked with magazines and papers.

Chee considered himself fairly adept at guessing the ages of males and fairly poor with females. Ms. Sam he thought must be in her late sixties—give or take five or ten years. She did her hair bound up in the traditional style, wore the voluminous long skirt demanded by traditional modesty, and had a television set on a corner table tuned to a morning talk show. It was one of the sleazier ones—a handsome young woman named Ricki something or other probing into the sexual misconduct, misfortune, hatreds, and misery of a row of retarded-looking guests, to the amusement of the studio audience. But Chee was distracted from this spectacle by what was sharing table space with the television set.

It was a telescope mounted on a short tripod and aimed through the window at the world outside. Chee recognized it as a spotting scope—the sort the marksmanship instructor had peered through on the police recruit firing range to tell him how far he'd missed the bull's-eye. This one looked like an older, bulkier model, probably an artillery observer's range-finding scope and probably bought in an army surplus store.

Ms. Sam had placed her book, a black ledger that looked even older than the scope, on the table. She settled a pair of bifocals on her nose and opened it.

"I haven't seen much since you asked me to be watching," she said to Officer Manuelito. "I mean I haven't seen much that you'd want to arrest somebody for." She looked over the bifocals at Chee, grinning. "Not unless you want to arrest that lady that used to work at the Red Rock trading post for fooling with somebody else's husband."

Officer Manuelito was grinning, too. Chee apparently looked blank, because Ms. Sam pointed past the telescope and out the window.

"Way over there toward Rock with Wings," she explained. "There's a nice little place down there. Live spring there and cottonwood trees. I was sort of looking around through the telescope to see if any trucks were parked anywhere and I see the lady's little red car just driving up toward the trees. And then in a minute, here comes Bennie Smiley's pickup truck. Then, quite a little bit later, the truck comes out over the hill again, and then four or five minutes, here comes the little red car."

She nodded to Chee, decided he was hopeless, and looked at Manuelito. "It was about an hour," she added, which caused Officer Manuelito's smile to widen.

"Bennie," she said. "I'll be darned."

"Yes," Ms. Sam said.

"I know Bennie," Officer Manuelito said. "He used to be my oldest sister's boyfriend. She liked him but then she found out he was born to the Streams Come Together clan. That's too close to our 'born to' clan for us."

Ms. Sam shook her head, made a disapproving sound. But she was still smiling.

"That lady with the red car," Manuelito said. "I wonder if I know her, too. Is that Mrs.—"

Chee cleared his throat.

"I wonder if you noticed any pickups, anything you could haul a load of hay in, stopped over there on the road past the Rattlesnake pumping station. Probably a day or so before the snow." He glanced at Officer Manuelito, tried to read her expression, decided she was either slightly abashed for gossiping instead of tending to police business, or irritated because he'd interrupted her. Probably the latter.

Ms. Sam was thumbing through the ledger, saying, "Let's see now. Wasn't it Monday night it started snowing?" She thumbed past another page, tapped the paper with a finger. "Big fifthwheel truck parked there beside Route 33. Dark blue, and the trailer he was pulling was partly red and partly white, like somebody was painting it and didn't get it finished. Had Arizona plates. But that was eight days before it snowed."

"That sounds like my uncle's truck," Manuelito said. "He lives over there at Sanostee."

Ms. Sam said she thought it had looked familiar. And, no, she hadn't noticed any strange trucks the days just before the storm, but then she'd gone into Farmington to buy groceries and was gone one day. She read off the four other entries she'd made since getting Manuelito's request. One sounded like Dick Finch's truck with its bulky camper. None of the others would mean anything unless and until some sort of pattern developed. Pattern! That made him think of the days he'd worked for Leaphorn. Leaphorn was always looking for patterns.

"How did you know it was an Arizona license?" Chee asked. "The telescope?"

"Take a look," Ms. Sam said, and waved at the scope.

Chee did, twiddling the adjustment dial. The mountain jumped at him. Huge. He focused on a slab of basalt fringed with mountain oak. "Wow," Chee said. "Quite a scope."

He turned it, brought in the point where Navajo Route 33 cuts through the Chinese Wall of stone that wanders southward from the volcano. A school bus was rolling down the asphalt, heading for Red Rock after taking kids on their fifty-mile ride into high school at Shiprock.

"We bought it for him, long time ago when he started getting sick," Ms. Sam said—using the Navajo words that avoided alluding directly to the name of the dead. "I saw it in that big pawnshop on Railroad Avenue in Gallup. Then he could sit there and watch the world and keep track of his mountain."

She produced a deprecatory chuckle, as if Chee might think this odd. "Every day he'd write down what he saw. You know. Like which pairs of kestrels were coming back to the same nests. And where the red-tailed hawks were hunting. Which kids were spray-painting stuff on that old water tank down there, or climbing the windmill. That sort of thing."

She sighed, gestured at the talk show. "Better than this stuff. He loved his mountain. Watching it kept him happy."

"I heard he used to come down to Shiprock, to the police station, and report people trespassing and climbing Tse´ Bit´ a´í," Chee said. "Is that right?"

"He wanted them arrested," she said. "He said it was wrong, those white people climbing a mountain that was sacred. He said if he was younger and had some money he would go back East and climb up the front of that big cathedral in New York." Ms. Sam laughed. "See how they liked that."

"What sort of things did he write in the book?" Chee asked, thinking of Lieutenant Leaphorn and feeling a twinge of excitement. "Could I see it?"

"All sorts of things," she said, and handed it to him. "He was in the marines. One of the code talkers, and he liked to do things the way they did in the marines."

The entries were dated with the numbers of day, month, and year, and the first one was 25/7/89. After the date Hosteen Sam had written in a tiny, neat missionary-school hand that he had gone into Farmington that day and bought this book to replace the old one, which was full. The next entry was dated 26/7/89. After that Sam had written: "Redtail hawks nesting. Sold two rams to D. Nez."

Chee closed the book. What was the date Breedlove had vanished? Oh, yes.

He handed Ms. Sam the ledger.

"Do you have an earlier book?"

"Two of them," she said. "He started writing more after he got really sick. Had more time then." She took two ledgers down from the top of the cabinet where she stored canned goods and handed them to Chee. "It was something that kills the nerves. Sometimes he would feel pretty good but he was getting paralyzed."

"I've heard of it," Manuelito said. "They say there's no cure."

"We had a sing for him," Ms. Sam said. "A Yeibichai. He got better for a little while."

Chee found the page with the day of Hal Breedlove's disappearance and scanned the dates that followed. He found crows migrating, news of a coyote family, mention of an oil field service truck, but absolutely nothing to indicate that Breedlove or anyone else had come to climb Hosteen Sam's sacred mountain.

Disappointing. Well, anyway, he would think about this. And he'd tell Lieutenant Leaphorn about the book. That thought surprised him. Why tell Leaphorn? The man was a civilian now. It was none of his business. He didn't exactly like Leaphorn. Or he hadn't thought he did. Was it respect? The man was smarter than anybody Chee had ever met. Damn sure smarter than Acting Lieutenant Jim Chee. And maybe that was why he didn't exactly like him.

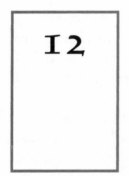

12

FOR THE FIRST time in his life that metaphor whites use about money burning a hole in your pocket had taken on meaning for Joe Leaphorn. The heat had been caused by a check for twenty thousand dollars made out to him against an account of the Breedlove Corporation. Leaphorn had endorsed it and exchanged it for a deposit slip to an account in his name in the Mancos Security Bank. Now the deposit slip resided uneasily in his wallet as he waited for Mrs. Cecilia Rivera to finish dealing with a customer and talk to him. Which she did, right now.

Leaphorn rose, pulled back a chair for her at the lobby table where she had deposited him earlier. "Sorry," she said. "I don't like to keep a new customer waiting." She sat, examined him briefly, and got right to the point. "What did you want to ask me about?"

"First," Leaphorn said, "I want to tell you what I'm doing here. Opening this account and all."

"I wondered about that," Mrs. Rivera said. "I noticed your address was Window Rock, Arizona. I thought maybe you were going into some line of business up here." That came out as a question.

"Did you notice who the check was drawn against?" Leaphorn asked. Of course she would have. It was a very small bank in a very small town. The Breedlove name would be famous here, and Leaphorn had seen the teller discussing the deposit with Mrs. Rivera. But he wanted to make sure.

"The Breedloves," Mrs. Rivera said, studying his face. "It's been a few years since we've seen a Breedlove check but I never heard of one bouncing. Hal's widow banked here for a little while after he—after he disappeared. But then she quit us."

Mrs. Rivera was in her mid-seventies, Leaphorn guessed, thin and sun-wrinkled. Her bright black eyes examined him through the top half of her bifocals with frank curiosity.

"I'm working for them now," Leaphorn said. "For the Breedloves." He waited.

Mrs. Rivera drew in a long breath. "Doing what?" she asked. "Would it be something to do with that moly mine project?"

"It may be that," Leaphorn said. "To tell the truth, I don't know. I'm a retired policeman." He extracted his identification case and showed it to her. "Years ago when Hal Breedlove disappeared, I was the detective working that case." He produced a deprecatory expression. "Obviously I didn't have much success with it, because it took about eleven years to find him, and then it was by accident. But anyway, the family seems to have remembered."

"Yes," Mrs. Rivera said. "Young Hal did like to climb up onto the mountains." A dim smile appeared. "From what I read in the *Farmington Times*, I guess he needed more studying on how to climb down off of them."

Leaphorn rewarded this with a chuckle.

"In my experience," he said, "bankers are like doctors and lawyers and ministers. Their business depends a lot on keeping confidences." He looked at her, awaiting confirmation of this bit of misinformation. Leaphorn had always found bankers wonderful sources of information.

"Well, yes," she said. "Lot of business secrets come floating around when you're negotiating loans."

"Are you willing to handle another one?"

"Another secret?" Mrs. Rivera's expression became avid. She nodded.

And so Lieutenant Joe Leaphorn, retired, laid his cards on the table. More or less. It was a tactic he'd used for years—based on his theory that most humans prefer exchanging information to giving it away. He'd tried to teach Jim Chee that rule, which was: Tell somebody something interesting and they'll try to top it. So now he was going to tell Mrs. Rivera everything he knew about the affair of Hal Breedlove, who had been by Four Corners standards her former neighbor and was her onetime customer. In return he expected Mrs. Rivera to tell him something she knew about Hal Breedlove, and his ranch, and his business. Which was why he had opened this account here. Which was what he had decided to do yesterday when, after long seconds of hesitation, he had accepted the check he had never expected to receive.

They had met again yesterday at the Navajo Inn—Leaphorn, McDermott, and George Shaw.

"If I take this job," Leaphorn had said, "I will require a substantial retainer." He kept his eyes on Shaw's face.

"Substantial?" said McDermott. "How sub—"

"How much?" asked Shaw.

How much, indeed, Leaphorn thought. He had decided he would mention a price too large for them to pay, but not ludicrously overdone. Twenty thousand dollars, he had decided. They would make a counteroffer. Perhaps two thousand. Two weeks pay in advance. He would drop finally to, say, ten thousand. They would counter. And finally he would establish how important this affair was to Shaw.

"Twenty thousand dollars," Leaphorn said.

McDermott had snorted, said, "Be serious. We can't—"

But George Shaw had reached into his inside coat pocket and extracted a checkbook and a pen.

"From what I've heard about you we won't need to lawyer this," he said. "The twenty thousand will be payment in full, including any expenses you incur, for twenty weeks of your time or until you develop the information we need to settle this business. Is that acceptable?"

Leaphorn hadn't intended to accept anything—certainly not to associate himself with these two men. He didn't need money. Or want it. But Shaw was writing the check now, face grim and intent. Which told Leaphorn there was much more involved here than he'd expected.

Shaw had torn out the check, handed it to him. A little piece of the puzzle that had stuck in Leaphorn's mind for eleven years—that had been revived by the shooting of Hosteen Nez—had clicked into place. Unreadable yet, but it shed a dim light on the effort to kill Nez. If twenty thousand dollars could be tossed away like this, millions more than that must be somehow involved. That told him hardly anything. Just a hint that Nez might still be, to use that white expression, "worth killing." Or for Shaw, perhaps worth keeping alive.

He had held the check a moment, a little embarrassed, trying to think of what to say as he returned it. He knew now that he would try again to find a way to solve this old puzzle, but for himself and not for these men. He extended the check to Shaw, said, "I'm sorry. I don't think—"

Then he had seen how useful that check could be. It would give him a Breedlove connection. He wasn't a policeman any longer. This would give him the key he'd need to unlock doors.

And this morning, in this small, old-fashioned bank lobby, Leaphorn was using it.

"This is sort of hard to explain," he told Mrs. Rivera. "What I'm trying to do for the Breedlove family is vague. They want me to find out everything about the disappearance of Hal Breedlove and about his death on Ship Rock."

Mrs. Rivera leaned forward. "They don't think it was an accident?"

"They don't exactly say that. But it was a pretty peculiar business. You remember it?"

"I remember it very well," Mrs. Rivera said, with a wry laugh. "The Breedlove boy did his banking here—like the ranch always had. He was my customer and he was four payments behind on a note. We'd sent him notices. Twice, I believe it was. And the next thing you know, he's vanished."

Mrs. Rivera laughed. "That's the sort of thing a banker remembers a long, long time."

"How was it secured? I understand he didn't get title to the ranch until his birthday—just before he disappeared."

Mrs. Rivera leaned back now and folded her arms. "Well, now," she said. "I don't think we want to get into that. That's private business."

"No harm me asking, though," Leaphorn said. "It's a habit policemen get into. Let me tell you what I know, and then you decide if you know anything you would be free to add that might be helpful."

"That sounds fair enough," she said. "You talk. I'll listen."

And she did. Nodding now and then, sometimes indicating surprise, enjoying being an insider on an investigation. Sometimes indicating agreement as Leaphorn explained a theory, shaking her head in disapproval when he told her how little information Shaw and McDermott had given him to work on. As Leaphorn had hoped, Mrs. Rivera had become a partner.

"But you know how lawyers are," he said. "And Shaw's a lawyer, too. I checked on it. He specializes in corporate tax cases. Anyway, they sure didn't give me much to work with."

"I don't know what I can add," she said. "Hal was a spendthrift, I know that. Always buying expensive toys. Snowmobiles, fancy cars. He'd bought himself a—can't think of the name—one of those handmade Italian cars, for example. A Ferrari, however you pronounce that. Cost a fortune and then he drove it over these old back roads and tore it up. He'd worked out some sort of deal with the trust and got a mortgage on the ranch. But then when they sold cattle in the fall and the money went into the ranch account he'd spend it right out of there instead of paying his debts."

She paused, searching for something to add. "Hal always had Sally get him first-class tickets when he flew—Sally has Mancos Travel—and first class costs an arm and a leg."

"And coach class gets there almost as quick," Leaphorn said.

Mrs. Rivera nodded. "Even when they went places together Sally had her instructions to put Hal into first class and Demott in coach. Now what do you think of that?"

Leaphorn shook his head.

"Well, I think it's insulting," Mrs. Rivera said.

"Could have been Demott's idea," Leaphorn said.

"I don't think so," Mrs. Rivera said. "Sally told—" She cut that off.

"I talked to Demott when I was investigating Breedlove's disappearance," Leaphorn said. "He seemed like a solid citizen."

"Well, yes. I guess so. But he's a strange one, too." She chuckled. "I guess maybe we all get a little odd. Living up here with mountains all around us, you know."

"Strange," Leaphorn said. "How?"

Mrs. Rivera looked slightly embarrassed. She shrugged. "Well, he's a bachelor for one thing. But I guess there's a lot of bachelors around here. And he's sort of a halfway tree-hugger. Or so people say. We have some of those around here, too, but they're mostly move-ins from California or back East. Not the kind of people who ever had to worry about feeding kids or working for a living."

"Tree-hugger? How'd he get that reputation?" Leaphorn was thinking of a favorite nephew, a tree-hugger who'd gotten himself arrested leading a noisy protest at a tribal council meeting, trying to stop a logging operation in the Chuskas. In Leaphorn's opinion his nephew had been on the right side of that controversy.

"Well, I don't know," Mrs. Rivera said. "But they say Eldon was why they didn't do that moly operation. Up there in the edge of the San Juan National Forest."

Leaphorn said, "Oh. What happened?"

"It was years ago. I think the spring after Hal went missing. We weren't in on the deal, of course. This bank is way too little for the multimillion-dollar things like that. A bank up in Denver was involved I think. And I think the mining company was MCA, the Moly Corp. Anyway, the way it was told around here, there was some sort of contract drawn up, a mineral lease involving Breedlove land up the canyon, and then at first the widow was going to handle it, but Hal legally was still alive and she didn't want to file the necessary papers to have the courts say he was dead. So that tied it up. People say she stalled on that because Demott was against it. Demott's her brother, you know. But to tell the truth, I think it was her own idea. She's loved that place since she was a tot. Grew up on it, you know."

"I don't know much about their background," Leaphorn said.

"Well, it used to be the Double D ranch. Demott's daddy owned it. The price of beef was way down in the thirties. Lot of ranches around here went at sheriff's auction, including that one. Old Edgar Breedlove bought it, and he kept the old man on as foreman. Old Breedlove didn't care a thing about ranching. One of his prospectors had found the moly deposit up the headwaters of Cache Creek and that's what he wanted. But anyway, Eldon and Elisa grew up on the place."

"Why didn't he mine the molybdenum?" Leaphorn asked.

"War broke out and I guess he couldn't get the right kind of priority to get the manpower or the equipment." She laughed. "Then when the war ended, the price of the ore fell. Stayed down for years and then went shooting up. Then Hal got himself lost and that tied it all up once again."

"And by the time she had Breedlove declared dead, the price of ore had gone down. Is that right?"

"Right," Mrs. Rivera said. And looked thoughtful.

"And now it's up again," Leaphorn said.

"That's just what I was thinking."

"You think that might be why the Breedlove Corporation would pay me the twenty thousand?"

She looked over her glasses at him. "That's an unkind thought," she said, "but I confess it occurred to me."

"Even though Hal's widow owns the place now?"

"She owns it, unless they can prove she had something to do with killing him. We had our lawyer look into that. She wanted to extend a mortgage on the place." She looked mildly apologetic. "Can't take chances, you know, with your investors' money."

"Did you extend the mortgage?"

Mrs. Rivera folded her arms again. But finally she said, "Well, yes, we did."

Leaphorn grinned. "Could I guess then that you don't think she had anything to do with killing Breedlove? Or anyway, nobody is ever going to prove it?"

"I just own a piece of this bank," Mrs. Rivera said. "There's people I'm responsible to. So I'd have to agree with you. I thought the loan was safe enough."

"Still do?"

She nodded, remembering. Then shook her head.

"When it happened, I mean when he just disappeared like that, I had my doubts. I always thought Elisa was a fine young lady. Good family. Raised right. She used to help take care of her grandmother when the old lady had the cancer. But you know, it sure did look suspicious. Hal inherits the Lazy B and then the very same week—or pretty close to that, anyway—he's gone. So you start thinking she might of had herself another man some-where and—well, you know."

"That's what I thought, too," Leaphorn said. "What do you think now?"

"I was wrong," she said.

"You sound certain," Leaphorn said.

"You live in Window Rock," she said. "That's a little town like Mancos. You think some widow woman there with a rich husband lost somewhere could have something going with a boyfriend and everybody wouldn't know about it?"

Leaphorn laughed. "I'm a widower," he said. "And I met this nice lady from Flagstaff on some police work I was doing. The very first time I had lunch with her, when I got back to the office they were planning my wedding."

"It's the same way out here," Mrs. Rivera said. "About the time everybody around here decided that Hal was gone for good, they started marrying Elisa off to the Castro boy."

Leaphorn smiled. "You know," he said, "we cops tend to get too high an opinion of ourselves. When I was up here asking around after Hal disappeared I went away thinking there wasn't a boyfriend in the background."

"You got here too quick," Mrs. Rivera said. "Here at Mancos we let the body get cold before the talking starts."

"I guess nothing came of that romance," Leaphorn said. "At least she's still a widow."

"From what I heard, it wasn't from lack of Tommy Castro's trying. About the time she got out of high school everybody took for granted they were a pair. Then Hal showed up." Mrs. Rivera shrugged, expression rueful. "They made a kind of foursome for a while."

"Four?"

"Well, sometimes it was five of 'em. This George Shaw, he'd come out with Hal sometimes and Eldon would go. He and Castro were the old heads, the coaches. They'd go elk hunting together. Camping. Rock climbing. Growing up with her dad raising her, and then her big brother, Elisa was quite a tomboy."

"What broke up the group? Was it the country boy couldn't compete with the big-city glamour?"

"Oh, I guess that was some of it," she said. "But Eldon had a falling-out with Tommy. They're too much alike. Both bull-headed."

Leaphorn digested that. Emma's big brother hadn't liked him, either, but that hadn't bothered Emma. "Do you know what happened?"

"I heard Eldon thought Tommy was out of line making a play for his little sister. She was just out of high school. Eight or ten years between 'em, I guess."

"So Elisa was willing to let big brother monitor her love life," Leaphorn said. "I don't hear about that happening much these days."

"Me neither," Mrs. Rivera said, and laughed. "But you know," she said, suddenly dead serious, "Elisa is an unusual person. Her mother died when she was about in the second grade, but Elisa takes after her. Has a heart big as a pumpkin and a cast-iron backbone, just like her mother. When old man Demott was losing the ranch it was Elisa's mama who held everything together. Got her husband out of the bars, and out of jail a time or two. One of those people who are aways there in the background looking out for other people. You know?"

Mrs. Rivera paused at this to see what Leaphorn thought of it. Leaphorn, not sure of where this was leading, just nodded.

"So there Elisa was after Hal was out of the picture. Tommy was beginning to court her again, and Eldon wanted to run him off. They even got into a yelling match down at the High Country Inn. So there's Elisa with two men to take care of—and knowing how she is I have a theory about that." She paused again. "It's just a theory."

"I'd like to hear it," Leaphorn said.

"I think she loved them both," Mrs. Rivera said. "But if she married the Castro boy, what in the wide world was Eldon going to do? It was her ranch now. Eldon loved it but he wouldn't stay around and work for Tommy, and Tommy wouldn't want him to." She sighed. "If we had a Shakespeare around here, they could have made a tragedy out of it."

"So this Castro was a rock climber, too," Leaphorn said. "Does he still live here?"

"If you got gas down at the Texaco station you might have seen him. That's his garage."

"What do you think? Did this affection for Castro linger on after she married Hal?"

"If it did, she didn't let it show." She thought about that awhile, looked sad, shook her head. "Far as you could tell being an outsider, she was the loyal wife. I couldn't see much to love in Hal myself but every woman's different about that and Elisa was the sort who—the more that was wrong with a man, the more she'd stand behind him. She mourned

for him. Matter of fact, I think she still does. You hardly ever see her looking happy."

"How about her brother, then? You said he was sort of strange."

She shrugged. "Well, he liked to climb up cliffs. To me, that's strange."

"Somebody said he taught Hal the sport."

"That's not quite the way it was. After old Edgar got the place away
from Demott's daddy, Hal and Shaw would come out in the summers.
Shaw had been climbing already. So he didn't need much teaching. And
Demott and Castro were already into climbing some when they had time.
Eldon was about six or eight years older than Hal and more of an athlete.
From what I heard he was the best of the bunch."

A customer came in and the cool smell of autumn and the sound of
laughter followed him through the doorway from the street. Leaphorn
could think of just one more pertinent question.

"You mentioned Hal Breedlove had overdue note payments when he
disappeared. How'd that get paid off?"

It was the sort of bank business question he wasn't sure she would
answer. Neither was she. But finally she shook her head and laughed.

"Well, you sort of guessed right about not having it secured the way
we should have. Old family, and all. So we weren't pressing. But we'd sold
off another loan to a Denver bank. Made it to a feedlot operator who liked
to go off to Vegas and try to beat the blackjack tables. With people like
that you make sure you have it secured. Wrote it on sixty-two head of
bred heifers he had grazing up in a Forest Service lease. The Denver people foreclosed on it and they called us for help on claiming the property."

She laughed. "Those Denver people had sixty-two head of cows out in
the mountains grazing on a Forest Service lease and not an idea in the
world about what to do with them. So I told 'em Eldon Demott might
round them up for 'em and truck them over to Durango to the auction
barn. And he did."

"He got paid enough for that to pay off Breedlove's note?"

She laughed again. "Not directly. But I mentioned we made the loan
on bred heifers. So we sold the Denver bank a mortgage on sixty-two head,
but when Demott went to get 'em, they weren't pregnant anymore. They
were mama cows."

She paused, wanting to see if Leaphorn understood the implications of this. Leaphorn said: "Ah, yes. He didn't get back from Las Vegas to brand 'em."

"Ah, yes, is right," Mrs. Rivera said. "In fact he didn't get back at all. The sheriff has a warrant out for him. So there was Eldon with sixty-two cows loaded up and all those calves left over. They were all still slicks. Not any of 'em branded yet. Nobody in the world had title to 'em. Nobody owned 'em but the Lord in heaven."

"Enough to pay off the note?"

"He might've had a little bit left over," she said, and looked at Leaphorn over her glasses. "Wait a minute now," she said. "Don't you get any wrong ideas. I don't actually know what in the world happened to those calves. And I've been talking way too much and it's time to get some work done."

Back at his car, Leaphorn fished his cellular telephone from the glove compartment, dialed his Window Rock number, and punched in the proper code to retrieve any messages accumulated by his answering machine. The first call was from George Shaw, asking if he had anything to report and saying he could be reached at room 23, Navajo Inn. The second call was from Sergeant Addison Deke at the Chinle police station.

"Better give me a call, Joe," Deke said. "It probably doesn't amount to anything but you asked me to sort of keep an eye on Amos Nez and you might like to hear about this."

Leaphorn didn't check on whether there was a third call. He dialed the Arizona area code and Chinle police department number. Yes, Sergeant Deke was in.

He sounded apologetic. "Probably nothing, Joe," he said. "Probably wasting your time. But after we talked, I told the boys to keep it in their minds that whoever shot Nez might try it again. You know, keep an eye out. Be looking." Deke hesitated.

Leaphorn, who almost never allowed impatience to show, said, "What did they see?"

"Nothing, actually. But Tazbah Lovejoy came in this morning—I don't think you know him. He's a young fellow out of recruit training two years ago. Anyway Tazbah told me he'd run into one of those Resource Enforcement Agency rangers having coffee, and this guy was telling him about seeing a poacher up on the rim of Canyon del Muerto yesterday."

Sergeant Deke hesitated again. This time Leaphorn gave him a moment to organize his thoughts.

"The ranger told Tazbah he was checking on some illegal firewood cutting, and he stopped at that turnout overlook down into del Muerto. Wanted to take a leak. He was getting that done, standing there, looking out across the canyon, and he kept seeing reflections off something or other across the canyon. No road over there, you know, and he wondered about it. So he went to his truck and got his binoculars to see what he could see. There was a fellow over there with binoculars. The reflections turned out to be coming off the lenses, I guess. Anyway, he had a rifle, too."

"Deer hunter, maybe," Leaphorn said.

Deke laughed. "Joe," he said. "How long's it been since you've been deer hunting? That'd be out on that tongue of the plateau between del Muerto and Black Rock Canyon. Nobody's seen a deer over there since God knows when."

"Maybe it was an Anglo deer hunter then. Did he get a good look at him?"

"I don't think so. The ranger thought it was funny. Hunter over there and nothing to hunt. But I guess he was going to call it attempted poaching, or conspiracy to poach. So he drove back up to Wheatfields campground and tried to get back in there as far as he could on that old washed-out track. But he gave up on it."

"Did he get a good enough look to say man or woman?"

"I asked Tazbah and he said the ranger didn't know for sure. He said they were thinking man, on grounds a woman wouldn't be stupid enough to go hunting where there wasn't anything to shoot at. I thought you'd like to know about it because it was just up the canyon a half mile or so from where that sniper shot old Amos."

"Which would put it just about right over the Nez place," Leaphorn said.

"Exactly," Deke said. "You could jump right down on his roof."

13

ACTING LIEUTENANT JIM Chee was parked at sunrise on the access road to Beclabito Day School because he wanted to talk to Officer Teddy Begayaye at a private place. Officer Begayaye would be driving to the office from his home at Tec Nos Pos. Chee wanted to tell him that vacation schedules were being posted today, that he was getting the Thanksgiving week vacation time he had asked for. He wanted Begayaye to provide him some sort of justification (beyond his twelve years of seniority) for approving it. Another member of Chee's criminal investigation squad wanted the same days off, namely, Officer Manuelito. She had applied for them first, and Chee wanted to give her some reason (beyond her total lack of seniority) why she didn't get it—thereby avoiding friction in the department. Thus Chee had parked where Begayaye could see him instead of hiding his patrol car behind the day school sign in hope of nabbing a speeder.

But now Chee wasn't thinking of vacation schedules. He was thinking of the date he had tonight with Janet Pete, back from whatever law business had taken her to Washington. Janet shared an apartment at Gallup with Louise Guard, another of the DNA lawyers. Chee had hopes that Louise, as much as he liked her, would be away somewhere for the evening (or, better, had found herself another apartment). He wanted to show Janet a videotape he'd borrowed of a traditional Navajo wedding. She had more or less agreed, with qualifications, that they would do the ceremony the Navajo way and that he could pick the haatalii to perform it. But she clearly had her doubts about it. Janet's mother had something more so-cially correct in mind. However, if he lucked out and Ms. Guard actually had shoved off for somewhere, he would hold the videotape for another evening. He and Janet hadn't seen each other for a week and there were better ways to occupy the evening.

The vehicle rolling down U.S. 64 toward him was a camper truck, dirty and plastered with tourist stickers. Dick Finch's vehicle. It slowed to a crawl, with Finch making a series of hand signals. Most of them were meaningless to Chee, but one of them said "follow me."

Chee started his engine and followed, driving eastward on 64 with Finch speeding. Chee topped the ridge. Finch's truck had already disap-peared, but a plume of dust hanging over the dirt road that led past the Rattlesnake pump station betrayed it. Chee made the left turn into the dust—thinking how quickly this arid climate could replace wet snow with blowable dirt. Just out of sight of the highway the camper was parked, with Finch standing beside it.

Finch walked over, smiling that smile of his. Lots of white teeth.

"Good morning," Chee said.

"Captain Largo wants us to work together," Finch said. "So do my people. Get along with the Navajos, they tell me. And the Utes and the Zunis, Arizona State Police, the county mounties, and everybody. Good policy, don't you think?"

"Why not?" Chee said.

"Well, there might be a reason why not," Finch said, still smiling, waiting for Chee to say, "Like what?" Chee just looked at him until Finch tired of the game.

"For example, somebody's been taking a little load of heifers now and then off that grazing lease west of your Ship Rock mountain. They're owned by an old codger who lives over near Toadlena. He rents grass from a fella named Maryboy, and his livestock is all mixed up with Maryboy's and nobody keeps track of the cattle."

Finch waited again. So did Chee. What Finch was telling him so far was common enough. People who had grazing leases let other people use them for a fee. One of the problems of catching cattle thieves was the animals might be gone a month before anyone noticed. Finally Chee said: "What's your point?"

"Point is, as we say, I've got reason to believe that the fella picking up these animals is this fella I've been trying to nail. He comes back to the mountain about every six months or so and picks up a load. Does the same thing over around Bloomfield, and Whitehorse Lake, and Burnham, and other places. When I catch him, a lot of this stealing stops. My job gets easier. So a couple of months ago, I found where he got the last ones he took from that Ship Rock pasture. The son of a bitch was throwing hay over a fence at a place where he could back his truck in. Chumming them up like he was a fisherman. I imagine he'd blow his horn when he threw the hay over. Cows are curious. Worse than cats. They'd come to see about it. And they've got good memories. Do it about twice, and when they hear a horn they think of good alfalfa hay. Come running."

Finch laughed. Chee knew exactly where this was leading.

"Manuelito spotted that hay, too," Chee said. "She noticed how the fence posts had been dug up there, loosened so they can be pulled up. She took me out to show me."

"I saw you," Finch said. "Watched you through my binoculars from about two miles away. Trouble is, our cow thief was probably watching, too. He's baited that place three times now. No use wasting any more hay. It's time to collect his cows."

Finch stared at Chee, his smile still genial. Chee felt his face flushing, which seemed to be the reaction Finch was awaiting.

"But he ain't going to do it now, is he? You can bet your ass he's got a set of binoculars every bit as good as mine, and he's careful. He sees a police car parked there. Sees a couple of cops tromping around. He's gone and he won't be back and a lot of my hard work is down the goddamn tube."

"This suggests something to me," Chee said.

"I hoped it would. I hoped it would make you want to learn a little more about this business before you start practicing it."

"Actually it suggests that you screwed up. You had about four hours of talking to me on that ride up to Mancos, with me listening all the way. You told me about this Zorro you're trying to catch—and I guess this is him. But you totally forgot to tell me about this trap you were going to spring so we could coordinate. How could you forget something like that?"

Finch's face had also become a little redder through its windburn. The smile had gone away. He stared at Chee. Looked down at his boots. When he looked up he was grinning.

"Touché! I got a bad habit of underestimating folks. You say that woman cop with you noticed the fence posts had been dug loose. I missed that. Good-looking lady, too. You give her my congratulations, will you. Tell her any old time she wants to work alongside of me, or under me either, she's more than welcome."

Chee nodded, started his engine.

"Hold it just a minute," Finch said, his smile looking slightly more genuine. "I didn't stop you just to start an argument. Wondered if I could get you to be a witness for something."

Chee left the motor running. "For what?"

"There's five Angus calves at a feedlot over by Kirtland. Looks like they were branded through a wet gunnysack, like the wise guys do it, but they're still so fresh they haven't even scabbed over yet. And the fellow that signed the bill of sale hasn't got any mother cows. He claimed he sold 'em off—which we can check on. On the other hand, a fellow named Bramlett is short five Angus calves off some leased pasture. I'm going over and see if there's five wet cows there. If there is I call the feedlot and they bring the calves over and I turn on my video camera and get a tape of the mama cows saying hello to their missing calves. Letting 'em nurse, all that."

"So what do you need me for?"

"It'd be a mostly Navajo jury, and the cow thief—he's a Navajo," Finch said. "Be good to have a Navajo cop on the witness stand."

Chee looked at his watch. By now Teddy Begayaye would be at the office celebrating getting his requested vacation time, and Manuelito would be sore about it. Too late for any preventive medicine there. But he had, after all, ruined Finch's trap. Besides, it would give him another hour away from the office and something positive for a change to report to Captain Largo on the cow-theft front.

"I'll follow you," Chee said, "and if you speed, you get a ticket."

Finch sped, but kept it within the Navajo Tribal Police tolerance zone. He parked beside the fence at the holding pasture at just about nine A.M. It was bottomland here, a pasture irrigated by a ditch from the San Juan

River, and it held maybe two hundred head of Angus—young cows and their calves—last spring's crop but still nursing. Chee parked as Finch was climbing the fence, snagging his jeans on the barbed wire.

"I think I saw a wet one already," he shouted, pointing into the herd, which now was moving uneasily away. "You stay back by your car."

Wet one? Chee thought. He'd been raised with sheep, not cows. But "wet" must be what you called a cow with a painfully full udder. A cow whose nursing calf was missing. Finch had been right about cow memories. Their memory connected men on foot with being roped, bulldogged, and branded. They were scattering away from Finch. So the question was, how was Finch going to locate five such cows in that milling herd and know he hadn't just counted the same cow five times?

Finch picked himself a spot free of cow manure, dropped to his knees, and rolled over on his back. He folded his arms under his head and lay motionless. The cows, which had shied fearfully away from him, stopped their nervous milling. They stared at Finch. He yawned, squirmed into a more comfortable position. A heifer, head and ears stretched forward, moved a cautious step toward him. Others followed, noses pointed, ears forward. The calves, with no memory of branding to inhibit them, were first. By eleven minutes after nine, Finch was surrounded by a ring of Angus cattle, sniffing and staring.

As for Finch, only his head was moving, and he made an udder inspection. He arose, creating a panic, and walked through the scattering herd, already dialing his portable telephone, talking into it as he climbed the fence. He closed it, walked up to Chee's window.

"Five wet ones," he said. "They're going to bring the calves right out. I'm going to videotape it, but it'd help if you'd stick around so you can testify. You know, tell the jury that the calves ran right up to their mamas and started nursing, and their mamas let 'em do it."

"That was pretty damn clever," Chee said.

"I told you about cows being curious," Finch said. "They're scared of a man standing up. Lay down and they say, 'What the hell's going on here?' and come on over to take a look." He brushed off his jeans. "Drawback is you're likely to get manure all over yourself."

"Well, it's a lot quicker than chasing them all over the pasture, trying to get a look."

Finch was enjoying this approval.

"You know where I learned that trick? I was in the dentist's office at Farmington waiting to get a root canal. Picked up a *New Yorker* magazine and there was an article in there about a Nevada brand inspector name of Chris Collis. It was a trick he used. I called him and asked him if it really worked. He said sure."

Finch fished his video camera out of the truck cab, fiddled with it. Chee radioed his office, reported his location, collected his messages. One was from Joe Leaphorn. It was brief.

A truck from the feedlot arrived bearing two men and five terrified Angus calves. Each was ear-tagged with its number and released into the pasture. Each ran, bawling, in search of its mother, found her, underwent a maternal inspection, was approved and allowed to nurse while Finch videotaped the happy reunions.

But Chee wasn't paying as much attention as he might have been. While Finch was counting turgid udders, Chee had checked with his office. Leaphorn wanted to talk to him again about the Fallen Man. He said he was working for the Breedlove family now.

14

THE QUESTION NAGGING at Jim Chee wasn't the sort he wanted to explore on the Tribal Police radio band. He stopped at the Hogback trading post, dropped a quarter in the pay phone, and called the number Leaphorn had left. It proved to be the Anasazi Inn in Farmington, but the front desk said Leaphorn had checked out. Chee dropped in another quarter and called his own office. Jenifer answered. Yes, Leaphorn had called again. He said he was on his way back from Farmington to Window Rock and he would drop by and try to catch Chee at his office.

Chee got there about five minutes faster than the speed limit allowed. Leaphorn's car was in the parking lot. The man himself was perched, ramrod straight, on a chair in the waiting room, reading yesterday's copy of *Navajo Times.*

"If you have a couple of minutes, I want to pass on some information," Leaphorn said. "Otherwise, I can catch you when you have some time."

"I have time," Chee said, and ushered him into his office.

Leaphorn sat. "I'll be brief. I've taken a retainer from the Breedlove Corporation. Actually, it's really the family, I guess. They want me to sort of reinvestigate the disappearance of Hal Breedlove." He paused, awaited a reaction. If he was reading Chee's studiously blank expression properly, the young man didn't like the arrangement.

"So it's official business for you now," Chee said. "At least unofficially official."

"Right," Leaphorn said. "I wanted you to know that because I may be bothering you now and then. With questions." He paused again.

"Is that it?" Chee asked. If it was, he had some questions of his own.

"There's something else I wanted to tell you. I think it's pretty clear the family thinks Hal was murdered. If they have any evidence of that they're not telling me. Maybe it's just that they want it to be murder. And they want to be able to prove it. They want to regain title to the ranch."

"Oh," Chee said. "Did they tell you that?"

Leaphorn hesitated, his expression quizzical. What the devil was bothering Chee? "I was thinking that would be the most likely motive," he said. "What do you think?"

Chee nodded noncommittally.

"Can you tell me who you made the deal with?" he asked.

"You mean the individual?" Leaphorn said. "I think private detectives are supposed to have a thing about client confidentiality, but I haven't learned to think like a private eye. Never will. This is my one and only venture. George Shaw handed me my check." He laughed, and told Chee how he'd outsmarted himself, trying to learn how big a deal this was for the Breedlove Corporation.

"So Hal's cousin signed the check, but the lawyer with him, you remember his name?"

"McDermott," Leaphorn said. "John McDermott. He's the lawyer handling it. He called me and arranged the meeting. Works for a Washington firm, but I think he used to have an office in Albuquerque. And—" He stopped, aware of Chee's expression. "You know this guy?"

"Indirectly," Chee said. "He was sort of an Indian affairs specialist for an Albuquerque firm. I think he represented Peabody Coal when they were negotiating one of the coal contracts with us, and a couple of pipeline companies dealing with the Jicarillas. Then he moved to Washington and is doing the same thing on that level. I think it's with the same law firm."

Leaphorn looked surprised. "You know a lot more about him than I do," he said. "How's his reputation? It okay?"

"As a lawyer? I guess so. He used to be a professor."

"He struck me as arrogant. Is that your impression?"

Chee shrugged. "I don't know him. I just know a little about him."

"Well, he didn't make a good first impression."

"Could you tell me when he called you? I mean made the first contact."

The question obviously surprised Leaphorn. "Let's see," he said. "Two or three days ago."

"Was it last Tuesday?"

"Tuesday? Let's see. Yeah. It was a call on my answering machine. I returned it."

"Morning or afternoon?"

"I don't know. It could have been either one. But it's still on the recording. I think I could find out."

"I'd appreciate that," Chee said.

"Will do," Leaphorn said, and paused. "I'm trying to place the date. That would have been about the day after you got the skeleton identified. Right?"

Chee sighed. "Lieutenant Leaphorn," he said, "you already know just what I'm thinking, don't you?"

"Well, I'd guess you're wondering how that lawyer found out so quickly that the skeleton had turned out to be somebody so important to his client. No announcement had been made. Nothing in the papers until a day or so later and I don't think it ever made the national news. Just a little story around here, and about three paragraphs in the *Albuquerque Journal*, and a little bit more in the *Rocky Mountain News*."

"That's what I'm thinking," Chee said.

"But you're ahead of me on something else. I don't know why it's important."

"You couldn't guess," Chee said. "It's something personal."

"Oh," Leaphorn said. He ducked his head, shook it, and said, "Oh," again. Sad, now. And then he looked up. "You know, they could have had this thing staked out, though. An important client. Maybe they had some law firm out here retained to tip them off if anything turned up that would bear in any way at all on this son-and-heir being missing. They knew he was a mountain climber. So when an unidentified body turns up . . ." He shrugged. "Who knows how law firms operate?" he said, not believing it himself.

"Sure," Chee said. "Anything's possible."

Leaphorn was leaving, hat in hand, but he stopped in the doorway and turned.

"One other thing that might bear on all this," he said. He told Chee of Sergeant Deke's account of the man with the binoculars and the rifle on the canyon rim. "Deke said he's going up the canyon and warn Nez that somebody may still be trying to kill him. I hope we can figure this out before they do it."

Chee sat for a moment looking at the closed door, thinking of Leaphorn, thinking of Janet Pete, of John McDermott back in New Mexico. Was he back in her life? Apparently he was. For the first time, the Fallen Man became more than an abstract tragedy in Chee's mind. He buzzed Jenifer.

"I'm taking off now for Gallup," he said. "If Largo needs me—if anybody calls—tell them I'll be back tomorrow."

"Hey," Jenifer said, "you have two meetings on the calendar for this afternoon. The security man from the community college and Captain Largo was—"

"Call them and tell them I had to cancel," Chee said, forgetting to say please, and forgetting to say thanks when he hung up. Captain Largo wouldn't like this. But then he didn't particularly like Captain Largo and he sure as hell didn't like being an acting lieutenant.

15

LOUISE GUARD'S FORD Escort was not in the driveway of the little
house she shared with Janet Pete in Gallup. Good news, but not as
good as it would have seemed when Jim Chee was feeling better about life.
This evening his mood had been swinging back and forth between a sort
of grim anger at the world that Janet occupied and self-contempt for his
own immature attitude. It hadn't taken long for Chee, who was good at
self-analysis, to determine that his problem was mostly jealousy. Maybe
it was 90 percent jealousy. But even so, that left 10 percent or so that
seemed legitimate.

He gave the door of his pickup the hard slam required to shut it and
walked up the pathway with the videotape of the traditional wedding
clutched in one hand and the other holding a pot of some sort of autumn-
blooming flowers he'd bought for her at Gallup Best Blossoms. It wasn't a
very impressive floral display, but what could you expect in November?

"Ah, Jim," Janet said, and greeted him with such a huge and enthusiastic hug that it left him helpless—tape in one hand and flowerpot in the
other. It also left him feeling guilty. What the devil was wrong with him?
Janet was beautiful. Janet was sweet. She loved him. She was wearing a set
of designer jeans that fit her perfectly and a blouse of something that shim-
mered. Her black hair was done in a new fashion he'd been observing on
the nighttime soap opera shows. It made her look young and jaunty and

like someone the muscular actor in the tank top would be laughing with at the fancy party in a Coca-Cola commercial.

"I'd almost forgotten how beautiful you are," Chee said. "Just back from Washington, you should be looking tired."

Janet was in the kitchen by then, watering whatever it was he'd brought her, opening the refrigerator and fixing something for them.

"It wasn't tiresome," she shouted. "It was lots of fun. The people in the BIA were on their very best behavior, and the people over at Justice were reasonable for a change. And there was time to see a show some German artist had going in the National Gallery. It was really interesting stuff. Partly sculpture and partly drawings. And then there was the concert I told you about. The one in the Library of Congress hall. It was partly Mozart. Really great."

Yes. The concert. He'd thought about that before. Maybe too much. In Washington and at the Library of Congress it wouldn't be a public event. It would be exclusive. Some sort of high-society fund-raiser. Shaking down the social set for some worthy literacy cause, probably. Almost certainly it would be by invitation only. Or just members and guests for the big-money patrons of library projects. She'd mentioned some ambassador being there. He had thought, once, that John McDermott might have taken her. But that was crazy. She detested the man. He had taken advantage of the leverage a distinguished professor has over his students. He'd seduced Janet. He'd taken her to Albuquerque as his live-in intern, had taken her to Washington as his token Indian. She had come back to New Mexico ashamed and brokenhearted when she realized what he was doing. There were a dozen ways McDermott could have learned the Fallen Man had been identified. Leaphorn, as usual, was right. McDermott's firm probably had connections with lawyers in New Mexico. Of course they would. They would be working with Arizona and New Mexico law firms on Indian business. Anyway, he damn sure wasn't going to bring it up. It would be insulting.

From the kitchen the sound of something clattering, the smell of coffee. Chee inspected the room around him. Nothing different that he could see except for something or other on the mantle over the gas-log fireplace. It was made of thin stainless steel tubing combined with shaped Plexiglas in three or four colors held together by what seemed to be a mixture of aluminum wiring and thread. Most peculiar. In fact, weird. Chee grinned at it. Something Louise had found somewhere. A conversation piece. Louise haunted garage sales, and in Gallup, garage sales were always offering odd harvests.

Janet emerged with a cup of coffee for him—fragile china on a thin-as-paper saucer—and a crystal goblet of wine for herself. She snuggled onto the sofa beside him, clicked glass against cup, smiled at him, and said, "To your capture of a whole squadron of cattle rustlers, your promotion to commander in chief of the Navajo police, chief honcho of the Federal Bureau of Ineptitude, and international boss of Interpol."

"You forgot my busting up the Shiprock graffiti vandals and election as sheriff of San Juan County and bureaucrat in chief of the Drug Enforcement Agency."

"All that, too," Janet said, raised her glass again, and sipped. She picked up the videocassette and inspected it. "What's this?"

"Remember?" Chee said. "My paternal uncle's niece was having a traditional wedding at their place north of Little Water. I got him to get me a copy of the videotape they had made."

Janet turned it over and inspected the back, which was just as black and blank as the other side. "You want me to look at it?"

"Sure," Chee said, his good feelings fading fast. "Remember? We talked about that." They had argued a little, actually. About cultures, and traditions, and all that. It wasn't that Janet was opposed, but her mother wanted a huge ceremony in an Episcopal cathedral in Baltimore. And Janet had agreed, or so he thought, that they would do both. "You said you had never been to a regular Navajo wedding with a shaman and the entire ceremony. I thought you'd be interested."

"Louise described it to me," Janet said, and put the videotape on the coffee table in a way that made Chee want to change the subject. Suddenly Louise's peculiar purchase seemed useful.

"I see Louise has been sailing the garage sales again. Quite an acquisition there," he said, nodding toward the thing. He laughed. "Louise is a wonderful lady, but I wonder about her taste sometimes."

Janet had no comment.

Chee said: "What's it for?" And waited, and belatedly understood that he should have kept his stupid mouth shut.

"It's called 'Technic Inversion Number Three, Side View,'" Janet said.

"Remarkable," Chee said. "Very interesting."

"I found it in the Kremont Gallery," Janet said, glum. "The artist is a man named Egon Kuzluzski. The critic at the *Washington Post* called him the most innovative sculptor of the decade. An artist who finds beauty and meaning in the technology which is submerging modern culture."

"Very complex," Chee said. "And the colors . . ." He couldn't think of a way to finish the sentence.

"I really thought you would like it," Janet said. "I'm sorry you don't."

"I do," Chee said, but he knew it was too late for that. "Well, not really. But I think it takes time to understand something that's so innovative. And then tastes vary, of course."

Janet didn't respond to that.

"It's the reason they have horse races," Chee said, and attempted a chuckle. "Differences of opinion, you know."

"I ran into something interesting in Washington," Janet said, in a fairly obvious effort to cut off this discussion. "I think it was why everybody was so cooperative with our proposals. Crime on Indian reservations has become very chic inside the Beltway. Everybody had read up on narcotics invading Indian territory, and Indian gang problems, Indian graffiti, Indian homicides, child abuse, the whole schmear. All very popular with the Beltway intelligentsia. We have finally made it into the halls of the mighty."

"I guess that would fall into the bad news, good news category," Chee said, grinning with relief at being let off the hook.

"Whatever you call it, it means everybody is looking for our expertise these days."

Chee's grin faded. "You got a job offer?"

"I didn't mean me. But one of the top assistants in BIA Law and Order wanted to let me know they're recruiting experienced reservation cops with the right kind of credentials for Civil Service, and I heard the same thing over at Justice." She smiled at him. "At Justice they actually asked me to be a talent scout for them, and when they told me what they wanted it sounded like they were describing you." She patted him on the leg. "I told 'em I'd already signed you up."

"Thank God for that," Chee said. "I did time in Washington a couple of times, remember? At the FBI academy for their training course, and once on an investigation." He shuddered, remembering. At the academy he had been the tolerated rube, one of "them." But they would, naturally, look on Janet as one of "us." It was a fact he'd have to find a way to deal with.

Janet removed her hand.

"Really, Jim, Washington's a nice place. It's cleaner than most cities, and something beautiful every place you look and there's always—"

"Beautiful what? Buildings? Monuments? There's too much smog, too much noise, too much traffic, too damn many people everywhere. You can't see the stars at night. Too cloudy to see the sunset." He shook his head.

"There's the breeze coming in off the Potomac," Janet said. "And the clean salty smell of the bay, and seafood fresh from the ocean and good wine. In April, the cherry blossoms, and the green, green hills, and the great art galleries, and theater, and music." She paused, waved her hands, overcome by the enormous glories of Washington's culture. "And the pay scales are about double what either one of us can make here—especially in the Justice Department."

"Working in the J. Edgar Hoover Building," Chee said. "That'd be a real kick. That old blackmailer should have been doing about twenty years for misuse of public records, but they named the building after him. At least it's an appropriately ugly building."

Janet let that one lie, sipped her wine, reminded Chee his coffee was getting cold. He tested it. She was right.

"Jim," she said, "that concert was absolutely thrilling. It was the Philadelphia Orchestra. The annual Founders Society affair. The First Lady was there, and all sorts of diplomats—all white tie and the best jewels dug out of the safety-deposit boxes. And Mozart. You like Mozart."

"I like a lot of Mozart," Chee said.

He took a deep breath. "It was one of those members-only things, I guess," he said. "Members and guests."

"Right," she said, smiling at him. "I was mingling with the *crème de la crème*."

"I'll bet your old law firm is a member," Chee said. "Probably a big donor."

"You betcha," Janet said, still smiling. Then she realized where Chee was headed. The smile went away.

"You're going to ask me who took me," she said.

"No, I'm not."

"I was a guest of John McDermott," she said.

Chee sat silent and motionless. He had known it, but he still didn't want to believe it.

"Does that bother you?"

"No," Chee said. "I guess not. Should it?"

"It shouldn't," she said. "After all, we go way back. He was my teacher. And then I worked with him."

He was looking at her. Wondering what to say. She flushed. "What are you thinking?" she said.

"I'm thinking I had it all wrong. I thought you detested the man for the way he treated you. The way he used you."

She looked away. "I did for a while. I was angry."

"But not now? No longer angry?"

"The Navajo way," she said. "You're supposed to get yourself back into harmony with the way the world is."

"Did you know he's out here again?"

She nodded.

"Did you know he's hired Joe Leaphorn to look into that Fallen Man business?"

"He told me he was going to try," she said.

"I wondered how he learned about the skeleton being identified as Harold Breedlove," Chee said. "It wasn't the sort of story that would have hit the *Washington Post*."

"No," she said.

"Did you tell him?"

"Why not?" she said, staring at him. "Why the hell not?"

"Well, I don't know. The man you're going to marry is on the telephone reminding you he loves you. And you ask him about a case he's working on, and so he sort of violates police protocol and tells you the skeleton has been identified." He stopped. This wasn't fair. He'd held this anger in for too many hours. He had heard his voice, thick with emotion.

She was still staring at him, face grim, waiting for him to continue.

"So?" she said. "Go on."

"So I'm not exactly sure what happened next. Did you call him right away and tell him what you'd learned?"

She didn't respond to that. But she edged a bit away from him on the sofa.

"One more question and then I'll drop it. Did that son of a bitch ask you to get that information out of me? In other words, I want to know whether he—"

Janet was on her feet.

"I think you'd better go now," she said.

He got up. His anger had drained away now. He simply felt tired and sick.

"Just one more thing I'd like to know," he said. "It would tell me something about just how important this business is to the Breedlove Corporation. In other words if you'd told him about the skeleton being found up there when you first got to Washington, it might naturally have reminded McDermott of Hal Breedlove disappearing. And he'd want to know who the skeleton belonged to. But if it was already on his mind even before that, if he brought it up instead of you, then it would mean a higher level of—it would mean they already—"

"Go away," Janet said. She handed him the videotape. "And take this with you."

He took the tape.

"Janet," he said. "Did you recommend that he hire Leaphorn to work for him?"

He asked that before he noticed the angry tears in Janet's eyes. She didn't answer and he didn't expect her to.

16

DECEMBER CAME TO the Four Corners but winter lingered up in the Utah mountains. It had buried the Wasatch Range under three feet and ventured far enough south to give Colorado's San Juans a snowcap. But the brief post-Halloween storm that had whitened the slopes of Ship Rock and the Chuskas proved to be a false threat. It was dry again across the Navajo Nation—skies dark blue, mornings cool, sun dazzling. The south end of the Colorado Plateau was enjoying that typically beautiful autumn weather that makes the inevitable first blizzard such a dangerous surprise.

Beautiful or not, Jim Chee was keeping himself far too busy to enjoy it—even if his glum mood would have allowed it. He had learned that he could handle administrative duties if he tried hard enough, and that he would never, ever enjoy them. For the first time in his life, he felt no sense of pleasure as he went to work. But the work got done. He made progress. The vacation schedules were established in a way that produced no serious discontent among the officers who worked with him. A system had been devised whereby whatever policemen who happened to be in the Hogback neighborhood would drop in on Diamonte's establishment for a friendly chat. This happened several times a week, thus keeping Diamonte careful and his customers uneasy without giving him any solid grounds for complaint. As a by-product, it had also produced a couple of arrests of young fellows who had been ignoring fugitive warrants.

On top of that, his budget for next year was about half finished and a plan had been drafted for keeping better track of gasoline usage and patrol car maintenance. This had produced an unusual (indeed, unprecedented in the experience of Acting Lieutenant Jim Chee) smile on the face of Captain Largo. Even Officer Bernadette Manuelito seemed to be responding to this new efficiency in Chee's criminal investigation domain.

This came about after the word reached the ear of Captain Largo (and very shortly thereafter the ear of Acting Lieutenant Chee) that Mr. Finch had nailed a pair of cattle-stealing brothers so thoroughly that they had actually admitted not just rustling five unweaned calves but also about six or seven other such larcenies from the New Mexico side of Chee's jurisdiction. So overwhelming was the evidence, the captain said, that they had plea-bargained themselves into jail at Aztec.

"Well, good," Chee had said.

"Well, goddammit," Largo replied, "why can't we nail some of those bastards ourselves?"

Largo's imperial "we" had actually meant him, Chee realized. He also realized, before this uncomfortable conversation ended, that Finch had revealed to Largo not only Chee's ignorance of heifer curiosity but how he and Officer Manuelito had screwed up Finch's trap out by Ship Rock. Chee had walked down the hall away from this meeting with several resolutions strongly formed. He would catch Finch's favorite cow thief before Finch could get his hands on him. Having beaten Finch at Finch's game, he would resign his role as acting lieutenant and go back to being a real policeman. There would be no more trying to be a bureaucrat to impress Janet. And to accomplish the first phase of this program he would shift Manuelito over to work on rustler cases—she and Largo being the only ones in the Shiprock District who took it seriously.

Officer Bernadette Manuelito responded to this shift in duties by withdrawing her request for a transfer. At least, that was Jim Chee's presumption. Jenifer had another notion. She had noticed that the frequent calls between the lady lawyer in Window Rock and the acting lieutenant in Shiprock had abruptly ceased. Jenifer was very good at keeping the Shiprock

District criminal investigation office running smoothly because she made it her business to know what the hell was going on. She made a couple of calls to old friends in the small world of law enforcement down at Window Rock. Yes, indeed. The pretty lawyer had been observed shedding tears while in conversation with a lady friend in her car. She had also been seen having dinner at the Navajo Inn with that good-looking lawyer from Washington. Things, it seemed, were in flux. Having learned this, it was Jenifer's theory that Officer Manuelito would learn of it, too—not as directly perhaps, or as fast, but she would learn of it.

Whatever her motives, Manuelito seemed to like her new duties. She stood in front of Chee's desk, looking excited, but not about rustling.

"That's what I said," she said. "They showed up at old Mr. Maryboy's place last night. They told him they wanted trespass permission on his grazing lease. They wanted to climb Ship Rock."

"And it was George Shaw and John McDermott?" Chee said.

"Yes, sir," Officer Manuelito said. "That's what they told him. They paid him a hundred dollars and said if they did any damage they'd pay him for that."

"My God," Chee said. "You mean those two lawyers are going to climb Ship Rock?"

"Old man Maryboy said the little one had climbed it before. Years ago. He said most of the white people just sneaked in and climbed it, but George Shaw had come to his house to get permission. He remembered that. How polite Shaw had been. But this time Shaw said they were bringing a team of climbers."

"So the tall one with the mustache probably isn't going up," Chee said, wondering if he sounded disappointed. But should he be disappointed? Would having McDermott fall off a cliff solve his problem with Janet? He didn't think so.

"They didn't say why they were going up there, I guess," Chee said.

"No, sir. I asked him about that. Mr. Maryboy said they didn't tell him why." She laughed, showing very pretty white teeth. "He said why do white men do anything? He said he knew a white fellow once who was trying to get a patent on a cordless bungee jumper."

Chee rewarded that with a chuckle. The way he'd heard it, it was a stringless yo-yo, but Maryboy had revised it to fit mountain climbers.

"But what I wanted to tell you about was business," Officer Manuelito said. "Mr. Maryboy told me he was missing four steers."

"Maryboy," Chee said. "Let's see. He has—"

"Yes, sir," she said. "That's his lease where we found the loose fence posts. Where somebody was throwing the hay over the fence. I went by his place to tell him about that. I was going to give him a notebook and ask him to keep track of strange trucks and trailers. He said I was a little late, but he took the notebook and said he'd help."

"Did he say how late?" Maryboy hadn't reported a cattle theft. Chee was sure of that. He checked on everything involving rustling every day. "Did he say why he hadn't reported the loss?"

"He said he missed 'em sometime last spring. He was selling off steers and came up short. And he said he didn't report it because he didn't think it would do any good. He said when it happened before, a couple of times, he went in and told us about it but he never did get his animals back."

That was one of the frustrations Chee had been learning to live with in dealing with rustling. People didn't keep track of their cattle. They turned them out to graze, and if they had a big grazing lease and reliable water maybe they'd only see them three or four times a year. Maybe only at calving time and branding time. And if you did see them, maybe you wouldn't notice if you were short a couple. Chee had spent his boyhood with sheep. He could tell an Angus from a Hereford but beyond that one cow looked a lot like every other cow. He could understand how you wouldn't miss a couple, and if you did, what could you do about it? Maybe the coyotes had got 'em, or maybe it was the little green men coming down in flying saucers. Whatever, you weren't going to get 'em back.

"So we put an X on our map and mark it 'unreported,'" Chee said, "which doesn't help much."

"It might," Officer Manuelito said. "Later on."

Chee was extracting their map from his desk drawer. He kept it out of sight on the theory that everyone in the office except Manuelito would think this project was silly. Or, worse, they would think he was trying to copy Joe Leaphorn's famous map. Everybody in the Tribal Police seemed to know about that and the Legendary Lieutenant's use of it to exercise his theory that everything fell into a pattern, every effect had its cause, and so forth.

The map was a U.S. Geological Survey quadrangle chart large enough in scale to show every arroyo, hogan, windmill, and culvert. Chee pushed his in basket aside, rolled it out and penned a tiny blue ? on the Maryboy grazing lease with a tiny 3 beside it. Beside that he marked in the date the loss had been discovered.

Officer Manuelito looked at it and said: "A blue three?"

"Signifies unreported possible thefts," Chee said. "Three of them." He waved his hand around the map, indicating a scattering of such designations. "I've been adding them as we learn about them."

"Good idea," Manuelito said. "And add an X there, too. Maryboy is going to be a lookout for us." She pulled up a chair, sat, leaned her elbows on the desk, and studied the chart.

Chee added the X. The map now had maybe a score of those, each marking the home of a volunteer equipped with a notebook and ballpoint pen. Chee had bought the supplies with his own money, preferring that to trying to explain this system to Largo. If it worked, which today didn't seem likely to Chee, he would decide whether to ask for a reimbursement of his twenty-seven-dollar outlay.

"Funny how this is already working out," Manuelito said. "I thought it would take months."

"What do you mean?"

"I mean the patterns you talked about," she said. "How those single-animal thefts tend to fall around the middle of the month."

Chee looked. Indeed, most of the 1s that marked single-theft sites were followed by midmonth dates. And a high percentage of those midmonth dates were clustered along the reservation border. But what did that signify? He said: "Yeah."

"I don't think we should concentrate on those," she said, still staring thoughtfully at the map. "But if you want me to, I could check with the bars and liquor stores around Farmington and try to work up a list of guys who come in about the middle of the month with a fresh supply of money." She shook her head. "It wouldn't prove anything, but it would give us a list of people to look out for."

About halfway through this monologue, Chee's brain caught up with Manuelito's thinking. The Navajo Nation relief checks arrived about the first of the month. Every reservation cop knew that the heavy workload produced by the need to arrest drunks tended to ease off in the second week when the liquor addicts had used up their cash. He visualized a dried-out drunk driving past a pasture and seeing a five-hundred-dollar cow staring through the fence at him. How could the man resist? And why hadn't he thought of that?

He thought of it now. Weeks compiling the list, weeks spent cross-checking, sorting, coming up finally with four or five cases, getting maybe two convictions resulting in hundred-dollar fines, which would be suspended, and thirty-day sentences, which would be converted to probation. Meanwhile, serious crime would continue to flourish.

"I think instead we'll sort those out and set them aside. Let's concentrate on solving the multiple thefts," Chee said.

"There's a pattern there, too, I think," Officer Manuelito said. "Am I right?"

Chee had noticed this one himself. The multiple thefts tended to show up in empty country—from grazing leases like Maryboy's where the owner might not see his herd for a month or so. They talked about that, which led them back to their growing list of rustler-watchers, which led them back to Lucy Sam.

"You looked through her telescope," Manuelito said. "Did you notice she could see that place where the fence posts were loose?"

Chee shook his head. He had been looking at the mountain. Thinking of the Fallen Man stranded on the cliff up there, calling for help.

"You could," Manuelito said. "I looked."

"I think I should go talk to her," Chee said. But he wasn't thinking of rustling when he said it. He was wondering what Lucy Sam's father might have seen all those years ago when Hal Breedlove had huddled on that little shelf waiting to die.

17

THE SOUND OF *bang, bang, bang, thud, thud* stopped Joe Leaphorn in his tracks. It came from somewhere up Cache Creek, nearby, just around the bend and beyond a stream-side stand of aspens. But it stopped him just for a moment. He smiled, thinking he'd spent too many years as a cop with a pistol on his hip, and moved up the path. The aspen trunks were wearing their winter white now, their leaves forming a yellow blanket on the ground around them. And through the barren branches Leaphorn could see Eldon Demott, bending over something, back muscles straining.

Doing what? Leaphorn stopped again and watched. Demott was stretching barbed wire over what seemed to be a section of aspen trunk. And now, with more banging, stapling the wire to the wood.

Something to do with a fence, he guessed. Here a cable had been stretched between ponderosas on opposite sides of the stream, and the fence seemed to be suspended from that. Leaphorn shouted, "Hello!"

It took Demott just a moment to recognize him but he did even before Leaphorn reminded him.

"Yeah," Demott said. "I remember. But no uniform now. Are you still with the Tribal Police?"

"They put me out to pasture," Leaphorn said. "I retired at the end of June."

"Well, what brings you all this way up the Cache? It wouldn't have something to do with finally finding Hal, would it? After all these years?"

"That's a good guess," Leaphorn said. "Breedlove's family hired me to go over the whole business again. They want me to see if I overlooked anything. See if I could find out where he went when he left your sister at Canyon de Chelly. See if anything new turned up the past ten years or so."

"That's interesting," Demott said. He retrieved his hammer. "Let me get done with this." He secured the wire with two more staples, straightened his back, and stretched.

"I'm trying to rig up something to solve a problem here," he explained. "The damned cows come to drink here, and then they move downstream a little ways—or their calves do—and they come out on the wrong side of the fence. We call it a water gap. Is that the term you use?"

"We don't get enough water down in the low country where I was raised to need 'em much," Leaphorn said.

"In the mountains, it's the snowmelt. The creek gets up, washes the brush down, it catches on the fence and builds up until it makes a dam out of it, and the dam backs up the water until the pressure tears out the fence," Demott said. "It's the same story every spring. And then you got cattle up and down the creek, ruining the stream banks, getting erosion started and everything silted up."

It was cool up here, probably a mile and a half above sea level, but Demott was sweating. He wiped his brow on his shirtsleeve.

"The way it's supposed to work, it's kinda like a drawbridge. You make a section of fence across the creek and just hang it from that cable with a dry log holding the bottom down. When the flood comes down, the log floats. That lifts the wire, the brush sails right by under it, and when the runoff season's over, the log drops back into place and you've got a fence again."

"It sounds pretty foolproof," Leaphorn said, thinking that it might work with snowmelt, but runoff from a male rain roaring down the side of a mesa would knock it into the next county and take the cable with it, and the trees, too. "Or maybe I should say cowproof."

Demott looked skeptical. "Actually, it just works until too much stuff catches on the log," he said. "Anyway, it's worth trying." He sat on a boulder, wiped his face again.

"What can I tell you?"

"I don't know," Leaphorn said. "But we wrote off this thing with your brother-in-law almost eleven years ago. It was just another adult missing person case. Another skip-out without a clue to where or why. So there's been a lot of time for you to get a letter, or hear some gossip, or find out that somebody who knew him had seen him playing the slots in Las Vegas. Something like that. There's no crime involved, so you wouldn't have had any reason to tell us about it."

Demott was wiping mud off the side of his hand on his pant leg. "I can tell you why they hired you," he said.

Leaphorn waited.

"They want this place back."

"I thought they might," Leaphorn said. "I couldn't think of another reason."

"The sons-a-bitches," Demott said. "They want to lease out the mineral rights. Or more likely, just sell the whole outfit to a mining company and let 'em wreck it all."

"That's the idea I got from the bank lady at Mancos."

"Did she tell the plan? They'd do an open pit operation on the molybdenum deposits up there." Demott pointed up Cache Creek, past the clusters of white-barked aspens, past the stately forest of ponderosa, into the dark green wilderness of firs. "Rip it all out," he said, "and then . . ."

The emotion in Demott's voice stopped him. He took a deep breath and sat for a moment, looking down at his hands.

Leaphorn waited. Demott had more than this to say. He wanted to hear it.

Demott gave Leaphorn a sidewise glance. "Have you seen the Red River canyon in New Mexico? Up north of Taos?"

"I've seen it," Leaphorn said.

"You seen it before and after?"

"I haven't been there for years," Leaphorn said. "I remember a beautiful trout stream, maybe a little bigger than your creek here, winding through a narrow valley. Steeper than this one. High mountains on both sides. Beautiful place."

"They ripped the top right off of one of those mountains," Demott said. "Left a great whitish heap of crushed stone miles long. And the holding ponds they built to catch the effluent spill over and that nasty stuff pours down into Red River. They use cyanide in some sort of solution to free up the metal and that kills trout and everything else."

"I haven't been up there for years," Leaphorn said.

"Cyanide," Demott repeated. "Mixed with sludge. That's what we'd have pouring down Cache Creek if the Breedlove Corporation had its way. That slimy white silt brewed with cyanide."

Leaphorn didn't comment on that. He spent a few minutes letting Demott get used to him being there, listening to the music of Cache Creek bubbling over its rocky floor, watching a puffy white cloud just barely making it over the ridge upstream. It was dragging its bottom through the tips of the fir trees, leaving rags of mist behind. A beautiful day, a beautiful place. A cedar waxwing flew by. It perched in the aspens across the creek and watched them, chirping bird comments.

Demott was watching him, too, still absently picking at the resin and dirt on his left hand. "Well, enough of that," he said. "I don't know what to tell you. I got no letters and neither did Elisa. If she had, I would have known it. We're a family that don't keep secrets, not from one another. And we didn't hear anything, either. Nothing."

"You'd think there'd be rumors," Leaphorn said. "You know how people are."

"I do," Demott said. "I thought it was strange, too. I'm sure there must have been a lot of talk about it up at Mancos and around. Hal disappearing was the most exciting thing that happened around here in years. I'm sure some people would say Elisa killed her husband so she could get the ranch, or she had a secret boyfriend do it, or I killed him so the ranch would come back into the Demott family."

"Yeah," Leaphorn said. "I'd think that would be the natural kind of speculation, considering the circumstances. But you didn't hear any of that kind of talk?"

Demott looked shocked. "Why, they wouldn't say things like that around me. Or Elisa either, of course. And you know, the funny thing was Elisa loved Hal, and I think folks around here understood that."

"How about you? What did you think of him?"

"Oh, I got pretty sick of Hal," Demott said. "I won't lie about it. He was a pain in the butt. But you know in a lot of ways I liked him. He had a good heart, and he was good for Elisa. Treated her like a quality lady, and that's what she is. And it made you feel sad, you know. I think he could have amounted to something if he'd been raised right."

Demott despaired of getting the hand suitably clean by rubbing at it. He got up, squatted by the stream, and washed it.

"I'm not sure I know what you mean," Leaphorn said. "What went wrong?"

Finished with his ablutions, Demott resumed his seat and thought about how to tell this.

"Hard to put it exactly," he said. "But when he was just a kid his folks would send him out here and we'd get him on a horse, and he'd do his share of work just like everybody else. Made a good enough hand, for a youngster. When we was baling hay, or moving the cows or anything, he'd do the twelve-hour day right along with us. And when the work was laid by, he'd go rock climbing with me and Elisa. In fact he got good at it before she did." Demott exhaled hugely, shook his head.

No mention of Tommy Castro. "Just the three of you?" Leaphorn asked.

Demott hesitated. "Pretty much."

"Tommy Castro didn't go along?"

Demott flushed. "Where'd you hear about him?"

Leaphorn shrugged.

Demott drew in a deep breath. "Castro and I were friends in high school and, yeah, he and I climbed together some. But then when Elisa got big enough to learn and she'd come along, Tommy began to make a move on her. I told him she was way too young and to knock it off. I put a stop to that."

"He still climb?"

"I have no idea," Demott said. "I stay away from him. He stays away from me."

"No problem with Hal, though."

"He was more her age and more her type, even though he was citified and born with the old silver spoon." Demott thought about that. "You know," he said, "I think he really did love this place as much as we did. He'd talk about getting his family to leave it to him as his part of the estate. Had it all figured out on paper. It wasn't worth near as much as the share he'd get otherwise, but it was what he wanted. That's what he'd say. Prettiest place on earth, and he'd make it better. Improve the stream where it was eroding. Plant out some ponderosa seedlings where we had a fire kill. Keep the herd down to where there wouldn't be any more overgrazing."

"I didn't see much sign of overgrazing now," Leaphorn said.

"Not now, you don't. But before Hal's daddy died he always wanted this place to carry a lot more livestock than the grass could stand. He was always putting the pressure on my dad, and after dad passed away, putting it on me. As a matter of fact he was threatening to fire me if I didn't get the income up to where he thought it ought to be."

"You think he would have done it?"

"We never will know," Demott said. "I wasn't going to overgraze this place, that's for damn sure. But just in time Breedlove had his big heart attack and passed away." He chuckled. "Elisa credited it to the power of my prayers."

Leaphorn waited. And waited. But Demott was in no hurry to interrupt his memories. A breeze came down the stream, cool and fresh, rustling the leaves behind Leaphorn and humming the little song that breezes sing in the firs.

"It's a mighty pretty day," Demott said finally. "But blink your eyes twice and winter will be coming over the mountain."

"You were going to tell me what went wrong with Hal," Leaphorn said.

"I got no license to practice psychiatry," Demott said. He hesitated just a moment, but Leaphorn knew it was coming. It was something Demott wanted to talk about—and probably had for a long, long time.

"Or theology, either," he continued. "If that's the word for it. Anyway, you know how the story goes in our Genesis. God created Adam and gave him absolutely everything he could want, to see if he could handle it and still be obedient and do the right thing. He couldn't. So he fell from grace."

Demott glanced at Leaphorn to see if he was following.

"Got kicked out of paradise," Demott said.

"Sure," Leaphorn said. "I remember it." It wasn't quite the way he'd always heard it, but he could see the point Demott might make with his version.

"Old Breedlove put Hal in paradise," Demott said. "Gave him everything. Prep school with the other rich kids, Dartmouth with the children of the ruling class—absolutely the very goddamn best that you can buy with money. If I was a preacher I'd say Hal's daddy spent a ton of money teaching his boy to worship Mammon—however you pronounce that. Anyway, it means making a god out of things you can buy." He paused, gave Leaphorn a questioning glance.

"We have some of the same philosophy in our own Genesis story," Leaphorn said. "First Man calls evil 'the way to make money.' Besides, I took a comparative religion course when I was a student at Arizona State. Made an A in it."

"Okay," Demott said. "Sorry. Anyway, when Hal was about a senior or so he flew into Mancos one summer in his own little airplane. Wanted us to grade out a landing strip for it near the house. I figured out how much it would cost, but his daddy wouldn't come up with the money. They got into a big argument over it. Hal had already been arguing with him about taking better care of this place, putting money in instead of taking it all out. I think it was about then that the old man got pissed off. He decided he'd give Hal the ranch and nothing else and let him see if he could live off it."

"Figuring he couldn't?"

"Yep," Hal said. "And of course the old man was right. Anyhow Breedlove eased up on the pressure for profits some and I got to put in a lot of fencing we needed to protect a couple of the sensitive pastures and get some equipment in there for some erosion control along the Cache. Elisa and Hal got married after that. Everything going smooth. But that didn't last long. Hal took Elisa to Europe. Decided he just had to have himself a Ferrari. Great car for our kind of roads. But he bought it. And other stuff. Borrowed money. Before long we weren't bringing in enough from selling our surplus hay and the beef to cover his expenses. So he went to see the old man."

At this point Demott's voice was thickening. He paused, rubbed his shirtsleeve across his forehead. "Warm for this time of year," he said.

"Yeah," Leaphorn said, thinking it was a cool, dry sixty degrees or so even with the breeze gone.

"Anyway, he came back empty. Hal didn't have much to say but I believe they must have had a big family fight. I know for sure he tried to borrow from George—that's George Shaw, his cousin who used to come out and climb with us—and George must have turned him down, too. I think the family must have told him they were going ahead with the moly strip mine deal, and to hell with him."

"But they didn't," Leaphorn said. "Why not?"

"I think it was because the old man had his heart attack a little bit after that. When he passed away it hung everything up in probate court for a while. This ranch was in trust for Hal. He didn't get it until he turned thirty, but of course the family didn't control it anymore. That's sort of where it stood for a while."

Demott paused. He inspected his newly washed hand. Leaphorn was thinking, too, about this friction between Hal and his family and what it might imply.

"When I had my visit with Mrs. Rivera at the bank," Leaphorn said, "she told me things were starting to brew on the moly mine development again just before Hal disappeared. But this time she thought it was going to be a deal with a different mining company. She didn't think the family corporation was involved."

Demott lost interest in his hand.

"She tell you that?"

"That's what she said. She said a Denver bank was involved in the deal somehow. It was way too big an operation for her little bank to handle the money end of it."

"With Mrs. Rivera in business we don't really need a newspaper around here," Demott said.

"So I was thinking that if the family told Hal they were going to run right over him, maybe he decided he'd screw them instead. He'd make his own deal and cut them out."

"I think that's probably about the way it was," Demott said. "I know his lawyer told him all he had to do was slow things down in court long enough to get to his birthday. Then he'd have clear title and he could do what he wanted. That's what Elisa wanted him to do. But Hal was a fella who just could not wait. There were things he wanted to buy. Things he wanted to do. Places he hadn't seen yet. And he'd borrowed a lot of money he had to pay back."

Demott produced a bitter-sounding laugh. "Elisa didn't know about that. She didn't know he could use the ranch as collateral when he didn't own it yet. Came as quite a shock. But he had his lawyer work out some sort of deal which put up some sort of overriding interest in the place as a guarantee."

"Lot of money?"

"Quite a bit. He'd gotten rid of that little plane he had and made a down payment on a bigger one. After he disappeared we let them take the plane back but we had to pay back the loan."

With that, Demott rose and collected his tools. "Back to work," he said. "Sorry I didn't know anything that would help you."

"One more question. Or maybe two," Leaphorn said. "Are you still climbing?"

"Too old for it," he said. "What's that in the Bible about it? About when you get to be a man you put aside the ways of the boy. Something like that."

"How good was Hal?"

"He was pretty good but he was reckless. He took more chances than I like. But he had all the skills. If he'd put his mind to it he could have been a dandy."

"Could he have climbed Ship Rock alone?"

Demott looked thoughtful. "I thought about that a lot ever since Elisa identified his skeleton. I didn't think so at first, but I don't know. I wouldn't even try it myself. But Hal . . ." He shook his head. "If he wanted something, he just had to have it."

"George Shaw went out to the Maryboy place the other day and got permission for a climb," Leaphorn said. "Next day or two. Any idea what he thinks might be found up there?"

"George is going to climb it?" Demott's tone was incredulous and his expression shocked. "Where'd you hear that?"

"All I know is that he told me he paid Maryboy a hundred dollars for trespass rights. Maybe he'll get somebody to climb it but I think he meant he was going up himself."

"What the hell for?"

Leaphorn didn't answer that. He gave Demott some time to answer it himself.

"Oh," Demott said. "The son of a bitch."

"I would imagine he thinks maybe somebody gave Hal a little push."

"Yeah," Demott said. "Either he thinks I did it, and I left something behind that would prove it—and he could use that to void Elisa's inheritance—or he did it himself and he remembers that he left something up there that would nail him and he wants to go get it."

Leaphorn shrugged. "As good a guess as any."

Demott put down his tools.

"When Elisa came back from having the bones cremated she told me none of them had been broken," he said. "Some of them were disconnected, you know. That could have been done in a fall, or maybe the turkey vultures pulled 'em apart. They're strong enough to do that, I guess. Anyway, I hope it was a fall, and he didn't just get hung up there to starve to death for water. He could have been a damn good man."

"I never knew him," Leaphorn said. "To me he was just somebody to hunt for and never find."

"Well, he was a good, kind boy," Demott said. "Big-hearted." He picked up his tools again. "You know, when the cop came up to show Elisa Hal's stuff I saw that folder he had with him. He had it labeled 'Fallen Man.' I thought, Yes, that described Hal. The old man gave him paradise and it wasn't enough for him."

18

L UCY SAM HAD seemed glad to see Chee.
"I think they're going to be climbing up Tse´ Bit´ a´i´ again," she
told Chee. "I saw a big car drive down the road toward Hosteen Maryboy's
place two days ago, and it stayed a long time, and when I saw it coming
back from there, I drove over there to see how he was doing and he told
me about it."

"I heard about it, too," Chee said, thinking how hard it was to keep secrets in empty country.

"The man paid Hosteen Maryboy a hundred dollars," she said, and
shook her head. "I don't think we should let them climb up there, even for
a thousand dollars."

"I don't think so either," Chee said. "They have plenty of their own
mountains to play around on."

"The one who lived here before," Lucy Sam said, using the Navajo cir-
cumlocution to avoid saying the name of the dead, "he'd say that it would
be like us Navajos climbing all over that big church in Rome, or getting up
on top of the Wailing Wall, or crawling all over that place where the Is-
lamic prophet went up to heaven."

"It's disrespectful," Chee agreed, and with that subject out of the way
he shifted the conversation to cattle theft.

Had Hosteen Maryboy mentioned to her that he'd lost some more cattle? He had, and he was angry about it. There would have been enough money in those cows to make the last payments on his pickup truck.

Had Ms. Sam seen anything suspicious since the last time he'd been here? She didn't think so.

Could he look at the ledger where she kept her notes? Certainly. She would get it for him.

Lucy Sam extracted the book from its desk drawer and handed it to Chee.

"I kept it just the same way," she said, tapping the page. "I put down the date and the time right here at the edge and then I write down what I see."

As he leafed backward through the ledger, Chee saw that Lucy Sam wrote down a lot more than that. She made a sort of daily journal out of it, much as her father had done. And she had not just copied her father's system, she also followed his Franciscan padres' writing style—small, neat lettering in small, neat lines—which had become sort of a trademark of generations of those Navajos educated at St. Michael's School west of Window Rock. It was easily legible and wasted neither paper nor ink. But readable or not, Chee found nothing in it very helpful.

He skipped back to the date when he and Officer Manuelito had visited the site of the loose fence posts. They had rated an entry, right after Lucy Sam's notation that, "Yazzie came. Said he would bring some firewood" and just before, "Turkey buzzards are back." Between those Lucy had written, "Police car stuck on road under Tse´ Bit´ a´i´. Truck driver helps." Then, down the page a bit: "Two truck gets police car." The last entry before the tow truck note reported, "That camper truck stopped. Driver looked around."

That camper truck? Chee felt his face flush with remembered embarrassment. That would have been Finch checking to see how thoroughly they had sprung his Zorro trap. He worked his way forward through the pages, learning more about kestrels, migrating grosbeaks, a local family of coyotes, and other Colorado Plateau fauna than he wanted to know. He also gained some insights into Lucy Sam's loneliness, but nothing that he could see would be useful to Acting Lieutenant Chee in his role as rustler hunter. If Zorro had come back to collect a load of Maryboy's cows from the place he'd left the hay, he'd done it when Lucy Sam wasn't looking.

But she was looking quite a lot. There was a mention of a "very muddy" white pickup towing a horse trailer on the dirt road that skirted Ship Rock, but no mention of it stopping. Chee made a mental note to check on that. About a dozen other vehicles had come in view of Lucy Sam's spotting scope, none of them potential rustlers. They included a Federal Express delivery truck, which must have been lost, another mention of Finch's camper truck, and three pickups that she had identified with the names of local-area owners.

So what was useful about that? It told him that if Manuelito's network of watchers would pay off at all, it would require patience, and probably years, to establish suspicious-looking patterns. And it told him that Mr. Finch looked upon him as a competitor in his hunt for the so-called Zorro. Finch wanted him to write off Maryboy's loose-fence-posts location, but Finch hadn't written it off himself. He was keeping his eye on the spot. That produced another thought. Maryboy had been losing cattle before. Had either Lucy Sam or her father noticed anything interesting in the past? Specifically, had they ever previously noticed that white truck pulling its horse trailer? He would page back through the book and check on that when he had time. And he would also look through the back pages for school buses. He'd noticed a Lucy Sam mention of a school bus stuck on that same dirt road, and the road wasn't on a bus route. She had also mentioned "that camper truck" being parked almost all day at the base of the mountain the year before. Her note said "Climbing our mountain?"

Chee put down the ledger. Lucy Sam had gone out to feed her chickens and he could see her now in her sheep pen inspecting a young goat that had managed to entangle itself in her fence. He found himself imagining Janet Pete in that role and himself in old man Sam's wheelchair. It didn't scan. The white Porsche roared in and rescued her. But that wasn't fair. He was being racist. He had been thinking like a racist ever since he'd met Janet and fallen in love with her. He had been thinking that because her name was Pete, because her father was Navajo, her blood somehow would have taught her the ways of the *Dine'* and made her one of them. But only your culture taught you values, and the culture that had formed Janet was blue-blooded, white, Ivy League, chic, irreligious, oldrich Maryland. And that made it just about as opposite as it could get from the traditional values of his people, which made wealth a symbol for selfishness, and had caused a friend of his to deliberately stop winning rodeo competitions because he was getting unhealthily famous and therefore out of harmony.

Well, to hell with that. He got up, refocused the spotting scope, and found the place where the posts had been loosened. That road probably carried no more than a dozen vehicles a week—none at all when the weather was wet. It was empty today, and there was no sign of anything around Mr. Finch's Zorro trap. Beyond it in the pasture he counted eighteen cows and calves, a mixture of Herefords and Angus, and three horses. He scanned across the Maryboy grassland to the base of Ship Rock and focused on the place where Lucy Sam had told him the climbing parties liked to launch their great adventures. Nothing there now but sage, chamisa, and a red-tailed hawk looking for her lunch.

Chee sat down again and picked up the oldest ledger. On his last visit he'd checked the entries on the days following Breedlove's disappearance but only with a casual glance. This time he'd be thorough.

Lucy Sam came in, washed her hands, and looked at him while she dried them.

"Something wrong?"

"Disappointed," Chee said. "So many details. This will take forever."

"He didn't have anything else to do," Lucy Sam said, voice apologetic. "After he got that sickness with his nerves, all he could do after that was get himself into his wheelchair. He couldn't go anyplace, he'd just sit there in the chair and sometimes he would read, or listen to the radio. And then he would watch through his telescope and keep his notes."

And he kept them very well, Chee noticed. Unfortunately they didn't seem to include what he wanted to find.

The date Hal Breedlove vanished came about midpoint in the old ledger. In Hosteen Sam's eyes it had been a windy day, cool, crows beginning to gather as they did when summer ended, flying in great, disorganized twilight flocks past Ship Rock to their roosting places in the San Juan River woods. Three oil field service trucks came down the road toward Red Rock and turned toward the Rattlesnake field. Some high clouds appeared but there had been no promise of rain.

The next day's entry was longer, devoted largely to the antics of four yearling coyotes who seemed to be trying to learn how to hunt in the prairie dog town down the slope. Interesting, but not what Chee was hoping for.

An hour and dozens of pages later, he closed the ledger, rubbed his eyes, and sighed.

"You want some lunch?" Lucy Sam asked, which was just the question Chee had been hoping to hear. Lucy had been there at the stove across the kitchen from him, cutting up onions, stirring, answering his questions about abbreviations he couldn't read or points he didn't understand, and the smell of mutton stew had gradually permeated the room and his senses—making this foolish search seem far less important than his hunger.

"Please," he said. "That smells just like the stew my mother used to make."

"Probably is the same," Lucy said. "Everybody has to use the same stuff—mutton, onions, potatoes, can of tomatoes, salt, pepper." She shrugged.

Like his mother's stew, it was delicious. He told Lucy what he was looking for—about the disappearance of Hal Breedlove and then his skeleton turning up on the mountain. He was looking for some idea of when Hal Breedlove returned to make his fatal climb.

"You find anything?"

"I think I learned that the man didn't come right back here after running away from his wife in Canyon de Chelly. At least there was no mention of anybody climbing."

"There would have been," she said. "How far did you get?"

"Just through the first eight weeks after he disappeared. It's going to take forever."

"You know, they always do it the same way. They start climbing just at dawn, maybe before. That's because they want to get down before dark, and because there's some places where that black rock gets terribly hot when the afternoon sun shines on it. So all you got to do is take a look at the first thing written down each day. He would always do the same every morning. He would get up at dawn and roll his wheelchair to the door. Then he would sing the song to Dawn Boy and bless the morning with his pollen. Next he would take a look at his mountain. If there was anything parked there where the climbers always left their cars, it would be the first thing he wrote down."

"I'll try that, then," he said.

On the page at which Chee reopened the ledger the first entry was marked 9/15/85, which was several pages and eight days too early. He glanced at the first line. Something about a kestrel catching a meadowlark. He paged forward, checking Lucy's advice by scanning down the first notes after dates.

Now he was at 9/18/85—halfway down the page. The first line read, "Climbers. Funny looking green van where climbers park. Three people going up. If Lucy gets back from Albuquerque I will get her to go into Shiprock and tell the police."

Chee checked the date again. September 18, 1985. That would be five days before Hal Breedlove disappeared from the Canyon de Chelly. He scanned quickly down the page, looking for other mentions of the climbers. He found two more on the same day.

The first said: "They are more than half way up now, creeping along under a cliff—like bugs on a wall." And the second: "The headlights turned on on the fancy green car, and the inside lights. I see them putting away their gear. Gone now, and the police did not come. I told Maryboy he should not let anyone climb Tse´ Bit´ a´i´ but he did not listen to me."

Lucy was washing dishes in a pan of water on the table by the stove, watching him while she worked. He took the ledger to her, pointed to the entry.

"Do you remember this?" Chee asked. "It would have been about eleven years ago. Three people came to climb Ship Rock in some sort of green van. Your father wanted you to go tell the police but you had gone to Albuquerque."

Lucy Sam put on her glasses and read.

"Now why did I take the bus to Albuquerque?" she asked herself. "Yes," she answered. "Irma was having her baby there. Little Alice. Now she's eleven. And when I came home he was excited about those climbers. And angry. He wanted me to take him to see Hosteen Maryboy about it. And I took him over there, and they argued about it. I remember that."

"Did he say anything about the climbers?"

"He said they were a little bit slow. It was after dark when they got back to the car."

"Anything about the car?"

"The car?" She looked thoughtful. "I remember he hadn't seen one like it before. He said it was ugly, clumsy looking, square like a box. It was green and it had a ski rack on top."

Chee closed the ledger and handed it to Lucy, trying to remember how Joe Leaphorn had described the car Hal Breedlove had abandoned after he had abandoned his wife. It was a recreational vehicle, green, something foreign-made. Yes. A Land-Rover. That would fit old man Sam's description of square and ugly.

"Thank you," he said to Lucy Sam. "I have to go now and see what Hosteen Maryboy can remember."

19

THE SUNSET HAD flared out behind Beautiful Mountain when Chee's patrol car bounced over Lucy Sam's cattle guard and gained the pavement. In the darkening twilight his headlights did little good and Chee almost missed the unmarked turnoff. That put him on the dirt track that led southward toward Rol Hai Rock, Table Mesa, and the infinity of empty country between these massive old buttes and the Chuska range.

Lucy Sam had told him: "Watch your odometer and in about eight miles from the turnoff place you come to the top of a ridge and you can see Maryboy's place off to the left maybe a mile."

"It'll be dark," Chee said. "Is the turnoff marked?"

"There's a little wash there, and a big cottonwood where you turn," she said. "It's the only tree out there, and Maryboy keeps a ghost light burning at his hogan. You can't miss it."

"Okay," Chee said, wishing she hadn't added that 'can't miss it' phrase. Those were the landmarks he always missed.

"There's a couple of places with deep sand where you cross arroyos. If you're going too slow, you might get stuck. But it's a pretty good road in dry weather."

Chee had been over this track a time or two when duty called, and did not consider it pretty good. It was bad. Too bad to warrant even one of those dim lines that were drawn on the official road map with an "unimproved" label and a footnoted warning. But Chee drove it a little faster than common sense dictated. He was excited. That boxy green vehicle must have been Hal Breedlove's boxy green Land-Rover—the same car he'd seen at the Lazy B. One of those three men who climbed out of it must have been Breedlove. Why not suspect that one of the other two was the man who had called Breedlove at the Thunderbird Lodge three or four days later and lured him away from his wife to oblivion? He would get a description from Maryboy if the old man could provide one. And he might be able to because those who live lonely lives where fellow humans are scarce tend to remember strangers—especially those on the strange mission of risking their lives on Ship Rock. Whatever, he would learn all he could and then he would call Leaphorn.

For a reason he didn't even try to understand, sitting across a table from the Legendary Lieutenant and telling him all this seemed extremely important to Chee. He had thought he was angry at Leaphorn for signing up with John McDermott. But Leaphorn's clear black eyes would study him with approval. Leaphorn's dour expression would soften into a smile. Leaphorn would think awhile and then Leaphorn would tell him how this bit of information had solved a terrible puzzle.

The odometer had clicked off almost exactly the eight prescribed miles from the turnoff and the track was topping the ridge. The moon was not yet up, but the ragged black shape of the Chuskas to the right and the flat-topped bulk of Table Mesa to the left were outlined against a sky a-dazzle with stars. Ahead an ocean of darkness stretched toward the horizon. Then the track curved past a hummock of Mormon tea, and there shone the Maryboy ghost light, punctuating the night with a bright yellow spot.

Chee made the left turn past the cottonwood Lucy Sam had described into two sandy ruts separated by a grassy ridge. They led him along a shallow wash toward the light. The track dipped down a slope and the bright spot became just a glow. He heard a thud from somewhere a long ways off. More like a sudden clapping sound. But he was too busy driving for the moment to wonder what caused it. The track had veered down the bank of the wash, tilting his police car. It entered a dense tangle of chaparral, converted by his headlights into a tunnel of brightness. He emerged from that.

The ghost light was gone.

Chee frowned, puzzled. He decided it must be just out of sight behind the screen of brush he was driving past. The track emerged from the brush into flat grassland where nothing grew higher than the sage. Still no ghost light. Why not? Maryboy had turned it off, what else? Or the bulb had burned out. Out here, Maryboy wouldn't be on a Rural Electrification Administration power line. He'd be running a windmill generator and battery system. Perhaps the batteries had gone dead. Nonsense. And yet the only reason one puts out a ghost light is because, for some reason, he believes he is threatened by the spirits of the dead. And if he believes that, why would he turn it off before Dawn Boy has restored harmony to the world? And why would he turn it off when he'd seen he had a visitor coming? Had Maryboy been expecting someone he would want to hide from?

Chee covered the last quarter mile slower than he would have had the light still been burning. His patrol car rolled past a plank stock pen with a loading ramp for cattle. His headlights reflected from the aluminum siding of a mobile home. Beyond it he could see the remains of a truck with its back wheels removed. Beyond that a fairly new pickup stood, and behind that, a small hogan, a small goat pen, a brush arbor, and two sheds. He parked a little further from the house than he would have normally and left the motor running a bit longer. And when he turned off the ignition he rolled down the window beside him and sat listening.

There was no light in the mobile home. Cold, dry December air poured through the truck window. It brought with it the smell of sage and dust, of dead leaves, of the goat pen. It brought the dead silence of a windless winter night. A dog emerged from one of the sheds, looking old, ragged, and tired. It limped toward his truck and stopped, the glare of his headlights reflecting from its eyes.

Chee leaned out of the window toward it. "Anybody home?" he asked. The dog turned and limped back into the shed. Chee switched off the car lights and waited, uneasy, for some sign of life from the house. Tapped his fingers on the steering wheel. Listened. From somewhere far away he heard the call of a burrowing owl hunting its prey. He thought. Someone turned off that damned ghost light. Therefore someone is here. I am absolutely not going back home and admit I came out here to talk to Maryboy and was too afraid of the dark to get out of the car.

Chee muttered an expletive, made sure that his official .38-caliber pistol was securely in its holster, took the flashlight from its rack, opened the car door, and got out—thankful for the policy that eliminated those dome lights that went on when the door opened. He stood beside the car, glad of the darkness, and shouted, "Hosteen Maryboy," and a greeting in Navajo. He identified himself by clan and family. He waited.

Only silence. But the sound of his own voice, loud and clear, had burst the bubble of his nervousness. He waited as long as politeness required, walked up to the entrance, climbed the two concrete block steps that led to the door, and tapped on the screen.

Nothing. He tapped again, harder this time. Again, no response. He tried the screen, swung it open. Tried the door. The knob turned easily in his hand.

"Hosteen Maryboy," Chee shouted. "You've got company." He listened. Nothing. And opened the door to total darkness. Flicked on his flash.

If time is measurable in such circumstances, it might have taken a few nanoseconds for Chee's flashlight beam to traverse this tiny room from end to end and find it unoccupied. But even while this was happening, his peripheral vision was telling him otherwise. He turned the flashlight downward.

The body lay on its back, feet toward the door, as if the man had come to answer a visitor's summons and then had been knocked directly backward.

In the moment that elapsed before Chee snapped off the flash and jumped into the darkness of the house he had reached several conclusions. The man had been shot near the center of the chest. He was probably, but not certainly, Mr. Maryboy. The claplike sound he had heard had been the fatal shot. Thus the shooter must be nearby. Having shot Maryboy, and seen Chee's headlights, he had switched off the ghost light. And, more to the immediate point, Acting Lieutenant Jim Chee was likely to get shot himself. He leaned against the wall beside the door, drew the pistol, cocked it, and made sure the safety was off.

Chee spent the next few minutes listening to the silence and thinking his situation through. Among the aromas that came from Hosteen Maryboy's kitchen he had picked up the acrid smell of burned gunpowder, confirming his guess that Maryboy had been shot only a few minutes ago. A frightening conclusion, it reinforced the evidence offered by the doused ghost light. The killer had not driven away. Chee would have met him on the access track. That he had walked away was possible but not likely. It would have meant abandoning his vehicle. Was it the pickup he'd noticed? Perhaps. But that was most likely Maryboy's. The killer, having seen him coming, would have had plenty of time to move his car but no way to drive out without meeting Chee on the track.

So what options did he have?

Chee squatted beside the body, felt for a pulse, and found none. The man was dead. That reduced the urgency a little. He could wait for daylight, which would even the odds. As it now stood the killer knew exactly where he was and he didn't have a clue. But waiting had a downside, too. It would occur to the killer sooner or later to fire a shot into the patrol car gas tank—or do something else to disable it. Then he could drive away unpursued. Or he might drain out some gasoline from any one of the vehicles, set this mobile home ablaze, and shoot Chee as he came out.

By now his eyes had adjusted to the darkness. Chee could easily see the windows. The starlight that came through them—dim as it was—allowed him to make out a chair, a couch, a table, and the door that led into the kitchen.

Could the killer be there? Or in the bedroom beyond it? Not likely. He sat against the wall, holding his breath, focusing every instinct on listening. He heard nothing. Still, he dreaded the thought of being shot in the back.

Chee picked up the flash, held it far from his body, pointed both his pistol and the flash at the kitchen doorway, and flicked it on. Nothing moved in the part of the room visible to him. He edged to the door, keeping the flash away from him. The kitchen was empty. And so, when he repeated that process, were the bedroom and the tiny bath behind it.

Back in the living room, Chee sat on the couch and made himself as comfortable as the circumstances permitted. He weighed the options, found no new ones, imagined dawn coming, imagined the sun rising, imagined waiting and waiting, imagined finally saying to hell with it and walking out to the patrol car. Then he would either be shot, or he wouldn't be. If he wasn't shot, he would have to get on the radio and report this affair to Captain Largo.

"When did this happen?" the captain would ask, and then, "Why did you wait all night to report it?" and then, "Are you telling me that you sat in the house all night because you were afraid to come out?" And the only answer to that would be, "Yes, sir, that's what I did." And then, a little later, Janet Pete would be asking why he was being dismissed from the Navajo Tribal Police, and he would say—But would Janet care enough to ask? And did it matter anyway?

Something mattered. Chee got up, stood beside the door, looking and listening—impressed with how bright the night now seemed outside the lightless living room. But he saw nothing, and heard nothing. He pushed open the screen and, pistol in hand, dashed to the patrol car, pulled open the door and slid in—crouched low in the seat, grabbed the mike, started the engine.

The night dispatcher responded almost instantly. "Have a homicide at the Maryboy place," Chee said, "with the perpetrator still in the area. I need—"

The dispatcher remembered hearing the sound of two shots, closely spaced, and of breaking glass, and something she described as "scratching, squeaking, and thumping." That was the end of the message from Acting Lieutenant Jim Chee.

20

A T FIRST CHEE was conscious only of something uncomfortable covering much of his head and his left eye. Then the general numbness of the left side of his face registered on his consciousness and finally some fairly serious discomfort involving his left ribs. Then he heard two voices, both female, one belonging to Janet Pete. He managed to get his right eye in focus and there she was, holding his hand and saying something he couldn't understand. Thinking about it later, he thought it might have been "I told you so," or something to that effect.

When he awoke again, the only one in the room was Captain Largo, who was looking at him with a puzzled expression.

"What the hell happened out there?" Largo said. "What was going on?" And then, as if touched by some rare sentiment, he said, "How you feeling, Jim? The doctor tells us he thinks you're going to be all right."

Chee was awake enough to doubt that Largo expected an answer and gave himself a few moments to get oriented. He was in a hospital, obviously. Probably the Indian Health Service hospital at Gallup, but maybe Farmington. Obviously something bad had happened to him, but he didn't know what. Obviously again, it had something to do with his ribs, which were hurting now, and his face, which would be hurting when the numbness wore off. The captain could bring him up to date. And what day was it, anyway?

"What the hell happened?" Chee asked. "Car wreck?"

"Somebody shot you, goddammit," Largo said. "Do you know who it was?"

"Shot me? Why would somebody do that?" But even before he finished the sentence he began to remember. Hosteen Maryboy dead on the floor. Getting back into the patrol car. But it was very vague and dreamlike.

"They shot you twice through the door of the patrol car," Largo said. "It looked to Teddy Begayaye like you were driving away from the Maryboy place and the perpetrator fired two shots through the driver's-side door. Teddy found the empties. Thirty-eights by the looks of them, and of what they took out of you. But you had the window rolled down, so the slugs had to get through that shatterproof glass after they punched through the metal. The doc said that probably saved you."

Chee was more or less awake now and didn't feel like anything had saved him. He felt terrible. He said, "Oh, yeah. I remember some of it now."

"You remember enough to tell me who shot you? And what the hell you were doing out at the Maryboy place in the middle of the night? And who shot Maryboy? And why they shot him? Could you give us a description? Let us know what the hell we're looking for—man, woman, or child?"

Chee got most of the way through answering most of those questions before whatever painkillers they had shot into him in the ambulance, and the emergency room, and the operating room, and since then cut in again and he started fading away. The nurse came in and was trying to shoo Largo out. But Chee was just awake enough to interrupt their argument. "Captain," he said, hearing his voice come out soft and slurry and about a half mile away. "I think this Maryboy homicide goes all the way back to that Hal Breedlove case Joe Leaphorn was working on eleven years ago. That Fallen Man business. That skeleton up on Ship Rock. I need to talk to Leaphorn about . . ."

The next time he rejoined the world of the living he did so more or less completely. The pain was real, but tolerable. A nurse was doing something with the flexible tubing to which he was connected. A handsome, middle-aged woman whose name tag said SANCHEZ, she smiled at him, asked him how he was doing and if there was anything she could do for him.

"How about a damage assessment?" Chee said. "A prognosis. A condition report. The captain said he thought I might live, but how about this left eye? And what's with the ribs?"

"The doctor will be in to see you pretty soon," the nurse said. "He's supposed to be the one to give the patient that sort of information."

"Why don't you do it?" Chee said. "I'm very, very interested."

"Oh, why not?" she said. She picked up the chart at the foot of his bed and scanned it. She frowned, made a disapproving clicking sound with her tongue.

"I don't like the sound of that," Chee said. "They're not going to decide I'm too banged up to be worth repairing?"

"We've got two misspelled words in this," she said. "They quit teaching doctors how to spell. But, no, I just wish I was as healthy as you are," she said. "I guess a body shop estimator would rate you as a moderately serious fender bender. Not bad enough to total you out, and just barely bad enough to cause the insurance company to send in its inspector and raise your premium rates."

"How about the eye?" Chee said. "It has a bandage over it."

"Because of "—she glanced down at the chart and read—" 'multiple superficial lacerations caused by glass fragments.' But from the looks of this, no damage was done where it might affect your vision. Maybe you'll have some bumpy shaving on that cheek for a while, and need to grow yourself about an inch of new eyebrow. But apparently no sight impairment."

"That's good to hear," Chee said. "How about the rest of me?"

She looked down at him sternly. "Now when the doctor comes in, you've got to act surprised. All right? Everything he tells you is news to you. And for God's sake don't argue with him. Don't be saying: 'That ain't what Florence Nightingale told me.' You understand?"

Chee understood. He listened. Two bullets involved. One apparently had struck the thick bone at the back of the skull a glancing blow, causing a scalp wound, heavy bleeding, and concussion. The other, apparently fired after he had fallen forward, came through the door. While the left side of his face was sprayed with debris, the slug was deflected into his left side, where it penetrated the muscles and cracked two ribs.

"I'd say you were pretty lucky," the nurse said, looking at him over the chart. "Except maybe in your choice of friends."

"Yeah," Chee said, wincing. "Does that chart show who sent me those flowers?"

There were two bunches of them, one a dazzling pot of some sort of fancy chrysanthemum and the other a bouquet of mixed blossoms.

The nurse extracted the card from the bouquet. "Want me to read it to you?"

"Please," Chee said.

"It says, 'Learn to duck,' and it's signed, 'Your Shiprock Rat Terriers.'"

"Be damned," Chee said, and felt himself flushing with pleasure.

"Friends of yours?"

"Yes, indeed," Chee said. "They really are."

"And the other card reads 'Get well quick, be more careful and we have to talk,' and it's signed 'Love, Janet.'" With that Nurse Sanchez left him to think about what it might mean.

The next visitor was a well-dressed young man named Elliott Lewis, whose tidy business suit and necktie proclaimed him a special agent of the Federal Bureau of Investigation. Nevertheless, he displayed his identification to Chee. His interest was in the wrongful death of Austin Maryboy, such felonious events on a federal reservation being under the jurisdiction of the Bureau. Chee told him what he knew, but not what he guessed. Lewis, in the best FBI tradition, told Chee absolutely nothing.

"This thing must have made some sort of splash in the papers," Chee said. "Am I right about that?"

Lewis was restoring his notebook and tape recorder to his briefcase. "Why you say that?"

"Because the FBI got here early."

Lewis looked up from the housekeeping duties in his briefcase. He suppressed a grin and nodded. "It made the front page in the *Phoenix Gazette*, and the *Albuquerque Journal*, and the *Deseret News*," he said. "And I guess you could add the *Gallup Independent*, *Navajo Times*, *Farmington Times*, and the rest of 'em."

"How long you been assigned out here?" Chee asked.

"This is week three," Lewis said. "I'm fresh out of the academy but I've heard about our reputation for chasing the headlines. And you'll notice I've already got the names of the pertinent papers memorized."

Which left Chee regretting the barb. What was Lewis but another young cop trying to get along? Maybe the Bureau would teach him its famous arrogance. But it hadn't yet, and maybe with the old J. Edgar Hoover gang fading away, it was dropping the superman pose. Chee had worked with both kinds.

Lewis was also efficient. He asked the pertinent questions, which made it apparent that the theory of the crime appealing to the Bureau was a motive involving cattle theft—of which Maryboy was known to be a victim. Chee considered introducing mountain climbing into the conversation but decided against it. His head ached. Life was already too complicated. And how the devil could he explain it anyway? Lewis closed his notebook, switched off his tape recorder, and departed.

Chee turned his thoughts to the note Janet had signed. Remembering earlier notes, it sounded cool, considering the circumstances. Or was that his imagination? And there she was now, standing in the doorway, smiling at him, looking beautiful.

"You want a visitor?" she said. "They gave the fed first priority. I had to wait."

"Come in," he said, "and sit and talk to me."

She did. But en route to the chair, she bent over, found an unbandaged place, and kissed him thoroughly.

"Now I have two reasons to be mad at you," she said.

He waited.

"You almost got yourself killed," she said. "That's the worst thing. Lieutenants are supposed to send their troops out to get shot at. They're not supposed to get shot themselves."

"I know," he said. "I've got to work on it."

"And you insulted me," she added. "Are you recovered enough to talk about that?" No more banter now. The smile was gone.

"Did I?" Chee said.

"Don't you think so? You implied that I had tricked you. You pretty well said that I had used you to get information to pass along to John."

Chee didn't respond to that. "John," he was thinking. Not "McDermott," or "Mr. McDermott," but "John."

He shrugged. "I apologize, then," he said. "I think I misunderstood things. I had the impression the son of a bitch was your enemy. Everything I know about the man is what you told me. About how he had used you, taken advantage of his position. You the student and the hired hand. Him the famous professor and the boss. That made him your enemy, and anyone who treats you like that is my enemy."

She sat very still, hands folded in her lap, while he said all that. "Jim," she began, and then stopped, her lower lip between her teeth.

"I guess it shocked me," he said. "There I was, the naive romantic, thinking of myself as Sir Galahad saving the damsel from the dragon, and I find out the damsel is out partying with the dragon."

Janet Pete's complexion had become slightly pink.

"I agree with some of that," she said. "The part about you being naive. But I think we'd better talk about this later. When you're better. I shouldn't have brought it up now. I wasn't thinking. I'm sorry. I want you to hurry up and get well, and this isn't good for you."

"Okay," Chee said. "I'm sorry I hurt your feelings."

She stopped at the door. "I hope one really good thing will come out of this," she said. "I hope this being almost killed will cure you of being a policeman."

"What do you mean?" Chee said, knowing full well what she meant.

"I mean you could stay in law enforcement without carrying that damned gun, and doing that sort of work. You could take your pick of half a dozen jobs in—"

"In Washington," Chee said.

"Or elsewhere. There are dozens of offices. Dozens of agencies. In the BIA, the Justice Department. I heard of a wonderful opening in Miami. Something involving the Seminole agency."

Chee's head ached. He didn't feel well. He said, "Thanks for coming, Janet. Thanks for the flowers."

And then she was gone.

Chee drifted into a shallow sleep punctuated by uneasy dreams. He was awakened to take antibiotics and to have his temperature and vital signs checked. He dozed again, and was aroused to eat a bowl of lukewarm cream of mushroom soup, a portion of cherry Jell-O, and some banana-flavored yogurt. He was reminded that he was supposed to rise from his bed now and walk around the room for a while to get everything working properly. While dutifully doing that, he sensed a presence behind him.

Joe Leaphorn was standing in the doorway, his face wearing that expression of disapproval that Chee had learned to dread when he was the Legendary Lieutenant's assistant and gofer.

21

 AREN'T YOU SUPPOSED to be in bed?" Leaphorn asked. He was wearing a plaid shirt and a Chicago Cubs baseball cap, but even that didn't minimize the effect. He still looked to Chee like the Legendary Lieutenant.

"I'm just doing what the doc told me to do," Chee said. "I'm getting used to walking so these ribs don't hurt." He was also getting used to looking at the image of himself in the mirror with one eye bandaged and the other one hideously black. But he wasn't admitting that to Leaphorn. In fact, he was disgusted with himself for explaining his conduct to Leaphorn. He should have told him to bug off. But he didn't. Instead he said, "Yes, sir. I'm being the model patient so they'll give me time off for good behavior."

"Well, I'm glad it's not as bad as I first heard it was," Leaphorn said, and helped himself to a chair. "I'd heard he almost killed you."

They dealt with all the facts of the incident then, quickly and efficiently—became two professionals talking about a crime. Chee eased himself back onto the bed. Leaphorn sat, holding his cap. His bristly short haircut was even grayer now than Chee had remembered.

"I'm not going to stay long," Leaphorn said. "They told me you're supposed to be resting. But I have something I wanted to tell you."

"I'm listening," Chee said, thinking, *You also have something you want to ask me.* But so what? That was the tried-and-true Leaphorn strategy. There was nothing underhanded about it.

Leaphorn cleared his throat. "You sure you don't want to get some rest?"

"To hell with resting," Chee said. "I want out of here and I think they may let me go this evening. The doc wants to change the bandages again and check everything."

"The quicker the better," Leaphorn said. "Hospitals are dangerous places."

Chee cut off his laugh just as it started. Leaphorn's wife had died in this very hospital, he remembered. A brain tumor removed. Everything went perfectly. The tumor was benign. But the staph infection that followed was lethal.

"Yes," he said. "I want to go home."

"I've done a little checking," Leaphorn said. He made an abashed gesture. "When you've been in the NTP as long as I was—and out of it just a little bit—then it seems people have trouble remembering you're just a civilian. That you're no longer official."

"Lieutenant," Chee said, and laughed. "I'm afraid you're always going to seem official to a lot of people. Including me."

Leaphorn looked vaguely embarrassed by that. "Well, anyway, things are going about the way you'd expect. It was a slim day for news, and the papers made a pretty big thing out of it. That brings the feds hurrying right in. You've seen the newspapers, I guess?"

"No," Chee said, and pointed to his left eye. "I haven't been in very sharp focus until today. But I've seen the fed."

"Well, you can't be surprised they're on it. Big headlines. Slayer shoots policeman at the scene of the murder. No suspect. No motive. Big mystery. Big headlines. So the Bureau moves in right away without requiring the usual prodding. They found out that Maryboy had been having some livestock stolen. They found out you'd gone out there to check on rustling. So they're working that angle some . . ." Leaphorn paused, gave Chee a wry grin. "You know what I mean?"

Chee laughed. "Unless they've reformed since day before yesterday it means they're having my friends in the NTP at Shiprock working on it, and the Arizona Highway Patrol, and the New Mexico State Police, and the San Juan and McKinley County sheriff's deputies."

Leaphorn didn't object to that analysis. "And then they think maybe there might be a drug angle, or a gang angle. All those good things," he added.

"No other theories?"

"Not from what I'm hearing."

"You're telling me something right now," Chee said, unable to suppress a grin, even though it hurt. "I think you're telling me that neither the feds nor anyone else has shown any interest in trying to tie an eleven-year-old runaway-husband case into this felony homicide. Am I right?"

Leaphorn was never very much a man for laughing, but his amusement showed. "That is correct," he said.

"I've been trying to visualize that," Chee said. "You've known Captain Largo longer than I have. But can you visualize him trying to explain to some special agent that I had actually gone out to interview Maryboy to see if he could identify who had climbed Ship Rock eleven years ago, because we were still working on a 1985 missing person case? Can you imagine Largo doing it? Trying to get the guy's attention, especially when Largo doesn't understand it himself."

The amusement had left Leaphorn's face.

"I guessed that's why you were out there," he said. "What'd you find out?"

Chee couldn't pass up this opportunity to needle the Legendary Lieutenant. Besides, Leaphorn was working for McDermott. So Chee said, "Nothing. Maryboy was dead when I got there."

"No. No." Leaphorn let his impatience show. "I meant what had you learned that caused you to go out there? In the night?"

The moment had come:

"I learned that on the morning of September 18, 1985, a dark green, square, ugly recreational vehicle with a ski rack on its roof was driven to the usual climbers' launch site on Maryboy's grazing lease. Three men got out and climbed Ship Rock. Maryboy had given them trespass permission. Now, to bring things up to date, I learned yesterday that John McDermott hands this same Hosteen Maryboy one hundred dollars for trespass rights for another climb. I presume that George Shaw and others intend to climb the mountain, probably just as quickly as they can get a party organized. So, I went out to learn if Hosteen Maryboy remembered who had paid him for climbing trespass rights back in 1985."

Chee recited this slowly, watching Leaphorn's face. It became absolutely still. Breathing stopped. The green vehicle was instantly translated into Breedlove's status truck, the date into a week before Hal had begun his vanishing act, and two days before his all-important thirtieth birthday. All that, and all the complex implications suggested, had been processed by the time Chee finished his speech. Leaphorn's first question, Chee knew, would be how he had learned this. Whether the source of this information was reliable. Well, let him ask it. Chee was ready.

Leaphorn sighed.

"I wonder how many people knew that George Shaw was looking for a team to climb that mountain with him," Leaphorn said.

Chee looked at the ceiling, clicked his tongue against his teeth, and said, "I have no idea." Why did he continue trying to guess how the Legendary Lieutenant's mind worked? It was miles and miles beyond him.

Leaphorn abruptly clapped his hands together.

"Now you've given us the link that can fit the pattern together," Leaphorn said, with rare exuberance. "Finally something to work with. I spent most of my time for months trying to think this case through and I didn't come up with this. Emma was still healthy then, and she thought about it, too. And I've spent a lot of thought on it since then, even though we officially gave up. And in—how many days was it?—less than ten, you come up with the link."

Chee found himself baffled. But Leaphorn was beaming at him, full of pride. That made it both better and worse.

"But we still don't know who killed Hosteen Maryboy," Chee said, thinking at least he didn't know.

"But now we have something to work on," Leaphorn said. "Another part of the pattern takes shape."

Chee said, "Umm," and tried to look thoughtful instead of confused.

"Breedlove's skeleton is found on Ship Rock," Leaphorn said, holding up a blunt trigger finger. "Amos Nez is promptly shot." Leaphorn added a second finger. "Now, shortly thereafter, just as arrangements are being made for another climb of Ship Rock, one of the last people to see Breedlove is shot." He added a third finger.

"Yes," Chee said. "If we have all the pertinent facts it makes for a short list of suspects."

"I can add a little light to that," Leaphorn said. "Actually, it's what I came in to tell you. Eldon Demott told me some interesting things about Hal. The key one was that he'd quarreled with his father, and his family. He had decided to cut the family corporation out of the mining lease as soon as he inherited the ranch."

"Did the family know that?"

"Demott presumed they did. So do I. He probably told them himself. Demott understood Hal had tried to get money out of his father, and got turned down, and came home defiant. But even if he tried to keep it secret, the money people seemed to have known about it. Hal was in debt. Borrowing money. And if the money people knew, I'm sure the word got back to the Breedlove Corporation."

"Ah," Chee said. "So we add George Shaw to the list of people who would be happy if Hal Breedlove died before he celebrated the pertinent birthday."

"Or even happier to prove that Hal Breedlove was murdered by his wife, which would mean she couldn't inherit. I would guess that would put the ranch back into probate. And the Breedlove family would be the heir."

They sat for a while, thinking about it.

"If you want a little bit more confusion, I turned up a possible boyfriend for Elisa," Leaphorn said. "It turns out their climbing team was once a foursome." He explained to Chee what Mrs. Rivera had told him of Tommy Castro and what Demott had added to it.

"Another rock climber," Chee said. "You think he killed Hal to gain access to the widow? Or the widow and Castro conspired to get Hal out of the way?"

"If so, they didn't do much about it. As far as we know, that is."

"How about Shaw as the man who left Breedlove dying on the ledge? Or maybe gave him a shove?"

Leaphorn shrugged. "I think I like one of the Demotts a little better."

"How about the shootings?"

"About the same," Leaphorn said.

They thought about it some more, and Chee felt himself being engulfed with nostalgia. Remembering the days he'd worked for Leaphorn, sat across the desk in the lieutenant's cramped second-floor office in

Window Rock trying to put the pieces of something or other together in order to understand a crime. Stressful as it had been, demanding as Leaphorn tended to be, it had been a joyful time. And damn little paperwork.

"Do you still have your map?" Chee asked.

If Leaphorn heard the question he didn't show it. He said, "The problem here is time."

Lost again, Chee said, "Time?"

"Think how different things would be if Hal Breedlove's thirtieth birthday had been a week after he disappeared, instead of a week before," Leaphorn said.

"Yeah," Chee said. "Wouldn't that have simplified things?"

"Then the presumption that went with his disappearance would have been foul play. A homicide to prevent the inheritance."

"Right," Chee said.

Leaphorn rose, recovered his Cubs cap from Chee's table.

"Do you think you can get Largo to make Ship Rock off limits to climbers for a few days?"

"Do I tell him why?" Chee asked.

"Tell him that mountain climbers have this tradition of leaving a record behind when they reach a difficult peak. Ship Rock is one of those. On top of it, there's a metal box—one of those canisters the army uses to hold belted machine gun ammunition. It's waterproof, of course, and there's a book in it that climbers sign. They jot down the time and the date and any note they'd like to leave to those who come later."

"Shaw told you that?"

"No. I've been asking around. But Shaw would certainly know it."

"You want to keep Shaw from going up and getting it," Chee said. "Didn't you tell me you were working for him?"

"He retained me to find out everything I could about what happened to Hal Breedlove," Leaphorn said. "How can I learn anything I can depend on from that book if Mr. Shaw gets it first?"

"Oh," Chee said.

"I want to know who was in that party of three who made the climb before Hal disappeared. Was one of them Hal, or Shaw, or Demott, or maybe even Castro? Three men, Hosteen Sam said. But how could he be sure of gender through a spotting scope miles away? Climbers wear helmets and they don't wear skirts. Was one of the three Mrs. Breedlove? If Hal was one of them and he got to the top, his name will be in the book. If it isn't, that might help explain why he went back after he vanished from Canyon de Chelly: to try again. If he got to the top that time, his name and the date will be there. I want to know when he made the climb that killed him."

"It wasn't in the first forty-three days after he disappeared," Chee said.

"What?" Leaphorn said, startled. "How do you know that?"

Chee described Hosteen Sam's ledger, his habit of rolling his wheelchair to the window each day after his dawn prayers and looking at the mountain. He described Sam's meticulous entry system. "But there was no mention of a climbing party from September eighteenth, when he watched the three climb it and then complained to Maryboy about it, through the first week of November. So if Hal climbed it in that period he had to somehow sneak in without old Sam seeing him. I doubt if that's possible, even if he knew Sam would be watching—which he wouldn't— or had some reason to be sneaky. I'm told that that's the starting point for the only way up."

"I think we need to keep that ledger somewhere safe," Leaphorn said. "It seems to be telling us that Breedlove was alive a lot longer than I'd been thinking."

"I'll call Largo and get him to stall off climbing for a while," Chee said. "And I'll call my office. Manuelito knows Lucy Sam. She can go out and take custody of that ledger for a little while."

"You take care of yourself," Leaphorn said, and headed for the door.

"Wait a second. If we get the climbing stopped, how are you going to get someone up there to look at the register?"

"I'm going to rent a helicopter," Leaphorn said. "I know a lawyer in Gallup. A rock climber who's been up Ship Rock himself. I think he'd be willing to go up with me and the pilot, and we put him down on the top, and he takes a look."

"And brings down the book."

"I didn't want to do that. I'm a civilian now. I don't want to tamper with evidence. We'll take along a camera."

"And make some photocopies?"

"Exactly."

"That's going to cost a lot of money, isn't it?"

"The Breedlove Corporation is paying for it," Leaphorn said. "I've got their twenty thousand dollars in the bank."

22

THE KOAT-TV WEATHER map the previous night had shown a massive curve of bitterly cold air bulging down the Rocky Mountains out of Canada, sliding southward. The morning news reported snow across Idaho and northern Utah, with livestock warnings out. The weather lady called it a "blue norther" and told the Four Corners to brace for it tomorrow. But at the moment it was a beautiful morning for a helicopter ride, if you enjoyed such things, which Leaphorn didn't.

The last time he'd ridden in one of these ugly beasts he was being rushed to a hospital to have a variety of injuries treated. It was better to go when one was healthy, he thought, but not much.

However, Bob Rosebrough seemed to be enjoying it, which was good because Rosebrough had volunteered to climb down the copter's ladder to the tip of Ship Rock, photograph the documents in the box there, and climb back up.

"No problem, Joe," he'd said. "Climbing down a cliff can be harder than climbing up it, but ladders are different. And I sort of like the idea of being the first guy to climb down onto the top of Ship Rock." Liking the idea meant he wouldn't accept any payment for taking the day off from his Gallup law practice. That appealed to Leaphorn. The copter rental was taking eight hundred dollars out of the Breedlove Corporation's twenty thousand retainer, and Leaphorn was beginning to have some ethical qualms about how he was using that fee.

The view now was spectacular. They were flying south from the Farmington Airport and if Leaphorn had cared to look straight down, which he didn't, he would have been staring into row after row of dragon's teeth that erosion had formed on the east side of the uplift known as the Hogback. The rising sun outlined the teeth with shadows, making them look like a grotesquely oversized tank trap—even less hospitable than they appeared from the ground. The slanting light was also creating a silver mirror of the surface of Morgan Lake to the north and converting the long plume of steam from the stacks of the Four Corners Power Plant into a great white feather. The scale of it made even Leaphorn, a desert rat raised in the vastness of the Four Corners, conscious of its immensity.

The pilot was pointing down.

"How about having to land in those shark's teeth?" he asked. "Or worse, parachuting down into it. Just think about that. It makes your crotch hurt."

Leaphorn preferred to think of something else, which in its way was equally unpleasant. He thought about the oddity of murder in general, and of this murder in particular. Hal Breedlove disappears. Ten quiet years follow. Then, rapidly, in a matter of days, an unidentified skeleton is found on the mountain, apparently a man who has fallen to his death in a climbing accident. Then Amos Nez is shot. Next the bones are identified as the remains of Hal Breedlove. Then Hosteen Maryboy is murdered. Cause and effect, cause and effect. The pattern was there if he could find the missing part—the part that would bring it into focus. At the center of it, he was certain, was the great dark volcanic monolith that was now looming ahead of them like the ruins of a Gothic cathedral built for giants. On top of it a metal box was cached. In the box would be another piece to fit into the puzzle of Hal Breedlove.

"The spire on the left is it," Rosebrough said, his voice sounding metallic through the earphones they were wearing. "They look about the same height from this vantage, but the one on the left is the one you have to stand on top of if you want to say you've climbed Ship Rock."

"I'm going to circle around it a little first," the pilot said. "I want to get a feeling for wind, updrafts, downdrafts, that sort of thing. Air currents can be tricky around something like this. Even on a calm, cool morning."

They circled. Leaphorn had been warned about what looking down while a copter is spiraling does to one's stomach. He folded his hands across his safety belt and studied his knuckles.

"Okay," Rosebrough said. "That's it just below us."

"It doesn't look very flat," the pilot said, sounding doubtful. "And how big is it?"

"Not very," Rosebrough said. "About the size of a desktop. The box is on that larger flattish area just below. I'll have to climb down to get it."

"You have twenty feet of ladder, but I guess I could get close enough for you to just jump down," the pilot said.

Rosebrough laughed. "I'll take the ladder," he said.

And he did.

Leaphorn looked. Rosebrough was on the mountain, standing on the tiny sloping slab that formed the summit, then climbing down to the flatter area. He removed an olive drab U.S. Army ammunition box from the crack, opened it, removed the ledger, and tried to protect it from the wind produced by the copter blades. He waved them away. Leaphorn, stomach churning, resumed the study of his knuckles.

"You all right?" the pilot asked.

"Fine," Leaphorn said, and swallowed.

"There's a barf bag there if you need it."

"Fine," Leaphorn said.

"He's taking the pictures now," the pilot said. "Photographing one of the pages."

"Okay," Leaphorn said.

"It'll just be a minute."

Leaphorn, busy now with the bag, didn't respond. But by the time the rhetorical minute had dragged itself past and Rosebrough was climbing back into the copter, he was feeling a little better.

"I took a bunch of different exposures so we'll have some good ones," he said, settling himself in his seat and fastening his safety belt. "And I shot the five or six pages before and after. That what you wanted?"

"Fine," Leaphorn said, his mind working again, buzzing with the questions that had brought them up here. "Did you find Breedlove's name?

And who else—" He stopped. He was breaking his own rule. Much better to let Rosebrough tell what he had found without intervention.

"He signed it," Rosebrough said, "and wrote 'vita brevis.'"

He didn't explain to Leaphorn that the inscription was Latin and provide the translation—which was one of the reasons Leaphorn liked the man. Why would Breedlove have bothered to leave that epigram? "Life is short." Was it to explain why he'd taken the dangerous way down in case he didn't make it? He'd worry about that later.

"Funny thing," Rosebrough said. "No one else signed it on that date. I told you I didn't think he could possibly climb it alone. But it looks like maybe I was wrong."

"Maybe the people with him had climbed it before," Leaphorn said.

"That wouldn't matter. You'd still want to have it on the record that you'd done it again. It's a hell of a hard climb."

"Anything else?"

"He said he made it up at eleven twenty-seven A.M. and under that he wrote, 'Four hours, twenty-nine minutes up. Now, I'm going down the fast way.'"

"Looks like he tried," the pilot said. "But it took him about eleven years to make it all the way to the bottom."

"Could he have climbed it that fast alone?" Leaphorn asked. "Is that time reasonable?"

Rosebrough nodded. "These days the route is so well mapped, a good, experienced crew figures about four hours up and three hours down."

"How about the fast way down?" Leaphorn asked. To him it sounded a little like a suicide note. "What do you think he meant by that?"

Rosebrough shook his head. "It took teams of good climbers years to find the way you can get from the bottom to the top. Even that's no cinch. It involves doing a lot of exposed climbing, with a rope to save you if you slip. Then you have to climb down a declivity to reach the face where you can go up again. That's the way everybody who's ever got to the top of Ship Rock got there. And as far as I know, that's the way everybody always got down."

"So there isn't any 'fast way down'?"

Rosebrough gave that some thought. "There has been some speculation of a shortcut. But it would involve a lot of rappelling, and I never heard of anyone actually trying it. I think it's way too dangerous."

They were moving away from Ship Rock now, making the long slide down toward the Farmington Airport. Leaphorn was feeling better. He was thinking that whatever Breedlove had meant by the fast way down, he had certainly done something dangerous.

"I'm thinking about that rappel route," Rosebrough said. "If he tried that by himself, that would help explain where they found the skeleton." He was looking at Leaphorn quizzically. "You're awfully quiet, Joe. Are you okay? You're looking pale."

"I'm feeling pale," Leaphorn said, "but I'm quiet because I'm thinking about the other two people who made the climb with him that day. Didn't they get all the way up? Or what?"

"Who were they?" Rosebrough asked. "I know most of the serious rock climbers in this part of the world."

"We don't know," Leaphorn said. "All we have are the notes of an old mountain watcher. Sort of shorthand, too. He just jotted down nine slash eighteen slash eighty-five and said three men had parked at the jump-off site and were climbing the—"

"Wait a minute," Rosebrough said. "You said nine eighteen eighty-five? That's not the date Breedlove wrote. He put down nine thirty eighty-five."

Leaphorn digested that. No thought of nausea now. "You're sure?" he asked. "Breedlove dated his climb September thirty. Not September eighteen."

"I'm dead certain," Rosebrough said. "That's what the photo is going to show. Was I confused or something?"

"No," Leaphorn said. "I was the one who was confused."

"You sure you feel all right?"

"I feel fine," Leaphorn said. Actually he was feeling embarrassed. He had been conned, and it had taken him eleven years to get his first solid inkling of how they had fooled him.

23

CHEE HAD DECIDED the grease in the frying pan was hot enough and was pulling the easy-open lid off the can of Vienna sausages when the headlight beam flashed across his window. He flicked off his house trailer's overhead light—something he wouldn't have considered doing a few days ago. But his cracked ribs still ached, and the person who had caused that was still out there somewhere. Possibly in the car that was now rolling to a stop under the cottonwood outside.

Whoever had driven it got out and walked into the headlights where Chee could see him. It was Joe Leaphorn, the Legendary Lieutenant, again. Chee groaned, said, "Oh, shit!" and switched on the light.

Leaphorn entered hat in hand. "It's getting cold," he said. "The TV forecaster said there's a snow warning out for the Four Corners. Livestock warning. All that."

"It's just about time for that first bad one," Chee said. "Can I take your hat?"

Which got Leaphorn's mind off the weather. "No. No," he said, looking apologetic. He regretted the intrusion, the lateness of the hour, the interruption of Chee's supper. He would only take a moment. He wanted Chee to see what they'd found in the ammunition box on top of Ship Rock. He extracted a sheaf of photographs from the big folder he'd been carrying and handed them to Chee.

Chee spread them on the table.

"Note the date of the signature," Leaphorn said. "It's the week after Breedlove disappeared from Canyon de Chelly."

Chee considered that. "Wow," he said. And considered it again. He studied the photograph. "Is this it? No one else signed the book that day?"

"Only Breedlove," Leaphorn said. "And I'm told that it's traditional for everyone in the climbing party to sign if they get to the top."

"Well, now," Chee said. He tapped the inscription. "It looks like Latin. Do you know what it means?"

Leaphorn told him the translation. "But what did he mean by it? Your guess is as good as mine." He explained to Chee what Rosebrough had told him about the 'fast way down' remark—that if Hal had tried this dangerous rappelling route it might explain how his body came to be on the ledge where it was found.

They stood at the table, Chee staring at the photograph and Leaphorn watching Chee. The aroma of extremely hot grease forced itself into Leaphorn's consciousness, along with the haze of blue smoke that accompanied it. He cleared his throat.

"Jim," he said. "I think I interrupted your cooking."

"Oh," Chee said. He dropped the photograph, snatched the smoking pan off the propane burner, and deposited it outside on the doorstep. "I was going to scramble some eggs and mix in these sausages," he said. "If you haven't eaten I can dump in a few more."

"Fine," said Leaphorn, who had deposited his breakfast in the barf bag, had been suffering too much residual queasiness for lunch, and had been too busy since to stop for dinner. In his current condition, even the smell of burning grease aroused his hunger.

They replaced the photos with plates, retrieved the frying pan, replenished the incinerated grease with a chunk of margarine, put on the coffeepot, performed those other duties required to prepare dinner in a very restricted space, and dined. Leaphorn had always tried to avoid Vienna sausages even as emergency rations but now he found the mixture remarkably palatable. While he attacked his second helping, Chee picked up the crucial photograph and resumed his study.

"I hesitate to mention it," Chee said, "but what do you think of the date?"

"You mean being a date when the keen eye of Hosteen Sam saw no one climbing Ship Rock?"

"Exactly," Chee said.

"I've reached no precise conclusion," Leaphorn said. "What do you think?"

"About the same," Chee said. "And how about nobody at all signing the book twelve days earlier? What do you think about that? I'm thinking that the three people who old man Sam saw climbing up there must not have made it to the top. Either that, or they were too modest to take credit for it. Or, if his ledger hadn't told me how exactly precise Sam was, I'd think he got his dates wrong."

Leaphorn was studying him. "You think there's no chance of that, then?"

"I'd say none. Zero. You should see the way he kept that ledger. That's not the explanation. Forget it."

Leaphorn nodded. "Okay, I will."

The entry signed by Breedlove was near the center of the page. Above it the register had been signed by four men, none with names familiar to Chee, and dated April 4, 1983. Below it, a three-climber party—two with Japanese names—had registered their conquest of the Rock with Wings on April 28, 1988.

"Skip back to September eighteenth," Leaphorn said. "Let's say that Hal was one of the three Hosteen Sam saw climbing. It sounds like the car they climbed out of was that silly British recreation vehicle he drove. And then let's say they didn't make it to the top because Hal screwed up. So Hal broods about it. He gets the call at Canyon de Chelly from one of his climbing buddies. He decides to go back and try again."

"All right," Chee said. "Then we'll suppose the climbing buddy went with him, they tried the dangerous way down. This time the climbing buddy—and let's call him George Shaw—well, George screws up and drops Hal down the cliff. He feels guilty and he figures Hal's dead anyway, so slips away and tells no one."

"Yeah," Leaphorn said. "I thought about that. Trouble is, why hadn't the climbing buddy signed the register before they started down?"

Chee shook his head, dealt Leaphorn some more of the Vienna-and-eggs mixture, and put down the pan.

"Modesty, you think?" Leaphorn said. "He didn't want to take the credit?"

"The only reason I can think of involves first-degree murder," Chee said. "The premeditated kind."

"Right," Leaphorn said. "Now, how about a motive?"

"Easy," Chee said. "It would have something to do with the ranch, and with that moly mine deal."

Leaphorn nodded.

"Now Hal has inherited. It's his. So let's say George Shaw figures Hal's going to keep his threat and do his own deal on the mineral lease, cutting out Shaw and the rest of the family. So Shaw drops him."

"Maybe," Leaphorn said. "One problem with that, though."

"Or maybe Demott's the climbing buddy. He knows Hal's going for the open strip mine, so he knocks him off to save his ranch. But what's the problem with the first idea?"

"Elisa inherits from Hal. Shaw would have to deal with her."

"Maybe he thought he could?"

"He says he couldn't. He told me this afternoon that Elisa was just as fanatical about the ranch as her brother. Said she told him there wouldn't be any strip-mining on it as long as she was alive."

"You saw Shaw today?" Chee sounded as much shocked as surprised.

"Sure," Leaphorn said. "I showed him the photographs. After all, I spent his money getting them."

"What'd he think?"

"He acted disappointed. Probably was. He'd like to be able to prove that Hal was dead about a week or so before he signed that register."

Chee nodded.

"There's a problem with your second theory, too."

"What?"

"I was talking with Demott on the telephone September twenty-fourth. Twice, in fact."

"You remember that? After eleven years?"

"No. I keep a case diary. I looked it up."

"Mobile phone, maybe?"

"No. I called him at the ranch. Elisa didn't remember the license number on the Land-Rover. I called him about the middle of the morning and he gave me the number. Then I called him again in the afternoon to make sure Breedlove hadn't checked in. And to find out if he'd had any other calls. Anything worthwhile."

"Well, hell," Chee said. "Then I guess we're left with Breedlove climbing up there alone, or with Shaw, and then taking the suicidal shortcut down."

Leaphorn's expression suggested he didn't agree with that conclusion, but he didn't comment on it directly.

"It also means I'm going to have to run down all these people who climbed up there in the next ten years and find out if any of them got off with a long piece of that climbing rope."

"Not necessarily," Leaphorn said. "You're forgetting our Fallen Man business is still not a crime. It's a missing person case solved by the discovery of an accidental death."

"Yeah," Chee said, doubtful.

"It makes me glad I'm a civilian these days."

The wind gusted, rattling sand against the aluminum side of Chee's home, whistling around its aluminum cracks and corners.

"So does the weather," Leaphorn said. "Everybody in uniform is going to be working overtime and getting frostbite this week."

Chee pointed to Leaphorn's plate. "Want some more?"

"I'm full. Probably ate too much. And I took too much of your time." He got up, retrieved his hat.

"I'm going to leave you these pictures," he said. "Rosebrough has the negatives. He's a lawyer. An agent of the court. They'll stand up as evidence if it comes to that."

"You mean if anyone gets up there and steals the ledger?"

"It's a thought," Leaphorn said. "What are you going to do tomorrow?"

Chee had worked for Leaphorn long enough for this question to produce a familiar uneasy feeling. "Why?"

"If I go up to the ranch tomorrow and show Demott and Elisa these pictures and ask her what she thinks about them, and ask her who was trying to climb that mountain on that September eighteenth date, then I think I could be accused of tampering with a witness."

"Witness to what? Officially there's no crime yet," Chee reminded him.

"Don't you think there will be one? Presuming we're smart enough to get this sorted out."

"You mean not counting Maryboy and me? Yeah. I guess so. But you could probably get away with talking to Elisa until the official connection is made. Now you're just a representative of the family lawyer. Perfectly legit."

"But why would Demott or the widow want to talk to a representative of the family's lawyer?"

Chee nodded, conceding the point.

"And I think there's something else I should be doing."

Chee let his stare ask the question.

"Old Amos Nez trusts me," Leaphorn said, and paused to consider it. "Well, more or less. I want to show him this evidence that Hal climbed Ship Rock just one week after he left the canyon and tell him about Maryboy being murdered, and ask him if Hal said anything about trying to climb Ship Rock just before he came to the canyon. Things like that."

"That could wait," Chee said, thinking of his aching ribs and the long painful drive up into Colorado.

"Maybe it could wait," Leaphorn said. "But you know the other afternoon you decided Hosteen Maryboy couldn't wait and you rushed right out there to see if he could identify those climbers for you. And you were right. Turned out it couldn't wait."

"Ah," Chee said. "But I'm not clear on what makes Amos Nez so important. You think Breedlove might have told him something?"

"Let's try another theory," Leaphorn said. "Let's say that Hal Breedlove didn't live until his thirtieth birthday. Let's say those people Hosteen Sam saw climbing on September eighteenth got to the top, or at least two of them did. One of the two was Hal. The other one—or maybe two—push him off. Or, more likely he just falls. Now he's dead and he's dead two days too soon. He's still twenty-nine years old. So the climber's register is falsified to show he was alive after his birthday."

Chee held up his hand, grinning. "Huge hole in that one," he said. "Remember Hal was prowling around the canyon with his wife and Amos Nez until the twenty-third of . . ." Chee's voice trailed off into silence. And then he said, "Oh!" and stared at Leaphorn.

Leaphorn was making a wry face, shaking his head. "It sure took me long enough to see that possibility," he said. "I never could have if you hadn't got into old man Sam's register."

"My God," Chee said. "If that's the way it worked, I can see why they have to kill Nez. And if they're smart, the sooner the better."

"I'm going to ask you to call the Lazy B and find out if Demott and the widow are there and then arrange to drive up tomorrow and talk to them about what we found on top of the mountain."

"What if they're not at home?"

"Then I think we ought to be doing a little more to keep Amos Nez safe," Leaphorn said. And he opened the door and stepped out into the icy wind.

24

E LISA BREEDLOVE HAD answered the telephone. And, yes, Eldon was home and they'd be glad to talk to him. How about sometime tomorrow afternoon?

So Acting Lieutenant Chee showed up at his office in Shiprock early to get his desk cleared and make the needed arrangements. He arrived with tape plastered over the stitches around his left eye and a noticeable shiner visible behind them. He lowered himself carefully into the chair behind the desk to avoid jarring his ribs and gave Officers Teddy Begayaye, Deejay Hondo, Edison Bai, and Bernadette Manuelito a few moments to inspect the damage. In Begayaye and Bai it seemed to provoke a mixture of admiration and amusement, well suppressed. Hondo didn't seem interested and Officer Bernie Manuelito's face reflected a sort of shocked sympathy.

With that out of the way, he satisfied their curiosity with a personal briefing of what actually happened at the Maryboy place, supplementing the official one they would have already received. Then down to business.

He instructed Bai to try to find out where a .38-caliber pistol confiscated from a Shiprock High School boy had come from. He suggested to Officer Manuelito that she continue her efforts to locate a fellow named Adolph Deer, who had jumped bond after a robbery conviction but was reportedly "frequently being seen around the Two Gray Hills trading post." He told Hondo to finish the paperwork on a burglary case that was about to go to the grand jury. Then it was Teddy Begayaye's turn.

"I hate to tell you, Teddy, but you're going to have to be taxi driver to-day," Chee said. "I have to go up to the Lazy B ranch on this Maryboy shooting thing. I thought I could handle it myself, but"—he lifted his left arm, flinched, and grimaced—"the old ribs aren't quite as good as I thought they were."

"You shouldn't be riding around in a car," Officer Manuelito said. "You should be in bed, healing up. They shouldn't have let you out of the hospital."

"Hospitals are dangerous," Chee said. "People die in them."

Edison Bai grinned at that, but Officer Manuelito didn't think it was funny.

"Something goes wrong with broken ribs and you have a punctured lung," she said.

"They're just cracked," Chee said. "Just a bruise." With that subject closed, he kept Bai behind for a fill-in about the pistol-carrying student. Typ-ically, Bai provided far more details than Chee needed. The boy had been in-volved in a joyride car theft during the summer. He was born to the Streams Come Together people, his mother's clan, and for the Salt clan, for his pater-nal people, but his father was also part Hopi. He was believed to be involved in the smaller and rougher of Shiprock's juvenile gangs. He was meanness on the hoof. People weren't raising their kids the way they used to. Chee agreed, put on his hat and hurried stiffly out the door into the parking lot. It had been chilly and clouding up when he came to work. Now there was solid overcast and an icy northwest wind swept dust and leaves past his ankles.

The gale was blowing Begayaye back toward him.

"Jim," he said. "I forgot. The wife made a dental appointment for me today. How about me switching assignments with Bernie? That Deer kid isn't going anywhere."

"Well," Chee said. Across the parking lot he saw Bernie Manuelito standing on the sheltered side of his patrol car, watching them. "Is it okay with Manuelito?"

"Yes, sir," Begayaye said. "She don't mind."

"By the way," Chee said, "I forgot to thank you guys for sending me those flowers."

Begayaye looked puzzled. "Flowers? What flowers?"

Thus it was that Acting Lieutenant Jim Chee headed north toward the Colorado border leaning his good shoulder against the passenger-side door with Officer Bernadette Manuelito behind the wheel. Chee, being a detective, had figured out who had sent him the flowers. Begayaye hadn't done it, and Bai would never think of doing such a thing even if he was fond of Chee—which Chee was pretty sure he wasn't. That left Deejay Hondo and Bernie. Which clearly meant Bernie had sent them and made it look like everybody did it so he wouldn't think she was buttering him up. That probably meant she liked him. Thinking back, he could remember a couple of other signs that pointed to that conclusion.

All things considered, he liked her, too. She was really smart, she was sweet to everybody around the office, and she was always using her days off to take care of an apparently inexhaustible supply of ailing and indigent kinfolks, which gave her a high score on the Navajo value scale. When the time came he would have to give her a good efficiency rating. He gave her a sidewise glance, saw her staring unblinkingly through the windshield at the worn pavement of infamous U.S. Highway 666. A very slight smile curved the corner of her lip, making her look happy, as she usually was. No doubt about it, she really was an awfully pretty young woman.

That wasn't the way he should be thinking about Officer Bernadette Manuelito. Not only was he her superior officer and supervisor, he was more or less engaged to marry another woman. And he was thinking that way, most likely, because he was having a very confusing problem with that other woman. He was beginning to suspect that she didn't really want to marry him. Or, at least, he wasn't sure she was willing to marry Jim Chee as he currently existed—a just-plain cop and a genuine sheep-camp Navajo as opposed to the more romantic and politically correct Indigenous Person. Making it worse, he didn't know what the hell to do about it. Or whether he should do anything. It was a sad, sad situation.

Chee sighed, decided the ribs would feel better if he shifted his weight. He did it, sucked in his breath, and grimaced.

"You all right?" Bernie asked, giving him a worried look.

"Okay," Chee said.

"I have some aspirin in my stuff."

"No problem," Chee said.

Bernie drove in silence for a while.

"Lieutenant," she said. "Do you remember telling us how Lieutenant Leaphorn was always trying to get you to look for patterns? I mean when you had something going on that was hard to figure out."

"Yeah," Chee said.

"And that's what you wanted me to try to find in this cattle-stealing business?"

Chee grunted, trying to remember if he had made any such suggestion.

"Well, I got Lucy Sam to let me take that ledger to that Quik-Copy place in Farmington and I got copies made of the pages back for several years so I'd have them. And then I went through our complaint records and copied down the dates of all the cattle-theft reports for the same years."

"Good Lord," Chee said, visualizing the time that would take. "Who was doing your regular work for you?"

"Just the multiple-head thefts," Officer Manuelito said, defensively. "The ones which look sort of professional. And I did it in the evenings."

"Oh," Chee said, embarrassed.

"Anyway, I started comparing the dates. You know, when Mr. Sam would write down something about a certain sort of truck, and when there would be a cattle theft reported in our part of the reservation."

Officer Manuelito had been reciting this very carefully, as if she had rehearsed it. Now she stopped.

"What'd you notice?"

She produced a deprecatory laugh. "I think this is probably really silly," she said.

"I doubt it," Chee said, thinking he would like to get his mind off of Janet Pete and quit trying to find a way to turn back the clock and make things the way they used to be. "Why don't you just go ahead and tell me about it."

"There was a correlation between multiple-theft reports and Mr. Sam seeing a big banged-up dirty white camper truck in the neighborhood," Manuelito said, looking fixedly at the highway center stripe. "Not all the time," she added. "But often enough so it made you begin to wonder about it."

Chee digested this. "The trailer like Mr. Finch's rig?" he said. "The New Mexico brand inspector's camper?"

"Yes, sir." She laughed again. "I said it was probably silly."

"Well, I guess our theft reports would be passed along to him. Then he'd come out here to see about it."

Officer Manuelito kept her eyes on the road, her lips opened as if she were about to say something. But she didn't. She simply looked disappointed.

"Wait a minute," Chee said, as understanding belatedly dawned. "Was Hosteen Sam seeing Finch's trailer after the thefts were reported? Or—"

"Usually before," Bernie said. "Sometimes both, but usually before. But you know how that is. Sometimes the cattle are gone for a while before the owner notices they're missing."

Bernie drove, looking very tense. Chee digested what she'd told him. Suddenly he slammed his right hand against his leg. "How about that?" he said. "That wily old devil."

Officer Manuelito relaxed, grinned. "You think so? You think that might be right?"

"I'd bet on it," Chee said. "He'd have everything going for him. All the proper legal forms for moving cattle. All the brand information. All the reasons for being where the cattle are. And all cops would know him as one of them. Perfect."

Bernie was grinning even wider, delighted. "Yes," she said. "That's sort of what I was thinking."

"Now we need to find out how he markets them. And how he gets them from the pasture to the feedlots."

"I think it's in the trailer," Bernie said.

"The trailer? You mean he hauls cattle in his house trailer?"

Chee's incredulous tone caused Bernie to flush slightly. "I think so," she said. "I couldn't prove it."

A few moments ago Acting Lieutenant Chee might have scoffed at this remarkable idea. But not now. "Tell me," he said. "How does he get them through the door?"

"It took me a long time to get the idea," she said. "I think it was noticing that now and then I'd see that trailer parked at the Anasazi Inn at Farmington, and I'd think it was funny that you'd drive that big clumsy camper trailer around if you didn't want to sleep in it. I thought, you know, well, maybe he just wants a hot bath, or something like that. But it stuck in my mind."

She laughed. "I'm always trying to understand white people."

"Yeah," Chee said. "Me too."

"So the other day when he parked the trailer in the lot at the station, when I walked past it I noticed how it smelled."

"A little whiff of cow manure," said Chee, who had walked behind it, too. "I just thought, you know, he's around feedlots all the time. Stepping in the stuff. Probably gets used to it. Doesn't clean his boots."

"That occurred to me, too," Bernie said. "But it was pretty strong. Maybe women are more sensitive to smells."

Or smarter, Chee thought. "Did you look inside?"

"He's got all the windows all stuck full of those tourist stickers, and they're high windows. I tried to take a peek but I didn't want him to see me snooping."

"I guess we could get a search warrant," Chee said. "What would you put on the petition? Something about the brand inspector's camper smelling like cow manure, to which the judge would say 'Naturally,' and about Finch not liking to sleep in it, which would cause the judge to say 'Not if it smells like cow manure.'"

"I thought about the search warrant," Bernie said. "Of course there's no law against hauling cows in your camper if you want to."

"True," Chee said. "Might be able to get him committed for being crazy."

"Anyway," Bernie said. "I called his office and I—"

"You *what!*"

"I just wanted to know where he was. If he answered I was going to hang up. If he didn't, I'd ask 'em where I could find him. He wasn't there, and the secretary said he'd called in from the Davis and Sons cattle-auction place over by Iyanbito. So I drove over there and his camper truck was parked by the barn and he was out in back with some people loading up steers. So I got a closer look."

"You didn't break in?" Chee asked, thinking she'd probably say she had. Nothing this woman did was going to surprise him anymore.

She glanced at him, looking hurt, and ignored the question.

"Maybe you noticed that camper has just a straight-up flat back. There's no door in it and no window. Well, all around that back panel it's sealed up with silvery duct tape. Like you'd maybe put on to keep the dust out. But when you get down and look under you can see a row of big, heavy-duty hinges."

Chee was into this now. "So you back your trailer up to the fence, pull off the duct tape, lower the back down, and that makes a loading ramp out of it. He probably has it rigged up with stalls to keep 'em from moving around."

"I guessed it would handle about six," Bernie said. "Two rows of cows, three abreast."

"Bernie," Chee said. "If my ribs weren't so sore, and it wasn't going to get me charged with sexual harassment and cause us to run off the road, I would reach over there and give you a huge congratulatory hug."

Bernie looked both pleased and embarrassed.

"You put a lot of work into this," he said. "And a lot of thought, too. Way beyond the call of duty."

"Well, I'm trying to learn to be a detective. And it got sort of personal, too," she said. "I don't like that man."

"I don't much either," Chee said. "He's arrogant."

"He sort of made a move on me," she said. "Maybe not. Not exactly."

"Like what?"

"Well, he gives you that 'doll' and 'cute' stuff, you know. Then he said how would I like to get assigned to work with him. But of course he said 'under' him. He said I could be Tonto to his Lone Ranger."

"Tonto?" Chee said. "Well, now. Here's what we do. We keep an eye on him. And when he's on the road with a load, we nail him. And when we do, you're the one who gets to put the handcuffs on him."

25

WHEN OFFICER BERNADETTE Manuelito parked Chee's patrol car at the Lazy B ranch Elisa Breedlove was standing in the doorway awaiting them—hugging herself against the cold wind. Or was it, Chee thought, against the news he might be bringing?

"Four Corners weather," she said. "Yesterday it was sunny, mild autumn. Today it's winter." She ushered them into the living room, exchanged introductions gracefully with Bernie, expressed the proper dismay at Chee's condition, wished him a quick recovery, and invited them to be seated.

"I saw the story about you being shot on television," she said. "Bad as you look, they made it sound even worse."

"Just some cracked ribs," Chee said.

"And old Mr. Maryboy being killed. I only met him once, but he was very nice to us. He invited us in and offered to make coffee."

"When was that?"

"Way back in the dark ages," she said. "When Hal and George would come out for the summer and Eldon and I would go climbing with them."

"Is your brother here now?" Chee asked. "I was hoping to talk to you both."

"He was here earlier, but one of the mares got herself tangled up in a fence. He went out to see about her. There's supposed to be a snowstorm moving in and he wanted to get her into the barn."

"Do you expect him back soon?"

"She's up in the north pasture," Elisa said. "But he shouldn't be long unless she's cut so badly he had to go into Mancos and get the vet. Would you two care for something to drink? It's a long drive up here from Shiprock."

She served them both coffee but poured none for herself. Chee sipped and watched her over the rim, twisting her hands. If she had been one of the three climbers that day, if she had reached the top, she should know what was coming now. He took out the folder of photographs and handed Elisa the one signed with her husband's name.

"Thanks," she said, and looked at it. Officer Manuelito was watching her, sitting primly on the edge of her chair, cup in saucer, uncharacteristically quiet. It occurred to Chee that she looked like a pretty girl pretending to be a cop.

Elisa was frowning at the photograph. "It's a picture of the page from the climbers' ledger," she said slowly. "But where—"

She dropped the picture on the coffee table, said, "Oh, God," in a strangled voice, and covered her face with her hands.

Officer Manuelito leaned forward, lips apart. Chee shook his head, signaled silence.

Elisa picked up the picture again, stared at it, dropped it to the floor and sat rigid, her face white.

"Mrs. Breedlove," Chee said. "Are you all right?"

She shook her head. Shuddered. Composed herself, looked at Chee.

"This photograph. That's all there was on the page?"

"Just what you saw."

She bent, picked up the print, looked at it again. "And the date. The date. That's what was written?"

"Just as you see it," Chee said.

"But of course it was." She produced a laugh on the razor edge of hysteria. "A silly question. But it's wrong, you know. It should have been— but why—" She put her hand over her mouth, dropped her head.

The noise the wind was making—rattles, whistles, and howls—filtered through windows and walls and filled the dark room with the sounds of winter.

"I know the date's wrong," Chee said. "The entry is dated September thirty. That's a week after your husband disappeared from Canyon de Chelly. What should—" He stopped. Elisa wasn't listening to him. She was lost in her own memory. And that, combined with what the picture had told her, was drawing her to some ghastly conclusion.

"The handwriting," she said. "Have you—" But she cut that off, too, pressed her lips together as if to keep them from completing the question.

But not soon enough, of course. So she hadn't known what had happened on the summit of Ship Rock. Not until moments ago when the forgery of her husband's signature told her. Told her exactly what? That her husband had died before he'd had a chance to sign. That her husband's death, therefore, must have been preplanned as well as postdated. The pattern Leaphorn had taught him to look for took its almost final dismal shape. And filled Jim Chee with pity.

Officer Manuelito was on her feet.

"Mrs. Breedlove, you need to lie down," she said. "You're sick. Let me get you something. Some water."

Elisa sagged forward, leaned her forehead against the table. Officer Manuelito hurried into the kitchen.

"We haven't checked the handwriting yet," Chee said. "Can you tell us what that will show?"

Elisa was sobbing now. Bernie emerged from the kitchen, glass of water in one hand, cloth in the other. She gave Chee a "How could you do this?" look and sat next to Elisa, patting her shoulder.

"Take a sip of water," Bernie said. "And you should lie down until you feel better. We can finish this later."

Ramona appeared in the doorway, wrapped in a padded coat, her face red with cold. She watched them anxiously. "What are you doing to her?" she said. "Go away now and let her rest."

"Oh, God," Elisa said, her voice muffled by the table. "Why did he think he had to do it?"

"Where can I find Eldon?" Chee asked.

Elisa shook her head.

"Does he have a rifle?" But of course he would have a rifle. Every male over about twelve in the Rocky Mountain West had a rifle. "Where does he keep it?"

Elisa didn't respond. Chee motioned to Bernie. She left in search of it.

Elisa raised her head, wiped her eyes, looked at Chee. "It was an accident, you know. Hal was always reckless. He wanted to rappel down the
cliff. I thought I had talked him out of it. But I guess I hadn't."

"Did you see it happen?"

"I didn't get all the way to the top. I was below. Waiting for them to
come down."

Chee hesitated. The next question would be crucial, but should he
ask it now, with this woman overcome by shock and grief? Any lawyer
would tell her not to talk about any of this. But she wouldn't be the one
on trial.

Bernie reappeared at the doorway, Ramona behind her. "There's a
triple gun rack in the office," she said. "A twelve-gauge pump shotgun in
the bottom rack and the top two empty."

"Okay," Chee said.

"And in the wastebasket beside the desk, there's a thirty-ought-six
ammunition box. The top's torn off and it's empty."

Chee nodded and came to his decision.

"Mrs. Breedlove. No one climbed the mountain on the date by your
husband's name. But on September eighteenth three people were seen
climbing it. Hal was one of them. You were one. Who was the third?"

"I don't want to talk to you anymore," Elisa said. "I want you to go."

"You don't have to tell us anything," Chee said. "You have the right to
remain silent, and to call your lawyer if you think you need one. I don't
think you've done anything you could be charged with, but you never really know what a prosecuting attorney will decide."

Officer Manuelito cleared her throat. "And anything you say can be
used against you. Remember that."

"I don't want to say any more."

"That's okay," Chee said. "But I should tell you this. Eldon isn't here
and neither is his rifle and it looks like he just reloaded it. If we have this
figured out right, Eldon is going to know there is just one man left alive
who could ruin this for him."

Chee paused, waiting for a response. It didn't come. Elisa sat as if
frozen, staring at him.

"It's a man named Amos Nez. Remember him? He was your guide in
Canyon de Chelly. Right after Hal's skeleton was found on Ship Rock last

Halloween, Mr. Nez was riding his horse up the canyon. Someone up on the rim shot him. He wasn't killed, just badly hurt."

Elisa sagged a little with that, looked down at her hands, and said, "I didn't know that."

"With a thirty-ought-six rifle," Chee added.

"What day was it?"

Chee told her.

She thought a moment. Remembering. Slumped a little more.

"If anyone kills Mr. Nez the charge will be the premeditated murder of a witness. That carries the death penalty."

"He's my brother," Elisa said. "Hal's death was an accident. Sometimes he acted almost like he wanted to die. No thrills, he said, if you didn't take a chance. He fell. When Eldon climbed down to where I was waiting, he looked like he was almost dead himself. He was devastated. He was so shaken he could hardly tell me about it." She stopped, looking at Chee, at Bernie, back at Chee.

Waiting for our reaction, Chee thought. *Waiting for us to give her absolution? No, waiting for us to say we believe what she is telling us, so that she can believe it again herself.*

"I think you were driving that Land-Rover," Chee said. "When police found it abandoned up an arroyo north of Many Farms they said there was a telephone in it."

"But what good would it have done to call for help?" Elisa asked, her voice rising. "Hal was dead. He was all broken to pieces on that little ledge. Nobody could bring him back to life again. He was dead!"

"Was he?"

"Yes," she shouted. "Yes. Yes. Yes."

And now Chee understood why Elisa had been so shocked when she learned the skeleton was intact—with not a bone broken. She didn't want to believe it. Refused to believe it still. That made the next question harder to ask. What had Eldon told her of the scene at the top? Had he explained why Hal had started his descent before he signed the book? Why he falsified the register? Had he—

Ramona rushed into the room, sat beside Elisa, hugged the woman to her. She glared at Chee. "I said go away now," she said. "Get out. No more. No more. She has suffered too much."

"It's all right," Elisa said. "Ramona, when you came in did you see the Land-Rover in the garage?"

"No," Ramona said. "Just Eldon's pickup truck."

Elisa looked at Chee, sighed, and said, "Then I guess he didn't go up to see about the mare. He would have taken his truck."

Chee picked up his hat and the photographs. He thanked Mrs. Breedlove for the cooperation, apologized for bringing her bad news, and hurried out, with Bernie trotting along behind him. The wind was bitter now, and carrying those dry-as-dust first snowflakes that were the fore-runners of a storm.

"I want to get Leaphorn on the radio," he said, as Bernie started the engine, "and maybe we'll have to make a fast trip to Canyon de Chelly."

Bernie was looking back at the house. "Do you think she will be all right?"

"I think so," Chee said. "Ramona will take good care of her."

"Ramona's pretty shaken up, too," Bernie said. "She was crying when she helped me look for the rifle. She said it was always the wrong men with Elisa—always having to take care of them. That Hal was a spoiled baby and Eldon was a bully. She said if it wasn't for Eldon she'd be married to a good man who wanted to take care of her."

"She say who?"

"I think it was Tommy Castro. Or maybe Kaster. Something like that. She was crying." Bernie was staring back at the house, looking worried.

"Bernie," Chee said. "It's starting to snow. It's probably going to be a bad one. Start the car. Go. Go. Go."

"You're worried about Amos Nez," Bernie said, starting the engine. "We can just call the station at Chinle and have them stop any Land-Rover driving in. Bet Mr. Leaphorn already did that."

"He said he would," Chee said. "But I want to get a message to him about Demott taking off with his thirty-ought-six loaded. Maybe Eldon won't be driving in. If you can climb seventeen hundred feet up Ship Rock, maybe you can climb down a six-hundred-foot cliff."

26

THEY DROVE INTO the full brunt of the storm halfway between Man-cos and Cortez, the wind buffeting the car and driving a blinding sheet of tiny dry snowflakes horizontally past their windshield.

"At least it's sweeping the pavement clear," Bernie said, sounding cheerful.

Chee glanced at her. She seemed to be enjoying the adventure. He wasn't. His ribs hurt, so did the abrasions around his eye, and he was not in the mood for cheer.

"That won't last long," he said.

It didn't. In Cortez, snow was driving over the curbs and the pavement was beginning to pack, and the broadcasts on the emergency channel didn't sound promising. A last gasp of the Pacific hurricane system was pushing across Baja California into Arizona. There it met the first blast of Arctic air, pressing down the east slope of the Rockies from Canada. In-terstate 40 at Flagstaff, where the two fronts had collided, was already closed by snow. So were highways through the Wasatch Range in Utah. Autumn was emphatically over on the Colorado Plateau.

They turned onto U.S. 666 to make the forty-mile run almost due south to Shiprock. With the icy wind pursuing them, the highway emp-tied of traffic by storm warnings, and speed limits ignored, Bernie outran the Canadian contribution to the storm. The sky lightened now. Far ahead, they could see where the Pacific half of the blizzard had reached the Chuska range. Its cold, wet air met the dry, warmer air on the New Mexico side at the ridgeline. The collision produced a towering wall of white fog, which poured down the slopes like a silent slow-motion Niagara.

"Wow," Bernie said. "I never saw anything quite like that before."

"The heavy cold air forces itself under the warmer stuff," said Chee, unable to avoid a little showing off. "I'll bet it's twenty degrees colder at Lukachukai than it is at Red Rock—and they're less than twenty miles apart."

They crossed the western corner of the Ute reservation, then roared into New Mexico and across the mesa high above Malpais Arroyo.

"Wow," Bernie said again. "Look at that."

Instead Chee glanced at the speedometer and flinched.

"You drive," he said. "I'll check the scenery for both of us." It was worth checking. They looked down into the vast San Juan River basin— dark with storm to the right, dappled with sunlight to the left. Ship Rock stood just at the edge of the shadow line, a grotesque sunlit thumb thrust into the sky, but through some quirk of wind and air pressure, the long bulge of the Hogback formation was already mostly dark with cloud shadow.

"I think we're going to get home before the snow," Bernie said.

They almost did. It caught them when Bernie pulled into the parking lot at the station—but the flakes blowing against Chee as he hurried into the building were still small and dry. The Canadian cold front was still dominating the Pacific storm.

"You look terrible," Jenifer said. "How do you feel?"

"I'd say well below average," Chee said. "Did Leaphorn call?"

"Indirectly," Jenifer said, and handed Chee three message slips and an envelope.

It was on top—a call from Sergeant Deke at the Chinle station confirming that Leaphorn had received Chee's message about Demott leaving his ranch with his rifle. Leaphorn had gone up the canyon to the Nez place and would either bring Nez out with him or stay, depending on the weather, which was terrible.

Chee glanced at the other messages. Routine business. The envelope bore the word "Jim" in Janet's hand. He tapped it against the back of his hand. Put it down. Called Deke.

"I've seen worse," Deke said. "But it's a bad one for this time of year. Still above zero but it won't be for long. Blowing snow. We have Navajo 12 closed at Upper Wheatfields, and 191 between here and Ganado, and 59 north of Red Rock, and—well, hell of a night to be driving. How about there?"

"I think we're just getting the edge of it," Chee said. "Did Leaphorn get my message?"

"Yep. He said not to worry."

"What do you think? Demott's a rock climber. Is Nez going to be safe enough?"

"Except for maybe frostbite," Deke said. "Nobody's going to be climbing those cliffs tonight."

And so Chee opened the envelope and extracted the note.

"Jim. Sorry I missed you. Going to get a bite to eat and will come by your place—Janet."

Her car wasn't there when he drove up, which was just as well, he thought. It would give him a little time to get the place a little warmer. He fired up the propane heater, put on the coffee, and gave the place a critical inspection. He rarely did. His trailer was simply where he lived. Sometimes it was hot, sometimes it was cold. But otherwise it was not something he gave any thought to. It looked cramped, crowded, slightly dirty, and altogether dismal. Ah, well, nothing to do about it now. He checked the refrigerator for something to offer her. Nothing much there in the snack line, but he extracted a slab of cheese and pulled a box of crackers and a bowl with a few Oreos in it off the shelf over the stove. Then he sat on the edge of the bunk, slumped, listening to the icy wind buffeting the trailer, too tired to think about what might be about to happen.

Chee must have dozed. He didn't hear the car coming down the slope, or see the lights. A tapping at the door awakened him, and he found her standing on the step looking up at him.

"It's freezing," she said as he ushered her in.

"Hot coffee," he said. Poured a cup, handed it to her, and offered her the folding chair beside the fold-out table. But she stood a moment, hugging herself and shivering, looking undecided.

"Janet," he said. "Sit down. Relax."

"I just need to tell you something," she said. "I can't stay. I need to get back to Gallup before the weather gets worse." But she sat.

"Drink your coffee," he said. "Warm up."

She was looking at him over the cup. "You look awful," she said. "They told me you'd gone up to Mancos. To see the Breedlove widow. You shouldn't be back at work yet. You should be in bed."

"I'm all right," he said. And waited. Would she ask him why he'd gone to Mancos? What he'd learned?

"Why couldn't somebody else do it?" she said. "Somebody without broken ribs."

"Just cracked," Chee said.

She put down her cup. He reached for it. She intercepted his hand, held it.

"Jim," she said. "I'm going away for a while. I'm taking my accrued leave time, and my vacation, and I'm going home."

"Home?" Chee said. "For a while. How long is that?"

"I don't know," she said. "I want to get my head together. Look forward and backwards." She tried to smile but it didn't come off well. She shrugged. "And just think."

It occurred to Chee that he hadn't poured himself any coffee. Oddly, he didn't want any. It occurred to him that she wasn't burning her bridges.

"Think?" he said. "About us?"

"Of course." This time the smile worked a little better.

But her hand was cold. He squeezed it. "I thought we were through that phase."

"No, you didn't," she said. "You never really stopped thinking about whether we'd be compatible. Whether we really fit."

"Don't we?"

"We did in this fantasy I had," she said, and waved her hands, mocking herself. "Big, good-looking guy. Sweet and smart and as far as I could tell you really cared about me. Fun on the Big Rez for a while, then a big job for you in someplace interesting. Washington. San Francisco. New York. Boston. And the big job for me in Justice, or maybe a law firm. You and I together. Everything perfect."

Chee said nothing to that.

"Everything perfect," she repeated. "The best of both worlds." She looked at him, trying to hold the grin and not quite making it.

"With twin Porsches in the triple garage," Chee said. "But when you got to know me, I didn't fit the fantasy."

"Almost," she said. "Maybe you do, really." Suddenly Janet's eyes went damp. She looked away. "Or maybe I change the fantasy."

He extracted his handkerchief, frowned at it, reached into the storage drawer behind him, extracted paper napkins, and handed them to Janet. She said, "Sorry," and wiped her eyes.

He wanted to hold her, very close. But he said, "A cold wind does that."

"So I thought maybe as time goes by everything changes a little. I change and so do you."

He could think of nothing honest to say to that.

"But after the other evening in Gallup, when you were so angry with me, I began to understand," she said.

"Remember once a long time ago you asked me about a schoolteacher I used to date? Somebody told you about her. From Wisconsin. Just out of college. Blonde, blue eyes, taught second grade at Crownpoint when I was a brand-new cop and stationed there. Well, it wasn't that there was anything much wrong with me, but for her kids she wanted the good old American dream. She saw no hope for that in Navajo country. So she went away."

"Why are you telling me this?" Janet said. "She wasn't a Navajo."

"But I am," he said. "So I thought, what's the difference? I'm darker. Rarely sunburn. Small hips. Wide shoulders. That's racial, right? Does that matter? I think not much. So what makes me a Navajo?"

"You're going to say culture," Janet said. "I studied social anthropology, too."

"I grew up knowing it's wrong to have more than you need. It means you're not taking care of your people. Win three races in a row, you better slow down a little. Let somebody else win. Or somebody gets drunk and runs into your car and tears you all up, you don't sue him, you want to have a sing for him to cure him of alcoholism."

"That doesn't get you admitted into law school," Janet said. "Or pull you out of poverty."

"Depends on how you define poverty."

"It's defined in the law books," Janet said. "A family of x members with an annual income of under y."

"I met a middle-aged man at a Yeibichai sing a few years ago. He ran an accounting firm in Flagstaff and came out to Burnt Water because his mother had a stroke and they were doing the cure for her. I said something about it looking like he was doing very well. And he said, 'No, I will be a poor man all my life.' And I asked him what he meant, and he said, 'Nobody ever taught me any songs.'"

"Ah, Jim," she said. She rose, took the two steps required to reach the bunk where he was sitting, put her arms carefully around him and kissed him. Then she pressed the undamaged side of his face against her breast.

"I know having a Navajo dad didn't make me a Navajo," she said. "My culture is Stanford sorority girl, Maryland cocktail circuit, Mozart, and tickets to the Met. So maybe I have to learn not to think that being ragged, and not having indoor plumbing, and walking miles to see the dentist means poverty. I'm working on it."

Chee, engulfed in Janet's sweater, her perfume, her softness, said something like "Ummmm."

"But I'm not there yet," she added, and released him.

"I guess I should work on it from the other end, too," he said. "I could get used to being a lieutenant, trying to work my way up. Trying to put some value on things like—" He let that trail off.

"One thing I want you to know," she said. "I didn't use you."

"You mean—"

"I mean deliberately getting information out of you so I could tell John."

"I guess I always knew that," he said. "I was just being jealous. I had the wrong idea about that."

"I did tell him you'd found Breedlove's body. He invited Claire and me to the concert. Claire and I go all the way back to high school. And we were remembering old times and, you know, it just came out. It was just something interesting to tell him."

"Sure," Chee said. "I understand."

"I have to go now," she said. "Before you guys close the highway. But I wanted you to know that. Breedlove had been his project when the widow filed to get the death certified. It looked so peculiar. And finally, now, I guess it's all over."

Her tone made that a question.

She was zipping up her jacket, glancing at him.

"Lieutenant Leaphorn gave Mr. Shaw that photograph of the climber's ledger," she said.

"Yeah," Chee said. The wind buffeted the trailer, made its stormy sounds, moved a cold draft against his neck.

"She must have thought that terribly odd—for him to just leave her at the canyon, and then abandon their car, and go back to Ship Rock to climb it like that."

Chee nodded.

"Surely she must have had some sort of theory. I know I would have had if you'd done something crazy like that to me."

"She cried a lot," Chee said. "She could hardly believe it."

And in a minute Janet was gone. The goodbye kiss, the promises to write, the invitation to come and join her. Then holding the car door open for her, commenting on how it always got colder when the snowing stopped, and watching the headlights vanish at the top of the slope.

He sat on the bunk again then, felt the bandages around his eye, and decided the soreness there was abating. He probed the padding over his ribs, flinched, and decided the healing there was slower. He noticed the coffeepot was still on, got up, and unplugged it. He switched on the radio, thinking he would get some weather news. Then switched it off again and sat on the bed.

The telephone rang. Chee stared at it. It rang again. And again. He picked it up.

"Guess what?" It was Officer Bernadette Manuelito.

"What?"

"Begayaye just told me," she said. "He detoured past Ship Rock today. The cattle were crowded around our loose-fence-post place, eating some fresh hay."

"Well," Chee said, and gave himself a moment to make the mental transition from Janet Pete to the Lone Ranger competition. "I'd say this would be a perfect time for Mr. Finch to supplement his income. The cops all away working weather problems, and everybody staying home by the fire."

"That's what I thought," she said.

"I'll meet you there a little before daylight. When's sunup these days?"

"About seven."

"I'll meet you at the office at five. Okay?"

"Hey," Bernie said. "I like it."

27

I'M GOING TO show you some pictures," Leaphorn said to Amos Nez, and he dug a folder out of his briefcase.

"Pretty women in bikinis," old man Nez said, grinning at his mother-in-law. Mrs. Benally, who didn't much understand English, grinned back.

"Pictures which I should have showed you eleven years ago," Leaphorn said, and put a photograph on the arm of the old sofa where Nez was sitting. The old iron stove that served for heating and cooking in the Nez hogan was glowing red from the wood fire within it. Cold was in the canyon outside; Leaphorn was sweating. But Nez had kept his sweater on and Mrs. Benally had her shawl draped over her shoulders.

Nez adjusted his glasses on his nose. Looked. He smiled at Leaphorn, handed him back the print. "That's her," he said. "Mrs. Breedlove."

"Who's the man with her?"

Nez retrieved the print, studied it again. He shook his head. "I don't know him."

"That's Harold Breedlove," Leaphorn said. "You're looking at a photograph the Breedloves had taken at a studio in Farmington on their wedding anniversary—the summer before they came out here and got you to guide them."

Nez stared at the photograph. "Well, now," he said. "It sure is funny what white people will do. Who is that man she was here with?"

"You tell me," Leaphorn said. He handed Nez two more photographs. One was a photocopy he'd obtained, by imposing on an old friend in the Indian Service's Washington office, of George Shaw's portrait from the Georgetown University School of Law alumni magazine. The others had been obtained from the photo files of the *Mancos Weekly Citizen*—mug shots of young Eldon Demott and Tommy Castro wearing Marine Corps hats.

"I don't know this fella here," Nez said, and handed Leaphorn the Shaw photo.

"I didn't think you would," Leaphorn said. "I was just making sure."

Nez studied the other photo. "Well, now," he said. "Here's my friend Hal Breedlove."

He handed Leaphorn the picture of Eldon Demott.

"Not your friend now," Leaphorn said, and tapped Nez's leg cast. "He's the guy that tried to kill you."

Nez retrieved the photo, looked at it, and shook his head. "Why did he do—" he began, and stopped, thinking about it.

Leaphorn explained about ownership of the ranch depending on the date of Breedlove's death, and now depending upon continuing the deception. "There were just two people who knew something that could screw this up. One of them knew the date Hal Breedlove and Demott climbed Ship Rock—a man named Maryboy who gave them permission to climb. Demott shot him the other day. That leaves you."

"Well, now," Nez said, and made a wry face.

"A policeman who is looking into all this sent me a message that Demott loaded up his rifle this morning and headed out. I guess he'd be coming out here to see if he could get another shot at you."

"Why don't they arrest him?"

"They have to catch him first," Leaphorn said, not wanting to get into the complicated explanation of legalities—and the total lack of any concrete evidence that there was any reason to arrest Demott. "My idea was to take you and Mrs. Benally into Chinle and check you into the motel there. The police can keep an eye on you until they get Demott locked up."

Nez gave himself some time to think this over. "No," he said. "I'll just stay here." He pointed to the shotgun in the rack on the opposite wall. "You just take old lady Benally there. Look after her."

Mrs. Benally may not have been able to translate "bikini" into Navajo, but she had no trouble with "motel."

"I'm not going into any motel," she said.

For practical purposes, that ended the argument. Nobody was moving.

Leaphorn wasn't unprepared for that. Before he'd parked at the Nez hogan, he had scouted up Canyon del Muerto, examining the south-side cliff walls below the place where the ranger had reported seeing the man with the rifle. Sergeant Deke had said it was just five or six hundred yards up-canyon from the Nez place. Leaphorn had seen no location within rifle range where the top of the south cliff offered a fair shot at the Nez hogan. But about a quarter mile up-canyon a huge slab of sandstone had given way to the erosion undercutting it.

The cliff had split here. The slab had separated from the wall. He'd studied it. Someone who knew rock climbing, had the equipment, and didn't mind risking falling off a forty-story building could get down here. This must have been what Demott had been doing here—if it was De-mott. He was looking for a way in and out that avoided the bottleneck entrance.

It was certainly conveniently close for a climber. Or a bird. Being nei-ther meant Leaphorn would have to drive about fifteen miles down Canyon del Muerto to its junction with Canyon de Chelly, then another five or six to the canyon mouth to reach the pavement of Navajo Route 64. Then he'd have to reverse directions and drive twenty-four miles north-eastward along the north rim of del Muerto, turn southwestward maybe four miles toward Tsaile, then complete the circle down the brushy dirt-and-boulder track that took those foolhardy enough to use it down that finger of mesa separating the canyons. The last six or seven miles on that circuit would take about as long as the first fifty.

Leaphorn hurried. He wanted enough daylight left to check the place carefully—to either confirm or refute his suspicions. More important, if Demott was coming Leaphorn wanted to be there waiting for him.

He seemed to have managed that. He stopped across the cattle guard where the unmarked track connected with the highway, climbed out, and made a careful inspection. The last vehicle to leave its tracks here had been coming out, and that had been shortly after the snowfall began. Eight or nine jolting miles later, he pulled his car off the track and left it concealed behind a cluster of junipers. The wind was bitter now, but the snow had diminished to occasional dry flakes.

The west rim of Canyon del Muerto was less than fifty yards away over mostly bare sandstone. If he had calculated properly, he was just about above the Nez home site. In fact, he was perhaps a hundred yards below it. He stood a foot or two back from the edge looking down, confirming that the Nez hogan was too protected by the overhang to offer a shot from here. He could see the track where Nez drove in his truck, but the hogan itself and all of its outbuildings except a goat pen were hidden below the wall. But he could see from here the great split-off sandstone slab, and he walked along the rim toward it. He was almost there when he heard an engine whining in low gear.

Along the cliff here finding concealment was no problem. Leaphorn moved behind a great block of sandstone surrounded by piñons. He checked his pistol and waited.

The vehicle approaching was a dirty, battered, dark green Land-Rover. It came almost directly toward him. Stopped not fifty feet away. The engine died. The door opened. Eldon Demott stepped out. He reached behind him into the vehicle and took out a rifle, which he laid across the hood. Then he extracted a roll of thin, pale yellow rope and a cardboard box. These two also went onto the hood. From the box he took a web belt and harness, a helmet, and a pair of small black shoes. He leaned against the fender, removed a boot, replaced it with a shoe, and repeated the process. Then he put on the belt and the climbing harness. He looked at his watch, glanced at the sky, stretched, and looked around him.

He looked directly at Joe Leaphorn, sighed, and reached for the rifle.

"Leave it where it is," Leaphorn said, and showed Demott his .38 revolver.

Demott took his hand away from the rifle, dropped it to his side.

"I might want to shoot something," he said.

"Hunting season is over," Leaphorn said.

Demott sighed and leaned against the fender. "It looks like it is."

"No doubt about it. Even if I get careless and you shoot me, you can't get out of here anyway. Two police cars are on their way in after you. And if you climb down, well, that's hopeless."

"You going to arrest me? How do you do that? You're retired. Or is it a citizen's arrest?"

"Regular arrest," Leaphorn said. "I'm still deputized by the sheriff in this county. I didn't get around to turning in the commission."

"What do you charge me with—trespass?"

"Well, I think more likely it will start out being attempted homicide of Amos Nez, and then after the FBI gets its work done, the murder of Hosteen Maryboy."

Demott was staring at him, frowning. "That's it?"

"I think that would do it," Leaphorn said.

"Nothing about Hal."

"Nothing so far. Except that Amos Nez thinks you're him."

Demott considered that. "I'm getting cold," he said, and reopened the car door. "Going to get out of the wind."

"No," Leaphorn said, and shifted the pistol barrel before him.

Demott stopped, shut the door. He smiled at Leaphorn, shook his head. "Another weapon in there, you think?"

Leaphorn returned the smile. "Why take chances?" he said.

"Nothing about Hal," he said. "Well, I'm glad of that."

"Why?"

Demott shrugged. "Because of Elisa," he said. "The other cop, Jim Chee I think it was, he was coming up to see us. He said you had looked at the climber register. What did Elisa say about that?"

"I wasn't there. Chee showed her the page with Hal's name on it, and the date. He said she sort of went to pieces. Cried." Leaphorn shrugged. "About what you'd expect, I guess."

Demott slumped against the fender. "Ah, hell," he said, and slammed his fist against the hood. "Damn! Damn! Damn! Damn!"

"It made it look premeditated, of course," Leaphorn said.

"Of course," Demott said. "And it wasn't."

"An accident. If it wasn't, it may be hard to keep her out of it."

"She was still in love with the bastard. Didn't have a damn thing to do with it."

"I'm not surprised," Leaphorn said. "But considering what's involved, the Breedloves will probably hire a special prosecutor and they'll be aimed at getting the ranch back. Voiding the inheritance."

"Voiding the inheritance? What do you mean? Wouldn't that sort of be automatic? I mean, with what you said about Nez knowing . . . You know, Hal didn't inherit until he was thirty. The way the proviso read, if he didn't reach that birthday, everything was voided."

"Nez thinking you were Hal isn't the only evidence that he lived past that birthday," Leaphorn said. "There's his signature in the climbers' register. That's dated September thirty. You know of any evidence that he died before that?"

Demott was staring at Leaphorn, mouth partly open. "Wait a minute," he said. "Wait. What are you saying?"

"I guess I'm saying that I think there's sometimes a difference between the law and justice. If there's justice here, you're going to spend life in prison for the premeditated murder of Mr. Maryboy, with maybe an add-on twenty years or so for the attempted murder of Amos Nez. I think that would be about right. But it probably won't work quite like that. Your sister's probably going to be charged with accessory to murder—maybe as a conspirator and certainly as an accessory after the fact. And the Breedloves will get her ranch."

Demott inhaled a deep breath. He looked down at his hands, rubbed at his thumb.

"And Cache Creek will be running water gray with cyanide and mining effluent."

"Yeah," Demott said. "I really screwed it up. Year after year you're nervous about it. Sunny day you think you're clear. Nothing to worry about. Then you wake up with a nightmare."

"What happened up there?" Leaphorn said.

Demott gave him a questioning look. "You asking for a confession?"

"You're not under arrest. If you were, I'd have to tell you about your rights not to say anything until you get your lawyer. Elisa told Chee she didn't get all the way to the top. Is that right?"

"She didn't," Demott said. "She was getting scared." He snorted. "I should say sensible."

Leaphorn nodded.

"This birthday was a big deal for Hal," Demott said. "He'd say, Lord God Almighty, I'll be free at last, and get all excited thinking about it. And he'd invited this guy he'd known at Dartmouth to bring his girlfriend to see Canyon de Chelly and Navajo National Monument, the Grand Canyon, all that. Meet him and Elisa at the canyon for a birthday party for starters.

But first he wanted to climb Ship Rock before he was thirty. That proved something to him. So we climbed it. Or almost."

Demott looked away. Deciding how much of this he wants to tell me, Leaphorn thought. Or maybe just remembering.

"We stopped in Rappel Gulch," Demott said. "Elisa had dropped out about an hour before that. Said she would just wait for us. So Hal and I were resting for that last hard climb. He had been talking about how the route up involves so much climbing up and then climbing back down to get to another up-route. He said there surely had to be a better way with all the good rappelling equipment we had now. Anyway, he edged out on the cliff. He said he wanted to see if there was a faster way down."

Demott stopped. He sat on the fender, studying Leaphorn.

"I take it there was," Leaphorn said.

Demott nodded. "Partway."

"Gust of wind caught him. Something like that?"

"Why are you doing this?"

"I like your sister," Leaphorn said. "A kind, caring woman. And besides, I don't like strip miners ruining the mountains."

The wind was blowing a little harder now, and colder. It came out of the northwest, blowing the hair away from Demott's face and dust around the tires of the Land-Rover.

"How does this come out?" Demott said. "I don't know much about the law."

"It will depend mostly on how you handle it," Leaphorn said.

"I don't understand."

"Here's where we are now. We have three felonies. The Maryboy homicide and the related shooting of a Navajo policeman. The FBI is handling that one. Then there is the assault upon Amos Nez, in which the FBI has no interest."

"Hal?"

"Officially, formally, an accident. FBI's not interested. Nobody else is, except the Breedlove Corporation."

"Now what happens?"

"Depends on you," Leaphorn said. "If I were still a Navajo Tribal Policeman and working this case, I'd take you in on suspicion of shooting Amos Nez. The police do a ballistics check on that rifle of yours and if the bullets match the one they got from Nez's horse, then they charge you with attempted murder. That gets Nez on the witness stand, which makes Elisa an accessory after the fact but probably indicted as coconspirator. That leads the Breedloves to file legal papers to void the inheritance. And what Nez says wakes up the FBI and they make the Maryboy connection. The ballistics test on whatever you shot him with, which I suspect we'll find either in your glove compartment or under the front seat, nails you on that one. I'd say you do life. Elisa? I don't know. Much shorter."

Demott had been following this intently, nodding sometimes. Sometimes frowning.

"But why Elisa?"

"If they can't make the jury believe she helped plan it, you can see how easy it is to prove she helped cover it up. Just get Nez and some of the people at the Thunderbird Lodge under oath. They saw you there with her."

"You mentioned an option. Said it depends on me. How could it?"

"We go into Gallup. You turn yourself in. Say you want to confess to the shooting of Hosteen Maryboy and Jim Chee. No mention of Nez. No mention of Hal. No mention of climbing Ship Rock."

"And what do you say? I mean about where you found me. And why and all that."

"I'm not there," Leaphorn said. "I park where I can see you walk into the police station and wait awhile and when you don't come out, I go somewhere and get something to eat."

"Just Maryboy, then, and Chee?" Demott said. "And Elisa wouldn't get dragged into it?"

"Without Nez involved, how would she?"

"Well, that other cop. The one I shot. Doesn't he have a lot of this figured out?"

"Chee?" Leaphorn chuckled. "Chee's a genuine Navajo. He isn't interested in revenge. He wants harmony."

Demott's expression was skeptical.

"What would he do?" Leaphorn asked. "It's obvious why you shot Chee. You were trying to escape. But you have to give them some plausible reason for shooting Maryboy. Chee isn't going to rush in and say the real motive was some complicated something or other to cover up not reporting that Hal Breedlove fell off the mountain eleven years ago. What's to be gained by it? Except a lot of work and frustration. Either way, you are going to do life in prison."

"Yes," Demott said, and the way he said it caused Leaphorn to lose his cool.

"And you damn sure deserve it. And worse. Killing Maryboy was cold-blooded murder. I've seen it before but it was always done by psychopaths. Emotional cripples. I want you to tell me how a normal human can decide to go shoot an old man to death."

"I didn't," Demott said. "They found the skeleton. Then they identified Hal. The nightmare was coming true. I got panicky. Nobody knew I'd climbed up there with Hal and Elisa that day but the old man. We went to ask him about trespassing, but that was eleven years ago. I didn't think he'd remember. But I had to find out. So I drove down there that evening, and knocked on the door. If he didn't recognize me, I'd go away and forget it. He opened the door and I told him I was Eldon Demott and heard he had some heifers to sell. And right away I could see he knew me. He said I was the man who'd climbed up there with Mr. Breedlove. He got all excited. He asked how I could have gone off and left a friend up there on the mountain. And now that he knew who I was, he was going to tell the police about it. I went out and got into the car and there he was coming out after me, carrying a thirty-thirty, and wanted me to go back into the house. So I got my pistol out of the glove box and put it in my coat pocket. He went into his house and put on his coat and hat, and he was going to take me right into the police station at Shiprock. And, you know . . ."

"That's how it was, then?"

"Yeah," Demott said. "But if I can just keep Nez out of it, maybe we save Elisa?"

Leaphorn nodded.

Demott reached his hand slowly toward the rifle.

"What I'd like to do is slip the bolt out of this thing so it's harmless."

"Then what?"

"Then I walk five steps over there to the cliff, and I toss it down into that deepest crack where nobody could ever find it."

"Do it," Leaphorn said. "I won't look."

Demott did it. "Now," he said. "I want just a few minutes to write Elisa a little letter. I want her to know I didn't kill Hal. I want her to know that when I climbed on up there and signed that register for him, it was just so she wouldn't lose her ranch."

"Go ahead."

"Got to get my notebook out of the glove box then."

"I'll watch," Leaphorn said. He moved around to where he could do that.

Demott dug out a little spiral notebook and a ballpoint pen, closed the box, backed out of the vehicle, and used the hood as a writing desk. He wrote rapidly, using two pages. He tore them out, folded them, and dropped them on the car seat.

"Now," he said, "let's get this over with."

"Demott," Leaphorn shouted. "Wait!"

But Eldon Demott had already taken the half dozen running steps to the rim of Canyon del Muerto and jumped, arms and legs flailing, out into empty space.

Leaphorn stood there a while listening. And heard nothing but the wind. He walked to the rim and looked. Demott had apparently hit the stone where the cliff bulged outward, down some two hundred feet. The body bounced out and landed on the stony talus slope just beside the canyon road. The first traveler to come along would see it.

Demott had left the door open on the Land-Rover. Leaphorn reached in and picked up the letter, holding it by its edges.

Dear Sister:

The first thing you do when you read this is call Harold Simmons at his law office don't tell anyone anything until you talk it over with him. I've made an awful mess of things, but I'm out of it now and you can still have a good life taking care of the ranch. But I want you to know that I didn't kill Hal. I'm ashamed to tell you a lot of this but I want you to know what happened.

About a week after Hal disappeared from the canyon I got a call from him. He was in a motel in Farmington. He wouldn't tell me where he had been, or why he was doing this, but he said he wanted to climb Ship Rock right away, before it got too cold. I said hell no. He said if I didn't I was fired. I wouldn't anyway. Then he said if I would and I didn't say anything to you, he would decide against signing that strip mining contract and put it off for another full year. He said he wanted to explain everything to you after we got down. So I said okay and I picked him up at the motel about five the next morning. He wouldn't tell me a word about where he'd been and he was acting strange. But we climbed it, up to Rappel Gulch, and there he insisted on edging out on the cliff face to see if there was a way good hands with rope could get down. A gust of wind caught him and he fell.

That's it, Elisa. I've been too ashamed to tell you all these years and I'm ashamed now. I think it's made me crazy. Because when I went to see Mr. Maryboy about his stock getting onto our grazing over on the Checkerboard Reservation, we got to yelling at one another and he got his rifle down and I shot him and then I shot the policeman to get away. I checked on the penalty I can expect and it's life in prison, so I'm going to take the quick way out of it and set an all-time record getting down that 800-foot cliff into Canyon del Muerto.

Remember I love you. I just got crazy.

Your big brother, Eldon

Leaphorn read it again, refolded it carefully, replaced it on the seat. He took out his handkerchief, pushed down the lock lever, wiped off the leather seat where he might have touched it, and slammed the door.

He drove a little faster than was smart down the track, anxious to get out before somebody spotted Demott's body. He didn't want to meet a police car coming in, and if he didn't, the dry snow now being carried by the wind would quickly eliminate any clue that Demott had had company. He was almost back to Window Rock before a call on his police monitor let him know that the body of a man had been found up Canyon del Muerto.

He turned up the thermostat beside his front door, heard the floor furnace roar into action, put on the coffeepot, and washed his face and hands. That done, he checked his telephone answering machine, punched the button and listened to the first words of an insurance agent's sales pitch, and hit the erase button. Then he took his coffee mug off the hook, got out the sugar and cream, poured himself a cup, and sat beside the telephone.

He sipped now, and dialed Jim Chee's number in Ship Rock.

"Jim Chee."

"This is Joe Leaphorn," he said. "Thanks for the message you sent me. I hope I'm not calling at a bad time."

"No. No," Chee said. "I've been wondering. And I've been wanting to tell you about an arrest we made today in our cattle-rustling case. But by the way, have you heard they found a man's body in Canyon del Muerto? Deke said it was near the Nez place. He said it's Demott."

"Heard a little on my scanner," Leaphorn said.

Brief silence. Chee cleared his throat. "Where are you calling from? Was it Demott? Were you there?"

"I'm at home," Leaphorn said. "Are you off duty?"

"What do you mean? Oh. Well, yes. I guess so."

"Better be sure," Leaphorn said.

"Okay," Chee said. "I'm sure. I'm just having a friendly talk with an unidentified civilian."

"Tomorrow, you're going to get the word that Demott killed himself. He jumped off the cliff above the Nez place. About like diving off a sixty-story building. And he left a suicide note to his sister. In it he said he got into a quarrel with Mr. Maryboy over some cattle and shot him. Shot you while escaping. He told Elisa that he didn't kill Hal. He said Hal had called him from Farmington a week after vanishing from his birthday party, offered to delay signing the mining lease he had cooking for a year if Demott would climb Ship Rock with him the next day. Demott agreed. They climbed. Hal fell off. Demott said he kept it a secret because he was ashamed to tell her."

Silence. Then Chee said, "Wow!"

Leaphorn waited for the implications to sink in.

"I'm not supposed to ask you how you know all this?"

"That is correct."

"What did he say about Nez?"

"Who?"

"Amos Nez," Chee repeated. "Oh, I guess I see."

"Saves you a lot of work, doesn't it?"

"Sure does," Chee said. "Except for when they find the rifle. Body near the Nez place, rifle nearby I guess. Nez recently shot. Two and two make four and the ballistics test raises a problem. Even the FBI won't be able to shrug that off."

"I think the rifle doesn't exist," Leaphorn said.

"Oh?"

"It's my impression that Demott didn't want to involve his sister. So he didn't want the Nez thing connected to the Maryboy thing because with Nez, you have his sister indicted as an accessory."

"I see," Chee said, a little hesitantly. "But how about Nez? Won't he be talking about it?"

"Nez isn't much for talking. And he's going to think I pushed Demott off the cliff to keep Demott from shooting him."

"Yeah. I see that."

"I think Demott did this partly to keep the Breedlove Corporation from strip-mining the ranch. Ruining his creek. So he left the world a suicide letter certifying that he was on Ship Rock with Hal a week after the famous birthday. Add that to Hal signing the register a week after the same birthday."

"One's as phony as the other," Chee said.

"Is that right?" Leaphorn said. "I would like to sit there and listen while you try to persuade the agent in charge that he should reopen his Maryboy homicide, throw away a written point-of-death confession on grounds that Demott was lying about his motive. I can just see that. 'And what was his real motive, Mr. Chee?' His real motive was trying to prove that accidental death that happened eleven years ago actually happened on a different weekend, and then—"

Chee was laughing. Leaphorn stopped.

"All right," Chee said. "I get your point. All it would do is waste a lot of work, maybe get Mrs. Breedlove indicted for something or other, and give the ranch back to the Breedlove Corporation."

"And get a big commission to the attorney," Leaphorn added.

"Yeah," Chee said.

"Tomorrow, when the news is out, I'll send Shaw details about the suicide note. And give him back what's left of his money. Now, what were you going to tell me about cattle rustling?"

"It sounds trivial after this," Chee said, "but Officer Manuelito arrested Dick Finch today. He was loading Maryboy heifers into his camper."

The First Eagle

Acknowledgments

A LL CHARACTERS IN this work are fictional. Especially let it be known that Pamela J. Reynolds and Ted L. Brown, vector control specialists of the New Mexico Department of Public Health, did not model for the two vector control characters in *The First Eagle*—being too amiable and generous for those roles. They did try to educate me on how they track the viruses and bacteria that plague our mountains and deserts and even modeled PAPRS for me. Thanks, too, to Patrick and Susie McDermott, Ph.D. and M.D. respectively in microbiology and neurology, who tried to keep my speculation about drug-resistant microbes close to reality. Dr. John C. Brown of the University of Kansas Department of Microbiology provided a reading list and good advice. Robert Ambrose, a falconer and trainer of raptors, informed me about eagles. My friend Neal Shadoff, M.D., helped make the medical professionals involved sound professional, and Justice Robert Henry of the U.S. Tenth Circuit Court of Appeals advised me relative to the federal death penalty law. I thank them all.

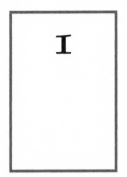

I

THE BODY OF Anderson Nez lay under a sheet on the gurney, waiting. From the viewpoint of Shirley Ahkeah, sitting at her desk in the Intensive Care Unit nursing station of the Northern Arizona Medical Center in Flagstaff, the white shape formed by the corpse of Mr. Nez reminded her of Sleeping Ute Mountain as seen from her aunt's hogan near Teec Nos Pos. Nez's feet, only a couple of yards from her eyes, pushed the sheet up to form the mountain's peak. Perspective caused the rest of the sheet to slope away in humps and ridges, as the mountain seemed to do under its winter snow when she was a child. Shirley had given up on finishing her night shift paperwork. Her mind kept drifting away to what had happened to Mr. Nez and trying to calculate whether he fit into the Bitter Water clan Nez family with the grazing lease adjoining her grandmother's place at Short Mountain. And then there was the question of whether his family would allow an autopsy. She remembered them as sheep camp traditionals, but Dr. Woody, the one who'd brought Nez in, insisted he had the family's permission.

At that moment Dr. Woody was looking at his watch, a black plastic digital job that obviously hadn't been bought to impress the sort of people who are impressed by expensive watches.

"Now," Woody said, "I need to know the time the man died."

"It was early this morning," Dr. Delano said, looking surprised. It surprised Shirley, too, because Woody already knew the answer.

"No. No. No," Woody said. "I mean exactly when."

"Probably about two A.M.," Dr. Delano said, with his expression saying that he wasn't used to being addressed in that impatient tone. He shrugged. "Something like that."

Woody shook his head, grimaced. "Who would know? I mean, who would know within a few minutes?" He looked up and down the hospital corridor, then pointed at Shirley. "Surely somebody would be on duty. The man was terminal. I know the time he was infected, and the time he began registering a fever. Now I need to know how fast it killed him. I need every bit of information I can get on processes in that terminal period. What was happening with various vital functions? I need all that data I ordered kept when I checked him in. Everything."

Odd, Shirley thought. If Woody knew all that, why hadn't Nez been brought to the hospital while there was still some hope of saving him? When Nez was brought in yesterday he was burning with fever and dying fast.

"I'm sure it's all there," Delano said, nodding toward the clipboard Woody was holding. "You'll find it there in his chart."

Now Shirley grimaced. All that information wasn't in Nez's chart. Not yet. It should have been, and would have been even on this unusually hectic shift if Woody hadn't rushed in demanding an autopsy, and not just an autopsy but a lot of special stuff. And that had caused Delano to be summoned, looking sleepy and out of sorts, in his role as assistant medical superintendent, and Delano to call in Dr. Howe, who had handled the Nez case in ICU. Howe, she noticed, wasn't letting Woody bother him. He was too old a hand for that. Howe took every case as his personal *mano-a-mano* battle against death. But when death won, as it often did in ICU units, he racked up a loss and forgot it. A few hours ago he had worried about Nez, hovered over him. Now he was simply another of the battles he'd been fated to lose.

So why was Dr. Woody causing all this excitement? Why did Woody insist on the autopsy? And insist on sitting in on it with the pathologist? The cause of death was clearly the plague. Nez had been sent to the Intensive Care Unit on admission. Even then the infected lymph glands were swollen, and subcutaneous hemorrhages were forming their splotches on his abdomen and legs, the discolorations that had given the disease its "Black Death" name when it swept through Europe in the Middle Ages, killing tens of millions.

Like most medical personnel in the Four Corners country, Shirley Ahkeah had seen Black Death before. There'd been no cases on the Big Reservation for three or four years, but there were three already this year. One of the others had been on the New Mexico side of the Rez and hadn't come here. But it, too, had been fatal, and the word was that this was a vintage year for the old-fashioned bacteria—that it had flared up in an unusually virulent form.

It certainly had been virulent with Nez. The disease had gone quickly from the common glandular form into plague pneumonia. The Nez sputum, as well as his blood, swarmed with the bacteria, and no one went into his room without donning a filtration mask.

Delano, Howe, and Woody had drifted down the hall beyond Shirley's eavesdropping range, but the tone of the conversation suggested an agreement of some sort had been reached. More work for her, probably. She stared at the sheet covering Nez, remembering the man under it racked by sickness and wishing they'd move the body away. She'd been born in Farmington, daughter of an elementary schoolteacher who had converted to Catholicism. Thus she saw the Navajo "corpse avoidance" teaching as akin to the Jewish dietary prohibitions—a smart way to prevent the spread of illnesses. But even without believing in the evil *chindi* that traditional Navajos knew would attend the corpse of Nez for four days, the body under the sheet provoked unhappy thoughts of human mortality and the sorrow death causes.

Howe reappeared, looking old and tired and reminding her as he always did of a plumper version of her maternal grandfather.

"Shirley, darlin', did I by any chance give you a long list of special stuff we were supposed to do on the Nez case? One thing I remember was he wanted a bunch of extra blood work. Wanted measurement of the interleukin-six in his blood every hour, for one thing. And can't you just imagine the screaming fit the Indian Health Service auditors would have if we billed for that?"

"I can," Shirley said. "But nope. I didn't see any such list. I would have remembered that interleukin-six." She laughed. "I would have had to look it up. Something to do with how the immune system is working, isn't it?"

"It's not my field either," Howe said. "But I think you're right. I know it shows up in AIDS cases, and diabetes, and the sort of situations that affect immunity. Anyway, we shall let the record show that the list didn't reach your desk. I think I must have just wadded it up and tossed it."

"Who is this Dr. Woody anyway?" Shirley asked. "What's his specialty? And why did it take so long to get Nez in here? He must have been running a fever for days."

"He's not a doctor at all," Howe said. "I mean he's not a practicing physician. I think he has the M.D. degree, but mostly he's the Ph.D. kind of doc. Microbiology. Pharmacology. Organic chemistry. Writes lots of papers in the journals about the immune system, evolution of pathogens, immunity of microbes to antibiotics, that sort of stuff. He did a piece for *Science* magazine a few months ago for the layman to read, warning the world that our miracle medicines aren't working anymore. If the viruses don't get us, the bacteria will."

"Oh, yeah," Shirley said. "I remember reading that article. That was his piece? If he knows so much, how come he didn't see that fever?"

Howe shook his head. "I asked him. He said Nez just started showing the symptoms. Said he had him on preventive doxycycline already because of the work they do, but he gave him a booster shot of streptomycin and rushed him right in."

"You don't believe that, do you?"

Howe grimaced. "I'd hate to," he said. "Good old plague used to be reliable. It'd poke along and give us time to treat it. And, yeah, that was Woody's article. Sort of don't worry about global warming. The tiny little beasties will get us first."

"Well, as I remember it, I agreed with a lot of it," Shirley said. "It's downright stupid the way some of you doctors prescribe a bunch of antibiotics every time a mama brings her kid in with an earache. No wonder—"

Howe held up a hand.

"Save it, Shirley. Save it. You're preaching to the choir here." He nodded toward the sheet on the gurney. "Doesn't Mr. Nez there just prove we're breeding a whole new set of drug-resistant bugs? The old *Pasteurella pestis*, as we used to call it in those glorious primitive days when drugs worked, was duck soup for a half dozen antibiotics. Now, whatever they call it these days, *Yersinia pestis* I think it is, just ignored everything we tried on Mr. Nez. We had us a case here where one of your Navajo curing ceremonials could have done Nez more good than we did."

"They just brought him in too late," Shirley said. "You can't give the plague a two-week head start and hope to—"

Howe shook his head. "It wasn't two weeks, Shirley. If Woody knows what the hell he's talking about, it was more like just about one day."

"No way," Shirley said, shaking her head. "And how would he know, anyway?"

"Said he picked the flea off of him. Woody's doing a big study of rodent host colonies. National Institutes of Health money, and some of the pharmaceutical companies. He's interested in these mammal disease reservoirs. You know. Prairie dog colonies that get the plague infection but somehow stay alive while all the other colonies are wiped out. That and the kangaroo rats and deer mice, which aren't killed by the hantavirus. Anyway, Woody said he and Nez always took a broad-spectrum antibiotic when there was any risk of flea bites. If it happened, they'd save the flea so he could check it and do a follow-up treatment if needed. According to Woody, Nez found the flea on the inside of his thigh, and almost right away he was feeling sick and running a fever."

"Wow," Shirley said.

"Yeah," Howe agreed. "Wow indeed."

"I'll bet another flea got him a couple of weeks ago," she said. "Did you agree on the autopsy?"

"Yeah again," Howe said. "You said you know the family. Or know some Nezes, anyway. You think they'll object?"

"I'm what they call an urban Indian. Three-fourths Navajo by blood, but I'm no expert on the culture." She shrugged. "Tradition is against chopping up bodies, but on the other hand it solves the problem of the burial."

Howe sighed, rested his plump buttocks against the desk, pushed back his glasses and rubbed his hand across his eyes. "Always liked that about you guys," he said. "Four days of grief and mourning for the spirit, and then get on with life. How did we white folks get into this corpse worship business? It's just dead meat, and dangerous to boot."

Shirley merely nodded.

"Anything hopeful for that kid in Room Four?" Howe asked. He picked up the chart, looked at it, clicked his tongue and shook his head. He pushed himself up from the desk and stood, shoulders slumped, staring at the sheet covering the body of Anderson Nez.

"You know," he said, "back in the Middle Ages the doctors had another cure for this stuff. They thought it had something to do with the sense of smell, and they recommended people stave it off by using a lot of perfume and wearing flowers. It didn't stop everybody from dying, but it proved humans have a sense of humor."

Shirley had known Howe long enough to understand that she was now supposed to provide a straight line for his wit. She wasn't in the mood, but she said: "What do you mean?"

"They made an ironic song out of it—and it lived on as a nursery rhyme." Howe sang it in his creaky voice:

Ring around with roses,
pockets full of posies.
Ashes. Ashes.
We all fall down.

He looked at her quizzically. "You remember singing that in kindergarten?"

Shirley didn't. She shook her head.

And Dr. Howe walked down the hall toward where another of his patients was dying.

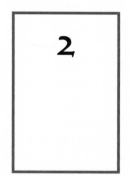

2

ACTING LIEUTENANT JIM Chee of the Navajo Tribal Police, a "traditional" at heart, had parked his trailer with its door facing east. At dawn on July 8, he looked out at the rising sun, scattered a pinch of pollen from his medicine pouch to bless the day and considered what it would bring him.

He reviewed the bad part first. On his desk his monthly report for June—his first month as administrator in charge of a Navajo Police subagency unit—awaited him, half-finished and already overdue. But finishing the hated paperwork would be fun compared to the other priority job—telling Officer Benny Kinsman to get his testosterone under control.

The good part of the day involved, at least obliquely, his own testosterone. Janet Pete was leaving Washington and coming back to Indian country. Her letter was friendly but cool, with no hint of romantic passion. Still, Janet was coming back, and after he finished with Kinsman he planned to call her. It would be a tentative exploratory call. Were they still engaged? Did she want to resume their prickly relationship? Bridge the gap? Actually get married? For that matter, did he? However he answered that question, she was coming back and that explained why Chee was grinning while he washed the breakfast dishes.

The grin went away when he got to his office at the Tuba City station.

Officer Kinsman, who was supposed to be awaiting him in his office, wasn't there. Claire Dineyahze explained it.

"He said he had to run out to Yells Back Butte first and catch that Hopi who's been poaching eagles," Mrs. Dineyahze said.

Chee inhaled, opened his mouth, then clamped it shut. Mrs. Dineyahze would have been offended by the obscenity Kinsman's action deserved.

She made a wry face and shook her head, sharing Chee's disapproval.

"I guess it's the same Hopi he arrested out there last winter," she said. "The one they turned loose because Benny forgot to read him his rights. But he wouldn't tell me. Just gave me that look." She put on a haughty expression. "Said his informant was confidential." Clearly Mrs. Dineyahze was offended by this exclusion. "One of his girlfriends, probably."

"I'll find out," Chee said. It was time to change the subject. "I've got to get that June report finished. Anything else going on?"

"Well," Mrs. Dineyahze said, and then stopped.

Chee waited.

Mrs. Dineyahze shrugged. "I know you don't like gossip," she said. "But you'll probably hear about this anyway."

"What?"

"Suzy Gorman called this morning. You know? The secretary in the Arizona Highway Patrol at Winslow. She said one of their troopers had to break up a fight at a place in Flagstaff. It was Benny Kinsman and some guy from Northern Arizona University."

Chee sighed. "They charge him?"

"She said no. Professional courtesy."

"Thank God," Chee said. "That's a relief."

"May not be over, though," she said. "Suzy said the fight started because Kinsman was making a big move on a woman and wouldn't stop, and the woman said she was going to file a complaint. Said he'd been bothering her before. On her job."

"Well, hell," Chee said. "What next? Where's she work?"

"Works out of that little office the Arizona Health Department set up here after those two bubonic plague cases. They call 'em vector control people." Mrs. Dineyahze smiled. "They catch fleas."

"I've got to get that report out by noon," Chee said. He'd had all the Kinsman he wanted this morning.

Mrs. Dineyahze wasn't finished with Kinsman. "Did Bernie talk to you about Kinsman?"

"No," Chee said. She hadn't, but he'd heard a rumble on the gossip circuit.

"I told her she should tell you, but she didn't want to bother you."

"Tell me what?" Bernie was Officer Bernadette Manuelito, who was young and green and, judging from gossip Chee had overheard, had a crush on him.

Mrs. Dineyahze looked sour. "Sexual harassment," she said.

"Like what?"

"Like making a move on her."

Chee didn't want to hear about it. Not now. "Tell her to report it to me," he said, and went into his office to confront his paperwork. With a couple of hours of peace and quiet he could finish it by lunchtime. He got in about thirty minutes before the dispatcher buzzed him.

"Kinsman wants a backup," she said.

"For what?" Chee asked. "Where is he?"

"Out there past Goldtooth," the dispatcher said. "Over near the west side of Black Mesa. The signal was breaking up."

"It always does out there," Chee said. In fact, these chronic radio communication problems were one thing he was complaining about in his report. "We have anyone close?"

"Afraid not."

"I'll take it myself," Chee said.

A few minutes after noon, Chee was bumping down the gravel trailing a cloud of dust looking for Kinsman. "Come in, Benny," Chee said into his mike. "I'm eight miles south of Goldtooth. Where are you?"

"Under the south cliff of Yells Back Butte," Kinsman said. "Take the old Tijinney hogan road. Park where the arroyo cuts it. Half mile up the arroyo. Be very quiet."

"Well, hell," Chee said. He said it to himself, not into the mike. Kinsman had gotten himself excited stalking his Hopi poacher, or whatever he was after, and had been transmitting in a half-intelligible whisper. Even more irritating, he was switching off his receiver lest a too-loud response alert his prey. While this was proper procedure in some emergency situations, Chee doubted this was anything serious enough to warrant that sort of foolishness.

"Come on, Kinsman," he said. "Grow up."

If he was going to be backup man on whatever Benny was doing, it would help to understand the problem. It would also help to know how to find the road to the Tijinney hogan. Chee knew just about every track on the east side of the Big Rez, the Checkerboard Rez even better, and the territory around Navajo Mountain fairly well. But he'd worked out of Tuba City very briefly as a rookie and had been reassigned there only six weeks ago. This rugged landscape beside the Hopi Reservation was relatively strange to him.

He remembered Yells Back Butte was an outcrop of Black Mesa. Therefore it shouldn't be too difficult to find the Tijinney road, and the arroyo, and Kinsman. When he did, Chee intended to give him some very explicit instructions about how to use his radio and to behave himself when dealing with women. And, come to think of it, to curb his anti-Hopi attitude.

This was the product of having his family's home site added to the Hopi Reservation when Congress split the Joint Use lands. Kinsman's grandmother, who spoke only Navajo, had been relocated to Flagstaff, where almost nobody speaks Navajo. Whenever Kinsman visited her, he came back full of anger.

One of those scattered little showers that serve as forerunners to the desert country rainy season had swept across the Moenkopi Plateau a few minutes before and was still producing rumbles of thunder far to the east. Now he was driving through the track the shower had left and the gusty breeze was no longer engulfing the patrol car in dust. The air pouring through the window was rich with the perfume of wet sage and dampened earth.

Don't let this Kinsman problem spoil the whole day, Chee told himself. Be happy. And he was. Janet Pete was coming. Which meant what? That she thought she could be content outside the culture of Washington's high society? Apparently. Or would she try again to pull him into it? If so, would she succeed? That made him uneasy.

Before yesterday's letter, he had hardly thought about Janet for days. A little before drifting off to sleep, a little at dawn while he fried his breakfast Spam. But he had resisted the temptation to dig out her previous letter and reread it. He knew the facts by heart. One of her mother's many well-placed friends reported that her job application was "favorably considered" in the

Justice Department. Being half-Navajo made her prospects for an assignment in Indian country look good. Then came the last paragraph.

"Maybe I'll be assigned to Oklahoma—lots of legal work there with
that internal fight the Cherokees are having. And then there's the rumble
inside the Bureau of Indian Affairs over law enforcement that might keep
me in Washington."

Nothing in that one that suggested the old prequarrel affection. It had
caused Chee to waste a dozen sheets of paper with abortive attempts to
frame the proper answer. In some of them he'd urged her to use the experience she'd gained working for the Navajo tribe's legal aid program to
land an assignment on the Big Rez. He'd said hurry home, that he'd been
wrong in distrusting her. He had misunderstood the situation. He had
acted out of unreasonable jealousy. In others he'd said, Stay away. You'll
never be content here. It can never be the same for us. Don't come unless
you can be happy without your Kennedy Center culture, your Ivy League
friends, art shows, and high-fashion and cocktail parties with the celebrity
set, without the snobbish intellectual elite. Don't come unless you can be
happy living with a fellow whose goals include neither luxury nor climbing
the ladder of social caste, with a man who has found the good life in a
rusty trailer house.

Found the good life? Or thought he had. Either way, he knew he was finally having some luck forgetting her. And the note he'd eventually sent
had been carefully unrevealing. Then came yesterday's letter, with the last
line saying she was "coming home!!"

Home. Home with two exclamation points. He was thinking of that
when Kinsman's silly whispering had jarred him back to reality. And now
Kinsman was whispering again. Unintelligible muttering at first, then:
"Lieutenant! Hurry!"

Chee hurried. He'd planned to pause at Goldtooth to ask directions,
but nothing remained there except two roofless stone buildings, their
doorways and windows open to the world, and an old-fashioned round
hogan that looked equally deserted. Tracks branched off here, disappearing through the dunes to the right and left. He hadn't seen a vehicle since
he'd left the pavement, but the center track bore tire marks. He stayed
with it. Speeding. He was out of the shower's path now and leaving a roos-
ter tail of dust. Forty miles to the right the San Franciscos dominated the

horizon, with a thunderstorm building over Humphrey's Peak. To the left rose the ragged shape of the Hopi mesas, partly obscured at the moment by the rain another cloud was dragging. All around him was the empty wind-shaped plateau, its dunes held by great growths of Mormon tea, snakeweed, yucca, and durable sage. Abruptly Chee again smelled the perfume that showers leave behind them. No more dust now. The track was damp. It veered eastward, toward mesa cliffs and, jutting from them, the massive shape of a butte. The tracks leading toward it were hidden behind a growth of Mormon tea and Chee almost missed them. He backed up, tried his radio again, got nothing but static, and turned onto the ruts toward the butte. Short of the cliffs he came to the washout Kinsman had mentioned.

Kinsman's patrol car was parked by a cluster of junipers, and Kinsman's tracks led up the arroyo. He followed them along the sandy bottom and then away from it, climbing the slope toward the towering sandstone wall of the butte. Kinsman's voice was still in Chee's mind. To hell with being quiet. Chee ran.

Officer Kinsman was behind an outcrop of sandstone. Chee saw a leg of his uniform trousers, partly obscured by a growth of wheatgrass. He began a shout to him, and cut it off. He could see a boot now. Toe down. That was wrong. He slid his pistol from its holster and edged closer.

From behind the sandstone, Chee heard the sound boots make on loose gravel, a grunting noise, labored breathing, an exclamation. He thumbed off the safety on his pistol and stepped into the open.

Benjamin Kinsman was facedown, the back of his uniform shirt matted with grass and sand glued to the cloth by fresh red blood. Beside Kinsman a young man squatted, looking up at Chee. His shirt, too, was smeared with blood.

"Put your hands on top of your head," Chee said.

"Hey," the man said. "This guy . . ."

"Hands on head," Chee said, hearing his own voice harsh and shaky in his ears. "And get facedown on the ground."

The man stared at Chee, at the pistol aimed at his face. He wore his hair in two braids. A Hopi, Chee thought. Of course. Probably the eagle poacher he'd guessed Kinsman had been trying to catch. Well, Kinsman had caught him.

"Down," Chee ordered. "Face to the ground."

The young man leaned forward, lowered himself slowly. Very agile, Chee thought. His torn shirt sleeve revealed a long gash on the right forearm, the congealed blood forming a curved red stripe across sunburned skin.

Chee pulled the man's right hand behind his back, clicked the handcuff on the wrist, cuffed the left wrist to it. Then he extracted a worn brown leather wallet from the man's hip pocket and flipped it open. From his Arizona driver's license photo the young man smiled at him. Robert Jano. Mishongnove, Second Mesa.

Robert Jano was turning onto his side, pulling his legs up, preparing to rise.

"Stay down," Chee said. "Robert Jano, you have the right to remain silent. You have the right to . . ."

"What are you arresting me for?" Jano said. A raindrop hit the rock beside Chee. Then another.

"For murder. You have the right to retain legal counsel. You have the right—"

"I don't think he's dead," Jano said. "He was alive when I got here."

"Yeah," Chee said. "I'm sure he was."

"And when I checked his pulse. Just thirty seconds ago."

Chee was already kneeling beside Kinsman, his hand on Kinsman's neck, first noticing the sticky blood and now the faint pulse under his fingertip and the warmth of the flesh under his palm.

He stared at Jano. "You sonofabitch!" Chee shouted. "Why did you brain him like that?"

"I didn't," Jano said. "I didn't hit him. I just walked up and he was here." He nodded toward Kinsman. "Just lying there like that."

"Like hell," Chee said. "How'd you get that blood all over you then, and your arm cut up like—"

A rasping shriek and a clatter behind him cut off the question. Chee spun, pistol pointing. A squawking sound came from behind the outcrop where Kinsman lay. Behind it a metal birdcage lay on its side. It was a large cage, but barely large enough to hold the eagle struggling inside it. Chee lifted it by the ring at its top, rested it on the sandstone slab and stared at Jano. "A federal offense," he said. "Poaching an endangered species. Not as bad as felony assault on a law officer, but—"

"Watch out!" Jano shouted.

Too late. Chee felt the eagle's talons tearing at the side of his hand.

"That's what happened to me," Jano said. "That's how I got so bloody."

Icy raindrops hit Chee's ear, his cheek, his shoulder, his bleeding hand. The shower engulfed them, and with it a mixture of hailstones. He covered Kinsman with his jacket and moved the eagle's cage under the shelter of the outcrop. He had to get help for Kinsman fast, and he had to keep the eagle under shelter. If Jano was telling the truth, which seemed extremely unlikely, there would be blood on the bird. He didn't want Jano's defense attorney to be able to claim that Chee had let the evidence wash away.

3

THE LIMO THAT had parked in front of Joe Leaphorn's house was a glossy blue-black job with the morning sun glittering on its polished chrome. Leaphorn had stood behind his screen door watching it—hoping his neighbors on this fringe of Window Rock wouldn't notice it. Which was like hoping the kids who played in the schoolyard down his gravel street wouldn't notice a herd of giraffes trotting by. The limo's arrival so early meant the man sitting patiently behind the wheel must have left Santa Fe about 3:00 A.M. That made Leaphorn ponder what life would be like as a hireling of the very rich—which Millicent Vanders certainly must be.

Well, in just a few minutes he'd have a chance to find out. The limo now was turning off a narrow asphalt road in Santa Fe's northeast foothills onto a brick driveway. It stopped at an elaborate iron gate.

"Is this it?" Leaphorn asked.

"Yep," the driver said, which was about the average length of the answers Leaphorn had been getting before he'd stopped asking questions. He'd started with the standard break-the-ice: gasoline mileage on the limo, how it handled, that sort of thing. Went from that into how long the driver had worked for Millicent Vanders, which proved to be twenty-one years. Beyond that point, Leaphorn's digging ran into granite.

"Who is Mrs. Vanders?" Leaphorn had asked.

"My boss."

Leaphorn had laughed. "That's not what I meant."

"I didn't think it was."

"You know anything about this job she's going to offer me?"

"No."

"What she wants?"

"It's none of my business."

So Leaphorn dropped it. He watched the scenery, learned that even the rich could find only country-western music on their radios here, tuned in KNDN to listen in on the Navajo open-mike program. Someone had lost his billfold at the Farmington bus station and was asking the finder to return his driver's license and credit card. A woman was inviting members of the Bitter Water and Standing Rock clans, and all other kinfolk and friends, to show up for a *yeibichai* sing to be held for Emerson Roanhorse at his place north of Kayenta. Then came an old-sounding voice declaring that Billy Etcitty's roan mare was missing from his place north of Burnt Water and asking folks to let him know if they spotted it. "Like maybe at a livestock auction," the voice added, which suggested that Etcitty presumed his mare hadn't wandered off without assistance. Soon Leaphorn had surrendered to the soft luxury of the limo seat and dozed. When he awoke, they were rolling down I-25 past Santa Fe's outskirts.

Leaphorn then had fished Millicent Vanders's letter from his jacket pocket and reread it.

It wasn't, of course, directly from Millicent Vanders. The letterhead read Peabody, Snell and Glick, followed by those initials law firms use. The address was Boston. Delivery was FedEx's Priority Overnight.

Dear Mr. Leaphorn:

This is to confirm and formalize our telephone conversation of this date. I write you in the interest of Mrs. Millicent Vanders, who is represented by this firm in some of her affairs. Mrs. Vanders has charged me with finding an investigator familiar with the Navajo Reservation whose reputation for integrity and circumspection is impeccable.

You have been recommended to us as satisfying these requirements. This inquiry is to determine if you would be willing to meet with Mrs. Vanders at her summer home in Santa Fe and explore her needs with her. If so, please call me so arrangements can be made for her car to pick you up and for your financial reimbursement. I must add that Mrs. Vanders expressed a sense of urgency in this affair.

Leaphorn's first inclination had been to write Christopher Peabody a polite "thanks but no thanks" and recommend he find his client a licensed private investigator instead of a former cop.

But...

There was the fact that Peabody, surely the senior partner, had signed the letter himself, and the business of having his circumspection rated impeccable, and—most important of all—the "sense of urgency" note, which made the woman's problem sound interesting. Leaphorn needed something interesting. He'd soon be finishing his first year of retirement from the Navajo Tribal Police. He'd long since run out of things to do. He was bored.

And so he'd called Mr. Peabody back and here he was, driver pushing the proper button, gate sliding silently open, rolling past lush landscaping toward a sprawling two-story house—its tan plaster and brick copings declaring it to be what Santa Feans call "Territorial Style" and its size declaring it a mansion.

The driver opened the door for Leaphorn. A young man wearing a faded blue shirt and jeans, his blond hair tied in a pigtail, stood smiling just inside the towering double doors.

"Mr. Leaphorn," he said. "Mrs. Vanders is expecting you."

Millicent Vanders was waiting in a room that Leaphorn's experience with movies and television suggested was either a study or a sitting room. She was a frail little woman standing beside a frail little desk, supporting herself with the tips of her fingers on its polished surface. Her hair was almost white and the smile with which she greeted him was pale.

"Mr. Leaphorn," she said. "How good of you to come. How good of you to help me."

Leaphorn, with no idea yet whether he would help her or not, simply returned the smile and sat in the chair to which she motioned.

"Would you care for tea? Or coffee? Or some other refreshment? And should I call you Mr. Leaphorn, or do you prefer 'Lieutenant'?"

"Coffee, thank you, if it's no trouble," Leaphorn said. "And it's mister. I've retired from the Navajo Tribal Police."

Millicent Vanders looked past him toward the door: "Coffee then, and tea," she said. She sat herself behind the desk with a slow, careful motion that told Leaphorn his hostess had one or other of the hundred forms of arthritis. But she smiled again, a signal meant to be reassuring. Leaphorn detected pain in it. He'd become very good at that sort of detection while he was watching his wife die. Emma, holding his hand, telling him not to worry, pretending she wasn't in pain, promising that someday soon she'd be well again.

Mrs. Vanders was sorting through papers on her desk, arranging them in a folder, untroubled by the lack of conversation. Leaphorn had found this unusual among whites and admired it when he saw it. She extracted two eight-by-ten photographs from an envelope, examined one, added it to the folder, then examined the other. A thump broke the silence—a careless piñon jay colliding with a windowpane. It fled in wobbling flight. Mrs. Vanders continued her contemplation of the photo, lost in some remembered sorrow, undisturbed by the bird or by Leaphorn watching her. An interesting person, Leaphorn thought.

A plump young woman appeared at his elbow bearing a tray. She placed a napkin, saucer, cup, and spoon on the table beside him, filled the cup from a white china pot, then repeated the process at the desk, pouring the tea from a silver container. Mrs. Vanders interrupted her contemplation of the photo, slid it into the folder, handed it to the woman.

"Ella," she said. "Would you give this, please, to Mr. Leaphorn?"

Ella handed it to Leaphorn and left as silently as she had come. He put the folder on his lap, sipped his coffee. The cup was translucent china, thin as paper. The coffee was hot, fresh, and excellent.

Mrs. Vanders was studying him. "Mr. Leaphorn," she said, "I asked you to come here because I hope you will agree to do something for me."

"I might agree," Leaphorn said. "What would it be?"

"Everything has to be completely confidential," Mrs. Vanders said. "You would communicate only to me. Not to my lawyers. Not to anyone else."

Leaphorn considered this, sampled the coffee again, put down the cup. "Then I might not be able to help you."

Mrs. Vanders looked surprised.

"Why not?"

"I've spent most of my life being a policeman," Leaphorn said. "If what you have in mind causes me to discover anything illegal, then—"

"If that happened, I would report it to the authorities," she said rather stiffly.

Leaphorn allowed the typical Navajo moments of silence to make certain that Mrs. Vanders had said all she wanted to say. She had, but his lack of response touched a nerve.

"Of course I would," she added. "Certainly."

"But if you didn't for some reason, you understand that I would have to do it. Would you agree to that?"

She stared at Leaphorn. Then she nodded. "I think we are creating a problem where none exists."

"Probably," Leaphorn said.

"I would like you to locate a young woman. Or, failing that, discover what happened to her."

She gestured toward the folder. Leaphorn opened it.

The top picture was a studio portrait of a dark-haired, dark-eyed woman wearing a mortarboard. The face was narrow and intelligent, the expression somber. Not a girl who would have been called "cute," Leaphorn thought. Nor pretty either, for that matter. Handsome, perhaps. Full of character. Certainly it would be an easy face to remember.

The next picture was of the same woman, wearing jeans and a jean jacket now, leaning on the door of a pickup truck and looking back at the camera. She had the look of an athlete, Leaphorn thought, and was older in this one. Perhaps in her early thirties. On the back of each photograph the same name was written: Catherine Anne.

Leaphorn glanced at Mrs. Vanders.

"My niece," she said. "The only child of my late sister."

Leaphorn returned the photos to the folder and took out a sheaf of papers, clipped together. The top one had biographical details.

Catherine Anne Pollard was the full name. The birthdate made her thirty-three, the birthplace was Arlington, Virginia, the current address Flagstaff, Arizona.

"Catherine studied biology," Mrs. Vanders said. "She specialized in mammals and insects. She was working for the Indian Health Service, but actually I think it's more for the Arizona Health Department. The environment division. They call her a 'vector control specialist.' I imagine you would know about that?"

Leaphorn nodded.

Mrs. Vanders made a wry face. "She says they actually call her a 'flea-catcher.'"

"I think she could have had a good career as a tennis player. On the tour, you know. She always loved sports. Soccer, striker on the college volleyball team. When she was in junior high school she worried about being bigger than the other girls. I think excelling in sports was her compensation for that." .

Leaphorn nodded again.

"The first time she came to see me after she got this job, I asked for her job title, and she said 'fleacatcher.'" Mrs. Vanders's expression was sad. "Called herself that, so I guess she doesn't mind."

"It's an important job," Leaphorn said.

"She wanted a career in biology. But 'fleacatcher'?" Mrs. Vanders shook her head. "I understand that she and some others were working on the source of those bubonic plague cases this spring. They have a little laboratory in Tuba City and check places where the victims might have picked up the disease. Trapping rodents." Mrs. Vanders hesitated, her face reflecting distaste. "That's the flea catching. They collect the fleas from them. And take samples of their blood. That sort of thing." She dismissed this with a wave of the hand.

"Then last week, early in the morning, she went to work and never came back."

She let that hang there, her eyes on Leaphorn.

"She left for work alone?"

"Alone. That's what they say. I'm not so sure."

Leaphorn would come back to that later. Now he needed basic facts. Speculation could wait.

"Went to work where?"

"The man I called said she just stopped by the office to pick up some of the equipment she uses in her work and then drove away. To someplace out in the country where she was trapping rodents."

"Was she meeting anyone where she was going to be working?"

"Apparently not. Not officially anyway. The man I talked to didn't think anyone went with her."

"And you think something has happened to her. Have you discussed this with the police?"

"Mr. Peabody discussed it with people he knows in the FBI. He said they would not be involved in something like this. They would have jurisdiction only if it involved a kidnapping for ransom, or"—she hesitated, glanced down at her hands—"or some other sort of felony. They told Mr. Peabody there would have to be evidence that a federal law had been violated."

"What evidence was there?" He was pretty sure he knew the answer. It would be none. Nothing at all.

Mrs. Vanders shook her head.

"Actually, I guess you would say the only evidence is that a woman is missing. Just the circumstances."

"The vehicle. Where was it found?"

"It hasn't been found. Not as far as I have been able to discover." Mrs. Vanders's eyes were intent on Leaphorn, watching for his reaction.

Had they not been, Leaphorn would have allowed himself a smile—thinking of the hopeless task Mr. Peabody must have faced in trying to interest the federals. Thinking of the paperwork this missing vehicle would cause in the Arizona Health Department, of how this would be interpreted by the Arizona Highway Patrol if a missing person report had been filed, of the other complexities. But Mrs. Vanders would read a smile as an expression of cynicism.

"Do you have a theory?"

"Yes," she said, and cleared her throat. "I think she must be dead."

Mrs. Vanders, who had seemed frail and unhealthy, now looked downright sick.

"Are you all right? Do you want to continue this?"

She produced a weak smile, extracted a small white container from the pocket of her jacket and held it up.

"I have a heart condition," she said. "This is nitroglycerin. The prescription used to come in little tablets, but these days the patient just sprays it on the tongue. Please excuse me. I'll feel fine again in a moment."

She turned away from him, held the tube to her lips for a moment, then returned it to her pocket.

Leaphorn waited, reviewing what little he knew about nitro as a heart medication. It served to expand the arteries and thus increase the blood flow. Neither of the people he'd known who used it had lived very long. Perhaps that explained the urgency Peabody mentioned in his letter.

Mrs. Vanders sighed. "Where were we?"

"You'd said you thought your niece must be dead."

"Murdered, I think."

"Did someone have a motive? Or did she have something that would attract a thief?"

"She was being stalked," Mrs. Vanders said. "A man named Victor Hammar. A graduate student she'd met at the University of New Mexico. A fairly typical case, I'd guess, for this sort of thing. He was from East Germany, what used to be East Germany that is, with no family or friends over here. A very lonely man, I would imagine. And that's the way Catherine described him to me. They had common interests at the university. Both biologists. He was studying small mammals. That caused them to do a lot of work in the laboratory together. I suppose Catherine took pity on him."

Mrs. Vanders shook her head. "Losers always had a special appeal to her. When her mother was going to buy her a dog, she wanted one from the pound. Something she could feel sorry for. But with that man . . ." She grimaced. "Well, anyway, she couldn't get rid of him. I suspected she dropped out of graduate school to get away from him. Then, after she took the job in Arizona, he would turn up at Phoenix when she was there. It was the same thing when she started working at Flagstaff."

"Had he threatened her?"

"I asked her that and she just laughed. She thought he was perfectly harmless. She told me to think of him as being like a little lost kitten. Just a nuisance."

"But you think he was a threat?"

"I think he was a very dangerous man. Under the right circumstances anyway. When he came here with her once, he seemed polite enough. But there was a sort of—" She paused, looking for the way to express it. "I think a lot of anger was right under that nicey-nicey surface ready to explode."

Leaphorn waited for more explanation. Mrs. Vanders merely looked worried.

"I told Catherine that even with kittens, if you hurt one it will scratch you," she said.

"That's true," Leaphorn said. "If I decide I can be of any help on this, I'll need his name and address." He thought about it. "And I think finding that vehicle she was driving is important. I think you should offer a reward. Something substantial enough to attract attention. To get people talking about it."

"Of course," Mrs. Vanders said. "Offer whatever you like."

"I'll need all the pertinent biographical information about her. People who might know her or something about her habits. Names, addresses, that sort of thing."

"All I have is in the folder you have there," she said. "There's a report about what a lawyer from Mr. Peabody's office found out, and a report from a lawyer he hired in Flagstaff to collect what information he could. It wasn't much. I'm afraid it won't be very helpful."

"When was the last time she saw this Hammar?"

"That's one reason I suspect him," Mrs. Vanders said. "It was just before she disappeared. He'd come out to Tuba City where she was working. She'd called to tell me she was coming to see me that weekend. That Hammar man was there at Tuba City when she called."

"Did she say anything that made you think she was afraid of him?"

"No." Mrs. Vanders laughed. "I don't think Catherine's ever been afraid of anything. She inherited her mother's genes."

Leaphorn frowned. "She said she was coming to see you but she disappeared instead," he said. "Did she say why she was coming? Just social, or did she have something on her mind?"

"She was thinking of quitting. She couldn't stand her boss. A man named Krause." Mrs. Vanders pointed at the folder. "Very arrogant. And she disapproved of the way he ran the operation."

"Something illegal?"

"I don't know. She said she didn't want to talk about it on the telephone. But it must have been pretty serious to make her think about leaving."

"Something personal, you think? Did she ever suggest sexual harassment? Anything like that?"

"She didn't exactly suggest that," Mrs. Vanders said. "But he was a bachelor. Whatever he was doing it was bad enough to be driving her away from a job she loved."

Leaphorn questioned that by raising his eyebrows.

"She was excited by that job. She's been working for months to find the rodents that caused that last outbreak of bubonic plague on your reservation. Catherine has always been obsessive, even as a child. And since she took this health department job her obsession has been the plague. She spent one entire visit telling me about it. About how it killed half the people in Europe in the Middle Ages. How it spreads. How they're beginning to think the bacteria are evolving. All that sort of thing. She's on a personal crusade about it. Almost religious, I'd say. And she thought she might have found some of the rodents it spreads from. She'd told this Hammar fellow about it and I guess he used that as an excuse to come out."

Mrs. Vanders made a deprecating gesture. "Being a student of mice and rats and other rodents, that gives him an excuse, I guess. She said he might go out there with her to help her with the rodents. Apparently he wasn't with her when she left Tuba City, but I thought he might have followed her. I guess they trap them or poison them or something. And she said it was a hard-to-get-to place, so maybe she would want him to help her carry in whatever they use. It's out on the edge of the Hopi Reservation. A place called Yells Back Butte."

"Yells Back Butte," Leaphorn said.

"It seems a strange name," Mrs. Vanders said. "I suspect there's some story behind it."

"Probably," Leaphorn said. "I think it's a local name for a little finger sticking out from Black Mesa. On the edge of the Hopi Reservation. And when was she going out there?"

"The day after she called me," Mrs. Vanders said. "That would be a week ago next Friday."

Leaphorn nodded, sorting out some memories. That would be July 8, just about the day—No. It was exactly the day when Officer Benjamin Kinsman had his skull cracked with a rock somewhere very near Yells Back Butte. Same time. Same place. Leaphorn had never learned to believe in coincidences.

"All right, Mrs. Vanders," Leaphorn said, "I'll see what I can find out."

4

CHEE WAS NOT standing at the waiting room window just to watch the Northern Arizona Medical Center parking lot and the cloud shadows dappling the mountains across the valley. He was postponing the painful moment when he would walk into Officer Benjamin Kinsman's room and give Benny the foredoomed official "last opportunity" to tell them who had murdered him.

Actually, it wasn't murder yet. The neurologist in charge had called Shiprock yesterday to report that Kinsman had become brain-dead and procedures could now begin to end his ordeal. But this was going to be a legally complicated and socially sensitive process. The U.S. Attorney's office was nervous. Converting the charge against Jano from attempted homicide to murder had to be done exactly right. Therefore, J. D. Mickey, the acting assistant U.S. attorney charged with handling the prosecution, had decided that the arresting officer must be present when the plug was pulled. He wanted Chee to testify that he was available to receive any possible last words. That meant that the defense attorney should be there, too.

Chee had no idea why. Everybody involved had the same boss. As an indigent, Jano would be represented by another Justice Department lawyer. Said lawyer being—Chee glanced at his watch—eleven minutes late. But maybe that was his vehicle pulling into the lot. No. It was a pickup truck. Even in Arizona, Justice Department lawyers didn't arrive in trucks.

In fact, it was a familiar truck. Dodge Ram king cab pickups of the early nineties looked a lot alike, but this one had a winch attached to the front bumper and fender damage covered with paint that didn't quite match. It was Joe Leaphorn's truck.

Chee sighed. Fate seemed to be tying him to his former boss again, endlessly renewing the sense of inferiority Chee felt in the presence of the Legendary Lieutenant.

But he felt a little better after he thought about it. There was no way the murder of Officer Kinsman could involve Leaphorn. The Legendary Lieutenant had been retired since last year. As a rookie, Kinsman had never worked for him. There were no clan relationships that Chee knew about. Leaphorn must be coming to visit some sick friend. This would be one of those coincidences that Leaphorn had told him, about a hundred times, not to believe in. Chee relaxed. He watched a white Chevy sedan, driving too fast, skid through the parking lot gate. A federal motor-pool Chevy. The defense lawyer finally. Now the plugs could be pulled, stopping the machines that had kept Kinsman's lungs pumping and his heart beating for all these days, since the wind of life that had blown through Benny had left, taking Benny's consciousness on its last great adventure.

Now the lawyers would agree, in view of the seriousness of the case, to ignore the objections the Kinsman family might have and conduct a useless autopsy. That would prove that the blow to the head had caused Benny's death and therefore the People of the United States could apply the death penalty and kill Robert Jano to even the score. The fact that neither the Navajos nor the Hopis believed in this eye-for-an-eye philosophy of the white men would be ignored.

Two floors below him the white Chevy had parked. The driver's-side door opened, a pair of black trouser legs emerged, then a hand holding a briefcase.

"Lieutenant Chee," said a familiar voice just behind him. "Could I talk to you for a minute?"

Joe Leaphorn was standing in the doorway, holding his battered gray Stetson in his hands and looking apologetic.

So much for coincidences.

5

SOMEPLACE QUIETER, MAYBE," Leaphorn had said, meaning a place where no one would overhear him. So Chee led him down the hall to the empty orthopedic waiting room. He pulled back a chair by the table and motioned toward another one.

"I know you just have a minute," Leaphorn said, and sat down. "The defense attorney just drove up."

"Yeah," Chee said, thinking that Leaphorn not only had managed to find him in this unlikely place but knew why he was here and what was going on. Probably knew more than Chee did. That irritated Chee, but it didn't surprise him.

"I wanted to ask if the name Catherine Anne Pollard meant anything to you. If a missing persons report was filed on her. Or a stolen vehicle report? Anything like that?"

"Pollard?" Chee said. "I don't think so. It doesn't ring a bell." Thank God Leaphorn wasn't involving himself in the Kinsman business. It was already complicated enough.

"Woman, early thirties, working with the Indian Health Service," Leaphorn said. "In vector control. Looking for the source of that bubonic plague outbreak. Checking rodents. You know how they work."

"Oh, yeah," Chee said. "I heard about it. When I get back to Tuba I'll check our reports. I think somebody in environmental health or the Indian

Health Service called Window Rock about her not coming back from a job and they passed it along to us." He shrugged. "I got the impression they were more worried about losing the department's Jeep."

Leaphorn grinned at him. "Not exactly the crime of the century."

"No," Chee said. "If she was about thirteen you'd be checking the motels. At her age, if she wants to run off somewhere, that's her business. As long as she brings back the Jeep."

"She didn't, then? It's still missing?"

"I don't know," Chee said. "If she returned it, APH forgot to tell us."

"That wouldn't be unusual," Leaphorn said.

Chee nodded, and looked at Leaphorn. Wanting an explanation for his interest in something that seemed both obvious and trivial.

"Somebody in her family thinks she's dead. Thinks somebody killed her." Leaphorn let that hang a moment, made an apologetic face. "I know that's what kinfolks usually think. But this time there's a suspicion that a would-be boyfriend was stalking her."

"That's not unusual either," Chee said. He felt vaguely disappointed. Leaphorn had done some private detecting right after he'd retired, but that had been to tie up a loose end from his career, close out an old case. This sounded purely commercial. Was the Legendary Lieutenant Leaphorn reduced to doing routine private detective stuff?

Leaphorn took a notebook out of his shirt pocket, looked at it, tapped it against the tabletop. It occurred to Chee that this was embarrassing Leaphorn, and that embarrassed Chee. The Legendary Lieutenant, totally unflappable when he'd been in charge, didn't know how to handle being a civilian. Asking favors. Chee didn't know how to handle it either. He noticed that Leaphorn's burr-cut hair, long black-salted-with-gray, had become gray-salted-with-black.

"Anything I can do?" Chee asked.

Leaphorn put the notebook back in his pocket.

"You know how I am about coincidences," he said.

"Yep," Chee said.

"Well, this one is so strained I hate to even mention it." He shook his head.

Chee waited.

"From what I know now, the last time anyone heard of this woman, she was heading out of Tuba City checking on prairie dog colonies, looking for dead rodents. One of the places on her list was that area around Yells Back Butte."

Chee thought about that a moment, took a deep breath, thinking he'd been too optimistic. But "that area around Yells Back Butte" didn't make it much of a coincidence with his Kinsman case. That "around" could include a huge bunch of territory. He waited to see if Leaphorn was finished. He wasn't.

"That was the morning of July eighth," Leaphorn said.

"July eighth," Chee said, frowning. "I was out there that morning."

"I was thinking that you were," Leaphorn said. "Look, I'm headed to Window Rock now and all I know now is from some preliminary checking a lawyer did for Pollard's aunt. I couldn't reach Pollard's boss on the telephone and soon as I do, I'll go to Tuba and talk to him. If I learn anything useful, I'll let you know."

"I'd appreciate that," Chee said. "I'd like to know some more about this."

"Probably absolutely no connection with the Kinsman case," Leaphorn said. "I don't see how there could be. Unless you know some reason to feel otherwise. I just thought—"

A loud voice from the doorway interrupted him.

"Chee!" The speaker was a beefy young man with reddish-blond hair and a complexion that suffered from too many hours of dry air and high-altitude sun. The coat of his dark blue suit was unbuttoned, his necktie was slightly loose, his white shirt was rumpled and his expression was irritated. "Mickey wants to get this damned thing over with," he said. "He wants you in there."

He was pointing at Chee, a violation of the *Dine'* rules of courtesy. Now he beckoned to Chee with his finger—rude in a multitude of other cultures.

Chee rose, his face darkened a shade.

"Mr. Leaphorn," Chee said, motioning toward the man, "this gentleman is Agent Edgar Evans of the Federal Bureau of Investigation. He was assigned out here just a couple of months ago."

Leaphorn acknowledged that with a nod toward Evans.

"Chee," Agent Evans said, "Mickey is in a hell of a—"

"Tell Mr. Mickey I'll be there in a minute or so," Chee said. And to Leaphorn: "I'll call you from the office when I know what we have."

Leaphorn smiled at Evans and turned back to Chee.

"I am particularly interested in that Jeep," Leaphorn said. "People don't just walk away from good trucks. It's odd. Someone sees it, mentions it to someone else, the word gets around."

Chee chuckled. (More, Leaphorn suspected, for Evan's benefit than his own.) "It does," Chee said. "And pretty soon people begin deciding no one wants it anymore, and parts of it begin showing up on other people's trucks."

"I'd like to spread the word that there's a reward for locating that Jeep," Leaphorn said.

Evans cleared his throat loudly.

"How much?" Chee asked.

"How does a thousand dollars sound?"

"About right," Chee said, turning toward the door. He motioned to Agent Evans. "Come on," he said. "Let's go."

Officer Benjamin Kinsman's room was lit by the sun pouring through its two windows and a battery of ceiling fluorescent lights. Entering involved slipping past a burly male nurse and two young women in the sort of pale blue smocks doctors wear. Acting Assistant U.S. Attorney J. D. Mickey stood by the windows. The shape of Officer Kinsman lay at rigid attention in the center of the bed, covered with a sheet. One of the vital signs monitors on the wall above the bed registered a horizontal white line. The other screen was blank.

Mickey looked at his watch, then at Chee, glanced at the doors and nodded.

"You're the arresting officer?"

"That's correct," Chee said.

"What I want you to do is ask the victim here if he can tell you anything about who killed him. What happened. All that. We just want to get it on the record in case the defense tries something fancy."

Chee licked his lips, cleared his throat, looked at the body.

"Ben," he said. "Can you tell me who killed you? Can you hear me? Can you tell me anything?"

"Pull the sheet down," Mickey said. "Off of his face."

Chee shook his head. "Ben," he said. "I'm sorry I didn't get there quicker. Be happy on your journey."

Agent Evans was pulling at the sheet, drawing it down to reveal Benjamin Kinsman's waxen face.

Chee gripped his wrist. Hard. "No," he said. "Don't do that." He pulled the sheet back in place.

"Let it go," Mickey said, looking at his watch again. "I guess we're done here." He turned toward the door.

Standing there, looking in at Chee, at all of them, was Janet Pete.

"Better late than never," Mickey said. "I hope you got here early enough to know all your client's legal rights were satisfied."

Janet Pete, looking very pale, nodded. She stood aside to let them pass.

Behind Chee the medical crew was working fast, disconnecting wires and tubes—starting the bed rolling toward the side exit. There, Chee guessed, Officer Benjamin Kinsman's kidneys would be salvaged, perhaps his heart, perhaps whatever else some other person could use. But Ben was far, far away now. Only his *chindi* would remain here. Or would it follow the corpse into other rooms? Into other bodies? Navajo theology did not cover such contingencies. Corpses were dangerous, excepting only those of infants who die before their first laugh, and people who die naturally of old age. The good of Benjamin Kinsman would go with his spirit. The part of the personality that was out of harmony would linger as a *chindi*, causing sickness. Chee turned away from the body.

Janet was still standing at the door.

He stopped.

"Hello, Jim."

"Hello, Janet." He took a deep breath. "It's good to see you."

"Even like this?" She made a weak gesture at the room and tried to smile.

He didn't answer that. He felt dizzy, sick, and depleted.

"I tried to call you, but you're never home. I'm Robert Jano's counsel," she said. "I guess you knew that?"

"I didn't know it," Chee said. "Not until I heard what Mr. Mickey said."

"You're the arresting officer, as I heard? Is that right? So I need to talk to you."

"Fine," Chee said. "But I can't do it now. And not here. Somewhere away from here." He swallowed down the bile. "How about dinner?"

"I can't tonight. Mr. Mickey has us all conferring about the case. And, Jim, you look exhausted. I think you must be working too hard."

"I'm not," he said. "And you look great. Will you be here tomorrow?"

"I have to drive down to Phoenix."

"How about breakfast then? At the hotel."

"Good," she said, and they set the time.

Mickey was standing down the hallway. "Ms. Pete," he called.

"Got to go," she said, and turned, then turned back again. "Jim," she said, "tired or not, you look fine."

"You, too," Chee said. She did. The classic, perfect beauty you see on the cover of *Vogue*, or on any of the fashion magazines.

Chee leaned against the wall and watched her walk down the hall, around the corner and out of sight, wishing he had thought of something more romantic to say than "You, too." Wishing he knew what to do about her. About them. Wishing he knew whether he could trust her. Wishing life wasn't so damned complicated.

6

IT SEEMED OBVIOUS to Leaphorn that the person most likely to tell him something useful about Catherine Anne Pollard was Richard Krause, her boss and the biologist in charge of rooting out the cause of the reservation's most recent plague outbreak. A lifetime spent looking for people in the big emptiness of the Four Corners and several futile telephone calls had taught Leaphorn that Krause would probably be off somewhere unreachable. He had tried to call him as soon as he returned to Window Rock from Santa Fe. He'd tried again yesterday before driving back from Flagstaff. By now he had the number memorized as well as on the redial button. He picked up the telephone and punched it.

"Public Health," a male voice said. "Krause."

Leaphorn identified himself. "Mrs. Vanders has asked me—"

"I know," Krause said. "She called me. Maybe she's right. To start getting worried, I mean."

"Miss Pollard's not back yet, then?"

"No," Krause said. "Miss Pollard still hasn't shown up for work. Nor has she bothered to call in or communicate in any way. But I have to tell you that's what you learn to expect from Miss Pollard. Rules were made for other people."

"Any word on the vehicle she was driving?"

"Not to me," Krause said. "And to tell the truth, I'm getting a little bit concerned myself. At first I was just sore at her. Cathy is a tough gal to work with. She's very into doing her own thing her own way, if you know what I'm saying. I just thought she'd seen something that needed doing worse than what I'd told her to do. Sort of reassigned herself, you know."

"I know," Leaphorn said, thinking back to when Jim Chee had been his assistant. Still, as much trouble as Chee had been, it had been a pleasure to see him yesterday. He was a good man and unusually bright.

"You still think that might be a possibility? That Pollard might be off working on some project of her own and just not bothering to tell anyone about it?"

"Maybe," Krause said. "It wouldn't bother her to let me stew awhile, but not this long." He'd be happy to tell Leaphorn what he knew about Pollard and her work, but not today. Today he was tied up, absolutely snowed under. With Pollard away, he was doing both their jobs. But to-morrow morning he could make some time—and the earlier the better.

Which left Leaphorn with nothing to do but wait for Chee's promised call. But Chee would be driving back to Tuba City from Flag this morning, and then he wouldn't get into his files until he dealt with whatever prob-lems had piled up in his absence. If Chee found something interesting in the files, he'd probably call after noon. Most likely there'd be no reason to call.

Leaphorn had never been good at waiting for the telephone to ring, or for anything else. He toasted two slices of bread, applied margarine and grape jelly, and sat in his kitchen, eating and staring at the Indian Country map mounted on the wall above the table.

The map was freckled with the heads of pins—red, white, blue, black, yellow, and green, plus a variety of shapes he'd reverted to when the colors available in pinheads had been exhausted. It had been accumulating pins on his office wall since early in his career. When he retired, the fellow who took over his office suggested he might want to keep it, and he'd said he couldn't imagine why. But keep it he had, and almost every pin in it re-vived a memory.

The first ones (plain steel-headed seamstress pins) he'd stuck in to keep track of places and dates where people had reported seeing a missing aircraft, the problem that then had been occupying his thoughts. The red ones had been next, establishing the delivery pattern of a gasoline tanker truck that was also hauling narcotics to customers on the Checkerboard Reservation. The most common ones were black, representing witchcraft reports. Personally, Leaphorn had lost all faith in the existence of these skinwalkers in his freshman year at Arizona State, but never in the reality of the problem that belief in them causes.

He'd come home for the semester break, full of new-won college sophistication and cynicism. He'd talked Jack Greyeyes into joining him to check out a reputed home base of skinwalkers and thus prove themselves liberated from tradition. They drove south from Shiprock past Rol-Hay Rock and Table Mesa to the volcanic outcrop of ugly black basalt where, according to the whispers in their age group, skinwalkers met in an underground room to perform the hideous initiation that turned recruits into witches. It was a rainy winter night, which cut the risk that someone would see them and accuse them of being witches themselves. Now, more than four decades later, winter rains still produced memorial shivers along Leaphorn's spine.

That night remained one of Leaphorn's most vivid memories. The darkness, the cold rain soaking through his jacket, the beginnings of fear. Greyeyes had decided when they'd reached the outcrop's base that this was a crazy idea.

"I'll tell you what," Greyeyes had said. "Let's not do it, and say we did."

So Leaphorn had taken custody of the flashlight, watched Greyeyes fade into the darkness, and waited for his courage to return. It didn't. He had stood there looking up at the great jumbled hump of rock. Suddenly he had been confronted with both nerve-racking fear and the sure knowledge that what he did now would determine the kind of man he would be. He'd torn his pant leg and bruised his knee on the way up. He'd found the gaping hole the whispers had described, shone his flash into it without locating a bottom, and then climbed down far enough to see where it led. The rumors had described a carpeted room littered with the fragments of corpses. He had found a drifted collection of blown sand and last summer's tumbleweeds.

That had confirmed his skepticism about skinwalker mythology, just as his career in the Navajo Tribal Police had confirmed his belief in what the evil skinwalkers symbolized. He'd lost any lingering doubts about that in his

rookie year. He had laughed off a warning that a Navajo oil-field pumper believed two neighbors had witched his daughter, thus causing her fatal illness.

As soon as the four-day mourning period tradition decrees had ended,
the pumper had killed the witches with his shotgun.

He thought about that now as he chewed his toast. Eight black pins
formed a cluster in the general vicinity of that north-reaching outcrop of
Black Mesa that included Yells Back Butte. Why so many there? Probably
because that area had twice been the source of bubonic plague cases and
once of the deadly hantavirus. Witches offer an easy explanation for unex-
plained illnesses. To the north, Short Mountain and the Short Mountain
Wash country had attracted another cluster of black pins. Leaphorn was
pretty sure that was due to John McGinnis, operator of the Short Mountain Trading Post. Not that the pins meant more witch problems around
Short Mountain. They represented McGinnis's remarkable talent as a col-
lector and broadcaster of gossip. The old man had a special love for skinwalker tales, and his Navajo customers, knowing his weakness, brought him
all the skinwalker sightings and witching reports they could collect. But any
sort of gossip was good enough for the old man. Thinking that, Leaphorn
reached for his new edition of the Navajo Communications Company telephone directory.

The Short Mountain Trading Post number was no longer listed. He
dialed the Short Mountain Chapter House. Was the trading post still operating? The woman who had picked up the telephone chuckled. "Well,"
she said, "I'd guess you'd say more or less."

"Is John McGinnis still there? Still alive?"

The chuckle became a laugh. "Oh, yes indeed," she said. "He's still going strong. Don't the *bilagaana* have a saying that only the good die
young?"

Joe Leaphorn finished his toast, put a message on his answering machine for Chee in case he did call, and drove his pickup out of Shiprock
heading northwest across the Navajo Nation. He was feeling much more
cheerful.

The years that had passed since he'd visited Short Mountain hadn't
changed it much—certainly not for the better. The parking area in front
was still hard-packed clay, too dry and dense to encourage weeds. The old
GMC truck he'd parked next to years ago still rested wheelless on blocks,

slowly rusting away. The 1968 Chevy pickup parked in the shade of a juniper at the corner of the sheep pens looked like the one McGinnis had always driven, and a faded sign nailed to the hay barn still proclaimed THIS STORE FOR SALE, INQUIRE WITHIN. But today the benches on the shady porch were empty, with drifts of trash under them. The windows looked even dustier than Leaphorn remembered. In fact, the trading post looked deserted, and the gusty breeze chasing tumbleweeds and dust past the porch added to the sense of desolation. Leaphorn had an uneasy feeling, tinged with sadness, that the woman at the chapter house was wrong. That even tough old John McGinnis had proved vulnerable to too much time and too many disappointments.

The breeze was the product of a cloud Leaphorn had been watching build up over Black Mesa for the last twenty miles. It was too early in the summer to make a serious rain likely but—as bad as the road back to the highway was—even a shower could present a problem down in Short Mountain Wash. Leaphorn climbed out of his pickup to the rumble of thunder and hurried toward the store.

John McGinnis appeared in the doorway, holding the screen door open, staring out at him with his shock of white hair blowing across his forehead and looking twenty pounds too thin for the overalls that engulfed him.

"Be damned," McGinnis said. "Guess it's true what I heard about them finally getting you off the police force. Thought I had me a customer for a while. Didn't they let you keep the uniform?"

"Ya'eeh te'h," Leaphorn said. "It's good to see you." And he meant it. That surprised him a little. Maybe, like McGinnis, the loneliness was beginning to get to him.

"Well, damnit, come on in so I can get this door closed and keep the dirt from blowing in," McGinnis said. "And let me get you something to wet your whistle. You Navajos act like you're born in a barn."

Leaphorn followed the old man through the musty darkness of the store, noticing that McGinnis was more stooped than he had remembered him, that he walked with a limp, that many of the shelves lining the walls were half-empty, that behind the dusty glass where McGinnis kept pawned jewelry very little was being offered, that the racks that once had displayed an array of the slightly gaudy rugs and saddle blankets that the

Short Mountain weavers produced were now empty. Which will die first, Leaphorn wondered, the trading post or the trader?

McGinnis ushered him into the back room—his living room, bedroom and kitchen—and waved him into a recliner upholstered with worn red velour. He transferred ice cubes from his refrigerator into a Coca-Cola glass, filled it from a two-liter Pepsi bottle, and handed it to Leaphorn. Then he collected a bourbon bottle and a plastic measuring cup from his kitchen table, seated himself on a rocking chair across from Leaphorn, and began carefully pouring himself a drink.

"As I remember it," he said while he dribbled in the bourbon, "you don't drink hard liquor. If I'm wrong about that, you tell me and I'll get you something better than soda pop."

"This is fine," Leaphorn said.

McGinnis held the measuring cup up, examined it against the light from the dusty window, shook his head, and poured a few drops carefully back into the bottle. He inspected the level again, seemed satisfied, and took a sip.

"You want to do a little visiting first?" McGinnis asked. "Or do you want to get right down to what you came here for?"

"Either way," Leaphorn said. "I'm in no hurry. I'm retired now. Just a civilian. But you know that."

"I heard it," McGinnis said. "I'd retire myself if I could find somebody stupid enough to buy this hellhole."

"Is it keeping you pretty busy?" Leaphorn asked, trying to imagine anyone offering to buy the place. Even tougher trying to imagine McGinnis selling it if someone did. Where would the old man go? What would he do when he got there?

McGinnis ignored the question. "Well," he said, "if you came by to get some gasoline, you're out of luck. The dealers charge me extra for hauling it way out here and I have to tack a little bit on to the price to pay for that. Just offered gasoline anyway to convenience these hard cases that still live around here. But they took to getting their tanks filled up when they get to Tuba or Page, so the gas I got hauled out to make it handy for 'em just sat there and evaporated. So to hell with 'em. I don't fool with it anymore."

McGinnis had rattled that off in his scratchy whiskey voice—an explanation he'd given often enough to have it memorized. He looked at Leaphorn, seeking understanding.

"Can't say I blame you," Leaphorn said.

"Well, you oughtn't to. When the bastards would forget and let the gauge get down to empty, they'd come in, air up their tires, fill the radiator with my water, wash their windshield with my rags, and buy two gallons. Just enough to get 'em into one of them discount stations."

Leaphorn shook his head, expressing disapproval.

"And want credit for the gas," McGinnis said, and took another long, thirsty sip.

"But I noticed driving in that you still have a tank up on your loading rack. With a hand pump on it. You keep that just for your own pickup?"

McGinnis rocked a little while, considering the question. And probably wondering, Leaphorn thought, if Leaphorn had noticed that the old man's pickup was double-tanked, like most empty-country vehicles, and wouldn't need many refills.

"Well, hell," McGinnis said. "You know how folks are. Come in here with a dry tank and seventy miles to a station, you got to have something for 'em."

"I guess so," Leaphorn said.

"If you haven't got any gas to give 'em, then they just hang around and waste your time gossiping. Then they want to use your telephone to get some kinfolks to come and bring 'em a can."

He glowered at Leaphorn, took another sip of bourbon. "You ever know a Navajo to be in a hurry? You got 'em underfoot for hours. Drinking up your water and running you out of ice cubes."

McGinnis's face was slightly pink—embarrassment caused by his admission of humanity. "So finally I just quit paying the bills and the telephone company cut me off. I figured keeping a little gasoline was cheaper."

"Probably," Leaphorn said.

McGinnis was glowering at him again, making sure that Leaphorn wouldn't suspect some socially responsible purpose in this decision.

"What'd you come out here for anyway? You just got a lot of time to waste now you're not a cop?"

"I wondered if you ever had any customers named Tijinney?"

"Tijinney?" McGinnis looked thoughtful.

"They had a place over in what used to be the Joint Use Reservation.

Over by the northwest corner of Black Mesa. Right on the Navajo–Hopi border."

"I didn't know there was any of that outfit left," McGinnis said. "Sickly bunch, as I remember it. Somebody always coming in here for me to take 'em to the doctor over at Tuba or the clinic at Many Farms. And they did a lot of business with old Margaret Cigaret and some of the other shamans, getting curing ceremonials done. They was always coming in here trying to get me to donate a sheep to help feed folks at the sings."

"You remember that map I used to keep?" Leaphorn asked. "Where I'd record things I needed to remember? I looked at it this morning and I noticed I'd marked down a lot of skinwalker gossip over there where they lived. You think all that sickness would account for that?"

"Sure," McGinnis said. "But I got a feeling I know what this is leading up to. That Kinsman boy the Hopi killed, wasn't that over there on the old Tijinney grazing lease?"

"I think so," Leaphorn said.

McGinnis was holding his measuring cup up to the light, squinting at the level. He poured in another ounce or two of bourbon. "Just 'think so'?" he said. "I heard the federals had that business all locked up. Didn't that young cop that used to work with you catch the man right when he did it? Caught him right in the act, the way I heard it."

"You mean Jim Chee? Yeah, he caught a Hopi named Jano."

"So what are you working on out here?" McGinnis asked. "I know you ain't just visiting. Aren't you supposed to be retired? What're you up to? Working the other side?"

Leaphorn shrugged. "I'm just trying to understand some things."

"Well, now, is that a fact?" McGinnis said. "I was guessing you were trying to find some way to prove that Hopi boy didn't do the killing."

"Why would you think that?"

"Cowboy Dashee was in here just the other day. You remember Cowboy? Deputy with the sheriff's office?"

"Sure."

"Well, Cowboy says the Jano boy didn't do it. He says Chee got the wrong fella."

Leaphorn shrugged, thinking that Jano was probably kinfolks with

Dashee, or a member of his kiva. The Hopis lived in a much smaller world than the Navajos. "Did Cowboy tell you who was the right fella?"

McGinnis had stopped rocking. He was staring at Leaphorn, looking puzzled.

"I was guessing wrong, wasn't I? Are you going to tell me what you're up to?"

"I am seeing if I can find out what happened to a young woman who worked for the Indian Health Service. She was checking on plague cases. Drove out of Tuba City more than a week ago and she still hasn't come back."

McGinnis had been rocking, holding his measuring cup in his left hand, left elbow on the rocker's arm, his forearm moving just enough to compensate for the motion—keeping the bourbon from splashing, keeping the surface level. But he wasn't watching his drink. He was staring out the dusty window. Not out of it, Leaphorn realized. McGinnis was watching a medium-sized spider working on a web between the window frame and a high shelf. He stopped rocking, pushed himself creakily out of the chair. "Look at that," he said. "The sonsabitches are slow learners."

He walked to the window, crumpled a handkerchief from his overalls pocket, chased the spider across the web with it, folded the cloth carefully around the insect, opened the window screen, and shook it out into the yard. Obviously the old man had a lot of practice capturing such insects. Leaphorn remembered once seeing McGinnis capture a wasp the same way, evicting it unharmed through the same window.

McGinnis retrieved his drink and lowered himself, groaning, back into his chair.

"Sonofabitch will be right back first time he sees the door open," he said.

"I've known people to just step on them," Leaphorn said, but he remembered his mother dealing with spiders in the same way.

"I used to do that," McGinnis said. "Even had some bug spray. But you get older, and you look at 'em up close and you get to thinking about it. You get to thinking they got a right to live, too. They don't kill me. I don't kill them. You step on a beetle, it's like a little murder."

"How about eating sheep?" Leaphorn asked.

McGinnis was rocking again, ignoring him. "Very small murders, I guess you'd have to say. But one thing leads to another."

Leaphorn sipped his Pepsi.

"Sheep? I quit eating meat awhile back," McGinnis said. "But you didn't drive all the way in here to talk about my diet. You want to talk about that Health Department girl that run off with their truck."

"You hear anything about that?" Leaphorn asked.

"Woman named Cathy something or other, wasn't it?" McGinnis said. "The Fleacatcher, the folks out here call her, because she collects the damned things. She was in here a time or two, asking questions. Wanted to get some gas once. Bought some soda pop, some crackers. Can of Spam, too. And it wasn't a truck, either, now I think of it. It was a Jeep. A black one."

"About that black Jeep. The family's offering a thousand-dollar reward to anybody who finds it."

McGinnis took another sip, savored it, stared out the window.

"That don't sound like they think she eloped."

"They don't," Leaphorn said. "They think somebody killed her. What sort of questions was she asking when she was in here?"

"About sick folks. Where they might have got the fleas on 'em to get the plague. Did they have sheepdogs? Anybody notice prairie dogs dying? Or dead squirrels? Dead kangaroo rats?" McGinnis shrugged. "Strictly business, she was. Seemed like a mighty tough lady. No time for kidding around. Hard as nails. And I noticed when she was walking around, she was looking at the floor all the time. Looking for rat droppings. And that pissed me off some. And I said, 'Missy, what are you looking for back there behind the counter? You lose something?' And she said, 'I'm looking for mice manure.'" McGinnis produced a rusty laugh and slapped the arm of his rocker. "Came right out with it without a blink and kept right on looking. Quite a lady she is."

"You heard anything about what might have happened to her?"

McGinnis laughed, took another sip of his bourbon. "Sure," he said. "It gives folks something to talk about. Heard all kinds of things. Heard she might have run off with Krause—that fellow she works with." McGinnis chuckled. "That'd be like Golda Meir running off with Yasser Arafat. Heard she might have run off with another young man who was out here with her a time or two. Some sort of student scientist, I think he was. He seemed kind of strange to me."

"Sounds like you don't think she and her boss got along."

"They was in here just twice that I remember," McGinnis said. "First time they never said a word to each other. I guess that's all right if you're stuck in the same truck all day. Second time it was snarling and snapping. Hostile-like."

"I'd heard she didn't like him," Leaphorn said.

"It was mutual. He was paying for some stuff he got, and she walked past him out the door and he said 'Bitch.' "

"Loud enough for her to hear him?"

"If she was listening."

"You think he might have knocked her on the head and dumped her somewhere?"

"I figure him for being hell on rodents and fleas, things like that. Not humans," McGinnis said. He thought about that for a moment and chuckled again. "Of course, couple of my customers figure the skinwalkers got off with her."

"What do you think of that?"

"Not much," McGinnis said. "Skinwalkers get a lot of blame around here. Sheepdog dies. Car breaks down. Kid gets the chicken pox. Roof leaks. Skinwalkers get the blame."

"I heard she had driven out toward Yells Back Butte to do some work out there," Leaphorn said. "There always seemed to be a lot of witching talk around there."

"Lot of talk about that place," McGinnis said. "Had its own legend. Old Man Tijinney was supposed to be a witch. Had a bucket of silver dollars buried somewhere. A tub full, the way some told it. When the last of that outfit died off people dug holes all around out there. Some of the city kids didn't even respect the death hogan taboo. I heard they dug in there, too."

"Find anything?"

McGinnis shook his head, sipped his drink. "You ever run into that Dr. Woody fella out there? He comes in here a time or two just about every summer. Working on some sort of a rodent research project here and there, and I think he has some sort of setup near the butte. He was in three or four weeks back to get some stuff and telling me another skinwalker story. I think it's a kind of hobby of his. Collects them. Thinks they're funny."

"Who's he get 'em from?" Leaphorn asked. It was a rare Navajo who'd pass along a skinwalker report to anyone he didn't know pretty well.

McGinnis obviously knew exactly what Leaphorn was thinking.

"Oh, he's been coming out here for years. Long enough to speak good Navajo. Comes and goes. Hires local folks to collect rodent information for him. Friendly guy."

"And he told you a fresh skinwalker story? Something that happened out near Yells Back?"

"I don't know how fresh it was," McGinnis said. "He said Old Man Saltman told him about seeing a skinwalker standing by a bunch of boulders at the bottom of the butte a little bit after sundown, and then disappearing behind them, and when he came out he turned into an owl and went flopping away like he had a broken wing."

"Turned from what into an owl?"

McGinnis looked surprised by the question. "Why, from a man. You know how it goes. Hosteen Saltman said the owl kept flopping around as if he wanted to be followed."

"Yeah," Leaphorn said. "And he didn't follow, of course. That's how the story usually goes."

McGinnis laughed. "I remember about the first or second time I saw you, I asked if you believed in skinwalkers, and you said you just believed in people who believed in 'em, and all the trouble that caused. Is that still the case?"

"Pretty much," Leaphorn said.

"Well then, let me tell you one I'll bet you haven't heard before. There's an old woman who comes in here after shearing time every spring to sell me three or four sacks of wool. Sometimes they call her Grandma Charlie, I think it is, but I believe her name is Old Lady Notah. She was in here just yesterday telling me about seeing a skinwalker."

McGinnis raised his glass in a toast to Leaphorn. "Now listen to this one. She said she was out looking after a bunch of goats she has over by Black Mesa—right on the edge of the Hopi Reservation—and she notices somebody down the slope messing around with something on the ground. Like hunting for something. Anyway, this fella disappears behind the junipers for a minute or two and then emerges, and now he's different. Now he's bigger, and all white with a big round head, and when he turned her way, his whole face flashed."

"Flashed?"

"She said like the flash thing on her daughter's little camera."

"What did the man look like when he quit being a witch?"

"She didn't stick around to see," McGinnis said. "But wait a minute. You ain't heard all of it yet. She said when this skinwalker turned around he looked like he had an elephant's trunk coming out of his back. Now how about that?"

"You're right," Leaphorn said. "That's a new one."

"And come to think of it, you can add that one to your Yells Back Butte stories. That's about where Old Lady Notah has her grazing lease."

"Well, now," Leaphorn said, "I think I might want to talk to her about that. I'd like to hear some more details."

"Me, too," McGinnis said, and laughed. "She said the skinwalker looked like a snowman."

7

THEY'D AGREED TO meet for breakfast, early because Janet had to
drive south to Phoenix and Chee had to go about as far north to
Tuba City. "Let's make it seven on the dot, and not by Navajo time," Janet
had said.

There he was, a little before seven, waiting for her at a table in the hotel coffee shop, thinking about the night he'd walked into her apartment
in Gallup. He'd been carrying flowers, a videotape of a traditional Navajo
wedding and the notion that she could explain away the way she had used
him, and—

He didn't want to think about that. Not now and not ever. What
could change that she'd gotten information from him and tipped off the
law professor, the man she'd told Chee she hated?

Before he'd finally slept, he decided he would simply ask her if they
were still engaged. "Janet," he would say. "Do you still want to marry me?"
Get right to the point. But this morning, with his head still full of gloomy
thoughts, he wasn't so sure. Did he really want her to say yes? He decided
she probably would. She had left her high-society inside-the-Beltway life
and come back to Indian Country, which said she really loved him. But
that would carry with it, in some subtle way, her understanding that he
would climb the ladder of success into the social strata where she felt at
home.

There was another possibility. She had taken her first reservation job to escape her law professor lover. Did this return simply mean she wanted the man to pursue her again? Chee turned away from that thought and remembered how sweet it had been before she had betrayed him (or, as she saw it, before he had insulted her because of his unreasonable jealousy). He could land a federal job in Washington. Could he be happy there? He thought of himself as a drunk, worthless, dying of a destroyed liver. Was that what had killed Janet's Navajo father? Had he drowned himself in whiskey to escape Janet's ruling-caste mother?

When he'd exhausted all the dark corners that scenario offered, he turned to an alternative. Janet had come back to him. She'd be willing to live on the Big Rez, wife of a cop, living in what her friends would rate as slum housing, where high culture was a second-run movie. In that line of thought, love overcame all. But it wouldn't. She'd yearn for the life she'd given up. He would see it. They'd be miserable.

Finally he thought of Janet as court-appointed defense attorney and of himself as arresting officer. But by the time she walked in, exactly on time, he was back to thinking of her as an Eastern social butterfly, and that thought gave this Flagstaff dining room a worn, grungy look that he'd never noticed before.

He pulled back a chair for her.

"I guess you're used to classier places in Washington," he said, and instantly wished he hadn't so carelessly touched the nerve of their disagreement.

Janet's smile wavered. She looked at him a moment, somberly, and looked away. "I'll bet the coffee is better here."

"It's always fresh anyway," he said. "Or almost always."

A teenage boy delivered two mugs and a bowl filled with single-serving-size containers labeled NON-DAIRY CREAMER.

Janet looked over her mug at him. "Jim."

Chee waited. "What?"

"Oh, nothing. I guess this is a time to talk business."

"So we take off our friend hats, and put on adversary hats?"

"Not really," Janet said. "But I'd like to know if you're absolutely certain Robert Jano killed Officer Kinsman."

"Sure I'm certain," Chee said. He felt his face flushing. "You must have read the arrest report. I was there, wasn't I? And what do you do with it if I say I'm not sure? Do you tell the jury that even the arresting officer told you that he had reasonable doubts?"

He'd tried to keep the anger out of his voice, but Janet's face told him he hadn't managed it. Another raw nerve touched.

"I'd do absolutely nothing with it," she said. "It's just that Jano swears he didn't do it. I'll be working with him. I'd like to believe him."

"Don't," Chee said. He sipped his coffee and put down the mug. It occurred to him that he hadn't noticed how it tasted. He picked up one of the containers: " 'Non-dairy creamer,' " he read. "Produced, I understand, on non-dairy farms."

Janet managed a smile. "You know what? Doesn't this episode we're having here remind you of the first time we met? Remember? In the holding room at the San Juan County Jail in Aztec. You were trying to keep me from bonding out that old man."

"And you were trying to keep me from talking to him."

"But I got him out." Janet was grinning at him now.

"But not until I got the information I wanted," Chee said.

"Okay," Janet said, still grinning. "We'll call that one a tie. Even though you had to cheat a little."

"How about our next competition," Chee said. "Remember the old alcoholic? You thought Leaphorn and I were picking on him. Until your client pleaded guilty."

"That was a sad, sad case," Janet said. She sipped her coffee. "Some things about it still bother me. Some things about this one bother me, too."

"Like what? Like the fact Jano is a Hopi and the Hopis are peaceful people? Nonviolent?"

"There's that, of course," Janet said. "But everything he told me has a sort of logic to it and a lot of it can be checked out."

"Like what? What can be checked?"

"Like, for example, he said he was going to collect an eagle his kiva needed for a ceremonial. His brothers in his religious group can confirm that. That made it a religious pilgrimage, on which no evil thoughts are allowed."

"Such as thoughts of revenge? Such as getting even with Kinsman for the prior arrest? The kind of thoughts the D.A. will want to suggest to the jury if he's going for malice, premeditation. The death penalty stuff."

"Right," she said.

"They would confirm why he was going for the eagle, and the prosecution would concede it," Chee said. "But how do you prove that deep down Jano didn't want to even the score?"

Janet shrugged.

"J. D. Mickey will probably state that in his opening. He'll say that Jano had gone onto the Navajo reservation to poach an eagle—a crime in itself. He'll say that Officer Benjamin Kinsman of the Navajo Tribal Police had previously arrested him doing the same crime last year and that Jano got off on some sort of technicality. He'll say that when he saw Kinsman was after him again, Jano was enraged. So instead of releasing the bird, getting rid of the evidence and trying to escape, he let Kinsman catch him, caught him off-guard and brained him."

"Is that the way Mickey is planning it?"

"I'm just guessing," Chee said.

"I have no doubt at all that Mickey will go for death. It would be the first one since the 1994 Congress allowed federal death penalties and there would be a media coverage circus." Janet doctored her coffee with the non-dairy creamer, tasted it. "Mickey for Congress," she intoned. "Your law-and-order candidate."

"That's the way I see it," Chee said. "But the courts would have to rule that Kinsman was a federal officer."

"People in criminal justice say he was."

Chee shrugged. "Probably."

"Which led the U.S. Department of Justice to unplug him from the various life support machines," Janet said. "So Benjamin Kinsman could hurry up and be a murder victim instead of the subject of criminal assault. Thereby simplifying the paperwork."

"Come on, Janet," Chee said. "Be fair. Ben was already dead. The machines were breathing for him, making his heart pump. Kinsman's spirit had gone away."

Janet was sipping her coffee. "You're right about one thing," she said. "This is good fresh java. Not that weird perfumed stuff the yuppie bars sell for four dollars a cup."

"What else could be checked out?" Chee asked. "In Jano's version."

Janet raised her hand. "First something else," she said. "How about that autopsy? The law requires one in homicides, sort of, but a lot of Navajos don't like the idea and sometimes they're skipped. And I heard one of the docs saying something about organ donations?"

"Kinsman was a Mormon. So were his parents. He'd had a donor card registered," Chee said, studying her as he said it. "But you already knew that. You were changing the subject."

"I'm the defense attorney," she said. "You think my client is guilty. I've got to be careful what I tell you."

Chee nodded. "But if there's something that can be checked out that I'm missing, something that could help his case, then I ought to know about it. I'm not going to go out there and destroy the evidence. Don't you—"

He had started to say: "Don't you trust me?" But she would have said she did. And then she would have returned the question, and he had no idea how he could answer it.

She was leaning forward, elbows on table, chin resting on clasped hands, waiting for him to finish.

"End of statement," he said. "Sure, I think he's guilty. I was there. Had I been a little faster, I would have stopped it."

"Cowboy doesn't think he's guilty."

"Cowboy? Cowboy Dashee?"

"Yes," Janet said. "Your old friend, Deputy Sheriff Cowboy Dashee. He told me Jano is his cousin. He's known him since childhood. They were playmates. Close friends. Cowboy told me that thinking Robert Jano would kill somebody with a rock is like thinking Mother Teresa would strangle the Pope."

"Really?"

"That's what he said. His exact words, in fact."

"How come you got in touch with Cowboy?"

"I didn't. He called the D.A.'s office. Asked who'd be assigned to handle Jano's defense. They told him a new hire would be assigned to it, and he left a message for whoever that would be to give him a call. It was me, so I called him."

"Well, hell," Chee said. "How come he didn't contact me?"

"I don't have to explain that, do I? He was afraid you'd think he was trying—"

"Sure," Chee said. "Of course."

Janet looked sympathetic. "That makes it worse for you, doesn't it? I know you guys go way back."

"Yeah, we do," Chee said. "Cowboy's about as good a friend as I ever had."

"Well, he's a cop, too. He'll understand."

"He's also a Hopi," Chee said. "And some wise man once told us that blood's thicker than water." He sighed. "What did Cowboy tell you?"

"He said Jano had caught his eagle. He was coming home with it. He heard noises. He checked. He found the officer on the ground, head bleeding."

Chee shook his head. "I know. That's the statement he gave us. When he finally decided to talk about it."

"It could be true."

"Sure," Chee said. "It could be true. But how about the slash on his forearm, and his blood mixed with Ben's? And no blood on the eagle? And where's the perpetrator, if it wasn't Jano? Ben Kinsman didn't hit himself on the head with that rock. It wasn't suicide."

"The eagle flew away," Janet said. "And don't be sarcastic."

That stopped Chee cold. He sat for a long moment, just staring at her. She looked puzzled. "What?"

"He told you the eagle flew away?"

"That's right. When he caught it, Jano was under some brush or something," she said. "A blind, I guess, with something on a cord for bait. He tried to grab the eagle by the legs and just got one of them, and it slashed him on the arm and he released it."

"Janet," Chee said. "The eagle didn't fly away. It was in a wire cage just about eight or ten feet from where Jano was standing over Kinsman."

Janet put down her coffee cup.

Chee frowned. "He told you it got away? But he knew we had it. Why would he tell you that?"

She shrugged. Looked down at her hands.

"And it didn't have any blood on its feathers. At least, I didn't see any. I'm sure the lab would check for it.

"If you think I'm lying, look." He held out his hand, displaying the still healing slash on its side. "I picked up the cage to move it. That's where its talon caught me. Ripped the skin."

Janet's face was flushed. "You didn't have to show me anything," she said. "I didn't think you were lying. I'll ask Jano about it. Maybe I misunderstood. I must have."

Chee saw Janet was embarrassed. "I'll bet I know what happened," he said. "Jano didn't want to talk about the eagle because it got too close to violating kiva secrecy rules. I think it would become a symbolic messenger to God, to the spirit world. Its role would be sacred. He just couldn't talk about it, so he said he turned it loose."

"Maybe so," she said.

"I'll bet he just wanted to divert you. To talk about something besides a touchy religious subject."

Janet's expression told him she doubted that.

"I'll ask him about it," Janet repeated. "I really haven't had much chance to talk to him yet. Just a few minutes. I just got here."

"But he told you he didn't kill Kinsman. Did he tell you who did?"

"Well," Janet said, and hesitated. "You know, Jim, I have to be careful talking about this. Let me just say that I guess whoever it was who had hit Officer Kinsman with the rock must have heard Jano coming and went away. Jano said it started raining about the time you got there. By the time you had him handcuffed in the patrol car, and called in for help, and tried to make Kinsman comfortable, any tracks would have been washed away."

Chee didn't comment on that. He had to be careful, too.

"Don't you think so? Or did you find other tracks?"

"You mean other than Jano's?"

"Of course. Did you have a chance to look for any before it started raining?"

Chee considered the question, why she had asked it and whether she already knew the answer.

"You want some more coffee?"

"Okay," Janet said.

Chee signaled the waiter, thinking about what he was about to do. It was fair, if her effort to get him to state that he hadn't looked for other tracks was fair.

"Janet, Jano told you how he got those deep slashes on his forearm. Did he mention exactly when he got scratched?"

The boy brought the coffee, refilled their cups, asked if they were ready to order breakfast.

"Give us another minute," Chee said.

"When?" Janet said. "Isn't that obvious? It would have been either while he was catching the eagle or when he was putting it in the cage. Or somewhere in between. I didn't quiz him about it."

"But did he say? Specifically when?"

"You mean in relation to what?" she asked, grinning at him. "Come on, Jim. Say it. The police lab people have told you that Jano's blood is mixed with Kinsman's on Kinsman's shirt. The lab is probably doing some of their new molecular magic to tell them if Jano's blood had been exposed to the air longer than Kinsman's, and how much longer, and all that."

"Can they do that now?" he asked, wishing he hadn't been pressing her on this, making her angry for no reason. "They probably would if they could, because the official, formal theory of the crime will be that Jano struggled with Kinsman and got his arm slashed on Kinsman's belt buckle."

"Can they do it? I don't know. Probably. But how can you get cut on a belt buckle?"

"Kinsman liked to bend the rules when he could. Put a feather in his uniform hat, that sort of thing. He put a fancy buckle on his belt to see how long it would be before I told him to take it off. Anyway, that's why the timing seems to be important."

"Well, go ahead then. Ask me. Just exactly to the minute, when did Jano get his arm slashed?"

"Okay," Chee said. "Exactly, precisely when?"

"Ha!" Janet said. "You're treading on client confidentiality."

"Whaddaya mean?"

"You know what I mean. I see J. D. Mickey with a new hundred-dollar haircut and an Italian silk suit addressing the jury. 'Ladies and gentlemen. The defendant's blood was found mixed with the blood of the victim on Officer Kinsman's uniform.' And then he gets into all the blood chemistry stuff." Janet raised her hand, dropped her voice—providing a poor imitation of Mickey's courtroom dramatics. " 'But! But! He told an officer of this court that he suffered the cut later. After he had moved Officer Kinsman.' "

"So I guess you're not going to tell me," Chee said.

"Right," Janet said. She put down her menu, studied him. Her expression was somber. "A little while ago, I might have."

Chee let his expression ask the question.

"How can I trust you when you don't trust me?"

Chee waited.

She shook her head. "I'm not just a shyster trying for a reputation with some sort of cheap acquittal," she said. "I really want to know if Robert Jano is innocent. I want to know what happened."

She put down her menu and stared at him, inviting a response.

"I understand that," Chee said.

"I respect—" she began. Her voice tightened. She paused, looked away from him. "When I asked you about the tracks, I wasn't trying to trick you," she said. "I asked because I think if somebody else had been there and left any traces you would have found them. That is, if anybody in the world could have found them. And if there weren't any, then maybe I'm wrong and maybe Robert Jano did kill your officer, and maybe I should be trying to talk him into a plea bargain. So I ask you, but you don't trust me, so you change the subject."

Chee had put down his menu to listen to this. Now he picked it up, opened it. "And now, once again, I think we should change the subject. How were things in Washington?"

"I'm really not going to have time for breakfast." She put down her menu, said, "Thanks for the coffee," and walked out.

8

"THERE'S JUST ONE thing I can tell you and feel absolutely certain about it," said Richard Krause without looking up from the box full of assorted stuff he was picking through. "Cathy Pollard didn't just run off with our Jeep. Something happened to her. But don't ask me what."

Leaphorn nodded. "That's what my client believes," he said. My client. It was the first time he'd used that term, and he didn't like the sound of it. Was this what he was making of himself? A private investigator?

Krause was probably in his late forties, Leaphorn guessed, big-boned, lean and gristly, probably an athlete in college, with a shock of blondish hair just showing signs of gray. He was sitting on a high stool behind a table in a faded green work shirt, dividing his attention between Leaphorn and stacks of transparent Ziploc bags that seemed to contain small dead insects—fleas or lice. Or maybe ticks.

"I guess you're working for her family," Krause said. He opened another bag, extracted a flea, and put it on a slide, which he placed in a binocular microscope. "Do they have any theories?"

"Ideas float around," Leaphorn said, asking himself if the ethics of private investigators, presuming they had them, allowed one to reveal the identity of clients. He'd deal with that when circumstances required. "The obvious ones. A sex crime. A nervous breakdown. A rejected boyfriend. Things like that."

Krause adjusted the microscope's focus, stared into the lenses, grunted and removed the slide. In its former existence this temporary lab had been a low-down-payment double-wide mobile home, and the heat of the summer sun radiated through its aluminum roof. The swamp-cooler fan roared away at its highest setting, mixing damp air into the dry heat. The rows of specimen jars on the shelf behind Krause were sweating. So was Krause. So was Leaphorn.

"I really doubt there's a boyfriend involved in this," he said. "She didn't seem to have one. Never talked about it anyway." He transferred the flea into another Ziploc bag, wrote something on an adhesive tag, and stuck it in place. "Of course, there could be a jilted one floating around somewhere in the past. That wouldn't be the sort of thing Cathy would have chatted about, even if she chatted. Which she didn't do much."

The cluttered, makeshift laboratory was reminding Leaphorn of his student career at Arizona State, which in those long-ago days required a mix of natural science courses even if your major was anthropology. Then he realized it wasn't as much what he was seeing as what he was smelling—those tissue-preserving, soap-defying chemicals that drove the scent of death deep into the pores of even the cleanest students.

"Cathy was a very serious lady. Focused. Just talked about business," Krause was saying. "She had a thing about bubonic plague. Thought it was downright criminal that we protect the middle-class urbanites from these communicable diseases and let the vectors do their thing out here in the boondocks where nobody gets killed except the working class. Cathy sounded like one of those old-fashioned Marxists sometimes."

"Tell me about the Jeep," Leaphorn said.

Krause stopped what he'd been doing, stared at Leaphorn, frowning. "The Jeep? What's to tell?"

"If there's foul play involved in this, the truck will probably be how the case gets broken."

Krause shook his head. Laughed. "It was just a black Jeep. They all look alike."

"It's harder to dispose of a vehicle," Leaphorn said.

"Than a body?" Krause said. "Sure. I see what you mean. Well, actually it was a pretty fancy model. We heard it was one of those seized by the DEA guys in a drug bust and turned over to the Health Department. Had a white pinstripe. Very hi-fi radio with special speakers. Telephone installed. The cowboy model. No top. Roll bars. Winch on the front. Tow-chain hooks and a trailer hitch on the back. I think it was three years old, but you know they don't change those models much. I drove it myself some until Cathy got it away from me."

"How'd that happen?"

"What Cathy wanted, Cathy got." He shrugged. "Actually, she had a good argument for it. Spent more time out in the bad country while I was doing the paperwork in here."

"I'm trying to get the word around that there's a reward out for whoever finds that vehicle. A thousand dollars."

Krause raised his eyebrows. "The family sounds serious then," he said, grinning. "What if she just drives in here and parks it? Can I call in and collect?"

"Probably not," Leaphorn said. "But I'd appreciate the call."

"I'll be happy to let you know."

"How about a man named Victor Hammar?" Leaphorn asked. "I'm told they knew each other. You wouldn't put him in the boyfriend category?"

Krause looked surprised. "Hammar? I don't think so." He shook his head, grinning.

"One of the theories has it that Hammar was in love with her. The way it's told, she didn't share the sentiment, but she couldn't get rid of him."

"Naw," Krause said. "I don't think so. Matter of fact, she invited him out here awhile back. He's working on his doctorate in vertebrate biology. He's interested in what we're doing."

"Just in what you're doing? Not in the woman who's doing it?"

"Oh, they're friends," Krause said. "And he probably feels those glandular urges. Young male, you know. And he likes her, but I think that was because she sort of gave him a little mothering when he was new in the country. He has a sort of funny accent. No friends in the department, I'll bet. From what I've seen of him, probably not many friends anywhere else either. So along comes Cathy. She's like a lot of these kids who grow up rich. They like doing good for the working-class losers. So she helped him along. Makes 'em feel less guilty about being part of the parasitic privileged class."

"When you think about it, though," Leaphorn said, "what you de-scribed is sort of typical of these stalker homicides. You know, the kind-hearted girl takes pity on the poor nerd and he thinks it's love."

"I guess you could ask him. He's out here again and said he was com-ing in to get copies of some of our mortality statistics."

"Mortality?"

"In fact, he's late," Krause said, looking at his watch. "Yeah, mortality. Die-offs among mammal communities in plague outbreaks, rabbit fever, hantavirus, that sort of thing. How many kangaroo rats survive compared with ground squirrels, pack rats, prairie dogs, so forth. But my point is, it's the data that brings him out, not Cathy. Take today, for example. He knows Cathy's not here, but he's coming anyway."

"He knew she was missing?"

"He called a couple of days after she didn't show up. Wanted to talk to her."

Leaphorn considered this.

"How well do you remember that conversation?"

Krause looked surprised, frowned. "What do you mean?"

"You know: 'he said,' and 'I said,' and 'he said.' That sort of thing. How did he react?"

Krause laughed. "You're hard to convince, aren't you?"

"Just curious."

"Well, first he asked whether we'd wrapped up the work on the plague cases. I said no, we still didn't know where the last one got it. I told him Cathy was still working on that one. Then he asked if we'd found any live kangaroo rats up around the Disbah place. That's one of the places where a hantavirus case had turned up. I told him we hadn't."

Krause tore off a sheet from a roll of paper towels and swabbed the sheen of perspiration from his forehead. "Let's see now. Then he said he had some time and thought he'd come out and maybe go along with Cathy if she was still chasing down prairie dogs and plague fleas. He wanted to ask her if she'd mind. I said she wasn't here. He said when'll she be back. So I told him about her not coming to work. Couple of days I guess it was by then."

Leaphorn waited. Krause shook his head. Went back to sorting through his bags. Now the chemical smell reminded Leaphorn of the Indian Health

Service Hospital at Gallup, of the gurney rolling down the hallway carry-ing Emma away from him. Of the doctor explaining—He drew a deep breath, wanting to finish this. Wanting out of this laboratory.

"She didn't tell you she was taking off?"

"Just left a note. Said she was going back up to Yells Back to collect some fleas."

"Nothing else?"

Krause shook his head.

"Could I see the note?"

"If I can find it. It probably went in the wastebasket but I'll look for it."

"How did Hammar react to what you told him?"

"I don't know. I think he said something like, whaddaya mean? Where did she go? What did she tell you? Where'd she leave the truck? That sort of thing. Then he seemed worried. What did the police say? Was anybody looking for her? So forth."

Leaphorn considered. That response seemed normal. Or well re-hearsed.

There was the sound of tires crunching over gravel, a car door slam-ming.

"That's probably Hammar," Krause said. "Ask him yourself."

9

ABOUT A MONTH into his first semester at Arizona State, Leaphorn had overcome the tendency of young Navajos to think that all white people look alike. But the fact was that Victor Hammar looked a lot like a bigger, less sun-baked weightlifter version of Richard Krause. At second glance Leaphorn noticed Hammar was also several years younger, his eyes a paler shade of blue, his ears a bit flatter to his skull, and—since cops are conditioned to look for "identifying marks"—a tiny scar beside his chin had defied sunburning and remained white.

Hammar showed less interest in Leaphorn. He shook hands, displayed irregular teeth with a perfunctory smile, and got down to business.

"Is she back yet?" he asked Krause. "Have you heard anything from her?"

"Neither one," Krause said.

Hammar issued a violent non-English epithet. A German curse, Leaphorn guessed. He sat on a stool across from Leaphorn, shook his head, and swore again—this time in English.

"Yeah," Krause said. "It's worrying me, too."

"And the police," Hammar said. "What are they doing? Nothing, I think. What do they tell you?"

"Nothing," Krause said. "I think they put the Jeep on the list to be watched for and—"

"Nothing!" Hammar said. "How could that be?"

"She's a full-grown woman," Krause said. "There's no evidence of any crime, except maybe for getting off with our vehicle. I guess—"

"Nonsense! Nonsense! Of course something has happened to her. She's been gone too long. Something happened to her."

Leaphorn cleared his throat. "Do you have any theories about that?"

Hammar stared at Leaphorn. "What?"

Krause said, "Mr. Leaphorn here is a retired policeman. He's trying to find Catherine."

Hammar was still staring. "Retired policeman?"

Leaphorn nodded, thinking Hammar would have no idea of what he knew and what he didn't and trying to decide how he would lead into this.

"Do you remember where you were July eighth? Were you here in Tuba then?"

"No," Hammar said, still staring.

Leaphorn waited.

"I'd already gone back. Back to the university."

"You're on a faculty somewhere?"

"I am just a graduate assistant. At Arizona State. I had lectures that day. Introduction to the laboratory for freshmen." Hammar grimaced. "Introduction to Biology. Awful course. Stupid students. And why are you asking me these questions? Do you—"

"Because I was asked to help find the woman," Leaphorn said, thereby violating his rule and Navajo courtesy by interrupting a speaker. But he wanted to cut off any questions from Hammar. "I will just collect a little more information and be out of here so you gentlemen can get back to your work. I wonder if Miss Pollard might have left any papers in the office here. If she did, they might be helpful."

"Papers?" Krause said. "Well, she had sort of a ledger and she kept her field notes in that. Is that what you mean?"

"Probably," Leaphorn said.

"Her aunt called me from Santa Fe yesterday and told me you'd come by," Krause said, shuffling through material stacked on a desk in the corner of the room. "I think her name is Vanders. Something like that. Cathy was planning to visit her last weekend. I thought maybe that's where she'd gone."

"You're working for old Mrs. Vanders," Hammar said, still staring at Leaphorn.

"Here's the sort of stuff that might be useful," Krause said, handing Leaphorn an accordion file containing a jumble of papers. "She's going to need it if she comes back."

"When she gets back," Hammar said. "When."

Leaphorn flipped through the papers, noticing that most of the entries Catherine had made were in a small irregular scribble, hard to read and even harder for a layman to interpret. Like his own notes, they were a shorthand that communicated only to her.

"Fort C," Leaphorn said. "What's that?"

"Centers for Disease Control," Krause said. "The feds who run the lab at Fort Collins."

"IHS. That's Indian Health Service?"

"Right," Krause said. "Actually, that's who we're working for here, but technically for the Arizona health people. Part of the big, complicated team."

Leaphorn had skipped to the back.

"Lots of references to A. Nez," he said.

"Anderson Nez. One of the three fatalities in the last outbreak. Mr. Nez was the last one, and the only one we haven't found the source for," Krause said.

"And who's this Woody?"

"Ah," said Hammar. "That jerk!"

"That's Albert Woody," Krause said. "Al. He's into cell biology, but I guess you'd call him an immunologist. Or a pharmacologist. Microbiologist. Or maybe a—I don't know." Krause chuckled. "What's his title, Hammar? He's closer to your field than mine."

"He's a damned jerk," Hammar said. "He has a grant from the Institute of Allergy and Immunology, but they say he also works for Merck, or Squibb, or one of the other pharmaceutical firms. Or maybe for all of them."

"Hammar doesn't like him," Krause said. "Hammar was trapping rodents somewhere or other this summer and Woody accused him of interfering with one of his own projects. He yelled at you, didn't he?"

"I should have kicked his butt," Hammar said.

"He's on this plague project, too?"

"No. No. Not really. He's been working out here for years, since we had an outbreak in the nineteen-eighties. He's studying how some hosts of vectors—like prairie dogs, or field mice, and so forth—can be infected by bacteria or viruses and stay alive while others of the same species are killed. For example, plague comes along and wipes out about a billion rodents, and you've got empty burrows and nothing but bones for a hundred miles. But here and there you find a colony still alive. They carry it, but it didn't kill them. They're sort of reservoir colonies. They breed, renew the rodent population, and then the plague spreads again. Probably from them, too. But nobody really knows for sure how it works."

"It's the same with snowshoe rabbits in the north of Finland," Hammar said. "And in your Arctic Alaska. Different bacteria but the same business. It's a seven-year cycle with that, regular as a clock. Everywhere rabbits, then the fever sweeps through and nothing but dead rabbits and it takes seven years to build back up and then the fever comes and wipes them out again."

"And the drug companies are paying Woody?"

"Wasting their money," Hammar said. He walked to the door, opened it, and stood looking out.

"It's more like they're looking for the Golden Fleece," Krause said. "I just have a sort of hazy idea of what Woody's doing, but I think he's trying to pin down what happens inside a mammal so that it can live with a pathogen that kills its kinfolks. If he learns that, maybe it's just a little step toward understanding intercellular chemistry. Or maybe it's worth a mega-trillion dollars."

Leaphorn let that hang while he sorted through what he remembered of Organic Chemistry 211 and Biology 331 from his own college days. That was vague now, but he recalled what the surgeon who'd operated on Emma's brain tumor had told him as if it were yesterday. He could still see the man and hear the anger in his voice. It was just a simple staph infection, he'd said, and a few years ago a dozen different antibiotics would have killed the bacteria. But not now. "Now the microbes are winning the war," he'd said. And Emma's small body, under the sheet on the gurney rolling down the hallway, was the proof of that.

"Well, maybe that's exaggerating," Krause said. "Maybe it would be just a few hundred billion."

"You're talking about a way to make better antibiotics?" Leaphorn said. "That's what Woody's after?"

"Not exactly. More likely he'd like to find the way a mammal's immune system is being adjusted so that it can kill the microbe. It would probably be more like a vaccine."

Leaphorn looked up from the journal. "Miss Pollard seems to connect him to Nez," he said. "The note says: 'Check Woody on Nez.' Wonder what that would mean."

"I wouldn't know," Krause said.

"Maybe Nez was that guy Woody had working for him," Hammar said. "Sort of a smallish fellow, with his hair cut real short. He'd put out traps for Woody and help him take blood samples from the animals. Things like that."

"Maybe so," Krause said. "I know that over the years Woody has located a bunch of prairie dog colonies that seem to resist the plague. And he was also collecting kangaroo rats, field mice, and so forth. The sort of rodents that spread the hantavirus. Cathy said he's been working with one near Yells Back Butte. That might be why Cathy was going up there. If Nez had been working for Woody, maybe she was going up there to see if he knew where Nez was when he got infected."

"Could Mr. Nez have been bitten up there?" Leaphorn asked. "I understand there'd been a couple of plague victims from that area in the past."

"I don't think so," Krause said. "She had pretty well pinned down where Nez had been during the period he was infected. It was mostly up south of here. Between Tuba and Page."

Krause had been sorting slides while he talked. Now he looked up at Leaphorn. "You know much about bacteria?"

"Just the basic stuff. Freshman-level biology."

"Well, with plague, the flea just puts a tiny bit in your bloodstream, and then it usually takes five or six days, sometimes longer, for the bacteria to multiply enough so you start showing any symptoms, usually a fever. Or maybe if you get bitten by a bunch of fleas, or they're loaded with some really virulent stuff, then it's quicker. So you skip back a few days from when the fever showed up and find out where the victim's been from that date to maybe a week earlier. When you know that, then you start checking those places for dead mammals and infected fleas."

Hammar was still looking out the door. He said: "Poor Mr. Nez. Killed by a flea. Too bad the flea didn't bite Al Woody."

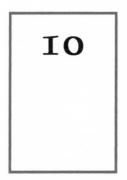

10

EAPHORN BLAMED IT on being lonely—this bad habit he'd developed of talking too much. And now he was paying the price. Instead of waiting until he'd arrived at Louisa Bourebonette's little house in Flagstaff to tell her of his adventures, the empty silence in his Tuba City motel room had provoked him into babbling away on the telephone. He'd told her about his visit with John McGinnis and his talk with Krause. He had given her a thumbnail sketch of Hammar and asked if she could think of an easy, make-no-waves way to check on his alibi.

"Can't you just call the police in Tempe and have them do it? I thought that's what was done."

"If I was still a cop I could, providing we had any evidence a crime had been committed and some reason to believe Mr. Hammar was a suspect in this crime."

"Lieutenant Chee would do it."

"If he would, that would take care of problem one. We'd still have problems two and three," Leaphorn said. "How is Chee going to explain to the Tempe police why he wants them to poke into the life of a citizen when there's not even a crime to suspect him of committing?"

"Yeah," Louisa said. "I see it. Academics can be touchy about things like that. I'll handle it myself."

Which left Leaphorn merely breathing into the phone for a moment or two. Then he said: "What?"

"Hammar was supposed to be teaching a lab class July eighth, isn't that what he said? So I have a friend over in our biology department who knows people in biology down at ASU. He calls somebody in his good-old-boy network down at Tempe and they ask around and if Mr. Hammar cut his lab class that day—or got somebody to handle it—then we know it. That sound okay?"

"That sounds great," Leaphorn said. It would also have been a great place to end the conversation, just to tell Louisa he'd be there for dinner tonight and say good-bye. But, alas, he kept on talking.

He told her about Dr. Woody and his project. Even though Louisa's field was ethnology and, even worse, mythology—on the extreme opposite end of the academic spectrum from microbiology—Louisa had heard of Woody. She said the fellow she'd ask to make the call to Tempe for her sometimes worked with the man, doing blood and tissue studies in his microbiology lab at the NAU.

Thus the restful evening Leaphorn had yearned for with Louisa had turned into a threesome with Professor Michael Perez invited to join them.

"He's one of the brighter ones," Louisa had said, thereby separating him from a good many of the hard science faculty, whom she found too narrow for her taste. "He'll be interested in what you're doing, and maybe he can tell you something helpful."

Leaphorn doubted that. In fact, he was wondering if he would ever learn anything helpful about Catherine Pollard. He'd classified what McGinnis had told him as no higher than interesting, and yesterday had left him wondering why he was wasting so much energy on what seemed more and more like a hopeless cause. He'd spent weary hours locating the sheep camp where Anderson Nez resided during the grazing months. As expected, he found the Navajo taboo against talking about the dead adding to the usual taciturnity of rural folks dealing with a citified stranger. Except for a teenager who remembered Catherine Pollard coming by earlier collecting fleas off their sheepdogs, checking rodent burrows and quizzing everyone about where Nez might have been, he learned just about nothing at the camp beyond confirming what Hammar had told him. Yes indeed,

Nez had worked part-time for several summers helping Dr. Woody catch rodents.

He arrived at Louisa's house just before sunset with the high dry-weather ice crystals dusted across the stratosphere reflecting red. The spot where he usually parked his pickup in her narrow driveway was occupied by a weather-beaten Saab sedan. Its owner was standing beside Louisa in the doorway as Leaphorn came up the steps—a lanky man with a narrow face and a narrow white goatee whose bright blue eyes were inspecting Leaphorn with undisguised curiosity.

"Joe," Louisa said. "This is Mike Perez, who'll tell us both more about molecular biology than we want to know."

They shook hands.

"Or about bacteria, or virology," Perez said, grinning. "We don't understand the virus end of it yet, but that doesn't keep us from pretending we do."

Louisa had presumed that Leaphorn, being Navajo, enjoyed mutton so the entree was lamb chops. Having been raised a sheep-camp Navajo, Leaphorn was both thoroughly tired of mutton and far too polite to say so. He ate his lamb chop with green mint jelly and listened to Professor Perez discuss Woody's work with rodents. Two or three questions early in the meal had established that Perez seemed to know absolutely nothing that would connect him to Catherine Pollard. But he knew an awful lot about the career and personality of Dr. Albert Woody.

"Mike thinks Woody's going to be one of the great ones," Louisa said. "Nobel Prize winner, books written about him. The Man Who Saved Humanity. A giant of medical science. That sort of thing."

Perez looked embarrassed by that. "Louisa tends to exaggerate. It's an occupational hazard of mythologists, you know," he said. "Hercules wasn't really any stronger than Gorgeous George, and Medusa just had her hair done in cornrows, and Paul Bunyan's blue ox was really brown. But I do think that Woody has a shot at it. Maybe one chance in a hundred. But that's better odds than Speed Ball lottery."

Louisa offered Leaphorn another chop. "Everyone in the hard sciences is making the headlines these days," she said. "It's 'breakthrough of the month' season. If it isn't a new way to clone toe-jam fungus, it's rediscovering life on Mars."

"I saw something about that life-on-Mars business," Leaphorn said. "It sounded like that molecules-in-the-asteroid discovery back in the sixties. Didn't the geologists discredit that?"

Perez nodded. "This one is a NASA publicity ploy. They'd been having their usual run of fiascoes and blunders, so they dug out an asteroid with the proper minerals in it and conned the reporters again. New generation of science writers, nobody remembered the old story, and it looked better on TV than the footage of astronauts demonstrating their bigger bubblegum bubbles, and that other sophomoric stuff they're always bragging about."

Louisa laughed. "Mike resents NASA because it siphons federal research money away from his microbiology research. It must have some purpose."

Perez looked slightly offended. "I don't resent our Clowns in Space program. It provides entertainment. But what Woody's working on is dead serious."

"Like recording the blood pressure of prairie dogs," Louisa said.

Leaphorn watched her pass Perez the bowl of boiled new potatoes. He had decided to drop out of this conversation and be a spectator.

Perez took a small potato. Looked at Louisa thoughtfully. Took another one.

"I just read a paper this morning from one of the microbiologists at NIH," Perez said, pausing to sample the potato. "NIH." He grinned at Louisa. "For you mythologists, that's the National Institutes of Health."

Louisa tried to let that pass but didn't manage it. "Not affiliated with the UN then," she said. "For you biologists, that's United Period Nations."

Perez laughed. "Okay," he said. "Peace be with us all. My point is, this guy was reporting dreadful stuff. For example, remember cholera? Virtually wiped out back in the sixties. Well, there were almost a hundred thousand new cases in South America alone in the past two years. And TB, the old 'white plague,' which we finally eliminated about 1970. Well, now the world death rate from that is up to three million per annum again— and the pathogen is a DR mycobacterium."

Louisa gave Leaphorn a wry look. "I listen to this guy a lot and learn his jargon. He's trying to say the TB germ has become drug-resistant."

"What we'd call the perpetrator," Leaphorn said.

"Great subject for dinner conversation," Louisa said. "Cholera and TB."

"More cheerful, though, than telling you about the summer-session papers I've been grading," Perez said. "But I'd like to hear from Mr. Leaphorn about this vanished biologist he's looking for."

"There's not much to tell," Leaphorn said. "She's a vector control person for the Indian Health Service, or maybe it's the Arizona Health Department. They sort of operate together. She's been working out of Tuba City. About two weeks ago she drove out in the morning to check on rodent burrows and didn't come back."

He stopped, waiting for Perez to ask the standard questions about boyfriend, stalker, nervous breakdown, job stress, et cetera.

"I'd guess that's why Louisa wanted me to find out whether the Hammar boy was teaching his lab on July eighth," Perez said. "Was that the day?"

Leaphorn nodded.

"Mike Devente handles those lab programs," Perez said. "He said Hammar was sick. Had food poisoning or something."

"Sick," Leaphorn said.

Perez laughed. "Or called in sick, anyway. With teaching assistants, sometimes there's a difference."

Perez sampled his second potato, said: "Is he a suspect?"

"He might be if we had a crime," Leaphorn said. "All we have is a woman who drove off in an Indian Health Service vehicle and didn't come back."

"Louisa said this Pollard lady was checking sources for this latest *Yersinia pestis* outbreak. Is that why you are interested in Woody?"

Leaphorn shook his head. "I never heard of him before today. But they're both interested in prairie dogs, pack rats and so forth and in the same territory. Not many people are, so maybe their paths crossed. Maybe he saw her somewhere. Maybe she told him where she was going."

Perez looked thoughtful. "Yeah," he said.

"They're working in the same field, so he'd probably know about her," Leaphorn said. "But in such a big country it's not likely they'd meet, and if they did, why is she going to tell a virtual stranger that she's going to run off with a government vehicle?"

"Mutual interests, though," Perez said. "They cut pretty deep. How often do you find someone who wants to talk to you about fleas on prairie dogs? And Woody is a downright fanatic about his work. Run him into another human with any knowledge of infectious diseases, immunology, any of that, and he's going to tell 'em a lot more about it than they'll want to know. He's obsessed by it. He thinks the bacteria are going to eliminate mammals unless we do something about it. And if they don't get us, the viruses will. He feels this need to warn everybody about it. Jeremiah complex."

"I can sympathize with that," Leaphorn said. "I'm always talking about what's wrong with the War on Drugs. Until I notice everybody is yawning."

"Same problem with me," Perez said. "I'll bet you're not very interested in discussing molecular mineral transmission through cell walls."

"Only if you explained it so I could understand it," Leaphorn said. He wished he hadn't mentioned Woody to Louisa, wished she hadn't invited Perez, wished they could just be having a relaxing evening together. "And first I guess you'd have to explain why I should care about it."

It was the wrong thing to say, inspiring Dr. Perez to defend pure science and orate on the need to collect knowledge merely for the sake of knowledge. Leaphorn nibbled at the second chop. He down-rated his character for lacking the courage to refuse it. He examined his semihostile reaction to Perez. It had begun when he saw the Saab parked where he liked to park in Louisa's driveway and worsened when he saw the man standing beside her in the doorway, grinning at him. And it clicked up another notch when he noticed that Perez seemed to be looking upon him as a rival. Perez was jealous, he concluded. But then what about Joe Leaphorn? Was Joe Leaphorn jealous? It was an unsettling thought, and he took another bite of the lamb chop to drive it away.

Perez had completed his account of how pure science had led to the discovery of penicillin and the whole arsenal of antibiotics, which had pretty well wiped out infectious diseases. Now he digressed into how stupid misuse of those drugs had turned victory into defeat and how the killer bugs were mutating furiously into all sorts of new forms.

"Mom brings her kid in with a runny nose. The doc knows a virus is causing it, and antibiotics won't touch the virus, but the kid is crying, and

Mom wants a prescription, so he gives her his pet antibiotic and tells Mama to give it to the kid for eight days. And then two days later, the immune system deals with the virus, and she stops the medicine. But two days of the antibiotic"—Perez paused, took a long sip from his wineglass, wiped his mustache—"has slaughtered all the bacteria in the kid's bloodstream except—" Perez paused again, waved his hand. "Except the few freaks who happened to be resistant to the drug. So, with the competition wiped out, these freaks multiply like crazy, and the kid is full of drug-resistant bacteria. And then—"

"And then it's time for dessert," Louisa said. "How about some ice cream? Or brownies?"

"Or maybe both," Perez said. "Anyway, just a few years ago about ninety-nine-point-nine percent of *Staphylococcus aureus* was killed by penicillin. Now it's down to about four percent. Only one of the other antibiotics works on the stuff now, and sometimes it doesn't work."

Louisa's voice came from the kitchen. "Enough! Enough! No more doomsday talk." She emerged, carrying dessert. "And now thirty percent of the people who die in hospitals die of something they didn't have when they came in." She laughed. "Or is it forty percent? I've heard this lecture before, but mythologists aren't good with numbers."

"It's about thirty percent," Perez said, looking miffed. A bowl of ice cream and two brownies later, Perez pleaded the need to finish grading papers and rolled his Saab out of Leaphorn's place in the driveway.

"An interesting man," Leaphorn said, stacking saucers on plates, and cutlery atop that, and heading for the kitchen.

"Have a seat," Louisa said. "I can take care of the cleanup."

"Widowers get awfully good at this. I want to demonstrate my skills." Which he did, until he noticed Louisa rearranging the plates he'd put into the washer.

"Wrong way?" he asked.

"Well," she said, "if you put them in with the food side facing inward, then the hot water spray hits that. It gets 'em cleaner."

So Leaphorn sat and wondered if Perez had actually been jealous of him and what that might imply, and tried to think of a way to bring up the subject. He drew a blank. A few moments later the clattering in the kitchen stopped. Louisa emerged and sat on the sofa across from him.

"Wonderful dinner," Leaphorn said. "Thank you."

She nodded. "Michael really is an interesting man," she said. "He was way too talky tonight, but that was because I told him you were interested in what Professor Woody was doing." She shrugged. "He was just trying to be helpful."

"I sort of got the feeling he didn't care too much for me."

"That was jealousy. He was showing off a little bit. The male territorial imperative at work."

Leaphorn had not the slightest idea how to react to that. He opened his mouth, took a breath, said "Aah," and closed it.

"We go way back. Old friends."

"Aah," Leaphorn said again. "Friends." He had left the question off the sound of that, but it didn't fool Louisa.

"He wanted to marry me once, long ago," Louisa said. "I told him I'd tried getting married once when I was young and I hadn't cared much for it."

Leaphorn considered this. Now was one of those times when you wished you hadn't quit smoking. Lighting up a cigarette gave you time for thought. "You never told me you'd been married," he said.

"There really wasn't any reason to," she said.

"I guess not," he said. "But I'm interested."

She laughed. "I really ought to tell you it's none of your business. But I think I'll put on a pot of coffee and decide what I'm going to say."

When she came back with two steaming cups, she handed one to Leaphorn with a broad smile.

"I decided I'm glad you asked," she said, sat down, and told him about it. They had both been graduate students, and he was big, hand-some, and sort of out of it and always needed help with his classes. She'd thought that was charming at the time, and the charm had lasted about a year.

"It took me that long to understand that he'd been looking for a sec-ond mother. You know, somebody to take care of him."

"Lots of men like that," Leaphorn said, and since he couldn't think of anything to add to that, he switched the subject over to Catherine Pollard and his meeting with Mrs. Vanders.

"I wondered why you decided to take that on," she said. "It sounds hopeless to me."

"It probably is," Leaphorn said. "I'm going to give it a couple more days and if it still looks hopeless, I'll call the lady and tell her I failed." He finished his coffee and stood. "It's eighty miles back to Tuba City—actually eighty-two to my motel—and I've got to get going."

"You're too tired to make that drive," she said. "Stay here. Get some sleep. Drive it in the morning."

"Um," Leaphorn said. "Well, I wanted to try to find this Woody and see if he can tell me anything."

"He'll keep," Louisa said. "It won't take any longer to drive it in the morning."

"Stay here?"

"Why not? Use the guest bedroom. I have a nine-thirty lecture. But if you want a real early start there's an alarm clock on the desk in there."

"Well," Leaphorn said, digesting this, and recognizing how tired he was, and the nature of friendship. "Yes. Well, thank you."

"There's some sleeping stuff in the chest. Nightgowns and so forth in the top drawer and pajamas in the bottom one."

"Men's?"

"Men's, women's, what have you. Guests can't be too particular about borrowed pajamas."

Louisa, taking their empty cups into the kitchen, stopped in the doorway.

"I'm still wondering why you took the job," she said. "It surprises me."

"Me, too," Leaphorn said. "But I'd been thinking about that Navajo policeman killed up near Yells Back Butte, and it turns out Catherine Pollard disappeared the same day, and she was supposed to be going to check on rodent burrows about the same place."

"Ah," Louisa said, smiling. "And if I remember what you've told me, Joe Leaphorn never could believe in coincidence."

She stood holding the cups, studying him. "You know, Joe, if I didn't have to work tomorrow I'd invite myself along. I'd like to meet this Woody fellow."

"You'd be welcome," Leaphorn said.

And more than welcome. He'd been dreading tomorrow, doing his duty, keeping a promise he'd made for no particular reason to an old woman he didn't even know without any real hope of learning anything useful.

Louisa still hadn't moved from the doorway.

"Would I be?"

"It would make my day," Leaphorn said.

11

A HIGH-PITCHED METHODICAL whimpering sound intruded into Joe Leaphorn's dream and jerked him abruptly awake. It came from a strange-looking white alarm clock on a desk beside his bed, which was also strange—soft and warm and smelling of soap and sunshine. His eyes finally focused and he saw a ceiling as white as his own, but lacking the pattern of plaster cracks he had memorized through untold hours of insomnia.

Leaphorn pushed himself into a sitting position, fully awake, with his short-term memories flooding back. He was in Louisa Bourebonette's guest bedroom. He fumbled with the alarm clock, hoping to shut off the whimpering before it awakened her. But obviously it was too late for that. He smelled coffee brewing and bacon frying—the almost forgotten aromas of contentment. He stretched, yawned, settled back against the pillow. The crisp, fresh sheets reminded him of Emma. Everything did. The morning breeze ruffled the curtains beside his head. Emma, too, always left their windows open to the outside air until Window Rock's bitter winter made it impractical. The curtains, too. He had teased her about that. "I didn't see window curtains in your mother's hogan, Emma," he'd said. And she rewarded him with her tolerant smile and reminded him he'd moved her out of the hogan, and Navajos must remain in harmony with houses that needed curtains. That was one of the things he loved about her. One of the many. As numerous as the stars of a high country midnight.

He'd persuaded Emma that she should marry him two days before he was to take the Graduate General Examination for his degree at Arizona State. The degree was in anthropology, but the dreaded GGE covered the spectrum of the humanities and he'd been brushing up on his weak points—which had led him into a quick scan of Shakespeare's "most likely to be asked about on GGE" plays and hence to Othello's discourse about Desdemona. He still remembered the passage, although he wasn't sure he had it quite right: "She loved me for the dangers I had passed, and I loved her that she did pity them."

"Leaphorn, are you up? If you're not, your eggs are going to be overhard."

"I'm up," Leaphorn said, and got up, grabbed his clothes and hurried into the bathroom. The point Othello was trying to make, he thought, was that he loved Desdemona because she loved him. Which sounded simple enough, but actually was a very complicated concept.

Louisa's guest bathroom was equipped with a guest toothbrush, and Leaphorn, being blessed with the Indian's sparse and slow-growing beard, didn't miss a razor. ("No whiskers is proof," his grandfather had told him, "that Navajos are evolved further from the apes than those hairy white men.")

Despite the threat, Louisa had actually delayed cracking the breakfast eggs until he appeared in the kitchen doorway.

"I hope you meant it when you said you'd be happy to have me along today," she said as they started breakfast. "If you did, I can come."

Leaphorn was buttering his toast. He'd already noticed that Professor Bourebonette was not wearing the formal skirt and blouse that were her teaching attire. She was clad in jeans and a long-sleeved denim shirt.

"I meant it," he said. "But it'll be boring, like about ninety-nine percent of this kind of work. I was just going to see if I could find this Woody, find out if he'd seen Catherine Pollard and if he could tell me anything helpful. Then I was going to drive back to Window Rock and call Mrs. Vanders, report no progress and—"

"Sounds all right," she said.

Leaphorn put down his fork. "How about your class?"

It wasn't really the question he wanted to ask. He wanted to know what her plans were when the day's duties were done. Did she expect him to bring her back to Flagstaff? Did she intend to stay in Tuba City? Or accompany him home to Window Rock? And if so, what then?

"All I have today is one meeting of my ethnology course," Louisa said. "I'd already scheduled David Esoni to do his lecture on Zuni teaching stories. I think you met him."

"He's the professor from Zuni? I thought he taught chemistry."

Louisa nodded. "He does. And every year I get him to talk to my entry-level class about Zuni mythology. And culture in general. I called him this morning. The class expects him and he said he could introduce himself."

Leaphorn nodded. Cleared his throat, trying to phrase the question. He didn't need to.

"I'll drop off when we get to Tuba. I want to see Jim Peshlakai—he teaches the traditional cultural stuff at Grey Hills High School there. He's going to set up interviews for me with a bunch of his students from other tribes. Then he's coming down to Flag tonight for some work in the library. I'll ride back with him."

"Oh," Leaphorn said. "Good."

Louisa smiled. "I thought you'd say that," she said. "I'll fix a thermos of coffee. And a little snack, just in case."

So nothing remained but to check his telephone answering service. He dialed the number and the code. Two calls. The first was from Mrs. Vanders. She still had heard nothing from Catherine. Did he have anything to tell her?

The second was from Cowboy Dashee. Would Mr. Leaphorn please call him as soon as possible. He left his number.

Leaphorn hung up and listened to the noises Louisa was causing in the kitchen while he stared at the telephone, getting Cowboy Dashee properly placed. He was a cop. He was a Hopi. A friend of Jim Chee. A Coconino County deputy sheriff now, Leaphorn remembered. What would Dashee want to talk about? Why try to guess? Leaphorn dialed the number.

"Cameron Police Department," a woman's voice said. "How may I be of service?"

"This is Joe Leaphorn. I just had a call from Deputy Sheriff Dashee. He left this number."

"Oh, yes," the woman said. "Just a moment. I'll see if he's still here."

Clicking. Silence. Then: "Lieutenant Leaphorn?"

"Yes," Leaphorn said. "But it's mister now. I got your message. What's up?"

Dashee cleared his throat. "Well," he said. "It's just that I need some advice." Another pause.

"Sure," Leaphorn said. "It's free and you know what they say about free advice being worth what it costs you."

"Well," Dashee said. "I have a problem I don't know how to handle."

"You want to tell me about it?"

Another clearing of throat. "Could I meet you someplace where we could talk? It's kind of touchy. And complicated."

"I'm calling from Flag and just getting ready to drive up to Tuba City. I'll be coming through Cameron in maybe an hour."

"Fine," Dashee said, and suggested a coffee shop beside Highway 89.

"I'll have an NAU professor with me," Leaphorn said. "Will that be a problem?"

A long pause. "No, sir," Dashee said. "I don't think so."

But by the time they'd reached Cameron and pulled up beside the patrol car with the Cononino County Sheriff's Department markings, Louisa had decided she should wait in the car.

"Don't be silly," she said. "Of course he'd say it would be no problem to have me listening in. What else could he say when he's asking you for a favor." She opened her purse and extracted a paperback and showed it to Leaphorn. "*Execution Eve*," she said. "You ought to read it. The son of a former Kentucky prison warden remembering the murder case that turned his dad against the death penalty."

"Oh, come on in. Dashee won't mind."

"This book's more interesting," she said, "and he would mind."

And of course she was right. When they parked, Leaphorn had seen Deputy Sheriff Albert "Cowboy" Dashee sitting in a booth beside the window looking out at them, his expression glum. Now, as he sat across from Dashee, watching him order coffee, Leaphorn was remembering that this Hopi had struck him as a man full of good humor. A happy man. There was no sign of that this morning.

"I'll get right to the point," Dashee said. "I need to talk to you about Jim Chee."

"About Chee?" This wasn't what Leaphorn had expected. In fact, he'd had no idea what to expect. Something about the Hopi killing the Navajo policeman, perhaps. "You two are old friends, aren't you?"

"For a long, long time," Dashee said. "That makes this harder to deal with."

Leaphorn nodded.

"Jim always considered you a friend, too," Dashee said. He grinned ruefully. "Even when he was sore at you."

Leaphorn nodded again. "Which was fairly often."

"The thing is, Jim got the wrong man in this Benjamin Kinsman homicide. Robert Jano didn't do it."

"He didn't?"

"No. Robert wouldn't kill anyone."

"Who did?"

"I don't know," Dashee said. "But I grew up with Robert Jano. I know you hear this all the time, but—" He threw up his hands.

"I know people myself who I just can't believe would ever kill anyone—no matter what. But sometimes something snaps, and they do it. Temporary insanity."

"You'd have to know him. If you did, you'd never believe it. He was always gentle, even when we were kids trying to be tough. Robert never seemed to really lose his temper. He liked everybody. Even the bastards."

Leaphorn could see Dashee was hating this. He'd pushed his uniform cap back on his head. His face was flushed. His forehead was beaded with perspiration.

"I'm retired, you know," Leaphorn said. "So all I get is the second-hand gossip. But what I hear is that Chee caught the man red-handed. Jano was supposed to be leaning over Kinsman, blood all over him. Some of the blood was Jano's. Some of the blood was Kinsman's. Was that about it?"

Dashee sighed, rubbed his hand across his face. "That's the way it must have looked to Jim."

"You talked to Jim?"

Dashee shook his head. "That's the advice I wanted. How do I go about that? You know how he is. Kinsman was one of his people. Somebody kills him. He must feel pretty strong about that. And I'm a cop, too.

It's not my case. And being a Hopi. The kind of anger that's grown up between us and you Navajos." He threw up his hands again. "It's such a damned complicated situation. I want him to know it's not just sentimental bullshit. How can I approach him?"

"Yeah," Leaphorn said, thinking that everything Dashee had said did indeed sound like sentimental bullshit. "I understand your problem."

The coffee arrived, reminding Leaphorn of Louisa waiting outside. But she had the thermos they'd brought and she would understand. Just as Emma always understood. He sipped the coffee without noticing anything, except that it was hot.

"Did they let you talk to Jano?"

Dashee nodded.

"How'd you manage that?"

"I know his lawyer," Dashee said. "Janet Pete."

Leaphorn grunted, shook his head. "I was afraid of that," he said. "I saw her at the hospital the day Kinsman died. The prosecution bunch was gathering and she showed up, too. I'd heard she's been appointed as a federal defender."

"That's it," Dashee said. "She'll do a good job for him, but it sure as hell won't make dealing with Jim any easier."

"They were about to get married once, I think," Leaphorn said. "And then she went back to Washington. Is that on again?"

"I hope not," Dashee said. "She's a city gal. Jim's always going to be a sheep-camp Navajo. But whatever, it's going to make him touchy as hell, being on opposite sides of this. He'll be hard to deal with."

"But Chee was always reasonable," Leaphorn said. "If it was me, I'd just go and lay it out for him. Just make the best case you can."

"You think it will do any good?"

"I doubt it," Leaphorn said. "Not unless you give him some sort of evidence. How could it? If what I hear at Window Rock is right, Jano had a motive. Revenge as well as avoiding arrest. Kinsman had already nailed him before for poaching an eagle. He got off light then, but this would be a second offense. More important, I understand there was no other possible suspect. Besides, even if you persuade Chee he's wrong, what can he do about it now?"

Dashee hadn't touched his coffee. He leaned across the table. "Find the person who actually killed Kinsman," Dashee said. "I want to ask him to do that. Or help me do it."

"But as I understand the situation, only Jano and Kinsman were there, until Chee came along answering Kinsman's call for some backup."

"There was a woman up there," Dashee said. "A woman named Catherine Pollard. Maybe other people."

Leaphorn, caught in the process of raising his cup for another sip, said, "Ah," and put down the cup. He stared at Dashee for a moment. "How do you know that?"

"I've been asking around," Dashee said, and produced a bitter laugh. "Something Jim should be doing." He shook his head. "He's a good man and a good cop. I'm asking you how I can get him moving. If he doesn't, I think Jano could get the death penalty. And one day Jim's going to know they gassed the wrong man. And then you might as well kill him, too. Chee would never get over that."

"I know something about Catherine Pollard," Leaphorn said.

"I know," Dashee said. "I heard."

"If she was there—and I understand that's where she was supposed to be going that day—how could she fit into this? Except, of course, as a potential witness."

"I'd like to give Jim another theory of the crime," Dashee said. "Ask him to look at it for a while as a substitute for 'Jano kills Kinsman to avoid arrest.' It goes like this: Pollard goes up to Yells Back Butte to do her thing. Kinsman is up there looking for Jano, or maybe he's looking for Pollard. One way, he runs across her. The other way, he finds her. Just a couple of nights earlier, Kinsman was in a bistro off the interstate east of Flag, and he saw Pollard and tried to take her away from the guy she was with. A fight started. An Arizona highway patrolman broke it up."

Leaphorn turned the cup in his hand, considering this. No reason to ask Dashee how he knew this. Cop gossip travels fast.

Dashee was watching him, looking anxious. "What do you think?" he said. "Kinsman has a reputation as a woman-chaser. He's attracted and now he's angry, too. Or maybe he thinks she'll file a complaint and get him suspended." He shrugged. "They struggle. She whacks him on the head with a rock. Then she hears Jano coming and flees the scene. Does that sound plausible?"

"A lot would depend on whether you have a witness who would testify they saw her there. Do you? I mean, beyond that being where she told her boss she'd be working that day?"

"I got it from Old Lady Notah. She keeps a bunch of goats up there. She remembers seeing a Jeep driving up that dirt road past the butte about daylight that morning. I understand Pollard was driving a Jeep." Dashee looked slightly abashed. "Just circumstantial evidence. She couldn't identify the driver. Not even the gender."

"Still, it was probably Pollard," Leaphorn said.

"And I understand the Jeep is still missing. And so is Pollard."

"Right again."

"And you've been offering a thousand-dollar reward for anyone who can find it."

"True," Leaphorn said. "But if Pollard did it, and Pollard was fleeing the scene, why didn't Chee see her? Remember, he got there just a few minutes after it happened. Kinsman's blood was still fresh. There's just that one narrow dirt road into there, and Chee was driving up it. Why didn't he—"

Dashee held up his hand. "I don't know, and neither do you. But don't you think it could have happened?"

Leaphorn nodded. "Possibly."

"I don't want to get out of line with this, or sound offensive, but let me add something else to my theory of the crime. Let's say that Pollard got out of there, got to a telephone, called somebody and told them her troubles and asked for help. Let's say whoever it was told her where to hide and they'd cover her trail for her."

Leaphorn asked: "Like who and how?" But he knew the answer.

"Who? I'd say somebody in her family. Probably her daddy, I'd say. How? By giving the impression that she's been abducted. Been murdered."

"And they do that by hiring a retired policeman to go looking for her," Leaphorn said.

"Somebody respected by all the cops," Dashee said.

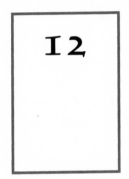

12

THE ROCK UPON which Chee had so carelessly put his weight tumbled down the slope, bounced into space, struck an obtruding ledge,
touched off a clattering avalanche of stone and dirt and disappeared amid
the weeds far below. Chee shifted his body carefully to his right, exhaled a
huge breath and stood for a moment, leaning against the cliff and letting
his heartbeat slow a little. He was just below the tabletop of Yells Back
Butte, high on the saddle that connected it with Black Mesa. It wasn't a
difficult climb for a young man in Chee's excellent physical shape, and not
particularly dangerous if one kept focused on what he was doing. Chee
hadn't. He'd been thinking of Janet Pete, facing the fact that he was wasting his day off just because she'd implied he hadn't done a proper job of
checking the Kinsman crime scene.

   Now, with both feet firmly placed and his shoulder leaning into the
cliff wall, he looked down at where the boulder had made its plunge and
thought about that chronic problem of the Navajo Tribal Police—lack of
backup. Had he not caught himself, he'd be down there in the weeds with
broken bones and multiple abrasions and about sixty miles from help. He
was thinking of that as he scrambled up the last fifty feet of talus and
crawled over the rim. Kinsman would be alive if he hadn't been alone. The
story was the same for the two officers killed in the Kayenta district. A
huge territory, never enough officers for backup, never enough budget for

efficient communications, never what you needed to get the job done. Maybe Janet had been right. He'd take the FBI examination, or accept the offer he'd had from the BIA law-and-order people. Or maybe, if all else failed, consider signing on with the Drug Enforcement Agency.

But now, standing on the flat stone roof of Yells Back Butte, he looked westward and saw the immense sky, the line of thunderheads building over the Coconino Rim, the sunlight reflecting off the Vermillion Cliffs below the Utah border, and the towering cauliflower shape of the storm already delivering a rain blessing upon the San Francisco Peaks, the Sacred Mountain marking the western margin of his people's holy land. Chee closed his eyes against that, remembering Janet's beauty, her wit, her intelligence. But other memories crowded in: the dreary skies of Washington, the swarms of young men entombed in three-piece suits and subdued by whatever neckties today's fashion demanded; remembering the clamor, the sirens, the smell of the traffic, the layers upon layers of social phoniness. A faint breeze stirred Chee's hair and brought him the smell of juniper and sage, and a chittering sound from far overhead that reminded him of why he was here.

At first glance he thought the raptor was a red-tailed hawk, but when it banked to repeat its inspection of this intruder Chee saw it was a golden eagle. It was the fourth one he'd seen today—a good year for eagles and a good place to find them—patrolling the mesa rimrock where rodents flourished. He watched this one circle, gray-white against the dark blue sky, until it satisfied its curiosity and drifted eastward over Black Mesa. When it turned, he noticed a gap in its fan of tail feathers. Probably an old one. Tail feathers aren't lost to molting.

Even with Janet's directions, it took Chee half an hour to find Jano's blind. The Hopi had roofed a crack in the butte's rimrock with a network of dead sage branches and covered that with foliage cut from nearby brush. Much of that was broken and scattered now. Chee climbed into the crack, squatted, and examined the place, reconstructing Jano's strategy.

He would have first assured himself that the eagle he wanted routinely patrolled this place. He would have probably come in the evening to prepare his blind—or more likely to repair one members of his kiva had been using for centuries. If he'd changed anything noticeable, he would have waited a few days until the eagle had become accustomed to this variation in his landscape. That done, Jano would have returned early on the morning he was fated to kill Ben Kinsman. He would have brought a rabbit with him, tied a cord to the rabbit's leg and put it atop the blind's roof. Then he would have waited, watching through the cracks for the eagle to appear. Since the eyes of raptors detect motion far better than any radar, he would have made sure the rabbit moved when the proper moment came. When the eagle seized it with its talons, he'd pull the rabbit downward, throw his coat over the bird to overpower it, and push it into the cage he'd brought.

Chee checked the ground around him, looking for any proof that Jano had been there. He didn't expect to find anything, and he didn't. The rock where Jano must have sat while he waited for his eagle was worn smooth. Anyone might have sat there that day, or no one. He found not a trace of the bloodstains Jano might have left here had the eagle gashed him as he caught it. The rain might have washed blood away, but it would have left a trace in the grainy granite. He climbed out of the crack, bringing with him only a bedraggled eagle feather from the sandy floor of the blind and a cigarette butt that looked like it had weathered much more than last week's shower. The feather was from the body—not one of the strong wingtip or tail feathers valued for ceremonial objects. And neither the feather nor the butt showed any sign of bloodstains. He tossed them back into the blind.

Chee spent another hour or so making an equally fruitless check around the butte. He came across another blind a half mile down the rim, and several places where stones had been stacked with little painted prayer sticks placed among them and feathers tied to nearby sage branches. Clearly the Hopis considered this butte part of their spiritual homeland, and it probably had been since their first clans arrived about the twelfth century. The federal government's decision to add it to the Navajo Reservation hadn't changed that, and never would. The thought made him feel like a trespasser on his own reservation and did nothing good for Chee's mood. It was time to say to hell with this and go home.

The desk work required of an acting lieutenant had not helped the muscle tone in Jim Chee's legs, nor his lungs. He was tired. He stood at the rim, looking across the saddle, dreading the long climb down. An eagle soared over Black Mesa and the shape of another was outlined against the clouds far to the south over the San Francisco Peaks. This was eagle country and always had been. When the first Hopi clans founded their villages on the First Mesa, the elders had assigned eagle-collecting territory just as they'd assigned cornfields and springs. And when the Navajos came along a couple of hundred years later they, too, soon learned that one came to Black Mesa when one's medicine bundle required eagle feathers.

Chee took out his binoculars and tried to locate the bird he'd seen against the cloud. It was gone. He found the one hunting over the mesa and focused on it—thinking it might be the one he'd watched earlier. It wasn't. This one had a complete fan of tail feathers. He swung the binoculars downward, focused on the place where he'd found Jano beside Ben Kinsman's dying body and tried to re-create how that tragedy must have happened.

Jano might not have seen Kinsman below, because Kinsman would have concealed himself. But looking down from here, he could hardly have missed noticing Kinsman's patrol car where he'd left it down the arroyo. Jano had been arrested once for poaching an eagle. He would have been nervous, and careful.

So why climb down to be captured? Probably because he had no choice. But why not just release the eagle, hide the cage, climb down and tell the cop he was up here meditating and saying his prayers? Jano's faded red pickup had been parked below the low point of the saddle and Kinsman had left his patrol car near the arroyo maybe a half mile away. Even without binoculars, Jano would have seen that Kinsman had his escape route blocked.

Chee scanned the valley again, picking up the ruins of what must have been the tumbled stones that once formed the walls of the Tijinney hogan, its sheep pens and its fallen brush arbor. Beyond the hogan site, a glint of reflected sunlight caught his eye. He focused on the spot. The side mirror of some sort of van parked in a cluster of junipers. What would that be doing up here? Two of last spring's plague victims had come from this quadrant of the reservation. The van might be Arizona Health Department people collecting rodents and checking fleas. He remembered Leaphorn had told him the woman he was looking for had come up this way working on a plague case.

On the opposite side of the saddle, away from the van, the Tijinney "death hogan" and the murder site, motion caught Chee's peripheral vision. He focused on it. A black-and-white goat grazing on a bush. And not just one. He counted seven, but there might be seventeen or seventy scattered through that rough area.

While counting them, he found the track. Actually, two tracks, probably formed by the vehicle of whomever held this grazing lease and drove in now and then to see about his flock.

It was not something even a sheep-camp Navajo would dignify by calling a road, but as Chee traced the track back toward the access road through his binoculars, he realized its importance. Jano did have a way out—a way to avoid capture without giving up his eagle. He could have slipped down the other side of the saddle, invisible to the officer waiting to arrest him. He could have left the eagle in some safe place, made the easy climb over the low point of the saddle with nothing to incriminate him. Then he could have recovered his pickup truck, driven back to the gravel road, followed it a mile or two back toward Tuba City, and then circled back on this goatherd's track to recover his captive bird.

Jano would have known about this track. These were his eagle-catching grounds. He could have escaped easily. Instead he chose the path that led him directly to where Kinsman was waiting.

Chee started his descent carefully, remembering the dislodged stone that had almost sent him tumbling down the slope. It had been a bad day so far. He'd climbed the saddle thinking that Jano was a man who had killed in what probably had been a frantic effort to avoid arrest and then made up unlikely lies to save himself from prison. At the foot of the saddle, Chee stood for a moment to catch his breath. He glanced at his watch. He'd locate the van now, find out if whoever was with it had been here on the fateful day and—if they had been—whether they'd seen anything. If they hadn't, that, too, could be useful as a sort of negative evidence.

When he'd climbed Yells Back Butte he had nursed a vague, ambiguous hope that maybe he could find something to suggest Jano wasn't lying, that Jano wouldn't have to face the death penalty or (worse, in Chee's opinion) life in prison. To be honest, he had wanted to discover something that would restore his prestige in the eyes of Janet Pete. But now he knew that the murder of Benjamin Kinsman had been a deliberate, premeditated, and savage act of revenge.

13

THE VAN WAS parked on the sandy bed of a shallow wash, partly shaded by a cluster of junipers and screened by a growth of four-winged saltbush. No one was visible, but what looked like an oversized air-conditioning unit was purring away on its roof. Chee stood on the fold-down step beside its door and rapped on the metal, then rapped again, and—harder this time—once again. No response. He tried the doorknob. Locked. He leaned his ear against the door and listened. Nothing at first, except the vibrations from the air conditioner, then a faint, rhythmic sound.

Chee stepped back from the van and inspected it. It had a custom-made body mounted on a heavy GMC truck chassis with dual rear wheels. It looked expensive, fairly new and—judging from the dents and abrasions—heavily (or carelessly) used in rough country. Except for the lack of a door, nothing was different on the driver's side. Built against the rear was a fold-down metal ladder to provide access to the roof and a rack, which now held a dirt bike, a folding table and two chairs, a five-gallon gasoline can, a pick, a shovel, and an assortment of rodent traps and cages. There were no windows on the rear and the only side windows were high on the wall. Placed high, Chee guessed, to allow more space for storage cabinets.

He knocked again, rattled the knob, shouted, received no response, put his ear against the door again. This time he heard another faint sound. Something scratching. A tiny squeak, like chalk on a blackboard.

Chee folded down the access ladder, climbed onto the roof, dropped to his stomach, and secured a firm grip on the air-conditioner engine mount. Then he squirmed over the edge and leaned down to look into the high windows. All he saw was darkness and a streak of light reflecting from a white surface.

"Ho, there," a voice shouted. "Whatcha doing?"

Chee jerked his head up. He looked down into a face staring up at him, expression quizzical, bright blue eyes, dark, sun-peeled face, tufts of gray hair protruding from under a dark blue cap that bore the legend SQUIBB. The man carried what looked like a shoebox containing what seemed to be a dead prairie dog inside a plastic sack.

"Is that your car I saw back there?" the man asked. "The Navajo Tribal Police car?"

"Yeah," Chee said, trying to scramble to his feet without further loss of dignity. He pointed down to the roof under his boots. "I heard something in there," he stammered. "Thought I did, anyway. Something squeaking. And I couldn't raise anyone, so—"

"Probably one of the rodents," the man said. He put down the shoe-box, extracted a key ring from a pocket and unlocked the doors. "Come on down. How about a drink of something?"

Chee scrambled down the ladder. The man under the Squibb cap was holding the door open for him. Cold air rushed out.

"My name's Chee," he said, extending a hand. "With the Navajo Tribal Police. I guess you're with the Arizona Health Department."

"No," the man said. "I'm Al Woody. I'm working on a research project up here. For the National Institutes of Health, Indian Health Service, so forth. But come on in."

Inside Chee turned down a beer and accepted a glass of water. Woody opened the door of a built-in floor-to-ceiling refrigerator and brought out a bottle white with frost. He scraped away the ice crystals and showed Chee a Dewar's scotch label.

"Antifreeze," he said, laughing, and began pouring himself a drink. "But once I was preserving some tissue and turned the fridge down so low that even the whiskey froze up on me."

Chee sipped his water, noticing it was stale and had a slightly unpleasant taste. He searched his brain for a proper apology for trying to peek into the man's window. He decided there wasn't one. He'd just forget it and let Woody think whatever he wanted to think.

"I'm doing some back-checking on a homicide case we had up here," Chee said. "It was July eighth. One of our officers was killed. Hit on the head with a rock. You probably heard about it on the radio or saw it in the paper. We're trying to find any witnesses we might have overlooked."

"I heard about that," Woody said. "But the man down at the trading post told me you'd caught the killer right in the act."

"Who told you?"

"That grouchy old man at the Short Mountain Trading Post," Woody said, frowning. "I think his name was Mac something. Sounded Scotch. Did he have it wrong?"

"About as close as you can get," Chee said. "The smoking gun was a bloody rock."

"The old man said it was a Hopi and the cop had arrested the same guy before," Woody said, looking pensive. Then he nodded, understanding it. "But out here you'd get Hopis on the jury. So you're trying not to leave them any grounds for reasonable doubts."

"Yeah," Chee said. "I guess that about sums it up. Were you working up here that day? If you were, did you see anybody? Or anything? Or hear anything?"

"July eighth, was it?" He punched buttons on his digital watch. "That would make it a Friday," he said, and frowned, thinking about it. "I drove down to Flagstaff, but I think that was Wednesday. I think I was up here Tuesday early, and then I drove over to Third Mesa. That's one of the prairie dog colonies I'm watching. Over there by Bacavi. That and some Kangaroo rats."

"It rained that day," Chee said. "Thundershower. Little bit of hail."

Woody nodded. "Yeah, I remember," he said. "I'd stopped at the Hopi Cultural Center to get some coffee, and you could see a lot of lightning over that side of Black Mesa and southwest over the San Francisco Peaks, and it looked like it was pouring down at Yells Back Butte. I was feeling glad I got down that road before it got muddy."

"Did you see anybody when you were driving out? Meet anyone coming in?"

Woody had been unzipping the plastic bag while he talked, and a puff of escaping air added another unpleasant aroma to the room. Now he pulled out the prairie dog, stiff with rigor mortis, and laid it carefully on the tabletop. He stared at it, felt its neck, groin area and under the front legs. He looked thoughtful. Then he shook his head, dismissing some troublesome notion.

"Going out?" he said. "I think I saw that old lady that herds her goats over on the other side of the butte. I think that was Tuesday I saw her. And then, when I was turning out onto the gravel, I remember seeing a car coming from the Tuba City direction."

"Was it a police car?"

Woody looked up from the prairie dog. "It might have been. It was too far away to tell. But, you know, he never did pass me. Maybe he turned in toward the butte. Maybe that was your policeman. Or maybe the Hopi."

"Possibly," Chee said. "About when was it?"

"Morning. Fairly early."

Woody reclosed the bag, shook it vigorously, reopened it, and poured its contents onto a white plastic sheet on the table.

"Fleas," he said. He selected stainless-steel tweezers from a tray on a lab table, picked up a flea and showed it to Chee. "Now, if I'm lucky, the blood in these fleas is laced with *Yersinia pestis* and"—Woody poked the prairie dog with the tweezers—"so is the blood of our friend here. And if I'm very lucky, it will be *Yersinia X*, the new, modified, recently evolved fast-acting stuff that kills mammals much quicker than the old stuff." He redeposited the flea among its brethren on the plastic, grinned at Chee. "Then, if fortune continues to smile on me, the autopsy I'm about to do on this dog here will confirm what not finding any swollen glands suggests. That this fellow here didn't die of bubonic plague. He died of something old-fashioned."

Chee frowned, not quite understanding Woody's excitement. "So he died of what?"

"That's not the question. Could be old age, any of those ills that beset elderly mammals. Doesn't matter. The question is, why didn't the plague kill him?"

"But that's nothing new, is it? Haven't you guys known for years that when the plague comes through, it always leaves behind a colony here and there that's immune or something? And then the stuff spreads again, from them? I thought—"

Woody had no patience for this. "Sure, sure, sure," he said. "Reservoir colonies. Host colonies. They've been studied for years. How come their immune system blocks the bacteria? If it kills the bacteria, how come the toxin released doesn't kill the dog? If our friend here just has the original version of *Pasteurella pestis*, as we used to call it, then he just gives us another chance to poke around in the blind alley. But if he has—"

It had been a hard and disappointing day for Chee, and this interruption rankled him. He interrupted Woody:

"If he has developed immunity to this new fast-acting germ, you can compare—"

"Germ!" Woody said, laughing. "I don't hear that good old word much these days. But yes. It gives us something to check against. Here's what we know about the blood chemistry of the dogs who survived the old plague." He suggested a big box with his hands. "Now we know this modified bacteria is also killing most of those survivors. We want to know the difference in the chemistry of those who survived the new stuff."

Chee nodded.

"You understand that?"

Chee grunted. He'd taken six hours of biology at the University of New Mexico to help meet the science requirement for his degree in anthropology. The teacher had been a full professor, an international authority on spiders who had made no effort to hide his boredom with basic undergraduate courses nor his disdain for the ignorance of his students. He'd sounded a lot like Woody.

"That's easy enough to understand," Chee said. "So when you solve the puzzle, you develop a vaccine and save untold billions of prairie dogs from the plague."

Woody had done something to the flea that produced a brownish fluid and put a bit of it into a petri dish and a drop on a glass slide. He looked up. His face, already unnaturally flushed, was now even redder.

"You think it's funny?" he said. "Well, you're not the only one who does. A lot of the experts at the NIH do, too. And at Squibb. And the *New England Journal of Medicine*. And the American Pharmaceutical Association.

The same damn fools who thought we won the microbe war with peni-cillin and the streptomycin drugs."

Woody slammed his fist on the countertop, his voice rising. "So they misused them, and misused them, and kept on misusing them until they'd evolved whole new variations of drug-resistant bacteria. And now, by God, we're burying the dead! By the tens of thousands. Count Africa and Asia and its millions. And these damn fools sit on their hands and watch it get worse."

Chee was no stranger to anger barely under control. He'd seen it while breaking up bar fights, in domestic disputes, in various other ugly forms. But Woody's rage had a sort of fierce, focused intensity that was new to him.

"I didn't mean to sound flippant," Chee said. "I'm just not familiar with the implications of this sort of research."

Woody took a sip of his Dewar's, his face flushed. He shook his head, studied Chee, recognized repentance.

"Sorry I'm so damned touchy about this," he said, and laughed. "I think it's because I'm scared. All the little beasties we had beaten ten years ago are back and meaner than ever. TB is an epidemic again. So is malaria. So is cholera. We had the staph bacteria whipped with nine different an-tibiotics. Now none of 'em work on some of it. And then there's the same story with viruses. Viruses. They're what makes this most important. You know that Influenza A, that Swine Flu that came out of nowhere in 1918 and killed maybe forty million people in just a few months. That's more than were killed in four years of war. Viruses scare me even more than bac-teria."

Chee raised his eyebrows.

"Because nothing stops them except your immune system. You don't cure a viral sickness. You try to prevent it with a vaccine. That's to prepare your immune system to deal with it if it shows up."

"Yeah," Chee said. "Like polio."

"Like polio. Like some forms of influenza. Like a lot of things," Woody said. He refilled his whiskey glass. "Are you familiar with the Bible?"

"I've read it," Chee said.

"Remember what the prophet says in the Book of Chronicles? 'We are powerless against this terrible multitude that will come against us.'"

Chee wasn't sure how to take this. "Do you read that as an Old Testament prophet warning us against viruses?"

"As it stands now, they are a terrible multitude and we are damn near powerless against them," Woody said. "Not as well prepared as some of these rodents are anyway. Some of these prairie dogs here somehow have had their immune systems modified to deal with this evolved bacteria. And some of the kangaroo rats have learned to live with the hantavirus. We have to find out how."

Woody's discourse had restored his good temper. He grinned at Chee. "We don't want the rodents outlasting the humans."

Chee nodded. He slid off the stool, picked up his hat. "I'll let you get back to work. Thanks for the time. And the information."

"I just had a thought," Woody said. "The Indian Health Service has had people up here the last several weeks working through this area. Doing the vector control cleanup on that plague outbreak. You might ask them if they had anyone out there on that day."

"They did," Chee said. "I was just going to get into that. One of their people was supposed to be checking on rodents around here the day Kinsman was killed. I was going to ask you if you'd seen her. And then I was going to be on my way."

"A woman? Did she notice anything helpful?"

"Nobody even knows for sure if she got here. She's missing," Chee said. "So is the vehicle she was driving."

"Missing?" Woody said, startled. "Really? You think there could be some connection with the attack on your policeman?"

"I don't see how there could be," Chee said. "But I'd like to talk to her. I understand she's a sturdy-looking brunette, about thirty, named Catherine Pollard."

"I've seen some of those Arizona public health people here and there. That sounds like one of them," Woody said. "But I don't know her name."

"You remember the last time you saw her? And where she was?"

"Nice-looking woman, was she?" Woody said, and glanced up at Chee, not wanting to give the wrong impression. "I don't mean pretty, but good bone structure." He laughed. "Looked like she might have been an athlete."

"She was around here?"

"I think it was over at Red Lake that I saw her. Filling the gas tank on a Health Service Jeep, if that's the right woman. She asked me about the van, if I was the man doing rodent research on the reservation. She asked me to let them know if I saw any dead rodents. Let her know if I saw anything that suggested the plague was killing the rodents."

He pushed himself up from the cot. "By golly, I think she gave me a card with a phone number on it." He sorted through a box labeled OUT on his desk, said "Ah," and read: " 'Catherine Pollard, Vector Control Specialist, Communicable Disease Division, Arizona Department of Public Health.' "

He handed the card to Chee, grinned, and said: "Bingo."

"Thanks," Chee said. It didn't sound like bingo to him.

"And, hey," Woody added. "If the time's important you can check on it. When I drove up there was a Navajo Tribal Police car there and she was talking to the driver. Another woman." Woody grinned. "That one you really could call cute. Had her hair in a bun and the uniform on, but she was what we used to call a dish."

"Thanks again," Chee said. "That would be Officer Manuelito. I'll ask her."

But he wouldn't. The timing didn't matter, and if he asked Bernie Manuelito about it, he'd have to ask her why she hadn't reported that Kinsman had been hitting on her. That was a can of worms he didn't want to dig into. Claire Dineyahze, who as secretary in Chee's little division, always knew such things, had already told him. "She doesn't want to cause you any trouble," Claire had said. Chee had asked her why not, and Claire had given him one of those female "you moron" looks and said: "Don't you know?"

14

A S THEY DROVE northward out of Cameron, Leaphorn explained to Louisa what was troubling Cowboy Dashee.

"I can see his problem," she said, after spending awhile staring out the windshield. "Partly professional ethics, partly male pride, partly family loyalty, partly because he feels Chee is going to think he's trying to use their friendship for a personal reason. Is that about it? Have you decided what you're going to do about it?"

Leaphorn had pretty much decided, but he wanted to give it some more thought. He skipped past the question.

"It's all of that, I guess. But it's even more complicated. And why don't you pour us some coffee while we're thinking about it."

"Didn't you just drink about two cups in there?" Louisa asked. But she reached back and extracted her thermos from the lunch sack.

"It was pretty weak," Leaphorn said. "Besides, I believe the caffeine helps my mind work. Didn't I read that somewhere?"

"Maybe in a comic book," she said. But she poured a cup and handed it to him. "What's the more complicated part that I'm missing?"

"Another friend of Cowboy Dashee's is Janet Pete. She's been assigned as Jano's public defender. Janet and Chee were engaged to be married a while back and then they had a falling-out."

"Ouch," Louisa said, and grimaced. "That does complicate matters some."

"There's more," Leaphorn said, and sipped his coffee.

"It's starting to sound like a soap opera," Louisa said. "Don't tell me that the deputy sheriff was the third party in a love triangle."

"No. It wasn't that."

He took another sip, gestured out of the windshield at the cumulus clouds, white and puffy, drifting on the west wind away from the San Francisco Peaks. "That's our sacred mountain of the west, you know, made by First Man himself, but—"

"He built it with earth brought up from the Fourth World in the usual version of the myth," Louisa said. "But if it wasn't that, then what was it?"

"I was going to tell you that in the stories told out here on the west side of the reservation, some of the clans also call it 'Mother of Clouds.'" He pointed through the windshield. "You can see why. When there's any humidity, the west winds hit the slopes, rise, the moisture cools with altitude, the clouds form, and the wind drifts them, one after another, out over the desert. Like a cat having a litter of kittens."

Louisa was smiling at him. "Mr. Leaphorn, am I to conclude that you don't want to tell me what it was with Miss Pete and Jim Chee if it wasn't another man?"

"I'd just be passing along gossip. That's all I have. Just guesswork and gossip."

"You don't start something like that with someone and just leave it hanging. Not if you're going to be trapped in the front seat with them all day. They'll nag you. They'll get mad and surly."

"Well, then," Leaphorn said, "maybe I better make up some sort of a story."

"Do it."

Leaphorn sipped coffee, handed her the empty cup.

"Miss Pete's half Navajo. On the paternal side. Her dad's dead and her mother's a socialite rich lady. Ivy League type. Janet came out here to work for DNA after quitting a job with some big Washington law firm, which handled tribal legal work. Now we get to the gossipy part."

"Good," Louisa said.

"The way the gossips tell it, she and one of the big-shot lawyers were very good friends, and she quit the job because they had a breakup, and she was very, very, very angry with the guy. She was sort of his protégée from way back when he was a professor and she was his law student."

Leaphorn stopped talking and glanced at Louisa. He found himself thinking how much he had come to like this woman. How comfortable he felt with her. How much more pleasant this drive was because she was there on the seat beside him.

"You enjoying this so far?"

"So far, so good," she said. "But I wonder if it's going to have a happy ending."

"I don't know," Leaphorn said. "I doubt it. But anyway. Out here, she and Jim meet because she's defending Navajo suspects and he's arresting them. They get to be friends and—"

Leaphorn paused, gave Louisa a doubtful look. "Now this is about fifthhand. Pure hearsay. Anyway, the gossips had it that what Miss Pete had told Chee about her ex-boss and boyfriend had Jim hating the guy, too. You know, thinking he was a real gold-plated manipulative jerk who had simply used Janet. Understand?"

"Sure," Louisa said. "Probably true, too."

"Understand, it's just gossip."

"Get on with it," Louisa said.

"So Chee tells her some of the information he's learned in a case he's working on. It involved a client of her old Washington law firm and her old boyfriend. So she passes it along to her old boyfriend. Jim figures she's betrayed him. She figures he's being unreasonable, that she was just being friendly and helpful. No harm done, she says. Chee's just being jealous. They have an angry row. She moves back to Washington with no more talk of marriage."

"Oh," Louisa said. "And now she's back."

"It's all just gossip," Leaphorn said. "And you didn't get any of it from me."

"Okay," Louisa said, and shook her head. "Poor Mr. Dashee. What did you tell him?"

"I told him I'd talk to Jim the first chance I get. Probably today." He made a face. "That won't be so easy either, talking to Chee. I'm his ex-boss and he's sort of touchy with me. And, after all, it's none of my business."

"Well, it shouldn't be."

Leaphorn took his eyes off the road long enough to study her expression. "What do you mean by that?"

"You should have just told Mrs. Vanders you were too busy. Or something like that."

Leaphorn let that pass.

"You're retired, you know. The golden years. Now's the time to travel, do all those things you wanted to do."

"That's true," Leaphorn said. "I could trot down to the senior center and play—whatever they do down there."

"You're not too old to get into golf."

"I already did that," Leaphorn said. "At a federal law-enforcement seminar in Phoenix. The feds stay at those three-hundred-dollar-a-night resort places with the big golf courses. I went out with some FBI agents and knocked the ball in all eighteen holes. It wasn't hard, but once you've done it, I don't know why you'd want to do it again."

"You think you're going to like this being a private detective any better?"

Leaphorn smiled at her. "I think it may be a lot harder to get the hang of than golf," he said. "Even the FBI agents mastered golf. They don't have much luck at detecting."

"You know, Joe, I have a feeling that Mr. Dashee might be right about what Pollard's aunt has in mind. I think the old lady might not really want you to find her niece."

"You may be right about that," Leaphorn said. "But still, that would make it a lot more interesting than knocking a golf ball around. Why don't we find Chee and see what he thinks."

They spent the rest of the drive to Tuba City with Louisa plowing through Catherine Pollard's hodgepodge of papers.

Leaphorn had already gone through them once, quickly. Pollard wrote fast, producing a tiny, erratic script in which all vowels looked about the same, and an *h* might be a *k*, or an *l*, or perhaps another of her many uncrossed *t*'s. This unintended code was made worse by a personal shorthand, full of abbreviations and cryptic symbols. Not knowing what he was looking for, he'd found nothing helpful.

Now Louisa read and he listened, amazed. "How can you decipher that woman's handwriting?" he said. "Or are you just guessing at it?"

"Schoolteacher skill," Louisa said. "Most students give you computer printouts for the long papers these days, but in olden times you got a lot of practice plowing through bad penmanship. Repetition develops skill." She went slowly through the papers, translating.

The first fatal case this spring had been a middle-aged woman named Nellie Hale, who lived north of the Kaibito chapter house and who had died in the hospital at Farmington the morning of May 19, ten days after being admitted. Pollard's notes were mostly information collected from family and friends about where Nellie Hale had been during the first weeks of May and the last few days of April. They reported checks made around the Hale hogan, the examination of a prairie dog town near Navajo National Monument where the victim had visited her mother (the dogs had fleas but neither fleas nor dogs had the plague), and the discovery of a deserted colony at the edge of the Hale grazing permit. Fleas collected from the burrows were carrying the plague. The burrows were dusted with poison and the case of Nellie Hale put on the back burner.

That brought them to Anderson Nez. Pollard's notes showed the date he died as June 30 in the hospital at Flagstaff, with "date of admission?" followed by "find out!" She had filled the rest of the page with data accumulated from quizzing family and friends about where his prior travels had taken him. This showed he left home on May 24 en route to Encino, California, to visit his brother. He had returned on June 22. Here Louisa paused.

"I can't make this out," she said, pointing.

He looked at the page. "It's 'i g h,'" he said. "I think I'd figure out that's short for 'in good health.' Notice she underlined it. I wonder why?"

"Double underlines," Louisa said, and resumed reading. Anderson Nez had left the next afternoon for the Goldtooth area and "job with Woody," according to Pollard's notes. "Did you notice he was working for Dr. Woody?" Louisa asked. Then she looked embarrassed. "Of course you did."

"Sort of ironic, isn't it?"

"Very," Louisa said. "Did you notice those dates? She was looking for sources of infection starting back three weeks or so before the dates of the deaths. Is that how long it takes for the bacteria to kill you?"

"I think that's the usual time range that's been established, and I guess that explains why she underlined the 'i g h.' In good health on the twenty-second. Dead on the thirtieth," Leaphorn said. "Anything more about Nez?"

"Not on this page," she said. "And I haven't found any mention of that third case you mentioned."

"That was a boy over in New Mexico," Leaphorn said. "They wouldn't handle that here."

They rolled past the Hopi outpost village of Moenkopi and into Tuba City and parked on the packed-dirt lot of the Navajo Tribal Police station. There Leaphorn found Sergeant Dick Roanhorse and Trixie Dodge, old friends from his days in the department, but not Jim Chee. Roanhorse told him Chee had headed out early for the Kinsman homicide crime scene and hadn't called in. He took Leaphorn into the radio room and asked the young man in the dispatcher's chair to try to get Chee on the radio. Then it was nostalgia time.

"You remember when old Captain Largo was out here, and the trouble he had with you?" Trixie asked.

"I'm trying to forget that," Leaphorn said. "I hope none of you people are giving Lieutenant Chee that kind of headache."

"Not that kind. But he's got one," Roanhorse said, and winked.

"Well, now," Trixie said. "If you mean Bernie Manuelito, I wouldn't call that trouble."

"You would if you were her supervisor," Roanhorse said, and noticed Leaphorn's uncomprehending look. "Bernie has what we used to call a crush on the lieutenant, and I guess he's more or less engaged to this woman lawyer, and everybody around here knows it. So he has to walk on eggs all the time."

"Yeah," Leaphorn said. "I'd call that a problem." He remembered now that when the word came on the grapevine at Window Rock that Chee was transferred from Shiprock to Tuba, people thought that was ironic. When he asked why, the answer was that when Officer Manuelito heard Chee was going to marry Janet Pete, she'd gotten herself transferred to Tuba to get away from him.

The dispatcher came to the door. "Lieutenant Chee said he'd be waiting for you," the young man said. "You take U.S. 264 seven miles south from the 160 junction, then turn right on the dirt road that connects there, and then about twenty miles down the dirt. There's a track that connects there leading back toward Black Mesa. Lieutenant Chee said he'll be parked there."

"Okay," Leaphorn said, thinking that would be the old road across the Moenkopi Plateau to Goldtooth, where nobody lived anymore, and on into the empty northwestern edge of the Hopi reservation to Dinnebito Wash and Garces Mesa. It was a drive you didn't start without a full tank of gasoline and air in your spare tire. Maybe it was better now. "Thank you."

"You think you can find it?"

Sergeant Roanhorse laughed and whacked Leaphorn on the back. "How soon they forget you," he said.

But Trixie hadn't exhausted the unrequited romance business as yet. "Bernie's been worried all week about whether she should invite him to a *kinaalda* her family's having for one of her cousins. She invited everybody else but would it be, you know, pushy or something if she invited the boss? Or would he feel hurt if she didn't? Can't make up her mind."

"Is that why she's been so hard to get along with the last day or two?" Roanhorse asked.

"What do you think?" she said. And grinned at him.

15

ACTING LIEUTENANT JIM Chee sat on a sandstone slab in the shade of a juniper awaiting the arrival of Joe Leaphorn, Former Boss, Former Mentor, and, as far as Chee was concerned, Perpetual Legendary Lieutenant. He admired Leaphorn, he respected him, he even sort of liked him. But for some reason, an impending meeting with the man had always made him feel uneasy and incompetent. He'd thought he'd get over that when Leaphorn was no longer his supervisor. Alas, he hadn't.

This afternoon he didn't need a Leaphorn conversation to make him feel like a rookie. He'd learned very little prowling around Yells Back, mostly negative, reinforcing what he already knew. Jano had hit Ben Kinsman on the head with a rock. He'd found no trace of blood at the blind where Jano had caught the bird to suggest that Jano's arm had been slashed by the eagle's talons. Nor had he turned up any evidence that he was overlooking any possible witnesses to the crime. He reconsidered what Dr. Woody had told him. Woody had recalled seeing a car coming from the north as he emerged from the track that led toward Yells Back Butte. Possibly it had been Kinsman en route to meet his destiny. Possibly it was the person who had killed Kinsman following him. Or possibly Woody's memory was faulty, or Woody was lying for some reason Chee couldn't fathom. Whatever the case, Chee had this uneasy feeling that he was missing something and that Leaphorn, in his gentle way, would point it out.

Well, now he'd find out. The cloud of dust coming down the road from the north would be the Legendary Lieutenant. Chee got up, put on his hat, and walked down the hill to where his patrol car had been baking in the sun beside the road. The pickup pulled up beside it and two people emerged—Leaphorn and a stocky woman wearing a straw hat, jeans, and a man's shirt.

"Louisa," Leaphorn said. "This is Lieutenant Chee. I think you met him in Window Rock. Jim, Professor Bourebonette."

"Yes," Chee said as they shook hands, "it's good to see you again." But it wasn't. Not now. He just wanted to know why Leaphorn was looking for him. He didn't want any complications.

"I hope this isn't causing you any inconvenience," Leaphorn said. "I told Dineyahze we'd just wait there at the station if you were coming in."

"No problem," Chee said, and stood there waiting for Leaphorn to get on with it.

"I'm still trying to find Catherine Pollard," Leaphorn said. "I wondered if you've turned up anything."

"Nothing helpful," Chee said.

"She wasn't here the day Kinsman was attacked?"

"Nope. At least, she wasn't until later in the day," Chee said. "I don't have to tell you how long it takes to get an ambulance into a place like this. By the time the criminalistics team got its photographs and all that, it was late afternoon. But she could have shown up after that."

Leaphorn was waiting for him to add something. But what could he add?

"Oh," Chee said. "Of course, she could have gotten here earlier."

That seemed to be what Leaphorn wanted him to think. The Legendary Lieutenant nodded.

"I ran into Cowboy Dashee at Cameron today," Leaphorn said. "He'd heard I was looking for Pollard. Knew about the reward we were offering for the Jeep she was driving. He told me a woman who keeps some goats up here had seen a Jeep going up that old road to the Tijinney place before sunrise that morning. He asked me to pass it along to you. In case it might be useful."

"He did?"

Leaphorn nodded. "Yeah. He said you had a tough one with this Kinsman homicide. He said he wished he could help you."

"Jano is his cousin," Chee said. "I think they were childhood buddies. Cowboy thinks I've got the wrong man. Or so I hear."

"Well, anyway, he thought you might want to talk to the woman. He told me they call her Old Lady Notah," Leaphorn said.

"Old Lady Notah," Chee said. "I think I saw some of her goats up there by the butte today. I'll go talk to her."

"Might be wasting your time," Leaphorn said.

"Or might not be," Chee said. He looked back toward the butte. "And, hey," he added. "Would you tell Cowboy I said thanks?"

"Sure," Leaphorn said.

Chee was still looking away from Leaphorn. "Did Cowboy have any other tips?"

"Well, he has his own theory of the crime."

Chee turned. "Like what?"

"Like Catherine Pollard did it."

Chee frowned, thinking about it. "Had he worked out the motive? The opportunity? All that?"

"More or less," Leaphorn said. "He has her coming up here on her vector control job. She runs into Kinsman, he makes a move on her. She resists. They struggle. She bangs him on the head and flees the scene." Leaphorn gave Chee awhile to consider that. Then he said: "But then why didn't you see her driving out while you were driving in?"

"That's what I was thinking. And if she's on the run, why did her family—" He stopped, looking abashed.

Leaphorn grinned. "If Cowboy is guessing right, the family hired me to look for her thinking that would make it look like she'd been abducted. Or killed or something like that."

"That doesn't make sense," Chee said.

"Well, it sort of does, actually," Leaphorn said. "The lady who hired me struck me as a mighty shrewd woman. I told her I didn't see how I could be of any help. She didn't seem to care."

Chee nodded. "Yeah, I guess so. I can see it."

"Except how did she get the Jeep out of here? The TV commercials make them look like they can drive up cliffs, but they can't."

"There's a way, though," Chee said. "There's another way in here if you don't mind doing a little scrambling. An old trail comes up the other side of Yells Back toward Black Mesa. I think the lady with the goats might use it. You could drive the Jeep up there, park it, climb over the saddle, do your deed, and then climb back over the saddle and drive out on the goat path."

Chee stopped. "There's trouble with that, though."

"You mean she wouldn't do that unless she knew in advance that she was going to need an escape route?"

"Exactly," Chee said. "How could she have known that?"

Louisa had been listening, looking thoughtful. Now she said: "Do you professionals object if an amateur butts in?"

"Be our guest," Leaphorn said.

"I find myself wondering just why Pollard was coming up here any-way," Louisa said. She looked at Leaphorn. "Didn't you tell me she was looking for the place where Nez was infected? Where the flea bit him?"

"Right," Leaphorn said, looking puzzled.

"And isn't the period between infection and death—I mean in cases where treatment doesn't effect a cure—doesn't that range just a couple of weeks?" Louisa made one of those modifying gestures with her hands. "I mean, usually. Statistically. Often enough so that when vector control peo-ple are looking for the source, they're looking for places the victim had been during that period. And what Miss Pollard was writing in her notes suggested that she was always trying to find out where the victim was in that period before their death."

"Ah," Leaphorn said. "I see."

Chee, whose interest in plague and vector control people who hunted it extended back only a few minutes, had little idea what any of this was about.

He said: "You mean she knew Nez couldn't have been around Yells Back in that time frame? How would—?"

"Pollard's notes show where he was. They show—" She stopped in midsentence. "Just a minute. I don't want to be wrong about this. The book's in the car."

She found it on the dashboard, extracted it, leaned against the fender, and flipped through the pages.

"Here," she said. "Under her Anderson Nez heading. It shows that he was visiting his brother in Encino, California. He came home to his mother's hogan four miles southwest of Copper Mine Trading Post on June twenty-third. The next afternoon, he left to go to his job with Woody near Goldtooth."

"June twenty-fourth?" Leaphorn said thoughtfully. "Right?"

"And six days later he dies in the hospital at Flag." She checked back in the notes. "Actually more like five days. Pollard says in here somewhere he died just after midnight."

"Wow," Leaphorn said. "Are we sure he died of plague?"

"Slow down," Jim Chee said. "Explain this date business to me."

Louisa shook her head, looking doubtful. "I guess the point is that Pollard knows a lot more about plague than we do. So she would have known that Nez didn't get his infected flea up here. Plague doesn't kill that fast. So she didn't have any reason to come up here flea hunting when she did."

"That's the question," Leaphorn said. "If that wasn't her reason, what was? Or did she tell Krause she was coming, and not come? Or did Krause lie about it?"

Louisa was reading from another section of the notebook. She held up her hand.

"Pollard must have been thinking something was funny. She went back out to the Nez place near Copper Mine Mesa. Rechecking.

" 'Mom says Nez dug postholes, stretched sheep fencing to expand pens. Family dogs wearing flea collars and sans fleas. No cats. No prairie dog towns in vicinity. No history of rats or rat sign found. Nez drove to Page with mother, buying groceries. No headache. No fever.' " She closed the notebook, shrugged.

"That's it?" Chee asked.

"There's a marginal note for her to check sources at Encino," Louisa said. "I guess to see if he was sick when he was there."

Chee said, "But she told her boss she was coming up to Yells Back to check for fleas here. Or at least he says she did. I think I've met that guy." He looked at Leaphorn. "Big, raw-boned guy named Krause?"

"That's him."

"What else did she tell him?"

"Krause said she came by early that day before he got to work. He didn't see her. She just left him a note," Leaphorn said. "I didn't see it, but Krause said that she just reported she was going up to Yells Back to collect fleas."

"By the way," Chee asked, "with Pollard missing, as well as the Jeep she was driving, how did you get her notebook?"

"I guess we should call it a journal," Leaphorn said. "It was with a folder full of stuff her aunt's lawyer collected from her motel room in Tuba. It looks like she took the notes she jotted down in the field and converted them into sort of a report when she got home with her comments."

"Like a diary?" Chee asked.

"Not really," Leaphorn said. "There's nothing very personal or private in it."

"That was the last entry about Nez?" Chee asked.

"No," Louisa said. She flipped back through the pages.

" 'July 6. Krause says he heard Dr. Woody checked Nez into the hospital. Krause not answering his telephone. Will get to Flag mañana and see what I can learn.'

" 'July 7. Can't believe what I heard at Flag today. Somebody is lying. Yells Back Butte mañana, collect fleas, find out.' "

Louisa shut the notebook. "That's it. The final entry."

16

"IT'S FUNNY," LEAPHORN said, "how you can look at something a half dozen times and not see it."

Louisa waited for him to explain that, decided he didn't intend to and said, "Like what?"

"Like what Catherine Pollard wrote in that journal," Leaphorn said. "I should have noticed the pattern. The incubation period of that bacteria. I should have wondered why she would be coming up here."

They were jolting up the rocky tracks that had once given the Tijinney family access to the world outside the shadow of Yells Back Butte and Black Mesa. Over Black Mesa afternoon clouds were forming, hinting that the rainy season might finally begin.

"How?" Louisa said. "Did you know when Mr. Nez died?"

"I could have found out," Leaphorn said. "That would have been as easy as making a telephone call."

"Oh, knock it off," Louisa said. "I've noticed males have this practice of entertaining themselves with self-flagellation. Mea culpa, mea culpa, mea maxima culpa. We females find that habit tiresome."

Leaphorn considered that awhile. Grinned.

"You mean like Jim Chee blaming himself for not getting up here quick enough to keep Kinsman from getting himself hit on the head."

"Exactly."

"Okay," Leaphorn said. "You're right. I guess I couldn't have known."

"On the other hand, you shouldn't get too complacent," Louisa said. "I hope you noticed that I figured it out pretty quick."

He laughed. "I noticed it. It took me awhile to deal with that. Then two thoughts occurred. You could translate Pollard's scribbles and I couldn't, and you were paying attention while Professor Perez was educating us about pathogenic bacteria last night and I was just sitting there letting my mind wander. I decided that you just have a much higher tolerance for boredom than I do."

"Academics have to be boredom-invulnerable," Louisa said. "Otherwise we'd walk out of faculty meetings, and if you do that, you don't get tenure. You have to go get real jobs."

Leaphorn shifted into second and followed the established tire tracks through the arroyo where Chee had left his car that fatal day. They ran out of old tracks on the little hump of high ground that overlooked what was left of the old Tijinney place. Leaphorn stopped and turned off the ignition, and they sat looking down on the abandoned homestead.

"Mr. Chee said Woody had his van parked over closer to the butte," Louisa said. "Over there where all those junipers are growing by the arroyo."

"I remember," Leaphorn said. "I just wanted to take a look." He waved at the ruined hogan, its door missing, its roof fallen, its north wall tumbled. Beyond it stood the remains of a brush arbor, a sheep pen formed of stacked stones, two stone pylons that once would have supported timbers on which water storage barrels had rested. "Sad," he said.

"Some people would call it picturesque."

"People who don't understand how much work went into building all that. And trying to make a living here."

"I know," Louisa said. "I was a farm girl myself. Lots of work, but Iowa had rich black dirt. And enough rain. And indoor plumbing. Electricity. All that."

"Old Man McGinnis told me kids had vandalized this place. It looks like it."

"Not Navajo kids, I'll bet," she said. "Isn't it a death hogan?"

"I think the old lady died in it," Leaphorn said. "You notice the north wall's partly knocked down."

"The traditional way to take out the body, isn't it? North, the direction of evil."

Leaphorn nodded. "But McGinnis was complaining that a lot of young Navajos, not just the city ones, don't respect the old ways these days. They ignore the taboos, if they ever heard of them. He thinks some of them tore into this place, looking for stuff they could sell. He said they even dug this deep hole where the fire pit was. Apparently they thought something valuable was buried there."

Louisa shook her head. "I wouldn't think there would be anything very valuable left in that hogan. And I don't see any sign of a big deep hole."

Leaphorn chuckled. "I don't either. But then McGinnis never certifies the accuracy. He just passes along the gossip. And as for the value, he said they were looking for ceremonial stuff. When that hogan was built, the owner probably had a place in the wall beside the door where he kept his medicine bundle. Minerals from the sacred mountains. That sort of thing. Some collectors will pay big money for some of that material, and the older it is the better."

"I guess so," Louisa said. "Collecting antiques is not my thing."

Leaphorn smiled at her. "You collect everybody's antique stories. Even ours. That's how I met you, remember. One of your sources was in jail."

"Collect them and preserve them," she said. "Remember when you were telling me about how First Man and First Woman found the baby White Shell Girl on Huerfano Mesa and you had it all wrong?"

"I had it exactly right," Leaphorn said. "That's the version we hold to in my Red Forehead Clan. That makes it correct. The other clans have it wrong. And you know what, I'm going to take a closer look at that hogan. Let's see if McGinnis knew what he was talking about."

She walked down the slope with him. There was nothing left of the hogan building but the circle of stacked stone that formed a wall around the hard-packed earth of the floor, and the ponderosa poles and shreds of tar paper that had formed its collapsed roof.

"There was a hole there once," Louisa said. "Mostly filled in, though."

They were in cloud shadow now, and the thunderhead over the mesa made a rumbling noise. They climbed the slope back to the truck.

"I wonder what they found?"

"In the hole?" Leaphorn said. "I'd guess nothing. I never heard of a

Navajo burying anything under his hogan fire pit. But of course McGinnis had an answer for that. He said Old Man Tijinney was a silversmith. Had a lard bucket full of silver dollars."

"Sounds more logical than ceremonial things," Louisa said.

"Until you ask why bury a bucket when there's a million places you could hide it. And hoarding wealth isn't part of the Navajo Way anyway. There're always kinfolks who need it."

She laughed. "You tell McGinnis that?"

"Yeah, and he said, 'You're supposed to be the goddamn detective. You figure it out.' So I figured out there wasn't any bucket. You notice I never came up here with my pick and shovel to check it out."

"I don't know," she said. "You're the tidiest man I ever knew. Just the kind of looter who'd push the dirt back in the hole."

They found Dr. Albert Woody's van just where Chee had said it would be. Woody was standing in the doorway watching them park. To Leaphorn's surprise, he looked delighted to see them.

"Two visitors on the same day," he said as they got out of the truck. "I've never been this popular."

"We won't take much of your time," Leaphorn said. "This is Dr. Louisa Bourebonette, I'm Joe Leaphorn and I presume you must be Dr. Albert Woody."

"Exactly," Woody said. "And glad to meet you. What can I do for you?"

"We're trying to locate a woman named Catherine Pollard. She's a vector control specialist with the Arizona Health Department, and—"

"Oh, yes," Woody said. "I met her over near Red Lake some time ago. She was looking for sick rodents and infected fleas. Looking for the source of a plague case. In a way we're in the same line of work."

He looked very excited, Leaphorn thought. Wired. Ready to burst. As if he were high on amphetamines.

"Have you seen her around here?"

"No," Woody said. "Just over at the Thriftway station. We were both buying gasoline. She noticed my van and introduced herself."

"She's working out of that temporary laboratory in Tuba City," Leaphorn said. "On the morning of July eighth she left a note for her boss saying she was coming up here to collect rodents."

"There was a Navajo Tribal policeman up here talking to me this morning," Woody said. "He asked me about her, too. Come in and let me give you something cold to drink."

"We didn't intend to take a lot of your time," Leaphorn said.

"Come in. Come in. I've just had something great happen. I need somebody to tell it to. And Dr. Bourebonette, what is your specialty?"

"I'm not a physician," Louisa said. "I'm a cultural anthropologist at Northern Arizona University. I believe you know Dr. Perez there."

"Perez?" Woody said. "Oh, yes. In the lab. He's done some work for me."

"He's a great fan of yours," Louisa said. "In fact, you're his nominee for the next Nobel Prize in medicine."

Woody laughed. "Only if I'm guessing right about the internal working of rodents. And only if somebody in the National Center for Emerging Viruses doesn't get it first. But I'm forgetting my manners. Come in. Come in. I want to show you something."

Woody was twisting his hands together, grinning broadly, as they went past him through the doorway.

It was almost cold inside, the air damp and clammy and smelling of animals, formaldehyde, and an array of other chemicals that linger forever in memory. The sound was another mixture—the motor of the air-conditioner engine on the roof, the whir of fans, the scrabbling feet of rodents locked away somewhere out of sight. Woody seated Louisa in a swivel chair near his desk, motioned Leaphorn to a stool beside a white plastic working surface, and leaned his lanky body against the door of what Leaphorn presumed was a floor-to-ceiling refrigerator.

"I've got some good news to share with Dr. Perez," he said. "You can tell him we've found the key to the dragon's cave."

Leaphorn shifted his gaze from Woody to Louisa. Obviously she didn't understand that any better than he did.

"Will he know what that means?" she asked. "He understands you're hunting for a solution to drug-resistant pathogens. Do you mean you've found it?"

Woody looked slightly abashed.

"Something to drink," he said, "and then I'll try to explain myself." He opened the refrigerator door, fished out an ice bucket, extracted three stainless-steel cups from an overhead cabinet and a squat brown bottle, which he displayed. "I only have scotch."

Louisa nodded. Leaphorn said he'd settle for water.

Woody talked while he fixed their drinks.

"Bacteria, like about everything alive, split themselves into genera. Call it families. Here we're dealing with the *Enterobacteriaceae* family. One branch of that is *Pasteurellaceae*, and a branch of that is *Yersinia pestis*—the organism that causes bubonic plague. Another branch is *Neisseria gonorrhoeae*, which causes the famous venereal disease. These days, gonorrhea is hard to treat because—" Woody paused, sipping his scotch.

"Wait," he said. "Let me skip back a little. Some of these bacteria, gonorrhea for example, contain a little plasmid with a gene in it that codes for the formation of an enzyme that destroys penicillin. That means you can't treat the disease with any of those penicillin drugs. You see?"

"Sure," Louisa said. "Remember, I'm a friend of Professor Perez. I get a lot of this sort of information."

"We now understand that DNA can be transferred between bacteria—especially between bacteria in the same family."

"Kissing cousins," Louisa said. "Like incest."

"Well, I guess," Woody said. "I hadn't thought of it like that."

Leaphorn had been sampling his ice water, which had the ice cube flavor plus staleness, plus an odd taste that matched the aroma of the van's air supply. He put down the cup.

Leaphorn had been doing some reading. He said: "I guess we're talking about a mixture of plague and gonorrhea—which would make the plague microbe resistant to tetracycline and chloramphenicol. Is that about right?"

"About right," Woody said. "And possibly several other antibiotic formulations. But that's not the point. That's not what's important."

"It sounds important to me," Louisa said.

"Well, yes. It makes it terribly lethal if one is infected. But what we have here is still a blood-to-blood transmission. It requires a vector—such as a flea—to spread it from one mammal to another. If this evolution converted it directly into an aerobic form—a pneumonic plague spread by coughing or just breathing the same air—we'd have cause for panic."

"No panic then?"

Woody laughed. "Actually, the epidemic trackers might even be happier with this form. If a disease kills its victims fast enough, they don't have time to spread it."

Louisa's expression suggested she took no cheer from this. "What is important then?"

Woody opened the door of a bottom cabinet, extracted a wire cage, and displayed it. A tag with the name CHARLEY printed on it was tied to the wire. Inside was a plump brown prairie dog, apparently dead.

"Charley, this fellow here, and his kith and kin in the prairie dog town where I trapped him, are full of plague bacteria—both the old form and the new. Yet he's alive and well, and so are his relatives."

"He looks dead," Louisa said.

"He's asleep," Woody said. "I took some blood and tissue samples. He's still recovering from the chloroform."

"There's more to it than this," Leaphorn said. "You've known for years that when the plague sweeps through it leaves behind a few towns where the bacteria doesn't kill the animals. Host colonies. Or plague reservoirs. Isn't that what they're called?"

"Exactly," Woody said. "And we've studied them for years without finding out what happens in the one prairie dog's immune system to keep it alive while a million others are dying." He stopped, sipped scotch, watched them over the rim of his cup, eyes intense.

"Now we have the key." He tapped the cage with his finger. "We inject this fellow's blood into a mammal that has resisted the standard infection and study the immune reaction. We inject it into a normal mammal and make the same study. See what's happening to white blood cell production, cell walls, so forth. All sorts of new possibilities are open."

"And what you learn from the rodent immune system applies to the human system."

"That's been the basis of medical research for generations," Woody said. He put down his cup. "If it doesn't work this time, we can quit worrying about global warming, asteroids on collision courses, nuclear war, all those minor threats. The tiny little beasties have neutralized our defenses. They'll get us first."

"That sounds extreme," Louisa said. "After all, the world has had these sweeping epidemics before. Humanity survived."

"Before fast mass transportation," Woody said. "In the old days a disease killed everybody in an area, then died out because there was nobody left to pass it around. Now airlines can have it spread planetwide before the Centers for Disease Control knows it's happening."

That produced a moment of thoughtful silence, which Woody ended after mixing another drink.

"Let me show you what had me so excited when you drove up," he said after Louisa declined a refill. He pointed to the larger of his two microscopes. Louisa looked first.

"Notice the clusters of ovoid cells, very regular shapes. Those are the *Yersinia*. See the rounder ones? They're darker because they take the dye differently. They look a lot like what you find in a gonorrhea victim. But not quite. They also have some of the *Yersinia* characteristics."

"You couldn't prove it by me," Louisa said. "When I look into one of these things, I always think I'm seeing my eyelashes."

Leaphorn took his turn. He saw the bacteria and what he guessed were blood cells. Like Louisa, they told him nothing except that he was wasting time. He had come up here to find out what had happened to Catherine Pollard.

"Very interesting," Leaphorn said. "But we're taking too much of your time. About two or three more questions and we'll go. I guess Lieutenant Chee told you that Miss Pollard was trying to find the source of Mr. Nez's infection. Did Nez work for you?"

"Yes. Part-time for several years. He'd put out the traps, and check them, and collect the rodents. Take care of all such things."

"I understand you checked him into the hospital. Did you tell the people there where Nez was infected?"

"I didn't know."

"Not even a general idea?"

"Not even that," Woody said. "He'd been in several places. Here and there. Fleas get into people's clothing. You carry them around. You're not sure when you get bit."

Leaphorn weighed that against his own experience. He had been bitten by fleas more than once. Not very painful, but something you noticed.

"When did you notice he was sick?"

"It would have been the evening before I checked him in. He had driven in that morning to do some things, and after we ate our supper he said he had a headache. No other symptoms and no temperature, but you don't take chances in this business. I gave him a dose of doxycycline. Next morning, he still had a headache, and he was also running a temp. It was a hundred and three. I took him right to the hospital."

"How long does it usually take between the infected flea bite and those sort of symptoms?"

"Usually about four or five days. The longest I know of is sixteen days."

"What was the shortest?"

Woody thought. "I've been told of a two-day case, but I have my doubts. I think an earlier flea bite caused that one." He paused. "Here," he said. "Let me show you another slide."

He opened a filing case, pulled out a box of slides, selected one and inserted it into the microscope.

"Take a look at this."

Leaphorn looked. He saw the ovoid cells of the plague bacteria and the rounder specimens of the evolved bacteria. Only the blood cells looked different.

"It looks almost the same," he said.

"You have a good eye," Woody said. "It is almost the same. But this slide is from a blood sample I took from Nez when I took his temperature."

"Oh," Leaphorn said.

"Two things are important here. From the onset of the fever to death was less than three days. That's far too short a time for the standard *Yersinia* bacteria to kill. And the second—" Woody paused for effect, grinning at Leaphorn.

"Charley is still alive," he said.

17

I T HAD TAKEN Acting Lieutenant Jim Chee about a year to learn the three ways of getting things done in the Navajo Tribal Police. Number one was the official system. The word, neatly typed on an official form, worked its way up through the prescribed channels to the correct level, and then down again to the working cops. In number two, the midlevel bureaucrat whom Chee had now become telephoned friends at the Window Rock headquarters and the various substations, explained what he needed done, and either called in IOUs or asked for a favor.

Chee learned quickly that number three was the fastest. There, one outlined the problem to the proper woman in the office and asked her for help. If the asker had earned the askee's respect, she would get the really savvy folks at work on the project—the female network.

Since racing back to his Tuba City office from his meeting with the Legendary Lieutenant Leaphorn, Chee was using all three systems to make sure that if Catherine Pollard's missing Jeep could be found, it would be found in a hurry. Until it was—in fact, until Pollard herself was found—Chee knew he wouldn't have a comfortable moment. He'd be haunted by the thought that he might be hanging Jano for a crime he hadn't committed. Jano had done it, of course. He'd seen him do it. Or practically had, and there was no alternative. But what had been an open-and-shut case in his mind now had a crack in it. He had to close it.

Therefore, when he walked into the Tuba City station, he went directly to the office of Mrs. Dineyahze and explained to her how important it was to find the vehicle. "All right," she said, "I'll call around. Get some people off their rear ends."

"I'd appreciate it," Chee said. He didn't explain to Mrs. Dineyahze what should be done, which was one of the reasons she liked him.

He hadn't noticed that Officer Bernadette Manuelito had come through the open door of the secretary's office and was standing behind him.

She said, "Can I help?" which was exactly what Bernie often said. Nor did how she looked surprise him, which was shirt wrinkled, hair sort of disheveled, lipstick slightly askew and—despite all that—very feminine and very pretty.

Chee looked at his watch. "Thanks, but you're off-duty now, Bernie. And tomorrow's your day off."

He didn't think that would have much effect, since Bernie did pretty much what she wanted to do. But he could hear the telephone clamoring for attention in his office, and so was the stack of paperwork he'd abandoned this morning. He headed for the door.

"Lieutenant," Bernie said. "My family is having a *kinaalda* starting next Saturday for Emily—that's my cousin. Over at Burnt Water. You'd be welcome."

"Golly, Bernie, I'd like to. But I don't think I can get away from here." Bernie looked downcast. "Okay," she said.

The telephone call was to remind him not to be late for a coordination meeting with people from the BIA Law and Order staff, the Coconino County Sheriff's Office, the Arizona Highway Patrol, the FBI and the Drug Enforcement Agency. While he listened, he could overhear Mrs. Dineyahze discussing the impending puberty ceremonial with Bernie—Mrs. D. sounding cheerful, Ms. Manuelito sounding sad. As for Chee, he felt repentant. He hated hurting Bernie's feelings.

When he returned from the coordination meeting about sundown, his IN basket held a report from Mrs. Dineyahze with a note clipped to it. The report assured him that the right people in the state police and highway patrols of Arizona, New Mexico, Utah, and Colorado now had all the needed data on the missing Jeep. More important, they knew why it was needed. A brother cop had been killed. Finding that Jeep was part of the investigation. The same information had gone to police departments in reservation border towns and to sheriff's offices in relevant county seats.

Chee leaned back in his chair, feeling better. If that Jeep was rolling down a highway anywhere in the Four Corners there was a fair chance it would be spotted. If a city cop saw it parked somewhere, there was a good chance the license plate would be checked. He unclipped the note, which was handwritten. By Mrs. Dineyahze's standards, untyped meant unofficial.

"Lt. Chee: Bernie called the Arizona State motor pool and got all the specifications on the Jeep. It had been impounded in a drug bust and had a lot of fancy add-ons, which are listed below. Also note battery and tire types, rims, other things that Bernie thought might turn up at pawnshops, etc. She relayed the list to shops in Gallup, Flag, Farmington, etc., and also called Thriftway people in Phoenix and asked them to ask their stores on reservation to be alert." This was signed "C. Dineyahze."

Far below this signature, which made it not only unofficial but off the record, Mrs. Dineyahze had scrawled:

"Bernie is a good girl."

Chee already knew that. He liked her. He admired her. He thought she was a very neat lady. But he also knew that Bernadette Manuelito had a crush on him, and almost everybody else in the extended family of the Navajo Tribal Police seemed to know it, too. That made Bernie a pain in the neck. In fact, that was how Chee, who wasn't very good at under-standing women, had come to notice Bernie had her eye on him. He'd started being kidded about it.

But there was no time to think of that now. Nor about her idea—which was smart. If the Jeep had been abandoned somewhere on the Big Rez or in the border country, the odds were fairly good that it would be stripped—especially since it had been loaded with expensive, easily stolen stuff. Now he was hungry and tired. None of the frozen dinners awaiting him in the little refrigerator in his trailer home had any appeal for him to-night. He'd go by the Kentucky Fried Chicken place, pick up a dinner with biscuits and gravy, go home, dine, kick back, finish *Meridian*, the Norman Zollinger novel he was reading, and get some sleep.

He was finishing a thigh and the second biscuit when the phone rang.

"You said to call you if anything turned up on the Jeep," the dispatcher said.

"Like what?"

"Like a guy came into the filling station at Cedar Ridge last Monday and tried to sell the clerk a radio and tape player. It was the same brand that was in that Jeep."

"They have an identification?"

"The clerk said it was a kid from a family named Pooacha. They have a place over on Shinume Wash."

"Okay," Chee said. "Thanks." He looked at his watch. It would have to wait until morning.

By midafternoon the next day the Jeep was found. If you discount driving about two hundred miles back and forth, and some of it over roads far too primitive even to be listed as primitive on Chee's AAA Indian Country road map, the whole project proved to be remarkably easy.

Since Officer Manuelito had provided the idea that made it possible, and had the day off anyway, Chee could think of no way to discourage Bernie from coming along. In fact, he didn't even try. He enjoyed her company when she had her mind on business instead of on him. They drove first to the Cedar Ridge trading post, talked to the clerk there, learned the would-be radio salesman was a young man named Tommy Tsi, and got directions to the Pooacha place, where he lived. They took the dusty washboard gravel of Navajo Route 6110 westward to Blue Moon Bench, turned south on the even rougher Route 6120 along Bekihatso Wash, and found the track that wandered through the rocks and saltbush to the Pooacha establishment.

At this intersection a cracked old boot was stuck atop the post beside the cattle guard.

"Well, good," said Bernie, pointing to the boot. "Somebody's home."

"Somebody is," Chee agreed, "unless the last one out forgot to take the boot down. And in my experience, when the road's as bad as this one, the somebody who's there isn't the one you're looking for."

But Tommy Tsi, a very young Pooacha son-in-law, was home—and very nervous when he noticed the uniform Chee was wearing and the

Navajo Tribal Police decal on his car. No, he didn't still have the radio and tape player. It belonged to a friend who had asked him to try to sell it for him. The friend had reclaimed it, Tsi said, rubbing his hand uneasily over a very sparse mustache as he spoke.

"Give us the friend's name," Chee said. "Where can we locate him?"

"His name?" Tommy Tsi said. And thought a while. "Well, he's not exactly a close friend. I met him in Flag. I think they call him Shorty. Or something like that."

"And how were you going to get his money back to him when you sold his stuff?"

"Well," Tommy Tsi said. And hesitated again. "I'm not sure."

"That's a shame," Bernie said. "If you could find him we want you to tell him we're not much interested in the radio stuff. We want to find the Jeep. If he can show us where the Jeep is, then he gets to collect the reward."

"Reward? For the Jeep?"

"A thousand bucks," Bernie said. "Twenty fifty-dollar bills. The family of the woman who was driving the Jeep put it up."

"Really," Tsi said. "A thousand bucks."

"For finding the Jeep. That's what this guy did, you know. Found an abandoned vehicle. No law against that, is there?"

"Right," Tommy Tsi agreed, nodding and looking much more cheerful.

"If he told you where the Jeep is, then you could take us there. We could arrange for you to get the money. Then if you can find him again, you could share it with him."

"Yes," Tsi said. "Let me get my hat."

"Tell you what," Chee said. "Bring the radio stuff along, too. We might need that for fingerprints."

"Mine?" Tsi looked startled.

"We know yours are on it," Chee said. "We're thinking of whoever drove it where you found it."

And so they had jolted back down 6120, to 6110, to Cedar Ridge, and thence southward on the pavement past Tuba City and through Moenkopi, and back onto the dusty road past the abandoned Goldtooth trading post, and then a left turn over a cattle guard onto dirt tracks that led up the slope of Ward Terrace. Where the track crossed a shallow wash, Tommy Tsi said, "Here," and pointed down it.

The Jeep had been left mid-wash around a bend some fifty yards downstream. They left Tsi in the car and walked along the edge of the streambed, careful not to mar any tracks that might still be there. There was no sign of foot traffic up the sand. Much of the Jeep's tire marks had already been erased by the pickup Tsi had been driving, and the wind had softened the edges of what few remained. But enough had survived to add one bit of information. Bernie noticed it, too.

"That little rainstorm came through just after you found Ben, didn't it?" And she pointed to a protected place where the Jeep tires had left their imprint in sand that obviously had been damp.

"How far is this from where that happened?"

"I'd say maybe twenty miles as the crow flies," Chee said. "And no rain since, I think that tells us a little something."

The Jeep itself told them little else. They stood back from it, examining the ground. The sand around the driver's side had been churned, presumably by Tsi's boots, as he got in and out looking for something easy to loot, and while he pried out the radio.

From the passenger's door, one could step directly onto the stony slope of the arroyo bank. If the occupant had left that way, it made tracking this many days later virtually hopeless.

"What's that stuff in the backseat?" Bernie asked. "I guess the equipment for the job."

"I see some traps," Chee said. "And cages. That canister is probably for poison they blow into burrows to kill the fleas."

He took out his pocketknife, used it to depress the button to open the passenger-side door, then used it to swing the door open.

"Looks like nothing much here," Bernie said, "unless we find something in the litter bag."

Chee wasn't ready to concede that. Leaphorn had once told him that you're more likely to find something if you're not looking for anything in particular. "Just keep an open mind and see what you see," Leaphorn liked to say. Now Chee saw a dark stain on the leather upholstery on the Jeep's passenger seat.

He pointed at it.

"Oh," Bernie said, and made a wry face.

The stain streaked downward, almost black.

"I'd guess dried blood," Chee said. "Let's get the crime scene people out here."

18

ID YOU NOTICE his face when he said that?" Leaphorn asked. "Said 'Mr. Nez is dead. Charley is still alive.' The damn prairie dog is still alive. Like it was the best news possible."

"I don't think I've ever seen you really angry before," Louisa said.

"I try not to let things get to me," Leaphorn said. "You really can't if you're a cop. But that was a little too damn coldhearted for me."

"I've seen a few of the real superbrains act like that before," she said. "He was making a point, of course. The dog's immune system had modified to deal with the new bacteria forms, and nothing mattered except the research. No such luck with Nez. So now he thinks he'll have a whole prairie dog colony full of test subjects. So it's Nez died but the rodent lived. Hip, hip, hooray. And aren't you driving too fast for this road?"

Leaphorn slowed a little, enough so the following breeze engulfed them in dust but not enough to stop the jolting the car was taking. "Weren't you going to have dinner with Mr. Peshlakai and set up interviews with some students? I don't want you to miss that and we're running late."

"Mr. Peshlakai and I always operate on Navajo time," she said. "No such thing as late. We meet when I get there and he gets there. What's got you in such a rush?"

"I'm going on back down to Flag," Leaphorn said. "I want to go to the hospital and talk to the people there and try to find out what Pollard learned that made her so angry."

"You mean that 'Somebody is lying' note in her journal?"

"Yeah. That seemed to explain why she was going back up to Yells Back Butte. To find out for herself."

"Lying about what?" Louisa said, mostly to herself.

"I'd guess she meant about where Nez picked up his lethal flea. That was her job, and from what I've heard, she took it very seriously." He shook his head. "But who knows? I don't. This is getting hard to calculate."

Louisa nodded.

"Find out for herself?" Leaphorn repeated. "And how does she do that? We know she drove up to Yells Back bright and early either to talk to Woody about where he had Nez working on the day the flea got onto him. Or maybe to collect some rodents or fleas from around there for herself. But she didn't go talk to Woody. Or so he tells us. And if she collected fleas she sure must have done it fast, because she drove right out again."

"Any idea now where she drove?"

"Well, she didn't go back to her motel room to pack up for a trip. Her stuff was still there. And none of the people there had seen her."

"Which doesn't sound good."

"We've got to find that Jeep," Leaphorn said. "And meanwhile I'll try to find out who she talked to at the hospital. It could be helpful."

They jolted off the gravel onto Navajo Route 3 and skirted past Moenkopi to U.S. Highway 160 and Tuba City.

"Where do I drop you?"

"At the filling station right here," Louisa said, "but just long enough to use the telephone. I'm going to call Peshlakai and cancel. Tell him I'll get with him later."

Leaphorn stared at her.

"This is getting too interesting," she said. "I don't want to quit now."

It was after nine when they got back to Flag. They stopped for a fast snack at Bob's Burgers and decided to check at the hospital on the chance a doctor who knew something about the Nez case might be working the night shift.

The doctor proved to be a young woman who had completed intern training at Toledo in March and was doing her residency duties at the Flagstaff hospital in a deal with the Indian Health Service—paying off her federal medical school loan.

"I don't think I ever saw Mr. Nez," she said. "Dr. Howe probably handled him in the Intensive Care Unit. Or maybe the nurse on that floor would know something helpful. Tonight it would be Shirley Ahkeah."

Shirley Ahkeah remembered Mr. Nez very well. She also remembered Dr. Woody. Even better, she remembered Catherine Pollard.

"Poor Mr. Nez," she said. "Except for Dr. Howe, it didn't seem like the others cared about him after he was dead."

"I'm not sure I know what you mean," Leaphorn said.

"Forget it," she said. "It wasn't fair to say it. After all, it was Dr. Woody who checked him in. And Miss Pollard was just doing her job—trying to find out where he picked up the infected flea. Did she ever find out?"

"We don't know," Leaphorn said. "The morning after she left here she left a note for her boss. It just said that she was driving up to where Dr. Woody had his mobile laboratory and checking for plague carriers around there. Dr. Woody tells us she never arrived at his lab. She didn't go back to her office or to the motel where she was staying. Nobody has seen her since."

Shirley's face registered a mixture of shock and surprise.

"You mean—has something happened to her?"

"We don't know," Leaphorn said. "Her office reported her disappearance to the police. And the vehicle she was driving is missing, too."

"You think I was the last one to talk to her? Nobody has seen her since she left here?"

"We don't know. No one that we can locate. Did she say anything to you about where she was going? Anything that would give us a hint of what was going on with her?"

Shirley shook her head. "Nothing that you don't already know. All she talked about here was Mr. Nez. She wanted to know how he'd been infected. Where and when."

"Did you tell her?"

"Dr. Delano told her we didn't know for sure. That Nez had a high fever and fully developed plague symptoms—the black splotches under the skin where the capillaries have failed, and the swollen glands—he already had all that when we got him up here in Intensive Care, and they brought him right up. She asked Delano a lot of questions, and he told her that Dr. Woody had said that Nez had been bitten by the flea the evening before he brought him in. And she said that wasn't what Dr. Woody had told her, and Delano—"

"Wait a second," Louisa said. "She had already talked to Woody about Nez?"

Shirley chuckled. "Apparently. She said something about a lying sonofabitch. And Delano, he's sort of touchy and he seemed to think that Miss Pollard was accusing him of lying. So then she said something to make it clear she had meant Woody. And Delano said he wasn't certifying what Woody had told him, because he didn't think it was true either. He said Nez couldn't possibly have developed a fever that high and the other plague symptoms so quickly."

Shirley shrugged. End of explanation.

Leaphorn frowned, digesting this. He said: "Do you think Dr. Delano could have misunderstood him? About when Nez was infected?"

"I don't see how," Shirley said. She pointed. "They were standing right there and I heard it all myself. Delano had told Woody that Nez had died sometime after midnight. And Woody said he wanted to know just exactly when Nez died. Exactly. He said the flea had bitten Nez on the inside of his thigh the evening before he brought him in. Woody was very emphatic about the time. He told Delano he'd left a list of symptoms and so forth that he wanted timed and charted as the disease developed. He wanted an autopsy scheduled and he wanted to be there when it was done."

"Was it done?"

"So I hear," Shirley said. "Nurses aren't included in the circuit of information at that level, but the word gets around."

Louisa chuckled at that. "Hospitals and universities. About the same story."

"What did you hear?" Leaphorn asked.

"Mostly that Woody had more or less tried to take over the procedure, and the pathologist was sore as hell. Otherwise, I guess it was just a finding of another death from bubonic plague. And Woody had a lot of tissue and some of the organs preserved."

Neither Leaphorn nor Louisa had much to say on their way back to his truck. Settled in their seats, Louisa said they were probably lucky Delano hadn't been there. "He might have known a little more, but he probably wouldn't have told us much. Professional dignity involved, you know."

"Yeah," Leaphorn said, and started the engine.

"You're not very talkative," Louisa said. "Did that answer any questions for you?"

"Well, now we know for sure who Miss Pollard thought had been lying to her," Leaphorn said. "And of course that raises the next question."

"Which is why would Woody lie to her? And for that matter, he must have lied to us, too."

"Exactly," Leaphorn said.

"We should go up there again and confront him with it. See what he says."

"Not yet," Leaphorn said. "I think he'd just insist he wasn't lying. He'd come up with some sort of explanation. Or he'd tell me to bug off. Quit wasting his time."

"I guess he could, couldn't he."

"We're just two nosy civilians," Leaphorn said, wondering if that sounded as sad as it felt.

"So what are you going to do?"

"I'm going to call Chee in the morning. See if anything new has turned up on Pollard or her Jeep. And then I'll return Mrs. Vanders's call and tell her what little we know. And then I want to go see Krause."

"And see if he knows more than he's told you?"

"I didn't know what questions to ask," Leaphorn said. "And I'd like to get a look at that note Pollard left for him."

Louisa's expression asked him why.

Leaphorn laughed. "Because I spent too many years being a cop, and I can't get over it. I ask him to see the note, so what happens? Possibility A. He finds a reason not to show it to me. That makes me wonder why not."

"Oh," Louisa said. "You think he might, ah, be involved?"

"I don't think that now, but I might if he refused to let me see the note. But on to possibility B. He shows me the note. The handwriting obviously doesn't match her script in the journal. That raises all sorts of possibilities. Or C. He hands me the note, and it has information on it that he didn't think was important enough to mention. Possibility C is the best bet. Even that's unlikely, but it doesn't cost anything to try."

"Are you going to invite me along again?"

"I'm counting on it, Louisa. Instead of the job just being a grind, you make it fun."

She sighed. "I can't go tomorrow. I'm chairing a committee meeting, and it's my project and my committee."

"I'll miss you," Leaphorn said. And he knew he would.

19

CHEE HAD STARED at the telephone with distaste, dreading this call. Then he picked it up, took a deep breath and dialed Janet Pete's office at the federal building in Phoenix. Ms. Pete was not in. Did he want her voice mail? He didn't. Where could he reach her? Was this matter urgent?

"Yes," Chee said. Janet might not agree, but it was urgent for him. He couldn't focus on anything else until the genie that Cowboy's "Pollard did it" theory had released was securely back in the bottle. Chee's "yes" earned him a number in Flagstaff, which proved to be the telephone on a desk in a multiple-users' office assigned to public defenders in the courthouse at Flagstaff.

The very familiar voice of many happy memories said: "Hello, Janet Pete."

"Jim Chee," he said. "Do you have some time to talk, or should I call you back?"

Brief silence. "I have time." The voice was even softer now, or was it his imagination? "Is this about business?"

"Alas, it's business," Chee said. "I've heard Cowboy Dashee's theory of what happened to Kinsman and we've been checking on it. I need to talk to your client. Is he still being held there at Flag? And would you be willing to get me in to talk to him?"

"Yes, on the first one," Janet said. "He's still there because I couldn't get bail for him. Mickey opposed it and I think that's stupid. Where could Jano hide?"

"It is stupid," Chee agreed. "But Mickey wants to go for the death penalty, I guess. If he didn't fight bond, even for a Hopi who sure as hell isn't going to run, then you could use it to prove even the U.S. attorney didn't really believe Jano is dangerous."

Even as he was finishing the sentence, Chee was wondering why he always seemed to begin conversations with Janet like this—as if he were trying to start a fight. The silence at the other end of the line suggested she was having the same thought.

"What do you want to talk to Mr. Jano about?"

"I understand he saw the Jeep Ms. Pollard was driving."

"He saw a Jeep. Have you picked her up yet?"

More adversarial than "Have you found her?" Chee closed his eyes, remembering how it had been once.

"We haven't located her," he said.

"It may not be easy," Janet said. "She's had a long time to hide, and I understand she has plenty of money to make that easy."

"We didn't make the connection until—" He stopped. He wasn't going to apologize. None was needed. Janet had worked as a defense attorney long enough to know how the police operated. How they couldn't possibly investigate every time someone drove off without telling anyone where they were going. Why explain what she already knew?

"Look, Jim," she said. "I'm the man's defense attorney. Unless you can let me see how he—how justice would benefit by letting you cross-examine him, then I can't do it. Tell me what good it would do him."

Chee sighed. "We found the Jeep," he said. "The passenger-side seat was smeared with dried blood. There's evidence it was abandoned within an hour or so after Jano—after Kinsman was hit on the head."

Silence. Then Janet said: "Blood. Whose was it? But you haven't had time for any lab work yet, I guess. Is Jano a suspect in this, too?"

"I don't see how he could be. I know exactly where he was when the Jeep was being abandoned."

"Where was it?"

"About twenty miles southwest. Down an arroyo."

"You think Jano might have seen something, or heard something, that would help you find Catherine Pollard?"

"I think he might have. Slim chance, but we don't have anything else to go on. Not now, anyway. Maybe we will when the crime scene crew and the lab people finish with the Jeep."

"Okay then," Janet said. "You know the rules. I'm there, and if I cut off the questions, that ends it. You want to do it today?"

"Fair enough," Chee said. "And the sooner the better. I'll leave Tuba City as soon as I hang up."

"I'll meet you at the jail," she said. "And, Jim, let's try not to make each other mad all the time." She didn't wait for a response.

Janet was waiting in the interrogation room—a small dingy space with two barred windows looking out at nothing. She was sitting across a battered wooden table from Robert Jano. She talked quietly. Jano listened intently. Glanced up as Chee appeared in the doorway. Examined Chee with mild, polite curiosity. Chee nodded to him, suddenly aware that when he had caught Jano with his hands still red with Kinsman's blood he hadn't—in his shock and rage—really studied the man. He studied him now. This handsome, polite young killer whom Chee was trying to give a place in history. The first man strapped into a gas chamber under the new federal reservation death sentence law.

Chee nodded to Janet, said: "Thanks."

"You two have met," Janet said, with no sign that she appreciated the irony of that. They nodded. Jano smiled, then seemed embarrassed that he had.

"Have a seat," Janet said, "and I'll go over the rules. Mr. Chee here will ask a question. And, Robert, you won't answer it until I say it's okay. All right?"

Jano nodded. Chee looked at Janet, who returned the look with no trace of warmth. She'd learned a lot, he thought, since he'd first met her in the interrogation room at the San Juan County Jail in Aztec. Many happy times ago.

"Okay," Chee said. He looked at Jano. "That morning I arrested you, did you see a young woman anywhere around there?"

"I saw—" he began, but Janet interrupted.

"Just a moment," she said, and took a tape recorder from her purse, put it on the table, set up a microphone and switched it on. "Okay," she said.

"I saw a black Jeep," Jano said. "I didn't see who was driving it."

"When did you see it, and where were you?"

Jano looked at Janet. She nodded.

"I had climbed the butte and was walking along the rim to where I have a blind for catching eagles. I looked down and saw a black Jeep parked on that rise near the abandoned hogan."

"No one was in it?"

Jano glanced at Janet. She nodded.

"No."

"Did you see Officer Kinsman's car driving in?"

Jano glanced at Janet.

"What's the purpose of that question?"

"I want to find out if the Jeep was still there when Kinsman arrived."

Janet thought about it. "Okay."

"I saw him coming in, yes. And the Jeep was still there."

Chee looked at Janet. "So," he said, "if Pollard was the Jeep driver, she was in the vicinity when Kinsman was killed."

"Injured," Janet said. "But yes, she was."

"I intend to ask your client to just re-create what he saw and heard and did that morning," Chee said.

She thought. "Go ahead. We'll see."

Jano said he arrived about dawn, parked his pickup, unloaded his eagle cage with the rabbit in it that he'd brought along as bait and climbed the saddle to the rim of the butte. He heard an engine sound, watched and saw the Jeep arriving, but he couldn't see who got out of it because of where it had been parked. He had settled himself into the blind and put the rabbit, secured with a cord on the brush, on top of it. Then he had waited about an hour. The eagle came circling over, in its hunting pattern. It saw the rabbit, dived, and caught it. He had caught the eagle by one leg and its tail. It had slashed his forearm with its other talon. "Then I turned the eagle loose and—"

"Just a second," Chee said. "You had the eagle in the cage when I arrested you. The cage was beside the rocks, just a few feet away. Remember?"

"That was the second eagle," Jano said.

"You're saying you caught an eagle, released it and then caught a second one?"

"Yes," Jano said.

"Will you tell me why you released the first one?"

Jano looked at Janet.

"No, he won't," she said.

"He'll be asked at the trial," Chee said.

"If it goes to trial, he will say his reason involves religious beliefs that he is not free to discuss outside his kiva. He may say that two of its tail feathers were pulled out in the struggle, eliminating its ritual use. And then, if I have to do it, I will call in an authority on the Hopi religion who will also explain why a eagle thus stained by bloody violence could not be used in the role assigned to it in this religious ceremonial."

"Okay," Chee said. "Please continue, Mr. Jano. What happened next?"

"I took the rabbit and walked maybe two miles down the rim of the butte to where another eagle has its hunting ground, got into the blind there and waited. Then the eagle you saw came for the rabbit and I caught it."

Jano stopped, looked at Chee as if waiting for an argument and then went on.

"This time I was more careful." He smiled and displayed his forearm. "No injury this time."

Jano said he had seen the Navajo Tribal Police car driving up the trail while he was carrying the eagle down the saddle toward his truck. He said he'd hidden behind an outcrop of rock for a while, hoping the policeman would leave, and then had crept down the rest of the way, thinking he had not been seen.

"Then I heard a loud voice. I think it was the policeman. I heard him several times. And then—"

Chee held up his hand. "Hold it there. Did you hear a response from the person he was talking to?"

"I just heard that one voice," Jano said.

"A man's voice?"

"Yes. It sounded like he was giving orders to someone."

"Orders? What do you mean?"

"Yelling. Like he was arresting someone. You know. Ordering them around."

"Could you tell where the voices were coming from?"

"Just one voice," Jano said. "From about over where I found Mr. Kinsman."

"I want you to skip back a little," Chee said. "When you were climbing down the saddle, was the Jeep still parked where you first saw it parked?"

Jano nodded, then looked at the microphone and said: "Yes, the Jeep was still there."

"Okay. Then what did you do when you heard the voice?"

"I hid behind a juniper for a while, just listening. I could hear what sounded like walking. You know, boots on rocky ground and sort of coming in my direction. Then I heard a voice saying something. And then I heard a sort of a thumping sound."

Jano paused, looking at Chee. "I think it might have been Mr. Kinsman being hit on the head with something. And then there was a clatter."

Jano paused again, pursed his lips, seemed to be remembering the moment.

"Then what?" Chee asked.

"I just waited there behind the juniper. And after it was silent awhile, I went to look. And there was Mr. Kinsman on the ground, with the blood running out of his head." He shrugged. "Then you walked up and pointed your gun at me."

"Did you recognize Kinsman?"

Janet Pete said: "Hold it. Hold it." She frowned at Chee. "What are you trying to do, Jim? Establish malice?"

"The D.A. will establish that Kinsman had arrested Mr. Jano before," Chee said. "I wasn't trying anything tricky."

"Maybe not," she said. "But this looks like a good place to cut this off."

"Just one more question," Chee said. "Did you see anyone else when you were there? Anyone at all? Or anything? Going in, or coming out, or anything?"

"I saw a bunch of goats over on the other side of the saddle," Jano said. "Lot of trees over there. I couldn't tell for sure. But maybe there was somebody with them."

"Okay," Janet said. "Mr. Jano and I have some things to talk about. Good-bye, Jim."

Chee stood, took a step toward the door, turned back. "Just one more thing," he said. "I found a blind at the rim of Yells Back where you may have caught an eagle." He described the location and the blind. "Is that right?"

Jano looked at Janet, who looked at Chee. She nodded.

"Yes," Jano said.

"The first eagle, or the second one?"

"The second one."

"Where did you catch the first eagle?"

Jano didn't glance at Janet this time for permission to answer. He sat, eyes on Chee, looking thoughtful.

He won't tell me, Chee thought, because there was only one eagle, or he won't tell me because he isn't willing to reveal the location of another of his kiva's hidden hunting blinds.

Janet cleared her throat, rose. "I'm going to cut this off," she said. "I think—"

Jano held up a hand. "Stand there on the rim at the top of the saddle. Look directly at Humphrey's Peak in the San Franciscos. Walk straight toward it. About two miles you come to the rim again. It's a place there where a slab tilted down and left a gap."

"Thank you," Chee said.

Jano smiled at him. "I think you know eagles," he said.

20

LEAPHORN AWOKE IN a silent house, with the early sun shining on his face. He had built their house in Window Rock with their bedroom window facing the rising sun because that pleased Emma. Therefore, both the sun and the emptiness were familiar. Louisa had left a note on the kitchen table, which began: "Push ON button on the coffee maker," and went on to outline the availability of various foods for breakfast and concluded on a more personal note.

"I have errands to run before class. Good hunting. Please call and let me know what luck you're having. I enjoyed yesterday. A LOT. Louisa."

Leaphorn pushed the ON button, dropped bread into the toaster, got out a plate, cup, knife and the butter dish. Then he went to the telephone, began dialing Mrs. Vanders's number in Santa Fe, then hung up. First he would call Chee. Perhaps that would give him something to tell Mrs. Vanders besides that he had nothing at all to tell her.

"He hasn't arrived yet, Lieutenant Leaphorn," the station secretary said. "Do you want his home number?"

"It's 'Just call me mister' now," Leaphorn said. "And thanks, but I have it."

"Wait a minute. Here he comes now."

Leaphorn waited.

"I was just going to call you," Chee said. "We found the Jeep." He gave Leaphorn the details.

"You said the tire tracks showed the sand was still wet when it got there?"

"Right."

"So it got there after Kinsman was hit."

"Right again. And probably not long after. It wasn't a very wet rain."

"I guess it's too early to have anything much from the crime lab about prints or—" Leaphorn paused. "Look, Lieutenant, I keep forgetting that I'm a civilian now. Just say no comment or something if I'm overstepping."

Chee laughed. "Mr. Leaphorn," he said. "I'm afraid you're always going to be Lieutenant to me. And they said they found a lot of prints everywhere matching the guy who stole the radio. But there was no old latent stuff in the obvious places. The steering wheel, gearshift knob, door handles—all those places had been wiped. Very thoroughly."

"I don't like the sound of that," Leaphorn said.

"No," Chee said. "Either she's on the run and wanted to leave the impression she'd been abducted, or she actually was taken by someone who didn't want to be identified. Take your pick."

"Probably number two if I had to guess. But who knows? And I guess it's way too early to know anything about the blood," Leaphorn said.

"Way too early."

"Is there any chance you could find any samples of Pollard's blood anywhere? Was she a blood bank donor? Or was she scheduled for any surgery that she'd stockpile blood for?"

"That was one reason I was about to call you," Chee said. "We can get next of kin and so forth from her employer, but it would be quicker to call that woman who hired you. Was it Vanders?"

Leaphorn provided the name, address and telephone number.

"I'm going to call her right now and tell her the Jeep was found and to expect a call from you," Leaphorn added. "Anything you've told me that you want withheld?"

A moment of silence while Chee considered. "Nothing I can think of," he said. "You know any reason we should?"

Leaphorn didn't. He called Mrs. Vanders.

"Give me a moment to get ready for this," she said. "People who call early in the morning usually have bad news."

"It might be," Leaphorn said. "The Jeep she was driving has been located. It had been abandoned in an arroyo about twenty miles from where she said she was going. There was no sign of an accident. But some dried blood was found on the passenger-side seat. The police don't know yet how long the blood was there, whether it was hers or where it came from."

"Blood," Mrs. Vanders said. "Oh, my."

"Dried," Leaphorn said. "Perhaps from an old injury, an old cut. Do you remember if she ever told you of hurting herself? Or of anyone being hurt in that vehicle?"

"Oh," she said. "I don't think so. I can't remember. I just can't make my mind work."

"It's too early to worry," Leaphorn said. "She may be perfectly all right." This was not the time to tell her the Jeep had been wiped clean of fingerprints. He asked her if Catherine might have been a blood bank donor, if she had scheduled any surgery for which she would have stockpiled blood. Mrs. Vanders didn't remember. She didn't think so.

"You'll be getting a call this morning from the officer investigating the case," Leaphorn told her. "A Lieutenant Jim Chee. He'll tell you if anything new has developed."

"Yes," Mrs. Vanders said. "I'm afraid something terrible has happened. She was such a headstrong girl."

"I'm going now to talk to Mr. Krause," Leaphorn said. "Maybe he can tell us something."

Richard Krause was not in his temporary laboratory at Tuba City, but a note was thumbtacked to the door: "Out mouse hunting. Back tomorrow. Reachable through Kaibito Chapter House."

Leaphorn topped off his gasoline tank and headed northeast—twenty miles of pavement on U.S. 160 and then another twenty on the washboard gravel of Navajo Route 21. Only three pickups rested in the Chapter House parking lot, and none of them belonged to the Indian Health Service. Discouraging news.

But inside Leaphorn found Mrs. Gracie Nakaidineh in charge of things.

Mrs. Nakaidineh remembered him from his days patrolling out of Tuba City long, long ago. And he remembered Gracie as one of those women who always do what needs to be done and know what needs to be known.

"Ah," Gracie said after they had gotten through the greeting ritual common to all old-timers, "you mean you're looking for the Mouse Man."

"Right," Leaphorn said. "He left a note on his door saying he could be contacted here."

"He said if anyone needed to find him, he'd be catching mice along Kaibito Creek. He said he'd be about where it runs into Chaol Canyon."

That meant leaving washboard gravel and taking Navajo Route 6330, which was graded dirt circling up onto the Rainbow Plateau for twenty-six bumpy empty miles. Leaphorn avoided much of that journey. About eight miles out, he spotted an Indian Health Service pickup parked in a growth of willows. He pulled off onto the shoulder, got out his binoculars and tried to make out enough of the symbol painted on its dusty, brush-obscured door to determine whether it was the Indian Health Service or something else. Failing that, he scanned the area for Krause.

A figure, clad head to foot in some sort of shiny white coverall, was moving through the brush toward the truck, carrying plastic sacks in both hands. Krause? Leaphorn couldn't even tell whether it was a man or woman. Whoever was wearing the astronaut's suit stopped beside the truck and began removing shiny metal boxes from the sacks, placing them in a row in the shade behind the vehicle. That done, he took one of the boxes to the truck bed, put it into another plastic sack, sprayed something from a can into the bag, and then began arranging a row of flat square pans on the tailgate.

It must be Krause on his mouse-hunting expedition, and now he was performing whatever magic biologists perform with mice. He was working with his back to Leaphorn, revealing a curving black tube that extended from a black box low on his back upward into the back of his hood. Here was what Mrs. Notah had seen behind the screen of junipers at Yells Back Butte. The witch who looked part snowman and part elephant.

As that thought occurred to Leaphorn, Krause turned, and as he took the box from the sack, sunlight reflected off the transparent face shield— completing Mrs. Notah's description of her skinwalker. He turned to watch Leaphorn approaching.

Leaphorn restarted the engine and rolled his truck down the slope. He parked, got out, slammed the door noisily behind him.

Krause spun around, yelling something and pointing to a hand-lettered sign on the pickup: IF YOU CAN READ THIS YOU'RE TOO DAMNED CLOSE.

Leaphorn stopped. He shouted: "I need to talk to you."

Krause nodded. He held up a circled thumb and finger, and then a single finger, noted that Leaphorn understood the signals, and turned back to his work—which involved holding a small rodent in one hand over a white enamel tray and running a comb through its fur with the other. That job done, he held up the tiny form of a mouse, dangling it by its long tail, for Leaphorn to see. He dropped the animal into another of the traps, peeled off a pair of latex gloves, disposed of them in a bright red canister beside the truck. He walked toward Leaphorn, pushing back his hood.

"Hantavirus," he said, grinning at Leaphorn. "Which we used to call, in our days of cultural insensitivity, the Navajo Flu."

"A name which we didn't like any better than the American Legion liked your name for Legionnaire's disease."

"So now we give both of them their dignified Greek titles, and everybody is happy," Krause said. "And anyway, what I was doing was separating the fleas from the fur of a *Peromyscus*, actually a *Peromyscus maniculatus*, and ninety-nine-point-nine chances out of a hundred, when we test both fleas and mammal, the tests will show I have murdered a perfectly healthy deer mouse who never hosted a virus in his life. But we won't know until we get the lab work done."

"Are you finished here now?" Leaphorn asked. "Do you have time for some questions?"

"Some," Krause said. He turned and waved at the row of metal boxes in the shade. "But before I can peel off this uniform—which is officially called a Positive Air Purifying Respirator Suit, or PAPRS, in vector controller slang—I've got to finish with the mice in those traps. Separate the fleas and then it's slice and dice for the poor little deer mice."

"I have plenty of time," Leaphorn said. "I'll just watch you work."

"From a distance, though. It's probably safe. As far as we know, hantavirus spreads aerobically. In other words, it's carried in the mouse urine, and when that dries, it's in the dust people breathe. The trouble is, if it infects you, there's no way to cure it."

"I'll stay back," Leaphorn said. "And I'll hold my questions until you get out of that suit. I'll bet you're cooking."

"Better cooked than dead," Krause said. "And it's not as bad as it looks. The air blowing into the hood keeps your head cool. Stick your hand close here and feel it."

"I'll take your word for it," Leaphorn said.

He watched while Krause emptied the box traps one at a time, combed the fleas out of the fur into individual bags and then extracted the pertinent internal organs. He put those in bottles and the corpses into the disposal canister. He peeled off the PAPR and dropped it into the same can.

"Runs the budget up," he said. "When we're hunting plague, we don't use the PAPRS when we're just trapping. And after we've done the slice-and-dice work, we save 'em for reuse, unless we slosh prairie dog innards on them. But with hantavirus you don't take any chances. But what can I tell you that might be useful?"

"Well, first let me tell you that we found the Jeep Miss Pollard was driving. It had been left in an arroyo down that road that leads past Goldtooth."

"Well, at least she was going in the direction she told me she was going," Krause said, grinning. "No note left for me about taking an early vacation or anything like that?"

"Only a little smear of blood," Leaphorn said.

Krause's grin vanished.

"Oh, shit," he said. "Blood. Her blood?" He shook his head. "From the very first, I've been taking for granted that one day she'd either call or just walk in, probably without even explaining anything until I asked her. You just don't think something is going to happen to Cathy. Nothing that she doesn't want to happen."

"We don't know that it has," Leaphorn said. "Not for sure."

Krause's expression changed again. Immense relief. "It wasn't her blood?"

"That brings us to my question. Do you have any idea where we might find a sample of Miss Pollard's blood? Enough for the lab to make a comparison?"

"Oh," Krause said. "So you just don't know yet? But who else could it belong to? There was no one with her."

"You sure of that?"

"Oh," Krause said again. "Well, no, I guess I'm not. I didn't see her that morning. But she didn't say anything in the note about having company. And she always worked alone. We often do on this kind of work."

"Any possibility that Hammar could have been with her?"

"Remember? Hammar said he was doing his teaching work back at the university that day."

"I remember," Leaphorn said. "That hasn't been checked yet as far as I know. When the lab tells the police it's Miss Pollard's blood in the Jeep, then the alibis get checked."

"Including mine?"

"Of course. Including everybody's."

Leaphorn waited, giving Krause time to amend what he'd said about that morning. But Krause just stood there looking thoughtful.

"Had she cut herself recently? Donated any blood? Any idea where some could be found for the lab?"

Krause closed his eyes, thinking. "She's careful," he said. "In this work you have to be. Hard as hell to work with, but skillful. I don't ever remember her cutting herself in the lab. And in a vector control lab getting cut is a big deal. And if she was a blood donor, she never mentioned it."

"When you came in that morning, where did you find her note?"

"Right on my desk."

"You were going to see if you could find it. Any luck?"

"I've been busy. I'll try," Krause said.

"I'll need a copy," Leaphorn said. "Okay?"

"I guess so," Krause said, and Leaphorn noticed that some of his cordiality had slipped away. "But you're not a policeman. I'll bet the cops will want it."

"They will," Leaphorn said. "I'd be satisfied with a Xerox. Can you remember exactly what it said? Every word of it?"

"I can remember the meaning. She wouldn't be in the office that day. She was taking the Jeep and heading southeast, over toward Black Mesa and Yells Back Butte. Working on the Nez plague fatality."

"Did she say she'd be trapping animals? Prairie dogs or what?"

"Probably. I think so. Either she said it or I took it for granted. I don't think she was specific, but she'd been working on plague. She still hadn't pinned down where Mr. Nez got his fatal infection."

"And that would have been from a prairie dog flea?"

"Well, probably. That *Yersinia pestis* is a bacteria spread by fleas. But some of the *Peromyscus* host fleas, too. We got two hundred off one rock squirrel once."

"Would she have had a PAPRS with her?"

"She carries one with her stuff in the Jeep. Was it still there when they found the vehicle?"

"I don't know," Leaphorn said. "I'll ask. And I have one more question. In that note, did she tell you why she planned to quit?"

Krause frowned. "Quit?"

"Her job here."

"She wasn't going to quit."

"Her aunt told me that. In a call Pollard made just before she disappeared, she said she was quitting."

"Be damned," Krause said. He stared at Leaphorn, biting his lower lip. "She say why?"

"I think it was because she couldn't get along with you."

"That's true enough," Krause said. "A hardheaded woman."

21

SUMMER HAD ARRIVED with dreadful force in Phoenix, and the air-conditioning in the Federal Courthouse Building had countered the dry heat outside its double glass windows by producing a clammy chill in the conference room. Acting Assistant U.S. Attorney J. D. Mickey had assembled the assorted forces charged with maintaining law and order in America's high desert country to decide whether to go for the first death penalty under the new congressional act that authorized such penalties for certain crimes committed on federal reservations.

Acting Lieutenant Jim Chee of the Navajo Tribal Police was among those assembled, but being at the bottom level of the hierarchy, he was sitting uncomfortably in a metal folding chair against the wall with an assortment of state cops, deputy sheriffs, and low-ranking deputy U.S. marshals. It had been clear to Chee from the onset of the meeting that the decision had been long since made. Mr. Mickey was serving on some sort of temporary appointment and intended to make the most of it while it lasted. The timing of the death of Benjamin Kinsman opened a once-in-a-lifetime window of opportunity. National—or at least congressional district regional—publicity was there for the grabbing. He'd go for the historic first. What was happening here was known in upper-level civil service circles as "the CYA maneuver," intended to Cover Your Ass by diluting the blame when things went wrong.

"All right then," Mickey was saying. "Unless anyone has more questions, the policy will be to charge this homicide as a capital crime and impanel a jury for the death sentence. I guess I don't have to remind any of you people here that this will mean a lot more work for all of us."

The woman in the chair to Chee's right was a young Kiowa-Comanche-Polish-Irish cop wearing the uniform of the Law Enforcement Services of the Bureau of Indian Affairs. She snorted, "Us!" and muttered, "Means more work for us, all right. Not him. He means he guesses he don't have to remind us he's running for Congress as the law-and-order candidate."

Now Mickey was outlining the nature of this extra work. He introduced Special Agent in Charge John Reynald. Agent Reynald would be coordinating the effort, calling the signals, running the investigation.

"There'll be no problem getting the conviction," Mickey said. "We caught the perpetrator literally red-handed with the victim. What makes it absolutely iron-clad is having Jano's blood mixed with the victim's on both of their clothing. The best the defense can come up with is a story that the eagle he was poaching slashed him."

This produced a chuckle.

"Trouble is, the eagle didn't cooperate. There wasn't a trace of Jano's blood on it. What we'll need to get the death penalty is evidence of malice. We'll want witnesses who heard Mr. Jano talking about his previous arrest by Officer Kinsman. We need to find people who can remember hearing him talk about revenge. Talking about how badly Kinsman handled him during that first arrest. Even bad-mouthing Navajos in general. That sort of thing. Check out the bars, places like that."

"Where'd this jerk come from?" the LES woman asked Chee. "He sure doesn't know much about Hopis."

"Indiana, I think," Chee said. "But I guess he's been in Arizona long enough to establish residency for a federal office election."

Mickey was closing down the meeting, shaking hands with the proper people. He stopped Chee at the door.

"Stick around a minute," Mickey said. "I want to have a word or two with you."

Chee stuck around. So did Reynald and Special Agent Edgar Evans, who closed the door behind the last departee.

"There're several points I want to make," Mickey said. "Point one is that the victim in this case may not have had a perfect personal record, you know what I mean, being a healthy young man and all. If there's any talk going around among his fellow officers that the defense might use to dirty his name, then I want that stopped. Going for the death penalty, you understand why."

"Sure," Chee said, and nodded.

"I'll get right to the second point then," Mickey said. "The gossip has it that you're engaged to this Janet Pete. The defense attorney. Either that, or used to be."

Mickey had phrased it as a question. He and Reynald and Evans waited for an answer.

Chee said: "Really?"

Mickey frowned. "In a case like this one, in a touchy business like this, culturally sensitive, the press looking over our shoulders, we have to watch out for anything that might look like a conflict of interest."

"That sounds sensible to me," Chee said.

"I don't think you're understanding me," Mickey said.

"Yes, sir," Chee said. "I understand you."

Mickey waited. So did Chee. Mickey's face turned slightly pink.

"Well, then, goddamnit, what's with this gossip? You got something going with Ms. Pete or what?"

Chee smiled. "I had a wise old maternal grandmother who used to teach me things. Or try to teach me when I was smart enough to listen to her," Chee said. "She told me that only a damn fool pays attention to gossip."

Mickey's complexion turned redder. "All right," he said. "Let's get one thing straight. This case is about the murder of a law officer in the performance of his duty. One of your own men. You're part of the prosecution team. Ms. Pete runs the defense team. You're no lawyer, but you've been in the enforcement business long enough to know how things work. We got the disclosure rule, so the criminal's team gets to know what we're putting into evidence."

He paused, staring at Chee. "But sometimes justice requires that you don't show your hole card. Sometimes you have to keep some of your plans and your strategy in the closet. You understand what I'm telling you?"

"I think you're telling me that if this gossip is true, I shouldn't talk in my sleep," Chee said. "Is that about right?"

Mickey grinned. "Exactly."

Chee nodded. He'd noticed that Reynald was following this conversation intently. Agent Evans looked bored.

"And I might add," Mickey added, "that if somebody else talks in their sleep, you might just give a listen."

"My grandmother had something else to say about gossip," Chee said. "She said it doesn't have a long shelf life. Sometimes you hear the soup's on the table and it's too hot to eat, and by the time the news gets to you it's in the freezer."

Mickey's beeper began chirping as Chee was ending that observation. Whatever the call was about, it broke up the cluster without the ritual shaking of hands that convention required.

Chee hadn't lucked into a shady place to leave his car. He used his handkerchief to open the door without burning his hand, started the engine, rolled down all the windows to let the ovenlike heat escape, turned the air conditioner to maximum and then slid off the scorching upholstery to stand outside until the interior became tolerable. It gave him a little time to plan what he'd do. He'd call Joe Leaphorn from here to see if anything new had developed. He'd call his office to learn what awaited him there, and then he'd head for the north end of the Chuska Mountains, the landscape of his boyhood, and the sheep camp where Hosteen Frank Sam Nakai spent his summers.

From Phoenix, from almost anywhere, that meant a hell of a long drive. But Chee was a man of faith. He did his damnedest to maintain within himself the ultimate value of his people, the sense of peace, harmony and beauty Navajos call *hozho*. He badly needed Hosteen Nakai's counsel on how to deal with the death of a man and the death of an eagle.

Hosteen Nakai was Chee's maternal granduncle, which gave him special status in Navajo tradition. He had given Chee his real, or war, name, which was "Long Thinker," a name revealed only to those very close to you and used only for ceremonial purposes. Circumstances, and the early death of Chee's father, had magnified Nakai's importance to Chee—making him mentor, spiritual adviser, confessor and friend. By trade he was a rancher and a shaman whose command of the Blessing Way ceremonial and a half dozen other curing rituals was so respected that he taught them to student *bataalii* at Navajo Community College. If anyone could tell Chee the wise way to handle the messy business of Kinsman, Jano and Mickey, it would be Nakai.

More specifically, Nakai would advise him on how he could deal with the problem posed by the first eagle. If it existed and he caught it, it would die. He had no illusions about its fate in the laboratory. There was a chant to be sung before hunting, asking the prey to know it was respected and to understand the need for it to die. But if Jano was lying, then the eagle he would try to lure to that blind would die for nothing. Chee would be violating the moral code of the *Dine'*, who did not take lightly the killing of anything.

No telephone line came within miles of the Nakai summer hogan, but Chee drove along Navajo Route 12 with not a doubt that his granduncle would be there. Where else would he be? It was summer. His flock would be high in the mountain pastures. The coyotes would be waiting in the fringes of the timber, as they always were. The sheep would need him. Nakai was always where he was needed. So he would be in his pasture tent near his sheep.

But Hosteen Nakai wasn't in his tent up in the high meadows.

It was late twilight when Chee pulled his truck off the entry track and onto the hard-packed earth of the Nakai place. His headlight beams swept across the cluster of trees beside the hogan. They also caught the form of a man, propped on pillows in a portable bed, the sort medical supply companies rent. Chee's heart sank. His granduncle was never sick. Having the bed outside was an ominous sign.

Blue Lady was standing in the hogan doorway, looking out at Chee as he climbed out of the truck, recognizing him, running toward him, saying: "How good. How good. He wanted you to come. I think he sent out his thoughts to you, and you heard him."

Blue Lady was Hosteen's second wife, named for the beauty of the turquoise she wore with her velvet blouse when her *kinaalda* ceremony initiated her into womanhood. She was the younger sister of Hosteen Nakai's first wife, who had died years before Chee was born. Since Navajo tradition is matrilineal and the man joined his bride's family, practice favored widowers marrying one of their sisters-in-law, thereby maintaining the same residence and the same mother-in-law. Nakai, being most traditional and already studying to be a shaman, had honored that tradition. Blue Lady was the only Nakai grandmother Chee had known.

Now she was hugging Chee to her. "He wanted to see you before he dies," she said.

"Dies? What is it? What happened?" It didn't seem possible to Chee that Hosteen Nakai could be dying. Blue Lady had no answer to that question. She led him over to the trees and motioned him into a rocking chair beside the bed.

"I will get the lantern," she said.

Hosteen Nakai was studying him. "Ah," he said, "Long Thinker has come to talk to me. I had hoped for that."

Chee had no idea what to say. He said: "How are you, my father? Are you sick?"

Nakai produced a raspy laugh, which provoked a racking cough. He fumbled on the bedcover, retrieved a plastic device, inserted it into his nostrils and inhaled. The tube connected to it disappeared behind the bed. Connected, Chee presumed, to an oxygen tank. Nakai was trying to breathe deeply, his lungs making an odd sound. But he was smiling at Chee.

"What happened to you?" Chee asked.

"I made a mistake," Nakai said. "I went to a *bilagaana* doctor at Farmington. He told me I was sick. They put me in the hospital and then they broke my ribs, and cut out around in there and put me back together." His voice was trailing off as he finished that, forcing a pause. When he had breath again, he chuckled. "I think they left out some parts. Now I have to get my air through this tube."

Blue Lady was hanging a propane lantern on the limb overhanging the head of the bed.

"He has lung cancer," she said. "They took out one lung, but it had already spread to the other one."

"And all sorts of other places, too, that you don't want to even know about," Nakai said, grinning. "When I die, my *chindi* will be awful mad. He'll be full of malignant tumors. That's why I made them move my bed out here. I don't want that *chindi* to be infecting this hogan. I want it out here where the wind will blow it away."

"When you die, it will be because you just got too old to want to live anymore," Chee said. He put his hand on Nakai's arm. Where he had always felt hard muscle, he now felt only dry skin between his palm and the bone. "It will be a long time from now. And remember what Changing Woman taught the people: If you die of natural old age, you don't leave a *chindi* behind."

"You young people—" Nakai began, but a grimace cut off the words. He squeezed his eyes shut, and the muscles of his face clenched and tightened. Blue Lady was at his side, holding a glass of some liquid. She gripped his hand.

"Time for the pain medicine," she said.

He opened his eyes. "I must talk a little first," he said. "I think he came to ask me something."

"You talk a little later. The medicine will give you some time for that." And Blue Lady raised his head from the pillow and gave him the drink. She looked at Chee. "Some medicine they gave him to let him sleep. Morphine maybe," she said. "It used to work very good. Now it helps a little."

"I should let him rest," Chee said.

"You can't," she said. "Besides, he was waiting for you."

"For me?"

"Three people he wanted to see before he goes," she said. "The other two already came." She adjusted the oxygen tube back into Nakai's nostrils, dampened his forehead with a cloth, bent low and put her lips to his cheek, and walked back into the hogan.

Chee stood looking down at Nakai, remembering boyhood, remembering the winter stories in his hogan, the summer stories at the fire beside the sheep-camp tent, remembering the time Nakai had caught him drunk, remembering kindness and wisdom. Then Nakai, eyes still closed, said: "Sit down. Be easy."

Chee sat.

"Now, tell me why you came."

"I came to see you."

"No. No. You didn't know I was sick. You are busy. Some reason brought you here. The last time it was about marrying a girl, but if you married her you didn't invite me to do the ceremony. So I think you didn't do it." Nakai's words came slowly, so softly Chee leaned forward to hear.

"I didn't marry her," Chee said.

"Another woman problem then?"

"No," Chee said.

The morphine was having its effect. Nakai was relaxing a little. "So you came all the way up here to tell me you have no problems to talk to me about. You are the only contented man in all of Dinetah."

"No," Chee said. "Not quite."

"So tell me then," Nakai said. "What brings you?"

So Chee told Hosteen Frank Sam Nakai of the death of Benjamin Kinsman, the arrest of the Hopi eagle poacher, of Jano's unlikely story of the first and second eagles. He told him of the death sentence and even of Janet Pete. And finally Chee said: "Now I am finished."

Nakai had listened so silently that at times Chee—had he not known the man so well—might have thought he was asleep. Chee waited. Twilight had faded into total darkness while he talked and now the high, dry night sky was a-dazzle with stars.

Chee looked at them, remembered how the impatient Coyote spirit had scattered them across the darkness. He hunted out the summer constellations Nakai had taught him to find, and as he found them, tried to match them with the stories they carried in their medicine bundles. And as he thought, he prayed to the Creator, to all the spirits who cared about such things, that the medicine had worked, that Nakai was sleeping, that Nakai would never awaken to his pain.

Nakai sighed. He said: "In a little while I will ask you questions," and was silent again.

Blue Lady came out with a blanket, spread it carefully over Nakai and adjusted the lantern. "He likes the starlight," she said. "Do you need this?"

Chee shook his head. She turned off the flame and walked back into the hogan.

"Could you catch the eagle without harming it?"

"Probably," Chee said. "I tried twice when I was young. I caught the second one."

"Checking the talons and the feathers for dried blood, would the laboratory kill it then?"

Chee considered, remembering the ferocity of eagles, remembering the priorities of the laboratory. "Some of them would try to save it, but it would die."

Nakai nodded. "You think Jano tells the truth?"

"Once I was sure there was only one eagle. Now I don't know. Probably he is lying."

"But you don't know?"

"No."

"And never would know. Even after the federals kill the Hopi you would wonder."

"Of course I would."

Nakai was silent again. Chee found another of the constellations. The small one, low on the horizon. He could not remember its Navajo name, nor the story it carried.

"Then you must get the eagle," Nakai said. "Do you still keep your medicine *jish*? You have pollen?"

"Yes," Chee said.

"Then take your sweat bath. Make sure you remember the hunting songs. You must tell the eagle, just as we told the buck deer, of our respect for it. Tell it the reason we must send it with our blessings away to its next life. Tell it that it dies to save a valuable man of the Hopi people."

"I will," Chee said.

"And tell Blue Lady I need the medicine that makes me sleep."

But Blue Lady had already sensed that. She was coming.

This time there were pills as well as a drink from the cup.

"I will try to sleep now," Nakai said, and smiled at Chee. "Tell the eagle that he will also be saving you, my grandson."

22

WHERE WAS ACTING Lieutenant Jim Chee? He'd gone to Phoenix yesterday and hadn't checked in this morning. Maybe he was still there. Maybe he was on his way back. Check later. Leaphorn hung up and considered what to do. First he'd take a shower. He flicked on the television, still tuned to the Flagstaff station he'd been watching before sleep overcame him, and turned on the shower.

They had good showerheads in this Tuba City motel, a fine, hard jet of hot water better than the one in his bathroom. He soaped, scrubbed, listened to the voice of the television newscaster reporting what seemed to be a traffic death, then a quarrel at a school board meeting. Then he heard "—murder of Navajo policeman Benjamin Kinsman." He turned off the shower and walked, dripping soapy water, to stand before the set.

It seemed that Acting Assistant U.S. Attorney J. D. Mickey had held a press conference yesterday evening. He was standing behind a battery of microphones at a podium with a tall, dark-haired man stationed uneasily slightly behind him. The taller man was clad in a white shirt, dark tie and a well-tailored dark business suit, which caused Leaphorn to immediately identify him as an FBI agent—apparently a new one to this part of the world, since Leaphorn didn't recognize him, and probably a special agent in charge, since he had come to take credit for whatever discoveries had been made in an affair that produced the sort of headlines upon which the Bureau fed.

"The evidence the FBI has collected makes it clear that this crime was not only a murder done in the commission of a felony, which would make it a capital crime under the old law, but that it fits the intent of Congress in the passage of the legislation allowing the death penalty for such crimes committed on federal reservations." Mickey paused, looked at his notes, adjusted his glasses. "We didn't decide to seek the death penalty casually," Mickey continued. "We considered the problem confronting the Navajo Tribal Police, and the police of the Hopis and Apaches and all the other reservation tribes, and the same problems shared by the police of the various states. These men and women patrol vast distances, alone in their patrol cars, without the quick backup assistance that officers in the small, more populous states can expect. Our police are utterly vulnerable in this situation, and their killers have time to be miles away before help can arrive. I have the names of the officers who have been killed in just—"

Leaphorn switched off the mortality list and ducked back into the shower. He had known several of those men. Indeed, six of them were Navajo policemen. And it was a story that needed to be told. So why did he resent hearing Mickey tell it? Because Mickey was a hypocrite. He decided to skip breakfast and wait for Chee at the police station.

Chee's car was already in the parking lot, and Acting Lieutenant Chee was sitting behind his desk, looking downcast and exhausted. He looked up from the file he was reading and forced a smile.

"I'll just ask a couple of questions and then I'll be out of here," Leaphorn said. "The first one is, do you have a report yet from the crime scene people? Did they list what they found in the Jeep?"

"This is it," Chee said, waving the file. "I just got it."

"Oh," Leaphorn said.

"Sit down," Chee said. "Let me see what's in it."

Leaphorn sat, holding his hat in his lap. It reminded him of his days as a rookie cop, waiting for Captain Largo to decide what to do with him.

"No fingerprints except the radio thief," Chee said. "I think I already told you that. Good wiping job. There were prints on the owner's manual in the glove box, presumed to be Catherine Pollard's." He glanced up at Leaphorn, turned a page and resumed reading.

"Here's the list of items found in the Jeep," he said, and handed it across the desk to Leaphorn. "I didn't see anything interesting on it."

It was fairly long. Leaphorn skipped the items in the glove box and door pockets and started with the backseat. There the team had found three filter-tip Kool cigarette butts, a Baby Ruth candy wrapper, a thermos containing cold coffee, a cardboard box containing fourteen folded metal rodent traps, eight larger prairie dog traps, two shovels, rope, and a satchel that contained five pairs of latex gloves and a variety of other items that, while the writer could only guess at their technical titles, were obviously the tools of the vector control trade.

Leaphorn looked up from the list. Chee was watching him.

"Did you notice the spare tire, the jack and the tire tools were all missing?" Chee asked. "I guess our radio thief didn't limit himself to that and the battery."

"This is all of it?" Leaphorn asked. "Everything that they found in the Jeep?"

"That's it," Chee said, frowning. "Why?"

"Krause said she always carried a respirator suit in the Jeep with her."

"A what?"

"They call 'em PAPRS," Leaphorn said. "For Positive Air Purifying Respirator Suit. They look a little like what the astronauts wear, or the people who make computer chips."

"Oh," Chee said. "Maybe she left it at her motel. We can check if you think it's important."

The telephone on Chee's desk buzzed. He picked it up, said, "Yes." Said, "Good, that's a lot faster than I expected." Said, "Sure, I'll hold."

He put his hand over the receiver. "They've got the report on the bloodwork."

Leaphorn said: "Fine," but Chee was listening again.

"That's the right number of days," Chee told the telephone, and listened again, frowned, said: "It wasn't? Then what the hell was it?" Listened again, then said: "Well, thanks a lot."

He put down the telephone.

"It wasn't human blood," Chee said. "It was from some sort of rodent. He said he'd guess it was from a prairie dog."

Leaphorn leaned back in his chair. "Well now," he said.

"Yeah," Chee said. He tapped his fingers on the desktop a moment, then picked up the telephone, punched a button and said: "Hold any calls for a while, please."

"Did you see the dried blood on the seat?" Leaphorn asked.

"I did."

"How'd it look? I mean, had it been spilled there, or smeared on, or maybe an injured prairie dog had been put there, or dripped, or what?"

"I don't know," Chee said. "I know it didn't look like somebody had been stabbed, or shot, and bled there. It didn't really look natural—like what you expect to see at a homicide scene." He grimaced. "It looked more like it had been poured out on the edge of the leather seat. Then it had run down the side and a little onto the floor."

"She would have had access to blood," Leaphorn said.

"Yeah," Chee said. "I thought of that."

"Why do it?" Leaphorn laughed. "It suggests she didn't have a very high opinion of the Navajo Tribal Police."

Chee looked surprised, saw the point. "You mean we'd just take for granted it was her blood and wouldn't check." He shook his head. "Well, it could happen. And then we'd be looking for her body instead of for her."

"If she did it," Leaphorn said.

"Right. If. You know, Lieutenant, I sort of wish we were back in Window Rock right now, with that map of yours on the wall, and you'd be putting your pins in it." He grinned at Leaphorn. "And explaining to me what happened."

"You're thinking about where the Jeep was left? So far from anywhere?"

"I was," Chee said.

"Way too far to walk to Tuba City. Too far to walk back to Yells Back Butte. So somebody had to meet her, or whoever drove the Jeep there, and give them a lift," Leaphorn said.

"Like who?"

"Did I tell you about Victor Hammar?"

"Hammar? If you did, I don't remember."

"He's a graduate student at Arizona State. A biologist, like Pollard. They were friends. Mrs. Vanders had him pegged as a stalker, a threat to her niece. He'd been out here just a few days before she disappeared, working with her. And he was out here the day I showed up to start my little search."

Chee's expression brightened. "Well now," he said, "I think we should talk to Mr. Hammar."

"The trouble is he told me he was teaching his lab course at ASU the day she vanished. Actually he wasn't. He called in sick. Haven't checked beyond that."

Chee nodded and grinned again. "I have a map." He pulled open his desk drawer, rummaged, and pulled out a folded Indian Country map. "Just like yours." He spread it on the desktop. "Except it's not mounted so I can stick pins in it."

Leaphorn picked up a pencil, leaned over the map, and made some quick additions to terrain features. He drew little lines to mark the cliffs of Yells Back Butte and the saddle linking it to Black Mesa. A dot indicated the location of the Tijinney hogan. With that Leaphorn stopped.

"What do you think?" Chee asked.

"I think we're wasting our time. We need a larger map scale."

Chee extracted a sheet of typing paper from his desk and penciled in the area around the butte, the roads, and the terrain features. He drew a tiny *b* for the Tijinney hogan, an *l* for Woody's lab, a faint irregular line from the hogan to represent the track in from the dirt road, and a little *j* and *k* for where Jano and Kinsman had left their vehicles. He examined his work for a moment, then added another faint line from the saddle back to the road.

Leaphorn was watching. "What's that?"

"I saw a flock of goats on the wrong side of the saddle and a track leading in. I think it's a shortcut the goatherd uses so he doesn't have to climb over," Chee said.

"I didn't know about that," Leaphorn said. He took the pencil and added an *x* near the Yells Back cliffs. "And here is where an old woman McGinnis called Old Lady Notah told people she had seen a snowman. The same woman? Probably."

"Snowman? When was that?"

"We don't know the day. Maybe the day Miss Pollard disappeared. The day Ben Kinsman got hit on the head." Leaphorn leaned back in his chair. "She thought she'd seen a skinwalker. First it was a man, then it walked behind a bunch of junipers and when she saw it again it was all white and shiny."

Chee rubbed a finger against his nose, looked up at Leaphorn. "Which is why you were asking me about that filter respirator suit, isn't it? You thought Pollard was wearing it."

"Maybe Miss Pollard. Maybe Dr. Woody. I'll bet he has one. Or maybe somebody else. Anyway, I'm going to go talk to that old lady if I can find her," Leaphorn said.

"Dr. Woody, he'd have access to animal blood, too," Chee said. "And so would Krause, for that matter."

"And so would Hammar, our man with the bum alibi. Now I think it might be worth the time to look into that."

They considered this for a while.

"Did you know Frank Sam Nakai?" Chee asked.

"The *bataalii*?" Leaphorn asked. "I met him a few times. He taught curing ceremonials at the college at Tsali. And he did a *yeibichai* sing for one of Emma's uncles after he had a stroke. A fine old man, Nakai."

"He's my maternal granduncle," Chee said. "I went to see him last night. He's dying of cancer."

"Ah," Leaphorn said. "Another good man lost."

"Did you see the TV news this morning? The press conference J. D. Mickey called in Phoenix?"

"Some of it," Leaphorn said.

"He's going for the death penalty, of course. The sonofabitch."

"Running for Congress," Leaphorn said. "What he said about cops out here having no backup help, lousy radio communications, all that's true enough."

"It's a funny thing," Chee said. "I catch Jano practically red-handed standing over Kinsman. He was there, and nobody else was around. He had a fine revenge motive. And then there's Jano's blood mixed with Kinsman's on the front of Kinsman's uniform—just about where he would have cut himself on Kinsman's buckle if they'd been struggling. You have a dead-cinch conviction—and all Jano can do is come up with a daydream story about the eagle he poached slashing him—and there's the eagle right there with no blood on it, so he says not that eagle. That's the second eagle, he says. I caught one earlier and turned it loose." Chee shook his head. "And yet, I'm beginning to have some doubts. It's crazy."

Leaphorn let that all pass without comment.

"That other eagle story is so phony that I'm surprised Janet's not too embarrassed to give it to the jury."

Leaphorn made a wry face, shrugged.

"Jano claims he pulled out a couple of the first eagle's tail feathers," Chee said. "I saw one circling up there over Yells Back with a gap in its tail plume."

"So what are you going to do?" Leaphorn asked.

"Jano told me how to locate the blind where he caught the first eagle. I'm going to get myself a rabbit as eagle bait and go up there tomorrow and catch the bird. Or shoot it if I can't catch it. If there's no old blood in the grooves in its talons, or in its ankle feathers, then I don't have any more doubts."

Leaphorn considered this. "Well," he said. "Eagles are territorial hunters. It would probably be the same bird. But the blood could be from a rodent it caught."

"If there's dried blood anywhere, I'll take it in and let the lab decide. You want to come along?"

"No thanks," Leaphorn said. "I'm going to go find the lady with the goats and learn about that snowman she saw."

23

ACTING LIEUTENANT JIM Chee reached Yells Back Butte early and well prepared. He climbed the saddle while the light of dawn was just brightening the sky over Black Mesa, carrying his binoculars, an eagle cage, his lunch, a canteen of water, a quart thermos of coffee, a rabbit and his rifle. He found the tilted slab of rimrock just where Jano said it would be, straightened out the disordered brush that formed the blind's roof. He took out his medicine bag and removed from the doeskin pouch the polished stone replica of a badger, which Frank Sam Nakai had given him as his hunting fetish, and an aspirin bottle, which held pollen. He put the fetish in his right hand and sprinkled a pinch of pollen over it. Then he faced the east and waited. Just as the rim of the sun appeared, he sang his morning song and sprinkled an offering of pollen from the bottle. That done, he shifted into the hunting chant, telling the eagle of his respect for it, asking it to come and join in this sacrifice that would send it into its next life with his blessing and, perhaps, save the life of the Hopi whose arm it had slashed.

Then he climbed down into the blind.

By 10:00 A.M. he had watched two eagles patrolling the rim of the butte to the west of his position, neither the one he wanted. He'd found the feather he'd left behind on his original visit to the blind, retrieved it, wrapped it in his handkerchief and laid it aside. He'd consumed about fifty percent of his coffee and the apple from his lunch sack, and read two more chapters of *Execution Eve*, the Bill Buchanan book he'd brought along to pass the time. At 10:23, the eagle he wanted showed up.

It came from the east, drifting over Black Mesa in lazy circles that brought it nearer and nearer. Through gaps in the blind's brush roofing, Chee followed it through the binoculars, confirming the irregularity in its fan of tail feathers. He lifted the struggling rabbit out of the eagle cage, made sure the nylon cord on its leg was secure and waited until the bird's hunting circle was taking it away. Then he put the rabbit on the roof, squirmed into his best watching position and waited.

On its next circle it swept southward, lost altitude and patrolled over the rolling sagebrush desert away from the butte, disappearing from Chee's view. He put the rifle in a handier place and waited, tense. A moment later, the eagle reappeared, rising on an updraft just a few yards above the rim of the butte and not fifty yards from the blind, then soared above him to the left.

The rabbit had long since given up its struggles and sat motionless on the roof. Chee stirred the brush supporting it with the rifle barrel. Startled, it scrambled to the end of the cord, jerked at it, sat again. The eagle turned, tightened its circle directly overhead. Chee jerked the cord, provoking a fresh flurry of struggles.

And then the eagle produced a raucous whistle and swept down.

Chee pulled the rabbit back toward the center of the blind. As he did, the eagle struck it with a crash, blanking out the sky with extended wings. Chee tugged at the cord, pulling against the thrust of beating wings, reaching for the eagle's legs.

He was lucky. When it struck, the eagle had locked both sets of talons, one through the rabbit's back, the other on its head. Chee grabbed both legs and brought bird, rabbit, and much of the brush roof falling down on him. He dragged his jacket over the eagle, folded it over head and wings and inspected the bird's legs. He saw fresh blood on its talons. At the base of the ruff feathers on its left leg, he found something black and brittle. Dried blood. Old rabbit blood, perhaps. Or Jano's. The lab would decide. Either way, Chee could rest now.

He pushed bird, rabbit, and jacket into the eagle cage and secured the door. Then he leaned back against the stone, poured himself the last of the coffee, and inspected the damage to himself. It was minimal—just a single cut across the side of his left hand, where the eagle's beak had caught him.

The eagle extricated itself from his jacket, unlocked its talons from the rabbit, and battled frantically against the stiff metal wires that formed the cage.

"First Eagle," Chee said. "Be calm. Be peaceful. I will treat you with respect." The eagle stopped its struggles and fixed Chee with an unblinking stare. "You will go where all eagles go," Chee said, but he was sad when he said it.

Back at the Tuba City police station, Chee parked in the shade. He brought the eagle cage in and put it beside Claire Dineyahze's desk.

"Wow," Claire said. "He looks mean enough. What's he charged with?"

"Resisting arrest and biting a cop," Chee said, displaying the cut on his hand.

"Ugh. You ought to put some disinfectant on that."

"I will," Chee said. "But first I've got to report this capture to the Federal Bureau of Ineptitude in Phoenix. Could you get 'em for me?"

"Sure." She started dialing. "On line three."

He picked up the telephone on the adjoining desk.

The receptionist at the FBI office said that Agent Reynald was busy and would he leave a message.

"Tell him it concerns the Benjamin Kinsman case," Chee said. "Tell him it's important." He waited.

"Yes," the next voice said. "This is Reynald."

"Jim Chee," Chee said. "I want to tell you we have the other eagle in the Jano case."

"Who?"

"Jano," Chee said. "The Hopi who—"

"I know who Jano is," Reynald snapped. "I mean who is the person I'm talking to."

"Jim Chee. Navajo Tribal Police."

"Oh, yes," Reynald said. "Now what's this about an eagle?"

"We caught him today. Where do you want him delivered for the blood testing?"

"We already have the eagle," Reynald said. "Remember? The arresting

officer impounded it when he took the perp into custody. It tested negative. No blood was on it."

"This is the other eagle," Chee said.

Silence. "Other eagle?"

"Remember?" Chee said, trying to include in the question the same
measure of impatience that Reynald had used when he'd asked it. "The
suspect's case will be based in part on his claim that the slash on his arm
was caused by a first eagle, which he then released," Chee said, reciting it
at about the rate a teacher might read a difficult passage to a remedial class.
"Whereupon Jano claims he caught a second eagle, which he contends
was the bird the arresting officer impounded. He contends that the
blood—"

"I know what he contends," Reynald said, and laughed. "I didn't
dream you guys—or anybody, for that matter—was taking that seriously."

While Reynald was enjoying his laugh, Chee signaled Claire to listen
and to flick on the recording machine.

"Serious or not," Chee said, "we have the eagle now. When the FBI
lab checks it for human blood in the talon grooves or the leg ruff feathers,
it's either there or it isn't. That takes care of that."

Reynald chuckled. "I can't believe this," he said. "You mean you fellas
actually went out and caught yourself a bird to run through the lab?
What's that supposed to prove? The lab finds nothing, so you keep catching eagles until you run out of them, and then you tell the jury Jano must
have made it up."

"On the other hand, if Jano's blood—"

But Reynald was laughing. "And then the defense attorney will say
you missed the one he released. Or, better still, the defense catches one for
itself, and they put some of Jano's blood on it and present it as evidence."

"Okay," Chee said. "But I want to be clear about this. How does the Federal Bureau of Investigation want me to dispose of this eagle I have here?"

"Whatever you like," Reynald said. "Just don't dump it on me. I'm al-
lergic to feathers."

"All right then, Agent Reynald," Chee said. "It's been a pleasure working with you."

"Just a second," Reynald said. "What I want you to do with that bird is get rid of it. All it can possibly do is complicate this case, and we don't want it complicated. You understand? Get rid of the damned thing."

"I understand," Chee said. "You're telling me to get rid of the eagle."

"And get to work on what you're supposed to be doing. Are you making any progress finding witnesses who can testify that Jano wanted some revenge on Kinsman? People who can swear he was angry about that original arrest?"

"Not yet," Chee said. "I've been busy trying to catch that first eagle."

That out of the way, Chee called the federal public defender's office and asked for Janet Pete. She was in.

"Janet, we have the first eagle."

"Really?" She sounded incredulous.

"At least I'm almost certain it's the right one. A couple of its tail feathers are missing, which matches what Jano told us."

"But how did you get it?"

"The same way Jano did. Used the same blind, in fact. Only the decoy rabbit was different."

"Has it gone to the lab yet? When will we know what they find?"

"It hasn't gone to the lab. Reynald didn't want it."

"He what? He said that? When?"

"I called him just a little while ago. He said what it boiled down to was nobody would believe Jano's story and if we dignified it by checking another eagle for his blood, you'd just say we'd caught the wrong eagle and want us to go out and keep catching them. And so forth."

"The sonofabitch," Janet said. There was silence while she thought about it. "But I guess I can see his logic. A negative find wouldn't help his case. Finding Jano's blood on that bird might hurt it. So it would be either no help or a loss for him."

"Unless he wanted justice."

"Well, I don't think he has any doubt Jano killed Kinsman. You don't, do you?"

"I didn't."

"You do now? Really?"

"I want to know if he's telling the truth."

"You may have to let a jury decide."

"Janet, twist Reynald's arm. Tell him you insist on it. Tell him if he won't have the tests done you'll petition the court to order it."

Long silence. "Who caught the eagle? How many people know it's caught?"

"I caught it," Chee said. "Claire Dineyahze has it sitting beside her desk right now. That's it."

"Was there dried blood on the feathers? Anywhere else?"

"Not that I could be sure of," Chee said. "Something dried on its feathers. Tell the bastard if he won't order the lab work you'll get it done yourself."

"Jim, it's not that simple."

"Why not?"

"A lot of reasons. In the first place, I won't even know about the eagle until Reynald tells me. If he doesn't think it has any importance, he won't."

"But there's the evidence disclosure rule. Mickey has to tell the defense attorney what evidence he has."

"Not if it's not important enough for him to use. Mickey will say he didn't even intend to mention the eagle in connection with the blood on Kinsman. The defense can use it if it likes. He'll say he considers it too foolish to require any response."

"All that's probably right. So you tell him that you know the eagle was caught, tell him—"

"And he says, How do you know this? Who told you?"

"And you say, A confidential informant."

"Come on, Jim," Janet said impatiently. "Don't sound naive. The federal criminal justice world is small and the acoustics are good. How long do you think it took me to know that Mickey had been warning you about leaking stuff to me? My confidential informant said she got it thirdhand, but she said Mickey called it 'pillow talk.' Did he?"

"That's what he called it. But do it anyway."

Chee listened while Janet outlined the sort of trouble this would cause for Acting Lieutenant Jim Chee. True, he wasn't a federal employee, but the links between the U.S. justice system and the Tribal Justice operations were strong, close and often personal. And it meant a headache for her, too. She badly wanted to win this case, at the very least to save Jano from the death penalty. It was her first in this new job and she wanted it to be clean, neat and tidy, not a messy affair with her looking like an inept loose cannon who didn't understand the system. And so forth. And while he listened, Chee knew what he had to do. And how to do it. And that the effects might change the direction of his life.

"Tell you what," he said. "You tell Mickey that you have access to a tape recording, with two credible witnesses to certify it's genuine. Tell him that on this tape, the FBI agent whom Mr. Mickey put in charge of the Jano case can be clearly heard ordering a policeman to get rid of evidence that might be beneficial to the defense."

"My God!" Janet said. "That's not true, is it?"

"It's true."

"Did you tape a telephone call with Reynald? When you told him you had the eagle? Surely he didn't give you permission to tape something like that. If he didn't, that's a federal offense."

"I didn't ask him," Chee said. "I just taped it, with a witness listening in."

"That's against the law. You could go to jail. You'll surely lose your job."

"You're being naive now, Janet. You know how the FBI feels about bad publicity."

"I won't have anything to do with this," Janet said.

"That's fair enough," Chee said. "And I want to be fair with you, too. Here's what I'll have to do now. I'll get on the telephone and find out how I can get the necessary laboratory work done. Maybe at the lab at Northern Arizona University or Arizona State. I have to be here at the office until noon tomorrow. I'll check with you then—or you can call me here—so I'll know what's going on. Then I'll take the bird on to the lab and I'll have them send you a copy of their report."

"No, Jim. No. They'll charge you with evidence tampering. They'll think of something. You're being crazy."

"Or maybe just stubborn," Chee said. "Anyway, give me a call tomorrow."

Then he sat back and thought about it. Had he been bluffing? No, he'd do it if he had to. Leaphorn's lady friend would know someone on the NAU biology faculty who could run the tests—and do it right so it would hold water in court. And if they found it wasn't Jano's blood, then maybe Jano was just a damn liar.

But Chee wasn't kidding himself about his motivation. One of the reasons he'd told Janet about the tape was to give her a weapon if she needed it. But part of that was purely selfish—the kind of reason Frank Sam Nakai had always warned him against. He wanted to find out how Janet would use this weapon he'd handed her.

For that, he'd have to wait until tomorrow. Maybe a few days more, but he thought tomorrow would tell him.

24

CHEE SLEPT FITFULLY, the darkness in his little trailer full of bad dreams. He got to his office early, thinking he would get a stack of paperwork out of the way. But the telephone was at his elbow and concentration was hard.

It first rang at eighteen minutes after eight. Joe Leaphorn wanted to know if he could get a copy of the list of items found in Miss Pollard's Jeep.

"Sure," Chee said. "We'll Xerox it. You want it mailed?"

"I'm in Tuba," Leaphorn said. "I'll pick it up."

"You on to something I should know about?"

"I doubt it," Leaphorn said. "I want to show the list to Krause and see if he notices anything funny. Something missing that should be there. That sort of thing."

"Did you locate Mrs. Notah?"

"No. I found some of her goats. Somebody's goats, anyway. But she wasn't around. After I waste some of Krause's time this morning, I think I'll go there and look again. See if she can add anything to what she told McGinnis about the skinwalker who looked like a snowman. Did the FBI pick up that eagle?"

"They didn't want it," Chee said, and told Leaphorn what Reynald had said without mentioning taping the call.

"I'm not too surprised," Leaphorn said. "But you can't blame the people.

I've known a lot of good agents. It's the system you get with political police. I'll let you know if Mrs. Notah saw anything useful."

The next two calls were routine business. When call number four arrived, Claire didn't just buzz him. She waved and wrote FBI in the air with
her finger.

Chee took a long breath, picked up the telephone, said, "Jim Chee."

"This is Reynald. Do you still have that eagle?"

"It's here," Chee said. "What do—"

"Agent Evans is en route to pick it up," Reynald said. "He'll be there
about noon. Be there, because he'll need you to sign a form."

"What are you—" Chee began, but Reynald had hung up.

Chee leaned back in his chair. One question was now answered, he
thought. Janet had told Reynald she knew about the eagle, prodding him
into action, or she had told J. D. Mickey, who had told Reynald how to react. That solved the first part of the problem. The FBI would have the lab
test the eagle. He would know sooner or later whether Jano had lied. That
left the second question. How had Janet used the club he'd handed her?

In the periods between his bad dreams the night before, he had worked
out three scenarios for Janet. In the first, she would simply stand aside, as
she had suggested she would, and see what happened. If nothing happened, when he appeared on the witness stand as Jano's arresting officer,
she would lead him to the eagle during cross-examination.

"Lieutenant Chee," she would say, "is it true that you were told by
Mr. Jano that he had caught a second eagle after the first one slashed his
arm, and that you made an attempt to recapture that first eagle?" To which
he would have to say: "Yes."

"Did you capture it?"

"Yes."

"Did you then take the eagle to the laboratory at Northern Arizona
University and arrange for an examination to be made to determine if it
had Mr. Jano's blood on its talons or feathers?"

"Yes."

"And what did that report show?"

The answer to that, of course, would depend on the laboratory report.

He could now rule out that scenario. She hadn't stood aside. She had
intervened. But how?

nario two, the one for which he ardently longed, Janet went to
one of the key federals, told him she had reason to believe the first eagle
had been caught, and demanded to see the results of the blood testing.
Mickey or Reynald, or both, would evade, deny, argue that her request was
ridiculous, imply that she was ruining her career in the Department of Justice if she was too stupid to understand that, demand to know the source
of this erroneous leak, and so forth. Janet would bravely stand her ground,
threaten court action or a leak to the press. And he would love her for her
courage and know that he was wrong in not trusting her.

In scenario three, the cause of the previous night's bad dreams, Janet
went to Mickey, told Mickey that he had a problem—that Lieutenant Jim
Chee had gone out and captured an eagle that he insisted was the same eagle her client would testify had slashed his arm and he had then released.
She would recommend that he take custody of said eagle and have tests
done to determine if Jano's blood was on it. Whereupon Mickey would tell
her to just relax and let the FBI handle collection of evidence in its routine
manner. Then Janet would say the FBI had decided against checking the
eagle. And Mickey would ask her if Reynald had told her that. And she'd
say no. And he'd say how did you find out then. And she would say Lieutenant Chee had told her. And he'd say Chee was misleading her, trying
to cause trouble. And about there Janet would realize that she had already
caused career-blighting trouble in Mickey's mind and the only way that
could be fixed was by using Chee's secret weapon. She would then
pledge Mickey to secrecy. She would let him know that in telling Chee he
wouldn't get the eagle tested, Reynald had carelessly allowed his telephone
conversation to be taped and that on that tape Agent Reynald could
be heard imprudently ordering Chee to get rid of the eagle and thus the
evidence.

What would this prove? He knew, but he didn't want to admit it or
think about it. And he wouldn't have to until Agent Evans arrived to pick
up the bird. And not even then, if Evans's conduct didn't somehow tip
him off.

Edgar Evans arrived at eleven minutes before noon. Through his
open office door Chee watched him come in, watched Claire point him
to the eagle cage in the corner behind her, watched her point him to Chee's
office.

"Come in," Chee said. "Have a seat."

"I'll need you to sign this," Evans said, and handed Chee a triplicate form. "It certifies that you transferred evidence to me. And I give you this form, which certifies that I received it."

"This makes it awful hard for anything to get lost," Chee said. "Do you always do this?"

Evans stared at Chee. "No," he said. "Not often."

Chee signed the paper.

"You need to be careful with that bird," he said. "It's vicious and that beak is like a knife. I have a blanket out in the car you can put over it to keep it quiet."

Evans didn't comment.

He was putting the cage in the backseat of his sedan when Chee handed him the blanket. He spread it over the cage.

"I thought Reynald had decided against this," Chee said. "What made him change his mind?"

Evans slammed the car door, turned to Chee.

"You mind if I pat you down?"

"Why?" Chee asked, but he held out his hands.

Evans quickly, expertly felt along his belt line, checked the front of his shirt, patted his pockets, stepped back.

"You know why, you bastard. To make sure you're not wearing a wire."

"A wire?"

"You're not as stupid as you look," Evans said. "And not half as smart as you think you are."

With that, Evans got into his car and left Jim Chee standing in the parking lot looking after him, knowing which tactic Janet had used and feeling immensely sad.

25

FOR LEAPHORN IT was a frustrating day. He'd stopped at Chee's office and picked up the list. He studied it again and saw nothing on it that told him anything. Maybe Krause would see something interesting. Krause wasn't at his office and the note pinned to his door said: "Gone to Inscription House, then Navajo Mission. Back soon." Not very soon, Leaphorn decided, since the round trip would be well over a hundred miles. So he drove to Yells Back Butte, parked, climbed over the saddle and began his second hunt for Old Lady Notah.

After much crashing around the goats again, twenty-one in all unless he had counted some twice (easy to do with goats) or missed some others, he didn't find Mrs. Notah. Recrossing the saddle required much huffing and puffing, a couple of rest stops, and produced a resolution to watch his diet and get more exercise. Back at his truck, he drank about half the water in the canteen he'd carelessly left behind, and then just rested awhile. This cul-de-sac walled in by the cliffs of Yells Back and the mass of Black Mesa was a blank spot for all radio reception except, for reasons far beyond Leaphorn's savvy in electronics, KNDN, Gallup's Navajo-language Voice of the Navajo Nation.

He listened to a little country-western music and the Navajo-language open-mike segment, and while he listened he sorted out his thoughts. What would he tell Mrs. Vanders when he called her this evening? Not much, he decided. Why was he feeling illogically happy? Because the tension was gone with Louisa. No more feeling that he was betraying Emma or himself. Or that Louisa was expecting more from him than he could possibly deliver. She'd made it clear. They were friends. How had she put it about marriage? She'd tried it once and didn't care for it. But enough of that. Back to Cathy Pollard's Jeep. That presented a multitude of puzzles.

The Jeep had come here early, as the note from Pollard suggested. Jano said he had seen it arrive, and he had no reason Leaphorn could think of to lie about that. It must have left during the brief downpour of hail and rain, not long after Chee had arrested Jano. Earlier, Chee would have heard it. Later, it wouldn't have left the tire prints in the arroyo sand where it had been abandoned. So that left the question of who was driving it, and what he or she had done after parking it. No one had come down the arroyo to pick up the driver. But an accomplice might have parked near the point where the access road crossed the arroyo and waited for the Jeep's driver to walk back to join him or her along the rocky slope.

That required some sort of partnership, not a sudden panicky impulse. Leaphorn's imagination couldn't produce a motive for such a conspiracy. But he came up with another possibility. No cinch, but a possibility. He started the engine and drove off in search of Richard Krause.

A stopoff at Tuba showed Krause's office still empty with the same note on the door. Leaphorn refilled his gasoline tank and started driving. Krause wasn't at Inscription House. The woman who responded to Leaphorn's knock at the Navajo Mission office door said the Health Department man had left about thirty minutes earlier. Going where? He hadn't said.

So Leaphorn made the long, long drive back to Tuba City, writing off the day as a loser, watching the sunset backlight the towering thunderheads on the western horizon and turn them into a kind of beauty only nature can produce. By the time he reached his motel, he was more than ready to call it quits. Calling Mrs. Vanders could wait. Tomorrow he'd rise earlier and catch Krause before he left his office.

Wrong again. The note on the door the next morning suggested that Krause would be working in the arroyo west of the Shonto Landing Strip. An hour and sixty miles later Leaphorn spotted Krause's truck from the road, and Krause on his knees apparently peering at something on the ground. He heard Leaphorn coming, got to his feet, dusted off his pant legs.

"Collecting fleas," he said, and shook hands.

"It looked like you were blowing into that hole," Leaphorn said.

"Good eye," Krause said. "Fleas detect your breath. If something is killing their host mammal and they're looking for a new host, they're very sensitive to that. You blow into the hole and they come to the mouth of the tunnel." He grinned at Leaphorn. "Some say they prefer garlic on your breath, but I like chili." He stared at the tunnel month. Pointed. "See 'em?"

Leaphorn squatted and stared. "Nope," he said.

"Little black specks. Put your hand down there. They'll jump on it."

"No thanks," Leaphorn said.

"Well, what can I do for you?" Krause said. "And what's new?"

He removed a flexible metal rod from the pickup bed and unfurled the expanse of white flannel cloth attached to the end of it.

"I'd like you to take a look at this list of stuff found in the Jeep," Leaphorn said. "See if it's missing anything that should be there, or if there's anything on it that tells you anything."

Krause had folded the flannel around the rod. Now he pushed it slowly into the rodent hole, deeper and deeper. "Okay," he said. "I'll just give 'em a minute to collect on the flannel. Then when I pull it out, the flannel pulls off the rod and folds over the other way and traps a bunch of fleas."

Krause slipped the flannel off the rod, dropped it into a Ziploc bag, closed it, then checked himself for fleas, found one on his wrist, and disposed of it.

Leaphorn handed him the list. Krause put on a pair of bifocals and studied it. "Kools," he said. "Cathy didn't smoke so those must be from somebody else."

"I think it notes they were old," Leaphorn said. "Could have been there for months."

"Two shovels?" Krause said. "Everybody carries one for the digging we do. Wonder why she had the other one?"

"Let me see it," Leaphorn said, and took the list. Under "on floor behind front seat" it listed "long-handled shovel." Under "rear luggage space," it also listed "long-handled shovel."

"Maybe a mistake," Krause said, and shrugged. "Listing the same shovel twice."

"Maybe," Leaphorn said, but he doubted it.

"And here," Krause said. "What the hell was she doing with this?" He pointed to the rear luggage space entry, which read: "One small container of gray powdery substance labeled 'calcium cyanide.'"

"Sounds like a poison," Leaphorn said.

"It damn sure is," Krause said. "We used to use it to clean out infected burrows. You blow that dust down it and it wipes out everything. Pack rats, rattlesnakes, burrowing owls, earthworms, spiders, fleas, anything alive. But it's dangerous to handle. Now we use 'the pill.' It's phostoxin, and we just put it in the ground at the mouth of a burrow and it gets the job done."

"So where would she get this cyanide stuff?"

"We still have a supply of it. It's on a shelf back in our supply closet."

"She'd have access to it?"

"Sure," Krause said. "And look at this." He pointed to the next entry: "'Air tank with hose and nozzle.' That's what we used to use to blow the cyanide dust back into the burrow. It was in the storeroom, too."

"What do you think it means—her having that in the Jeep?"

"First, it means she was breaking the rules. She doesn't take that stuff out without checking with me and explaining what she wants it for, and why she's not using the phostoxin instead. And second, she wouldn't be using it unless she wanted to really sterilize burrows. Zap 'em. Something big like prairie dogs. Not just to kill fleas."

He returned the list to Leaphorn.

"Anything else on there you'd wonder about?"

"No, but there's something that should be on that list that isn't. Her PAPRS."

"You always have that with you?"

"No, but you'd damn sure have it if you were going to use that calcium cyanide dust." Krause made a wry face. "They say the warning is you smell almonds, but the trouble is, by the time you smell it, it's already too late."

"Not something you'd use casually then."

Krause laughed. "Hardly. And before I forget it, I found that note

Cathy left me. Made a copy for you." He fished out his wallet, extracted a much-folded sheet of paper, and handed it to Leaphorn. "I don't see anything helpful on it, though."

The note was written in Pollard's familiar semilegible scrawl:

Boss—Heard stuff about Nez infection at Flag. Think we've been lied to. Going to Yells Back, collect fleas and find out—Will fill you in on it when I get back. Pollard.

Leaphorn looked up from the note at Krause, who was watching his reaction, looking penitent.

"Knowing what I know now, I can see I should have got worried quicker when she didn't get back. But, hell, she was always doing things and then explaining later. If at all. For example, I didn't know where she was the day before. She didn't tell me she was driving down to Flag. Or why." He shrugged, shook his head. "So I just thought she'd gone tearing off somewhere else."

"I wonder why she didn't tell you she was quitting," Leaphorn said.

Krause stared at him. "I don't think she was. Did she tell her aunt why?"

"I gather it was something about you."

Krause had spent too many summers in the sun to look pale. But he did look tense.

"What about me?"

"I don't know," Leaphorn said. "She didn't get specific."

"Well, we never did get along very well," Krause said, and began putting his equipment in the truck. The legend on his sweat-soaked T-shirt said, SUPPORT SCIENCE: HUG A HERPETOLOGIST.

26

TWO TELEPHONE NOTES were stuck on his spindle when Chee got to his office. One was from Leaphorn, asking Chee to call him at his motel. The second was from Janet Pete. It said: "The eagle's being tested today. Please call me."

Chee wasn't quite ready for that. He dialed Leaphorn's number first. Yesterday the Legendary Lieutenant had wanted to show Krause the list of stuff found in the Jeep. Maybe that had developed into something.

"You had breakfast?" Leaphorn asked.

"I'm not much for eating breakfast," Chee said. "What's on your mind?"

"How about joining me for coffee then at the motel diner? I want to go back out to Yells Back Butte. Can you get away? I think I should have an officer along."

An officer along! "Oh," Chee said. He felt elation, quickly tinged with a little disappointment. The Legendary Lieutenant had done it again. Had unraveled the puzzle of who had abandoned the Jeep. Had maintained the legend. Had again outthought Jim Chee. "Sure. I'll be there in ten minutes."

Leaphorn was sitting at a window table, putting butter on a stack of pancakes. He put the note on the table in front of Chee and smoothed it out.

"I showed the list to Krause," he said. "There were a couple or three surprises."

"Oh," Chee said, feeling slightly defensive. He hadn't noticed anything amiss.

"Mostly technical stuff way over our heads," Leaphorn said. "This blower here, for example, and the container of calcium cyanide. I figured that was just one of their flea killers. Turns out they don't use it these days except in some sort of unusual circumstances." He looked up at Chee. "Like, let's say they needed to wipe out a whole colony of prairie dogs."

Chee leaned back in his chair, understanding again why he admired Leaphorn instead of resenting him. The man was giving him a chance to figure it out for himself. And of course he had.

"Like, let's say, the colony Dr. Woody is working with."

Leaphorn was grinning. "That occurred to me, too," he said. "I don't think Woody would have wanted that to happen."

Chee nodded. And waited. He could tell from Leaphorn's expression that more was coming.

"And then there's this," Leaphorn said. "I asked Krause why there would be two of these long-handled shovels in that Jeep. He said everybody carried one because of the digging they do, besides getting stuck in the sand. But just one."

Chee leaned back again, considering that. "Be useful to have one if you wanted to dig a grave."

Leaphorn nodded. "That also occurred to me. Maybe toss it in, not knowing there was already one in the Jeep."

"So somewhere between Yells Back Butte and where the Jeep was left we might be checking on easy places to dig and looking for freshly dug dirt."

"I'd suggest that," Leaphorn said.

"I'm also asking people to check for bicycle tracks along the Goldtooth road. But there's not much chance they'll find any. Too dry."

This caused Leaphorn's eyebrows to rise. "Bicycle?"

"I noticed Woody had a bicycle rack bolted to the back of that mobile lab truck," Chee said. "There wasn't a bike on it."

Leaphorn slammed his hand on the tabletop, rattling his plate. "I must be getting old," he said. "Why didn't I think of that?"

"It wouldn't be a hard bike ride," Chee said, "from where the Jeep was left back to Yells Back. He could have stepped out of the Jeep onto rocks, lifted the bike out, and carried it back to the road."

"Sure," Leaphorn said. "Sure he could. But it would have been clumsy to carry the shovel, too. I've had my brain turned off."

Chee doubted that. It reminded Chee of watching the Easter egg hunt on the White House lawn on television. Seeing the big brother overlook an egg so the little kid could find it.

The waitress arrived and offered refills. But now both of them were in a hurry.

They took Chee's patrol car, roared down Arizona 264, turned right onto the road to Goldtooth, jolted over the washboard bumps.

"Seems like old times," Leaphorn said. "Us working together."

"You miss it? I mean, being a cop?"

"I miss this part of it. And the people I worked with. I don't miss the paperwork. I'll bet you wouldn't, either."

"I hate that part of it," Chee said. "I'm not good at it, either."

"You're acting now," Leaphorn said. "Usually after you've done that a while, they offer you the permanent position. Would you take it?"

Chee drove for a while without answering. Clouds were building up already, fleets of great white ships against the dark blue sky. By late evening yesterday they had towered high enough to produce a few drops of rain here and there. By this afternoon the monsoon rains might actually begin. Long overdue.

"No," Chee said. "I guess not."

"When I heard you'd applied for the promotion, I sort of wondered why," Leaphorn said.

Chee glanced at him, saw only a profile. Leaphorn was staring at the clouds. "I imagine you could make a pretty good guess. Part prestige, mostly the money's better."

"What do you need it for? You still live in that rusty old trailer, don't you?"

Chee decided to turn the cross-examination around.

"You think they'll offer me the job?"

Long silence. "Probably not."

"Why's that?"

"I suspect the powers that be will get the impression that you would not be a proper team player. You wouldn't cooperate well with other law enforcement agencies," Leaphorn said.

"Any agency in particular?"

"Well, maybe the FBI."

"Oh," Chee said. "What have you heard?"

"It has been said that the FBI would hesitate to handle sensitive business with you over the telephone."

Chee laughed. "Man, oh man," he said. "How fast the word does travel. Did you hear that this morning?"

"Last night already," Leaphorn said.

"Who?"

"Kennedy called me from Albuquerque. Remember him? We worked with him a time or two, and then the Bureau transferred him. He was asking me about a thing we were looking into just before I retired. He's retiring himself at the end of the year and he wanted to know how I liked being a civilian. Asked about you, too. And he said you had made yourself some enemies. So I asked him how you managed that."

"And he said I'd taped a telephone call without permission," Chee said. "Thereby violating a federal statute."

"Yeah," Leaphorn said. "Did he have it right?"

Chee nodded.

"It's nice you don't want that promotion then," Leaphorn said. "Had you decided that before or after you turned on the tape recorder?"

Chee thought for a moment. "Before, I guess. But I didn't really realize it."

They turned up the track toward Yells Back Butte, circled around a barrier of tumbled boulders and found themselves engulfed in goats. And not just the goats. There, beside the track was an aged woman on a large roan horse watching them.

"Lucked out," Leaphorn said. He climbed out of the patrol car, said "Ya'eeh te'h" to Old Lady Notah and introduced himself, reciting his membership in his born to and born for clans. Then he introduced Jim Chee, by maternal and paternal clans and as a member of the Navajo Tribal Police at Tuba City. The horse stared at Chee suspiciously, the goats milled around, and Mrs. Notah returned the courtesy.

"It is a long way to Tuba City," Mrs. Notah said. "And I have seen you here before. I think it must be because the other policeman was killed here. Or because the Hopi came to steal our eagles."

"It is even more than that, mother," Leaphorn said. "A woman who worked with the health department came here the day the policeman was killed. No one has seen her since. Her family asked me to look for her."

Mrs. Notah waited a bit to see if Leaphorn had more to say. Then she said: "I don't know where she is."

Leaphorn nodded. "They say you saw a skinwalker somewhere near here. Was that the day the policeman was killed?"

She nodded. "Yes. It was that day it rained. Now I think it might have been somebody who helps the man who works in that big motor home."

Chee sucked in his breath.

Leaphorn said: "Why do you think that?"

"After that day I saw that man come out of his place carrying a white suit. He walked way up the slope with it, and through the junipers, and then he put it on and put a white hood over his head." She laughed. "I think it is something to keep the sickness off of them. I saw something like that on television."

"I think that's right," Leaphorn said. And then he asked Mrs. Notah to try to tell them everything she had seen or heard around Yells Back Butte that morning. She did, and it took quite awhile.

She had risen before dawn, lit her propane burner, warmed her coffee and ate some fry bread. Then she saddled her horse and rode there. While she was rounding up the goats, she heard a truck coming up the track toward the butte. About sunup, she had seen a man climb up the saddle and disappear over the rim onto the top of the butte.

"I thought it must be one of the Hopi eagle-catchers come to get one. They used to come out here a lot before the government changed the boundary, and I had seen this same man the afternoon before. Just looking around," she said. "That's the way they used to work. Then they would come back before daylight the next morning and go up and catch one."

Chee asked: "Did you tell anyone about this?"

"I was down by the road when a police car came by. I told him I thought the Hopis were going to steal an eagle again."

Chee nodded. Mrs. Notah had been Kinsman's confidential source.

Next in Mrs. Notah's narration was the arrival of the black Jeep.

"It was going too fast for those rocks," Mrs. Notah said. "I thought it would be the young woman with the short hair, but I couldn't see who it was."

"Why the woman with the short hair?" Leaphorn asked.

"I have seen her driving that car before. She drives too fast." Mrs. Notah emphasized her disapproval with a negative shake of her head. "Then I had to go get that goat there." She pointed at a black-and-white male that had wandered far down the track. "Maybe a half-hour later, when I moved the goats back up near the butte, I saw somebody moving behind the trees, and then I saw the thing in the white suit."

She paused, rewarded them with a wry smile. "I went away for a while then, and on the way back to the goats, I heard a car coming, very, very slowly, up the trail. It was a police car, and I thought, That policeman knows how to drive over rocks. When I came back to the goats, I saw the man who works in that motor home was over at the old Tijinney hogan. He was right in there, and I thought *bilagaana* don't know about death hogans, or maybe that's the skinwalker. A witch, well, he don't care about *chindis*."

"What was he doing?" Leaphorn asked.

"I couldn't see much over the wall from where I was," she said. "But when he came out, I could see he was carrying a shovel."

Chee parked his patrol car on the hump overlooking the Tijinney place. They walked down together, Chee carrying the shovel from the trunk of his car, and stood looking over the tumbled stone. The hard-packed earthen floor was littered with pieces of the fallen roof, blown-in tumbleweeds, and the debris vandals had left. It was flat and smooth except for a half dozen holes and the filled-in excavation where the fire pit had been.

"That's where it would be," Chee said, pointing.

Leaphorn nodded. "I've been doing nothing for about a week but sitting in a car seat. Give me the shovel. I need a little exercise."

"Well, now," Chee said, but he surrendered the shovel. For a Navajo as traditional as Chee, digging for a corpse in a death hogan wasn't a task done lightly. It would require at least a sweat bath and, more properly, a curing ceremony, to restore the violator of such taboos to *hozho*.

"Easy digging," Leaphorn said, tossing aside his sixth spadeful. A few moments later he stopped, put aside the shovel, squatted beside the hole. He dug with his hands.

He turned and looked at Chee. "I guess we have found Catherine Pollard," he said. He pulled out a forearm clad in the white plastic of her PAPR suit and brushed away the earth. "She's still wearing her double set of protective gloves."

27

DR. WOODY OPENED his door at the second knock. He said: "Good morning, gentlemen," leaned against the doorway and motioned them in. He was wearing walking shorts and a sleeveless undershirt. It seemed to Leaphorn that the odd pink skin color he'd noticed when he'd first met the man was a tone redder. "I think this is what they call serendipity, or a fortunate accident. Anyway, I'm glad you're here."

"And why is that?" Leaphorn asked.

"Have a seat first," Woody said. He swayed, supported himself with a hand against the wall, then pointed Leaphorn to the chair and Chee to a narrow bed, now folded out of the wall. He seated himself on the stool beside the lab working area. "Now," he said, "I'm glad to see you because I need a ride. I need to get to Tuba City and make some telephone calls. Normally, I would drive this thing. But it's hard to drive. I'm feeling pretty bad. Dizzy. Last time I took my temp it was almost one hundred and four. I was afraid I wouldn't make it out."

"We'll be glad to take you," Chee said. "But first we need to get answers to some questions."

"Sure," Woody said. "But later. After we get going. And one of you will have to stay here and take care of things." He leaned forward over the table and ran his hand over his face. Leaphorn now noticed a dark discoloration under his arm, spreading down the rib cage under the undershirt.

"Hell of a bruise there on your side," Leaphorn said. "We should get you to a hospital."

"Unfortunately, it's not a bruise. It's the capillaries breaking down under the skin. Releases the blood into the tissue. We'll go to the Medical Center at Flagstaff. But first I have to do some telephoning. And someone should stay here. Look after things. The animals in the cages. The files."

"We found the body of Catherine Pollard buried out there," Chee said, "Do you know anything about that?"

"I buried her," Woody said. "But, damnit, we don't have time to talk about that now. I can tell you about it while we're driving to Tuba City. But I've got to get there before I'm too sick to talk, and these cell phones won't work out here."

"Did you kill her?"

"Sure," Woody said. "You want to know why?"

"I think I could guess," Chee said.

"Silly woman didn't give me a choice. I told her she couldn't exterminate that dog colony and I told her why. They might hold the key to saving millions of lives." Woody laughed. "She said I'd lied to her once and that was all she allowed."

"Lied," Chee said. "You told her the rodents weren't infected. Was that it?"

Woody nodded. "She put on her protective suit and was getting ready to pump cyanide dust into the burrow when I stopped her. And then the cop saw me burying her."

"You killed him, too?" Chee said.

Woody nodded. "Same problem. Exactly the same. I can't let anything interfere with this," he said, gesturing around the lab. Then he produced a weak chuckle, shook his head. "But something is. It's the disease itself. Isn't that ironic? This new, improved, drug-resistant version of *Yersinia pestis* is making me another lab specimen."

He was reaching into a drawer as he said that. When his hand came out it held a long-barreled pistol. Probably .22 caliber, Chee guessed. The right size for shooting rodents, but not something anyone wanted to be shot with.

"I just don't have time for this," Woody said. "You stay here," he said to Leaphorn. "Look after things. I'll ride with Lieutenant Chee. We'll send somebody back to take over when I get to the telephone."

Chee looked at the pistol, then at Woody. His own revolver was in the holster on his hip. But he wasn't going to need it.

"I'll tell you what we're going to do," Chee said. "We're going to take Mr. Leaphorn with us. As soon as we get out of this radio blind spot, we'll call an ambulance to meet us. I'll send out a patrolman to take care of this place. We'll turn on the siren and get to Tuba City fast."

Chee stood and took a step toward the door and opened it. "Come on," he said to Woody. "You're looking sicker and sicker."

"I want him to stay," Woody said, and waved the pistol toward Leaphorn. Chee reached and grabbed the gun out of Woody's hand and handed it to Leaphorn. "Come on," he said. "Hurry."

Woody was in no condition to hurry. Chee had to half-carry him to the patrol car.

They raised the dispatcher just as they bounced away from the radio shadow of Yells Back Butte. Chee told him to send an ambulance down the road to Goldtooth and an officer to guard Woody's mobile lab at the butte. Leaphorn sat in the back with Woody, and Woody talked.

He'd found two fleas in his groin area when he awakened the day before and immediately redosed himself with an antibiotic, hoping the fleas, if infected at all, were carrying the unmutated bacteria. By this morning a fever had developed. He knew then that he had the form that resisted medication and had killed Nez so quickly. He had hurriedly compiled his most recent notes in readable form, put away breakable items, stored the blood samples he'd been working on in the refrigerator for preservation and started the engine. But by then he felt so dizzy that he knew he couldn't drive the big vehicle out. So he'd begun a note explaining where he stood in the project, to be passed along to an associate at the Center for Control of Infectious Diseases.

"It's there in the folder on the desk with his name on it—a microbiologist named Roy Bobbin Hovey. But I forgot to mention that he'll want an autopsy. The name and number are in my wallet in case I'm out of it before we get to a telephone. Tell him to do the autopsy. He'll know what organs to check."

"Your organs?" Leaphorn asked.

Woody's chin had dropped down to his breastbone. "Of course," he mumbled. "Who else?"

Chee was driving far too fast for the washboard road and watching in the rearview mirror.

"How were you able to hit Officer Kinsman on the head?" he asked. "Why didn't he cuff you?"

"He was careless," Woody said. "I said, Aren't you going to put those handcuffs on me, and when he twisted around to reach for them, that's when I hit him."

"Then when we left with Kinsman, you drove the Jeep out and abandoned it and poured the blood on the seat so it would look like a murder-kidnapping? Right? And took your bicycle along so you could ride it back from there? Is that right?"

But by then, Dr. Woody had drifted off into unconsciousness. Or perhaps he didn't think the answer mattered.

They met the ambulance about ten miles from Moenkopi, warned the attendants that Woody was probably in the final stages of bubonic plague and sent it racing off toward the Northern Arizona Medical Center. At his station, Chee fished out the note from Woody's wallet, left Leaphorn talking with Claire, and disappeared into his office to make the telephone call.

He emerged looking angry, flopped into a chair across from Leaphorn, wiped his forehead, and said: "Whew, what a day."

"Did you get the man?" Leaphorn asked.

"Yeah. Dr. Hovey said he'll fly out to Flagstaff today."

"Quite a shock, I guess," Leaphorn said. "Learning your associate is a double murderer."

"That didn't seem to bother him. He asked about Woody's condition, and his notes, and who was looking after his papers, and where he could pick them up, and were they being cared for, and how about the animals he was working with, and was the prairie dog colony safe."

"Like that, huh?"

"Pissed me off, to tell the truth," Chee said. "I said I hoped we could keep the sonofabitch alive until we can try him for killing two people. And that irritated him. He sort of snorted and said: 'Two people. We're trying to save all of humanity.' "

Leaphorn sighed. "Matter of fact, I think Woody *was* trying to save humanity."

28

FOR CHEE, THE next hours were occupied by the work of wrapping it up. He called the Northern Arizona Medical Center, got the emergency room supervisor, and told the woman Woody was en route in an ambulance and what to expect. Then he called the FBI office in Phoenix. Agent Reynald was occupied. He got Agent Edgar Evans instead.

"This is Jim Chee," he said. "I want to report that the man who killed Officer Ben Kinsman is in custody. His name is Woody. He is a medical doctor, and a—"

"Hold it! Hold it!" Evans said. "What're ya talking about?"

"The arrest this morning of the man who killed Kinsman," Chee said. "You better take notes because your boss will be asking questions. After being read his rights, Dr. Woody made a full confession of the assault on Kinsman to me, in the presence of Joe Leaphorn. He also confessed to the murder of Catherine Pollard, a vector control specialist employed by the Indian Health Service. Woody is critically ill and is now en route to the hospital at Flag in an amb—"

"What the hell is this?" Evans said. "Some kind of joke?"

"In an ambulance," Chee continued. "I recommend you pass this information along to Reynald, so he can get it to Mickey, so Mickey can drop the charges against Jano," Chee said. "If you want to do a television spectacular with this, the Navajo Police office at Tuba City can tell you where you can find the Pollard body and the details you need about how you, the FBI, solved this crime."

"Hold it, Chee," Evans said. "What kind of—"

"No time for silly questions," Chee said, and hung up.

Next he worked his way down the list of law enforcement agencies put to work by J. D. Mickey on the Kinsman case and gave them the pertinent information. Then he called the Public Defender Service in Phoenix. He got the office secretary. Ms. Pete was not in. Ms. Pete had left about an hour ago en route to Tuba City. Yes, there was a telephone in her car. Yes, she would notify Ms. Pete that she should contact him at Tuba City to receive information critical to the Jano case.

"I think she was going to Tuba to talk to you, Lieutenant Chee," the secretary said. "But this 'critical information.' She'll ask me about that."

"Tell Ms. Pete she was right about the Kinsman case. I arrested the wrong man. Now we have the right one."

Then he called Leaphorn's room at the motel. No answer. He called the desk.

"He's over at the diner," the clerk said. "He said if you called to come on over and join him."

Leaphorn had been busy, too. First he had called the law firm of Peabody, Snell and Glick and persuaded a receptionist that he should be allowed to talk to Mr. Peabody himself. He'd told Peabody the circumstances and suggested that, in view of Mrs. Vanders's fragile health, someone close to her should break the news to her. He'd explained that Miss Pollard's body would not be released to the family until the crime scene crew exhumed it properly and the required autopsy had been completed. He'd given him the names of those who could provide further information.

That done, he had called Louisa and recited into her answering machine the details of what had happened. He'd told her he was checking out, would drive back to Window Rock, and would call her from there tomorrow. Then he'd taken a shower, rescued what was left of the soap and shampoo from the bathroom to add to his emergency supply, packed, left a message for Chee at the desk, and strolled over to the diner to eat.

He was enjoying the diner's version of a Navajo taco and watching a Nike commercial on the wall-mounted television when Lieutenant Chee walked in, spotted Leaphorn and came over. He moved Leaphorn's bag from a chair and sat.

"You leaving town?"

"Home to Window Rock," Leaphorn said. "Back to washing my own dishes, doing the laundry, being a housewife." He had to speak up because the Nike ad had been followed by a used-car commercial, which involved noise and shouting.

"I wanted to thank you for the help," Chee said.

Leaphorn nodded. "I thank you in return. It was mutual. Like old times."

"Anyway, if I can ever—"

But now he was talking over a promo for what the Phoenix station called a news break. A pretty young man was telling them there had been a startling development in the Ben Kinsman murder case and he would take them to Alison Padilla, who was "live at the federal building."

Alison was not as pretty as the anchorman, but she seemed competent. She told them that Acting Assistant U.S. Attorney J. D. Mickey had called a press conference a bit earlier. She would let him speak for himself. Mr. Mickey, looking stern, got right to the point.

"The Federal Bureau of Investigation has taken into custody a suspect in the homicide of Officer Benjamin Kinsman and in the death of an Indian Health Service employee who has been missing for several days. The FBI has also developed information which verifies statements made by Robert Jano, who had previously been arrested by the Navajo Tribal police and charged with the Kinsman murder. Charges against Mr. Jano will now be dismissed. More information will be released as details become available."

While Mickey was reading this, Officer Bernadette Manuelito walked in. Chee waved her over, pointed to a seat. Mickey was now waving off questions and ending the conference, and the camera switched back to Ms. Padilla, who began providing background information.

"Lieutenant," Officer Manuelito said. "Mrs. Dineyahze asked me to tell you the U.S. Attorney's office is trying to reach you." She pointed to the screen. "Him."

"Okay," Chee said. "Thanks."

"And the U.S. Public Defender Service. They said it was urgent."

"Okay," Chee said again. "And, Bernie, you remember Mr. Leaphorn, don't you? From when we were both working at Shiprock? Have a seat. Join us."

Bernie smiled at Leaphorn and said she had to get back to the station. "But did you hear what that man said? I think that's awful. He made it sound like we screwed up."

Chee shrugged.

"It's not fair," she said.

"They tend to do that," Leaphorn said. "That's why a lot of the real cops resent the federals."

"Well, anyway, I just think—" Bernie paused, looking for the words to express her indignation.

Chee wanted to change the subject. He said: "Bernie, when did you say they were having the *kinaalda* for your cousin? Now that we have the FBI handling the Kinsman case, I'm not going to be so busy. Would it still be okay if I came?"

The beeper in her belt holster made its unpleasant noise. "It would be okay," Bernie said, and hurried out the door.

Leaphorn picked up his check, looked at it, fished out his wallet and dropped a dollar tip on the table. "That drive from here to Window seems to get longer and longer," he said. "Got to get moving."

But at the door he paused to shake hands with a woman coming in and chat for a moment. He pointed back into the room and disappeared. Janet Pete had arrived from Phoenix.

She stood in the doorway a moment, scanning the tables. She wore boots and a long skirt with a patterned blouse, and her silky hair was cut short like the chic women on the television shows wore theirs these days. She looked tired, Chee thought, and tense, but still so beautiful that he closed his eyes for a moment and looked away.

When he looked again, she was walking toward him, her expression saying she was glad she had found him. But it revealed nothing else.

Chee stood, pulled back a chair for her and said: "I guess you got the message."

"The message, but not the meaning." She sat, adjusted her skirt. "What does it mean?"

Chee told her how they had found Pollard's body, about Woody's confession that he had killed Kinsman when Kinsman found him burying the woman, about Woody's desperate sickness. She listened without a word.

"Mickey was just on television announcing the murder charge against your client is being dropped," Chee said. "Nothing left now but the 'poaching an endangered species' charge. It's a second offense, done while on probation for the first one. But under the circumstances I'd imagine the judge will just sentence Jano to the time he's already spent locked up waiting for the big trial."

Janet was looking at her hands folded on the table in front of her. "Nothing left but that," she said. "That and the wreckage."

He waited for an explanation. None came. She simply looked at him quizzically.

"Let me get you a cup," Chee said. He pushed back his chair, but she shook her head. "I got your call about the eagle being tested," Chee said. "I intended to call you back, but things got too busy. How did it come out? Mickey made it sound like they found blood."

"It doesn't matter now, does it?"

"Well, sure," Chee said. "It would be nice to know Mr. Jano wasn't lying to us."

"I haven't seen the report yet," Janet said.

He sipped his coffee, watching her. The ball was in her court.

She took a deep breath.

"Jim. How long had you known about this Woody? That he'd killed Kinsman?"

"Not very long," Chee said, wondering where this was leading.

"Before you told me about catching the eagle?"

"No. Not until this morning."

She looked down at her hands again. Calculating all this, he thought. Adding it up. Searching for a conclusion. She found it.

"I want to know why you told me you'd taped Reynald's telephone call."

"Why not?"

"Why not!" The anger showed in her face as well as her voice. "Because as you certainly knew I am a sworn officer of the court in this case. You tell me you have committed a crime." She threw up her hands. "What did you think I would do?"

Chee shrugged.

"No. Don't just kiss it off. I'm serious. You must have had a reason for telling me. What did you think I would do?"

Chee considered that. By traditional Navajo ethical standards he wouldn't be required to tell the absolute truth unless she asked the question a fourth time. This was time two.

"I thought you'd either push the FBI to get the eagle tested or you'd handle it yourself."

"That's not what I meant. What would I do about the taped call? And for that matter about the agent in charge asking you to destroy evidence."

"I thought the information would be useful. Give you leverage if you needed it," Chee said, thinking: That's the third time.

She stared at him, sighed. "You're not good at pretending to be naive, Jim. I know you too well. You had a reason—"

Chee held up his hand, ending this just short of the fourth question. Why make her ask it? He spoke carefully.

"I thought you would go to Mickey and tell him that you had learned Jano's first eagle had been caught, that the FBI declined to test it on grounds that it would be a waste of time and money and had ordered the eagle disposed of. I presumed that if you did this, Mickey would tell you he agreed with the FBI. He would suggest that you, a rookie member of the federal justice family, should be part of the team and drop the issue. Then you would either agree or you would defy Mickey and tell him you would have the eagle tested yourself."

He paused, then drew a deep breath, looked away.

Janet waited.

Chee sighed. "Or you might start by telling Mickey that you had become aware of a potential risk to the case. The Navajo Police had caught the eagle, the FBI agent representing Mickey had ordered it destroyed and the telephone call during which he had done this had been taped. Therefore you would urgently recommend that he order the first eagle tested immediately and make the results public."

Janet's face was flushed. She looked away from him, shook her head, looked back.

"And what would I say when Mickey asked who had made this unauthorized felonious tape? And what would I tell the grand jury when Mickey called it to investigate?"

"He wouldn't call a grand jury," Chee said. "That would drag Reynald in, Reynald would pass the buck back to Mickey, and then Mickey's political hopes are down the tube. Besides, he'd have no trouble at all figuring out who taped the telephone call."

"And you certainly knew that. So what did you do? You deliberately wrecked your career in law enforcement. You put me in an intolerable position. What happens if there is a grand jury? What do I testify?"

"You'd have to tell the simple truth. That I had told you I had illegally taped Reynald's call. But Mickey will never call the jury."

"And what if he doesn't? There's still the fact that you admitted a felony to me and I, also an officer of the court, failed in my duty to report it."

"And the FBI knows you failed to report it. But the FBI knew it, too, and didn't report it either."

"Not yet," she said.

"They won't."

"And if they do, what then?"

"You say that Jim Chee told you he had, without authorization, taped a telephone call from Agent Reynald." Chee paused. "And that you had believed him."

She stared at him. "Had believed him?"

"Then you say that after you had reported this to the assistant U.S. attorney, Jim Chee informed you that while Reynald had made the remarks exactly as reported, Chee had no such tape."

Janet was rising from her chair. She stood looking down at him. How long? Five or six seconds, but memory doesn't operate on conscious time. And Chee was remembering the happiest day of his life—the moment when their romance had become a love affair. He had imagined their love could blend oil and water. She would become a Navajo in more than name and work on the reservation. She would forget the glitter, power, and prestige of the affluent Washington society that produced her. He would set aside his goal of becoming a shaman. He would become ambitious, compromise with materialism enough to keep her content with what he knew she must see as poverty and failure. He'd been young enough to believe that. Janet had believed it, too. Believed the impossible. She could no more reject the only value system she'd ever known than he could abandon the Navajo Way. He hadn't been fair to her.

"Janet," he said, and stopped, not knowing what else to say.

She said: "Damn you, Jim," and walked away.

Chee finished his coffee, listened to her car starting up and rolling across the parking-lot gravel. He felt numb. She had loved him once, in her way. He knew he'd loved her. Probably he still did. He'd know more about that tomorrow when the pain began.

Hunting Badger

For Officer Dale Claxton
Who died doing his duty, bravely and alone.

Author's Note

O N MAY 4, 1998, Officer Dale Claxton of the Cortez, Colorado, police stopped a stolen water truck. Three men in it killed him with a fusil-lade of automatic-weapons fire. In the ensuing chase, three other officers were wounded, one of the suspects killed himself, and the two survivors vanished into the vast, empty wilderness of mountains, mesas, and canyons on the Utah-Arizona border. The Federal Bureau of Investigation took over the manhunt. Soon it involved more than five hundred officers from at least twenty federal, state, and tribal agencies, and bounty hunters attracted by a $250,000 FBI reward offer.

To quote Leonard Butler, the astute Chief of Navajo Tribal Police, the search "became a circus." Sighting reports sent to the coordinator were not reaching search teams. Search parties found themselves tracking one another, unable to communicate on mismatched radio frequencies, local police who knew the country sat at roadblocks while teams brought in from the cities were floundering in canyons strange to them. The town of Bluff was evacuated, a brush fire was set in the San Juan bottoms to smoke out the fugitives, and the hunt dragged on into the summer. The word spread in July that the FBI believed the fugitives dead (possibly of laughter, one of my cop friends said). By August, only the Navajo Police still had scouts out looking for signs.

As I write this (July 1999) the fugitives remain free. But the hunt of 1998 exists in this book only as the fictional memory of fictional characters.

The characters in this book are fictional with the exception of Patti (P.J.) Collins and the Environmental Protection Agency survey team. My thanks to Ms. Collins for providing information about this radiation-mapping job, and to P.J. and the copter crew for giving Chee a ride up Gothic Canyon.

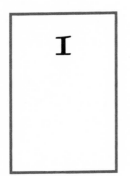

I

DEPUTY SHERIFF TEDDY Bai had been leaning on the doorframe looking out at the night about three minutes or so before he became
aware that Cap Stoner was watching him.

"Just getting some air," Bai said. "Too damn much cigarette smoke in
there."

"You're edgy tonight," Cap said, moving up to stand in the doorway
beside him. "You young single fellas ain't supposed to have anything worrying you."

"I don't," Teddy said.

"Except maybe staying single," Cap said. "There's that."

"Not with me," Teddy said, and looked at Cap to see if he could read
anything in the old man's expression. But Cap was looking out into the
Ute Casino's parking lot, showing only the left side of his face, with its
brush of white mustache, short-cropped white hair and the puckered scar
left along the cheekbone when, as Cap told it, a woman he was arresting
for Driving While Intoxicated fished a pistol out of her purse and shot
him. That had been about forty years ago, when Stoner had been with the
New Mexico State Police only a couple of years and had not yet learned
that survival required skepticism about all his fellow humans. Now Stoner
was a former captain, augmenting his retirement pay as a rent-a-cop security

director at the Southern Ute gambling establishment—just as Teddy was doing on his off-duty nights.

"What'd ya tell that noisy drunk at the blackjack table?"

"Just the usual," Teddy said. "Calm down or he'd have to leave."

Cap didn't comment. He stared out into the night. "Saw some lightning," he said, pointing. "Just barely. Must be way out there over Utah. Time for it, too."

"Yeah," Teddy said, wanting Cap to go away.

"Time for the monsoons to start," Cap said. "The thirteenth, isn't it? I'm surprised so many people are out here trying their luck on Friday the thirteenth."

Teddy nodded, providing no fodder to extend this conversation. But Cap didn't need any.

"But then it's payday. They got to get rid of all that money in their pay envelopes." Cap looked at his watch. "Three-thirty-three," he announced. "Almost time for the truck to get here to haul off the loot to the bank."

And, Teddy thought, a few minutes past the time when a little blue Ford Escort was supposed to have arrived in the west lot. "Well," he said, "I'll go prowl around the parking areas. Scare off the thieves."

Teddy found neither thieves nor a little blue Escort in the west lot. When he looked back at the EMPLOYEES ONLY doorway, Cap was no longer there. A few minutes late. A thousand reasons that could happen. No big deal. He enjoyed the clean air, the predawn high-country chill, the occasional lightning over the mountains. He walked out of the lighted area to check his memory of the midsummer starscape. Most of the constellations were where he remembered they should be. He could recall their American names, and some of the names his Navajo grandmother had taught him, but only two of the names he'd wheedled out of his Kiowa-Comanche father. Now was that moment his grandmother called the "deep dark time," but the late-rising moon was causing a faint glow outlining the shape of Sleeping Ute Mountain. He heard the sound of laughter from somewhere. A car door slammed. Then another. Two vehicles pulled out of the east lot, heading for the exit. Coyotes began a conversation of yips and yodels among the piñons in the hills behind the casino. The sound of a truck gearing down came from the highway below. A pickup pulled into the EMPLOYEES ONLY lot, parked, produced the clattering sound of something being unloaded.

Teddy pushed the illumination button on his Timex. Three-forty-six. Now the little blue car was late enough to make him wonder a little. A man wearing what looked like coveralls emerged into the light carrying an extension ladder. He placed it against the casino wall, trotted up it to the roof.

"Now what's that about?" Teddy said, half aloud. Probably an electrician. Probably something wrong with the air-conditioning. "Hey," he shouted, and started toward the ladder. Another pickup pulled into the employee lot—this one a big oversize-cab job. Doors opened. Two men emerged. National Guard soldiers apparently, dressed in their fatigues. Carrying what? They were walking fast toward the EMPLOYEES ONLY door. But that door had no outside knob. It was the accounting room, opened only from the inside and only by guys as important as Cap Stoner.

Stoner was coming out of the side entrance now. He pointed at the roof, shouted, "Who's that up there? What the hell—"

"Hey," Teddy yelled, trotting toward the two men, unsnapping the flap on his holster. "What's—"

Both men stopped. Teddy saw muzzle flashes, saw Cap Stoner fall backward, sprawled on the pavement. The men spun toward him, swinging their weapons. He was fumbling with his pistol when the first bullets struck him.

2

SERGEANT JIM CHEE of the Navajo Tribal Police was feeling downright fine. He was just back from a seventeen-day vacation. He was happily reassigned from an acting-lieutenant assignment in Tuba City to his old Shiprock home territory, and he had five days of vacation left before reporting back to work. The leftover mutton stew extracted from his little refrigerator was bubbling pleasantly on the propane burner. The coffeepot steamed—producing an aroma as delicious as the stew. Best of all, when he did report for work there wouldn't be a single piece of paperwork awaiting his attention.

Now, as he filled his bowl and poured his coffee, what he was hearing on the early news made him feel even better. His fear—his downright dread—that he'd soon be involved in another FBI-directed backcountry manhunt was being erased. The TV announcer was speaking "live" from the Federal Courthouse, reporting that the bad guys who had robbed the casino on the Southern Ute Reservation about the time Chee was leaving Fairbanks were now "probably several hundred miles away."

In other words, safely out of Shiprock's Four Corners territory and too far away to be his problem.

The theory of the crime the FBI had hung on this robbery, as the handsome young TV employee was now reporting on the seventeen-inch screen in Chee's trailer, went like this: "Sources involved in the hunt said the three bandits had stolen a small single-engine aircraft from a ranch south of Montezuma Creek, Utah. Efforts to trace the plane are under way, and the FBI asked anyone who might have seen the plane yesterday or this morning to call the FBI."

Chee sampled the stew, sipped coffee and listened to the announcer describe the plane—an elderly dark blue single-engine high-wing monoplane—a type used by the U.S. Army for scouting and artillery spotting in Korea and the early years of the Vietnam War. The sources quoted suggested the robbers had taken the aircraft from the rancher's hangar and used it to flee the area.

That sounded good to Chee. The farther the better. Canada would be fine, or Mexico. Anywhere but the Four Corners. In the spring of 1998 he'd been involved in an exhausting, frustrating FBI-directed manhunt for two cop killers. At its chaotic worst, officers from more than twenty federal, state, county and reservation agencies had floundered around for weeks in that one with no arrests made before the federals decided to call it off by declaring the suspects "probably dead." It wasn't an experience Chee wanted to repeat.

The little hatch Chee had cut into the bottom of the trailer door clattered behind him on its rubber hinges, which meant his cat was making an unusually early visit. That told Chee that a coyote was close enough to make Cat nervous or a visitor was coming. Chee listened. Over the sound of the television, now selling a cell-telephone service, he heard wheels on the dirt track that connected his home under the San Juan River cottonwoods to the Shiprock-Cortez highway above.

Who would it be? Maybe Cowboy Dashee, but this wasn't Cowboy's usual day off from his deputy sheriff's job. Chee swallowed another bite of stew, went to the door and pulled back the curtain. A fairly new Ford 150 pickup rolled to a stop under the nearest tree. Officer Bernadette Manuelito was sitting in it, staring straight ahead. Waiting, Navajo fashion, for him to recognize her arrival.

Chee sighed. He was not ready for Bernie. Bernie represented something he'd have to deal with sooner or later, but he preferred later. The gossip in the small world of cops had it that Bernie had a crush on him. Probably true, but not something he wanted to think about now. He'd wanted some time. Time to adjust to the joy of being demoted from acting lieutenant back to sergeant. Time to get over the numbness of knowing he'd finally burned the bridge that had on its other end Janet Pete—seductive, smart, chic, sweet and treacherous. He wasn't ready for another problem. But he opened the door.

Officer Manuelito seemed to be off-duty. She climbed out of her truck wearing jeans, boots, a red shirt and a Cleveland Indians baseball cap and looking small, pretty and slightly untidy, just as he remembered her. But somber. Even her smile had a sad edge to it. Instead of the joke he had ready for her, Chee simply invited her in, gesturing to his chair beside the table. He sat on the edge of his cot and waited.

"Welcome back to Shiprock," Bernie said.

"Happy to escape from Tuba," Chee said. "How's your mother?"

"About the same," Bernie said. Last winter, her mother's drift into the dark mists of Alzheimer's disease won Officer Manuelito a transfer back to Shiprock, where she could better care for her. Chee's was a late-summer transfer, caused by his reversion from acting lieutenant to sergeant. The Tuba City section didn't need another sergeant. Shiprock did.

"Terrible disease," Chee said.

Bernie nodded. Glanced at him. Looked away.

"I heard you went up to Alaska," Bernie said. "How was it?"

"Impressive. Took the cruise up the coast." He waited. Bernie hadn't made this call to hear about his vacation.

"I don't know how to do this," she said, giving him a sidelong glance.

"Do what?" Chee asked.

"You don't have anything to do with that casino thing, do you?"

Chee felt trouble coming. "No," he said.

"Anyway, I need some advice."

"I'd say just turn yourself in. Return the money. Make a full confession and . . ."

Chee stopped there, wishing he'd kept his mouth shut. Bernie was looking at him now, and her expression said this was not the time for half-baked humor.

"Do you know Teddy Bai?"

"Bai? Is that the rent-a-cop wounded in the casino robbery?"

"Teddy's a Montezuma County deputy sheriff," Bernie said, rather stiffly. "That was just a part-time temporary job with casino security. He was just trying to make some extra money."

"I wasn't—" Chee began and stopped. Less said the better until he knew what this was all about. So he said, "I don't know him." And waited.

"He's in the hospital at Farmington," Bernie said. "In intensive care. Shot three times. Once through a lung. Once through the stomach. Once through the right shoulder."

Clearly Bernie knew Bai pretty well. All he knew about this case personally was what he'd read in the papers, and he hadn't seen any of these details reported. He said, "Well, that San Juan Medical Center there has a good reputation. I'd think he'd be getting—"

"They think he was involved in the robbery," Bernie said. "I mean the FBI thinks so. They have a guard outside his room."

Chee said, "Oh?" And waited again. If Bernie knew why they thought that, she'd tell him. What he'd read, and what he'd heard, was that the bandits had killed the casino security boss and critically wounded a guard. Then, during their escape, they'd shot at a Utah Highway Patrolman who had flagged them for speeding.

Bernie looked close to tears. "It doesn't make any sense," she said.

"It doesn't seem to. Why would they want to shoot their own man?"

"They think Teddy was the inside man," Bernie said. "They think the robbers shot him because he knew who they were, and they didn't trust him."

Chee nodded. He didn't have to ask Bernie how she knew all this confidential stuff. Even if it wasn't her case, she was a cop, and if she really wanted to know, she'd know who to talk to. "Sounds pretty weak to me," he said. "Cap Stoner was shot, too. He was the security boss out there. You'd think they'd figure Stoner for the inside man."

He rose, poured a cup of coffee and handed it to Bernie, giving her a little time to think how she wanted to answer that.

"Everybody liked Stoner," she said. "All the old-timers anyway. And Teddy's been in trouble before," she said. "When he was just a kid. He got arrested for joyriding in somebody else's truck."

"Well it couldn't have been very serious," Chee said. "At least the county was willing to hire him as a deputy."

"It was a juvenile thing," Bernie said.

"Awful weak then. Do they have something else on him?"

"Not really," she said.

He waited. Bernie's expression told him something worse was coming. Or maybe not. Maybe she wouldn't tell him.

She sighed. "People at the casino said he'd been acting strange. They said he was nervous. Instead of watching people inside, he kept going out into the parking lot. When his shift was over, he stayed around. He told one of the cleanup crew he was waiting to be picked up."

"OK," Chee said. "I can see it now. I mean them thinking he was waiting for the gang to show up. In case they needed help."

"He wasn't, though. He was waiting for someone else."

"No problem, then. When he gets well enough to talk, he tells the feds who he was waiting for. They check, confirm it, and there's no reason to hold him," Chee said, thinking there was probably something else.

"I don't think he'll tell," Bernie said.

"Oh. You mean he was waiting for a woman then?" He didn't pursue that. Didn't ask her how she knew all this, or why she hadn't passed it along to the FBI. Didn't ask her why she had come here to tell him about it.

"I don't know what to do," Bernie said.

"Probably nothing," he said. "If you do, they'll want to know how you got this information. Then they'll talk to his wife. Mess up his marriage."

"He's not married."

Chee nodded, thinking there could be all sorts of reasons a guy wouldn't want the world to know about a woman picking him up at 4 A.M. He just couldn't think of a good one right away.

"They'll be trying to get him to tell who the robbers were," Bernie said. "They'll come up with some way to hold him until he tells. And he won't know who they are. So I'm afraid they'll find something to charge him with so they can hold him."

"I just got back from Alaska," Chee said, "so I don't know anything about any of this. But I'll bet they got a good idea by now who they're looking for."

Bernie shook her head. "No. I don't think so," she said. "I hear that's a total blank. They were talking at first like it was some of the right-wingers in one of the militia groups. Something political. But now I hear they don't have a clue."

Chee nodded. That would explain why the FBI had been so quick to announce the aircraft business. It took the heat off the area Agent in Charge.

"You're sure you know Bai was waiting for a woman? Do you know who?"

Bernie hesitated. "Yes."

"Could you tell the feds?"

"I guess I could. I will if I have to." She put the coffee cup on the table, untasted. "You know what I was thinking? I was thinking you worked here a long time before they shifted you to Tuba City. You know a lot of people. With the FBI thinking they already have the inside man they won't be looking for the real inside man. I thought maybe you could find out who really was their helper in the casino. If anybody can."

Now it was Chee's turn to hesitate. He sipped his coffee, cold now, and tried to sort out his mixture of reactions to all this. Bernie's confidence in him was flattering, if misguided. Why did the thought that Bernie was having an affair with this rent-a-cop disappoint him? It should be a relief. Instead it gave him an empty, abandoned feeling.

"I'll ask around," Chee said.

3

THE ONLY CLIENT in the dining room in Window Rock's Navajo Inn was sitting at a table in the corner with a glass of milk in front of him. He was wearing a droopy gray felt Stetson and reading the *Gallup Independent*. Joe Leaphorn stood at the entrance a moment studying him. Roy Gershwin, looking a lot older, more weather-beaten and worn-out than he'd remembered him. But then he hadn't seen him for years—not since Gershwin had helped him nail a U.S. Forest Service ranger who'd been augmenting his income by digging artifacts out of Anasazi burials on a Gershwin grazing lease. That had been at least six years ago, about the time Leaphorn had started thinking about retirement. But they went far back beyond that—back to Leaphorn's rookie years. Back to a summer when Leaphorn had arrested one of Gershwin's hired hands on a rape complaint—a bad start with a happy ending. That had been the first time he'd heard Gershwin's deep, gruff whiskey-ruined voice—an angry voice telling Leaphorn he'd arrested an innocent man. When he had answered the telephone this morning, he recognized that odd voice instantly.

"Lieutenant Leaphorn," Gershwin had said. "I hear you're retired now. Is that right? If it is, I guess I'm trying to impose on you."

"Mr. Gershwin," Leaphorn had replied. "It's Mr. Leaphorn now, and it's good to hear from you." He had heard himself saying that with a sort of surprise. This was what retirement was doing to him. And what lay ahead.

This old rancher had never really been a friend. Just one of those thousands of people you deal with in a lifetime spent as a cop. But here he was, genuinely happy to hear his telephone ring. Happy to have someone to talk to.

But Gershwin had stopped talking. Long silence. The sound of the man clearing his throat. Then: "I guess this ain't going to surprise you much. I mean to tell you I got myself a problem. I guess you've heard that from a lot of people. Being a policeman."

"Sort of goes with the job," Leaphorn said. Two years ago he would have grumbled about this sort of call. Today he didn't. Loneliness conditions.

"Well," Gershwin said, "I got something I don't know how to handle. I'd like to talk to you about it."

"Let's hear it."

"I'm afraid it's not something you can handle over the telephone," Gershwin replied.

So they arranged to meet at three at the Navajo Inn. It was now three minutes short of that. Gershwin looked up, noticed Leaphorn approaching, stood and motioned him to the chair across from him.

"Damn good of you to come," he said. "I was afraid you'd tell me you were retired now and I should worry somebody else with it."

"Glad to help if I can," Leaphorn said. They polished off the required social formalities faster than usual, discussing the cold, dry winter, poor grazing, risk of forest fires, agreed that last night's weather report sounded like the monsoon season was about to start and finally got to the point.

"And what brings you all the way down here to Window Rock?"

"I heard on the radio yesterday the FBI's got that Ute Casino robbery all screwed up. You know about that?"

"I'm out of the loop on crimes these days. Don't know anything about it. But it wouldn't be the first time an investigation went sour."

"The radio said they're looking for a damned airplane," Gershwin said. "None of them fellas could fly anything more complicated than a kite."

Leaphorn raised his eyebrows. This was getting interesting. The last he'd heard, those working the case had absolutely no identifications. But Gershwin had come here to tell him something. He'd let Gershwin talk.

"You want something to drink?" Gershwin waved at the waiter. "Too bad you fellows still have prohibition. Maybe one of those pseudo beers?"

"Coffee'd be good."

The waiter brought it. Leaphorn sipped. Gershwin sampled his milk.

"I knew Cap Stoner," Gershwin said. "They oughta not let them get away with killing him. It's dangerous to have people like that around loose."

Gershwin waited for a response.

Leaphorn nodded.

" 'Specially the two younger ones. They're half crazy."

"Sounds like you know them."

"Pretty well."

"You tell the FBI?"

Gershwin studied his milk glass again and found it about half empty. Swirled it. He had a long, narrow face that betrayed his seventy or so years of dry air, windblown sand and dazzling sun, with a mass of wrinkles and sunburn damage. He shifted his bright blue eyes from the milk to Leaphorn.

"There's a problem with that," he said. "I tell the FBI, and sooner or later everybody knows it. Usually sooner. They come up there to see me at the ranch, or they call me. I've got a radio-telephone setup, and you know how that is. Everybody's listening. Worse than the old party line."

Leaphorn nodded. The nearest community to the Gershwin ranch would be Montezuma Creek, or maybe Bluff if his memory served. Not a place where visits from well-dressed FBI agents would go unnoticed, or untalked about.

"You remember that deal in the spring of '98? The feds decided to announce those guys they were looking for are dead. But the folks who snitched on 'em, or helped the cops, they're damn sure keeping their doors locked and their guns loaded and their watchdogs out."

"Didn't the FBI say the gang in 1998 were survivalists? Is it the same people this time?"

Gershwin laughed. "Not if the feds had the names right the last time."

"I'll skip ahead a little," Leaphorn said, "and you tell me if I have it figured right. You want the FBI to catch these guys, but in case they don't, you don't want folks to know you turned them in. So you're going to ask me to pass along the—"

"Whether or not they catch them," Gershwin said. "They have lots of friends."

"The FBI said the 1998 bandits were part of a survivalist organization. Is that what you're saying about these guys?"

"I think they call themselves the Rights Militia. They're for saving the Bill of Rights. Making the Forest Service, and the BLM, and the Park Service people behave so folks can make a living out here."

"You want to give me these names, and I pass them along to the feds. What do I say when the feds ask where I got them?"

Gershwin was grinning at him. "You got it partly wrong," he said. "I've got the names on a piece of paper. I'm going to ask you to give me your word of honor that you'll keep me out of it. If you won't, then I keep the paper. If you promise, and we shake hands on it, then I'll leave the names on the table here and you can pick it up if you want to."

"You think you can trust me?"

"No doubt about it," Gershwin said. "I did before. Remember? And I know some other people who trusted you."

"Why do you want these people caught? Is it just revenge for Cap Stoner?"

"That's part of it," Gershwin said. "But these guys are scary. Some of them anyway. I used to have a little hand in this political stuff with the ones who started it. But then they got too wild."

Gershwin had been about to finish his milk. Now he put the glass down. "Bastards in the Forest Service were acting like they personally owned the mountains," he said. "We lived there all our lives, but now we couldn't graze. Couldn't cut wood. Couldn't hunt elk. And the Land Management bureaucrats were worse. We were the serfs, and they were the lords. We just wanted to have some sort of voice with Congress. Get somebody to remind the bureaucrats who was paying their salaries. Then the crazies moved in. EarthFirst bunch wanting to blow up the bridges the loggers were using. That sort of thing. Then we got some New Age types, and survivalists and Stop World Government people. I sort of phased out."

"So some of these guys did the casino job? Was it political?"

"What I hear, it was supposed to be to finance the cause. But I think some of them needed money to eat," Gershwin said. "If you're not working, I guess you could call that political. But maybe they did want to buy guns and ammunition and explosives. That sort of stuff. Anyway, that's what folks I know in the outfit say. Needed cash to arm themselves to fight off the federal government."

"I wonder how much they got," Leaphorn said.

Gershwin drained his milk. Got up and extracted a folded sheet of paper from his shirt pocket.

"Here it is, Joe. Am I safe to leave it with you? Can you promise you won't turn me in?"

Leaphorn had already thought that through. He could report this conversation to the FBI. They would question Gershwin. He'd deny everything. Nothing accomplished.

"Leave it," Leaphorn said.

Gershwin dropped it on the table, put a dollar beside his milk glass and walked out past the waiter arriving to refill Leaphorn's cup.

Leaphorn took a drink. He picked up the paper and unfolded it. Three names, each followed by a brief description. The first two, Buddy Baker and George Ironhand, meant nothing to him. He stared at the last one. Everett Jorie. That rang a faint and distant bell.

4

CAPTAIN LARGO LOOKED up from the paper he'd been reading, peered over his glasses at Sergeant Chee, and said, "You're a few days early, aren't you? Your calendar break?"

"Captain, you forgot to say, 'Welcome Home. Glad to have you back. Have a seat. Be comfortable.'"

Largo grinned, waved at a chair across from his desk. "I'm almost afraid to ask it, but what makes you so anxious to get back to work?"

Chee sat. "I thought I'd get back to speed gradually. Find out what I've been missing. How'd you get so lucky not to get us dragged into another big manhunt as bush beaters for the federals?"

"That was a relief, that airplane business," Largo said. "On the other hand, you hate to see people shooting policemen and getting away with it. Sets another bad example after that summer of '98 fiasco. You want some coffee? Go get yourself a cup, and we'll talk. I want to hear about Alaska after you tell me what you're doing here."

Chee returned with his coffee. He sipped, sat, waited. Largo outwaited him.

"OK," Chee said. "Tell me about the casino robbery. All I know is what I've seen in the papers."

Largo leaned back in his chair, folded his arms across his generous stomach. "Just before four last Saturday morning a pickup drives into the casino lot. Guy gets out, takes out a ladder, climbs up on the roof and cuts the power lines, telephone lines, everything. Another pickup pulls in while this is going on and two guys get out wearing camouflage suits. A Montezuma County deputy, guy named Bai, is standing out there. Then Cap Stoner comes running out, and they shoot both of 'em. You remember Stoner? He used to be a captain with the New Mexico State Police. Worked out of Gallup. Decent man. Then these two guys get into the cashier's room. The money's all sacked up to be handed to the Brinks truck. They make everybody lie down, walk out with the money bags and drive off. Apparently they drove west into Utah because about daylight a Utah Highway Patrolman tries to stop a speeding truck on Route 262 west of Aneth, and they shoot holes in his radiator. Pretty high-powered ammunition according to what Utah tells us."

Largo paused, pushed his bulky frame out of his swivel chair with a grunt. "Need some of my coffee, myself," he said, and headed for the dispenser in the front office.

Sort of good to be back working under Largo, Chee was thinking. Largo had been his boss in his rookie year. Cranky, but he knew his business. Then Largo was coming through the door, holding his cup, talking.

". . . with the lines out, and all the scared gamblers scrambling around trying to get away from the casino, or trying to grab some chips, or whatever you do when the lights go out at the craps table. Anyway, it took a while before anybody knew what the hell was going on and got the word out." Largo eased back into his chair. "I think just about every track you can drive on was blocked by sunup, but by then they had a hell of a lead. Next thing, maybe nine-thirty or so, the word went out somebody in a pickup had shot at the Utah trooper. That shifted the focus westward. The next day a couple of deputy sheriffs found a banged-up pickup abandoned up by the Arizona-Utah border south of Bluff. It fit the description."

"They find any tracks? Were they walking out, changing cars or what?"

"Two sets of tracks around the truck, but here came the feds in their copters"—Largo paused, waved his arms in imitation of helicopter rotors—"and blew everything away."

"Slow learners," Chee said. "That's the same way they fanned away the tracks we'd found across the San Juan in that big thing in '98."

"Maybe we ought to get the Federal Aviation Administration to order all those things grounded during manhunts," Largo said.

"They have anything to match them with? Did they find any tracks at the casino?"

Largo shook his head, paused to sip his coffee, shrugged. "It looked like we were going to have an encore performance of that 1998 business. The federals got a command post set up. Everybody was getting into the act. Regular circus. All we needed was the performing elephants. Had plenty of clowns."

Chee grinned.

"You'd have loved to come home to that."

"I'd have gone right back to Alaska," Chee said. "How'd the FBI find out about the airplane?"

"The owner called in to report it stolen. He said he'd been away up in Denver. When he got home he noticed somebody had broken into his barn, and the airplane he kept there was gone."

"Close to where the pickup was abandoned?"

"Mile and a half or so," Largo said. "Maybe two."

Chee considered that. Largo watched him.

"You're thinking they must have liked to walk."

"Well, there's that," Chee said. "But maybe they wanted to hide the truck. Or if it was found, keep it far enough from the barn so there wouldn't be a connection."

"Uh-huh," Largo said, and sipped coffee. "The FBI says the truck was disabled."

"Out there, it's easy enough to blow tires or bust an oil pan on the rocks if you want to," Chee said.

Largo nodded. "I remember back at Tuba City you did that to a couple of our units, and you claimed you weren't even trying."

Chee let that pass. "Anyway," he said, "I just hope that airplane had enough gas in it to get 'em out of our jurisdiction."

"Full tank, the owner said."

"Makes you think, doesn't it?" Chee said. "I mean how neat everything worked out on both ends of this business."

Largo nodded. "If this was my responsibility now, I'd be getting that rancher's fingerprints and checking out his record and seeing if he was maybe tied up with survivalists, or the Earth Liberation Front, or the tree-huggers, or one of the militia."

"I imagine the FBI is taking care of that. That's the part they're good at," Chee said. "And how about the casino end? What do you hear about that?"

"They think the rent-a-cop was part of the team. Filled 'em in on when the money was sacked up for the Brinks pickup. Which wires to cut, which security people had the evening off. All that."

"Any evidence?"

Largo shrugged. "Nothing much I know about. This Teddy Bai they're holding in the hospital, he had a juvenile record. Witnesses said he was acting skittish all evening. Waiting around out in the lot when he was supposed to be in watching the drunks."

"That's not much," Chee said.

"They probably have more than that," Largo said. "You know how they are. The feds don't tell us locals anything unless they have to. They think we might gossip about it and screw up the investigation."

Chee laughed. "What! Us gossip?"

Largo was grinning, too.

"Have they connected Bai with any of the suspects?"

Largo laughed. "That cold air up in Alaska made an optimist out of you. Not a hint far as I hear. There was some guessing that one of the militia did it to get money for blowing something up, or maybe it was the Earth Liberation Front, but I haven't heard Bai was in any of them. The Earth Liberation folks have been pretty quiet since they burned up all those buildings at the Vail ski resort. Anyway, if anything checked out, they haven't gotten around to informing the Navajo Tribal Police."

"What do you think, Captain? Has your own grapevine been sending any messages about Bai that you haven't gotten around to telling the feds about?"

Largo studied Chee, his expression suggesting he didn't like the tone of that, and he wasn't sure he would answer it. But he did.

"If Deputy Sheriff Bai is on the wrong side of this one, I haven't heard it," he said.

5

O FFICER BERNADETTE MANUELITO was absolutely correct when she reminded Chee that he knew a lot of people around Shiprock. That had paid off. A chat with a senior San Juan County undersheriff, a drop-in talk with an old friend in the county clerk's office at Aztec, a visit at the Farmington pool hall and another at the Oilmen's Bar and Grill had provided him with a headful of information about the Ute Casino in general and Teddy Bai in particular.

The casino came off better than he'd expected. There was the usual and automatic assumption that organized crime must have a finger in it somehow, but no one could offer any support for that. Otherwise, the people most likely actually to know anything considered it well run. No one had any specific notion about who might have been the robbery's inside man if Bai wasn't. There was agreement that Bai had been a wild kid and mixed opinion on his character in later life, with the consensus in favor of salvation. He had married a girl in the Streams Come Together Clan, but that hadn't lasted. One of the regulars at Oilmen's said since the divorce, Bai came in now and then with a young woman. Who? Chee asked. He didn't know her, but he described her as "cute as a bug's ear." It wasn't the metaphor Chee would have chosen, but it could fit Officer Bernadette Manuelito.

It was also at Oilmen's that he learned Bai had been taking flying lessons.

"Flying lessons?" Chee said. "Really? Where?"

Chee's source for this was a New Mexico State Police dispatcher named Alice Deal. She delayed taking the intended bite from her cheeseburger to wave the free hand toward the Farmington Airport, which sat, like the flight deck of an aircraft carrier, on the mesa looking down on the city.

The sign over the office door of Four Corners Flight declared it the source of charter flights, aircraft rentals, repair, sales, parts, supplies and FAA-certified flight instruction. It didn't appear to be busy in any of those categories when Chee walked into the front office. The only person on the premises was a woman in the manager's office. She interrupted her telephone conversation long enough to wave Chee in.

"Well, now," she was saying, "that's no way to behave. If Betty acts like that, I just wouldn't invite her anymore." She motioned Chee into a chair, listened a moment longer, said, "Well, maybe you're right. I've got a customer. Got to go," and hung up.

Chee introduced himself and his subject.

"Bai," she said. "He owes us for a couple of lessons. The FBI already talked to us about him."

"Could you—"

"Matter of fact, they wanted the names of everybody we'd been teaching from way back. Then they came back again to talk specifically about Teddy."

"Could you tell me if he had his license yet?"

"I doubt it. You're going to have to talk to Jim Edgar," she said. "He's out there talking to the people at the DOE copter, and if he's not there, he'll be working in the hangar."

The copter was a big white Bell with Department of Energy identification markings. Round white bathtub-size containers had been attached above the skids, and a woman in blue coveralls was doing something technical at one of them. The only others present were two men in the same sort of coveralls engaged in conversation. Probably pilot and copilot. Chee tried to guess what the big tubes would contain, with no luck. Obviously none of these people was Jim Edgar.

He found Edgar in the back of the hangar, muttering imprecations and doing something at a workbench to something that looked like a small electric engine. Chee stopped a polite distance away and stood waiting.

Edgar put down a small screwdriver, sucked at a freshly injured thumb and inspected Chee.

Chee explained himself.

"Teddy Bai," Edgar said, inspecting his thumb as he said it. "Well, he'd soloed, but he wasn't near ready to be licensed. He was sort of mediocre as a student. I already told the FBI fellas if he was going to be flying that old L-17, I didn't want to be along on the trip."

"That's the one that was stolen? Why not?"

"He was learning in a new Cessna. Everything modern. Tricycle landing gear. Power-assisted stuff. Different instrumentation. Piper built that L-17 thing for the army in World War Two. Easy enough to fly, I guess, if you understand it, but you'd do a lot of things different than that little Cessna he was learning in."

Edgar paused, seeking a way to explain this. "For example that was one of the first of that sort of plane to use wing flaps. But you can't use 'em on the L-17 if your airspeed is over eighty. And you have to set the tabs on the ground. Little things like that you have to know about."

"And more than fifty years old," Chee said. "Do you know anything about what shape it was in?"

Edgar laughed. "From what I heard on the television, the FBI thinks those casino robbers flew away in it. They better be lucky if they did. Unless Old Man Timms decided to spend some money on it since I saw it."

Chee found himself getting more and more interested in this conversation.

"Was that recently? What was wrong with it?"

Edgar grinned at him. "How much time you got?"

"Any serious stuff?"

"Well, he brought it in for an FAA inspection last autumn. Wanted to get the FAA airworthy certification renewed. Way overdue anyway for an overage plane like that one, and he could have gotten in trouble for just flying it. First thing I noticed he'd let the mice get into it. He keeps it in a barn out at his ranch, which ain't too uncommon out here. But if you do that, you've got to keep the rodents from chewing on things. Set the tail wheel in a bucket of kerosene, maybe. So the wiring and fabric needed inspection, and the engine was running sour. Then these things have twelve-gallon gasoline tanks built into each wing root, feeding into a header tank behind the engine fire wall. Had a little leak in one of the lines."

Edgar shrugged. "Other things, too."

"He got them fixed?"

"He got me to give him an estimate. Said it was way too damn high." Edgar chuckled. "Said he'd sell me the plane for half that. He was going to fly it up to Blanding and get the inspection done at CanyonAire up there. That's the last I saw of him."

"Would you have a phone number for Mr. Timms?" Chee asked. "Or his address?"

"Sure."

Edgar walked across the hangar to his desk and sorted through a Rolodex file. Chee stood watching, trying to understand his motive for what he was doing. What did this have to do with Bernie's boyfriend's problem? Had he spent so many hours fishing and fighting mosquitoes in Alaska that he yearned for some way to get himself into trouble? Was he hungering for some explanation of the wildly illogical way the casino bandits had managed their escape? Whatever his motive, Captain Largo would be very unhappy indeed if Largo learned that Chee had stuck his nose into FBI business and the FBI caught him at it.

Edgar interrupted these thoughts by handing him a copy of a Mountain Mutual Insurance claim form.

"He had me sign off on his insurance claim. He'd left the plane out in the weather and gotten some hail damage," Edgar said. "That was several years ago, but as far as I heard, he hasn't moved."

Chee jotted the information he wanted into his notebook, thanked Edgar and headed back to his truck. Then a sudden thought caused him to grin. With the plane now stolen, Timms would be filing another insurance claim.

"Mr. Edgar," he shouted. "Do you remember what you'd have had to charge Timms for those repairs? When he said he'd sell it for half your estimate?"

"I think the estimate was close to four thousand dollars," Edgar said. "But if I was stupid enough to want that thing, and made him an offer, he'd have said it was a valuable antique and asked for about thirty thousand."

Chee laughed. That, he thought, would probably be about what Timms would claim from his insurance company.

"How about using your telephone?" Chee asked. "And the directory."

He punched in the Mountain Mutual Insurance Farmington agent's number, identified himself, asked the woman who ran the place if she still handled Eldon Timms's insurance.

"Unfortunately," she said.

"His airplane, too?"

"Same answer," she said. "Or I guess you'd say the former airplane, the one those robbers stole?"

"Does he have another one?"

"Lordy, I hope not," she said.

"He file a claim on it?"

"Yes, indeedy, he did. Right away. I just heard about the robbers steal-ing a plane out there and flying off in it, and he's on the phone asking about getting his money. And I said, 'What's the hurry. They have to land someplace and the cops recover it and you get it back.' And he said, 'If that happens, we tear up the claim.'"

"How much was the insurance?"

"Forty thousand," she said. "He just jacked it up to that a couple of months ago."

"Sounds like quite a bit for a fifty-year-old aircraft," Chee said.

"I thought so," she said. "But no skin off my nose. Timms was the one paying the premium. He said it was an antique, a real rare airplane, and he was going to sell it to that military-aircraft museum in Tucson. I have a feeling he was using that higher insured value to sort of—you know—establish a sales price."

Edgar had been standing nearby, listening.

"That do it for you?"

"Yeah," Chee said, "and thanks. But by the way, what's that Energy Department helicopter doing here? And what's the DOE doing with those big white pods?"

"Actually, the pods aren't DOE, they're EPA," Edgar said. "You are looking at a rare case of inter-agency cooperation. The Environmental Protection bunch borrows the copter and the pilots from the DOE's Nevada test site. They got radiation detectors in those pods, and they use them to find old uranium mines. Get the hot stuff covered up."

After he left Four Corners Flight, Chee dropped in at the New Mexico

State Police office below the airport and made two more calls—the first one to the Air War Museum at Tucson. Yes, the manager told him, Mr. Timms had flown his L-17 down in June and offered it for sale. And, yes, they would have liked to add it to their collection, but they hadn't made an offer. Why not? The usual reason, said the manager. He wanted way too much for it. He was asking fifty thousand.

The second call was to Cowboy Dashee, his old friend from boyhood. But it wasn't just to reminisce. Deputy Sheriff Dashee worked for the Sheriff's Department of Apache County, Arizona, which meant the ranch of Eldon Timms—at least the south end of it—might be in Deputy Dashee's jurisdiction.

6

FOR NO REASON except habit born of childhood in a crowded hogan, Joe Leaphorn awoke with the first light of dawn. The bedroom he and Emma had shared for three happy decades faced both the sunrise and the noisy street. When Leaphorn had noted the noise disadvantage to Emma she had pointed out that the quieter bedroom had no windows facing the dawn. No further explanation was needed.

Emma was a true Navajo traditional with the traditional's need to greet the new day. That was one of the countless reasons Leaphorn loved her. Besides, while Leaphorn was no longer truly a traditional, no longer offered a pinch of pollen to the rising sun, he still treasured the old ways of his people.

This morning, however, he had a good reason for sleeping late. Professor Louisa Bourebonette was sleeping in the quieter bedroom, and Leaphorn didn't want to awaken her. So he lay under the sheet, watched the eastern horizon turn flame red, listened to the automatic coffeemaker go to work in the kitchen, and considered what the devil to do with the names Gershwin had given him. The three had stolen themselves an airplane and flown away, which took some of the pressure off. Still, if Gershwin was right, having their identities would certainly be useful to those trying to catch them.

Leaphorn yawned, stretched, smelled coffee, wondered if he could get to the kitchen and pour a cup quietly enough not to disturb Louisa.

Wondered, too, what solution she would offer for his dilemma if he presented it to her. Emma would have told him to forget it. Locking robbers in prison helped no one, she'd say. They should be cured of the disharmony that was causing this bad behavior. Prison didn't accomplish that. A Mountain Way ceremony, with all their friends and relatives gathered to support them, would drive the dark wind out of them and restore them to *hozho*.

A clatter in the kitchen interrupted that thought. Leaphorn jumped out of bed and put on his bathrobe. He found Louisa standing at the stove, fully dressed and cooking pancakes.

"I'm using your mix," she said. "They'd be a lot better if you had some buttermilk."

Leaphorn rescued his mug from the sink, rinsed it, poured himself a cup, and sat by the table watching Louisa, remembering the ten thousand mornings he had watched Emma from the same chair. Emma was shorter, slimmer, and always wore skirts. Louisa had on jeans and a flannel shirt. Her hair was short and gray. Emma's was long and a luminous black. That hair was her only source of vanity. Emma had hated to have it cut even for the brain surgery that killed her.

"You're up early," Leaphorn said.

"Blame it on your culture," Louisa said. "These old-timers I need to talk to have been up an hour already. They'll be in bed by sundown."

"How about your translator? Did you ever manage to get hold of him?"

"I'll try again after breakfast," Louisa said. "Young people have more normal sleeping habits."

They ate pancakes.

"Something's on your mind," Louisa said. "Right?"

"Why do you say that?"

"Because it's true," Louisa said. "I could tell last night when we were having dinner down at the Inn. Couple of times you started to say something, but you didn't."

True enough. And why hadn't he? Because it would have taken him too close to his relationship with Emma—this hashing over of something he was working on. But now in the light of morning he saw nothing wrong with it. He told Louisa about Gershwin, the three names and his promise—ambiguous and vague.

"Did you shake hands on it? Any of that male-chivalry stuff?"

Leaphorn grinned. Louisa's way of striking right to the heart of matters was something he liked about her.

"Well, we shook hands, but it was sort of a 'good-bye, glad to see you again' handshake. No cutting our wrists and mixing blood," he said. "He had the identification information written on a piece of paper, and he just left that on the table. With sort of an unspoken understanding that if I took it, I could do whatever I wanted with it. But promising him confidentiality was implied no matter what I did."

"And you took the paper?"

"Not exactly. I read it, then wadded it up and dropped it in the wastebasket."

She was smiling at him, shaking her head.

"You're right," he said. "Throwing it away didn't work. I'm still stuck with the promise."

She nodded, cleared her throat, sat very straight. "Mr. Leaphorn," she said, "I remind you that you are under oath to tell this grand jury the truth and the whole truth. How did you obtain this information?" Louisa stared over her glasses at him, her stern look. "Then you say you read it off a piece of paper left on a restaurant table, and the lawyer asks if you know who left the paper, and . . ."

Leaphorn raised his hand. "I know," he said.

"Two choices, really. After all, that Gershwin jerk was just trying to use you. You could just forget it. Or you could figure out some sneaky way to get the names to the FBI. How about an anonymous letter? In fact, don't you wonder why he didn't write one himself?"

"I guess it was timing. A couple of days pass before the letter gets delivered. Then if it's anonymous, it goes right to the bottom of the pile," Leaphorn said. "I guess he knew that. I think he's afraid these days. That the bandits know that he knows, and they don't trust him, and if they aren't caught, they'll be coming after him."

Louisa laughed. "I'd say they have pretty good reason not to trust him. You shouldn't, either."

"I thought about faxing it in from some commercial place where nobody knows me, or sending an e-mail. But just about everything is traceable these days. And now there's a reward out, so they'll be getting dozens of tips by now. Probably hundreds."

"I guess so," Louisa said. "Why don't you call one of your old FBI buddies? Do the same thing to them Gershwin's doing to you?"

Leaphorn laughed. "I tried that. I called Jay Kennedy. You remember me telling you about him? Used to be Agent in Charge at Gallup, and we worked on several things together. Anyway, he's retired over in Durango. So I tried it on him. No luck."

"What did he say?"

"Same thing you just told me. If he passes it along to the Bureau, they ask him where he got it. He tells 'em me. They ask me where I got it."

"So what's your solution? How about disguising your voice and giving them a telephone call?"

"I might try that. The FBI has them flying away. I could tell them one of the guys is a pilot. That would be easy for them to check, and if one of them happens to be a flier, then they'd be interested. But that's just half the problem." He paused to take another bite of pancake.

She watched him chew, waited, sighed. Said, "OK, what's the other half?"

"Maybe these three guys had nothing to do with it. Maybe Gershwin just wants them hassled for some personal reason, and if the robbers aren't caught, this would damn sure do that sooner or later."

She nodded. "I'll take it under advisement, then," she said, and left the kitchen to call her interpreter.

By the time Leaphorn had the dishes washed she was back, looking disheartened.

"Not only is he sick, he has laryngitis. He can hardly talk. I guess I'll head back to Flagstaff and try it later."

"Too bad," Leaphorn said.

"Another thing. He'd told them we were coming today. And no telephone, of course, to tell them we're not."

"Where do these guys live?"

Louisa's expression brightened. "Are you about to volunteer to interpret? The Navajo's a fellow named Dalton Cayodito and the address I have is Red Mesa Chapter House. The other one's a Ute. Lives at Towaoc on the Ute Mountain Reservation. How's your Ute?"

"Maybe fifty words or so," Leaphorn said. "But I could help you with Cayodito."

"Let's do it," Louisa said.

"I'm thinking that a couple of the men on that list are supposed to live up there in that border country. One of 'em's Casa Del Eco Mesa. That couldn't be too far from the chapter house."

Louisa laughed. "Mixing business with pleasure. Or I should say your business with my business. Or maybe my business with something that really isn't your business."

"The one who has a place up there—according to the notes on that paper anyway—is Everett Jorie. I can't place him but the name's familiar. Probably something out of the distant past. I thought we could ask around."

Louisa was smiling at him. "You've forgotten you're retired," she said. "For a minute there, I thought you were going along for the pleasure of my company."

Leaphorn drove the first lap—the 110 miles from his house to the Mexican Water Trading Post. They stopped there for a sandwich and to learn if anyone there knew how to find Dalton Cayodito. The teenage Navajo handling the cash register did.

"An old, old man," she said. "Did he used to be a singer? If that's him, he did the Yeibichai sing for my grandmother. Is that the one you're looking for?"

Louisa said it was. "We heard he lived up by the Red Mesa Chapter House."

"He lives with his daughter," the girl said. "That's Madeleine Horse-keeper, I think they call her. Her place is—" She paused, thought, made a gesture of frustration with her hands, penciled a map on a grocery sack and handed it to Louisa.

"How about a man named Everett Jorie?" Leaphorn said. "You know where to find him? Or Buddy Baker? Or George Ironhand."

She didn't, but the man who had been stacking Spam cans on shelves along the back wall thought he could help.

"Hey," he said. "Joe Leaphorn. I thought you'd retired. What you want Jorie for? If you got a law against being a damned nuisance, you oughta had him locked up long ago."

They left the trading post a quarter hour later armed with explicit in-structions on how to find the two places Jorie might be located, an addendum to the grocery-sack map outlining which turns to take from which roads to find Ironhand, and a vague notion that Baker might have moved into Blanding. Along with that they took a wealth of speculative gossip about Utah-Arizona borderland political ambitions, social activities, speculation about who might have robbed the Ute Casino, an account of the most recent outrages committed by the Forest Service, Bureau of Land Management, Bureau of Reclamation, Park Service, and other federal, state and county agencies against the well-being of various folks who lived their hardscrabble lives along the Utah border canyon country.

"No wonder the militia nuts can sign people up," Louisa said, as they drove away. "Is it as bad as that?"

"They're mostly just trying to enforce unpopular laws," Leaphorn said. "Mostly fine people. Now and then somebody gets arrogant."

"OK, now," Louisa said. "These guys you mentioned in there—Jorie and Ironhand and so forth. I guess they're the three who robbed the casino?"

"Or maybe robbed it," Leaphorn said. "If we believe Gershwin."

Louisa was driving and spent a few moments looking thoughtful.

"You know," she said, "as long as I've been out here I still can't get used to how everybody knows everybody."

"You mean that guy at the store recognizing me? I was a cop out here for years."

"But living where? About a hundred and fifty miles away. But I didn't mean just you. The cashier knew all about Everett Jorie. And people know about Baker and Ironhand living"—she waved an expressive hand at the window—"living way the hell out there someplace. Where I came from people didn't even know who lived three houses down the block."

"Lot more people in Baltimore," Leaphorn said.

"Not a lot more people on our block."

"More people in your block, I'll bet, than in a twenty-mile circle around here," Leaphorn said. He was remembering the times he'd spent in Washington, in New York, in Los Angeles, when he'd considered this difference between urban and rural social attitudes.

"I have a theory not yet endorsed by any sociologist," he said. "You city folks have so many people crowding you they're a bother. So you try to avoid them. We rural people don't have enough, so we're interested. We sort of collect them."

"You'll have to make it a lot more complicated than that to get the so-
ciologists to adopt it," Louisa said. "But I know what you're driving at."

"Out here, everybody looks at you," he said. "You're somebody different. Hey, here's another human, and I don't even know him yet. In the
city, nobody wants to make eye contact. They have built themselves a little privacy bubble—hard to get any privacy in crowded places—and if you
look at them, or speak on the street, then you're an intruder."

Louisa looked away from the road to give him a sidewise grin.

"I take it you don't care for the busy, exciting, stimulating city life," she
said. "I've also heard it put another way. Like 'rural folks tend to be nosy
busybodies.' "

They were still discussing that when they turned off the pavement of
U.S. 160 onto the dirt road that climbed over the Utah border onto the
empty, broken highlands of the Casa Del Eco Mesa. She slowed while
Leaphorn checked the map against the landscape. The clouds were climbing on the western horizon, and the outriders of the front were speckling
the landscape spreading away to the west with a crazy-quilt pattern of
shadows.

"If my memory's good, we hit an intersection up here about seven
miles," he said. "Take the bad road to the right, and it takes you to the Red
Mesa Chapter House. Take the worse road to the left, and it gets you to
Highway 191 and on to Bluff."

"There's the junction up ahead," she said. "We do a left? Right?"

"Left is right," Leaphorn said. "And after the turn, we're looking for a
track off to our right."

They found it, and a dusty, bumpy mile later, they came to the place of
Madeleine Horsekeeper, which was a fairly new double-wide mobile
home, with an attendant hogan of stacked stones, sheep pens, outhouse,
brush arbor and two parked vehicles—an old pickup truck and a new blue
Buick Regal. Madeleine Horsekeeper was standing in the doorway greeting them, with a stern-looking fortyish woman standing beside her. She
proved to be Horsekeeper's daughter, who taught social studies at Grey
Hills High in Tuba City. She would sit in on the interview with Hosteen
Cayodito, her maternal grandfather, and would make sure the interpreting
was accurate. Or do it herself.

Which was fine with Joe Leaphorn. He had thought of a way to spend the rest of this day that would be much more interesting than listening for modifications and evolutions in the legends he'd grown up with. That talk with Louisa about how folks in lonely country knew everything about their neighbors had reminded him of Undersheriff Oliver Potts, now retired. If anyone knew the three on Gershwin's list, it would be Oliver.

7

OLIVER POTTS'S MODEST stone residence was shaded by a grove of cottonwoods beside Recapture Creek, maybe five miles northeast of Bluff and a mile down a rocky road even worse than described at the Chevron station where Leaphorn had topped off his gas tank.

"Yes," said the middle-aged Navajo woman who answered his knock, "Ollie's in there resting his eyes." She laughed. "Or he's supposed to be, anyway. Actually he's probably reading, or studying one of his soap operas." She ushered Leaphorn into the living room, said, "Ollie, here's company," and disappeared.

Potts looked up from the television, examined Leaphorn through thick-lensed glasses. "Be damned. You look like Joe Leaphorn, but if it is, you're out of uniform."

"I've been out of uniform almost as long as you have," Leaphorn said, "but not long enough to watch the soap operas."

He took the chair Potts offered. They exhausted the social formalities, agreed retirement became tiresome after the first couple of months, and reached the pause that said it was time for business. Leaphorn recited Gershwin's three names. Could Potts tell him anything about them?

Potts hadn't seemed to be listening. He had laid himself back in his recliner chair, glasses off now and eyes almost closed, either dozing or thinking about it. After a moment he said, "Odd mix you got there. What kind of mischief have those fellows been up to?"

"Probably nothing," Leaphorn said. "I'm just checking on some gossip."

It took Potts a moment to accept that. His eyes remained closed, but a twist of his lips expressed skepticism. He nodded. "Actually, Ironhand and Baker fit well enough. We've had both of them in a time or two. Nothing serious that we could make stick. Simple assault, I think it was, on Baker, and a DWI and resisting arrest. George Ironhand, he's a little meaner. If I remember right, it was assault with a deadly weapon, but he got off. And then we had him as a suspect one autumn butchering time in a little business about whose steers he was cutting up into steaks and stew beef."

He produced a faint smile, reminiscing. "Turned out to be an honest mistake, if you know what I mean. And then, the feds got interested in him. Somebody prodded them into doing something about that protected antiquities law. They had the idea that his little bitty ranch was producing way too many of those old pots and the other Anasazi stuff he was selling. They couldn't find no ruins on his place, and the feds figured he was climbing over the fence and digging them out of sites on federal land."

"I remember that now," Leaphorn said. "Nothing came of it? Right?"

"Usual outcome. Case got dropped for lack of evidence."

"You said they fit better than Jorie. Why's that?"

"Well, they're both local fellas. Ironhand's a Ute and Baker's born in the county. Both rode in the rodeo a little, as I remember. Worked here and there. Probably didn't finish high school. Sort of young." He grinned at Leaphorn. "By our standards, anyway. Thirty or forty. I think Baker is married. Or was."

"They buddies?"

That produced another thoughtful silence. Then: "I think they both worked for El Paso Natural once, or one of the pipeline outfits. If it's important, I can tell you who to ask. And then I think both of them were into that militia outfit. Minutemen I think they called it."

Potts opened his eyes now, squinted, rubbed his hand across them, restored the glasses and looked at Leaphorn. "You heard of our militia?"

"Yeah," Leaphorn said. "They had an organizing meeting down at Shiprock last winter."

"You sign up?"

"Dues were too high," Leaphorn said. "But they seemed to be getting some recruits."

"We got a couple of versions up here. Militia to protect us from the Bureau of Land Management and the Forest Service and the seventy-two other federal agencies. Then the survivalists, getting us ready for when all those black helicopters swarm in to round us up for the United Nations concentration camps. And then for the rich kids, we have our Save Our Mountains outfit trying to fix it so the Ivy Leaguers don't have to associate with us redneck working folks when they want to get away from their tennis courts."

Potts had his eyes closed again. Leaphorn waited, Navajo fashion, until he was sure Potts had finished this speech. He hadn't.

"Come to think of it," Potts added, "maybe that's how you could tie in ole Everett Jorie. He used to be one of the militia bunch."

Potts sat up. "Remember? He used to run that afternoon talk show on one of the Durango radio stations. Right-winger. Sort of an intellectual version of what's his name? That fat guy. Ditto Head. Made him sound almost sane. Anyway, Jorie was always promoting the militia. He'd quote Plato and Shakespeare and read passages from Thoreau and Thomas Paine to do it. Finally got so wild the station fired him. I think he was a fairly big shot in the militia. I heard Baker was a member. At least I'd see him at meetings. I think I saw George at one, too."

"Jorie still in the militia?"

"I don't think so," Potts said. "Heard they had a big falling-out. It's all hearsay, of course, but the gossip was he wanted 'em to do less talking and writing to their congressman and things like that and get more dramatic."

Potts had his eyes wide open now, peering at Leaphorn, awaiting the question.

"Like what?"

"Just gossip, you know. But like blowing up a Forest Service office."

"Or maybe a dam?"

Potts chuckled. "You're thinking of that big manhunt a while back. When the guys stole the water truck and shot the policeman, and the FBI decided they were going to fill the truck with explosives, blow up the dam and drain Lake Mead."

"What's your theory on that one?"

"Stealing the water truck? I figured they needed it to water their marijuana crop."

Leaphorn nodded.

"FBI didn't buy that. I guess there was budget hearings coming up. They needed some terrorism to talk about, and if it's just pot farmers at work, that hands the ball to the Drug Enforcement folks. The competition. The enemy."

"Yeah," Leaphorn said.

"Now," Potts said, "it is time for you to tell me what you're up to. I heard you been working as a private investigator. Did the Ute Casino people sign you up to get their money back?"

"No," Leaphorn said. "Tell the truth I don't know what I'm up to myself. Just heard something, and had time on my hands, and got to wondering about it, so I thought I'd ask around."

"Just bored then," Potts said, sounding as if he didn't believe it. "Nothing interesting on TV, so you thought you'd just take a three-hour drive up here to Utah and do some visiting. Is that it?"

"That's close enough," Leaphorn said. "And I've got one more name to ask about. You know Roy Gershwin?"

"Everybody knows Roy Gershwin. What's he up to?"

"Is there anything to connect him to the other three?"

Potts thought about it. "I don't know why I want to tell you anything, Joe, when you won't tell me why you're askin'. But let's see. He used to show up at militia meetings a while back. He was fighting with the BLM, and the Forest Service, and the Soil Conservation Service, or whatever they call it now, over a grazing lease and over a timber-cutting permit, too, I think it was. That had gotten him into an antigovernment mood. I think Baker used to work for him once on that ranch he runs. And I think his place runs up against Jorie's, so that makes them neighbors."

"Good neighbors?"

Potts restored his glasses, sat up and looked at Leaphorn. "Don't you remember Gershwin? He wasn't the kind of fellow you were good neighbors with. And Jorie's even worse. As a matter of fact, I think Jorie was suing Roy over something or other. Suing people was one of Jorie's hobbies."

"About what?"

Potts shrugged. "This and that. He sued me once 'cause his livestock was running on my place, and I penned them up, and he wanted to take 'em back without paying me for my feed. With Gershwin, I don't remember. I think they were fighting over the boundaries of a grazing lease." He paused, considering. "Or maybe it was locking a gate on an access road."

"Were any of those three people pilots?"

"Fly airplanes?" Potts was grinning. "Like rob the Ute Casino and then stealing Old Man Timms's airplane to fly away? I thought you was retired from being a cop."

Leaphorn could think of no response to that.

"You think maybe those three guys did it?" Potts said. "Well, that's as good a guess as I could make. Why not? You have any idea where they'd fly to?"

"No ideas about anything much," Leaphorn said. "I'm just idling away some time."

"Several ranchers around here have their little planes," Potts said. "None of those guys, though. I remember hearing Jorie going on about flying for the navy on his talk show, but I know he didn't have a plane. And airplanes was one of the things Ironhand used to bitch about. People flying over his ranch. Said they scared his livestock. He thought it was people spying on him when he was stealing pots. Baker and Ironhand now. Far as I know, neither of them ever had anything better than a used pickup."

"You know where Jorie lives?" Leaphorn asked.

Potts stared at him. "You going to go see him? What you going to say? Did you rob the casino? Shoot the cops?"

"If he did, he won't be home. Remember? He flew away."

"Oh, right," Potts said, and laughed. "If the Federal Bureau of Ineptitude says it, it must be true." He pushed himself up. "Let me get myself a piece of paper and my pencil. I'll draw you a little map."

8

COWBOY DASHEE ROLLED down the window of Apache County Sheriff's Department Patrol Unit 4 as Chee walked up. He leaned out, staring at Chee.

"The cooler's in the trunk," Dashee said. "Dry ice in it, with room enough for about forty pounds of smoked Alaska salmon caught by my Navajo friend. But where's the damned fish?"

"I hate to tell you about that," Chee said. "The girls had this big welcome-home salmonfest for me at Shiprock. Dancing around the campfire down by the San Juan, swimming bareback in the river. Just me and nine of those pretty teachers from the community college." Chee opened the passenger-side door and slid in. "I should have remembered to invite you."

"You should have," Dashee said. "Since you're going to work me for some favor. From what you said on the telephone, you're going to try to get me in trouble with the FBI. What do you want me to do?"

They'd met at the Lukachukai Chapter House, Chee making the long drive from Farmington over the Chuska Mountains and Dashee up from his station at Chinle. Dashee arrived a little late. And now was accused by Chee of being corrupted from his stern Hopi ways and learning how to operate on "Navajo Time," which recognized neither late nor early. They wasted a few minutes exchanging barbs and grinning at one another as old friends do, before Chee answered Dashee's question.

"What I'd like you to do is help me get straightened out on that business with the stolen airplane," Chee said.

"Eldon Timms's airplane? What's to straighten out? The bandidos stole it and flew away. And thank God for that." Dashee made a wry face. "If you see it anywhere, just call the nearest office of the Federal Bureau of Investigation."

"You think that's what actually happened?"

Dashee laughed. "Let's just say I hope the feds got it right this time. Otherwise, we both ought to apply for a leave. I don't think I could stand a repeat of that Great Four Corners Manhunt of 1998. You want to go crashing around in the canyons again?"

"I could get along without that," Chee said, and told Dashee what he'd learned about the Timms L-17, and the insurance, and Timms's futile effort to sell it, and all the rest. "You mind us driving over there and showing me where the pickup was found, and the barn where Timms kept the plane? Just going over that part of it with me?"

Dashee studied him. "You're wanting to use your old buddy Cowboy because you're not back on duty yet, and don't have any business out there anyway even if you were. And me, being a deputy sheriff of Apache County, Arizona, could claim I had some legitimate reason to be butting in on a case the FBI has taken over. So if the feds get huffy about us nosy locals, they can blame me. Am I right?"

"That's about it," Chee said. "Does it make sense to you?"

Dashee snorted, started the engine. "Well, then, let's go. Let's get there while we still have a little daylight."

The sun was low when Dashee stopped the patrol car. The ragged top of Comb Ridge to the west was producing a zigzag pattern of light and shadow across the sagebrush flats of the Nokaito Bench. The Gothic Creek bottoms below were already a crooked streak of darkness. Dashee was pointing down into the canyon. "Down there but for the grace of God and Timms's convenient airplane go you and I," he said. "Once again testing the federal law-enforcement theory that to locate fugitives you send out local cops until the perps start shooting them, thereby giving away their location."

"It used to work in India when the nabobs were hunting tigers," Chee said. "Only they did it with beaters instead of deputy sheriffs. They'd send those guys in to provoke the animals."

"I thought they used goats."

"That was later," Chee said. "After the beaters joined the union. Now why not tell me why we're stopping here."

"High ground. You can see the lay of the land from here." Dashee pointed northeast. "Up there, maybe three miles, is the Timms place. You can't see it because it's beyond that ridge, down a slope." He pointed again. "This road we're on angles along the rim of the mesa over Gothic Creek, then swings back past the Timms place, and then sort of peters out at a widow woman's ranch up toward the San Juan. That's the end of it. The truck was abandoned about a mile and a half up ahead."

Chee hoisted himself onto the front fender. "All I know about this case is what I've heard since I got home. Fill me in. What's the official Theory of the Crime?"

Dashee grinned. "You think the feds would tell an Apache County deputy?"

"No. But somebody in the Denver FBI, or maybe the Salt Lake office, or Phoenix, or Albuquerque, fills in some state-level cop, and he tells somebody else, and the word spreads and pretty soon somebody else tells your sheriff, and—" Chee made an all-encompassing gesture. "So everybody knows in about three hours, and the federals maintain their deniability."

"OK," Dashee said. "What we hear goes like this. This Teddy Bai fella, the one the FBI is holding at the Farmington hospital, he tells some of the wrong people how easy it would be to rob the Ute Casino, and the word gets back to some medium-level hoods. Maybe Las Vegas hoods, maybe Los Angeles. I've heard it both ways, and it's just guesswork. Anyway, the theory is Bai gets contacted. He's offered a slice if he'll help with the details, like getting the timing just right, all the inside stuff they need to know. Who's on guard when. When the bank truck comes. How to cut off the power, telephones, so forth. Bai is a flier, he tells them that Timms has this old army short-takeoff recon airplane they can grab for the getaway. He'll fly it for them. But they know that Bai's local. He'll be missed. He'll be the way the hoods planning this can be traced. So they bring along their own pilot, shoot Bai, drive out to the Timms place, tear up the pickup truck so the cops will think they had to abandon it out here, steal the plane and"—Dashee flapped his arms—"away they go."

Chee nodded.

"You're thinking about Timms," Dashee said. "The theory is they planned to kill him, too. That would have given them more time. But he wasn't home. On his way home Timms heard about the robbery on the news and then found the lock on his barn busted, and his airplane gone, and he notified the cops. And since we're closest, we got sent to check it out."

Chee nodded again.

"You don't like that, either?"

"I'm just thinking," Chee said. "Show me where they left the truck."

Doing that took them into the rugged, stony treeless territory where no one except surveyors seems to know exactly where Arizona ends and Utah begins. It involved a descent on a bad dirt road from the mesa top and took them past a flat expanse of drought-dwarfed sage where a white tanker truck was parked with its door open and a man sitting in the front seat reading something.

Dashee waved at him. "Rosie Rosner," Dashee said. "Claims he has the easiest job in North America. Even easier than being a deputy. Three or four times a day an Environmental Protection Agency copter flies in here, he refuels it, and then nods off again until it comes back."

"I think I saw that copter at the Farmington Airport," Chee said. "Guy there said they're locating abandoned uranium mines. Looking for radioactive dumps."

"I asked the guy if he'd seen our bandidos driving in," Dashee said. "But no such luck. They started doing this the next day."

Dashee honked at the driver and waved. "Come to think of it, I guess the timing was pretty lucky for him."

About a mile beyond the refueling truck Dashee stopped again and got out.

"Take a look at this." He pointed to a black outcrop of basalt beside the track, partly hidden by an outstretched limb of a four-wing saltbush and a collection of tumbleweeds.

"Here's where they banged up their oil pan on the truck," he said. "Either they didn't know the road, or they weren't paying attention or they swerved just a little bit to do it on purpose."

"So we'd think they abandoned the truck because they didn't have any choice," Chee said.

"Maybe. You'd see they didn't drive it much farther."

After another few hundred yards Dashee turned off the packed earth of the unimproved road into an even vaguer track. He rolled the patrol car down a slope into a place where humps of blown sand supported a growth of Mormon tea and a few scraggly junipers.

"Here we are," he said. "I'm parking just about exactly where they left the pickup."

Chee climbed one of the mounds, looked down at the place the truck had been and all around.

"Could you see the truck from the track? Just driving past?"

"If you knew where to look," Dashee said. "And Timms would have noticed the oil leak, and the tracks turning off. He would have been looking."

"You find any tracks?"

"Sure," Dashee said. "Both sides of the truck where they got out. Two sets. Then somebody told the feds, and here comes the copters full of the city boys in their bulletproof suits."

"The copters blew away the tracks?"

Dashee nodded. "Just like they did it for us in the '98 business. When I called it in, I asked 'em to warn the feds about that." Dashee laughed. "They said that'd be like trying to tell the pope how to hear confessions. Anyway, the light wasn't too bad, and I took a roll of photographs. Boot prints and the places they put stuff they unloaded."

"Like what?"

"Mark left by a rifle butt. Something that might have been a box. Big sack. So forth." Dashee shrugged.

Chee laughed. "Like a sack full of Ute Casino money, maybe. By the way, how much did they get?"

"An 'undetermined amount,' according to the FBI. But the unofficial and approximate estimate I hear was four hundred and eighty-six thousand, nine hundred and eleven dollars."

Chee whistled.

"All unmarked money, of course," Dashee added. "And lots of pockets full of big-value chips which honest folks grabbed off the roulette tables while escaping in the darkness."

"Did the tracks head right off toward the Timms place? Or where?"

"We didn't have much time to look. The sheriff called right back and said the FBI wanted us not to mess around the scene. Just back off and guard the place."

"Not much time to look, huh?" Chee said. "What did you see when you did look? What was in the truck?"

"Nothing much. They'd stolen it off of one of those Mobil Oil pump jack sites, and it had some of those greasy wrenches, wipe rags, empty beer cans, hamburger wrappers, so forth. Stuff left under the seats and on the floorboards. Girlie magazine in a door side pocket, receipts for some gas purchases." Dashee shrugged. "About what you'd expect."

"Anything in the truck bed?"

"We thought we had something there," Dashee said. "A good-as-new-looking transistor radio there on the truck bed. Looked expensive, too." He shrugged. "But it was broken."

"Broken. It wouldn't play?"

"Not a sound," Dashee said. "Maybe the battery was down. Maybe it broke when whoever threw it back there."

"More likely they threw it back there because it was already broken," Chee said. He was staring westward, down into the wash, and past it into the broken Utah border country, the labyrinth of canyons and mesa where the Navajo Tribal Police, and police from a score of other state, federal and county agencies had searched for the killers in the '98 manhunt.

"You know, Cowboy," Chee said, "I've got a feeling we're a little bit north of your jurisdiction here. I think Apache County and Arizona stopped a mile or two back there and we're in Utah."

"Who cares?" Dashee said. "What's more interesting is you can't see the Timms place from here. It's maybe a mile down the track."

"Let's go take a look," Chee said.

It was, judging by the police car odometer, 1.3 miles. The road wandered down a slope into a sagebrush flat, to a pitched-roof stone house and a cluster of outbuildings. A plank barn with a red tar-paper roof dominated the scene. From a pole jutting above it a white wind sock dangled, awaiting a breeze to return it to duty. Chee noticed an east–west strip of the flat had been graded clear of brush. He also noticed that the road continued beyond this place, reduced to a set of parallel ruts and wandering across the flat to disappear over a ridge.

Chee pointed. "Where's it go?"

"Another three, four miles, there's another little ranch, the widow I told you about," Dashee said. "It dead-ends there."

"No outlet then? Back to the highway?"

"Unless you can fly," Dashee said.

"I had been thinking that maybe the perps had turned off on this road figuring they'd circle past a roadblock on U.S. 191 up toward Bluff. I guess that would mean they didn't know this country."

"Yeah," Dashee said, "I thought about that. The feds figured it means they knew the Timms airplane was there waiting for them."

"Or they knew a trail down into Gothic Canyon, and down that to the San Juan, and down the river to some other canyon."

"Oh, man," Dashee said. "Don't even think of that." And he pulled the car into Eldon Timms's dusty yard.

A woman was standing on the shady side of the house watching them. Wearing jeans, well-worn boots, a man's shirt with the sleeves rolled and a wide-brimmed straw hat. About middle seventies, Chee guessed. But maybe a little younger. Whites didn't have the skin to deal with this dry sunshine. They wrinkled up about ten years early. She was walking toward the car as Chee and Dashee got out, squinting at them.

"That's Eleanor Ashby," Dashee said. "Widow living over the hill there. She looks after Timms's livestock when he's away. She said they trade off."

"Sheriff," Eleanor Ashby said, "what brings you back over here? You forget something?"

"We were looking for Mr. Timms," Dashee said, and introduced Chee and himself. "I forgot some things I wanted to ask him."

"You needed to go to Blanding to do that," she said. "He headed up there this morning to talk to the insurance people."

"Well, it's nothing important. Just some details I needed to fill in for the paperwork. I forgot to ask him what time of day it was he got back here and found his airplane was missing. But it can wait. I'll catch him next time I get back up this way."

"Maybe I can help you with that," Eleanor said. "Let me think just for a minute, and I can get close to it. He was supposed to bring me some stuff from Blanding, and I thought I'd heard an airplane, so I came on over. Thinking he'd gotten home, but he wasn't back yet."

"About noon?" Chee asked. "You're lucky you weren't here when the bandits were."

"Don't I know it," Eleanor said. "They just might have shot me. Or taken me as a hostage. God knows what. Still scares me when I think about it."

"That plane you heard. You think that was the bandits flying off in Mr. Timms's airplane?"

"No. I just figured Timms had flown over to take a look, and then went on over to the other little place he has over by Mexican Water."

Chee looked at Dashee and found Dashee looking at him.

"Wait a minute," Dashee said. "You mean Timms had flown the plane up to Blanding?"

Eleanor laughed. "Course not," she said. "But that's what I was thinking. Sometimes he took the plane, if he could land where he was going. Sometimes he took his truck."

"But the plane was here when you came by at noon?" Chee asked.

She nodded. "Yeah. Locked in the barn."

"You saw it in there?"

"I saw that big old lock he uses on the door hasp." She chuckled. "You lock that old airplane in there, it can't get out."

"You didn't see his truck?" Chee asked.

"It wasn't here. He—" She frowned at Chee. "What do you mean? What are you thinking?"

"Does he just leave his truck out front?" Dashee asked. "Or somewhere you could have seen it?"

"He keeps it in that shed behind the house," Mrs. Eleanor Ashby said, and her expression suggested she suddenly was confronting a headful of questions.

"You weren't here when Timms finally did get home?" Dashee asked.

"I was back at my house. Then the next day, a car drove up with the two FBI men in it. They asked me if I'd heard an airplane flying over. I told them what I've told you. They wanted to know if anybody had come around the Timms place while I was there. I said no. That was about it."

That was about it for Dashee and Chee as well. They took a look at the barn, at the broken hasp, looked around for tracks and found nothing useful. Then they drove south through the dying red flare of twilight toward

Mexican Water, where Eldon Timms had his other little place, where they dearly hoped, prayed, in fact, they would not find an L-17 hidden.

"If it's there," Dashee said, "then I tell the sheriff, and he tells the FBI, and old Eldon Timms gets sent up for insurance fraud and what else? Obstruction of justice?"

"Probably," Chee said. But he was thinking of three men, nameless, faceless, utterly unidentified, armed with automatic rifles. They had already killed a policeman, wounded another and tried to kill a third. Three killers at large in the Four Corners canyon country. He was wondering how many more would die before this thing was over.

9

THE LITTLE MAP Potts had drawn for Leaphorn on a sheet of notepaper took him across the San Juan down the asphalt of Highway 35 into the Aneth Oil Field, and thence onto a dirt road which led up the slopes of Casa Del Eco Mesa. It wandered past the roofless, windowless stone buildings which Potts had said were the relics of Jorie's ill-fated effort to run a trading post. Two dusty, bumpy miles later it brought him to the drainage that Potts had labeled Desert Creek. Leaphorn stopped there, let the dust settle a moment and looked down the slope. He saw a crooked line of pale green cottonwoods, gray-green Russian olives and silver-gray chamisa brush marking the course of the creek, the red roof of a house, a horse corral, sheep pens, a stack of hay bales protected by a vast sheet of plastic, and a windmill beside the round galvanized-metal form of the tank that received its water. Snaking down the slope along the road was a telephone line, sagging along between widely spaced poles.

Memory clicked in. He'd been there before. Now he knew why Jorie's name had rung a bell. He'd come to this ranch at least twenty-five years ago to deal with a complaint from a rancher that Jorie was shooting at him when he flew his airplane over. Jorie had been amiable about it. He had been shooting at crows, he said, but he sure did wish that Leaphorn would tell the fellow that flying so low over his place bothered his cattle. And apparently that had ended that—just another of the thousands of jobs rural policemen get solving little social problems among people turned eccentric by an overdose of dramatic skyscapes, endless silence and loneliness.

Leaphorn fished his binoculars from the glove box for a closer look. Nothing much had changed. The windmill tower now also supported what seemed to be an antenna, which meant Jorie—like many empty-country ranchers living beyond the reach of even Rural Electrification Administration power lines—had invested in radio communication. And the windmill was also rigged to turn a generator to provide the house with some battery-stored electricity. A little green tractor, dappled with rust and equipped with a front-end loader, was parked in the otherwise empty horse corral. No other vehicle was visible, which didn't mean one wasn't sitting somewhere out of sight.

Leaphorn found himself surprised by this. He'd expected to see a pickup, or whatever Jorie drove, parked by the house and Jorie working on something by one of the outbuildings. He'd expected to confirm that Jorie had not flown away with the Ute Casino loot and that Gershwin had been using him in some sort of convoluted scheme. He leaned back on the truck seat, stretched out his legs, and thought the whole business through again. A waste of time? Probably. How about dangerous? He didn't think so, but he'd have an explanation for this visit handy if Jorie came to the door and invited him in. He shifted the truck back into gear, drove slowly down the slope, parked under the cottonwood nearest the front porch and waited a few moments for his arrival to be acknowledged.

Nothing happened. No one appeared at the front door to note his arrival. He listened and heard nothing. He got out of the truck, closed the door carefully and silently, and walked toward the house, up the stone front steps, and tapped his knuckles against the doorframe. No response. A faint sound. Or had he imagined it?

"Hello," Leaphorn shouted. "Anyone home?"

No answer. He knocked again. Then stood, ear to the door, listening. He tried the knob, gently. Not locked, which wasn't surprising and didn't necessarily mean Jorie was home. Locking doors in this empty country was considered needless, fruitless and insulting to one's neighbors. If a thief wanted in, it would be about as easy to break the glass and climb in through a window.

But what was he hearing now?

A dim, almost imperceptible high note. Repeated. Repeated. Then a different sound. Something like a whistle. Birdsong? Now a bit of the music meadowlarks make at first flight. Leaphorn moved down the porch to a front window, shaded the glass with his hands and peered in. He looked into a dark room, cluttered with furniture, rows of shelved books, the dark shape of a television set.

He stepped off the end of the porch, walked around the corner of the house and stopped at the first window. The front of a green Ford 150 pickup jutted out from behind the house. Jorie's? Or someone else's? Perhaps Buddy Baker. Or Ironhand. Or both. Leaphorn became abruptly conscious that he was a civilian. That he didn't have the .38-caliber revolver he would have had with him if he was a law officer on duty. He shook his head. This uneasiness was groundless. He walked to the corner of the house. The truck was an oversize-cab model with no one visible in it. He reached through the open window and pulled down the sunshade. Clipped on it was the required liability insurance certification in Jorie's name. The cab was cluttered with trash, part of a newspaper, an Arby's sandwich sack, a bent drinking straw, three red poker chips—the twenty-five-dollar denomination bearing the Ute Casino symbol—on the passenger-side seat.

Leaphorn considered the implications of that a moment, then walked back to the house, put his forehead against the glass, shaded his eyes and looked into what seemed to be a bedroom also used as an office.

Once again he heard the birdcalls, more distinct now. To his right, close to the window, a single bright spot in the darkness attracted his eye. What seemed to be a small television screen presented the image of a meadow, a pond, a shady woods, birds. His eyes adjusted to the dimness. It was a computer monitor. He was seeing the screen saver. As he looked the scene shifted to broken clouds, a formation of geese. The birdsong became honking.

Leaphorn looked away from the screen to complete a scanning of the room. He sucked in his breath. Someone was slumped in the chair in front of the computer, leaning away, against an adjoining desk. Asleep? He doubted it. The position was too awkward for sleep.

Leaphorn hurried back across the porch, opened the door, shouted, "Hello. Hello. Anyone home?," and trotted through the living room into the bedroom.

The form in the chair was a small, gray-haired man, wearing a white T-shirt with HANG UP AND DRIVE printed across the back, new-looking jeans and bedroom slippers. His left arm rested on the tabletop adjoining the computer stand, and his head rested upon it with his face illuminated by the light from the monitor. The light brightened as the screen saver presented a new set of birds. That caused the color of the blood that had seeped down from the hole above his right eye to change from almost black to a dark red.

Everett Jorie, Leaphorn thought. *How long have you been dead? And how many years as a policeman does it take for me to get used to this? And understand it? And where is the person who killed you?*

He stepped back from Jorie's chair and surveyed the room, looking for the telephone and seeing it behind the computer with two stacks of the red Ute Casino chips beside it. Jorie was irrevocably dead. Calling the sheriff could wait for a few moments. First he would look around.

A pistol lay partly under the computer stand, beside the dead man's foot—a short-barreled revolver much like the one Leaphorn had carried before his retirement. If there was a smell of burned gunpowder in the room, it was too faint for him to separate from the mixed aromas of dust, the old wool rug under his feet, mildew and the outdoor scents of hay, horse manure, sage and dry-country summer invading through the open window.

Leaphorn squatted beside the computer, took his pen from his shirt pocket, knelt, inserted it into the gun barrel, lifted the weapon and inspected the cylinder. One of the cartridges it held had been fired. He took out his handkerchief, pushed the cylinder release and swung it open. The cartridge over the chamber was also empty. Perhaps Jorie had carried the pistol with the hammer over a discharged round instead of an empty chamber, a sensible safety precaution. Perhaps he didn't. That was something to be left to others to determine. He returned the pistol to its position beside the victim's foot, slid out the ballpoint, then stood for a moment, holding the pen and studying the room.

It held a small, neatly made double bed. Beyond the bed, an automatic rifle leaned against the wall, an AK-47. A little table beside it held a lamp, an empty water glass and two books. One was *The Virtue of Civility*, with the subtitle "Selected Essays on Liberalism." The other lay on its back, open.

Leaphorn checked the page, used the pen to close it. The cover title read: *Cato's Letters: Essays on Liberty*. He flipped the book open again, remembering it from a political science course in his undergraduate days at Arizona State. Appropriate reading for someone trying to go to sleep. The bookshelves along the wall were lined with similar fare: J.F. Cooper's *The American Democrat*, Burke's *Further Reflections on the Revolution in France*, Sidney's *Discourses Concerning Government*, de Tocqueville's *Democracy in America*, along with an array of political biographies, autobiographies and histories. Leaphorn extracted *The Servile State* from its shelf, opened it and read a few lines for the sake of Hilaire Belloc's poetic polemics. He'd read that one and a few of the others thirty years or so ago in his period of fascination with political theory. Most of them were strange to him, but the titles were enough to tell him that he'd find no socialists among Jorie's heroes.

He located Jorie's telephone book in an out basket beside the phone, found he could still remember the proper sheriff's number and picked up the telephone receiver. From the computer came an odd gargling sound. The screen was displaying a long V of sandhill cranes migrating against a winter sky. Leaphorn put down the phone, took his ballpoint pen, and tapped the computer mouse twice.

The cranes and their gargling vanished—instantly replaced on the screen by text. Leaphorn leaned past the body and read:

NOTICE: To anyone who might care, if such person exists, I declare I am about to close in appropriate fashion my wasted life. Fittingly, it ends with another betrayal. The sortie against the Ute Casino, which I foolishly believed would help finance our struggle against federal despotism, has served instead to finance only greed—and that at the needless cost of lives.

My only profit from this note will be revenge, which the philosophers have told us is sweet. Sweet or not, I trust it will re- move from society two scoundrels, betrayers of trust, traitors to the cause of liberty and American ideals of freedom, civil rights and es- cape from the oppression of an arrogant and tyrannical federal gov- ernment.

The traitors are George (Badger) Ironhand, a Ute Indian who runs cattle north of Montezuma Creek, and Alexander (Buddy) Baker, whose residence is just north of the highway between Bluff and Mexican Hat. It was Ironhand who shot the two victims at the casino and Baker who shot at the policeman near Aneth. Both of these shootings were in direct defiance of my orders and in viola- tion of our plan, which was to obtain the cash collection from the casino without causing injury. We intended to take advantage of the confusion caused by the power failure and the darkness and to cause injury to no one. Both Ironhand and Baker were aware of the policy of gambling casinos, following the pattern set in Las Vegas, of instructing security guards not to use their weapons due to the risk of injury to clients and to the devastating publicity and loss of revenue such injuries would produce. Thus the deaths at the casino were unplanned, unprovoked, unnecessary and directly con- trary to my instructions.

By the time we reached the point where we had planned to aban- don the vehicle and return to our homes it had become clear to me that this violence had been privately planned by Ironhand and Baker and that their plan also included my own murder and their appro- priation of the proceeds for their private and personal use. There- fore, I slipped away at the first opportunity.

I have no apologies for the operation. Its cause was just—to fi- nance the continued efforts of those of us who value our political freedom more than life itself, to forward our campaign to save the American Republic from the growing abuses of our socialist gov- ernment, and to foil its conspiracy to subject American citizens to the yoke of a world government.

It would not serve our cause for me to stand the pseudo-trial which would follow my arrest. The servile media would use it to make patriots appear to be no more than robbers. I prefer to sentence myself to death rather than endure either a public execution or life imprisonment.

However, arrest of Ironhand and Baker and the recovery of the casino proceeds they have taken would demonstrate to the world that their murderous actions were those of two common criminals seeking their own profits and not the intentions of patriots. If you do not find them at their homes, I suggest you check Recapture Creek Canyon below the Bluff Bench escarpment and just south of the White Mesa Ute Reservation. Ironhand has relatives and friends among the Utes there, and I have heard him talking to Baker about a free-flowing spring and an abandoned sheepherder's shack there.

I must also warn that after the business was done at the casino, these two men swore a solemn oath in my presence not to be taken alive. They accused me of cowardice and boasted that they would kill as many policemen as they could. They said that if they were ever surrounded and threatened with capture, they would continue killing police under the pretext of surrendering.

Long Live Liberty and all free men. Long live America.

I now die for it.

Everett Emerson Jorie

Leaphorn read through the text again. Then he picked up the telephone, dialed the sheriff's office number, identified himself, asked for the officer in charge and described what he had found at the residence of Everett Jorie.

"No use for an ambulance," Leaphorn said. And yes, he would wait until officers arrived and make sure that the crime scene was not disturbed.

That done, Leaphorn walked slowly through the rest of Jorie's home—looking but not touching. Back in Jorie's office, the sandhill cranes were again soaring across the computer screen saver, projecting an odd flickering illumination on the walls of the twilight room. Leaphorn tapped the mouse with his pen again, and reread the text of Jorie's note a third time. He checked the printer's paper supply, clicked on the PRINT icon, and folded the printout into his hip pocket. Then he went out onto the front porch and sat, watching the sunset give the thunderclouds on the western horizon silver fringes and turn them into yellow flame and dark red, and fade away into darkness.

Venus was bright in the western sky when he heard the police cars coming.

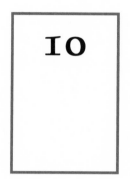

10

JIM CHEE TURNED down a side road on the high side of Shiprock and parked at a place offering a view of both the Navajo Tribal Police district office beside Highway 666 and his own trailer house under the cotton-woods beside the San Juan River. He got out, focused his binoculars and examined both locations.

As he feared, the NTP lot was crowded with vehicles, including New Mexico State Police black-and-whites, some Apache and Navajo County Sheriffs' cars, and three of those shiny black Fords instantly identifiable by all, cops and criminals alike, as the unmarked cars used by the FBI. It was exactly what the newscasts had led him to expect. The word was out that the missing L-17 had been found resting in a hay shed near Red Mesa. Thus the fervent hope of all Four Corners cops that the Ute Casino bandits had flown away to make themselves someone else's problem in another and far-distant jurisdiction had been dashed. That meant leaves would be canceled, everybody would be working overtime—including Sergeant Jim Chee unless he could keep out of sight and out of touch.

He focused on his own place. No vehicles were parked amid the cottonwoods that shaded his house trailer, so maybe no one was there waiting to order him back to duty. Chee had time left on his leave. He'd spent the morning making the long drive to the west slope of the Chuska range and then into high country to the place where Hosteen Frank Sam Nakai had always spent his summers tending his sheep, and where he now spent them doing the long slide into death by lung cancer. But Nakai wasn't there. And neither was his wife, Blue Woman, nor their truck.

Chee was disappointed. He'd wanted to tell Nakai that he'd been right about Janet Pete—that marriage with his beautiful, chic, brilliant silver-spoon socialite lawyer would never work. Either she would give up her ambitions, stay with him in *Dinetah* and be miserable, or he'd take the long bitter step out of the Land Between the Sacred Mountains and become a miserable success. In his gentle, oblique way, Nakai had tried to show him that, and he wanted to tell the man that he'd finally seen it for himself. Chee hung around for a while, thinking Nakai would be back soon. Even with his cancer in one of its periodic remissions, he wouldn't be strong enough for any extended travels. Certainly Nakai wouldn't be strong enough to conduct any of the curing ceremonial that his role as a *yataalii* required of him.

When the sun dipped behind the thunderheads over Black Mesa on the western horizon, Chee gave up and headed home. He would try again tomorrow unless Captain Largo located him. If that happened, he'd be spending what was left of his vacation trudging up and down canyons, serving as live bait for three fellows armed with automatic rifles and a demonstrated willingness to shoot cops.

Now he put his binoculars back into their case, drove down the hill and left his pickup behind a screen of junipers behind his trailer. A note was fastened to his screen door with a bent paper clip.

"Jim—The Captain says for you to report in right away."

Chee repinned it to the door and went in. The light on his telephone answering machine was blinking. He sat, took off his boots, and punched the answering-machine button.

The voice was Cowboy Dashee's:

"Hey, Jim. I filled the sheriff in on us finding Old Man Timms's airplane. He called the feds, they got me on the phone, too. (Sound of Cowboy chuckling) The agent quizzing me didn't want to believe it was the same airplane, and I don't blame him. I didn't want to believe it either. Anyway, they sent somebody down there to make sure us indigenous people can tell an old L-17 from a zeppelin, and now the same old manhunt circus is getting organized just like in '98. If you want to save what's left of your vacation, I'd recommend you keep a long way from your office."

The next call was brief.

"This is Captain Largo. Get your ass down here. The feds located that damned airplane, and we're going to be the beagles on one of their fox hunts again." Largo, who normally sounded grouchy, sounded even grouchier than usual.

The third call was his insurance dealer telling him he needed to add an uninsured motorists clause to his policy. The fourth and final one was Officer Bernadette Manuelito.

"Jim. I talked to Cowboy, and he told me what you did. And I want to thank you for that. But I was at the hospital in Farmington this morning, and they have Hosteen Nakai there. He's very sick, and he told me he needs to see you. I'm going to come by your place. It's ah, it's almost six. I should be there by six-thirty or so."

Chee spent a moment considering what Bernie had said. Then he erased calls one, three and four, leaving the Largo call (in case the captain needed to think he hadn't heard it). Why would Nakai be in the hospital? It was hard to imagine that. He was dying of lung cancer, but he would never, never want to die in a hospital. Nakai was an ultra-traditional. A famous *yataalii*, a shaman who sang the Blessing Way, the Mountain Top Chant, the Night Way, and other curing ceremonials. As the older brother of Chee's mother, he was Chee's "little father," the one who had given Chee his secret "war name," his mentor, the tutor who had tried to teach Chee to be a singer himself. Hosteen Nakai would hate being in a hospital. Dying in such a place would be intolerable for him. How could this have happened? Blue Woman was smart and tough. How could she have allowed anyone to take her husband from their place in the Chuska Mountains?

He was trying to think of an answer to that when he heard the sound of tires on gravel, looked up and saw through the screen door Bernie's pickup rolling to a stop. Maybe she could tell him.

She couldn't.

"I just happened to see him," Bernie said. "They rolled him up on a gurney to where I was waiting for the elevator, and I thought he looked like your uncle, so I asked him if he was Hosteen Nakai, and he nodded, and I told him I worked with you, and he reached out for my arm and said to tell you to come, and I said I would, and then he said to tell you to come right away. And then the elevator came, and they put him on it." Bernie shook her head, her expression sad. "He looked bad."

"That was all he said? Just for me to hurry and come?"

She nodded again. "I went back to the nursing station and asked. The nurse said they had put him in Intensive Care. She said it was lung cancer."

"Yes," Chee said. "Did she say how he got there?"

"She said an ambulance had brought him in. I guess his wife checked him in." She paused, looked at Chee, down at her hands and at him again. "The nurse said it was terminal. He had a tube in his arm and an oxygen thing."

"It's been terminal a long time," Chee said. "Cancer. Another victim of the demon cigarette. Last time I saw him they thought he had just a few weeks to live and that was—" He stopped, thinking it had been months. Far too long. He felt shame for that—for violating the bedrock rule of the Navajo culture and putting his own interests ahead of family needs. Bernie was watching him, awaiting the end of his sentence. Looking slightly un-tidy as usual, and worried, and a little shy, wearing jeans stiff with newness and a bit too large for her and a shirt which fit the same description. A pretty girl, and nice, Chee thought, and found himself comparing her with Janet. Comparing pretty with beautiful, cute with classy, a sheep-camp woman with high society. He sighed. "That was far too long ago," he concluded, and looked at his watch.

"They have evening visiting hours," he said, and got up. "Maybe I can make it by then."

"I wanted to tell you I talked to Cowboy Dashee," Bernie said. "He told me what you did."

"Did? You mean the airplane?"

"Yes," she said, looking embarrassed. "That was a lot of work for you. You were sweet to do all that."

"Oh," Chee said. "Well. It was mostly luck."

"I guess that was the big reason they were holding Teddy. Because he could fly. And he knew the man who had the plane. I owe you a big favor now. I didn't really mean to ask you to do all that work. I just wanted you to tell me what to do."

"I was going to ask why you were at the hospital. Seeing about Teddy Bai, I guess."

"He's better now," she said. "They moved him out of Intensive Care."

"I didn't know Bai knew Eldon Timms," Chee said. "Did you know that?"

"Janet Pete told me," Bernie said. "She was at the hospital. She was appointed to represent Teddy."

"Oh," Chee said. Of course. Janet was a lawyer in the federal court public defender's office. Bai was a Navajo. So was Janet, by her father's name and her father's blood if not by conditioning. Naturally, they'd give her Bai's case.

Bernie was studying him. "She asked about you,"

"Oh?"

"I told her you were on vacation. Just back from going fishing up in Alaska."

"Uh, what did she say to that?"

"She just sort of laughed. And she said she'd heard you had a hand in finding that airplane. Said she guessed you must have been doing that on your own time. I hadn't talked to Cowboy yet, and I didn't know about that, so I just said, well anyway you hadn't gone back to work yet. And she laughed again, and said she thought getting egg on the FBI's face had become sort of a hobby with you."

Chee picked up his hat. "It's not," he said. "Lot of good people in the Bureau. It's just they let the FBI get way too big. And the politicians get the promotions, and so they're the ones making the policies and calling the shots instead of the bright ones. And so a lot of stupid things happen."

"Like evacuating Bluff in that big manhunt of '98," Bernie said.

Chee held the door open for her.

Bernie stood there looking at him, in no hurry to leave.

"Would you like to go along?" Chee asked. "Go see Hosteen Nakai with me?"

Bernie's expression said she would.

"Could I help?"

"Maybe. Be good company anyway. And you could bring me up to date on what I've been missing here."

But Bernie wasn't very good company. As soon as she climbed into his pickup and shut the door behind her, he said, "You mentioned Janet asked about me at the hospital. What else did she say?"

Bernie looked at him a moment. "About you?"

"Yeah," Chee said, wishing he hadn't asked that question.

She thought for a moment, either about what Janet Pete had said about him, or about what she was willing to tell him.

"Just what I told you already, about you liking to embarrass the FBI," she said.

After that there wasn't much talking during the thirty-mile drive to the hospital.

Visiting hours were almost over when they pulled into the parking lot, and the traffic was mostly outgoing.

"I was noticing faces," Bernie said. "The ones who had good news and the ones who didn't. Not many of them looked happy."

"Yeah," Chee said, thinking of how he could apologize to Hosteen Nakai for neglecting him, trying to come up with the right words.

"Hospitals are always so sad," Bernie said. "Except for the maternity ward."

It took only a glance at the nurse manning the desk on the floor housing the Intensive Care ward to support Bernie's observation. She was talking on a desk telephone, a graying, middle-aged woman whose face and voice reflected sorrow.

"Did he say when? OK." She glanced up at Chee and Bernie, gave the "just a moment" signal, and said, "When he checks in tell him the Morris boy died." She hung up, made a wry face and replaced it with a question.

"We've come to see Mr. Frank Sam Nakai," Chee said.

"He may not be awake," she said, and glanced at the clock. "Visiting hours end at eight. You'll have to make it brief."

"He sent a message," Chee said. "He asked me to come right away."

"Let's see then," she said, and led them down the hall.

It was hard to tell whether Nakai was awake, or even alive. Much of his face was covered with a breathing mask, and he lay absolutely still.

"I think he's sleeping," Bernie said, and as she said it, Nakai's eyes opened. He turned his face toward them and removed the mask.

"Long Thinker has come," he said, in Navajo and in a voice almost too weak to be audible.

"Yes, Little Father," Chee said. "I am here. I should have come long ago."

A slender translucent tube connected Hosteen Nakai to a plastic container hung on a bedside stand. Nakai's fingers followed the tube along the sheet to his arm. Not the burly arm Chee remembered. Not much more than a bone covered with dry skin.

"I will go away soon," Nakai said. He spoke with his eyes closed, in slow, careful Navajo. "The instanding wind will be leaving me, and I will follow it to another place." He tapped his forearm with a finger. "Nothing will be left here but these old bones then. Before that, I must tell something. There is something I left unfinished. I must give you the last of your lessons."

"Lesson?" Chee asked, but instantly he knew what Nakai meant. Years ago, when Chee had still believed he could be both a Navajo Policeman and a *yataalii*, Nakai had been teaching him how to do the Night Way ceremony. Chee had memorized the actions of the Holy People involved in myth and how to reproduce this story in the sand paintings. He'd sung the chants that told the story. He'd learned the formula for the emetic required, how to handle the patient, everything required to produce the magic that would compel the Holy People to end the sickness and restore the harmony of natural life. Everything except the last lesson.

The tradition of Navajo shamanism required that. The teacher withheld the ultimate secret until he was certain the student was ready for it. For Chee, that moment had never come. Once he had gone away to Virginia to study at the FBI Academy, once he had flown to Los Angeles to work on a case, once he'd gone to Nakai's winter hogan to be tutored and Nakai had said the season and the weather were wrong for it. Finally, Chee had concluded that Nakai had seen that he would never be ready to sing the Night Way. He had been hurt by that. He had suspected that Nakai disapproved of assimilation of the white man's ways, of his plan to marry Janet Pete, had understood that having a Navajo father would never prepare her for the sacrifices required of a shaman's wife. Whatever the reason, Chee had respected Nakai's wisdom. He would have to forget that boyhood dream. He was not to be entrusted with the power to cure. He had come to accept that.

But now—? Had Nakai changed his mind? What could he say?

"Here?" he said. He gestured at the white, sterile walls. "Could you do that here?"

"A bad place," Nakai said. "Many people have died here, and many are sick and unhappy. I hear them crying in the hallway. And the *chindi* of the dead are trapped within its walls. I hear them, too. Even when they give me the medicine that makes me sleep, I hear them. What I must teach you should be done in a holy place, far away from evil. But we have no choice."

He replaced the mask over his face, inhaled oxygen, and removed it again.

"The *bilagaana* do not understand death," he said. "It is the other end of the circle, not something that should be fought and struggled against. Have you noticed that people die just at the end of night, when the stars are still shining in the west and you can sense the brightness of Dawn Boy on the eastern mountains? That's so the Holy Wind within them can go to bless the new day. I always thought I would die like that. In the summer. At our camp in the Chuskas. With the stars above me. With my instanding wind blowing free. Not dying trapped in—"

Nakai's voice had become so faint that Chee couldn't understand the last words. Then it faded into silence.

Chee felt Bernie's touch at his elbow.

"Jim. If this is something ceremonial, shouldn't I leave?"

"I guess so," Chee said. "I really don't know."

They stood, watching Nakai, his eyes closed now.

Chee replaced the oxygen mask over his face, felt Bernie's touch on his elbow.

"He hates this place," Bernie said. "Let's get him out of here."

"What do you mean?" Chee said. "How?"

"We tell the nurse we're taking him home. And then we take him home."

"What about all that?" Chee asked, pointing at the oxygen mask, the tubes that tied Nakai to life, and the wires that linked him to the computers which measured the Holy Wind within him and reduced it to electronic blips racing across television screens. "He'll die."

"Of course he'll die," Bernie said, her tone impatient. "That's what the nurse told us. He's dying right now. That's what he was telling you. But he doesn't want to die here."

"You're right," Chee said. "But how do—"

But Bernie was walking out. "First, I call the ambulance service," she said. "While they're coming I'll start trying to check him out."

It was not quite as simple as Bernie made it sound. The nurse was sympathetic but had questions to be answered. For example, where was Nakai's wife, whose name, but not her signature, was on the admissions form? By what authority were they taking Mr. Nakai off the life-support systems and out of the hospital? The doctor who had admitted Mr. Nakai had left for Albuquerque. That shifted responsibility to another doctor—now busy in the emergency room downstairs patching up a knifing victim. He arrived on the floor thirty minutes and two paging calls later, looking young and tired.

"What's this about?" he asked, and the nurse provided a fill-in that caused him to look doubtful. Meanwhile, the ambulance attendant emerged from the elevator, recognized Chee from working traffic accidents and asked him for instructions.

"I can't do it," the doctor said. "The patient's on life support. We need authorization from the next of kin. Lacking that, the admitting physician needs to sign him out."

"That's not really the question," Chee said. "We are taking Hosteen Nakai home tonight to be with his wife. Our question is how you can help us do this to minimize the trouble it might cause."

That produced a chilly but brief silence followed by the signing by Chee of a Released Against Advice of Physician form and a financial responsibility statement. Then Hosteen Frank Sam Nakai was free again.

Chee rode in the back of the ambulance with Nakai and the emergency medical technician.

"I guess you heard they got one of those casino bandits," the tech said. "It was on the six o'clock news."

"No," Chee said. "What happened?"

"The guy shot himself," the tech said. "It was that fella that used to have a radio talk show. Sort of a right-winger. News said he ran cattle up there south of Aneth. Married a Navajo woman and was using her grazing allotment up there."

"Shot himself? What'd they say about that?"

"Not much. It was at his house. I guess they were closing in on him, and he didn't want to get arrested. Fella named Everett Jorie. And now they know who the other two were. Said they're both from up there in Utah. Part of one of those militia bunches."

"Jorie," Chee said. "Never heard of him."

"He used to have a talk show on the radio. You know, all the nuts calling in and complaining about the government."

"OK. I remember him now."

"And they have the other two identified now. Man named George Ironhand and one named Buddy Baker. I think Ironhand's a Ute. Anyway, they said he used to work at the Ute Casino."

"I wonder how they got them identified."

"The TV said the FBI did it, but it didn't say how."

"Well, hell," Chee said. "I was hoping they'd catch them in Los Angeles, or Tulsa, or Miami, or anyplace a long ways from this place."

The ambulance tech chuckled. "You're not anxious to go prowling around in those canyons again. I wouldn't be, either."

Chee let that pass into silence.

Then Hosteen Nakai sighed, and said, "Ironhand." And sighed again.

Chee leaned over him, and said, "Little Father. Are you all right?"

"Ironhand," Nakai said. "Be careful of him. He was a witch."

"A witch? What did he do?"

But Hosteen Nakai seemed to be sleeping again.

11

THE HALF MOON was dipping behind the mountains to the west
when the ambulance, with Bernie trailing it in Chee's truck, rolled
down the track and stopped outside Hosteen Nakai's sheep-camp place in
the Chuskas. Blue Woman was standing in the doorway waiting. She ran
out to greet them, crying. At first the tears were for grief, thinking they
were bringing home her husband's body. Then she cried for joy.

They put him on his bed beside a piñon tree, rearranged his oxygen
supply and listened to Blue Woman's tearful explanation of how Hosteen
Nakai had come to be abandoned, as she saw it, in the Farmington hospital. Her niece had come to take her to have an infected tooth removed, and
to replenish the supply of the medicine which kept away the pain and let
her husband sleep. Nakai had been much better, had wanted to come
along and there had been no one to look after him at the sheep camp. But
at the dentist's office he had fainted, someone called 911, and an ambulance took him to the hospital. She had waited there, and waited, not
knowing what to do for him, and finally her niece had to go to care for her
children, and she had to go with her. There were stories that the rich
young people from the cities were putting wolves back in the mountains,
and there was no one at their place to protect their young lambs.

Nakai was awake now, listening to all this. When Blue Woman was
finished, he motioned to Chee.

"I have something to tell you," he said. "A story."

"We will make some coffee," Blue Woman said. She led Bernie away to the hogan, and as they left Nakai began his tale.

It would be long, Chee thought, involving the intricacies of Navajo theology, the relationship of the universal creator who set all nature in its harmonious motion to the spirit world of the Holy People, and to humanity, and when it was finished he would know the final secret that would qualify him as a shaman.

"I think you will be going into the canyon soon to hunt the men who killed the policemen," Nakai said. "I must tell you a story about Ironhand. I think you must be very, very careful."

Chee exhaled a long breath. *Wrong again*, he thought.

"A long time ago when I was a boy, and the winter stories were being told in the hogan, and people were talking about the great dam that was going to make Lake Powell, and how the water of the Colorado and the San Juan were backing up and drowning the canyons, the old men would talk about how the Utes and the Paiutes would come through the canyons in their secret ways, and steal the sheep and horses of our people, and kill them, too. And the worst of these was a Paiute they called Dobby, and the band that followed him. And the worst of the Utes was a man they called Ironhand."

Nakai replaced his oxygen mask and spent a few moments inhaling.

"Ironhand," Chee said, probably too softly for Nakai to hear him.

Nakai removed the mask again.

"They say Dobby and his people came out of the canyons at night and stole the sheep and horses at the place of woman of the *tl'igu dinee*, and they killed her and her daughter and two children. And the son-in-law of this old woman was a man they called Littleman, who married into the Salt Clan but was born to the Near the Water *Dine'*. And they say he forgot the Navajo Way and went crazy with his grief."

Nakai's voice grew weaker, and slower, as he related how Littleman, after years spent hunting and watching, had finally found the narrow trail the raiders had used and finally killed Dobby and his men.

"It took summer after summer for many years for the Salt Clan to catch Dobby," Nakai said. "But no one ever caught the Ute they called Ironhand."

The moon was down, the dark sky overhead adazzle with stars, and Chee was feeling the high-altitude chill. He leaned forward in his chair and tucked the blankets around Nakai's shoulders.

"Little Father," he said, "I think you should sleep now. Do you need more of the medicine for that?"

"I need you to listen," Nakai said. "Because while our people never caught Ironhand, we know now why we didn't. And we know he had a son and a daughter, and I think he must have a son or a grandson. And I think that is who you will be hunting, and what I will tell you will help."

Chee had to lean forward now, his ear close to Nakai's lips, to hear the rest of it. After two of his raids, the Navajos had managed to trace Ironhand and his men into the Gothic Creek Canyon, and then down Gothic toward the San Juan under the rim of Casa Del Eco Mesa. There tracks turned into a steep, narrow side canyon where the Utes and Mormon settlers from Bluff dug coal. They found a corpse in one of the coal mines. But the canyon was a dead end with no way out. It was as if Ironhand and his men were witches who could fly over the cliffs.

Nakai's voice died away. He replaced the mask, inhaled, and removed it again.

"I think if there is a young man named Ironhand, he robs and kills people, he would know where his grandfather hid in that canyon, and how he escaped from it.

"And now," Hosteen Nakai said, "before I sleep, I must teach you the last lesson so you can be a *yataalii*." He took a labored breath. "Or not be one."

To Chee, the old man seemed utterly exhausted. "First, Father, I think you should rest and restore yourself. You should—"

"I must do it now," Nakai said. "And you must listen. The last lesson is the one that matters. Will you hear me?"

Chee took the old man's hand.

"Know that it is hard for the people to trust outside their own family. Even harder when they are sick. They have pain. They are out of harmony. They see no beauty anywhere. All their connections are broken. That is who you are talking to. You tell them the Power that made us made all this above us and around us and we are part of the Power and if we do as we are taught we can bring ourselves back into *hozho*. Back into harmony. Then they will again know beauty all around them."

Nakai closed his eyes, gripped Chee's hand.

"That is hard to believe," he said. "Do you understand that?"

"Yes."

"To be restored, they must believe you."

Nakai opened his eyes, stared at Chee.

"Yes," Chee said.

"You know the chants. You sing them without a mistake. And your sand paintings are exactly right. You know the herbs, how to make the emetics, all that."

"I hope so," Chee said, understanding now what Hosteen Frank Sam Nakai was telling him.

"But you have to decide if you have gone too far beyond the four Sacred Mountains. Sometimes you can never come all the way back into *Dinetah* again."

Chee nodded. He remembered a Saturday night after he'd graduated from high school. Nakai had driven him to Gallup. They had parked on Railroad Avenue and sat for two hours watching the drunks wandering in and out of the bars.

He'd asked Nakai why he'd parked there, who they were looking for. Nakai hadn't answered at first, but what he said when he finally spoke Chee had never forgotten.

"We are looking for the *Dine'* who have left *Dinetah*. Their bodies are here, but their spirits are far beyond the Sacred Mountains. You can go east of Mount Taylor to find them, or west of the San Francisco Peaks, or you can find them here."

Chee had pointed to a man who had been leaning clumsily against the wall up the avenue from them, and who now was sitting, head down on the sidewalk. "Like him?" he asked.

Nakai had waved his hand in a motion that included the bar's neon Coors sign and the drunk now trying to push himself up from the pavement. But went beyond them to follow a polished white Lincoln Town Car rolling up the avenue toward them.

"Which one acts like he has no relatives?" Nakai had asked him. "The drunk who leaves his children hungry, or the man who buys that car that boasts of his riches instead of helping his brother?"

Nakai's eyes were closed now, and his efforts to breathe produced a faint groaning sound. Then he said, "To cure them you must make them believe. You must believe so strongly that they feel it. Do you understand?"

"Yes," Chee said. Nakai was telling him he had failed to meet Nakai's standards as a shaman whose conduct of the curing ways would actually cure. And Nakai was forgiving him—freeing him to be the sort of modern man he was becoming. There was a sense of relief in that, mixed with a dreary sense of loss.

12

IT WAS JUST a bit after noon when Captain Largo caught him.
Through his dreams Chee heard the sound of something thumping, which gradually became pounding, which suddenly was augmented by an angry shout.

"Damn it, Chee, I know you're in there. Unlock the door."

Chee unlocked the door and stood, naked except for boxer shorts and befuddled by sleep, staring at the captain.

"Where the hell have you been?" Largo demanded, pushing past Chee into the trailer. "And why don't you answer your telephone?"

The captain was staring at the telephone as he said it, noticing the little red light blinking on the answering machine.

"I've been away," Chee said. "Just got back, and I had a lot of family business to take care of."

He reached over, punched the button, awake enough now to be glad he'd been smart enough to erase the call from Cowboy Dashee. The machine reproduced the grouchy voice of Captain Largo saying: "This is Captain Largo. Get your ass down here. The feds located that damned airplane, and we're going to be the beagles on one of their fox hunts again."

The machine showed two other calls waiting and Chee clicked it off before they, whatever they were, got him into any trouble.

"I should have listened to that," he said. "But I just got in about nine this morning, and I was worn out." He told Largo how he and Officer Manuelito had brought his mother's oldest brother home from the hospital, about how the old man had managed to hold death at bay until he saw sunlight on the mountaintop, how Bernadette had gone to bring Blue Woman's sisters to help prepare the body for the traditional funeral. Under his uniform Largo was a traditional, a Standing Rock *Dine'*. He recalled the old man's fame as a singer and his wisdom and, like Chee himself, avoided speaking the name of the dead. He offered Chee his condolences, sat on the edge of Chee's fold-down cot, shook his head.

"I'd give you some time off if I could," he said, ignoring the fact that Chee was officially still on vacation, "but you know how it is. We've got everybody out looking for those bastards, so I'm just going to give you a minute to get your uniform on, and while you do that I'll fill you in, and then I want you out there getting things a little better organized."

"OK," Chee said.

A sudden and unpleasant thought struck the captain. "Manuelito was with you, then," Largo said, looking murderous. "She didn't bother to tell me, though. Did she bother to tell you I was looking all over for you?"

"I didn't ask her," Chee said, and busied himself getting his pants on, buttoning his shirt, hoping Largo wouldn't notice how he'd evaded the question, thinking of nothing to say to take the heat off Bernie, and now, happy to see the captain heading out the door.

"I'll bring you up to speed in my office," Largo said. "In exactly thirty minutes."

Approximately thirty minutes later Chee was sitting in the chair in front of Largo's desk, listening to the captain's end of a telephone conversation. "OK," the captain said. "Sure. I understand. Will do. OK." He hung up, sighed, looked at Chee and his watch. "All right," he said. "Here's the situation."

Largo was good at it. He named and described the surviving suspects. Nobody was at home at either man's residence. None of the neighbors had seen either man since before the robbery, which meant absolutely nothing in Ironhand's case because the nearest neighbor lived about four miles away. A horse trailer and two horses seemed to be missing from Ironhand's place. Since nobody could guess when or why, that might be equally meaningless. With their airplane-escape theory shot down, the feds had resumed custody of the manhunt operation, roadblocks were up and trackers were working over the area around the spot where the suspects had abandoned the escape vehicle.

"Pretty much Ringling Brothers, Barnum and Bailey again," Largo said. "Three sets of state police involved, three sheriff's departments, probably four, BIA cops, Ute cops, cops over from the Jicarilla Reservation, Immigration and Naturalization is sending up its Border Patrol trackers, federals galore, even Park Service security people. I'm putting you in Montezuma Creek. We have four people up there working with the FBI trying to locate some tracks. You're reporting to Special Agent"—Largo consulted a notepad on his desk—"named Damon Cabot. I don't know him."

"I've heard of him," Chee said. "You remember that old poem: 'The Lodges spoke only to Cabots, and the Cabots spoke only to God.'"

"No, I don't," Largo said, "and I hope you're not going up there with that smart-aleck attitude."

Chee looked at his watch. "You want me up there today?"

"I wanted you up there yesterday," Largo said. "Be careful and keep in touch."

"OK," Chee said, and headed for the door.

"And Chee," Largo said. "Use your head for once. Don't get crosswise with the Bureau again. Have some manners. Give 'em some respect."

Chee nodded.

Largo was grinning at him. "If you have trouble giving 'em respect, just remember they get paid about three times more than you do."

"Yeah," Chee said. "That'll help."

The gathering place for the manhunt was the conference room of the Montezuma Creek Chapter House. The parking lot was crowded with a varied assortment of police cars, most easily identified by jurisdiction by Chee. He spotted Cowboy Dashee's Apache County patrol unit resting off the gravel but under the shade of the lot's solitary tree, a couple NTP units, two of the shiny black Ford sedans the FBI used and an equally shiny green Land Rover. That, he concluded, would be far too expensive to be owned by any of the nonfederal agencies here. Probably it had been seized in a drug raid and driven down from Salt Lake or Denver by whichever Special Agent had been put in charge of this affair.

The conference room itself was as crowded as the lot and almost as hot. Someone had concluded that the feeble window-mounted air-conditioning unit wasn't handling the body heat produced by the crowd and had opened windows. A dozen or so men, some in camouflage outfits, some in uniforms, some in suits, were crowded around a table. Chee saw Dashee perched on a folding chair beside one of them, reading something.

Chee walked over. "Hey there, fella," he said to Dashee. "Are you the Special Agent in Charge?"

"Keep your voice down," Cowboy said. "I don't want the feds to know I associate with you. Not until this business is over, anyway. However, the man you want to report to is that tall guy with the black baseball cap with FBI on it. That doesn't stand for Full Blood Indian."

"He looks sort of young. Do you think he understands this country?"

Dashee laughed. "Well, he asked me about the trout fishing in the San Juan. He said somebody told him it was great. I think he's based in St. Louis."

"You tell him fishing was good?"

"Come on, Chee. Ease up. I just told him it was great about two hundred miles upstream before all the muddy irrigation water gets dumped in. He seems like a good guy. Said he was new out here. Didn't know whether to call a gully an arroyo, or a wash, or a cut, or a creek. His name's Damon Cabot."

Up close Damon Cabot looked even younger than he had from the back of the room. He shook hands with Chee, explained that other detachments were handling other aspects of the hunt and that this group was trying to collect all possible evidence from the area where the escape vehicle had been abandoned.

"Here's where we have you," he said, pointing to the map spread on the table and indicating a red X near the center of Casa Del Eco Mesa. "That's our Truck Base. Where the perps abandoned the pickup truck. Are you familiar with that area?"

"Just generally," Chee said. "I worked mostly out of Shiprock and in the Tuba City district. That's way west of here."

"Well, you know it a hell of a lot better than I do," Cabot said. "I just got reassigned from Philadelphia to Salt Lake City about a week ago. Did you work in that 1998 manhunt?"

Chee nodded.

"From what I've been overhearing, the Bureau didn't add any luster to its reputation with that one."

Chee shrugged. "Nobody did."

"What do you think? Are those two guys still out there?"

"From 1998? Who knows? But a lot of people around here think so," Chee said.

"I guess the Bureau decided they're dead," Cabot said. "I just wondered—" He cut that off, and shifted into telling Chee how the fugitives were thought to be armed: assault rifles and perhaps at least one scoped hunting rifle. Chee noticed that Special Agent Cabot seemed slightly downcast. The man had been trying to be friendly. The realization surprised Chee. It made him a bit ashamed of himself.

He brought that up with Cowboy as they drove in the deputy's patrol car to the meeting place on Casa Del Eco Mesa.

"Exactly what I've been telling you," Cowboy said. "You pick on the feds all the time. Hostile. I think it grows out of your basic and well-justified inferiority complex. There's a little envy mixed in there, too, I think. Healthy, good-looking guys, blow-dry haircuts, big salaries, good retirement, shiny shoes, Hollywood always making movies about them, heel-e-o-copters to fly around in, flak jackets, expense accounts, retirement pensions and"—Cowboy paused, gave Chee a sidewise glance—"and getting to associate with those real pretty Justice Department public-defender lawyers all the time."

Which was Cowboy's effort to open the subject of Janet Pete. Chee had once asked Cowboy to be his best man if Janet insisted on the white people's style of wedding Janet's mother wanted instead of the Navajo wedding Chee preferred. He never really explained to Cowboy how that affair had crashed and burned, and he wasn't going to do it now.

"How about you, Cowboy?" Chee said. "Nobody ever accused you of loving the federals. You're the one who told me the most popular course in the FBI Academy is Insufferable Arrogance 101."

"It's Arrogance 201 that's popular. They expect recruits to test out of 101. Anyhow, most of them are nice guys. Just a lot richer than us."

One of them was awaiting them at Truck Base, sitting in a black van, monitoring radio traffic with a book open on the seat beside him. He said the Special Agent running this part of the show had gone down in the canyon, and they were supposed to wait for instructions.

The radio tech pointed to the yellow police-line tape he'd parked beside.

"Don't go inside that," he said. "That's where the perps abandoned their truck. We can't have people messing that up until the crime-lab team signs off on it."

"OK," Cowboy said. "We'll just wait."

They leaned against Cowboy's patrol car.

"Why didn't you tell him you were the one who put up the tape?" Chee asked.

"Just being nice," Cowboy said. "You ought to try that. The feds respond well to kindness."

Chee let that one pass into a long silence, which he broke with a question.

"Have you heard how the Bureau got the perps identified? I know they announced it to the press, which means they're sure of 'em. So first I thought they'd found the inside man and got him to talk. This Teddy Bai guy they were holding at the hospital. Do you know if they got him to talk?"

"All I know is fourth-hand," Cowboy said. "I heard your old boss did it. Got the names for them."

"Old boss?"

"Joe Leaphorn," Dashee said. "The Legendary Lieutenant Leaphorn. Who else?"

"Be damned," Chee said. "How the devil could that have happened?" But he noticed that he wasn't really surprised.

"They said the sheriff got a call from some old friend from Aneth, or someplace like that—a former county cop named Potts. This Potts said Leaphorn came to his house and asked him about three men and then how to find this Jorie guy's place. Hour or so later Leaphorn calls the cops from Jorie's house and tells them Jorie's killed himself. That's all I know."

"Be damned," Chee said again. "How in hell does—"

"How long did you work for him?" Cowboy asked. "Three, four years?"

"Seemed longer," Chee said.

"So you know he's smart," Cowboy said. "Logical, thinks things out."

"Yeah," Chee said, sounding grumpy. "Everything fits into a pattern for him. Every effect has its cause. I told you about his map, didn't I? Full of different colored pins marking different sorts of things. He'd stick 'em in there marking off travel times, confluences, so forth. Looking for a pattern."

Chee paused, struck by a sudden thought. "Or lack of one," he added.

Cowboy looked at him. "Like what do you mean?"

"Like I just thought of something that doesn't fit here. Remember, you told me this truck abandoned here was an oversize cab job, right? And you found two sets of footprints around it. And three was the number of guys seen in the robbery."

"Right," Cowboy said. "So where's that leading?"

"So how did this Jorie get from here to his home up in Utah?"

Silence while Cowboy considered that. He sighed. "I don't know. How about they dropped him off at his house before they got here. Or how about he actually got out of the truck here, but he was very careful where he stepped."

"You think that's possible?"

"No. Not really. I'm pretty good at finding tracks."

The door of the communications van opened, and the tech leaned out.

"Cabot called in," he shouted. "Says you guys can take off now. He wants you back here in the morning. About daylight."

Dashee waved good-bye. The communications tech returned to his reading. Chee said, "Does this somehow remind you of our Great Manhunt of 1998?"

Dashee backed his car up to the track, turned it in the direction of the wandering road that would take them back to pavement.

"Hold it a minute," Chee said. "Let's sit here a little while where we can see the lay of the land and think about this."

"Think?" Dashee said. "You're not an acting lieutenant anymore. That thinking can get you in trouble." But he pulled the car off the track and turned off the ignition.

They sat. After a while Dashee said, "What are you thinking about? I'm thinking about how early we have to hit the floor tomorrow to get up by daylight. How about you?"

"I'm thinking this started out looking like a well-planned operation. Everything was timed out precisely." Chee looked at Dashee, meshed his fingers together. "Perfect precision," he said. "You agree."

Dashee nodded.

"The guy on the roof cuts the right wires at the right time. They use a stolen truck with the plates switched, shooting both of the competent security people. They leave total confusion behind, fixing it so they were far away from the scene before roadblocks were up, and so forth. Everything planned. Right?"

"And now this." Chee waved at the landscape in front of them, dunes stabilized by growths of Mormon tea, stunted junipers, needle grass, and then westward where the Casa Del Eco highlands dropped sharply away into a waste of eroded canyons.

"So?" Dashee asked.

"So why did they come here?"

"Tell me," Dashee said, "and then let's go back to Montezuma Creek and get a loaf of bread and some lunch meat at the store there and have our dinner."

"Well, first you think maybe they panicked. Figured they'd run into roadblocks if they stayed on the pavement, turned off here, found this old track dead-ended, and just took off."

"OK," Dashee said. "Let's go get something to eat."

"But that doesn't work because all three of them lived around here, and that Ironhand guy is a Ute. He'd know every road out here. They had a reason to come here."

"All right," Dashee said. "So they came here to steal Old Man Timms's airplane and fly out of our jurisdiction. The FBI liked that one. I liked that one. Everybody liked that one until you went and screwed it up."

"Call that reason number two, then, and mark it wrong. Now reason number three, currently in favor, is this is the place they had picked to climb down into the canyons and disappear."

Dashee restarted the engine. "Funny place for that, I'd say, but let's think about it while we eat."

"I'd guess this drainage wash here would take you down into Gothic Creek, and then you could follow it all the way down to the San Juan River Canyon, and then if you can get across the river you could go up Butler

Wash to just about anywhere. Or downstream a few miles and turn south again up the Chinle Canyon. Lots of places to hide out, but this is sort of an awkward, out-of-the-way place to start walking."

Dashee shifted into second as they rolled down a rocky slope where the track connected to what the map called "unimproved road."

"If they planned to hole up in the canyons, I'll bet you they knew what they were doing," Dashee said.

"I guess so. But then how about Jorie getting out of the truck here and going right home. That's a long way to walk."

"Drop it," Dashee said. "After I eat something and my stomach stops growling at me, I'll explain it all to you."

"I want to know how Lieutenant Leaphorn got those identities," Chee said. "I'm going to find out."

13

CHEE SCANNED THE tables in the Anasazi Inn dining room twice. He had looked right past the corner table and the stocky old duffer sitting there with a plump middle-aged woman without recognizing Joe Leaphorn. When he did recognize him on the second take, it came as a sort of a shock. He had seen the Legendary Lieutenant in civilian attire before, but the image he carried in his mind was of Leaphorn in uniform, Leaphorn strictly businesslike, Leaphorn deep in thought. This fellow was laughing at something the woman with him had said.

Chee hadn't expected the woman—although he should have. When he'd called Leaphorn's home the answering machine had said, "I'll be in the Anasazi Inn dining room at eight." No preamble, no good-bye, just the ten words required. The Legendary Lieutenant at his efficient best, expecting a call, unable to wait for it, rewording his answering machine answer to deal with the problem, handling an affair of the heart, if such it was, just as he'd handle a meeting with a district attorney. The woman dining with him he now recognized as the professor from Northern Arizona University with whom Leaphorn seemed to have something or other going. He wasn't accustomed to thinking of Leaphorn in any sort of romantic situation. Or to seeing him laughing. That was rare.

What wasn't rare was the effect this man had on him. Chee had considered it on the drive down to Farmington, had decided he was probably over it by now. He'd had the same feeling as a boy when Hosteen Nakai began teaching him about the Navajo relationship with the world, and at the University of New Mexico when in the presence of the famed Alaska Jack Campbell, who was teaching him early Athabascan culture in Anthropology 209.

He'd tried to describe it to Cowboy, and Cowboy had said, "You mean like a rookie reporting for basketball practice with Michael Jordan, or like a seminary student put on a committee with the pope." And, yes, that was close enough. And no, he hadn't quite gotten over it.

Leaphorn spotted him, got up, waved him over, said, "You remember Louisa, I'm sure," and asked him if he'd like something to drink. Chee, already wired with about six cups of coffee since breakfast, said he'd settle for iced tea.

"I figured out how you knew where to find me," Leaphorn said. "You called my house, and got my machine, and it played you the message I'd subbed in to tell Louisa where I'd meet her."

"Right," Chee said. "And that saved me about a hundred miles of driving. Getting all the way down to Window Rock. Two hundred, because I've got to get back to Montezuma Creek in the morning."

"We'll be going in that direction, too," Leaphorn said. "Professor Bourebonette's been using me as translator. She's interviewing an old woman over at the Beclabito Day School tomorrow."

They talked about that until the time came to order dinner.

"Did the desk give you the message I left for you?" Chee said.

"You want to know what I can tell you about the Ute Casino business," Leaphorn said. "Are you forgetting that I'm a civilian these days?"

"No," Chee said, and smiled. "Nor am I forgetting how you used to make your good-old-boy network deliver. And I hear it was you who provided the identification of those guys to the FBI."

"Where'd you hear that?"

"Got it from an Apache County deputy sheriff."

Leaphorn's expression suggested he knew which deputy.

"Anyway, it's like most rumors," Leaphorn said, and shrugged.

"You gentlemen want me to go powder my nose?" the professor asked. "Give you some privacy?"

"Not me," Leaphorn said, and Chee shook his head.

"What you mean is that it's partly true? According to the story I heard you went out to this Jorie fellow's place, found him dead, called in to report he'd committed suicide and gave the feds the names of his accomplices. Could you tell me how much of that is true?"

"You're working on this, I guess," Leaphorn said. "How much have they told you?"

"Not much," Chee said, and filled him in.

"They didn't tell you about the suicide note?"

"No," Chee said. "They didn't."

Leaphorn shook his head and looked disappointed. "Lot of good people work in the FBI," he said. "Lot of dumb ones, too, and the way it works as a bureaucracy gets bigger and bigger and bigger, the dumber you are the higher you rise. They get caught up in the Washington competition, where knowledge is power. That gets them obsessed with secrecy."

"I guess so," Chee said.

"This obsession for secrecy," Leaphorn said, shaking his head. "I used to work with a Special Agent named Kennedy," he added, no longer grinning. "A great cop, Kennedy. He explained to me how it grew out of the turf wars in Washington. The Bureau, and the Treasury cops, and CIA, and the Secret Service, and U.S. Marshal's Office, and the BIA, and Immigration and Naturalization cops, and about fifteen other federal law-enforcement agencies pushing and shoving each other for more money and more jurisdiction. 'Knowledge is Power,' Kennedy'd say, so you get conditioned not to tell anybody anything. They might steal the headlines, and the TV time, from your agency."

Chee nodded. "This suicide note," he said. "Anything in it I should know?" Leaphorn, he was thinking, must be showing his age, or too much living alone. He didn't used to ramble off into such digressions.

"Maybe. Maybe not. But how do you know if you don't know what's in it?"

"Well, I do have a question about this Jorie. I'd like to understand how he got home from where he and his buddies left their truck. And I'd like to know, if he was going home anyway, why he didn't just have them drop him off there?"

Leaphorn looked thoughtful.

"Just two men in the truck when it was abandoned, then? You found the tracks?"

"Not me," Chee said. "I wasn't back from vacation. Sheriff's department people. Cowboy Dashee, in fact. You remember him?"

"Sure," Leaphorn said. "And Cowboy said two sets of tracks around the truck?"

"He said two was all he found. He photographed them. One set of slick-soled boots with cowboy heels, one set that looked like those non-skid walking shoes."

Leaphorn thought about that. "What else did Dashee find?"

"Around the truck?"

"Or in it. Anything interesting."

"It was a stolen oil-field truck," Chee said. "Had all that sort of stuff in it. Wrenches, oily rags, so forth."

Leaphorn waited for more, made a wry, apologetic face.

"Remember how I used to be?" he said. "Always after you to give me all the details. Not leave anything out. Even if it didn't seem to mean anything."

Chee grinned. "I do," he said. "And I remember I used to resent it. Felt like it meant I couldn't do the thinking on my own. Come to think of it, I still do."

"It wasn't that," Leaphorn said, his face a little flushed. "It was just that a lot of times I'd have access to information you didn't have."

"Well, anyway, I didn't mention a girlie magazine in a door pocket, and some receipts for gasoline purchases, a broken radio in the truck bed, an oil-wipe rag and an empty Dr. Pepper can."

Leaphorn thought, said, "Tell me about the radio."

"The radio? Dashee said it wouldn't play. It looked new. Looked expensive. But it didn't work. He figured the battery must be dead."

Leaphorn thought again. "Seems funny they'd go off and leave something like that. They must have brought it along for a reason. Probably wanted to use it to keep track of what the cops were doing. Did it have a scanner, so they could monitor police radio traffic?"

"Damn," Chee said. "Dashee didn't say, and I didn't think to ask him."

Leaphorn glanced at Professor Bourebonette, looking apologetic.

"Go ahead," she said. "I always wondered how you guys do your work."

"Not in a restaurant usually," Leaphorn said. "But I wish I had a map."

"Lieutenant," Chee said, reaching for his jacket pocket, "can you imagine me coming in here to talk to you and not bringing a map?"

The waitress arrived while Leaphorn was spreading the map over the tablecloth. She made a patient face, took their orders and went away.

"OK," Leaphorn said. He drew a small, precise X. "Here we have Jorie's place. Now, where did the men get out of the pickup?"

"I'd say right here," Chee said, and indicated the spot with a tine of his fork.

"Right beside that unimproved road?"

"No. Several hundred yards down a slope. Toward that Gothic Creek drainage."

The map they were using was THE MAP, produced years ago by the Automobile Club of Southern California, adopted by the American Automobile Association as its "Guide to Indian Country" and meticulously revised and modified year by year as bankruptcy forced yet another trading post to close, dirt roads became paved, flash floods converted "unimproved" routes to "impassable," and so forth. Leaphorn refolded it now to the mileage scale, transferred that to the margin of his paper napkin and applied that to measure the spaces between X's.

"About twenty miles as the crow flies," Leaphorn said. "Make it thirty on foot because you have to detour around canyons."

"It seemed to me an awful long way to walk if you don't have to," Chee said. "And then there's more questions."

"I think I have the answer to one of them," Leaphorn said. "If you want to believe it."

"It's really a sort of bundle of questions," Chee said. "Jorie went home. So I guess we can presume he was sure the cops wouldn't be coming after him. Didn't have him identified. So forth. So how was he identified? And how did he know he'd been identified? And why didn't the other two members of the crew behave in the same way? Why didn't they go home? And—and so forth."

Leaphorn had extracted a folded paper from his jacket pocket. He opened it, glanced at it.

"That suicide note Jorie left," he said. "It seems to sort of explain some of that."

Chee, who had promised himself never to be surprised by Leaphorn again, was surprised. Had the Legendary Lieutenant just walked off with the suicide note? Surely the FBI wouldn't have given Leaphorn a copy. Chee tried to imagine that and failed. Legendary or not, Leaphorn was now a mere civilian. But the paper Leaphorn was handing him was indeed a suicide note, and the name on the bottom was Jorie's.

"No signature," Chee said.

"It was left on Jorie's computer screen," Leaphorn said. "This is a printout."

Yes, Chee could imagine Leaphorn doing that. Did the FBI know he'd done it? Highly unlikely. He read through it.

"Wow," Chee said. "This requires some new thinking." He glanced at Professor Bourebonette, who was watching him. Checking his reaction, Chee guessed. She'd read the note, too. Well, why shouldn't she?

"Some things are puzzling," Leaphorn said. "From what Dashee found—just two sets of footprints—Jorie seems to have gotten away from the two somewhere else. Near enough to his home to walk there? But if you look at the map, you see their escape route wouldn't take them there. It would be out of the way. He says in his note they were planning to kill him. That he slipped away. That suggests they stopped somewhere else. But where? And why?"

"Good questions," Chee said.

"I tried to re-create the situation from what little I knew," Leaphorn said. "Jorie, a sort of intellectual. Political idealogue. Fanatic. Doing a robbery to finance his cause. Then it goes sour on him. Unplanned killings. At least unplanned by him. Awareness that his recruits are going to take the loot. There must have been an argument. Or at least an angry quarrel. It must have occurred to Jorie that letting him split off represented a threat to them. How did he manage it?"

"No idea," Chee said.

"Let's say he was still with them when they left the truck. Do you think Dashee might have missed his tracks?"

"They'd stopped in a big flattish place. Mostly covered with old blow dirt. Dashee's good at his job, and it would be hard to miss fresh track in that."

"How about cover? A place to hide?"

"No," Chee said. "A cluster of junipers sort of screened the truck itself from the road. But I didn't see a good place to hide anywhere near. There wasn't one. Certainly not if they were looking for him."

"I presume he was armed," Leaphorn said. "Maybe he warned them away. You know: 'I'm out of here. Let me go or I'm shooting you.'"

"Could have been that," Chee said.

The waitress returned. Leaphorn moved the map to make space for the plates. He looked at Chee. "You had something you wanted to tell me."

"Uh, oh, yeah, I did. About Ironhand. How much do you know about him?"

"Very little."

Chee waited, hoping he'd add to that. From what Dashee had told him Leaphorn knew enough about George Ironhand to have him on the list of names he asked Potts about. But Leaphorn obviously wasn't going to explain that.

"They say a Ute by that same name, about ninety or so years ago, used to lead a little band of raiders down across the San Juan into our territory. Steal horses, sheep, whatever they could find, kill people, so forth. The Navajos would chase them, but they'd disappear in that rough country along the Nokaito Bench. Maybe into Chinle Wash or Gothic Creek. It started a legend that Ironhand was some sort of Ute witch. He could fly. Our people would see him down in the canyon bottom, and then they'd see him up on the rimrock, with no way to get there. Or sometimes the other way around. Top to bottom. Anyway, Ironhand was never caught."

Leaphorn took a small bite of the hamburger steak he'd ordered, and looked thoughtful.

"Louisa," he said, "have you ever picked up anything like that in your legend collecting?"

"I've read something sort of similar," Professor Bourebonette said. "A man they called Dobby used to raid across the San Juan about the same time. But that was farther west. Down into the Monument Valley area. I think that's more or less on the record. A Navajo named Littleman finally ambushed them in the San Juan Canyon. The way the story goes, he killed Dobby and two of the others. But they were Paiutes, and that happened earlier—in the eighteen nineties, I think it was."

Leaphorn nodded. "I've heard the old folks in my family talk about that. Littleman was Red Forehead *Dine'*, in my mother's clan."

"It produced a sort of witch story, too," Louisa said. "Dobby could make his men invisible."

Leaphorn put down his fork. "That old Ute you're interviewing at Towaoc tomorrow. Why not see what she remembers about the legendary Ironhand?"

"Why not," Professor Bourebonette said. "It's right down my scholarly alley. And the man you're after is probably Ironhand Junior. Or Ironhand the Second or Third."

She smiled at Chee. "Nothing changes. A century later and you have the same problem in the same canyons."

Chee nodded and returned the smile, but he was thinking there was one big difference. In the 1890s, or 1910s, or whenever it was, the local posse didn't have the FBI city boys telling them how to run their hunt.

14

F ROM WHERE JOE Leaphorn sat, he could see the odd shape of Sleeping
Ute Mountain out one window, and the Ute Casino about a mile
down the slope out of another. If he looked straight ahead, he could watch
Louisa and Conrad Becenti, her interpreter. They sat at a card table putting a new tape in their recording machine. Beyond them, on a sofa of bright
blue plastic against the wall, sat an immensely old and frail-looking Ute
woman named Bashe Lady, her plump and middle-aged granddaughter and a
girl about twelve who Leaphorn presumed was a great-granddaughter.
Leaphorn himself was perched upon a straight-backed kitchen chair,
perched far too long with no end in sight.

Only Bashe Lady and Louisa seemed to be enjoying this session—the
old woman obviously glorying in the attention, and Louisa in the role of
myth hunter happy with what she was collecting. Leaphorn was fighting
off sleep, and the occupants of the sofa had the look of those who had
heard all this before, and far too often.

They'd been hearing that Bashe Lady had been born into the
Mogche band of the Southern Utes but had married into the Kapot
band. With that out of the way, she had used the next hour or so
enthusiastically giving Louisa the origin story of both bands. Leaphorn
had been interested for thirty minutes or so, but mostly in Professor

Bourebonette's technical skills—the questions she chose to direct the interview and the way she made sure she understood what Becenti was telling her. Becenti was part Ute, part Navajo and probably part something else. He had studied mythology with Louisa at Northern Arizona and seemed to still maintain that awe-stricken student-to-teacher attitude.

Leaphorn squirmed into a slightly less uncomfortable position. He watched a truck towing a multisized horse trailer pull into the Ute Casino parking lot, watched its human occupants climb out and head for the gaming tables, noticed a long column of vehicles creeping south on U.S. 666, the cork in this traffic bottle being an overloaded flatbed hauling what seemed to be a well-drilling rig. He found himself wondering if the campaign by Biblical fundamentalists to have the highway number changed from "the mark of the Beast" to something less terrible (turning the signs upside down to make it 999 had been suggested) had any effect on patronage of the casino. Probably not. He shifted from that to trying to decide how the casino management dealt with the problem of chips that surely must have been snatched from roulette tables when the lights went off during the robbery. Probably they had borrowed a different set from another casino. But the discomfort inflicted by the wooden chair seat drove that thought away. He shifted into getting-up position and reached for his empty glass—intending to sneak into the kitchen with it without being rude.

No such luck. The great-granddaughter had been watching him, and apparently watching for her own excuse to escape. She leaped to her feet and confronted him.

"I'll get you some more iced tea," she said, snatched the glass and was gone.

Leaphorn settled himself again, and as he did, the interview got interesting.

". . . and then she said that in those days when the Bloody Knives were coming in all the time and stealing everything and killing people, the Mogches had a young man named Ouraynad, but people called him Ironhand, or sometimes The Badger. And he was very good at killing the Bloody Knives. He would lead our young men down across the San

Juan and they would steal back the cattle the Bloody Knives had stolen from us."

"OK, Conrad," Louisa said. "Ask her if Ouraynad was related to Ouray?"

Becenti asked. Bashe Lady responded with a discourse incomprehensible to Leaphorn, except for references to Bloody Knives, which was the Ute nickname for the hated Navajos. Leaphorn hadn't been bothered by that at first. After all, the Navajo curing ceremonial used the Utes to symbolize enemies of the people and the Hopi phrase for Navajos meant "head breakers," with the implication his forefathers killed people with rocks. But now Leaphorn had been hearing the translator rattle off uncomplimentary remarks about the *Dine'* for about two hours. He was beginning to resent it.

Bashe Lady stopped talking, gave Leaphorn an inscrutable look and threw out her hands.

"A lot of stuff about the heroism and bravery of the Great Chief Ouray," Becenti said, "but nothing that's not already published. Bottom line was she thought this Ironhand was related to Ouray in some way, but she wasn't sure."

Leaphorn leaned forward and interrupted. "Could you ask her if this Ironhand had any descendants with the same name?"

Becenti looked at Louisa. Louisa looked at Leaphorn, frowning. "Later," she said. "I don't want to break up her line of thought." And to Becenti: "Ask her if this hero Ironhand had any magical powers. Was he a witch? Anything mystical?"

Becenti asked, with Bashe Lady grinning at him. The grin turned into a cackling laugh, which turned into a discourse, punctuated by more laughter and hand gestures.

"She says they heard the Navajos (Becenti had stopped translating that into Bloody Knives in deference to Leaphorn sitting behind him) were fooled so often by Ironhand that they began believing he was like one of their witches—like a Skinwalker who could change himself into an owl and fly, or a dog and run under the bushes. She said they would hear stories the Navajos told about how he could jump from the bottom of the canyon up to the rim, and then jump down again. But she said the Mogche people knew he was just a man. Just a lot smarter than the Navajos who hunted him. About then they started calling him Badger. Because of the way he fooled the Navajos."

Leaphorn leaned forward into the silence which followed that, and began: "Ask her if this guy had a son."

Louisa looked over her shoulder at him, and said, "Patience. We'll get to that." But then she shrugged and turned back to Becenti.

"Ask her if Ironhand had any children."

He had several, both sons and daughters, Bashe Lady said. Two wives, one a Kapot Ute and the other a Paiute woman. While Becenti was translating that, she burst into enthusiastic discourse again, with more laughter and gestures. Becenti listened, and translated.

"She said he took this Paiute woman when he was old, after his first wife died, and she was the daughter of a Paiute they called Dobby. And Dobby was like Ironhand himself. He killed many Navajos, and they couldn't catch him either. And Ironhand, even when he was an old, old man, had a son by this Paiute woman, and this son became a hero, too."

Louisa glanced back at Leaphorn, looked at Becenti, said, "Ask her what he did to become a hero."

Bashe Lady talked. Becenti listened, inserted a brief question, listened again.

"He was in the war. He was one of the soldiers who wore the green hats. She said he shot a lot of men and got shot twice himself, and they gave him medals and ribbons," Becenti said. "I asked which war. She said she didn't know, but he came home about when they were drilling the new oil wells in the Aneth field. So it must have been Vietnam."

During all this, Great-Granddaughter emerged from the kitchen and handed Leaphorn his renewed glass of iced tea—devoid now of ice cubes. What Bashe Lady had been saying had brought Granddaughter out of lethargy. She listened intently to Becenti's translation, leaned forward. "He was in the army," she said. "In the Special Services, and they put him on the Cambodian border with the hill tribes. The Montagnards. And then they sent him over into Cambodia." She laughed. "He said he wasn't supposed to talk about that."

She paused, looking embarrassed by her interruption. Leaphorn took advantage of the silence. Granddaughter obviously knew a lot about this younger version of Ironhand. He put aside his manners and interjected himself into the program.

"What did he do in the army? Was he some sort of specialist?"

"He was a sniper," she told Leaphorn. "They gave him the Silver Star decoration for shooting fifty-three of the enemy soldiers, and then he was shot, so he got the Purple Heart, too."

"Fifty-three," Leaphorn said, thinking this had to be George Ironhand of the casino robbery, thinking he would hate to be prowling the canyons looking for him.

"Do you know where he lives?"

Granddaughter's expression suggested she didn't like this question. She studied Leaphorn, shook her head.

Becenti glanced back at him, said something to Bashe Lady. She responded with a few words and a couple of hand gestures. In brief she said Ironhand raised cattle at a place north of Montezuma Creek— approximately the same location Leaphorn had been given by Potts and had seen in Jorie's suicide note.

Leaphorn interrupted again.

"Louisa, could you ask her if anyone knows how the first Ironhand got away from the Navajos?"

Becenti was getting caught up in this, too. He didn't wait for approval. He asked. Bashe Lady laughed, answered, and laughed again. Becenti shrugged.

"She said the Navajos thought he got away like a bird, but he got away like a badger."

About then Granddaughter said something in rapid Ute to Bashe Lady, and Bashe Lady looked angry, and then abashed, and decided she knew absolutely nothing more about Ironhand.

When the interview was over and they were heading back toward Shiprock, Louisa wanted to talk about Ironhand Junior, as she had begun calling him. The session had gone well, she said. A lot of it was what had already been collected about Ute mythology, religion and customs. But some of it, as she put it, "cast some light on how the myths of preliterate cultures evolve with generational changes." And the information about Ironhand was interesting.

Having said that, she glanced at Leaphorn and caught him grinning.

"What?" she said, sounding suspicious.

The grin evolved into a chuckle. "No offense, but when you talk like that it takes me right back to Tempe, Arizona, and sleepy afternoons in the poorly air-conditioned classrooms of Arizona State, and the voices of my professors of anthropology."

"Well," she said, "that's what I am." But she laughed, too. "I guess it gets to be a habit. And it's getting even worse. Postmodernism is in the saddle now, with its own jargon. Anyway, Bashe Lady was a good source. If nothing else, it shows that hostility toward you Bloody Knives still lingers on like Serb versus Croat."

"Except these days we're far too civilized to be killing one another. We marry back and forth, buy each other's used cars, and the only time we invade them it's to try to beat their slot machines."

"OK, I surrender."

But Leaphorn was still a bit chafed from a long day listening to his people described as brutal invaders. "And as you know very well, Professor, the Utes were the aggressors. They're Shoshoneans. Warriors off the Great Plains moving in on us peaceful Athabascan farmers and shepherds."

"Peaceful shepherds who stole their sheep from who?" Louisa said. "Or is it whom? Anyway, I'm trying to calculate the chronology of this second Ironhand. Wouldn't he be too old now to be the bandit everyone is looking for?"

"Maybe not," Leaphorn said. "The first one would have been operating as late as 1910, which is when we started getting some fairly serious law and order out here. She said the current Ironhand was a child of his old age. Let's say Junior was born in the early forties. That's biologically possible, and that would have him the right age to be in the Vietnam War."

"I guess so. From what she said about him, if I was one of those guys out there trying to find him, I'd be hoping that I wouldn't."

Leaphorn nodded. He wondered how much the FBI knew about Ironhand. And if they did know, how much they had passed along to the locals. He thought about what Bashe Lady had said about how the original Ironhand had eluded the Navajos hunting him. Not like a bird, but like a badger. Badgers escaped when they didn't just stand and fight by diving into their tunnel. Badger tunnels had an exit as well as an entrance. When the hunting ground was canyon country and coal-mining country, that was an interesting thought.

15

ON THE MAPS drawn by geographers it's labeled the Colorado Plateau, with its eighty-five million acres sprawling across Arizona, Colorado, New Mexico and Utah. It is larger than any of those states; mostly high and dry and cut by countless canyons eroded eons ago when the glaciers were melting and the rain didn't stop for many thousand years. The few people who live on it call it the Four Corners, the High Dry, Canyon Land, Slick Rock Country, the Big Empty. Once a writer in more poetic times called it the Land of Room Enough and Time.

This hot afternoon, Sergeant Jim Chee of the Navajo Tribal Police had other names for it, all uncomplimentary and some, after he'd slid into a growth of thistles, downright obscene. He'd spent the day with Officer Jackson Nez, prowling cautiously along the bottom of one of those canyons, perspiring profusely under FBI-issued body armor, carrying an electronic satellite location finder and an infrared body-heat-detecting device and a scoped rifle. What weighed Chee down even more than all that was the confident knowledge that he and Officer Nez were wasting their time.

"It's not a total waste of time," Officer Nez said, "because when the federals can mark off enough of these canyons as searched, they can declare those guys dead and call this off."

"Don't count on it," Chee said.

"Or the perps see us coming and shoot us, and the feds watch for the buzzards, and when they find our bodies, they get their forensic teams in here, and do the match to decide where the shots came from, and then they find the bad guys."

"That makes me feel a little better," Chee said. "Nice to be working with an optimist."

Nez was sitting on a shaded sandstone slab with his body armor serving as a seat cushion while he was saying this. He was grinning, enjoying his own humor. Chee was standing on the sandy bottom of Gothic Creek, body armor on, tinkering with the location finder. Here, away from the cliffs, it was supposed to be in direct contact with the satellite and its exact longitude/latitude numbers would appear on its tiny screen.

Sometimes, including now, they did. Chee pushed the send switch, read the numbers into the built-in mike, shut the gadget off and looked at his watch.

"Let's go home," he said. "Unless you enjoy piling on a lot more overtime."

"I could use the money," Nez said.

Chee laughed. "Maybe they'll add it to your retirement check. We're still trying to collect our overtime for the Great Canyon Climbing Marathon of '98. Let's get out of here before it gets dark."

They managed that, but by the time Chee reached Bluff and his room at the Recapture Lodge, the stars were out. He was tired and dirty. He took off his boots, socks, shirt and trousers, flopped onto the bed, and unwrapped the ham-and-cheese sandwich he'd bought at the filling station across the highway. He'd rest a little, he'd take a shower, he'd hit the sack and sleep, sleep, sleep. He would not think about this manhunt, or about Janet Pete, or about anything else. He wouldn't think about Bernie Manuelito, either. He would set the alarm clock for 6 A.M. and sleep. He took a bite of the sandwich. Delicious. He had another sandwich in the sack. Should have bought a couple more for breakfast. He finished chewing, swallowed, yawned hugely, prepared for a second bite.

From the door the sound: *tap, tap, tap, tap.*

Chee lay still, sandwich raised, staring at the door. *Maybe a mistake,* he thought. *Maybe they will go away.*

Tap, tap, tap, followed by: "Jim. You home?"

The voice of the Legendary Lieutenant.

Chee rewrapped the sandwich, put it on the bedside table, sighed, limped over and opened the door.

Leaphorn stood there, looking apologetic, and beside him was the Woman Professor. She was smiling at him.

"Oops," Chee said, stepping out of her line of vision and reaching for his pants. "Sorry. Let me get some clothes on."

While he was doing that, Leaphorn was apologizing, saying they'd only be a minute. Chee waved them toward the room's two chairs, and sat on the bed.

"You look exhausted," the professor said. "The policewoman at your roadblock said you'd probably been searching in one of the canyons all day. But Joe learned something he felt you needed to know." She gave Chee a wry smile. "I told him you probably already knew it."

"Better safe than sorry," Chee said, and looked at Leaphorn, who was sitting uneasily on the edge of his chair.

"Just a couple of things about this George Ironhand," Leaphorn said. "I guess you knew he was a Vietnam veteran, but we heard today he was a Green Beret. Heard he was a sniper, won a Silver Star. Supposed to have shot fifty-three North Viet soldiers over in Cambodia."

Leaphorn stopped.

Chee thought about that for a moment.

"Fifty-three," he said finally. "I appreciate your telling me. I think if the FBI had let us in on that little secret, Officer Nez would have kept his body armor on in the canyon."

"I imagine the FBI would know this man was a veteran," Leaphorn said. "They're pretty thorough in checking records. But they might not know about the rest of it. To know that, they'd have to turn up the business about him getting decorated."

"Or pass it along if they did," Chee said, his voice now sounding more angry than tired. "We might leak it to the press; the feds wouldn't want the public to know we're chasing a certified official war hero."

"Well," Leaphorn said, "they probably didn't pick up the sniper bit. Army records would just show he received the decoration for something general. Risking his life beyond the call of duty. Something like that."

"OK," Chee said. "I guess I wasn't being fair."

"At least, though," said the professor, "I'd think they should have told you he was a combat veteran."

"Me, too," Chee said. "But I guess nobody's perfect. I know we weren't today. All we got was a lot of exercise."

"No tracks?"

Chee waved his hands.

"Lots of tracks. Coyotes, goats, rabbits, lizards, snakes, variety of birds every place there was a seep," Chee said. "But no sign of humans. We even picked up what might have been puma tracks. Either that or an over-size big-footed bobcat. One sign of porcupine, rodents galore, from kangaroo rats, to deer mice, to prairie dogs."

"Could you rule out humans?"

"Not really," Chee said. "Too much slick rock. We didn't find a single place in maybe five miles we covered where anybody careful couldn't find rocks to walk on."

"So the hunt goes nowhere," Leaphorn said. "I guess until someone comes up with a better reason for leaving that escape vehicle where it was left."

"You mean better than running down into Gothic Creek to hide?" Chee laughed. "Well, I guess that was better than the first idea. Thinking they trotted over to the Timms place to fly away in that old airplane of his." Chee paused. "Wait a minute. You said you had two things to tell me, Lieutenant. What's the second one. Do you have a better idea?"

Leaphorn looked a bit embarrassed, shook his head.

"Not really," he said. "Just more stuff about George Ironhand. Maybe it might mean something." He glanced at Louisa. "Where do I start?"

"At the beginning," Louisa said. "First tell him about the original Ironhand."

So he recounted the deeds of the legendary Ute hero/bandit, the futile efforts of the Navajos to hunt him down, describing Bashe Lady's account of how those hunting him thought he might be a witch because he seemed able to disappear from a canyon bottom and reappear magically on its rim.

"She said the Navajos thought he escaped like a bird, but actually he escaped like a badger." Leaphorn paused with that, watching for Chee's reaction.

Chee was rubbing his chin, thinking.

"Like a badger," Chee said. "Or a prairie dog. In one hole and out another. Did she give you any hint of where this was happening? Name a canyon, anything like that?"

"None," Leaphorn said.

"Do you think she knows?"

"Probably. At very least, I think she has a pretty good general idea. She knew a lot more than she was willing to tell us about that."

Professor Bourebonette was smiling. "She didn't show any signs of affection for you Navajos. You 'Bloody Knives.' I think that after about four hours of that, she was getting under Joe's skin a little. Right, Joe? Arousing your competitive, nationalistic macho instincts, maybe?"

Leaphorn produced a reluctant chuckle. "OK," he said. "I plead guilty. I was imagining Bashe Lady in one of those John-Wayne-type movies. Tepees everywhere, paint ponies standing around, dogs, cooking fires, young guys with Italian faces and Cheyenne war paint running around yipping and thumping drums, and there's Bashe Lady with a bloody knife in her hand torturing some tied-up prisoners. And I'm thinking of how it actually was in 1863, when these Utes teamed up with the U.S. Army, and the Hispanos and the Pueblo tribes and came howling down on us and—"

Professor Bourebonette held up her hand.

Leaphorn cut that off, made a wry face and a dismissing gesture. "Sorry," he said. "The old lady got on my nerves. And I'll have to admit I'd love to see the Navajo Tribal Police catch this new version of Ironhand and lock him up."

"The point of all this is that the George Ironhand you're looking for is probably the son of the original version," Professor Bourebonette said. "The first one took a new wife when he was old. The right time span for this guy. Right age to be in the Vietnam War."

Chee nodded. "So the man we're looking for would likely know how his daddy did the badger escape trick. And where he did it." He looked at Leaphorn. "Do you have any ideas about that?"

"Well, I was going to ask you if you had found any mine shafts down in Gothic Creek Canyon."

"We saw several little coal digs. What they call dog holes. None of them went in more than a few yards. Just people digging out a few sacks to get them through the winter. That creek cuts through coal seams in a lot of places, some of them pretty thick. But we didn't see anything that looked like commercial mining."

"Maybe Ironhand has himself a hidden route up some narrow side gulch," Leaphorn said. "From the way the old woman told the story there just had to be a quick way to get up and down the canyon wall. Did you see any little narrow cuts like that? Maybe even a crack a man could climb?"

"Not in the section we covered," Chee said. "Maybe we'll find one farther down toward the San Juan Canyon."

"If they had a secret hidey-hole, I think you'd find it not too far from where they left the truck. They'd be carrying a lot. Food and water probably, unless they stocked up in advance. And four hundred and something thousand dollars. From that casino it would be mostly in small bills. That would be a lot of weight. And then weapons. They apparently used assault rifles at the casino. They're heavy."

That triggered another thought in Chee—a worry that had been nagging for attention.

"You mentioned a roadblock on your way in from the Ute Reservation. An NTP block, I think you said. Talking to a policewoman."

"It was one of our patrol cars, but the man sitting in it was wearing a San Juan County deputy uniform. The woman was wearing a Navajo Police uniform. Up here it would probably be one of your people out of Shiprock."

Chee was doing a quick inventory of policewomen at Shiprock. There weren't many. "How old?" he asked. "How big?"

Leaphorn knew exactly what he was asking.

"I've only seen her a time or two," he said. "But I think it was Bernadette Manuelito."

"Son of a bitch," Chee said, voice vehement. "What are they using for brains?" He was pulling on his socks. "What the devil does she know about staying alive at a roadblock?"

16

THE ROADBLOCK AS Leaphorn described it was on Utah 163 about halfway between Recapture Creek and the Montezuma Creek Bridge. A sensible place to put it, Chee thought, since a fugitive who spotted it would have no side trails to detour onto. There was only the brush bosque of the San Juan River to the south and the sheer stone cliffs of McCracken Mesa to the north. What wasn't sensible was assigning Bernie to such dangerous duty. That was insane. Bernie would be working backup, surely. Even so, this would be a three-unit block at best. Whoever they had would be up against men who had already proved their willingness to kill and their ability to do it. They'd used an automatic rifle at the casino, and a rumor was afloat that they also had night-vision scopes missing from a Utah National Guard armory.

Chee imagined a bloody scene and drove the first eight miles of his trip much faster than the rules allowed. Then, abruptly, he slowed. A belated thought worked its way through his anger. What was he going to say when he got there? What would he say to the officer in charge? It would probably be a Utah state cop, or a San Juan County deputy. He tried to imagine the conversation. He'd introduce himself as NTP out of Shiprock, chat about the weather maybe, discuss the manhunt a minute or two. Then what? They'd want to know what he wanted. He'd tell 'em he didn't think Bernie had any roadblock training.

Down the slope, Chee's headlights illuminated a red REDUCE SPEED sign.

Then what would they say? Chee took his foot off the gas pedal, let the car roll, imagining a tough-looking Utah cop grinning at him, saying, "She's your lady? Well, then, we'll take good care of her for you." And a deputy sheriff standing behind him, chuckling. An even more dreadful thought emerged. The next step. They'd tell Bernie she had to stay in her car, run and hide anytime a stop seemed imminent. Bernie would be outraged, furious, terminally resentful. And justifiably so.

The car was rolling slowly now. Chee pulled it off onto the shoulder, slammed it into reverse, made a pursuit turn, and headed back toward Bluff, giving his idea of saving Officer Bernadette Manuelito more thought.

That thought was quickly interrupted. The sound of a siren in his ear, the blinking warning light atop a Utah State Police car reflecting off his rearview mirror. Chee grunted out the Navajo version of an expletive, slammed himself on the forehead with a free hand, and angled his car off on the shoulder. Of course. He'd done exactly what one does to trigger pursuit from every roadblock from Argentina to Zanzibar. He put on the parking brake, extracted his NTP identification, turned on the overhead light, did everything he could think of to make it easier for whichever cop would show up at his driver-side window.

He'd guessed right for once. It proved to be a Utah State Policeman.

He shined his flash on Chee, looked at the identification Chee was holding out, and said, "Out of the car, please," and stepped back.

Chee opened the door and got out.

"Face the car please, and put your hands on the roof."

Chee did so, happy he'd left his belt and holster on the motel bed, and was patted down.

"OK," the State Policeman said.

And then another voice, Bernie's voice, saying: "That's Sergeant Chee. Jim, what are you doing here?"

And Chee stood there, still leaning against the car, grimacing, wondering if there was any way things could possibly get any worse.

THE EASTERN SKY was glowing pink and red over the bluffs that gave
Bluff, Utah, its name when Officer Jim Chee climbed into his patrol
car. He inserted the key, started the engine, did what all empty-country
drivers habitually do: he checked the fuel gauge. The needle hovered between half and quarter full. Plenty to get back to the rendezvous point on
Casa Del Eco Mesa, where Nez and he were scheduled to resume the
search of their canyon. But not enough to feel comfortable when you're
going a long way from paved road and service stations. He glanced at his
watch, pulled out of the Recapture Lodge lot onto U.S. 163. The Chevron
station-diner he'd pass should be open about now. He'd stop, fill the tank,
buy a few emergency-ration candy bars to share with Nez and continue,
not thinking about how foolish he'd looked last night.

Good. The station must be open. He couldn't see whether the lights
were on, but a pickup was driving away. Chee stopped by the pumps, got
out. A man was sitting on the gravel beside the station's door, back against
the wall. If Chee had numbered the drunks he'd dealt with since he joined
the Navajo Tribal Police, this one would be about 999. He stepped out of the
car, wondering what the station operator was doing, and gave the drunk a
closer look.

Blood was trickling down the man's forehead. Chee squatted beside him. The man looked about sixty, hair graying, wearing a khaki shirt with LEROY DELL embroidered on it. The man was breathing heavily. The blood came from an abrasion cut over his right eye. Chee started for the car to radio this in and get an ambulance. Get a pursuit started.

"What? What are you doing? Oh!"

Chee spun around. The man was staring at him, eyes wild, getting up.

"What happened?" the man asked. "Where is he? Did he get away?"

Chee helped him to his feet. "You tell me who hit you," he said. "I'll radio it in and get you an ambulance and we'll see if we can catch him."

"The son of a bitch," the man said. He waved his hands. "Look at the mess he made."

On the other side of the entrance, under a sign reading REST ROOMS CUSTOMERS ONLY, a garbage can lay on its side, surrounded by a scattering of cans, bottles, newspapers, sacks, crumpled napkins—all those things people discard at service stations. Nearby, a newspaper-vending machine was on its back.

"Who was he?" Chee said. "I want to call it in. Give us a better chance to catch him."

"I don't know him," the man said. "He was a big Indian-looking guy. Navajo probably, or maybe a Ute. Tall. Maybe middle-aged, or so."

"Driving a blue pickup truck?"

"I didn't see the truck. Didn't notice it."

"Did he have a weapon?"

"That's what he hit me with. A pistol."

"OK," Chee said. "Why don't you go in and sit down. I'll get the police on it."

The dispatcher sounded sleepy until the pistol was mentioned.

"Call him armed and dangerous," Chee suggested. "You might mention this is in the area we're hunting the Ute Casino perps."

The dispatcher chuckled. "Those the perps the feds said were long gone. Flown away?"

"Don't we wish," Chee replied, and went back into the station to find out just what had happened.

Leroy Dell was sitting behind the cash register, holding his head.

"They'll be sending an ambulance," Chee said.

"Down from Blanding. About twenty-five miles from the clinic, and twenty-five back," Dell said. He groaned and grimaced and described to Chee what had happened. When he was walking from his house up behind the station to open the place he'd heard a sort of a crashing sound. He'd hurried around the corner and seen a man going through the trash. He had shouted at him, and the man had said he just wanted to get some old newspapers.

"Just newspapers?"

"That's what he said. And I said, 'Well you're going to have to clean up the mess, too.' And then I noticed the vending machine was turned over and went to look at that and I saw he'd broken into that. And I turned around and said he was going to have to pay for that and he had this gun in his hand and he hit me."

"What kind of gun?"

"Pistol. I don't know what kind. It wasn't a revolver."

"Anything missing?"

"I don't know," Dell said, grimacing again. "Tell the truth, I don't give a damn. I've got a hell of a headache. You take a look if you want to."

Chee looked. He opened the cash-register drawers.

"Empty."

"I take the money home at night," Dell said.

"You better call somebody to come down here and look after you," Chee said. "I'm going to get myself some gas and see if I can find that pickup truck."

Finding the truck occupied much of the day. A Bureau of Indian Affairs cop sent over from the Jicarilla Apache Reservation in New Mexico spotted it at the Aneth Oil Field about sundown. It was stuck in the sand of an arroyo bottom off an abandoned road. South of Montezuma Creek. West of Highway 35. Back on the emptiness of Casa Del Eco Mesa. Back within easy walking range of Gothic Canyon, or Desert Creek Canyon, or anyplace else for a man burdened only by an old newspaper.

It was farther, however, than Sergeant Jim Chee could have walked that evening. Chee had sprained his left ankle climbing down a rocky slope while on this fruitless hunt. It had been one of those no-brainer accidents. He'd put his weight on a protruding slab of sandstone that looked solid but wasn't. Then, instead of facing the inevitability of gravity and taking the tumble with a roll in the rocks, he'd tried to save his dignity, made an off-balance jump and landed wrong. That hurt, and it hurt even worse to require help from a deputy sheriff and an FBI agent to haul him back to his car.

18

THE VOICE ON the telephone was Captain Largo's, with no words
wasted.

Chee said, "No sir, I can't put any weight on it yet,"; listened a few moments, said, "Yes sir," listened again, another "Yes sir," and clicked off.
Total result: Largo wanted to know when Chee could resume his canyon-
combing duties, preferably immediately; Largo instructed him to fill out an
injury report form, and Largo had already sent somebody down to his
trailer with it. It should include name, phone number, etc., of the physician who had X-rayed the ankle. Chee should do this immediately and
send the report right back. Largo was shorthanded, and Chee should not
waste the messenger's time with a lot of conversation.

Chee adjusted the ice pack. He tried to think of the word, in either
Navajo or English, to describe the color the swelling had turned and settled on "plum-colored." He considered whether he should resent the lack
of either sympathy or confidence the captain's call had indicated. About
the time he'd decided to pass that off as part of Largo's natural-born
grumpiness, the messenger arrived.

"Come on in," Chee said, and Officer Bernadette Manuelito stepped
in, in full uniform and looking neater than usual.

"Wow," she said. "Look at that ankle." She made a wry face. "I'll bet it
hurts."

"Right," Chee said.

"You're lucky you didn't get shot," she said, her tone disapproving. "Barging right in like that."

"I didn't 'barge right in.' I drove up to get some gasoline. I noticed a pickup driving away. Then I saw the victim sitting by the wall. And weren't you supposed to bring me a report to fill in and then rush right back to the captain with it, with no time wasted talking?"

"I still think you were lucky," Manuelito said. "You're a fine one to be thinking I wasn't competent to work on a roadblock."

Chee was conscious of his face flushing. He looked at Bernie, found her expression odd but inscrutable—at least to him.

"Where'd you hear that?"

"Professor Bourebonette told me."

"I don't believe it," Chee said. "When did she say that? And why would she say anything like that?"

"At the roadblock. She and Lieutenant Leaphorn came through about an hour or so after you—" Bernie hesitated, seeking a way to describe Chee's arrival. "After you were there. They stopped and talked a while. That's when she said it. She asked me if you had come by, and I said yes, and she asked me what you'd said, and I said nothing much. And she acted surprised, and I asked why, and she said you'd gotten all angry and excited when they told you they'd seen me at the roadblock and ran right out and drove away."

Chee was still trying to read her expression. Was it fond, or amused? Or both.

"I didn't say you were incompetent."

Officer Manuelito said, "Well, OK," and shrugged.

"I just thought it was too dangerous. Those guys had already shot two cops, and shot at another one, and the Ironhand guy, he'd killed a lot more in Vietnam."

"Well, thanks then." Manuelito's expression was easy to read now. She was smiling at him.

"The captain said for you to rush that report right back to him," Chee said, and held out his hand.

She gave it to him, secured to a clipboard with a pen dangling.

"Which one was it? Ironhand or Baker?"

"A tall, middle-aged Indian," Chee said. "Sounds like Ironhand."

"And he just took newspapers? Like the radio said this morning?"

Chee was trying to fill in the form with the clipboard balanced on his right knee. "Apparently. The victim didn't think anything else was missing. But then he was still pretty stunned."

"I think you should call Lieutenant Leaphorn," Manuelito said. "It sounds awfully funny."

Chee looked up at her. "Why?"

"Because, you know, running that risk just to get a newspaper."

"I meant why call Leaphorn?"

"Well, you know, I think he'd be interested. At the roadblock he told us we should be extra careful because he guessed it would be about now those guys, if they were hiding in the canyons, about now they'd be making their move. And the deputy I was working with said he thought they'd be more likely to lie low until everybody got tired of looking before they made a run, and the lieutenant said, maybe so, but their radio was broken. They'd wouldn't know what was going on. They'd be getting desperate to know something."

"He said that?" Chee said, sounding incredulous. "About making their move now. How the devil could Leaphorn have guessed?" Manuelito shrugged.

"And that's why you think I should call him?"

Now it was Bernie's turn to look slightly embarrassed. She hesitated. "I like him," she said. "And he likes you. And I think he's a very lonely man, and—"

The buzz of the telephone cut her off. Captain Largo again.

"What the hell are you and Manuelito doing?" Largo said. "Get her back up here with that report."

"She just left a minute ago," Chee said. He clicked off, filled in the last space, signed the form, handed it to her. Leaphorn liked him? Nobody had ever suggested that before. He'd never even thought of it. Of Leaphorn liking anyone, for that matter. Leaphorn was—Well, he was just Leaphorn.

"You know, Bernie," he said. "I think I will call the lieutenant. I'd like to know what he's thinking."

19

HAVING RESIGNED HIMSELF to more long hours spent listening to elderly Utes recounting their tribal mythology, Joe Leaphorn was reaching for his cap when the phone rang.

"Hello," he said, sounding glum even to himself.

The voice was Jim Chee's. Leaphorn brightened.

"Lieutenant, if you have a minute or two, I'd like to fill you in on what happened at the Chevron station in Bluff yesterday. Have you heard about that? I'd like to find out what you think about it."

"I have time," Leaphorn said. "But all I know is what I got on the television news. A man shows up at the station around opening time. He knocks out the operator and drives off in a previously stolen pickup truck. The FBI presumes the man was one of the casino bandits. The newscaster said a Navajo Tribal Policeman was at the station buying gas when it happened, but the robber escaped. Is that about it?"

A moment of silence. "Well, I was the one buying the gas," Chee said, sounding somewhat defensive, "but I wasn't there until it had already happened. The perp was driving off as I drove up. But what's interesting is that all the man wanted was a newspaper. He took one from the rack, and when the operator got there and found him digging through the trash barrel, he said he was just hunting a newspaper.

Now it was Leaphorn's turn for a moment of silence.

"Just a newspaper," he said. "Just that. And he hadn't taken anything from inside the station. Food, cigarettes, anything like that?"

"The station was still locked up. I thought maybe the guy had taken the operator's keys after he hit him. Got in, looted the place, and then re-locked it—silly as that sounds—but apparently not."

"Well now," Leaphorn said, sounding thoughtful. "He just wanted a newspaper out of the rack."

"Or maybe another one. From what he'd scattered around out of the trash can, he was hunting something there, and he told the operator he was after a newspaper. I was guessing he wanted an older edition. One re-porting earlier stuff about the manhunt."

"Sounds reasonable. Where are you calling from?"

"My place in Shiprock. I hurt my ankle yesterday hunting the newspa-per bandit. I took a fall, and I'm homebound until I get the swelling down. I called your place in Window Rock and got another of those messages you leave on your answering machine. That's a good idea."

"Just a minute," Leaphorn said. He put his hand over the telephone and looked at Louisa, who was standing in the doorway, tape-recorder case over her shoulder, purse in hand, waiting and looking interested.

"It's Jim Chee at Shiprock," Leaphorn said. "You know that Chevron station robbery we were talking about. Chee said the only thing the man wanted was newspapers. Remember what I was saying about that bro-ken radio—"

"That sounds strange," Louisa said. "And look, unless you really want to come along and listen to this mythology cross-examination, why don't you drive over to Shiprock and talk to Chee? I'll ride with Mr. Becenti."

That was exactly the way Emma would have reacted, Leaphorn thought. And he noticed with a sort of joy that he could make such a com-parison now without feeling guilty about it.

The door of Chee's little house trailer was standing open as Leaphorn drove up, and he heard his "come on in" shout as he closed the door of his pickup. Chee was sitting beside the table, his left foot propped on a pillow on his bunk. As they exchanged the required greetings, the words of sym-pathy, the required disclaimer and disclaimer response, Leaphorn noticed the table was bare except for a copy of the Indian Country Map, unfolded to the Four Corners canyon country.

"I see you're ready for work," he said, tapping the map.

"My uncle used to tell me to use my head to save my heels," Chee said. "Since I have to save my ankle today, I'll have to think instead."

Leaphorn sat. "What have you come up with?"

"Nothing but confusion," Chee said. "I was hoping you could explain it all to me."

"It's as if we have a jigsaw puzzle with a couple of the central pieces missing," Leaphorn said. "But driving over from Farmington I began thinking how two of the pieces fit."

"The broken radio producing the need to get a paper to find out what the devil has been going on," Chee said. "Right?"

"Right. And that can tell us something."

Chee frowned. "Like they don't have another radio? Or any other access to news? Or something more than that?"

Leaphorn smiled. "I have an advantage in this situation, being able to sit by a telephone and tap into the retired-cops circuit while you're out working."

Chee leaned forward and readjusted his ice pack, engulfed in déjà—a sort of numb feeling of intellectual inadequacy. He'd heard this sort of preamble from Leaphorn often enough before to know where it led. It was the Legendary Lieutenant's way of leading into some disclosure without making Chee, the green kid who'd been assigned to be his gofer, feel more stupid than necessary. "To tell the truth, all this tells me is that these guys, without their radio, got desperate to find out what the devil was going on. They had to find out whether or not it was time to run."

"Exactly," Leaphorn said. "That's my conclusion, too. But let me add a little bit of information that wasn't available to you. I think I told you I might call Jay Kennedy to see if he could tell us what the FBI lab learned about that radio. Jay called back yesterday. He said his buddy back there told him the radio had been put out of commission deliberately."

Chee lost interest in realigning the ice pack. He stared at Leaphorn. Leaphorn said he'd asked Kennedy to "tell us."

"On purpose?" Chee said. "Why would they do that? Or, wait a minute. Let me restate that question. Make it which one did it, and why? And how could the Bureau determine it was done deliberately?"

"Never underestimate the Bureau's laboratory people. They took the radio apart to see if they could pick up any prints. The sort someone might leave changing batteries, or whatever. They noticed that a couple of the wire connections inside had been pried apart with something sharp. Knife point maybe."

Chee thought for a moment. "Fingerprints," he said. "Did they find any?" If they had, they would be Jorie's. Jorie, knowing he was being betrayed, doing a vengeful act of sabotage.

"Some partials," Leaphorn said. "But they belonged to nobody they had any record of."

Chee thought about that, noticed that Leaphorn was watching him, waiting his reaction. Whose prints would the FBI have on record? Jorie's of course, since they had his body. Perhaps Ironhand's, if they printed servicemen during the Vietnam War. Probably Baker's. He'd been arrested on minor stuff more than once.

"It could still be Jorie who sabotaged the radio," Chee said. "He could have had on gloves, used a handkerchief, been very careful with his knife."

Leaphorn nodded, smiling.

He's happy I thought it through, Chee thought. *Maybe Bernie was right. Maybe Leaphorn does like me.*

"I'd guess the prints don't mean much," Leaphorn said. "They'll belong to some clerk at a Radio Shack who put the battery in. I was thinking about Jorie, too. He still looks like the logical bet."

"He certainly had a motive. We have to presume he had access to the radio after he knew what they were planning."

Leaphorn nodded. "If he had decided to turn them in, he wouldn't want them to know the cops had them identified. Wouldn't want them to hear anything on the radio."

Chee nodded.

"There's a problem with that, though."

"Yeah," Chee said, wondering which problem Leaphorn saw. "Certainly a lot of unanswered questions left."

"Jorie must have thought he knew what he was talking about when he told the police in that suicide note where to find them. At their homes, he said, or that place up north. FBI went to get them, and they weren't there. Why not?" He looked at Chee to see if he would volunteer an answer.

"They didn't trust him," Chee said.

Leaphorn nodded. "They wouldn't. Not when they were double-crossing him." He tapped the map. "And next, why did they come up on this mesa?"

"I have two answers to that. Take your pick. One, I think they may have had a second escape vehicle hidden away someplace not far from where they ditched the pickup. Cowboy said they could find no trace of it, no tracks. Nothing. But in this country they could hide the tracks, knowing they had to, and taking their time to do it right."

Leaphorn acknowledged this with the barest hint of a nod.

"The second idea goes back to what you learned about Ironhand. He knew where his daddy hid during his career. How he managed his magical, mystical escapes. So I say that hiding place is around there someplace. The perps stocked it with food and water. And that's where they intend to hide until it's safe to make a run for it. That's why they drove the truck over the rock—ripped out the oil pan to make it appear to the FBI that they were forced to abandon it there. Then they hiked away to their hidey-hole."

Leaphorn's nod acknowledging this was a bit less languorous.

"But they didn't tell Jorie anything about this. It was their secret. Which means the double cross was planned far in advance of the crime."

"Sure," Chee said.

"I'm thinking of that second choice to look for them Jorie gave the police. That's way up toward Blanding. A long, long way from where they abandoned the pickup."

Chee sighed. "Wouldn't it be wonderful if Cowboy had found three sets of tracks at that damned truck."

Leaphorn laughed. "But let's set that aside for now and get back to your second idea. We'll say Baker and Ironhand had a place arranged to hide out. Jorie had parted company with them somehow before they got there. So Baker and Ironhand leave the truck and start walking. It wouldn't be a long walk because, if we can believe what Jorie said in that note, they must have been carrying a heavy load of paper money. Presuming they hadn't left it somewhere else, and why would they?"

"Heavy? I don't think of paper money as being heavy."

"I was guessing the Ute Casino wouldn't be using many hundred-dollar bills. I guessed a ten-dollar average, and came up with forty-five thousand pieces of paper."

"Be damned," Chee said. "That's a new factor to be thinking about."

"I'm remembering the old Ute lady said the Utes sometimes called the original Ironhand Badger. She said he'd disappear from the canyon bottom and reappear at the top. Or the other way around. Remember that? She said our people chasing him thought he could fly."

"Yes," Chee said. But he was thinking about a huge problem with the second idea. With both of them, in fact. Jorie. Given what he said in the suicide note about where to find his partners, he must have slipped away from them long before they abandoned the truck. The distances were simply too great. Especially if they were humping almost a hundred pounds of money as well as their weapons. But how could he have slipped away? Probably possible. But then, why would he believe his partners would be going home? Wouldn't he know they'd expect him to betray them?

Leaphorn was pursuing his own line of speculation. "Thinking of badgers got me to thinking of holes in the ground," he said. "Of old coal mines. This part of the world has far more than its share of those. Coal almost everywhere. And then when the uranium boom started in the forties, the geologists remembered how the coal veins were usually mixed with uranium deposits, and they were digging away again."

"Yeah," Chee said. "We noticed three or four old digs when we were looking for tracks down in the Gothic Creek Canyon."

Leaphorn looked very interested in that. "How deep? Real tunnels, or just places where people were taking a few wagonloads?"

"Nothing serious," Chee said. "Just a place where somebody got a sackful to heat the hogan."

"When the Mormon settlers moved in the middle of the nineteenth century they found the Navajos were already digging a little coal out of exposed seams. So were the Utes. But the Mormons needed a lot more to fire up smelters, so they developed some tunnel mines. Then the Aneth field development came, and there was natural gas to burn. The mines weren't economical any longer. Some of them were filled in, and some of them collapsed. But there must be some around there in one form or another."

"You're thinking they're hiding in a mine. I don't know. Where I grew up near Rough Rock people dug a little coal, but it was all just shallow stuff. We called them dog-hole mines. Nothing anyone could hide in."

"That's over in the Chuska Mountains," Leaphorn said. "Volcanic geology. Over by Gothic Creek Canyon it's mostly formed by sedimentation. Stratum after stratum."

"True."

"An old-timer in Mexican Water—old fella named Mortimer I think it was—told me there used to be a slide cut down the cliff on the south side of the San Juan across from Bluff. From the rimrock all the way down. He said his folks would dig the coal out of seams in the canyon, hoist it to the top, load it into oxcarts and then dump it down the slide into carts down by the river. Then they'd ferry it across on a cable ferry."

Chee was feeling a little less skeptical. "When was that?"

"It was about forty years ago when he told me, I'd guess, but he was talking about his parents when he was a child. I guess it was operating in the 1880s, or thereabouts. I'd like to take a look at that old mine if it still exists."

"You think we could still find it? Maybe locate the wagon tracks and trace them back? Trouble is, wagon tracks tend to get wiped out in a hundred years."

"I think we might find it another way," Leaphorn said. "Did you ever take a look at those notices posted on chapter-house bulletin boards? The Environmental Protection Agency put them up. They have maps on them showing where the EPA is going to be flying its copters back and forth making surveys of old mine sites."

"I've seen them," Chee said. "But they're surveying to map old uranium-mine sites. Trying to locate radioactive dumps."

"Basically, yes. But what the monitors show is spots with high radiation levels. Coal seams out here are often associated with uranium deposits, and the one Mortimer told me about must have been a pretty big operation. I don't have any business in this, but if I did, I'd call the EPA down in Flagstaff and see if they have a mine-waste map for that part of the Reservation."

"I guess I could do that," Chee said, sounding doubtful about it.

"Here's the reason I'd be hopeful," Leaphorn said. "Coal seams out here vary a lot in depth. Some right on the surface, some hundreds of feet down, and all depths between. You couldn't haul it down the canyon bottom to the river. Too rough. Too many barriers. I'm thinking the Mormons must have got tired of hauling it up to the top after digging it, and dug down to the seam from the top of the mesa. They hoisted it to the top with some sort of elevator like they still do in most tunnel mines."

"Which would explain how our Ironhand could fly from bottom to top," Chee said. "How our Badger could have two holes."

He picked up the telephone, dialed information, and asked for the Environmental Protection Agency number in Flagstaff.

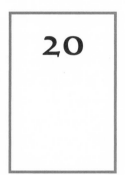

20

O N THE FOURTH call and after the sixth or seventh explanation of what he wanted to various people in various DOE and EPA offices in Las Vegas, Nevada, and Flagstaff, Arizona, Sergeant Jim Chee found himself referred to a New Mexico telephone number and enlightened.

"Call this number in Farmington," the helpful person in Albuquerque said. "That's the project's fixed base. Ask for either the fixed base operator or the project manager." That number took him right back to the Farmington Airport, no more than thirty miles or so from his aching ankle.

"Bob Smith here," the answering voice said.

Chee identified himself, rattled off what he was after. "Are you the project manager?"

"I'm a combination technical guy on the helicopter and driver of the refueling truck," Smith said. "And I'm the wrong guy to talk to for what you want. I'll try to get you switched to P.J. Collins."

"What's his title?"

"It's her," Smith said. "I think you'd call her the chief scientist on this job. Hold on. I'll get her."

P.J. answered the phone by saying, "Yes," in a tone that busy people use. Chee explained again, hurrying it a little.

"Does this involve that casino robbery? Shooting those policemen?"

"Well, yes," Chee said. "We're checking on places they might be hiding.

We know there's an old coal mine in Gothic Creek Canyon, abandoned maybe eighty or ninety years ago, and we thought that perhaps—"

"Good thinking," P.J. said. "Especially the 'perhaps' part. That coal up in that part of the world is uraniferous. Well, all coal tends to be a little radioactive, but that area is hotter than most. But that's a lot of years for the radioactive stuff to get washed away, or lose its punch. However, if you can give me a general idea of where the mine might be, I'll tell you if we've surveyed that area. If we have, I can get Jesse to check our maps in the van and see what hot spots showed up. If any."

"Great," Chee said. "We think this mine was dug into the east slope of Gothic Creek Canyon. It would be somewhere in a ten-mile stretch of the canyon from where it runs into the San Juan southward."

"Well, that's good," P.J. said. "That's on the Navajo Reservation, and that's what our contract covers. The Department of Energy has hired us to help 'em clean up the mess they left hunting uranium. They provide the copters and the pilots, and we provide the technicians."

"Do you think you've surveyed there yet?"

"Possibly today," she said. "We've been up there south of Bluff and Montezuma Creek this week. If they didn't cover that today, they probably will tomorrow."

Chee had been feeling foolish during most of his earlier telephone conversations, his skepticism about this idea reviving. Now he found himself getting excited. P.J. seemed to be taking the notion seriously.

"Can I give you my number? Have you call me back? I'll be reachable tonight and tomorrow and however long it takes."

"Where you calling from?"

"Shiprock."

"The copter will be coming in about an hour or so. Calling it quits for the day and downloading all the data they've collected. Why don't you drive on over and see for yourself?"

Why not, indeed. "I'll be there," he said.

Chee had given up on putting on his left sock, and was easing a sandal on that foot when he heard a vehicle bumping down his access road. It stopped, the west wind blew a puff of dust past his screen door, and a few moments later Officer Bernadette Manuelito appeared. She was carrying what seemed to be a tray covered with a white cloth, holding the cloth against the breeze with one hand, tapping on the screen with the other.

"Ya'eeh te'h," she said. "How's the ankle? Would you like something to eat?"

Chee said he would. But not right now. He had a can't-wait errand to run.

Bernie had been looking at the sandal on his left foot, frowning at it. It was not a pretty sight. She shook her head.

"You can't go anywhere," she said. "You can't drive. What do you think you're doing?" She put the tray on the table.

"It's just over to the Farmington Airport," Chee said. "Of course I can drive. Why not? You use your right foot for the gas pedal and the brake."

"Take off the sandal," Officer Manuelito said. "We'll wrap it up in the bandage again. If you think it can't wait, I'll drive you over there."

Which was, of course, what happened.

The woman who Chee presumed was P.J. turned out to be the same small, slightly sunburned blonde he'd noticed at the helicopter when he'd come to talk to Jim Edgar. She was standing beside the craft holding a black metal box, the box being linked by an insulated cable to the big white pod mounted on the copter's landing skid. When she noticed Chee limping up, her expression was skeptical. *Not surprising*, he thought. He was wearing his worn and wrinkled "stay at home" jeans and a blue T-shirt on which some of the mutton stew Bernie had brought him had splashed when she drove too fast over a bumpy place.

Chee introduced Officer Bernadette Manuelito, who looked uncharacteristically neat and spiffy in her uniform, and himself.

P.J. smiled. "I'm Patti Collins. Just a minute until I get this data unloaded."

Jim Edgar was leaning on the doorframe of his hangar watching them. He held up his hand in salute, shouted, "Heard you found Old Man Timms's airplane," and disappeared back in the direction of his workbench.

P.J. was unjacking the cable. "You got here fast," she said. "Let's take this into the lab and see what we have."

The lab was a standard-looking Winnebago mobile home, its white exterior badly in need of washing but the interior immaculate.

"Have a seat somewhere," P.J. said. She connected her black metal box to an expensive-looking console built into the back of the vehicle and did those incomprehensible things technicians do.

The console made computer sounds. The attached printer began spewing out a roll of paper. P.J. studied it. "Well, now," she said. "I don't know if this is going to help you much, but it's interesting." She detached a couple of feet of paper and laid it on a large scale U.S. Geological Survey map spread across the tabletop where Chee and Bernie were sitting.

"See this," she said, and traced her finger down a tight squiggle of lines on the computer printout. "That coordinates with this." She traced the same fingertip down Gothic Creek on the USGS map.

It was meaningless to Chee. He said, "Oh."

"It shows there's been a distribution of radioactive material downstream from here," P.J. said, tapping her finger on the *h* in Gothic Creek on the map legend.

"Would that suggest the mine waste dump might have been there?" Chee asked. "That would be interesting."

"Yeah," P.J. said, studying the printout again. "Now my problem is whether it's interesting enough to divert the copter a couple of miles tomorrow to get a closer scan."

"It would be a big help to us," Chee said.

"I'll talk to the pilots," P.J. said. "It would just take another twenty minutes or so. And if it's hot enough, we ought to get it on the map anyway."

"Would there be room for me to go along?"

P.J. looked at him skeptically. "You were limping along on that cane. What's the deal with your ankle?"

"I sprained it," Chee said. "It's just about healed."

She still looked skeptical. "You ridden in a copter before?"

"Twice," Chee said. "I didn't enjoy it either time, but I've got a good stomach for motion sickness."

"I'll let you know," she said. "Give me the number where you'll be tonight. If it's go, I'll call you and tell you where to meet the refueling truck."

21

FOR ONCE CHEE came out lucky with the timing. As promised, P.J. had
called him. Yes, they would revise their schedule for the next day a bit
and divert a few miles to do a follow-up low-level check of the Gothic
Creek drainage. He could go along. Everything had been more or less
cleared and approved. However, it was one of those "less said the better"
affairs. Why run the risk that some big shot far removed from the scene
might suspect this rational interpretation of regulations could cause trouble? The most economical and convenient time to do this diversion would
be the final flight of the day. Chee should be at the refueling truck at 2:40
P.M., at which time the truck would be at the same place Chee had seen it
previously, parked beside the road leading to the Timms place on Casa Del
Eco Mesa.

"Thanks," Chee said. "I'll be there waiting."

And he was. He'd gotten down to the office in the morning, caught up
on paperwork, handled some chores for Captain Largo, had lunch,
bought himself some snack stuff (including an extra apple to offer to Rosner) and headed west for the mesa. By two-fifteen, he and Rosner were
sitting in the shade of the truck snacking and watching the copter land. It
was the same big white Bell with radiation-sensor pods on its landing
skids, and the pilot put it down far enough away to avoid blasting them
with dust.

Rosner drove the truck over. He introduced Chee to pilot, copilot and technician, and started refueling.

"P.J. told me something about what you're looking for," the pilot said. "I'm not sure she had it right. Mine opening up on the canyon wall. Is that it?"

The pilot's name was Tom McKissack. He looked a weather-beaten sixty or so, and Chee remembered P.J. had said McKissack was one of those army pilots who'd survived the risky business of rescuing wounded Air Mobile Division grunts from various Vietnam battles. He introduced Chee to the copilot, a younger fellow named Greg DeMoss, another army copter veteran, and to Jesse, who would be doing the technical work. All three looked tired, dusty and not particularly thrilled by this detour.

"Sounds like P.J. had it right," Chee said. "We're trying to locate the mouth of an old Mormon coal mine abandoned back in the 1880s. We think it has a mouth fairly high up the canyon wall. Probably on a shelf of some sort. And then on top, maybe the remains of a tipple structure where they hoisted the coal up and dumped it."

McKissack nodded and looked at the Polaroid camera Chee was carrying. "They tell me those things are a lot better now," he said. He handed Chee a barf bag and a flight helmet, and explained how the intercom system worked.

"You'll be sitting on the right side behind DeMoss, which gives you a great view to the right, but nothing much to the front or the left. So if your mine is on the east side, your best chance to see it will be when we're going north, down the creek toward the river."

"OK," Chee said.

"We normally fly a hundred and fifty feet off the terrain, which means our equipment is scoping a swath three hundred feet wide. Down a canyon it may be lower, but we rarely get closer than fifty feet. Anyway, if you see something interesting, holler. If the situation is right, I can hover a minute so maybe you can get pictures."

McKissack started the rotors. "One more thing," he said, his voice coming through the intercom now. "We've been shot at a few times out here. Either people think we're the black helicopters the Conspiracy Commandos are taking over the world with, or maybe we're scaring their sheep. Who knows? Are we likely to get shot at in this canyon here?"

Chee considered that a moment and gave an honest answer. He said, "Probably not," and they took off in a chaos of dust, motor noise and rotor thumping.

Later Chee had very few memories of that flight, but the ones he retained were vivid.

The tableland was of multicolored stone, carved into a gigantic labyrinth by canyons, all draining eventually into the narrow green belt of the San Juan bottom. Multiple hundreds of miles of sculptured stone, cut off in the north by the blue-green of the mountains. The slanting afternoon sun outlined it into a pattern of gaudy red sandstone and deep shadows. The voice in Chee's ear saying: "You can see why the Mormons called the Bluff area 'The Hole in the Rock,'" and the tech saying: "If there was a market for rock, we'd all be rich."

Then they dropped into the Gothic Creek Canyon, flying slowly north, with the rimrock of Casa Del Eco Mesa above them and the great eroded hump of the Nokaito Bench to their left. The pilot's voice told Chee they were about two miles upcanyon from the point their sensor map had shown the streaks of migrated radiation along the canyon bottom.

"Be just a few minutes," McKissack said. "Let me know if you see anything interesting."

Chee was leaning his head against the Plexiglas window, seeing the stone cliffs slip slowly past. Here runoff erosion had sliced the sandstone. Here a rockslide had formed a semi-dam below. Here some variation of geology had caused a broad irregular bench to form. In places, the wall was almost sheer pink sandstone. In others, it was layered, marked with dark stripes of coal, the blue of shale, the red where iron ore had colored the rock.

"It ought to be close," McKissack said. "I think we can presume the radiation from the old tailings were washing downstream."

Gothic Creek Canyon had widened a little, and the copter was moving down it slowly and almost eye level with the rimrock to Chee's right. Chee could see another bench sloping up from the canyon floor, supporting a ragtag assortment of chamisa, snakeweed and drought-stunted saltbush. It angled upward toward the broad blackish streak of a coal seam. Then just a few yards ahead and just below Chee saw what he was hoping to see.

"There's a fair-size hole in that coal deposit up ahead," McKissack said. "You think that could be what you're looking for?"

"Could be," Chee said. They slid past the hole, with Chee taking pictures.

"Did you notice that structure above? Up on the mesa?" McKissack asked.

"Could you go up a little so I can get a picture of it?"

The copter rose. Almost directly above the mouth of the mine was the mostly roofless remains of a stone structure. Some of its walls had fallen, and a pyramid-shaped skeleton of pine timbers rose from its center.

"Well now," said McKissack, "does that do it for you?"

"I'm finished, and I thank you," Chee said.

"Unfortunately you're not quite finished," McKissack said. "We have to drag this all the way down to the San Juan, and then back, and then we go back over the mesa and finish our mapping there."

"About how long?"

"About one hour and thirty-four minutes of flying four miles north, making a sharp climbing turn, and flying four miles south, and making a sharp climbing turn and flying four miles north. Doing that until we have the quadrant covered. Then we land, get the tanks rejuiced and do it all over again. Except this time it will be quitting time and we'll knock off for the day."

The next voice was the technician's. "And then we come back tomorrow and do it all over again with another four-mile-by-four-mile quadrant. Only time the monotony gets broken is when somebody shoots at us."

22

JOE LEAPHORN CLEARED away his breakfast dishes, poured himself his second cup of coffee and spread his map on the kitchen table. He was studying it when he heard tires rolling onto the gravel in the parking space in front of his house. He pulled back the curtain and looked out at a dark green and dusty Dodge Ram pickup. The truck was strange to him, but the man who climbed out of it and was hurrying up his walk was Roy Gershwin. Gershwin's expression bespoke trouble.

Leaphorn opened the door, ushered him into the kitchen and said, "What brings you down to Window Rock so early this morning?"

"I got a telephone call last night," Gershwin said. "A threatening call. A man. Sounded like a fairly young man. He said they were going to come after me."

"Who? And come after you for what?"

Gershwin had slumped down in the kitchen chair with his long legs stretched under the table. He looked nervous and angry. "I don't know who," he said. "Well, maybe I could guess. His voice sounded familiar, but I think he had something over his mouth. Or he was trying to talk funny. If it was who I think it was, he's one of those damn militia people. Anyway, it was militia business. The fella said they'd heard I'd been snitching on 'em, and I was going to have to pay for that."

"Well, now," Leaphorn said, "it sounds like you were right to be worrying about those people. Let me get you a cup of coffee."

"I don't want any coffee," Gershwin said. "I want to know what you did to get me screwed like this."

"What I did?" Leaphorn diverted the coffeepot from the fresh cup and refilled his own. "Well, let's see. First, I just thought about what you were asking me to do for you. I couldn't think of any way to do it without getting into a crack—having a choice of either telling a judge you were my source or going to jail for contempt of a court order."

He sat across the table from Gershwin and sipped his coffee. "You sure you don't want a cup?"

Gershwin shook his head.

"So then I went up and talked to people around Bluff and around there about those men. I learned a little about all of them, but more about Jorie," Leaphorn said, watching Gershwin over the rim of his cup. "I decided I'd see if any of them were home. Jorie was."

"Killed himself. That right? So you're the one who found his body."

Leaphorn nodded.

"Paper said he left a suicide note. Is that right?"

"Yeah," Leaphorn said. "There it was." He wondered how he would answer when Gershwin asked him what was in it. But Gershwin didn't ask.

"I wonder why—" Gershwin began, but he cut off the sentence and started again. "The newspaper story sort of said the note was a confession. That he gave the names of the other two. That right?"

Leaphorn nodded.

"Then I don't see why those militia bastards are putting the blame on me." The tone of that was angry, and so was his stare.

"That's a puzzle," Leaphorn said. "Do you think they suspect you know a lot about the robbery plan and were giving that away? Any chance of that?"

"I don't see how that could be. When I was going to meetings, there was always somebody talking about doing something wild. Something to call attention to their little revolution. But nobody ever talked about robbery."

Leaphorn let it drop. He took another sip of coffee, looked at Gershwin, waited.

Gershwin slammed his fist on the table. "Damn it to hell," he said. "Why can't the cops catch those bastards? They're out there somewhere. They got their names. Know what they look like. Know where they live. Know their habits. It's just like that '98 mess. You got FBI agents swarming around everywhere. You Navajo cops, and the Border Patrol, and four kinds of state cops, and county sheriffs, and twenty other kinds of cops standing around and manning roadblocks. Why in hell can't they get the job done?"

"I don't know," Leaphorn said. "But there's enough canyons out there to swallow up ten thousand cops."

"I guess so. I guess I'm being unreasonable." He shook his head. "To be absolutely honest about it, I'm scared. I'll admit it. That guy that came to the filling station at Bluff the other morning, he could just as easy have come to my house. I could be dead right now. Dead in my bed. Just waiting for somebody to come wandering by and find my body."

Leaphorn tried to think of something reassuring to say. The best he could come up with was that he guessed the bandits would rather run than fight. It didn't seem to console Gershwin.

"You got any idea if the cops are closing in on them? Have they figured out where they might be?"

Leaphorn shook his head.

"If I knew that, I could sleep a little better. Now I can't sleep at all. I just sit in my chair with the lights off and my rifle on my lap." He gave Leaphorn a pleading look. "I'll bet you know something. Long as you was a cop, knowing all the other cops the way you do, and the FBI, they must tell you something."

"The last I heard is pretty much just common knowledge. That stolen truck was abandoned out there on the mesa south of the San Juan, and that's where I understand they're trying to pick up some tracks. South of Bluff and Montezuma Creek and over in the Aneth Oil—"

The buzz of his telephone interrupted him.

He picked it up off the table, said, "Leaphorn."

"This is Jim Chee. We found that mine." Chee's voice was loud with exuberance.

"Oh. Where?"

"You got your map there?"

"Just a minute." Leaphorn slid the map closer, picked up his pen. "OK."

"The mouth is not more than thirty feet below the canyon rim. About a hundred, hundred and ten feet up from the canyon bottom on a fairly wide shelf. And above it, there's the remains of what must have been a fairly large building. Most of the roof gone now, but a lot of the stone walls still standing. And the framework of what might have been some sort of a hoist sticking up."

"Sounds like what you were hoping to find," Leaphorn said.

"And the reason it fits the theory is you couldn't see the mouth of the mine from the bottom. It's maybe seventy feet up, and hidden by the shelf."

"How'd you find it?"

Chee laughed. "The easy way. Hitched a ride in the EPA helicopter."

Leaphorn still had the pen poised. "Where is it from the place they abandoned the truck?"

"About two miles north—maybe a little less than that."

Leaphorn marked one of his small, precise X's at the proper spot. He glanced at Gershwin.

"What's all this about?" Gershwin asked.

Leaphorn made one of those "just a second" gestures. "Have you notified the FBI?"

"I'm going to call Captain Largo right now," Chee said. "Let him explain it to the federals."

"That sounded interesting," Gershwin said. "Did they find something useful?"

Leaphorn hesitated. "Maybe. Maybe not. They've been looking for an old, long-abandoned mine out there. One of a thousand places people might hide."

"An old coal mine," Gershwin said. "There's lots of those around. You think it's something I could count on? Sleep easy again?"

Leaphorn shrugged. "You mean, would I bet my life on it?"

"Yeah," Gershwin said. "I guess that's what I mean." He stood, picked up his hat, looked down at the map. "Well, to hell with it. I think I owe you an apology, Joe, storming in here like I did. I'm just going to head on home, pack up my stuff and move out to a motel until this business is over with."

23

SERGEANT JIM CHEE limped into Largo's cluttered office feeling even more uneasy than he usually did when approaching the captain. And rightfully so. When he'd pulled into the Navajo Tribal Police parking lot he'd noticed two of the shiny black Ford Taurus FBI sedans. Chee's law-enforcement relationship with the world's largest police force had often been beset with friction. And Captain Largo's telephone call summoning him to this meeting had been even more terse than usual.

"Chee," Largo had said, "get your ass up here."

Now Chee nodded to Special Agent Cabot and the other well-dressed fellow sitting across the desk from the captain and took the chair to which Largo motioned him. He put his cane across his lap and waited.

"You already know Agent Cabot," Largo said. "And this gentleman is Special Agent Smythe." Mutual mumbles and nods followed.

"I've been trying to explain to them why you think this old mine you've found might be the place to look for Ironhand and Baker," Largo said. "They tell me they've already checked every mine deeper than a dog hole up on that mesa. If you've found one they missed, they want to know where it is."

Chee told them, estimating as closely as he could the distance of the mine's canyon mouth from the San Juan and the distance of the surface structure in from the canyon rim.

"You spotted this from a helicopter?" Cabot asked. "Is that correct?"

"That's correct," Chee said.

"Did you know we have prohibited private aircraft flights in that area?" Cabot said.

"I presumed you had," Chee said. "That was a good idea. Otherwise, you'll have those bounty hunters your reward offer is bringing in tying up the air lanes."

This caused a very brief pause while Cabot decided how to respond to this—a not very oblique reminder of the gales of laughter the Bureau had produced in its 1998 fiasco by offering a $250,000 reward one day, and promptly following that with an exhortation for swarms of bounty hunters the offer had attracted to please go away. They hadn't.

Cabot decided to ignore the remark.

"I'll need the name of the company that was operating this aircraft."

"No company, actually," Chee said. "This was a federal-government helicopter."

Cabot looked surprised.

"What agency?"

"It was a Department of Energy copter," Chee said. "I believe it's based at the Tonapaw Proving Grounds over in Nevada."

"Department of Energy? What business do the energy folks have out here?"

Chee had decided he didn't much like Special Agent Cabot, or his attitude, or his well-shined shoes and necktie, or perhaps the fact that Cabot's paycheck was at least twice as large as his, plus all those government perks. He said, "I don't know."

Captain Largo glowered at him.

"I understand the Department of Energy had leased the copter to the EPA," Chee said, and waited for the next question.

"Ah, let's see," said Cabot. "I will rephrase the question so you can understand it. What are the Environmental Protection people doing up here?"

"They're hunting old mines that might be a threat to the environment," Chee said. "Mapping them. Didn't the Bureau know about that?"

Cabot, used to asking questions and not to answering them, looked surprised again. He hesitated. Glanced at Captain Largo. Chee glanced at

Largo, too. Largo's almost-suppressed grin showed that he also knew what Chee was doing and wasn't as upset by it as it had seemed a moment ago.

"I'm sure we did," Cabot said, slightly flushed. "I'm sure if such mapping was in any way helpful to us in this case, it would be used."

Chee nodded. The ball was in the FBI court. He outwaited Cabot, who glanced at Largo again. Largo had found something interesting to look at out the window.

"Sergeant Chee," Cabot said, "Captain Largo told us you had some reason to suspect this particular mine might be used by the perpetrators of the Ute Casino robbery. Would you explain that, please?"

This was the moment Chee had dreaded. He could imagine the amused look on Cabot's face as he tried to explain that the idea came from a Ute tribal legend, trying to describe a hero figure who could jump from canyon bottoms to mesa rims. He took a deep breath and started.

Chee hurried through the relationship of George Ironhand with the original Ironhand, the account of how the Navajos couldn't catch the villain, the notion that since the man was called the Ute name for the badger he might have—like that animal—a hole to hide in with an exit as well as an entrance. As Chee had expected, both Cabot and his partner seemed amused by it. Captain Largo did not appear amused. No suppressed grin now. His expression was dour. Chee found himself talking faster and faster.

"So here was the EPA doing its survey, I hitchhiked a ride, and there it was. The old entrance on a shelf high up on the canyon wall and above it the ruins of the old surface mine. It made sense," Chee said. "I recommended to Captain Largo that it be checked out."

Cabot was studying him. "Let's see now," he said. "You think that the people digging coal out of the cliff down in the canyon decided to dig right on up to the top? If I know my geology at all, that would have them digging through several thick levels of sandstone and all sorts of other strata. Isn't that right?"

"Actually, I was thinking more of digging down from the top," Chee said.

"Can you describe the old mine structure?" Cabot asked. "The building?"

"I have pictures of it," Chee said. "I took my Polaroid camera along."

He handed Cabot two photos of the old structures, one shot from rim level and one from a higher angle.

Cabot looked at them, then handed them to his partner.

"Is that the one you thought it might be?" he asked.

"That's it," Smythe said. "We spotted that the day we found their truck. We put a crew in there that afternoon and searched it, along with all the other buildings on that mesa."

"What did you find?" asked Cabot, who obviously already knew the answer. "Did you see any sign that people might be hiding in the mine shaft?"

Smythe looked amused. "We didn't even see a shaft," he said. "Much less people. Just lots of rodent droppings, old, old trash, odds and ends of broken equipment, animal tracks, three empty Thunderbird wine bottles with well-aged labels. There was no sign at all of human occupancy. Not in recent years."

Cabot handed Chee the photographs, smiling. "You might want these for your scrapbook," he said.

24

As WAS HIS lifelong habit, Joe Leaphorn had gone to bed early. Professor Louisa Bourebonette had returned from her Ute-myth-collecting expedition late. The sound of the car door shutting outside his open window had awakened him. He lay listening to her talking to Conrad Becenti about some esoteric translation problem. He heard her coming in, doing something in the kitchen, opening and closing the door to what had been Emma's private working space and their guest bedroom, then silence. He analyzed his feelings about all this: having another person in the house, having another woman using Emma's space and assorted related issues. He reached no conclusions. The next thing he knew the sunlight was on his face, he heard his Mister Coffee making those strangling sounds signaling its work was done, and it was morning.

Louisa was scrambling eggs at the stove.

"I know you like 'em scrambled," she said, "because that's the way you always order them."

"True," Leaphorn said, thinking that sometimes he liked them scrambled, and sometimes fried, and rarely poached. He poured both of them a cup of coffee, and sat.

"I had a fairly productive day," she said, serving the eggs. "The old fellow in the nursing home at Cortez told us a version of the Ute migration story I've never heard before. How about you?"

"Gershwin came to see me."

"Really? What did he want?"

"To tell the truth, I've been wondering about that. I don't really know."

"So what did he say he wanted? I'll bet he didn't come just to thank you."

Leaphorn chuckled. "He said he'd had a threatening telephone call. Someone accusing him of tipping off the police. He said he was scared, and he seemed to be. He wanted to know what was being done to catch them. If the police had any idea where they were. He said he was going to move into a motel somewhere until this was over."

"Might be a big motel bill," Louisa said. "Those two guys from the 1998 jobs are still out there, I guess. I hear the FBI has quit suggesting they're dead."

"Yeah," Leaphorn said. He drank coffee, buttered his toast, ate eggs that were scrambled just a bit too dry for his taste and tried to decide what it was about Gershwin's visit that was bothering him.

"Something's on your mind," Louisa said. "Is it the crime?"

"I guess. It's none of my business anymore, but some things puzzle me."

Louisa had consumed only toast and was cleaning up around the stove.

"I'm heading south to Flagstaff," she said. "I'll go through all these notes. I'll take this wonderful old myth that has been floating around free as the air all these generations and punch it into my computer. Then one of these days I will call it up out of the hard disk and petrify it in a paper for whichever scholarly publication will want it."

"You don't sound very eager," Leaphorn said. "Why not let that wait another day and come along with me?"

Louisa had made her speech facing the sink, where she was rinsing his frying pan. Pan in hand, she turned.

"Where? Doing what?"

Leaphorn thought about that. A good question. How to explain?

"Actually doing what I do sometimes when I can't figure something out. I drive off somewhere, and walk around for a while, or just sit on a rock and hope for inspiration. Sometimes I get it, sometimes not."

Professor Bourebonette's expression said she liked the sound of that.

"Being a social scientist, I think I'd like to observe that operation," she said.

And so they left the professor's car behind and headed south in Leaphorn's pickup, taking Navajo Route 12 north, with the sandstone cliffs of the Manuelito Plateau off to their right, the great emptiness of Black Creek Valley on the left, and clouds lit by the morning sun building over the Painted Cliffs ahead of them.

"You said some things were bothering you," Louisa said. "Like what?"

"I called an old friend of mine up at Cortez. Marci Trujillo. She used to be with a bank up there that did business with the Ute Casino. I told her I thought that four-hundred-and-something-thousand-dollar estimate of the loot sounded a little high to me. She said it sounded just about right for an end-of-the-month payday Friday night."

"Wow," Louisa said. "And that mostly comes from people who can't afford to lose it. I think you Navajos were smart to say no to gambling."

"I guess so," Leaphorn said.

"On the other hand, in the old days when the Utes were stealing your horses they had to come down and get 'em. Now you drive up there and hand over the cash."

Leaphorn nodded. "So I told her I was guessing that the loot would be mostly in smaller bills. A very few hundreds or fifties, and mostly twenties, tens, fives, and ones. She said that was a good guess. So I asked her how much that would weigh."

"Weigh?"

"She said if we decide the median of bills in the loot was about ten dollars, which she thought would be close, that would be forty-five thousand bills. The weight of that would be just about one hundred and seven pounds and eleven ounces."

"I can't believe this," Louisa said. "Right off the top of her head?"

"No. She had to do some arithmetic. She said banks get their money supply in counted bundles. They put the bundles on special scales to make sure someone with sticky fingers isn't slipping a bill out here and there."

Louisa shook her head. "There's so much going on out in the real world we academics don't know about." She paused, thinking. "For example, now I'm wondering how any of this is causing you to get suspicious about Gershwin's visit."

"Ms. Trujillo once ran the bank Everett Jorie used. I asked her if she could tell me anything about Jorie's financial situation. She said probably not, but since Jorie was dead and his account frozen until an estate executor showed up, she could maybe give me some general hints. She said Jorie had both a checking and a savings account. He had 'some' balance in the first one and 'several thousand dollars' in the other. Plus a fine credit rating."

"Then why in the world—But he said it was to help finance their little revolution, didn't he? I guess that explains it. But it doesn't explain how you knew where Jorie did his banking."

"The checkbook was on Jorie's desk," Leaphorn said.

Louisa was grinning at him. "Oh, really," she said. "Right out there in plain sight just where people keep their checkbooks. Wasn't that convenient for you?"

Leaphorn chuckled. "Well, maybe I had to inch open a desk drawer a little. But anyway, then I asked if Ray Gershwin banked with her, and she said not now, but he used to. They'd turned him down for a loan last spring, and Gershwin had gotten sore about it and moved his business elsewhere. And did she know anything about Gershwin's current solvency. She laughed and said it was bad last spring, and she doubted if it was going to get any better. I asked why not, and she said Gershwin may lose his biggest grazing lease. Some sort of litigation is pending in federal court. So I called the district court clerk up in Denver to ask about that. He called me back and said the case was moot. The plaintiff had died."

Silence. Leaphorn angled to the right off of Navajo Route 12 onto New Mexico Highway 134.

"Now we cross Washington Pass," he said. "Named after the governor of New Mexico Territory who thought this part of the world was full of gold, silver and so forth and was an early believer in ethnic cleansing. He's the one who sent Kit Carson and the New Mexico Hispanos and the Utes to round us up and get rid of us—once and for all. The Tribal Council got the government to agree to change the name a few years ago, but everybody still calls it Washington Pass. I guess that proves we Navajos don't hold grudges. We're tolerant."

"I'm not," Louisa said. "I'm tired of waiting for you to tell me the name of the deceased plaintiff."

"I'll bet you've already guessed."

"Everett Jorie?"

"Right. Interesting, isn't it?"

"Yes. Let me think about it."

She did. "That could be a motive for murder, couldn't it?"

"Good enough I'd think."

"And lots of irony there," Louisa said, "if irony is the word for it. It reminds you of one of those awful wildlife films you're always seeing on television. The lions pull down the zebra, and then the jackals and the buzzards move in to take advantage. Only this time it's old Mr. Timms, trying to defraud his insurance company, and Mr. Gershwin, trying to get rid of a lawsuit."

"Doesn't do a lot for one's opinion of humanity," Leaphorn said.

Louisa was still looking thoughtful. "I'll bet you know this district court clerk personally, don't you? If I called the federal district court and asked for the court clerk, I'd get shifted around four or five times, put on hold, and finally get somebody who'd tell me he couldn't release that information, or I had to drive up to Denver and get it from the judge or something like that." Louisa was sounding slightly resentful. "This all-encompassing, eternal, universal, everlasting good-old-boy network. You do know him, don't you?"

"I confess," Leaphorn said. "But you know, it's a small world up here in this empty country. Work as a cop as long as I did, you know about everybody who has anything to do with the law."

"I guess so," Louisa said. "So he said he'd trot down and look it up for you?"

"I think it's just punch the proper keys on his computer and up comes Jorie, Everett, Plaintiff, and a list of petitions filed under that name. Something like that. He said this Jorie did a lot of business with the federal court. And he was also suing our Mr. Timms. Some sort of a claim he was violating rights of neighboring leaseholders by unauthorized use of BLM land for an airport."

"Well, now. That's nice. A Department of Defense spokesman would call that peripheral damage."

"Peripheral benefit in this case," Leaphorn said.

"It's collateral damage. But how about the suicide note?"

"Remember it wasn't handwritten on paper," Leaphorn said. "It was typed into a computer. Anyone could have done it. And remember that last manhunt. One of the perps turned up dead and the FBI declared him a suicide. That might have given somebody the idea that the feds would go for that notion again."

Louisa laughed. "You know what I'm wondering? Did the neat little trick Mr. Timms tried to pull off suggest to retired lieutenant Joe Leaphorn that Gershwin might have seen the same opportunity to deal with a lawsuit?"

Leaphorn grinned. "As a matter of fact, I think it did."

Near the crest of Washington Pass he pulled off the pavement onto a dirt track that led through a grove of Ponderosa pines. He pulled to a stop at the edge of a cliff and gestured northwest. Below them lay a vast landscape dappled with cloud shadows and late-morning sunlight and rimmed north and east by the shapes of mesas and mountains. They stood on the rimrock, just looking.

"Wow," Louisa said. "I never get enough of this."

"It's home country for me," Leaphorn said. "Emma used to get me to drive up here and look at it those times I was thinking of taking a job in Washington." He pointed northeast. "We lived right down there when I was a boy, about ten miles down between the Two Grey Hills Trading Post and Toadlena. My mother planted my umbilical cord under a piñon on the hill behind our hogan." He chuckled. "Emma knew the legend. That's the binding the wandering child can never break."

"You still miss her, don't you?"

"I will always miss her," Leaphorn said.

Louisa put her arm around him and hugged.

"Southeast," she said. "That hump of clouds. Could that be Mount Taylor?"

"It is, and that's why its other name—I should say one of its other names—is Mother of Rains. The westerlies are pushed up there, and the mist becomes rain in the colder air and then the clouds drift on, dumping the moisture before they get to Albuquerque."

"*Tsoodzil* in Navajo," Louisa said, "and the Turquoise Mountain when you translate it into English, and Dark Mountain for the Rio Grande Pueblos, and your Sacred Mountain of the East."

"And due north, maybe forty miles, there's Shiprock sticking up like a finger pointing at the sky, and, beyond, that blue bump on the horizon is the nose of Sleeping Ute Mountain."

"Scene of the crime," Louisa said.

Leaphorn said nothing. He was frowning, looking north. He drew in a deep breath, let it out.

"What?" Louisa said. "Why this sudden look of worry?"

He shook his head.

"I'm not sure," he said. "Let's drive on down to Two Grey Hills. I want to call Chee. I want to make sure the Bureau sent some people in to check out that old mine."

"I always wonder why you don't have a cell phone. Don't they work well out here?"

"Until I quit being a cop I had a radio in my vehicle," Leaphorn said. "When I quit being a cop, I didn't have anybody to call."

Which sounded sort of sad to Louisa. "What's this about a mine?" she asked, as they got back into the vehicle.

"Maybe I didn't mention that," Leaphorn said. "Chee was looking for an old Mormon coal mine, abandoned in the nineteenth century that maybe had a canyon entrance and another one from the top of the mesa. Where they could lift the coal out without climbing out of the canyon carrying it. I thought that might have been the hideout of Ironhand's dad. It would explain that business Old Lady Bashe was telling you about him disappearing in the canyon and reappearing on top."

"Yes," Louisa said. "You're thinking that's where those two are hiding now?"

"Yeah," Leaphorn said. "Just a possibility." He turned the truck left, down the bumpy dirt road and away from the highway. "This is rough going," he said. "But if you don't break something, its only about nine miles this way. If you go around by the highway, it's almost thirty."

"Which tells me you're in a hurry to make this telephone call. You want to tell me why?"

"I want to make sure he told the FBI," Leaphorn said, and laughed. "He's awful touchy about the Bureau. Gets his feelings hurt. And if he did tell them, I want to find out if they followed up on it."

Louisa waited, glanced at him, braced herself as the truck crossed a rocky washout and tilted down the slope.

"That doesn't tell me why you're worried. All of a sudden."

"Because I'm remembering how interested Gershwin was in the location of that mine."

She thought about that. "It seems reasonable. If somebody threatens you, you're going to wonder where they're hanging out."

"Right," Leaphorn said. "Probably nothing to worry about."

But he didn't slow down.

25

SERGEANT JIM CHEE was in his house-trailer home, sprawled in his chair with his foot perched on a pillow on his bunk and a Ziploc bag full of crushed ice draped over his ankle. Bernadette Manuelito was at the stove preparing a pot of coffee and being very quiet about it because Chee wasn't in the mood for conversation or anything else.

He had gone over everything that had happened in Largo's office, suffered again the humiliation of Cabot handing him his photos of the mine, Cabot's snide smile, being more or less dismissed by Captain Largo, slinking out of the room without a shred of dignity left. And then, his head full of outrage, indignation and self-disgust, not paying attention to where the hell he was walking, losing his balance tripping over something in the parking lot, and coming down full weight on his sprained ankle and dumping himself full length on the gravel.

And of course a swarm of the various sorts of cops working on the casino hunt had been there to see this—two of his NTP officers reporting in, the division radio gal coming out, three or four Border Patrol trackers up from El Paso, a BIA cop he'd once worked with, and a couple of the immense oversupply of FBI agents standing around picking their noses and waiting for Cabot to emerge. And of course, when he was pushing himself up—awkwardly trying to keep any pressure off the ankle—there was Bernie taking his arm.

And now here was Bernie in his trailer, puttering with his coffeepot. Largo had emerged and, despite Chee's objections, had dispatched Bernie to take him to the clinic to have the ankle looked after. She had done that, and brought him home, and now it was past quitting time for her shift but here she was anyway, measuring the coffee on her own time.

And looking pretty as she did it. He resisted thinking about that, unwilling to diminish the self-pity he was enjoying. But looking at her, as neat from the rear elevation as from the front, reminded him that he was comparing her with Janet Pete. She lacked Janet's high-gloss glamour, her physical perfection (depending, however, on how one rated that) and her sophistication. Again, how did one rate sophistication? Did you rate it by the standards of the Ivy League, Stanford and the rest of the politically correct privileged class, or by the Chuska Mountain sheep-camp society, where sophistication required the deeper and more difficult knowledge of how one walked in beauty, content in a difficult world? Such thoughts were causing Chee to feel better, and he turned his mind hurriedly back to the memory of Cabot returning his photographs, thereby restoking his anger.

Just then the telephone rang. It was the Legendary Lieutenant himself—the very one whose notions about Ute tribal legends was at the root of this humiliation.

"Did you report finding that mine to the Bureau?"

"Yes," Chee said.

Silence. Leaphorn had expected more than that.

"What's being done about it? Do you know?"

"Nothing."

"Nothing?" Leaphorn's tone said he couldn't believe that.

"That's right," Chee said. He realized he was playing the same childish game with Leaphorn that he had played with Cabot. He didn't like the feel of that. He admired Leaphorn. Leaphorn, he had to admit it, was his friend. So he interrupted the silence.

"The Special Agent involved said they'd already searched that mine. Nothing in it but animal tracks and mice droppings. He handed me back the photos I'd taken, and they sent me on my way."

"Be damned," Leaphorn said. Chee could hear him breathing for a while. "Did he say when they did their search?"

"He said right after the truck was found. He said they searched the whole area. Everything."

"Yeah," Leaphorn said. "How much structure was left on top of the mesa?"

"Some stone walls, partly fallen down, roof gone from part of it. Then there was a framework of timbers, sort of a triangle structure, sticking out of it."

"Sounds like the support for the tipple to lift the coal out and dump it."

"I guess so," Chee said, wondering about the point of all this. The feds had looked, and nobody was home.

"Searched the whole area, you said? That day?"

"Yeah," Chee said, sensing Leaphorn's point and feeling a faint stir of illogical optimism.

"Didn't Deputy Dashee say they found the truck about middle of the day?"

"Yeah," Chee said. "And they'd be searching the Timms place, house, barns, outbuildings, and all those roads wandering around to those Mobil Oil pump stations, and—" Chee ran out of other examples. Casa Del Eco Mesa was huge, but it was almost mostly empty hugeness.

"The best they would have had time to do would be to give it a quick glance," Leaphorn said.

"Well, yes. Wouldn't that be enough to show it was empty?"

"I think I'll take a drive up there and look around for myself. Is that area still roadblocked?"

"It was yesterday," Chee said. Then he added exactly what he knew the Legendary Lieutenant hoped he would add. "I'll go with you and show 'em my badge."

"Fine," Leaphorn said. "I'm calling from Two Grey Hills. Professor Bourebonette is with me, but she's run into a couple of her fellow professors dickering over a rug. Hold on. Let me find out if they can give her a ride back to Flagstaff."

Chee waited.

"Yep," Leaphorn said. "I'll pick you up soon as I can get there."

"Right. I'll be ready."

Bernadette Manuelito was staring at him. "Wait a minute," she said.

"Go where with whom? You can't go anywhere with that ankle. You're supposed to keep it elevated. And iced."

Chee relaxed, closed his eyes, recognized that he was feeling much, much better. Why did talking to Joe Leaphorn do that for him? And now this business with Bernie. Worrying about his ankle. Bossing him around. Why did that make him feel so much better? He opened his eyes and looked up at her. A very pretty young lady even when she was frowning at him.

26

SERGEANT JIM CHEE kept his ankle elevated by resting it on pillows on the rear seat of Officer Bernie Manuelito's battered old Unit 11. He kept it iced with a plastic sack loaded with ice cubes. The ankle was feeling better, and so was Chee. Going to the clinic and having it expertly wrapped and taped had done wonders for the injury. Having his old boss showing him some respect had been good for bruised morale.

Bernie was tooling westward on U.S. 160, past the Red Mesa School, heading toward the Navajo 35 intersection at Mexican Water. Chee was behind her, slumped against the driver's side of the car, watching the side of Leaphorn's graying burr haircut. The lieutenant was not nearly as taciturn as Chee remembered him. He was telling her of the names Gershwin had left on the note at the Navajo Inn coffee shop, and how that had led to Jorie's place and about learning Jorie was suing Gershwin and the rest of it. Bernie was hanging on every word, and Leaphorn was obviously enjoying the attention. He'd been explaining to her why he had always been skeptical of coincidence, and Chee had heard that so often when he was the man's assistant in the Window Rock office that he had it memorized. It was bedrock Navajo philosophy. All things interconnected. No effect without cause. The beetle's wing affects the breeze, the lark's song bends the warrior's mood, a cloud back on the western horizon parts, lets light of the setting sun through, turns the mountains to gold, affects the mood and decision of the Navajo Tribal Council. Or, as the Anglo poet had put it, "No man is an island."

And Bernie, in her kindly fashion, was recognizing a lonely man's need and asking all the right questions. What a girl. "Is that sort of how you use that map Sergeant Chee tells me about?" And of course it was.

"I think Jim's mind works about the way mine does," Leaphorn said. "And I hope he'll correct me if I'm wrong. This casino business, for example. The casino's by Sleeping Ute Mountain. The escape vehicle is abandoned a hundred miles west on Casa Del Eco Mesa. Nearby a barn with an aircraft in it. The same day the aircraft is stolen. Closeness in both time and place. Nearby is an old mine. The Ute legends suggest the father of one of the bandits used it as his escape route. A little cluster of coincidences."

Bernie said, "Yes," but she sounded doubtful.

"There are more," Leaphorn said. "Remember the Great 1998 Manhunt. Three men involved. Police shot, stolen vehicle abandoned. Huge hunt begins. The fellow believed to be the ringleader is found dead. The FBI rules it suicide. The other two men vanish in the canyons."

Now that his ankle was no longer painful, Chee was feeling drowsy. He let his head slide over against the upholstery. Yawned. How long had it been since he'd had a good sleep?

"Another coincidence," Bernie agreed. "You have your doubts about that one, too?"

"Jim suggested the first crime might have been the cause of the second one," Leaphorn said.

Chee was no longer sleepy. What did that mean? He couldn't remember saying that.

"Ah," Bernie said. "That's going to take some complicated thinking. And that could go for the other ones, too. For example, seeing the abandoned truck and hearing about the robbery on the radio, Mr. Timms saw a way to get rid of his airplane. He claimed it was stolen and filed an insurance claim."

"It would be cause and effect that way, too, of course," Leaphorn said. "Or perhaps the airplane was the reason the car was abandoned where it was, as the FBI originally concluded."

Chee sat up. *What the devil is Leaphorn driving at?*

"I'm afraid I'm lost," Bernie said.

"Let me give you a whole new theory of the crime," Leaphorn said. "Let's say it went like this. Someone up in this border country paid close attention to the 1998 crime, and it suggested to him the way to solve a problem. Actually two problems. It would supply him with some needed cash, and it would eliminate an enemy. Let's say this person has connections with the militia, or the survivalists, or EarthFirsters, or any of the radical groups. Let's say he recruits two or three men to help him, pretending they're going after the money to finance their political cause. He gets Mr. Timms involved. Either he leases the airplane in advance for a flight or he lets Timms in on the crime. Offers him a slice of the loot."

"You're talking about Everett Jorie," Bernie said.

"I could be, yes," Leaphorn said. "But in my proposal, Jorie has the role of the enemy to be eliminated."

Chee cleared his throat. "Wait a minute, Lieutenant," he said. "How about the suicide note? All that?"

Leaphorn looked around at Chee, gave him a wry look. "I had the advantage of being there. Seeing the man where he lived. Seeing what he read. His library. The sort of stuff he treasured, that made up his life. When I look back at it, it makes me think I'm showing my age. If you or Officer Manuelito had been the ones to find the body, to see it all, you would have gotten suspicious a long time before I did."

Chee was thinking he still didn't feel suspicious. But he said, "OK. How did it work?"

Bernie had slowed. "Is that where you want me to turn? That dirt road?"

"It's rough, but it's a lot shorter than driving down to 191 and then having to cut back."

"I'm in favor of short," Bernie said, and they were bumping off the pavement and onto the dirt.

"I'd guess this is the route the casino perps took," Leaphorn said. "They must have known this mesa, living out here, and they must have known it led them into a dead-end situation." He laughed. "Another argument for my unorthodox theory of the crime. Having them turn off 191 and get lost would be too much of a coincidence for my taste."

"Lieutenant," Chee said, "why don't you go ahead and tell us what happened at Jorie's place."

"What I think may have happened," Leaphorn said. "Well, let's say that our villain knocks on Jorie's door, points the fatal pistol at Jorie, marches him into Jorie's office, has Jorie sit in his computer chair, then shoots him point-blank so it will pass as a suicide. Then he turns on the computer, leans over the body, types out the suicide note, leaves the computer on, and departs the scene."

"Why?" Chee asked. "Actually about four or five whys. I think I can see some of the motives, but some of it's hazy."

"Jorie was one of these fellows who thrive on litigation. And being a lawyer and admitted to the Utah bar, he could file all the suits he liked without it costing him much. He had two suits pending against our man. He was even suing Timms. Claimed his little airplane panicked his cattle, causing weight loss, loss of calves, so forth. Another suit claimed Timms violated his grazing lease with that unauthorized landing strip. But Timms isn't my choice of villains. Another one of Jorie's suits was aimed at canceling our villain's Bureau of Land Management lease."

"We're talking about Mr. Gershwin, of course," Chee said. "Aren't we?"

"In theory, yes," Leaphorn said.

"All right," Chee said. "What's next?"

"Now he has eliminated one of his two problems—the enemy and his troublesome lawsuits. But not the other one."

"The money," Bernie said. "You mean he'd only get a third of that?"

"In my theory, I think it's a little more complicated," Leaphorn replied. He looked back at Chee. "You remember in that suicide note, how he told the FBI where to find his two partners, how he stressed that they had sworn never to be taken alive. If they were caught, they wanted to go into history for the number of cops they had killed."

"His plan to eliminate them," Chee said, and produced a wry laugh. "It probably would have worked. If those guys were militia members, they'd have their heads full of how the FBI behaved at Ruby Ridge and Waco. Frankly, if I was going in with the SWAT team, I think I'd be blazing away."

"There must have seemed to be a flaw in that plan, though. Our villain had to wonder how the suicide note would be found. No one had any reason to suspect Jorie. Not a clue to any of the identities. So our villain solved that by finding himself a not-very-bright retired cop who he could trust to tip off the FBI without getting him involved in it."

"I'll be damned," Chee said. "I wondered how you happened to be the one who found Jorie's body."

"What was the rush?" Bernie asked. "Sooner or later Jorie would have been missed. Somebody would have gone out to see about him. You know how people out here are."

"My theoretical villain didn't think he could wait for that. He didn't want to risk the cops catching his partners before the cops knew about their plan to go down killing cops. Captured alive, they'd know just exactly who'd turned them in. They'd even the score and get off easier by testifying against him."

"Yeah," Bernie said. "That makes sense."

Chee was leaning forward now. He tapped Leaphorn's shoulder. "Look. Lieutenant, I didn't mean that the way it sounded. Like I thought you weren't very bright."

"Matter of fact I wasn't. He got almost exactly what he wanted out of me."

Which was true, but Chee let that hang.

"The only thing that went wrong was his partners must have smelled something in the wind. They didn't go home like they were supposed to—safe in the notion that the police hadn't a clue to who they were. They didn't wait for the SWAT teams to arrive and mow them down. They slipped away and hid somewhere."

"The old Mormon mine," Chee said. "So why didn't the FBI find them there?"

"I don't know," Leaphorn said. "Maybe they were somewhere else when the federal agents took a look. Maybe they went home, as our villain probably told them to do, and then got uneasy and came back to Ironhand's dad's hideaway, to wait and see what happened. Or maybe the federals didn't look hard enough. They'd have had no way of knowing about the entrance down in the canyon."

"That's true," Chee said. "You couldn't see it from the bottom. And, of course, we don't know if the bottom mine connects to the top."

Bernie laughed. "I don't know," she said. "I like to believe in legends. Even if they're Ute legends."

"I've just been along for the ride," Chee said. "Just giving my ankle an airing. Now I'm wondering what the plan is. I hope it's not that we walk up to that mine and order Baker and Ironhand to come out with their hands up."

"No," Leaphorn said, and laughed.

"Bernie would have to handle that all by herself," Chee said. "You're a civilian. I'm on sick leave or something. Let's say I'm back on vacation."

"But you did bring your pistol, I'll bet," Bernie said. "You did, didn't you?"

"I think I've got it here somewhere. You know the rules. Don't leave home without it."

"What I'd like to do is drop in on Mr. Timms," Leaphorn said. "I think we can get him to cooperate. And if he does, and if I'm guessing right, then Officer Manuelito gets on her radio and summons reinforcements."

"Why couldn't we call in for a backup and then—" Chee cut off the rest of that. He imagined Leaphorn explaining his theory to Special Agent Cabot—asking backup to check a mine the FBI had already certified free of fugitives. He imagined Cabot's smirk. He switched to another question.

"Do you know Mr. Timms?" he asked. Another stupid question. Of course he did. Leaphorn knew everyone in the Four Corners. At least everyone over sixty.

"Not well," Leaphorn said. "Haven't seen him for years. But I think we can get him to cooperate."

Chee leaned back against the door and watched the desert landscape slide past. He imagined Timms telling them to go to hell. He imagined Timms ordering them off his property.

But then he relaxed. Retired or not, Leaphorn was still the Legendary Lieutenant.

27

BERNIE LET UNIT 11 roll to a stop just in front of the Timms front porch, and they sat for the few moments required by empty-country courtesy to give the occupant time to get himself decent and prepare to acknowledge visitors. The door opened. A tall, skinny, slightly stooped man stood in the doorway looking out at them.

Leaphorn got out, Bernie followed, and Chee moved his ankle off the pillow and onto the floor. It hurt, but not much.

"Hello, Mr. Timms," Leaphorn said. "I wonder if you remember me."

Timms stepped out onto the porch, the sunlight reflecting from his spectacles. "Maybe I do," he said. "Didn't you used to be Corporal Joe Leaphorn with the Navajo Police? Wasn't you the one who helped out when that fellow was shooting at my airplane?"

"Yes sir," Leaphorn said. "That was me. And this young lady is Officer Bernadette Manuelito."

"Well, come on in out of the sun," Timms said.

Chee couldn't stand the thought of missing this. He pushed the car door open with his good foot, got his cane and limped across the yard, eyes on the ground to avoid an accident, noticing that the bedroom slipper he was wearing on his left foot was collecting sandburrs. "And this," Leaphorn was saying, "is Sergeant Jim Chee. He and I worked together."

"Yes sir," Timms said, and held out his hand. The shake was Navajo fashion, less grip and more the gentle touch. An old-timer who knew the culture. And so nervous that the muscles in his cheek were twitching.

"Wasn't expecting company, so I don't have anything fixed, but I could offer you something cold to drink," Timms said, ushering them into a small, dark room cluttered with the sort of old mismatched furniture one collects from Goodwill Industries shops.

"I don't think we should accept your hospitality, Mr. Timms," Leaphorn said. "We came here on some serious business."

"On that insurance claim," Timms said. "I already sent off a letter canceling that. Already did that."

"I'm afraid it's a lot more serious than that," Leaphorn said.

"That's the trouble with getting old. You get so damned forgetful," Timms said, talking fast. "I get up to get me a drink of water and by the time I get to the icebox I forget what I'm in the kitchen for. I flew that old L-17 down there to do some work, and then a fella offered me a ride home and I went off and left it and then we were hearing about the robbery on the radio and when I got home and saw the barn open and my airplane gone I just thought—"

Timms stopped. He stared at Leaphorn. So did Bernie. So did Chee.

"More than that?" Timms asked.

Leaphorn stood silent, eyes on Timms.

"What more?" Timms asked. He slumped down into an overstuffed armchair, looking up at Leaphorn.

"You remember that fellow who was doing the shooting when you flew over his place? Everett Jorie."

"He quit doing that after you talked to him." Timms tried a smile, which didn't come off. "I appreciated that. Now he's turned into a bandit. Robbed that casino. Killed himself."

"It looked like that for a while," Leaphorn said.

Timms shrank into the chair. Raised his right hand to his forehead. He said, "You saying somebody killed him?"

Leaphorn let the question hang for a moment. Said: "How well do you know Roy Gershwin?"

Timms opened his mouth, closed it, and looked up at Leaphorn. Chee found himself feeling sorry for the man. He looked terrified.

"Mr. Timms," Leaphorn said, "you are in a position right now to help yourself a lot. The FBI isn't happy with you. Hiding that airplane, reporting it stolen, that slowed down the hunt for those killers a lot. It's not the sort of thing law enforcement forgets. Unless it has a reason to want to overlook it. If you're helpful, then the police tend to say 'Well, Mr. Timms was just forgetful.' If you're not helpful, then things like that tend to go to the grand jury to let the jury decide whether you were what they call an accessory after the fact. And that's not insurance fraud. That's in a murder case."

"Murder case. You mean Jorie?"

"Mr. Timms," Leaphorn said, "tell me about Roy Gershwin."

"He was by here today," Timms said. "You just missed him."

Now it was Leaphorn's turn to look startled. And Chee's.

"What did he want? What did he say?"

"Not much. He wanted directions to that old Latter-Day-Saints mine. The place those Mormons used to dig their coal. And I told him, and he run right out of here. In a big hurry."

"I think we'd better go," Leaphorn said, and started for the door.

Timms looked sick. He made a move to rise, sank back.

"You telling me Gershwin killed that Everett Jorie? Don't tell me that."

Leaphorn and Bernie were already out the door, and as Chee limped after them he heard Timms saying, "Oh, God. I was afraid of that."

28

IT WAS EASY enough to notice where Gershwin's pickup had turned off the track, easy to see the path it had left through the crusted blowsand and broken clusters of snakeweed. Following the tracks was a different matter. Gershwin's truck had better traction and much higher clearance than Bernie's Unit 11 patrol car, which, under its official paint, was still a worn-out Chevy sedan.

It lost traction on the side of one of those great humps that wind erosion drifts around Mormon tea in desert climates. It slid sideways, rear wheels down the slope. Leaphorn checked Bernie's instinct to gun the engine by a sharply whispered "No!"

"I think we're about as close as we want to drive," he said. "I'll take a look."

He took the unit's binoculars out of the glove box, opened the door, slid out, walked up the hummock, stood for a minute looking and then walked back.

"The mine structure is maybe a quarter mile," he said, pointing. "Over by the rimrock. Gershwin's truck is about two hundred yards ahead of us. It looks empty. It also looks like he left it where it couldn't be seen from the mine."

"So now what?" Chee said. "Do we radio in and ask for some backup?" Even as he asked, he was wondering how that call would sound. Imagining the exchange. An area rancher had driven his pickup over to an old mine site. Why do you need backup? Because we think the casino perps are hiding there. Which mine? One the FBI has already checked out and certified as empty.

Leaphorn was looking at him, quizzically.

"Or what?" Chee concluded, thinking that surely Leaphorn wouldn't propose they simply walk up, ask if anybody was inside and tell them to come out and surrender.

"We're on their blind side," Leaphorn said. "Why don't we get closer? See if we can learn what's going on."

"You brought your piece," Leaphorn said. "I'm going to borrow Officer Manuelito's pistol. Officer Manuelito, I want you to stay here close to the radio but get up on the hump there where you can see what's going on. We may need you to make some fast contacts. I'll borrow your sidearm."

"Give you my gun?" Bernie said, sounding doubtful.

Chee was easing himself out of the car, thinking that the Legendary Lieutenant had forgotten he was a civilian. He had unilaterally rescinded his retirement and resumed his rank.

"Your pistol," he said, holding out his hand. Bernie's expression switched from doubtful to determined.

"No, sir. That's one of the first things we learn. We keep our pistols."

Leaphorn stared at her. Nodded. "You're right," he said. "Hand me the rifle."

She pulled it out of the rack and handed it to him, butt first. He checked the chamber.

"In fact, Manuelito, I want you to get into radio contact now. Tell 'em where we are, precisely as you can, tell them that Sergeant Chee is checking an old mine building and we may need some support. Tell them you're going to be out of the car a few minutes to back him up and ask them to stand by. Then I want you on top of that hummock up there watching what's going on. Doing what needs to be done."

"Sergeant Chee should stay here," Bernie said. "He can't walk that far. I'll go with you. He can handle the radio."

Chee used his sergeant voice. "Manuelito, you'll do the radio. That's an order."

Whatever the reason, the excitement, the adrenaline pumping, per-haps the distracting notion that in a few minutes an award-winning Green Beret sniper might be shooting him, Chee limped up the hummock slope hardly aware of his bandaged ankle or the sand in his bedroom slipper. The ruined mine structure came into view, the back side of what he had photographed from the helicopter. As Leaphorn had said, this side pre-sented only a windowless stone wall.

Leaphorn pointed, noted the entrance door was probably to their left, pointed out the route down the gentle slope that Chee should take, noting the cover available in the event anyone came out of the structure. Any pre-tense of being a civilian, of being anything except the Navajo Tribal Police officer in charge, had ceased to exist.

"I'll move down to the right," Leaphorn concluded. "Watch for a sig-nal. If anyone comes out, we'll let them get far enough from the structure. They, or he, will probably be walking toward Gershwin's truck. We'll see what opportunity presents itself."

"Yes sir," Chee said. He rechecked his pistol and did exactly as told.

About five minutes, and fifty cautious yards later, Chee first heard a voice.

He stood, waved at Leaphorn, pointed to the wall and made talking motions with his hand. Leaphorn nodded.

A moment later, the sound of laughter.

Then the sharp door-slam sound of a pistol shot. Then another, and another.

Chee looked at Leaphorn, who was looking at him. Leaphorn signaled him to stay down. They waited. Time ticked past. Leaphorn signaled him to close in and moved slowly toward the wall. Chee did the same.

A tall, elderly man emerged from behind the wall. What seemed to be a student's backpack dangled from one hand. He was wearing a white shirt with the tail out, jeans and a tan straw hat. As Leaphorn had predicted, he walked toward Gershwin's truck.

Chee ducked back out of sight behind a growth of saltbush, following the man with his pistol. No more than twenty yards. An easy shot if a shooting was called for.

Leaphorn was standing in the open, the rifle cradled across his arm.

"Mr. Gershwin," he shouted. "Roy. What are you doing way out here?"

Gershwin stopped, stood frozen for a moment, then turned and looked at Leaphorn.

"Well now, I don't hardly know what to tell you about that. If I had noticed you first, I'd have asked you the same thing."

Leaphorn laughed. "I probably would have told you I'm out here hunting quail. But then you'd have noticed this is a rifle and not something you use to shoot birds. And you wouldn't have believed me."

"Prob'ly not," Gershwin said. "I'd guess you were thinking about all that money taken out of that casino and how it had to be hidden someplace and maybe this old mine was it."

"Well," Leaphorn said, "it's true that the Navajo Nation doesn't offer high retirement pay. How about you? You looking for some extra unmarked paper money?"

"Are you talking as an officer of the law, or are you still a civilian?"

"I'm the same civilian you brought your list of names to," Leaphorn said. "Once you're out they don't let you back in."

"Well, then, I hope you have better luck than I did. There's no money back there. I turned over every piece of junk. Nothing. Just a waste of time." Gershwin started walking again.

"I heard some shots fired," Leaphorn said. "What was that about?"

Gershwin turned around and started back toward the mine. "Come on," he said. "I'll show you. And I'll tell you, too. Remember me telling you I was pulling out. Going to move into a motel somewhere. Not wait around for those militia bastards to come after me. Well, I decided to hell with that. I'm too old a dog to let those punks run me out. I decided I'd have a showdown."

"Hold it a minute," Leaphorn said. "I want you to meet a friend of mine." He motioned to Chee.

Chee holstered his pistol, came out from behind the brush, raised a hand in greeting. If Gershwin was carrying a weapon it wasn't visible. If it was any size, he'd probably be carrying it under his belt, hidden by his shirt and not in a pocket. The sound of the gunshots suggested a serious weapon. Certainly not a pocket-size twenty-two.

"This is Sergeant Jim Chee," Leaphorn said. "Roy Gershwin."

Gershwin looked shocked. "Yes," he said, and nodded to Chee.

"Chee's short of money, too," Leaphorn said. "He's a single man, but he's trying to live on a police salary."

Gershwin gave Chee another look, nodded again, and resumed his walk toward the mine. "Well, as I was telling you, I drove out here thinking I was going to have it out with these bastards. Either take 'em in for the reward money, or run 'em off, or shoot 'em if I had to. That reward's supposed to be for dead or alive. I just decided not to run. I'm way too damned old to be running."

"You shot 'em?" Leaphorn asked.

"Just one. I shot Baker. George Ironhand, he got away."

They were in the structure by then, through a double doorway that pierced a partly tumbled wall and into the patterned light and darkness of a huge room. Sunlight streaming through gaps in its roof illuminated the cluttered earthen floor in streaks. It was about as Special Agent Cabot had described it. Empty except for a jumble of junk and scattered debris. Where the floor wasn't hidden by fallen roofing material and sheets of warped plywood, it was covered by layers of drifted sand, dust and trash drifted in by years of wind. Tumbleweeds were piled against the back wall, and beside them was the body of a man dressed in gray-green camouflage coveralls.

Gershwin gestured toward the body. "Baker," he said. "Son of a bitch tried to shoot me."

"Tell us about how it went," Leaphorn said.

"Well, I parked back there a ways so they wouldn't hear me coming. And walked up real quiet and looked in and that one"—Gershwin pointed to the body by the wall—"he seemed to be sleeping. The tall one was sitting over there, and when I came in he made a grab for his gun and I hollered for him to stop, but he got it, and then I shot him and he fell down. That woke up the other guy and he jumped up and pulled out a pistol and I hollered for him to drop it and he took a shot at me so I shot him, too."

"The first one you shot," Chee said. "Where did he go?"

"Be damned if I know," Gershwin said. "I thought he was down for good and I was busy with the other one, and when I was going to check on him, he wasn't there. I guess he just got out of here somehow. Didn't you fellas see him running away?"

"We didn't," Leaphorn said, "and we better be getting to our car. We need to call this in, and get the law out here to collect the body and get a search going for the one that got away."

"Surprised you didn't see him," Gershwin said.

"Where's your weapon?" Leaphorn asked. "You need to hand that over to Sergeant Chee here."

"I threw it away," Gershwin said. "I never had shot a man before, and when I realized what I'd done I just felt sick. Went to that side door over there and threw up and then I threw my pistol down in the canyon."

They had moved out through the broken doorway into the sunlight. Chee kept his hand near the butt of his pistol, thinking Leaphorn couldn't possibly believe that, thinking the weapon was probably a handgun and it was probably in the backpack Gershwin was carrying. Or perhaps stuck in Gershwin's belt, hidden by the shirt.

"It's a terrible feeling," Gershwin was saying, "shooting a man." And as he was saying that his hand flashed under the shirt and came out fumbling with a pistol.

Chee's pistol was pointed at Gershwin's chest. "Drop it," Chee said. "Drop it or I kill you."

Gershwin made an angry sound, dropped his pistol.

Leaphorn shouted, "Look out." There was a blast of sound from the darkness. Gershwin was knocked sprawling into the dirt.

"He's under that big sheet of plywood," Leaphorn shouted. "I saw a side of it rise. Then the muzzle flash."

The plywood was directly under the A-frame of timbers that rose through what was left of the building's roof. Chee and Leaphorn approached it as one approaches a prairie rattler, with caution. Chee did his stalking via the side door, a route with better cover. He got there first, motioned Leaphorn in. They stood on opposite sides of it, looking down at it.

"Gershwin is dead," Leaphorn said.

"I thought it looked like that," Chee said.

"If you pulled that plywood back, you'd expect to look right down into a vertical shaft," Leaphorn said. "But whoever pushed it up and stuck out that rifle barrel had to be standing on something."

"Probably some sort of rope ladder at least," Chee said. "Or maybe they dug out some sort of niche." He tried to visualize what would be under the plywood without much luck.

Leaphorn was studying him. "You want to pull it away and take a look?"

Chee laughed. "I think I'd rather just wait until Special Agent Cabot gets here with his people and let him do it. I wouldn't want to mess up the Bureau's crime scene."

29

J IM CHEE SPRAWLED across the rear seat of Unit 11, his throbbing ankle high on a pillow reminding him of what the doctor had said about putting weight on a sprain before it's healed. Otherwise, Chee was feeling no pain. He was at ease. He was content. True, George Ironhand was still at large in the canyons, either wounded or well, but he wasn't Chee's problem.

Chee relaxed, listened to the windshield wipers working against the off-and-on rain shower, eavesdropped now and then on the conversation the Legendary Lieutenant was having with Officer Manuelito (Leaphorn was calling her Bernie) and rehashing the events of a tense and tiring day.

The reinforcements had arrived a little before sundown. First came two big Federal Bureau of Investigation copters, hovering a while to find a place to put down among the hummocks of Mormon tea, the Special Agents swarming out, looking warlike in their official bulletproof costumes, pointing their automatic weapons at Leaphorn and looking miffed when Leaphorn ignored them. Then the business of trying to explain what had happened there. Explaining Gershwin to the Special Agent in Charge, who wanted to question everything, who wanted answers which would prove the Bureau was right in its Everett Jorie suicide/gang-leader conclusion, and who looked downright thunderstruck when he learned that the fellow instructing otherwise was just a civilian.

Chee grinned, remembering that. Leaphorn had cut off the SAC's arguments by suggesting he could end his doubts by sending a few of his troops over to Gershwin's truck and having them unpack some of the bundles, in which Leaphorn was confident they would find about one hundred seven pounds and eleven ounces of the paper money taken from the casino. The SAC did, and they did; some of the money was neatly double-sacked in eight of those Earth-Smart white-plastic kitchen trash bags stacked under Gershwin's luggage, and a bunch of the bigger bills was layered into the suitcases with his clothing. While that was happening the ground troops arrived—two sheriff's cars, a Utah State Police car and a BIA law-enforcement unit bringing an assortment of cops—including Border Patrol trackers with their dogs. The trackers nervously eyed the cumulus clouds, their tops backlit by the setting sun and their black bottoms producing lightning and promising the long-overdue rain. Trackers prefer daylight and dry ground and were making their preference obvious. Finally, the explaining stopped, an ambulance arrived to take away the much-photographed bodies, and now here Chee was, dry and comfortable, on his way home and an interested listener to the Legendary Lieutenant revealing a human side.

"I've only met her recently," Bernie was saying. "But she seemed very nice."

"An interesting person," Leaphorn said. "A real friend, I think." He chuckled. "At least she's willing to listen to me when I talk. When you're an old widower, and you haven't gotten used to living alone yet, that's something you need."

Which is why, Chee was thinking, *Leaphorn has been chattering like this.* He'd always thought of him as taciturn, hard to talk to. A silent man. But then Bernie was Bernie. He liked to talk to her, too. Or, come to think of it, he liked to talk while Bernie listened. He skipped backward into memories of conversations with Janet Pete. No problem there. Then came another memory, another comparison. Bernie putting ice on his swollen ankle, leaning over him, her soft hair brushing past his face. Janet kissing him. Janet's hair carried the perfume of flowers, Bernie's the scent of juniper and the wind.

"You don't seem old to me," Bernie was saying. "No older than my father, and he's still young."

"It's more than age," Leaphorn said. "Emma and I were married longer than you've been alive. One of those love-at-first-sight things when we were students at Arizona State. And when she died—" He didn't finish that.

The rain stopped. Bernie switched off the wipers. "I'll bet you she wouldn't have approved of you living alone, like a hermit. I'll bet she would want you to get married again."

Wow, Chee thought. *That took nerve. How will Lieutenant Leaphorn react to that?*

Leaphorn laughed. "Exactly. She did. But not Professor Bourebonette. At the hospital before her surgery she told me if anything went wrong, I should remember Navajo tradition."

"Marry her sister?" Bernie said. "You have a single sister-in-law?"

"Yep," Leaphorn said. "Emma almost always gave good advice, but her sister didn't like that idea any better than I did."

"I'll bet your wife would have approved of Professor Bourebonette," Bernie said. "I mean as your wife."

If Chee hadn't been watching while Bernie refused to surrender her sidearm to Leaphorn a few hours ago, he wouldn't have believed he was hearing this. He waited. Silence. Then Leaphorn said, "You know, Bernie, now you mention it, I'm sure she would."

What a woman, this Officer Bernadette Manuelito. Chee remembered the sort of subconscious uneasiness he'd felt when Bernie showed up at his trailer and asked him to help her wounded boyfriend. It was jealousy, of course, though he didn't want to admit it then. And he was feeling it again now.

"Bernie," Chee said, "what's the condition report on Teddy Bai?"

"Much better," Bernie said.

"Did you talk to him?"

"Rosemary did," she said. "She said he's going to be well enough so they won't have to postpone their wedding."

"Well, now," Chee said. "Wow. That's really good news." And he meant it.